MW01071688

A Death in the Family

James Agee. Photograph by Florence Homolka.

The Works of

James Agee

volume 1

General Editor
Michael A. Lofaro

Associate General Editor
Hugh Davis

A Death in the Family

A Restoration of the Author's Text

Edited by Michael A. Lofaro

The Works of

James Agee

volume 1

General Editor
Michael A. Lofaro

Associate General Editor
Hugh Davis

The University of Tennessee Press / Knoxville

Cloth: First printing, 2007; second printing, 2008.

Frontispiece: James Agee by Florence Homolka. Courtesy of and © Vincent Homolka and Laurence Homolka and courtesy of Special Collections, University of Tennessee Library.

This book is printed on acid-free paper.

Library of Congress Cataloging-in-Publication Data

Agee, James, 1909–1955.
A death in the family : a restoration of the author's text / edited by Michael A. Lofaro.
p. cm. — (Works of James Agee ; v. 1)
Includes bibliographical references and index.

ISBN-13: 978-1-57233-594-3 (hardcover : acid-free paper)
ISBN-10: 1-57233-594-7 (hardcover : acid-free paper)

1. Agee, James, 1909–1955. Death in the family.
2. Traffic accident victims—Fiction.
3. Knoxville (Tenn.)—Fiction.
4. Fathers and sons—Fiction.
5. Boys—Fiction.
6. Domestic fiction.
I. Lofaro, Michael A., 1948–
II. Title.

PS3501.G35D43 2007
813'.52—dc22 2007011564

For Nancy

Contents

Preface xi
General Textual Method xxiii
A James Agee Chronology xxix

James Agee's *A Death in the Family* 1
"towards the middle of the twentieth century" 3
"This little boy you live in": Perceptions c. 1911–1912 15
The Surprise: 1912 49
"Enter the Ford": Travel, 1913–1916 83
May 17, 1916: The Day Before 141
Daytime: May 18, 1916 181
Evening: May 18, 1916 203
Morning: May 19, 1916 283
"all the way home": The Last Day 311

Textual Commentary and Notes 357
Major Manuscript Variants 425
Marginal Notes 533
Word Choice Where No Preference Is Indicated 541
Paragraphing 547

Appendices
I. How to Read the Corrected McDowell Edition of *A Death in the Family* from This Text and a Chart of Substantive Corrections to the Library of America Edition of *A Death in the Family* 549
II. A Structural Comparison of the Restored and the McDowell Editions 563
III. "Knoxville: Summer of 1915" 565
IV. Agee's Memories of His Father's Accident and the Day Before 569

V. Unfinished Draft of Agee's Letter to His Father 573
VI. Unfinished Draft of Agee's Letter to His Mother 575
VII. Letter from Agee's Mother [Mrs. Erskine (Laura Tyler Agee) Wright] Concerning *A Death in the Family* 577
VIII. Outline and Possible Introduction to Agee's Massive Autobiographical Project and the Place of "This book" in It 579

Preface

When James Agee died of a heart attack at the age of forty-five in the back of New York City taxicab on May 16, 1955, he had essentially completed the handwritten manuscript of an untitled highly autobiographical novel of his first six and one-half years. For a small but rapidly growing cult of followers, he had also become an icon of the uncompromising artist, raging against the establishment, tragically out of step with his time. Feeding this myth was the fact that at the time of his death all his major works were out of print or not yet published; commercial failure represented the unimpeachable sign of unappreciated genius. With David McDowell's editing and publication of a distinctly altered version of the manuscript in 1957, under his title of *A Death in the Family,* and its subsequent winning of the Pulitzer Prize, however, the time for recognition had come.

As a direct result of McDowell's efforts as the head of the James Agee Trust, an entity designed to help support the three small children of Agee's third wife, Mia,[1] through the promulgation of his writing, the posthumous reconstruction of the Agee canon began in earnest. In addition to the reissuing of *Let Us Now Praise Famous Men,* which in 1960 found the audience that had eluded it in 1941, Agee's work was collected and interpreted over the next three decades by friends serving as editors to produce highly selective volumes of his screenplays, film criticism, poetry, short prose, letters, and journalism, along with scattered pieces of fiction and juvenilia.[2]

Despite the fact that Agee was a reasonably successful commercial writer and had turned more and more from elitist productions like *Let Us Now Praise Famous Men* to try to reach a wider audience through film criticism, writing screenplays for films such as *The African Queen* and *The Night of the Hunter,* and by focusing on an increasingly straightforward and direct prose style, his editors and critics generally ignored the shift. Dwight Macdonald even christened him a literary James Dean.[3] Eventually, the myth came to predominate, and Agee's work was judged, not solely on its merits, but more as a reflection of the various roles prescribed for him by his followers: rebel, poet, mystic, martyr.

In many ways Agee became the victim of having been loved not wisely but too well. The people most responsible for creating his legacy were long-time friends who wanted to ensure that his work would receive the attention it deserved by accentuating the ways it exemplified their views of contemporary aesthetic standards. But the creation of the legacy required selective destruction: Father James H. Flye burned the originals after editing Agee's letters to him; Robert Fitzgerald suppressed Agee's Marxist poetry in the service of aesthetic and political probity; and Dwight Macdonald shaped the facts of Agee's life and death to further his own ideas about cultural decline.

Perhaps the greatest posthumous change, however, was the result of David McDowell's treatment of the manuscripts of *A Death in the Family.* His altered version of the novel remained the standard until the present edition and became a classic of American literature. The most recent edition of *A Death in the Family,* published in 2005 by the Library of America, likewise uses the McDowell text as a base but attempts the minor correction of approximately eighty-five instances of errors in transcription.[4] All previous extant versions of the novel, however, remain unfaithful to Agee's original manuscript in major ways.

While scholars have long known that *A Death in the Family* had minor structural flaws and debated whether or not Agee's "Knoxville: Summer of 1915," published in the *Partisan Review* some nineteen years before the novel, should have been included as the work's introduction by the editors (primarily David McDowell), no one seriously questioned the editors' claim in the original preface, "A Note on this Book," that the work was essentially finished before Agee's death and needed only minor adjustments before publishing. According to this brief introduction, they simply printed "several scenes outside the time frame of the story . . . after Parts I and II [general divisions in the novel]" and added "Knoxville: Summer of 1915" as a prologue because, although it "was not a part of the manuscript which Agee left, . . . the editors would certainly have urged him to include it in the final draft." All these sections were printed in italics. They stated that the novel "is presented here exactly as he wrote it. There has been no re-writing, and nothing has been eliminated except for a few cases of first-draft material which he later reworked at greater length, and one section of seven-odd pages which the editors were unable satisfactorily to fit into the body of the novel."[5]

The issue remained relatively settled until the purchase of a collection of papers from the estate of the late David McDowell by the University of Tennessee in 1988. The collection made clear that the manuscript of the novel had undergone far more manipulation than the editors' preface implied. Permission to work with and publish these materials, however, had to wait until a change in directorship of the James Agee Trust in 2002.

Within these revelatory materials kept personally by McDowell and excluded from the archives of the trust were two lengthy and previously unknown named chapters of the novel—"Enter the Ford" and "Chilhowee Park"—as well as drafts, outlines, and correspondence. These manuscripts, which in essence completed those already available at the University of Texas, provided the key to unlocking the true structure of Agee's novel. Although Agee left a contiguous manuscript at the time of his death, it was subsequently scattered. The present restored edition therefore relies upon the coordination and transcription of the original holograph manuscripts of the novel held by the University of Texas at Austin, the University of Tennessee, and the James Agee Trust (now on deposit at the University of Tennessee).[6]

This edition also relies upon the author's manuscripts rather than attempting a correction or annotation of the first printed edition simply because the McDowell version and all those subsequently based upon it, such as the Library of America's, so substantially alter Agee's intent. These manuscripts exist in various states. Some are clearly final copies, often based upon multiple drafts since Agee was a constant reviser of his work, others exist in various states of correction, and all awaited whatever changes Agee might make when he would convert them into typescript. In each instance, the text printed here represents Agee's final effort.[7] For purposes of comparison, the first part of appendix I provides the reader with the McDowell text from this restored edition. This rendering allows access to McDowell's version of the novel, but with all necessary corrections to the text that he constructed. While retaining McDowell's editorial decisions, this process eliminates hundreds of instances of misreadings of words and phrases and remedies the accidental omission of Agee's words, phrases, and occasionally sentences. The second part of appendix I presents a chart of substantive corrections to the Library of America's edition. Previous editors and scholars nonetheless deserve substantial credit for their initial transcriptions and corrections of Agee's extraordinarily difficult handwriting.

The present edition restores *A Death in the Family* to the novel it was at the time of Agee's death. The restoration is clearly necessary. A three-year analysis of the author's original manuscripts has revealed that from its introduction, "Knoxville: Summer of 1915," through its entire text, McDowell's version of *A Death in the Family* was far more a construct of its editors than its author and a radically different book.

While beginning with Agee's holograph manuscript in final form, in addition to adding "Knoxville: Summer of 1915" to the work, the editors of the McDowell version deleted or did not use ten and one-third finished chapters, chose the wrong (i.e. earlier draft) versions of three other chapters, deliberately divided and interspersed others, and substantially altered the time sequence of the novel by creating the two blocks of three "italicized" chapters each from eight separate chapters which were deliberately fused together in a somewhat random, non-chronological order to serve as flashbacks.[8] Further degradation of the novel occurred in subsequent paperback editions which replaced chapter breaks between the italicized material in the first edition with a small space of several lines, an economy that further emphasized the distortion of chronology by compressing each section of McDowell's three italicized chapters into one.

When reordered and rejoined in the restored manuscript, these "italicized-flashback" sections, taken together with the omitted and final versions of chapters, comprise a new first one-third of the book and form a crucial part of the essentially straightforward chronological progression that was Agee's plan. He stated in his notes for the book: "Maximum simple: *Just the story of my relation with my father and, through that, as thorough as possible an image of him:* winding into other things on the way but never dwelling on them" (emphasis mine).[9] This information from the Texas materials is supported by notes in the Tennessee collection in which Agee records that *Death* was eventually intended as a part of a huge autobiographical project that was to proceed chronologically. His outline began with

> The Ancestors.
> (Culminate in my mother's and father's meeting in the dancing school.)
> The Father and Mother.
> (Ends with my birth: my father coming into the room for the first time.)
> *This book.*
> *(Begins with my first remembrance; ends the evening of his burial.)* [emphasis mine].[10]

While only a part of the evidence of Agee's true plan for "This book" (Agee never chose a title for his novel), these two items reveal the core of his chronological and autobiographical vision for the work, a vision to which the present text adheres. The book proper begins with his "first remembrance" and ends on "the evening of his [father's] burial."[11] In a draft letter to his mother, Agee reinforces the same plan: "I am trying to write a short book, a novel, beginning with the first things I can remember, and ending with my father's burial."[12] It also seems very unlikely that if he had lived Agee would ever have accepted McDowell's restructuring and editing of *A Death in the Family,* especially given how long and hard he fought to maintain his original artistic vision for his other major work, *Let Us Now Praise Famous Men.*[13]

Much of the material here incorporated into the novel for the first time deals precisely with the young Rufus' devotion to and developing relationship with his father, a relationship that in fact dominates the true introduction but is notably absent from "Knoxville: Summer of 1915." The restored text is in many ways a new novel. The new and reordered chapters and sections significantly alter the perceptions of the reader by providing Rufus with much more positive and caring interaction with his father, which clearly results in deeper memories and more powerful images of him. As Agee said in a draft letter to his dead father: "In trying to write about my first few years alive, I am bound to be writing, mainly, about you."[14] He also reminded himself in his notes on the novel to "concentrate more deeply & exclusively on my father" and that "long transitional & development sections is a kind of past imperfect, concentrated chiefly on him, and largely as seen through the child."[15] Similarly, the first category stated in other of Agee's notes, after listing his "new," far darker introduction, is "Episodes to build up chiefly my relation to him & the reader's liking for him."[16]

Agee also makes the father a vital and fully drawn character by demonstrating the tumult and strength in the love his parents have for each other in the restored novel. His notes foreground this intent: "Develop tension in her, *re*[garding] me & Emma & his drinking; school stuff; religion. Pleasures of marriage, home children, in them."[17] Agee also systematically prepares the reader for the father's death in the text with the previously unknown "Enter the Ford" chapter. His fatal automobile accident was never meant to be the *deus ex machina* or bolt out of the blue it was in the McDowell version. The bulk of the new chapters and a substantial amount of the italicized material actually belong before the previous chapter 1 (now chapter 17) and set the stage for a stronger and far more impressive narrative than that concocted by the former editors in which the father figured as an active character only in chapters 1, 2, 3, and 6. (He does appear as well in four of the six flashbacks, but their nature as remembrance does not support Jay Agee's active nature in the same way.) In this restored edition, Jay is alive and active for approximately one-half of the novel, as well as being the focal point of its introduction.

While the previous editors' reasons for manipulating the manuscript may never be fully known, it does seem likely that David McDowell, as editor and first trustee of the James Agee Trust, changed the novel to suit the popular tastes of the 1950s and increase the book's marketability. When James Agee died, he left only approximately $450 in a savings account for his family, and no life insurance, other indemnification, or support.[18] Part of McDowell's fiduciary duty as trustee was to maximize income to the trust to provide funds for the family's welfare. Another of his duties, however, was to ensure the accuracy of the texts published under Agee's name. McDowell's removal of the development of the character of the father and considerable amounts of related materials made the work more universal but quite vague, abruptly curtailing the lengthy depiction of Jay Agee as a complex, rugged, rural yet worldly paternal figure from the mountains of East Tennessee who spoke in a light dialect. With such substantial excision, the central and specific loving relationship with his son Rufus was also eliminated and the novel's significant theme of country life versus city life was considerably diminished.[19] While a questionable decision, it would simply be regarded as a choice within the posthumous purview of the editor-trustee if he had not so strongly asserted that he had not altered Agee's text in any appreciable way.

Overall, however, the changes are dramatic. Following Agee's structure, the restored novel is composed of a new introduction and forty-five chapters rather than "Knoxville: Summer of 1915" and the twenty chapters (and six unnumbered italicized sections) that McDowell published. The large number of shorter chapters following a structure of remembered episodes (scenes) might reflect Agee's career as a screenwriter; however, his notes reflect that he once considered writing the novel as "short stories, linked only by the main characters & a time-progression?"[20] The real names of the characters (which McDowell changed since so many were alive at the time of the book's publication) and of places are also restored, as are the punctuation and dialect spellings that Agee used so well to mimic local speech patterns and pronunciation. All are changes that enhance both the autobiographical base and the realism of the novel.

It is also hard to underestimate the effect of replacing McDowell's use of "Knoxville: Summer of 1915" with Agee's actual introduction to the novel. McDowell said of his use of "Knoxville: Summer of 1915" that "It was probably the most reckless piece of editorial judgment I ever made, but it is exactly what I would have advised Agee to do had he lived."[21] McDowell's substitution of that prose poem was in one way the most radical change to Agee's text because it set a completely contradictory tone for the work. Its rhapsodic, languorous prose creates a delightful reverie of southern summer sounds of locusts and crickets and children playing games and images of front porches and rocking chairs and quilts spread on lawns; all were delightful scenes but never intended as part of *A Death in the Family.*

In the restored version, the true introduction is a terrifying and revealing nightmare rather than an idyllic reverie, and it is clearly tied, both structurally and thematically, to the later chapters. One of Agee's outlines for the novel clearly supports the use of the nightmare and its immediate link to the next chapters in the restored edition. He begins the outline with

> Prologue.
> (Dream)
>
> 1. waking & songs.
> 2. establish family & family pleasures, Church Street; LaFollette.
> 3. develop image of father.

Agee then brackets the first two enumerated items and writes "or: start with father, then mother, then the 2 families," his eventual choice.[22]

Two other of Agee's outlines for the novel list "head, as now" and "head as now" as the first subject treated, and the nightmare/dream chapter moves the adult narrator Rufus, who is carrying the bleeding and then rotting corpse of a man murdered in the street and stripped bare by a mob, through a surreal adventure that culminates in the transformations of the by then detached head as it tries to elude capture.[23] The vacant lot to which the body is carried by the narrator in the nightmare is the place of true communion, solace, and bonding for father and son in the novel proper and ties this introduction directly to chapter 17.[24] Thus both the head and the vacant lot are major symbols that link this introduction to the body of the novel. The narrator's experiences in the nightmare range over an intermingling of self-analysis, guilt, religion, anger, doubt, and loneliness.[25] Ultimately, upon waking, the narrator finds the meaning of his search in the quest itself—a return to his earliest years—and begins, as Agee intended, a chronological progression that starts with his first memories, always vivid and sometimes unconnected, and ends with his father's funeral, all in a quest for self-discovery, understanding, and forgiveness.

A Death in the Family is indeed a masterpiece, one so well written that its prose cannot be obscured by past editorial decisions, inaccuracy, and deception. It is my opinion that James Agee's restored text successfully merges creative nonfiction with autobiography and provides readers and critics with an even firmer sense of his achievement as a novelist than the former version of his work that was awarded the Pulitzer Prize. Enjoy making your own judgments.

Notes

1. Personal communication (12/16/03) with Paul Sprecher, trustee, James Agee Trust, and TN 1A.2.2 (University of Tennessee, Special Collections Library, MS 1500 James Agee–David McDowell Papers, 1909–1985, Box 1A, Folder 2, p. 2). Subsequent references to this manuscript collection will be cited as TN 1A.2, [2]. References to other Tennessee manuscript collections will be labeled with that collection's number after the TN abbreviation but otherwise cited in the same manner. See note 15 below as an example.
2. Posthumously published works and collections of works by Agee include: *A Death in the Family* (New York: McDowell, Obolensky, 1957); *Agee on Film*, vols. 1 and 2 (New York: McDowell, Obolensky, 1958 and 1960); *Let Us Now Praise Famous Men*, intro. Walker Evans (Boston: Houghton Mifflin, 1960); *The Letters of James Agee to Father Flye*, ed. James H. Flye (New York: George Braziller, 1962); *The Collected Poems of James Agee*, ed. Robert Fitzgerald (Boston: Houghton Mifflin, 1968); and *The Collected Short Prose of James Agee*, ed. Robert Fitzgerald (Boston: Houghton Mifflin, 1968). Later works include *James Agee: Selected Journalism*, ed. Paul Ashdown (Knoxville: Univ. of Tennessee Press, 1985, rev. 2005); and *Agee: Selected Literary Documents*, ed. Victor A. Kramer (Troy: Whitson, 1996).
3. "In some literary circles, James Agee now excites the kind of emotion James Dean does in some nonliterary circles. There is already an Agee cult. This is partly because of the power of his writing and his lack of recognition—everyone likes to think he is on to a good thing the general public has not caught up with—but mainly because it is felt that Agee's life and

personality, like Dean's, were at once a symbolic expression of our time and a tragic protest against it" (150). Dwight Macdonald, "James Agee," in Macdonald, *Against the American Grain* (New York: Random House, 1962), pp. 143–59. This article was a reprinting of his "Death of a Poet," *New Yorker* 33 (November 16, 1957): pp. 204–21.

4. Michael Sragow, "Note on the Texts," ed., *James Agee:* Let Us Now Praise Famous Men, A Death in the Family, *and Shorter Fiction* (New York: Library of America, 2005), pp. 811–14. The other volume of the Library of America's edition is *James Agee: Film Writing and Selected Journalism* (New York: Library of America, 2005).
5. "A Note on this Book" precedes the table of contents in McDowell's edition of James Agee, *A Death in the Family.* The "seven-odd pages" cannot be identified since so much material was omitted from the novel, and the word "of" in "Knoxville: Summer of 1915" is subsequently dropped on the page that is the table of contents and when used as the title which heads the section on page 3. "Knoxville: Summer of 1915" first appeared in the *Partisan Review* V (August–September 1938): pp. 22–25. All references to *A Death in the Family* are cited parenthetically and are from McDowell's first edition, the second or later undesignated printing, which contains corrections to the first edition, first printing. For a more focused analysis of the problem of the introduction which combines the material found in various places in this edition, see Michael A. Lofaro, "Idyll or Terror? The True Introduction to Agee's *A Death in the Family,*" in Lofaro, ed., *Agee Agonistes: Essays on the Life, Legend, and Works of James Agee* (Knoville: University of Tennessee Press, 2007), pp. 238–49. See also "Textual Commentary and Notes," this volume, 2.1.
6. It relies as well on other primary materials held by these three groups, especially Agee's plans and notes on the novel located at the University of Texas, Agee's similar notes, unsent letters to his parents, and David McDowell's papers and correspondence at the University of Tennessee, as well as miscellaneous papers and manuscript chapters and fragments owned by the James Agee Trust.
7. The method of selection is outlined in the "General Textual Method" that follows this preface, and the particular evidence for each selection is presented in the "Textual Commentary and Notes" section of this book.
8. The ten and one-third deleted chapters are the introduction, chapters 5, 8, 9, 10, 11, 13, 14, 16, 23, and the middle one-third of chapter 15. Draft versions of chapters 1, 2, and 3 are printed in the McDowell edition.

   The materials italicized by McDowell aptly illustrate the extent of the alterations. The McDowell edition of the novel has three chapters in the first italicized section and three in the second. Since McDowell places these unnumbered italicized chapters after his chapters 7 and 13, I label them chapters 7.1, 7.2, 7.3, and 13.1, 13.2, 13.3 for clarity. His chapter 7.1 contains my chapters 1, 2, 3 (although McDowell incorrectly uses an earlier draft of each); his 7.2 is my chapter 4; his 7.3 is my chapter 7. McDowell's second italicized group of chapters is reorganized as follows: his 13.1 is my chapter 6; his 13.2 is my chapter 15 (McDowell again uses an earlier draft of part of this chapter); his 13.3 is my chapter 12. Other chapters are also presented out of order. For further information on the structure of Agee's manuscript and McDowell's version of the novel, see appendices I and II.

9. Ransom Humanities Research Center, University of Texas, James Agee Collection, Box 5, Folder 1, p. [15]. Subsequent references to these manuscripts will be cited as TX 5.1, [15]. Please note that these manuscript pages are unnumbered in each of the folders and are loose. Therefore the assigned page number(s) are accurate only insofar as no subsequent researcher has changed the order.

10. TN 1A.19, [4-1]. For Agee's complete outline and the apparent draft of his introduction to this large project, see appendix VIII. Both the outline and the introduction give additional general support to the correctness of a chronological approach as well as to the centrality of the figure of the father to the novel in Agee's mind: "This book is chiefly a remembrance of my childhood, and a memorial to my father; and I find that I value my childhood and my father as they were, as well and as exactly as I can remember and represent them, far beyond any transmutation of these matters which I have made, or might ever make, into poetry or fiction." The piece is published in Robert Fitzgerald, ed., *The Collected Short Prose of James Agee,* pp. 125–27; quoted material appears on pp. 125–26.

11. In another quite general outline that expands on "This book," Agee reinforces the chronological nature of the novel after describing its main characters:

> A soft and somewhat precocious child. A middle-class religious mother. A father of country background. Two sets of relatives: hers, middle-class, northern-born, more or less cultivated; his, of deep mountain country.
>
> Begin with complete security and the simple pleasures and sensations.
>
> Develop: the deficiency in the child which puts them at odds; the increasing need of the child for the father's approval.
>
> Interrupt with the father's sudden death. Here either, the whole family is involved, or it is told in terms of the child.
>
> At end: the child is in a sense & degree doomed, to religion & to the middle class. The mother: to religiosity. New strains develop, or are hinted between her & her family. (TX 5.1, [11])

Although general (Agee begins the outline under the heading "*Detachedly:*"), the order of the restored novel does conform well to this progression. For further support of Agee's chronological ordering of the novel, please see appendices V and VI.

12. TN 1A.19, [4-9]. See appendix VI for a transcription of the letter.
13. While there were many reasons for the delay in publishing the results of his initial assignment for *Fortune* magazine that he undertook in the summer of 1936 with Walker Evans, it was also clear that the delays leading to publication of *Let Us Now Praise Famous Men* in 1941 were due more to Agee than to negotiations over the rights of ownership to the material. After the legal and financial matters were settled by the end of 1937 and beginning of 1938, Edward Aswell, his editor at Harper's for the book, "discovered that Agee could not be hurried" and agreed to editorial suggestions with great reluctance and only when in dire need of money. After the ultimate rejection of the manuscript by Harper's, he placed it with Houghton Mifflin. While this arrangement did usher the volume into print in August 1941, the negotiations over artistry were still intriguing, with Agee finally agreeing to tone down the obscenities and his editor, Paul Brooks, stating that they would keep all the language that was legal in Massachusetts. But following up on his earlier ideas that the book be affordable for sharecroppers and cheaply made to echo their hardscrabble existence, Agee told Brooks that he wanted the volume printed on newsprint, a medium that would decay in several years. Brooks and a standard publishing format luckily won out. The longer version of this story is most accessible in Laurence Bergreen, *James Agee: A Life* (New York: E. P. Dutton, 1984). See especially pp. 217, 235–36, and 244.
14. TN 1A.19, [4-8]. See appendix V for a transcription of the letter.
15. TN MS 2730, 4.13, [10].
16. TX 5.1, [11].
17. TN MS 2730, 4.13, [3].
18. Bergreen, *James Agee,* p. 405.
19. Agee's notes reflect the powerful yet unconscious longing for the mountains that he builds into his father's character when he records Jay's "homesickness, which is in part a melancholy for lost life. W[oul]d he realize this at all clearly? I doubt it. For him it is in many ways elegiac, a reflection of lost or changed ambition; with her it is 'living,' taking what comes" (TN MS 2730, 4.13, [1]). Here, Agee again stresses the differing points of views of his parents.
20. TN MS 2730, 4.13, [10].
21. Scott Newton, "David McDowell on James Agee," *Western Humanities Review* 34 (Spring 1980): p. 124. McDowell interestingly says that there were "two versions of the nightmare scene . . . one longer than the other" (123). If so, only one complete version is presently known to survive. Two short fragments printed by Robert Fitzgerald in *The Collected Short Prose of James Agee,* pp. [121]–23, may be what McDowell is recalling. They are recorded in this volume under "Major Manuscript Variants," pp. 426–29.

    McDowell also saw the reverie-like nature of "Knoxville: Summer of 1915" quite differently from the present editor, noting: "there couldn't be a more appropriate tone to begin the novel" (p. 124). Of course, he refers to his edited version rather than Agee's intended text, and the use of "Knoxville: Summer of 1915" is somewhat less jarring due to his deletions from and manipulations of the original manuscript. The original version as published in the *Partisan Review* in 1938 is included here as appendix III. Victor A. Kramer has mentioned the possibility of the true introduction several times, most recently in 1996 in his *Agee: Selected Literary Documents,* pp. 260–61, and David McDowell defended his original rejection of it as late as 1980 in the interview with Newton noted above. For specific external and internal evidence in favor of the restored introduction, see the "Textual Commentary and Notes" for that section.

22. TN MS 2730, 4.13, [2]. Agee also incorporates some of the topics of his first outline.
23. TX 5.1, [10, 11]. See also note 5 above. For the depth of Agee's interest in surrealism and its interest in dreams, see Hugh Davis, "The Making of James Agee," Ph.D. dissertation, University of Tennessee, 2005, pp. 87–120.
24. For a full analysis of the evidence for the use of the nightmare introduction because of the images of the head and the vacant lot, see note 2.1 in "Textual Commentary and Notes." Examining TX 5.2, [31], a page of the correct version (the later text) of the third part of McDowell's chapter 7.1 (87–96), shows that Agee intensified the connection between the nightmare introduction and the novel proper in his revisions in regard to the image of the vacant lot. In the earlier draft that McDowell mistakenly prints, as Jay's mind drifts back to his own childhood home as he sings Rufus to sleep, he envisions "A great cedar and the colors of limestone and clay" (94). Agee's revised version in the restored chapter 3 elaborates this text: "If he was right there he couldn't have seen it any clearer. The big old shaggy cedar was blowing in the sunshine and it looked like it was full of sparks. He could see just how the limestone jutted out of the clay" (TX 5.2, [31]; page 28 this text). It provides a memory of Jay's boyhood home that places more emphasis upon the description of the tree and changes "the colors of limestone and clay" to "how the limestone jutted out of the clay," a far more direct parallel to the limestone outcrop of the vacant lot of the introduction and restored chapter 17. The revised text thus provides a stronger link between the nightmare introduction and the novel and reveals that the vacant lot in Knoxville may well be regarded as a diminished and possibly debased version of Jay's true home in the country.
25. For Agee's interest in Freudian and Jungian psychoanalysis, especially in relation to surrealism, see Davis, "The Making of James Agee," pp. 173–204. See also Bergreen, *James Agee,* pp. 82–83, 152–53, 374.

General Textual Method

This edition presents a "clean" text of Agee's novel by placing all notes, commentary, manuscript variants, and additional materials in the back matter of the volume. The intent is to present *A Death in the Family* as Agee's readers would have seen it without the distractions and interference of any of the scholarly apparatus that documents its restoration. Thus, no footnote or endnote numbers interrupt the text. All references are instead recorded at the rear of the book using page and line number(s). The text is also set in a larger typeface.

Another reason for the "clean" text approach is practical. The editorial material roughly equals the text of the novel in length. If footnotes were used, the amount of Agee's prose that appeared on a given page would be severely limited. Likewise, if chapter endnotes were used, the editorial material could not be well organized and would break the narrative and visual flow of the book. The incorporation of all the editorial material after the novel proper is designed to present the evidence and argument for the restored text in full in an organized and transparent manner for those who wish to examine all or part of the entire process.

By returning to the original manuscripts, this work corrects not only McDowell's structural changes and deletions but also the literally hundreds of errors in the transcription of Agee's notoriously crabbed pencil strokes, which sometimes occupied eight hundred words per standard size page. Agee's handwriting had proved a considerable problem for the original editors. The archives at Tennessee have an undated letter of McDowell to Frank Lorenz in which he writes, "I always had one devil of a time deciphering his script. . . . When I was trying to decipher the manuscript of *A Death in the Family,* there were times when neither Mia Agee [James's wife] nor I could make out certain words, and we had to get a *Time* staffer who had done a lot of typing for Jim to help out."[1] More help was needed. This restoration thus corrects the words that were still misread; incorporates the words, phrases, sentences, paragraphs, and sections that were omitted or missed; and rectifies the editors' occasional refusal to correct mistakes. In the Tennessee archives, for example, there are three letters to David McDowell from Father James H. Flye, Agee's friend and mentor, in regard to filling in a part of the manuscript that Agee had simply marked as a place to insert the last part of vespers. Flye insisted again and again that the passages he originally provided to fill in this section of McDowell's chapter 20 (now chapter 44) from *The Book of Common Prayer* were wrong. Once he saw the context, he knew that the prayers needed to be changed and even supplied McDowell with typed copies.[2] The change has never been made until now. Similarly, this edition rectifies the compounded errors made in subsequent editions of the novel over the years, as copyeditors viewed Agee's renderings of dialect as typographical errors and "corrected" their spellings, and rectifies as well the misreadings in the later published versions of some of the manuscript materials that McDowell chose not to include.[3]

Since Agee was an inveterate reviser, no editor then or now could assume to know his ultimate wishes for the novel. What is clear, however, is that the work can be brought far closer to such an ideal than the McDowell version falsely purports to do. Problems still exist. Despite the near final form of Agee's text, seldom are the chapters in finished final copy. Agee rarely bothered to transcribe his materials over as a copyist, instead preferring to produce that final version when the manuscript was typed. Agee's notes indicate that he intended to divide the work into sections, but since he apparently never arrived at a final decision, the nine major divisions and titles of these sections in the restored edition are those of the present editor. The very few necessary editorial clarifications in the text itself are enclosed by square brackets. Manuscript page number(s) cited in the "Textual Commentary and Notes" and elsewhere are likewise enclosed by square brackets since Agee seldom numbered his pages and, particularly in the larger gatherings of the Texas materials, it is quite easy for researchers inadvertently to change the order of individual pages or groups of pages.

Certain areas in Agee's manuscript do require minor correction. Most deal with simple proofreading and copyediting for matters of consistency in bringing together chapters composed and reworked over a total of nearly twenty years. This edition brings Agee's manuscripts through this normal process. Underlined words are rendered in italics. Agee's minor accidental errors such as irregular punctuation in regard to placing a comma or period outside end quotation marks rather than inside and erratic insertion of commas after question marks are likewise silently emended, since these would have been a normal part of Agee's own editing and that of his eventual copyeditor. In general, Agee's punctuation (or the lack of it) is designed to replicate the flow of speech and is retained. Misspellings, errors in other punctuation, and the omission of punctuation needed to determine meaning are all corrected and noted. Interlinear and marginal additions and revisions to the base text are included as Agee indicated with no special mention. Words or phrases directly written above a similar crossed-out word or section are regarded as replacements indicated by the author. However, no change is made for consistency in capitalization or in the spelling of words rendered in dialect or in punctuation in a character's speech or thoughts. Agee often used capitalization for emphasis and had a keen ear for replicating individual pronunciation and speech patterns. When no difference exists between the formation of his capital and lowercase letter, height and size of the letter are evaluated as well as overall usage. This method solves most cases, but if doubt still exists, Agee is given the benefit of the doubt in correctness, and the problem is noted.

In general, therefore, Agee's chapters are considered fair copy manuscripts and treated as such. His other orthographic quirks occasionally create initial confusion, but these problems do not usually affect meaning and are reconciled using the same method of analyzing size and usage and creating a note if a decision is not clear. Agee, like many writers, would sometimes lift his pencil in the middle of a word, creating a gap and two distinct words, or not lift it and run words together. Also, he would not always lift his pencil after ending a sentence, making a mark that could be either a period or a comma; similar habits affect the distinction between periods and dashes.

In attempting to be as true as reasonably possible to Agee's text, this edition thus makes changes in the manuscript in general only to avoid misreadings or confusion. Emendations strive to be conservative, consistent, grounded in available evidence, and made in accordance with Agee's stated or implied desires. Manuscript substantives in general present no significant difficulty. All editorial changes are recorded in the "Textual Commentary and Notes." These items include, among others, the need for occasional paragraphing other than for dialog and the removal of paragraph breaks, the explanation of Agee's rendering of text that might slightly alter or lead to ambiguity in the reading of the passage in some way, the explanation of the placement of an interlinear or marginal addition that was not clearly indicated by the author, and evidence for the selection, ordering, and division of chapters. End-line hyphens are nearly always created by the typesetting of Agee's manuscripts; any exceptions are noted. The "Textual Commentary and Notes" section also records small variant sections of the text (usually under one hundred words); larger variants are noted under the separate appendix entitled "Major Manuscript Variants." These are significant variants from the final text rather than minor or evolutionary variants (ones that are steps in the process of arriving at the final text). Agee often, for example, immediately redrafted a paragraph in the manuscript. Such a paragraph is deemed evolutionary and not recorded in the notes unless it is a significant variation. Similarly, words, paragraphs, and sections that are clearly crossed out or bracketed for deletion in the manuscript are generally not recorded. The crossing out of words and phrases that does not correctly extend through end punctuation or does so mistakenly is recorded if any ambiguity exists.

Given today's technology, in which the original manuscript itself could be rendered through digital imaging and placed online, it seems excessive to attempt to re-create all aspects of the manuscript in this text. Any additional notes called for concerning the major and minor variants included in this edition follow the texts of the variants themselves as a matter of convenience to the reader.

The process of restoring *A Death in the Family* is also documented in the "Textual Commentary and Notes" on a step-by-step basis and records the primary textual and physical evidence and the secondary sources such as correspondence used to determine the restored text when the author's intentions are not completely clear. Agee's notes on his novel often provide evidence or clues to the original order of the chapters and are cited when used. Agee, however, produced several outlines for his work, in total or in part, and did so at various times. Each of these tend to be exploratory and include more concepts and ideas than he eventually chose to treat. Thus his notes do not yield a final chapter outline for the novel, but do render a sound general sense of their intended progression.

Three areas of editorial information are presented separately to avoid further enlarging the "Textual Commentary and Notes" section and appear after "Major Manuscript Variants." These are: "Marginal Notes" (often Agee's directions, musings, or questions to himself), "Word Choice Where No Preference Is Indicated" (a list of Agee's undecided choices in an appendix that notes the alternative word or words that Agee recorded interlineally without indicating a final selection and the guidelines and reasons for the present editorial choices), and "Paragraphing" (a list of the paragraph breaks added to Agee's text, often for switches in dialog and speakers). Please see the headnotes of each of these sections for further elaboration of editorial methodology.

Other aids to the reader are included as appendices. Appendix I provides the instructions on "How to Read the Corrected McDowell Edition of *A Death in the Family* from This Text and a Chart of Substantive Corrections to the Library of America Edition of *A Death in the Family*" for those who wish to read McDowell's edition in either format. Appendix II gives "A Structural Comparison of the Restored and the McDowell Editions" to chart the differences in a more concise way than is possible in the "Textual Commentary and Notes." Appendix III contains Agee's "Knoxville: Summer of 1915" as it originally appeared in the *Partisan Review* in 1938, both to allow the complete reading of the McDowell edition and to facilitate comparison between it and the present introduction to the novel. Appendices IV through VIII are additional manuscript documents, four by Agee and one by his mother, that bear upon *A Death in the Family* and shed light upon his intentions and methods.

I wish to thank the libraries of the University of Tennessee and the Ransom Humanities Research Center of the University of Texas and the James Agee Trust for their permissions, which allow the use of all the Agee materials in this volume, and to thank their professional staffs for their kindness and untiring efforts on my behalf.

My work has greatly benefited from the time provided by the John C. Hodges Better English Fund of the Department of English and the financial support of the Senior Research and Creative Achievement Award of the College of Arts and Sciences, the Humanities Initiative, and the Office of Research, all of the University of Tennessee. It has likewise benefited from the encouragement and information provided by friends and colleagues over the years, of whom I here mention but a few. Deedee Agee, Paul Sprecher, Jackson R. Bryer, Hugh Davis, Emory Elliott, David Madden, Angie Maxwell, Thomas L. McHaney, John Seelye, Linda Wagner-Martin, John Wranovics, D. Strong Wyman, and John P. Zomchick all either made this volume possible or far better than it would have been. Any shortcomings or errors, however, are certainly my own. My wife Nancy and children Ellen and Christopher have been long in the storm of Agee, but always managed to muster an enthusiasm for it which energized me and my labors as a researcher and editor and made them truly enjoyable.

Notes

1. TN 1A.3.5.
2. The original letter is dated January 10, 1958. See TN 1A.2.23. The two subsequent letters are dated July 9, 1958 (TN 1A.2.23), and July 28, 1959 (TN 1A.2.24).
3. The true introduction to the novel that McDowell deleted serves as a case in point. Although Victor A. Kramer's transcription of the manuscript, which he entitles "Dream Sequence" (*Agee: Selected Literary Documents,* pp. 262–72), is generally accurate, especially when compared to the transcriptions David McDowell used for the chapters included in the novel, it still contains significant errors. A sample of the needed corrections of the manuscript (TX 5.2, [45–53]) is given below. None of the necessary corrections of punctuation or spacing is listed in this sample since they are recorded in the notes for this edition. Each entry below begins with the page and line number of Kramer's transcription, separated by a period. Thus a note concerning a word or phrase on page 262, line 4, of the text of his volume would be listed as 262.4. Line numbering does not count headings, titles, or spaces. Next, the correct reading of the manuscript is listed followed by the symbol "]" and then Kramer's transcription of the manuscript. 267.9–16 is a note on a necessary deletion from Kramer's version.

262.4	boiled] bore
262.8	iron and of] iron of
262.25	fun] just
262.29	relaxing] releasing
263.29	men] ones
263.35	conviction] convictions
266.33	harsh] hush
267.4	the] that
267.9–16	] The paragraph "But when he . . . with every second." is a draft of the section rewritten immediately below it on lines 17–25 (as was often Agee's method) and should be deleted.
267.11	clean] clear
267.28	to;] to do
268.7	two, and] two. And
268.24	just as in his] just as his
268.26	now were cut and bleeding] now were bleeding
269.29	striated] streaked
269.29	grainy] graying
269.32	must] might
270.1	gentle] jostle
270.9	curl up] curling
270.10	into] with
270.12–13	gently shoring] gently, sharing
270.19	organ] again
270.25	length] last when
270.38	son] Son
271.11	can] could
271.32	could] would
272.9	now] more
272.11	but it would] but would

While further correction of already printed transcriptions, whether those of McDowell or Kramer, is not the main purpose of this text since it returns to the original manuscripts as its source of authority, some additional information on such errors can be found in the "Textual Commentary and Notes" to this volume.

A James Agee Chronology

1909	James Rufus Agee is born November 27 to Laura Tyler Agee and Hugh James (Jay) Agee in Knoxville, Tennessee.
1912	Sister Emma born on June 22.
1916	Agee's father is killed in an automobile accident on Thursday, May 18. Jay Agee was 38 years old at the time of his death.
1919–24	Agee attends St. Andrew's School, near Sewanee, Tennessee, where he begins a lifelong friendship with Father James H. Flye.
1924	Agee returns to Knoxville and attends Knoxville High School. His mother marries Father Erskine Wright, who is part of the staff at St. Andrew's School, and moves with him to Rockland, Maine.
1925	After traveling with Father Flye in England and France during the summer, Agee enrolls in Phillips Exeter Academy in Exeter, New Hampshire.
1927	Agee is elected editor of the *Exeter Monthly* and president of the literary Lantern Club.
1928–32	Agee attends Harvard University.
1929	Agee spends the summer working as a migrant farm laborer in Nebraska and Kansas.
1930	Agee is introduced to the salon of Dr. Arthur Percy Saunders, whose home in Clinton, New York, is a center of culture, science, and art. Agee begins courting Dr. Saunders's daughter, Olivia.
1931	Agee is elected president of the *Harvard Advocate.*
1932	On the recommendation of Dwight Macdonald, Agee begins work as a reporter at *Fortune* magazine.
1933	Agee marries Olivia (Via) Saunders, January 28. Agee returns to Knoxville to do research and write about the Tennessee Valley Authority for *Fortune.*
1934	*Permit Me Voyage* is published in the Yale Series of Younger Poets with an introduction by Archibald MacLeish.

1935–36 On leave from *Fortune* from November 1935 to May 1936, Agee lives with Via in Anna Maria, off the west coast of Florida, and also visits New Orleans and St. Andrew's. He writes poetry and completes "Knoxville: Summer of 1915," eventually published in *Partisan Review* in 1938. Agee again returns to Knoxville to do more research and write about the Tennessee Valley Authority.

1936 On assignment for *Fortune*'s "Life and Circumstances" series, Agee travels with photographer Walker Evans to Mills Hill, Alabama, where he lives with a family of sharecroppers for eight weeks from June to August. *Fortune* rejects the article Agee produces on the experience.

1937 On assignment from *Fortune,* Agee and Walker Evans investigate Havana's tourist industry, as well as the steamship lines that connect Cuba to the United States; together with Via, the three spend six days on a cruise ship doing research for an article titled "Six Days at Sea," which is published in September. Agee begins an affair with Alma Mailman, a friend of the Saunders family.

1938 After his divorce from Via in November, Agee marries Alma on December 6. "Knoxville: Summer of 1915" is published in the *Partisan Review* V (August–September).

1939 Harper and Brothers rejects "Cotton Tenants: Three Families," Agee's revision and expansion of the *Fortune* sharecropper article. Agee begins reviewing books for *Time* magazine. Houghton Mifflin accepts "Three Tenant Families," now called *Let Us Now Praise Famous Men.* On assignment from *Fortune,* Agee writes a piece about Brooklyn. Ultimately the article is rejected, and Agee stops working for the magazine.

1940 Agee begins an affair with Mia Fritsch, a researcher at *Fortune.* Alma gives birth to his first son, Joel, on March 20. The annual *New Directions in Prose and Poetry* pairs excerpts from photo-texts by Wright Morris's *The Inhabitants* with excerpts from Walker Evans and James Agee's *Let Us Now Praise Famous Men* in an article titled "The American Scene."

1941 Houghton Mifflin publishes *Let Us Now Praise Famous Men.* Agee begins reviewing films for *Time.* Alma leaves Agee and goes with Helen Levitt to Mexico, taking Joel with her.

1942 In December Agee begins reviewing films for the *Nation,* and at *Time* Agee shifts from reviewing books to film criticism.

1943 Agee writes but does not publish "America! Look at Your Shame!"

1944 On July 30 Mia gives birth prematurely to a son, who dies soon afterward. Agee and Mia marry in late August. *Time* sends Agee to Hollywood.

1945 Agee begins writing features for *Time,* including pieces about the atomic bomb, the U.S. presence in Europe, and the death of Roosevelt; films *In the Street* with Janice Loeb and Helen Levitt.

1946 Mia gives birth to Julia Teresa (Deedee), Agee's first daughter, November 7.

1947 Agee begins, though never finishes, work on a film script, "Scientists and Tramps," about nuclear war, to feature Charlie Chaplin.

1947–48 Agee writes a substantial part of *A Death in the Family,* which is published posthumously.

1948 American composer Samuel Barber's *Knoxville: Summer of 1915,* for soprano and orchestra with text by Agee, debuts in Boston. Agee leaves *Time* and the *Nation* and writes his first full-length screenplay, an adaptation of Stephen Crane's "The Blue Hotel," under contract to Huntington Hartford.

1949 *The Quiet One,* a documentary film by Helen Levitt, for which Agee writes the narration, opens; it is named Best Film at the Venice Film Festival. His "Comedy's Greatest Era" appears in *Life* magazine (September 3).

1950 Agee's second daughter, Andrea Maria, is born on May 15. Agee goes to California to write the screenplay for John Huston's *The African Queen.* "Undirectable Director," Agee's portrait of Huston, appears in *Life* (September 18).

1951 On January 15 Agee suffers his first major heart attack and is hospitalized. Huston finishes the screenplay for *The African Queen;* the screenplay is nominated for an Academy Award. Houghton Mifflin publishes *The Morning Watch,* Agee's novella based on experiences at St. Andrew's. A sixty-page treatment focusing on the Civil War and set in Middle Tennessee, titled *Bloodline,* is submitted to Twentieth Century–Fox in September but is never filmed.

1952 On April 22 Agee signs a contract with the Ford Foundation to write a five-part series—running for two-and-a-half hours—on Abraham Lincoln for *Omnibus.* The script is completed in October; the program begins airing on November 16 and is broadcast every other week through February 8, 1953. Agee adapts another Stephen Crane story, "The Bride Comes to Yellow Sky," for

	Huntington Hartford, eventually incorporated as one half of *Face to Face,* directed by John Brahm and Bertaigne Windust.
1953	Agee writes the screenplay for *Noa Noa,* based on Paul Gauguin's diary.
1954	Agee meets Tamara Comstock on May 1, beginning an affair which would last through August. Their time together coincides with a period of great activity in Agee's writing of *A Death in the Family.* Agee writes the screenplay for *The Night of the Hunter,* directed by Charles Laughton. John Alexander, his second son, is born, September 6. Agee begins, but never completes, work on a script about the Tanglewood school for young musicians in collaboration with *New York Times* music critic Howard Taubman and director Fred Zinnemann. Agee offers ideas and lyrics for the Lillian Hellman–Leonard Bernstein musical *Candide.*
1955	Agee is commissioned to write a thirty-minute orientation film about colonial Williamsburg. On May 16 Agee dies of a heart attack in a New York City taxi. He is buried in Hillsdale, New York.
1956	The James Agee Trust is founded.
1957	*A Death in the Family,* edited by David McDowell, is published by McDowell, Oblensky.
1958	*A Death in the Family* wins the Pulitzer Prize for Fiction. McDowell, Oblensky publishes the first volume of *Agee on Film,* a collection of reviews and essays.
1960	McDowell, Oblensky publishes the second volume of *Agee on Film,* a collection of screenplays. Houghton Mifflin reissues *Let Us Now Praise Famous Men* with a new preface by Walker Evans and additional photographs. *All the Way Home,* Tad Mosel's stage adaptation of *A Death in the Family,* opens on Broadway; it later wins the Pulitzer Prize for Drama and a Drama Critics Award.
1962	George Braziller publishes *The Letters of James Agee to Father Flye.*
1963	The screen version of *All the Way Home,* starring Jean Simmons and Robert Preston, premieres in Knoxville.
1965	*A Way of Seeing,* a book of photographs by Helen Levitt with an essay by Agee, is published by Viking.
1968	Houghton Mifflin publishes *The Collected Poems of James Agee* and *The Collected Short Prose of James Agee,* both edited by Robert Fitzgerald.
1972	Agee Week is held at St. Andrews School, Mounteagle, Tennessee, in October.

1974 *Remembering James Agee,* edited by David Madden, is published by Louisiana State University Press.

1979 The James Agee Film Project produces *Agee,* a film by Ross Spears.

1984 Laurence Bergreen's *James Agee: A Life* is published.

1985 University of Tennessee Press publishes *James Agee: Selected Journalism,* edited by Paul Ashdown.

1988 Houghton Mifflin reissues *Let Us Now Praise Famous Men* with an introduction by John Hersey.

1992 *James Agee: Reconsiderations,* edited by Michael A. Lofaro, is published by University of Tennessee Press.

1996 *Agee: Selected Literary Documents,* edited by Victor A. Kramer, is published by Whitson Publishing Company.

1997 The second edition of *Remembering James Agee,* edited by David Madden and Jeffrey J. Folks, is published by Louisiana State University Press.

2003 A draft of Agee's *The Night of the Hunter* is discovered by Paul Sprecher.

2005 University of Tennessee Press publishes *James Agee Rediscovered: The Journals of* Let Us Now Praise Famous Men *and Other New Manuscripts,* edited by Michael A. Lofaro and Hugh Davis. James Agee's *Brooklyn Is Southeast of the Island: Travel Notes* is published by Fordham University Press with a preface by Jonathan Lethem. The Library of America publishes a two-volume set of *James Agee:* Let Us Now Praise Famous Men, A Death in the Family, *and Shorter Fiction;* and *James Agee: Film Writing and Selected Journalism.*

A Death in the Family

"towards the middle of the twentieth century"

Introduction

It was about noon, the lunch hour for clerks and for men in overalls, and for that hour the city, crowded as it was, was bemused and slack; a softly rattling, almost Sunday stillness. The sun boiled straight down without shadows. It was so hot that the air was a gunmetal haze, smelling of soft coal, live steam, and exhausts. In the shapeless part of town where he walked, there were more open yards than buildings, and the yards were full of old iron and of used and derelict cars; above them, the heat, like curling, just visible flame. Many were sitting, eating, in weak little edges of shade; nobody was walking who could help it, and those who walked went slowly.

He had thought that it was one of the streets of Chattanooga between the two depots, but now he began to realize that he was back home, in Knoxville, for he could see that the broken street thickened, far ahead of him, into the busiest blocks of Gay Street. He was both happy to be home, and wary, for he liked the Southerners who had never gone North but he knew if they knew his mind they would hate him. Two blocks ahead, a crowd was doing some terrible piece of violence, and the pit of his stomach went cold, yet now he felt really at home. He kept on walking towards it at his same pace, the loose stride inherited from the mountains, but a little more briskly than Southerners walked. He was pretty sure that the violence would be over, and the crowd drifted, by the time he got there; if it isn't, he thought, and they turn on me, that's all right too. Not fun exactly, but the way it was meant to be. He took care not to slow down, and not to hurry, for it was not his business to try to alter fate; and sure enough, by the time he was half a block away, the crowd was relaxing like a fist undoing, and the hunched men in shirtsleeves and in undershirts were moving away, and now he could see the man they had attacked, naked across the sidewalk, and even before he came up to him he knew that he was dead. He knew too that this man had stood in the street with furious eyes and had dared to shout into the noon hour, for everyone to hear, the truths and self-deceptions and the passionate beliefs and commitments which must certainly and always mean great danger to him and sooner or later, now at last, death. For just as he had begun to suspect, this was indeed John the Baptist. It was the first time he had seen him face to face, but he knew him.

The whole time, everywhere, was bursting with woe and fear and injustice and with this kind of passion and cruelty, and he was no longer of any side, no longer capable of any sufficient conviction except in the heroism, and meanness of soul, and blind hopelessness, of the whole gnashing machinery: one who could truly love liberty and honor must know that all those who tried to advance either, destroyed both. His most hopeful belief had been the belief for which John had died, and echoes of that hope and devotion returned to him now, quite hopelessly, as echoes of religious faith sometimes haunted him. He stood and looked down at the killed man and smiled, remembering, and cried quietly inside, dry crying, which hardly touched him. The old loudmouth, he thought with affection; the old ranter. He knew by heart the bawling cheapness, and the fierce-eyed frenzy, part real, part put-on, and he felt as much respect for it as dislike. It was from *way* back. Way back in the country, and in time, and in the human race. A stubborn, intrepid, archaic, insanely bigoted man, begging for trouble, begging for violence and for death until finally they gave it to him. A hero, not a neutral. Neutrals can die too, he reminded himself; caught in the crossfire from all the convinced ones; they are despised by all the convinced men, and by each other, and by themselves; and sooner or later that will happen. You have no more choice about neutrality, he told himself, than about partisanship. The only possible faithfulness is faithfulness to the best you can understand at the time.

Nevertheless he could only think ill of himself for his inevitable but convenient lack of conviction, as he looked down at the dead man; and this perhaps gave him more courage than he might otherwise have had. For even as he looked down he could see out of the ends of his eyes that the brutal and light-triggered nucleus of the crowd still lingered, not far away, and watched him, and even if he had not seen, he would have felt their eyes on him, and he knew very well the qualities which are uniquely to be feared in the eyes of the men of his part of the country: such still eyes, watching, with that terrifying whiteness increasing in them. The sons of bitches, he said to himself. The damned scum. The Common Man. It isn't enough to set on a man and beat him to death in the street (however obnoxiously he insulted them into martyring him); you strip him naked and you leave him where he lies as you wouldn't even leave a dead dog. No sense of honor towards a brave enemy. No sense of honor towards the dead. O sure I know, he reflected quickly; his crowd is no better than yours; and he thought of Mussolini and his girl, hung up like hogs at the filling station, and the falsely libertarian faces, goggling, he would have loved to have spit in. Nearly all, of every side, are just so many apes and cowards and vindictive swine, he thought; my own kind included; but on every side too there is devotion and the absolute honor that is in absolute courage: and this is how they recognize it and honor it. What they loathe and fear most of all. They beg so for the contempt of brave men that as a matter of fact they beg the brave crazy ones to beg them to kill them. To show one flicker of sympathy, he realized, is quite possibly just as dangerous as ranting. Hogs. Fools. Cowardly bullying bastards.

He straightened up and looked coolly around into one pair of eyes and then the next and at all of them, and they were all watching him and waiting for what he might do, and he did not lower his eyes or even blink, dry as his eyes were getting, and neither did they. He looked down again at the dead man and his heart spread and he loved the brave old bellower misled and misleading. Come on, John, he whispered, smiling again. We're going to find you a better place to rest than this. We're going to find you a place where you can lie out in the open, but in honor and in state. Laid out decently as a dead man ought to be. Where everyone who goes by can know you for a dead man and a hero. He squatted down and put his arms under the shoulders and under the knees and picked him up and carried him like a baby, but with the killed head lolling deep and heavy. The place you want to be, he whispered, as he started walking; and instantly he knew where that place was, and how to get there, though it was so many years now since he had been in Knoxville. He was pleased that he could remember the way so well. It was a certain corner, a certain vacant lot; he could already see it vividly in his mind's eye. That was where John wanted to lie for a while before burial and that was where he would bring him.

He crossed the street at his own pace through the traffic, and he looked into the eyes of those who lingered with cool arrogance. He could feel their eyes on him after he had passed and, knowing their kind, he knew that now quite possibly somebody would throw a rock or a tire-iron to jolt him or bring him down, or even that some ex-football star might clip him. He was braced for it, and he knew that he could not get rid of the dread of violence and of pain, but he was quietly happy to realize, all the same, how little he really cared what would happen to him; and he began looking forward to how much damage he might be able to do them before they should make that impossible. From the hips on up his back felt cold and tight, waiting. He came near the corner he should turn into, to take the corpse where it belonged; he knew the eyes were all still on him, but still nothing happened. Again he took care neither to slow down nor to speed up, thinking, it's not my business to tamper with it, and realizing, somewhat less clearly, that to keep the same pace was also the safest thing to do. A few steps from the corner he was tempted to keep on straight down the same street, to show them his contempt, but again he thought, my only business is John, it isn't my business to meddle; and turned west into the new street; and as he turned, realized, that thus to vanish might also be the thing which would bring them into action, or might be the safest thing; and kept on, taking care not to meddle. After a few seconds he could feel their eyes again, but after a few seconds more he became sure that they were only standing there; nobody was following, and nobody was going to throw anything or do anything. He was tempted to look back because he was sure that would insult and challenge them, or make them believe he was afraid; and because he was curious to satisfy and increase his contempt for them by seeing them gangling there, but he knew that it would be beneath the dignity of his action which, after all, needed all the dignity he could retain for it by now: for evidently there had been no danger after all, or at best it only required a show of courage and contempt to make them put their tails between their legs, or possibly the mere sight of respect for the dead, and for courage, had awakened what little capacity for shame and for honor might perhaps be left in even the meanest of spirit; anyhow he was certainly no hero in what he had done and was doing; very likely his neutrality stuck out all over him; possibly even the corpse they had made was a shield behind which he was hiding.

All right, he thought. All right. Let it be. All it is at best is a simple act of veneration for the dead who died bravely, a simple act of contempt for those who killed him and stripped him and let him lie where he fell. And he continued to look coolly into the eyes which met his, eyes of strangers to the action and to the meaning of what he was doing. There was clearly no further danger. His concern now was guardianship. To guard this violated man and to guard the meaning of both of them. He was contemptuous of all curiosity, and conjecture, and failure to understand, which he saw in these new eyes, and then he was contemptuous of his own contempt for how should they know, better than they happened to know, and it was, of course, an unlikely sight, even preposterous, possibly shocking. He began to feel almost kindly towards their innocence; and suddenly he became aware that in all this while since he had begun to carry him, he had been thinking only of himself and of the others, not of John at all. He was filled with shame. He found that the body had sagged clumsily during his carelessness, and he readjusted his hold, to carry it more decently, and looked down at the ruined body and down across his elbow at the head which hung so heavily, so deeply sunken into this death only a few minutes old, that he could see only the arched throat and the plowlike underside of the jaw and the chin through the pointed beard which stood straight upward like a spike. He shook his own head as he walked, continuing to gaze at that derangement of throat and jaw, and a certain darkness and stillness clouded his heart, yet chiefly he felt a kind of amused and reverent tenderness and whispered repeatedly to the yawing head, "Poor old boy. Poor old boy."

He was watching his burden so constantly now that he gave no heed to where he was going but he was sure he knew the way; without even seeing, he could see along his right the dying exquisite houses of the middle nineteenth century, furnished rooms, doctors' offices, and along his left a cold unhappy stillness, the harsh gray stone of the church in which he had been confirmed; on the feast of the conversion of St. Paul, he reflected idly. Then more of those intricate houses on both sides, an occasional face of limestone tracked with sooty marble; a few shade trees, few people, the silence of parked cars, the silent heat: God how it all came back. And now the second corner and the turn to the left and there was the corner he had in mind, exactly as he had remembered and foreseen it, though it must be twenty years; and as he came nearer that empty corner he knew that it was not the right one after all, and in the same instant he knew the one which was right. He was about equally amused by his stupidity and by his instant and now unquestionable knowledge of the somewhat similar corner he had really meant. Yes. Back down the street and across the other viaduct, not Clinch, Asylum;

on the far side: and again he could see it clearly, and all the streets between. He laid John down gently and in order, and took a breather. He had become quite heavy, the last block or so.

But when he leaned down low to take him up in his arms again, the corpse stank so that he had immediately to straighten up into the clean air. He stood there for a few seconds and tried to brace himself up to what he had to do, but his stomach kept knocking, and his mouth flooded saliva; the very hands with which he had just touched the body, felt nausea. The whole body had softened and was streaked with brown; he could see the brown streaks extend and widen even while he watched, and the stench became still more rotten with every second. To carry him now, decently and kindly, as he ought to be carried, was just more than he could do. For a little while he could not quite bring himself to do what he had to; then abruptly, turning his face away and holding his breath, he reached down with his right hand and caught the sharp bones of both ankles between his knuckles as if he were handling a baby, and turned his back, and began slowly to drag the body along the pavement like a sled. He tried to drag it respectfully, but one backward glance was enough to convince him that in what he was doing, there could be no respect. Again he wondered whether he could possibly carry him; but even as it was, the smell was as much as he could endure. It's all I can do under the circumstances, that's all, he thought. It's a hell of a way to treat anyone, but it'll have to do. And he set himself the modest goals of dragging the body gently, so as to hurt and bump it as little as possible, and of keeping his face clear of any show of disgust or even of doing anything out of the ordinary; and in the effort to look sober and stolid, he began to feel sober and stolid.

The town had certainly changed. It wasn't as he remembered it from childhood, nor did he like its looks as well as his memories of it; nor was it as he remembered it from the middle thirties; he didn't like its looks even as well as that; it was a blend of the two, and for every old sight which touched him and made him happy and lonely, there was something new which he disliked. Even the heat and sunlight of the weather was different, it was the weather of a bigger, worse, more proud and foolish city: ignored, as if it were possible to ignore, and complained about, as if proper legislation might improve it; and there was something else altered and odd about it. The light of the noon sun was as white as snow on the pavement and looking down, he saw that in fact it was snow and that his feet were numb with cold, and with good reason, for they were bare; and not only his feet; he was as naked as the man he dragged. Well I guess that's as it should be, he thought, accepting the new turn of fate with calm amusement; and again he became aware of the people in the streets, meeting their eyes with calm, and with a challenge behind the calm; but they took no special notice. He came down the little hill across from the Asylum and turned left into Asylum Avenue and he could see where the viaduct angled ahead, just as in his earliest memories of it, and now he was on the viaduct; and the pain in his feet, which by now were cut and bleeding as well as frozen, gave him back a sense of courage, difficulty, and dignity, so that he felt gravely cheerful, and knew there was a smile on his face. There were quite a few people along the viaduct and he was intensely interested in them because they were so uninterested in what they saw. It wasn't as if they did not see at all; without exception they saw this naked man dragging this naked corpse through the thin snow; they looked, with some interest; they even stopped in their tracks and looked after. But their interest was so strangely out of ratio to the thing they were looking at. It was about as if he were fully dressed, he realized, and was carrying something slightly outlandish, unwrapped, say, one of those fancy bridge lamps with a lot of beaded fringe, or maybe a watercloset bowl: something which might slightly amuse and interest you to see carried in the open through the streets, but you would subdue your interest and amusement out of a sort of amused sympathy for the man who had to carry it. Or of course, the times being what they were, very likely this weird mildness of curiosity was a measure of the commonness, by now, of just such things, mob murders, corpses of heroes dragged through the streets, the callousness, the anesthesia, which must have developed during the plagues of the Middle Ages. But these were all such well-meaning, comfortable, nominally safe and civilized people, and that was what made their casualness so amazing, and so amusing. He became more and more fond of them as they passed, and more and more amused by them and by the whole matter and by the world they all lived in, so touched, and so amused, by his sense of the absolute corruption of spirit and by his knowledge of doom, that suddenly he heard his soul exclaim in silence within him, delighted, sad, and in some way proud, "This could only happen in Alexandria!" But instantly he was aware that it was better even than that: for it was happening in Knoxville, in East Tennessee, in the middle of a day towards the middle of the twentieth century, and if this could only happen in Alexandria, then this was Alexandria now.

Without pausing in his walking he looked back to see how John was holding up: the snow had helped. There were blue streaks now as big as the brown, and they meant that the flesh was frozen, and would keep at least for a little while. The only trouble was the head. Through some kind of interplay between freezing and corruption, much of the head had become a kind of transparent gristle, yellowish and rubbery. He could see the thin dirty snow and the thin blue ice straight through it and, through the ice, the yellow and brown sand colors of the pavement, and all these colors of snow and ice and pavement were striated by the movement of the dragging into straight grainy streaks, and the trail the body had left in the snow was blue and brown. The head was not lasting at all well, it was only a question of time. He looked ahead to see how far they must still go, not far, he could remember, and sure enough he could see it, with a flinching deep within him of tenderness and joy and melancholy and great loneliness, he could see it, the very corner, the same outcrop of wrinkled limestone, like a lump of dirty laundry, the same tree even, and the tree had not even grown an inch. So shabby and sad; it had been waiting there all this time, and it had never changed, not a bit. So patient, and aloofly welcoming. Well. So you came back. His cold heart lifted in love and he walked more quickly, so quickly that a thud, striking him like a light blow in the stomach, just reminded him that he had neglected to gentle the body from the curb just opposite its corner; the head had struck hard, and looking back he could see, with sickness and grief, that now it hung to the body only by translucent shreds: and even as he looked, not yet having presence of mind to stop his dragging, the last shred broke and the head rolled clear, in a half circle, to a wobbling stop, cradling quietly in the middle of the street, so that with a groan of pity and shame he dropped the stony ankles and hurried to it and squatted to pick it up and saw it curl up swiftly upon itself like a jellyfish, an armadillo, into a shape roughly like a catcher's mitt, and twitch away from his reaching hand. He could not endure to chase and corner and trap it as if it were some frightened animal but gently shoring its escape with both hands, trying by the gentleness of his hands, without speaking, to assure it that it need not fear him, slid both hands beneath it and lifted its cold and gritty weight as if it were a Grail. By its withdrawal into itself it was no longer a head. It was a heavy rondure of tough jelly and of hair and beard and the hair sprang wild and radiant from his center where, meeting his eye, was one organ, so disfigured, that it was impossible to know whether it was a bloody glaring eye, or a mutely roaring mouth.

Waking, he felt none of the wise, sad amusement which had pervaded so much of his dream. His whole substance had become only horror and the coldest sorrow, so heavy and so still that when at length he was able to reflect, it was only to wonder, without caring, whether he could ever lift himself up from the bed or move again. Then slowly he began to realize a few of the things which, during the dream, had wholly evaded his notice. The church was the church of St. John the Baptist. The Asylum was the Asylum for the Deaf and Dumb. John: St. John: had not been killed by beheading; the head had come off just short of the corner, and it was he who was responsible. The corner was where he used to sit with his father and it was there of all times and places that he had known best that his father loved him, and had known not only that he loved him but that he was glad of his existence and that he thought well of him. And his father had come out of the wilderness, and it was there that the son had best known his homesickness for the wilderness.

So I suppose I'm Christ, he thought with self-loathing.

But which was John?

I've betrayed my father, he realized. Or myself. Or both of us.

How?

He thought of his father in his grave, over seven hundred miles away, and how many years. If he could only talk with him. But he knew that even if they could talk, they could never come at it between them, what the betrayal was.

He thought of the dream. He had no doubt of the terrifying magnitude of the dream, or that its meaning was the meaning he sought, but he doubted so thoroughly that the true meaning of any dream can ever be known, that he suspected that every effort to interpret a dream serves only to obscure and to distort what little of the true meaning may ultimately suggest itself.

He thought of all he could remember about his father and about his own direct relations with him. He could see nothing which even faintly illuminated his darkness, nor did he expect ever to see anything; yet if he could be sure of anything except betrayal and horror, he could be sure that that was where the dream indicated that he should go. He should go back into those years. As far as he could remember; and everything he could remember; nothing he had learned or done since; nothing except (so well as he could remember) what his father had been as he had known him, and what he had been as he had known himself, and what he had seen with his own eyes, and supposed with his own mind.

The more he thought of it the surer he became that there was nothing he could hope to understand out of it which was not already obvious to him. All the same, he could make the journey, as he had dreamed the dream, for its own sake, without trying to interpret; and if the journey was made with sufficient courage and care, very likely that of itself would be as near the answer as he could ever hope to get.

My father, he thought, not quite whispering the words. "My father," he whispered. And for a few moments it was as if his father were there in the room, not visible but clearly visible to the imagination, and his presence much more than imagination, a silent but almost unendurable power and aliveness: and he was not as the son could remember him, but was as he would have become by that time, by that morning of awakening from the dream: a strong, brave, sad old man, who also knew the dream, and no more knew or hoped ever to know its meaning, than the son. And even if they could have talked, there was not much they could have said to each other; but that was no great matter, for at last all was well. All his life, as he had begun during recent years to realize, had been shaped above all else by his father and by his father's absence. All his life he had fiercely loathed authority and had as fiercely loved courage and mastery. In every older man, constantly, he had looked for a father, or fought him, or both. And here he was, and all was well at last, and even though he was now rapidly fading, and most likely would never return, that was all right too. It might never be fully understood, but it would be all right from now on. From now on it was going to be all right. Thank you for coming, he said in silence. Goodbye. God keep you. Or whatever it is that keeps you.

His father did not say goodbye, anymore than the other time, but he knew of his brief smile, much as it had always been, and then he was gone.

He was alone again now, but that was no harm, for in a way in which he had been alone for so many years, he knew that he would never be alone again.

"This little boy you live in"
Perceptions c. 1911–1912

Chapter 1

He woke in darkness and knew only that he was wide awake and that he was breathing; then, leaning his head to the left, he saw the window. Curtains towered almost from the floor to the ceiling, tall and cloven. Transparent, manifold, waving along their inward edges like the valves of a sea creature, they moved on the air of the open window like breathing.

Where they were touched by the carbon glare of the street lamp they were as white as sugar. The exuberant flowers and tendrils which had been wrought into them by machinery showed even sharper white where the light touched; elsewhere they were black in the limpid cloth.

The light put the shadows of leaves against the curtains, which moved on the moving curtains and on the glass behind them, and on the bare glass between.

Where the light touched the leaves they seemed to burn, a bitter green. Elsewhere they were darkest gray and darker. Unnatural light or heavy darkness dwelt beneath each of these thousands of closely assembled leaves. Without touching each other all these leaves were stirred as the whole tree moved silently in its sleep.

Opposite his window was another. Behind this open window too there were curtains which moved, and the scattered shadows of leaves moved against them. Beyond these curtains and the bare glass between, the room was as dark as his own.

He heard the summer night.

The air vibrated like a fading bell with the last tired screaming of locusts. Couplings clashed and conjoined; a switch-engine breathed heavily. An auto engine bore beyond the edge of hearing the furious expletives of its incompetence. Hoofs broke along the hollow street with the lackadaisical rhythms of an exhausted clog-dancer; iron tires grinced continuously after. Along the sidewalks, with incisive heels and leathery shuffle, young men and women advanced, retreated.

A rocking chair betrayed reiterant strain, as of a defective lung. Like a single note from a stupendous guitar, the chain of a porch swing twanged.

Nearby, intimate to some damp inch of the grass between these homes, a cricket greeped, and was answered as if by his echo.

Humbled under the triumphant cries of children, which tore the whole darkness like streams of fire, the voices of men and women on their porches rubbed cheerfully against each other, and in the room next his own, like the laboring upward of laden windlasses and the calmest pouring out of fresh water, he heard in illegible antiphony the voices of the men and women he knew best. They groaned, rewarded; lifted, and spilled out: and watching the window, listening at the heart of the proud slowly quieting bell of darkness, he lay in perfect peace, breathing, without words,

Gentle gentle dark.

My darkness. Do you listen? O are you hollowed all one taking ear?

My darkness. Do you watch me? O are you rounded all one guardian eye?

O gentlest dark. Gentlest, gentlest night. My darkness. My dear darkness.

Under your shelter all things come and go.

Children are violent and valiant, they run and they shout like the winners of impossible victories, but before long now, even like me, they will be brought in to their sleep.

Those who are grown great talk quietly in their confidence and are skillful at all times to serve and to protect, but before long now they too, before long, even like me, they will be taken in and put to bed.

Soon come those hours when no one wakes. Even the locusts, even the crickets, shall be as still as frozen brooks.

In your great sheltering.

I hear my father. I need never fear.

I hear my mother. I shall never be lonely, or in want for love.

When I am hungry it is they who give me food: when I am sad it is they who fill me with comfort.

When I am dismayed it is they who make the weak ground sure beneath my soul: it is in them that I put my trust.

When I am sick it is they who send for the doctor: when I am well and happy it is in their eyes that I know I am loved: it is towards the shining of their smiles that I lift up my heart and in their laughter I know my delight.

I hear my father and my mother and they are my giants, my King and my Queen, and beside them there are no others so wise or worthy or honorable or brave or beautiful in this world.

O surely I need never fear: Surely fear can never enter me: nor ever shall I lack for loving kindness.

And those also who talk with them in that room beneath whose door the light lies like a guardian slave, like a bar of gold; my witty uncle, and my girlish aunt: I have yet to know them well, but they and my father and my mother are all fond of each other, and I like them, and I know that they like me.

I hear the easy changings of their four voices in their talking and I hear their pleased laughter.

But before long now they too will leave and the house will be almost silent after they have gone; and before long the darkness, for all its patience, will take my father and my mother by the hand and bring them, just as I have been brought, to bed and to sleep.

You come to us once each day and never a day rears up in its brightness but you stand behind it: you are upon us, you overwhelm us, all of each night. It is you who excuse from work, who bring parted families, and friends together, and who establish quiet and beauty for their gathering; and people for a little while are calm and free, and all at ease together: but before long, yes before long, all are brought down still as mountains

Under your sheltering darkness, your wide sheltering:

And all through that stillness you walk as if none but you had ever breathed, had ever dreamed, had ever been.

My darkness, are you lonesome?

Only listen, and I will listen to you.
Only watch me, and I will look into your eyes.
Only be my friend, and I will be your friend.
You need never fear; or ever be lonely; or in want for love.
Tell me your secrets: you can trust me.
Come near. Come very near.

Chapter 2

Darkness came near indeed. He could feel its breath like the breath of an iceberg. It buried its terrible eye so deeply against the eye of the child's own soul that the child knew that he would never move or breathe again.

Darkness whispered:

Had ever breathed. Had ever dreamed. Had ever been.

And even before the whispering continued, the child knew.

Darkness whispered:

Why yes. Of course. This little boy you live in: he isn't you at all. He thinks he is. But you Know better.

Do you know who you are? Do you know who you really are? Are you, at all?

What is it that you almost believe you can almost remember?

You will never remember it.

(In the corner, watching him constantly, a creature grew larger and larger.)

Darkness whispered:

It's nothing. It's only me.

(It grew larger and larger.)

Darkness whispered:

This man whose voice you hear, you think he is your father. How can you ever be afraid?

(Under the washstand, carefully, something moved.)

Listen to the woman who thinks you are her child.

(Beneath his prostrate head infinity opened.)

They know too. They only pretend they don't.

(He could hear how the man laughed at him; in what amusement the woman agreed.)

Darkness purred with delight and whispered:

Why, now, what's the matter?

Only a minute ago I was your friend.

Only a minute ago you wanted to know my secrets.

The curtain sighed as powers unspeakable passed though it and darkness, smiling, leaned ever more intimately inward upon him, laid open the huge, ragged mouth—

"*Ahhhhhhh*—"

Why child, what frightens you so?

Come near. Come very near.

"*Ohhhhhh*—"

Must you be naughty? It would vex me terribly to have to force you.

Be sensible. You know you can't get away. You don't even want to get away.

But with that the child was torn into two creatures, of whom one withdrew and watched, speechless and cold, and the other cried out for his father.

The shadows lay where they belonged, and he lay shaken in his tears. He watched the window, and waited.

Still the cricket chiseled; the voices persisted, placid as bran.

Behind his head, in that tall shadow his eyes could never reach, who could dare dream what abode its moment?

The voices chafed, untroubled: grumble and babble.

He cried out again more fiercely for his father.

There seemed a hollowing in the voices as if they crossed a high trestle. He knew they heard him.

Serenely the curtain dilated, serenely failed.

The shadows lay where they belonged but strain as he might he could not be sure what lay in the darkest of them.

The voices relaxed into their original heartlessness.

He turned his head as suddenly as he could and stared through the bars at the head of the bed. Whatever had been there, it had dodged: it stayed always at the back of his head, forever behind and beyond his hope of seeing.

He saw the wash-basin and it was only itself: but its eye was wicked ice.

Even the sugar curtains were evil, a senseless fumbling mouth, and the leaves, wavering, stifled their tree like an infestation.

Deadly, the opposite window returned his staring.

The cricket cherished what avaricious secret? patiently sculptured what effigy of dread?

The voices buzzed, pleased and oblivious as locusts. They cared nothing for him.

He screamed for his father.

Chapter 3

And now the voices changed. He could hear his father draw a deep breath and lock it against his palate, then let it out strong and harshly through his nose in annoyance. He heard how the chair creaked when his father stood up and he heard sounds from his mother which meant that she was made uneasy by his annoyance, almost frightened and defending and reproving, and that she would see to him, Jay. His uncle and his aunt made small polite noises and took no further part in the discussion and he heard his father's voice, less abrupt and unkind than the snort and the way he had gotten from his chair, but still annoyed; his father said: "Naw, he hollered for me. I'll see to him," and he could hear his tired, mastering approach. He was uneasy now, for he was no longer deeply frightened; he was glad he could show tears.

The room broke open full of gold and his father stooped through the door and shut it quietly, and quietly came to the bed. His leaning face was impatient but not unkind.

"'Ts wrong thyew," he asked, in his deepest voice.

"Daddy," the child said thinly. He sucked the phlegm from his nose and swallowed it.

The father's voice raised a little. "Why what's the trouble with my little boy," he said, and he got out his handkerchief and squatted by the bed. "Wuzza *matter!* What's he *crine* about!" The harsh cloth smelled of tobacco. "Blow," he said. "You know your mama don't like you to swaller that stuff." He felt the strong hand under his head and a sob overtook him as he blew.

"Why what's wrong," his father exclaimed; and now his voice was entirely kind. He lifted the child's head a little higher and looked carefully into his eyes; the child felt the strength of the other hand, covering his whole chest, patting gently. He tried for another sob, but the moment had departed.

"Bad dream?" the father asked; with his fingertips he removed tobacco crumbs from the damp face.

He shook his head, no.

"Then what's the trouble?"

He looked mournfully at his father. It had been something about him.

"Feared—fraid of the dark?"

He nodded. He could feel tears in his eyes.

"Nooooooo," his father soothed, pronouncing it like *do.* "You're a *big* boy now. *Big* boys don't git skeered of a little ole dark. *Big* boys don't cry."

He kept on looking at his father. I'm not so big, he thought.

"Where's the dark that skeered you? Over here?" With his head he indicated the darkest corner, where the thing had kept growing and growing. The child nodded. The father strode straight over there and with a beautiful striping and crackling noise struck a match on the seat of his pants.

Nothing there.

"Nothing there. Here?" He indicated the bureau. The child said "mm-hm" and began to suck at his lower lip. He watched with more idle interest while his father struck another match, just as admirably, and held it under the bureau and then under the washstand.

Nothing there.

"Nothing there."

There either.

"Here either. Ouch, God damn it." He shook out the match and threw it on the floor. "Anyplace else?"

The child turned and looked through the head of the bed. His father squatted with a new match. "Why there's poor ole Jackie!" he said; and sure enough there he was, deep in the corner.

He blew lint off the cloth dog and held it out. "You want Jackie?"

He shook his head.

"You don't want pore little ole Jackie? So lonesome? Layin' back there in the corner all this time?"

"Huh-uh."

"Gittn too big for Jackie?"

He nodded, but he was not sure that his father would believe him.

"Then you're gittn too big to cry."

He was puzzled, and felt alone.

"Pore ole Jackie."

Poor little ole Jackie. So lonesome.

He reached up and took him and as he comforted the little dog he began faintly to remember a towering multitude of firetipped candles, and a bristling smell of green, and a gaily colored and much larger dog, over which he puzzled, and his father's huge face, smiling, explaining, "it's a dog. A little dog;" while his father too remembered, how he had picked out the dog with such pleasure and had given it too soon, and how it was already too late. Lord how the time goes, he thought. No time at all, he'll be fishing.

Comforting the dog brought him comfort, and a deep yawn, taking him by surprise, was half out of him before he could try to hide it. He glanced anxiously at his father.

"Gittn sleepy, huh," his father said. It wasn't even a question.

He shook his head.

"Time you did. Time we all got to sleep."

He shook his head.

"Not skeered anymore are you?"

He considered lying, but he shook his head.

"Booger man's all gone, huh? All skeered away."

"Mm-hm."

"Now git on to sleep then, son," his father said. He almost never called him son; when he did, they both always felt shy and happy. He dawdled by the bed. He knew the child very much wanted him to stay and now it occurred to him that he could have lied and said he was still scared, as easy as not. He put his hand on his son's forehead. "You just don't want to be by yourself," he said tenderly. "Just like little ole Jackie. Just hate to be left all by your lonesome."

The child lay still.

"Tell you what," his father said. "I'll sing you one song. Then you be a good boy and git on to sleep. How about it." He pressed his forehead upward against the hard strong hand and nodded.

"What'll we sing?" his father asked.

"Froggy would a wooin go"; that was even longer than Jesse James.

"Hooo-*wee!*" his father exclaimed. "At's a *long* one. At's a *long old song*. You won't even stay awake that long, will you."

He nodded.

"Ah-right," his father said, and the child took a fresh hold on Jackie and settled back looking up at him. He sang very deep and just above a whisper, *Frog he would a-wooin go uh-hoo-oo-oo-oo!* and all about the clothes the frog rigged up in to go courting, and about the difficulties of the courtship and its ultimate success, and what several of the neighbors said and who the preacher would be who would marry them and what he said about the match, uh-hoo, and finally, what will the weddn supper be uh-hoo, three times over as in every verse, and then the answer once, catfish balls and sassafras tea, uh-hoo-oo-oo-oo, while he gazed into the wall and the child gazed up into the eyes which did not look at him and into the dark singing face in the dark. Every couple of verses or so the father glanced down but the child's eyes were as darkly and resolutely open at the end of the long song as at the beginning, though it was beginning to be an effort for him.

He was amused, and he was more pleased than impatient. Once he got started singing, he always loved to sing. There were ever so many of the old songs he knew, country songs and darky songs, and he liked them the best of all, but he also liked some of the popular songs; and although he would have been embarrassed and perhaps sore if he had been made conscious of it, he also enjoyed the sound of his own voice. "Ain't you asleep *yet?*" he exclaimed; but the child, hearing the amusement and satisfaction under the mock impatience, felt that now there was no danger of his leaving, and shook his head quite frankly.

"Sing Gallon," he said, for he liked the amusement he knew would come into his father's face, although he could never understand it. The amusement came, and his father struck up the song, still more quietly because such a fast, sassy tune might wake you up. He was amused because his son always mistook the words *gal an'* for *gallon,* and because he knew his wife and her relatives were not entirely amused by his amusement. He knew their feeling was that he was not a man to take the word *gallon* as a joke, and it always tickled him, as much as it riled him, to remember how uneasy they looked when he laughed about it—as if their eyes were going on tiptoes and their feet were cold. Not that liquor had been much of any problem, for a long time now. He was turning all this over idly in his mind while he sang it, and now he always sang it the child's way: "I got a gallon an a sugarbabe too my honey, my baby," and next time "my honey, my sweet thang," and next time, "I got a gallon an a sugarbabe too, Gal don't love me but my sugarbabe do dis mawnin, dis evenin, so soon": and then the two other verses he could remember; "when they kills a chicken she saves me the wing," three times over, then, "think I'm workin, ain't doin a thing; and every night about a ha' pas' eight, ye find me waitn at the white folks' gate dis mawnin, dis evenin, so soon."

The child still stared up at him; because there was so little light or it might be because he was so sleepy, his eyes looked very dark, although the father knew they were nearly as light as his own. He took his hand away and blew the moisture cool and dry on the child's forehead, and smoothed his hair away, and put his hand back. "What in the world you doin Google Eyes," he sang very slowly, while he and the child looked at each other. The child began to feel as if his eyes were very large and round as he listened, then even larger and even rounder so that they stuck out like the froggy would a wooin go uh-hoo, and by the time his father sang "You're the best there is and I need you in my biz, where did you get them great big Google Eyes," his eyes slowly closed, sprang open, almost in alarm, and closed again.

He waited. As stealthily as one who would not disturb a butterfly, he took his hand away. The child's eyes opened and he felt as if he had been caught at something. He touched the child's forehead again. "Go to sleep honey," he said. "Go on to sleep now." The child continued to look up at him and a tune came unexpectedly into his head. Lifting his voice almost to tenor he sang, just audibly, one of the slow, lonesome tunes he liked best: "*Ohhh,* I *hear* themm, *car*-wheells, a-*rum*blinn," with the unaccented syllables all on one note, a slow dreamy hum, and the short accented syllables on notes near to it: "*Annn',* they're *mighty, near* at, *hannnd, I, hear* that, *train* come, a-*rum*blin, *juss'* a-*rum*blin, *through,* the *lannn,"* and then the refrain, "Git on boa'd, little chilluns," three times over, "There's *room-forr, menn-*y *an', mo'."*

To the child it looked as if his father were gazing off into a great distance, and looking up into these eyes which looked so far away, he looked far away too: "Ohhh, I look uh way daown yonder," (so far you could hardly see at all), "Annn', uh wha' d'you, reckon I see," (I reckon so, what do you *reckon* I see? He knew what now, and it made the word *reckon* peaceful and shining, mysterious and happy); "A band uh, shinin, Angels" (shining like a brass band in the sunlight, shining like train windows in the night, far off across the country field but coming nearer, coming), "A-, comin, after, me," and then, hundreds, thousands of little children, and he was one of them, he was many of them, the angels reaching down their bright hands from the bright windows to help them, "Git on bode, little chilluns," he was a chilluns, "git on bode" meant get on board, climb up onto the train and sit down and take it easy, it was darky talk like Victoria, "Git on bode": and even nicer, "There's room for many an mo." He did not know just what "mo" meant but it was something to do with "many" and he liked it so he had never needed to ask. It always made him feel comfortable and warm and sleepy. His eyes closed.

The father did not look down; he kept looking straight on into the wall in silence and after a while he sang a slow, round wheeling song, at once dolorous and strangely cheerful, which was used by railroad men with heavy hammers when they were driving spikes: "Ohh *ev*-ry *time* the *sun* goes *down,* Dey's a *dol*-luh *saved* for *Bet*sy *Brown:* Sugah-Babe."

He looked down. He was almost sure now that the child was asleep. So much more quietly that he could scarcely hear himself, and that the sounds stole across the child's near-sleep like a band of shining angels, he went on: "They's a good ole sayin, as you all know, That you can't track a rabbit when they ain't no snow: Sugah-Babe."

Here again he waited, with his hand listening against the child, for he was so fond of the last verse that he always hated to have to come to it and be finished with it; but it was already in his mind, and it became so attractive to sing that finally he could not resist it any longer: "Oh it tain't agonna rain, an tain't agonn a snow": he felt coldness along his spine and saw the glistening as a great cedar moved, and tears came into his eyes: he went on, and it was a resolute and faithful statement from his heart: "But the sun's agoan ah shine, an the win's agoan a blow: Sugah-Babe."

If he was right there he couldn't have seen it any clearer. The big old shaggy cedar was blowing in the sunshine and it looked like it was full of sparks. He could see just how the limestone jutted out of the clay. He could even smell woodsmoke. He could see how the square logs of the wall lay on top of each other side by side, ever so sleepy-looking and stout and still in the shaky light of the fire and the dark brown light of the turned-down lamp. And there was his mother's face. It was young and round and it leaned over close above him.

He could feel her ridgy hand on his forehead, pushing back the hair and just stroking his forehead, easy, and she was talking real low, *don't you fret Jim, now don't you fret.* She was saying *git on to sleep now. They ain't nothing to be afeared about.* She was saying *Maw's right here son. Paw's right here. Now git on back to sleep now. Don't you fret,* and she was smiling.

She had a quilt pinned around her shoulders and it smelled of smoke, hickory, and oak, and pine.

Any house that didn't have that smoky smell, it just didn't smell like home.

He could see the chimney up against the end of the place and the fireplace inside, both at the same time. Some of the chimney was stone and rest was made of woven saplings and clay.

Her face was real young but it was already full of lines and gouges. Her hand was the gentlest there was but it felt raspy.

He could see the fire lazing in the stone fireplace and kind of cussing to itself under its breath, the way green wood does, and the sparks crawling along the soot at the back like a starry night.

Just sixteen when I was born.

He could see the humps of bread under the hot ashes. That's how bread tastes the best. Just blow the ashes off of it and eat it so hot it burns you.

He could see strings of peppers hanging from a rafter, and strings of corn. He could see the marks of the axe in the oak logs of the wall and a place where the clay chinking had worked out and a towsack had been prodded in.

Just a girl.

Don't you fret.

Wasn't hardly no time since she was just a baby.

Lord God and before his time, before he was ever dreamt of in this world, she must have laid like that under her own mother's hand or her daddy's, gentling her forehead. *Don't you fret.* And when they were younguns they looked up and saw faces he had never seen that were still young then and dead and gone now long ago.

And so on back with them too. A way on back through the mountains. A way on back through the years. Took you deeper on back than you could ever study.

Now don't you fret.

He looked around the dark room, and down at his son, and back into the wall. He shook his head once, very gravely.

Long ways.

Can't never get back.

Oh sure you can go back home. Good to go home and see the old folks.

All the places you used to know. The ones that stayed.

But if you ever leave it so much grows up between, you can't ever honestly get all the way back home in your life.

And what's the good of it.

All I aimed to make of myself. Left my people and sweat blood to get.

What's the good.

All that happens, you don't ever get what you started after, and you can't ever get back where you started.

Thought I hated it. Couldn't get away soon enough to suit me.

I sure did find out different.

Just one way.

You make you a home of your own and you get you a youngun, boy of your own, even a girl. And ever so often there's something they do, makes you remember. Even just some way they look or you know how they feel.

Then all of a sudden you know just exactly how it feels to be that young and ignorant. Look at the logs in a wall and don't even know they're logs or it's a wall.

Because you remember then.

How your folks felt to see you too, and you put them in mind of when they were younguns.

Because now you feel like they did then.

You even begin to know what it's going to feel like to get old.

Have grandchildren.

Die.

You know what it feels like to be so little and puny you can't do for yourself and it's pretty near the same as if you were your own self again, as little and far back as you can remember.

He looked down again at his son.

He could feel the breath of absolute coldness touch him, as if something stood just behind him. Sometimes it got all the way inside him and then sometimes for days on end he wasn't any good for anything. Just pitch-dark and ice cold straight through, and heavy as lead. So heavy he couldn't hardly say a word, or pick up one foot and put it in front of the other.

Times like that he just didn't want to be alive.

He didn't think it would get a hold on him like that, this time. He was feeling too good. He could stave it off all right, he knew he could.

But he sure could use a couple of slugs.

Imaginations of sneaking and deceit, and of brutal openness and anger and pride, immediately became clear to him, and he could taste in the lining of his mouth and feel it plumb down into his belly and right out his arms to the ends of his fingers, how good that would be. His jaws and then his whole body flinched.

Like hell I will, he said to himself with iron amusement. Like all hell.

He felt strong enough in body and in spirit to do anything.

In this excellent knowledge of his strength, firmly ignoring the insidious coldness and trying to recapture the moment of remembrance and the deep sad contentment it had brought him, he was staring into the dark wall almost without thinking when the door opened cautiously behind him, startling him. He was caught by a spasm of fury and by self-reproach.

She knew the fury in the darkness like an animal in a cave. "Jay," she called softly. "Isn't he asleep *yet?*"

"*Oh* yeah," he said. Standing up, his joints hurt.

"What was the matter with him?"

"Fraid of the dark, I reckon."

"He's all right? Before he went to sleep I mean?"

"Sure, *he's* all right."

"Hugh and Paula had to go," she whispered, tiptoeing over. She leaned past him and smoothed the sheet. "They said tell you goodnight." She put one hand under the child's head and lifted it while her husband, frowning, vigorously shook his head. "It's all right Jay he's *sound* asleep." With her other hand she smoothed the pillow.

"What you mean had to go?"

"Jay you were in there for *ever!* They waited. What on earth kept you?"

Lie to her. Couldn't get him to sleep.

"Reckon I was just studyin."

"For goodness sake what *about?*" she asked too quickly. Don't ask! Well and why in the world *shouldn't* I!

"Studyin, that's all," he said in the cold dark voice she had known he would use. She felt as if he had slammed a door in her face.

Jay I'm just simply not going to stand for this any longer, she wanted to say. But that had been often and uselessly said before. "Well let's get to bed," she said. "It's high time. You hungry?"

"Huhuh. No thanks Laura," he corrected himself.

"Well I'm going up then. Be sure and hook both doors."

He looked at her. He wanted to say, Dear I can do that without you telling me every time, but he couldn't feel quite friendly or amused enough, yet. He nodded. "I'll be right on up," he said.

Before long the lights were turned off downstairs, and before long the light upstairs was turned off too. Before much longer there were few lights left in all the city except those which burned at the corners of streets, and the country lay blind.

And all through that stillness you walk as if none but you had ever breathed, had ever dreamed, had ever been.

Chapter 4

His mother sang to him too. Her voice was soft and shining gray like her dear gray eyes. She sang, "Sleep baby sleep, Thy father watches the sheep," and he could see his father sitting on a hillside looking at a lot of white sheep in the darkness but why; "thy mother shakes the dreamland tree and down fall little dreams on thee," and he could see the little dreams floating down easily like huge flakes of snow at night and covering him in the darkness like babes in the wood with wide quiet leaves of softly shining light. She sang, "Go tell Aunt Rhoda," three times over, and then, "the old gray goose is dead," and then "She's worth the saving," three times over, and then "to make a featherbed," and then again, three times over, "Go tell Aunt Rhoda," and then again "the old gray goose is dead." He did not know what "She's worth the saving" meant, and it was one of the things he always took care not to ask, because although it sounded so gentle he was also sure that somewhere inside it there was something terrible to be afraid of exactly because it sounded so gentle, and he would become very much afraid instead of only a little afraid if he asked and learned what it meant. All the more, because when his mother sang this song he could always see Aunt Rhoda, and she wasn't at all like anybody else, she was like her name, mysterious and gray. She was very tall, as tall even as his father. She stood near a well on a big flat open place of hard bare ground, quite a way from where he saw her from, and even so he could see how very tall she was. Far back behind her there were dark trees without any leaves. She just stood there very quiet and straight as if she were waiting to be gone and told that the old gray goose is dead. She wore a long gray dress with a skirt that touched the ground and her hands were hidden in the great falling folds of the skirt. He could never see her face because it was too darkly within the shadow of the sunbonnet she wore, but from within that shadow he could always just discern the shining of her eyes, and they were looking straight at him, not angrily, and not kindly either, just looking and waiting. "She's worth the saving."

She sang, "Swing low, sweet cherryut," and that was the best song of all. "Comin for to care me home." So glad and willing and peaceful. A cherryut was a sort of a beautiful wagon because home was too far to walk, a long long way, but of course it was like a cherry, too, only he could not understand how a beautiful wagon and a cherry could be like each other, but they were. Home was a long long way. Much too far to walk and you can only come home when God sends the cherryut for you. And it would "care" him home. He did not even try to imagine what home was like except of course it was even nicer than home where he lived, but he always knew it was home. He always especially knew how happy he was in his own home when he heard about the other home because then he always felt he knew exactly where he was and that made it good to be exactly there.

His father loved to sing this song too and sometimes in the dark, on the porch, or lying out all together on a quilt in the back yard, they would sing it together. They wouldn't be talking, just listening to the little sounds, and looking up at the stars, and feeling ever so quiet and happy and sad at the same time, and all of a sudden in a very quiet voice his father sang out, almost as if he were singing to himself, "Swing low," and by the time he got to "cherryut" his mother was singing too, just as softly, and then their voices went up higher singing "comin for to carry me home," and looking up between their heads from where he lay he looked right into the stars, so near and friendly, with a great drift of dust like flour across the tip of the sky. His father sang it differently from his mother, more like Victoria. When she sang the second "Swing" she just sang "*swing low,*" on two notes, in a simple, clear voice, but he sang "*swing*" on two notes, sliding from the note above to the one she sang, and blurring his voice and making it more forceful on the first note, and springing it, dark and blurry, off the *l* in *low,* with a rhythm that made his son's body stir. And when he came to *tell all my friends I'm comin too,* he started four full notes above her, and slowed up a little, and sort of dreamed his way down among several extra notes she didn't sing, and some of these notes were a kind of blur, like hitting a black note and the next white one at the same time on Granma's piano, and he didn't sing *I'm comin'* but *I'm uh-comin,* and there too, and all through his singing, there was that excitement of rhythm that often made him close his eyes and move his head in contentment. But his mother sang the same thing clear and true in a sweet, calm voice, fewer and simpler notes. Sometimes she would try to sing it his way and he would try to sing it hers, but they always went back pretty soon to their own way, though he always felt they each liked the other's way very much. He liked both ways very much and best of all when they sang together and he was there with them, touching them on both sides, and even better, from when they sang *I look over Jordan what do I see,* for then it was so good to look up into the stars, and then they sang *A band of angels comin after me* and it seemed as if all the stars came at him like a great shining brass band so far away you weren't quite sure you could even hear the music but so near he could almost see their faces and they all but leaned down deep enough to pick him up in their arms. *Come for to care me home.*

They sang it a little slower towards the end as if they hated to come to the finish of it and then they didn't talk at all, and after a minute their hands took each other across their child, and things were even quieter, so that all the little noises of the city night raised up again in the quietness, locusts, crickets, footsteps, hoofs, faint voices, the shufflings of a switch-engine, and after a while, while they all looked into the sky, his father, in a strange and distant, sighing voice, said "Well . . . ," and after a little his mother answered, with a quiet and strange happy sadness, "Yes . . . ," and they waited a good little bit longer, not saying anything, and then his father took him up into his arms and his mother rolled up the quilt and they went in and he was put to bed.

He came right up to her hip bone; not so high on his father.

She wore dresses, his father wore pants. Pants were what he wore too, but they were short and soft. His father's were hard and rough and went right down to his shoes. The cloths of his mother's clothes were soft like his.

His father wore hard coats too and a hard celluloid collar and sometimes a vest with hard buttons. Mostly his clothes were scratchy except the striped shirts and the shirts with little dots or diamonds on them. But not as scratchy as his cheeks.

His cheeks were warm and cool at the same time and they scratched a little even when he had just shaved. It always tickled, on his cheek or still more on his neck, and sometimes hurt a little, too, but it was always fun because he was so strong.

He smelled like dry grass, leather and tobacco, and sometimes a different smell, full of great energy and a fierce kind of fun, but also a feeling that things might go wrong. He knew what that was because he overheard them arguing. Whiskey.

For awhile he had a big mustache and then he took it off and his mother said, "Oh Jay you look just *worlds* nicer, you have such a *nice* mouth, it's a *shame* to hide it." After awhile he grew the mustache again. It made him look much older, taller and stronger, and when he frowned the mustache frowned too and it was very frightening. Then he took it off again and she was pleased all over again and after that he kept it off.

She called it mstash´. He called it must´ash and sometimes mush´tash but then he was joking, talking like a darky. He liked to talk darky talk and the way he sang was like a darky too, only when he sang he wasn't joking.

His neck was dark tan and there were deep crisscross cracks all over the back of it.

His hands were so big he could cover him from the chin to his bath-thing. There were big blue strings under the skin on the backs of them. Veins, those were. Black hair even on the backs of the fingers and ever so much hair on the wrists; big veins in his arms, like ropes.

Chapter 5

It felt good to eat until there wasn't anything to eat. Then it felt bad.

It felt good to be warm and wet. Cold and wet felt bad.

It felt good to kick, and to suck his hands and feet. But eating was best of all until there wasn't any more.

She was the one who was so good to him. There there there she would say when he cried.

The other one liked him to smile and laugh but when he cried he sometimes got mad.

She was soft and warm in front and so was her neck. He nearly always saw her very close, leaning over him. Her eyes were soft and bright and often she was smiling.

Their faces were as big as skies and their hands were almost as big as he was. Their voices were different from each other and they smelled different.

The one with the deep voice was daddy. Smoke came out of his nose.

The one with the gentle voice was mama.

Sometimes daddy held him way up to the top of the room and laughed.

Mama was the one who washed him with the slippery soap.

Some of the time a clear light came into the room through wide glass holes. Other times these holes were black and then they were covered and the light was in the room, warm and yellow.

Sometimes he was out in the clear light and he could feel it move on his face and hands and feet. Things waved in the air. People and other things went back and forth and made sounds. Sometimes some of the people stopped and leaned over and put their faces close to his. They said things and smiled. Some said ahhh-*booo!* Some said kitchy kitchy kitchy and poked fingers at him.

People would bend over and say things and poke fingers at him and then suddenly they would go away.

People would pick him up and bounce him and laugh when he laughed and then suddenly they would put him down and go away.

He did not like them to go away.

Sometimes if he cried they came back. Sometimes not.

Sometimes daddy smiled and then it was nice. Sometimes he was mad and then it wasn't. When he said god damn it mama didn't like it. She said *Jay!*

That was her name for daddy.

His name for her was Laura.

They had other names for each other. Sweetheart. Darling. Dear.

Grampa had glass over his eyes and red and white hair all over his face and not much hair on top.

Granma had glass over her eyes too and she was deaf.

"Talk very loud Rufus, Granma doesn't hear very well."

"Talk right into her *trumpet* Rufus."

Ear trumpet. It sounded funny. The end she put to her ear was sticky and sour.

"*Rufus!* No-*no!*"

Why.

The legs of the furniture were dark brown with knobs on.

Some of the floor was hard and dark brown, some of it was soft and red and brown and blue and yellow.

The clothes of the people came down to their feet. Such big feet.

The things that waved in the clear light were leaves. They were on trees.

On the ground it was grass. Prickly and cool, a nice smell.

And flowers.

"Not by the *heads,* Rufus!"

"Not by the *roots,* Rufus!"

"Just leave them alone until you know how to pick them."

"How's he ever going to learn without trying."

The colors on the soft floor were flowers too.
Carpet.

When they said you they meant him. When they said me they meant themselves. And I. And we.

But when he said you, meaning himself, that wasn't it. And if he said me, meaning the other, or I, or we, that wasn't right either. They laughed sometimes but it was because he didn't say it right.

When he cried they said well well well *what's* the *matter!*

But then after while when he cried they said Rufus is a *big* boy now, *he* doesn't cry, though there he was, crying. Don't be a crybaby, they said.

The white in the glass was milk.
Mush. Soft and white and warm and sometimes molasses.

"*Eat* Rufus!"
"Don't dawdle."
"Eat your supper."

"Say please."
"Please."
"Say if you please."
"If you please."
"Say thank you."
"Thank you."
"Say thank you very much."
"Thank you very much."
"Don't talk with your mouth full Rufus."
"Don't sing at the table."
"Keep your mouth *closed* when you chew."
"When you make a noise like that say ex*cuse* me."
"Ex*cuse* me."
"Say may I leave the table please?"
"May I leave the table please?"

"Certainly Rufus."
"Now say thank you."
"Thank you."

After a while he could take the glass and suck it against his face so that it stuck there, under his chin and over his eyes, so he could look through it. If daddy laughed, mama said it isn't one bit funny Jay. If he dropped it and daddy got mad, she said Jay! even if she was mad herself.

He could put his spoon in his mouth and bend the handle up so that the other end touched his forehead and then flip the spoon out of his mouth with a popping sound and make it all go straight up so that that end was over his head.

They were the same about that.

If you can't eat decently Rufus you'll just have to eat by yourself.

But mama sometimes puffed out her cheek and hit it with a spoon and then that cheek went flat and the other cheek puffed out, and then she would hit that side with the spoon and the other side would puff out.

And daddy would take his nose in his hand and cover his mouth with the other hand and then twist his nose to one side with an awful cracking noise and then to the other side with the same noise.

Don't Jay, she would say. It sounds simply awful!

But no matter how hard he twisted his nose he could not make the awful sound.

"There now you see? Stop it Rufus. This *minute.* You'll *spoil* your nose."

"But daddy does it."

"Well daddy shouldn't. And *you mustn't,* no matter what daddy does."

"Aw Laura, don't be silly."

"I don't care. It's a horrid trick and I won't have him ruin his nose."

Sometimes daddy leaned over and spit neatly into the fireplace. When there was a fire it made a fine strong noise.

Once he leaned over and spit there and his mama said "why Rufus!" and then much more seriously, "Jay!"

Daddy turned dark red.

"A *fine* example," she said.

Then he looked mad and as if he would say something but he didn't say anything.

"I'm sorry Jay but *really!*" she said after a minute.

"Just let up on it Laura," he said.

"I just meant I was very sorry I embarrassed you dear. I mean specially in front of . . ." her voice trailed off and she nodded towards him.

"All right. Don't be sorry, I deserved it. But just let it go will you?"

"Of course Jay," she said very quietly. After that the air between them was stiff and they stayed quiet. Then after a while daddy looked at her and said "I'm sorry Laura." "So am I dear," she said, and they both smiled warmly.

It was then he realized that daddy never did it except when they were alone. So he took care that they were alone the next time he did it and his daddy let out the most surprising laugh and suddenly mussed up his hair but, still smiling, shook his head and said "uh-uh. Your mama's right," he said. "You mustn't do that. Me neither."

"It's all right up in the country," he said. "But in town people don't like it and we live in town."

He said "me neither" but sometimes he still did it all the same.

But only if they were by themselves.

"Hard to teach an old dog new tricks," he said.

Grampa called him Rambunctious. He liked to tickle.

Sometimes he talked in a sour voice about brats.

That meant him.

Grampa didn't like brats. "I can just about stand children," he said, "but deliver me from brats."

But he liked him. That's why he tickled.

Granma never said brats. She always smiled merrily when he tried to talk to her, even when she didn't hear what he said. She liked to rub her hand up and down his back and then slap it several times, but not like a spanking. While she was slapping she would cry, "Nice strong little back!" Then she would hug him.

They lived in the other house. It had a little glass house in front and there were flowers there. That was the green house.

Inside there was a green room. Things there were green.

They had a soft gray cat called Oliver. He had green eyes and if you scratched him very gently on the back, near the tail, he closed these eyes very slowly and stuck up his tail and made a happy sound. Purring.

He liked to walk into the room on his knuckles with his tail standing up and floating. Then Grampa would say "hahh, little cat" and slap his knee, and Oliver would jump up and stretch out.

He liked Grampa best of all and Grampa liked him better than any of the others did.

"He's independent," Grampa would say. "Not like a damned dog: excuse me for kicking your foot with my ribs, kick me again. He can take us or leave us alone. If he don't want to be petted he just turns on his heel and walks off. Kiss my ass."

"Papa!" mama whispered sharply, and the way she shook her head he knew she was talking about him.

Kiss my ass.

Then Oliver died. They all talked about it. He was very old, he had been with them since mama was just a girl. He didn't even get sick. He just curled up in his chair in the Green Room and went to sleep. The same as every night, and next morning there he was. He still looked just the same. Just as if he was asleep.

"He just knew when his time had come," daddy said.

Mama nodded gravely.

"So quiet," Grampa said. "No yowling. No deathbed scenes. Just plain tired. Just made up his mind he'd had a bellyful and went out just the way he'd walk out of a room."

They all nodded, even Rufus. They felt very sad and they knew Grampa felt saddest of all.

"Hope I have such luck," Grampa said.

"Me too," daddy said. "That's the way to go."

"You betcha," Grampa said.

"Let's not talk any more about it," mama said.

Grampa took a picture of him, just the way he lay there in his chair. It showed the pads on two of his paws and his tail lay over his paws, almost touching his neat gray nose. Then he made him a little box down at the shop and wrapped him in a pillowcase and buried him back in the garden.

"Dead," mother said, "meant when you're very old and tired and so God lets you go to sleep forever and ever, like Oliver."

"Does that mean if I should die before I wake?"

"Why n—why. Why yes Rufus but little *children* don't. It's just . . . that it *might* happen. That's why we all say that prayer.

"You see all of us die some day when God is ready for us to, so we all say that prayer, I pray the Lord my soul to take. But most of us don't till we're very old, and si—tired. So you see it isn't anything to *worry* about dear. You see?"

He nodded because she clearly wanted him to nod.

Worry about it?

He always liked to go to Grampa and Granma's because there were so many things there.

There was a big bay window with ferns and chairs and a table. There were white cloths pinned on the chairs and when he took the pins out the cloths fell down.

"*Don't* Rufus!"

"*Why* do you do that!"

"To see the cloth fall down."

"Well why on earth do you suppose Granma pins them *up?*"

?

"To *keep* them up, of *course!*"

All the same they looked nice, crumpling down.

"Now you just leave them *alone!*"

There was a picture with lions walking. It was dark and they padded along in the moonbeams. There were big stone stairs with weeds growing on them. There were big broken statues.

That was because it was a very very old city and nobody lived there any more. Everybody had gone away, long long ago. It was ruins. And that was why the lions could walk there, right in the street.

There was a thing all made of glass with glass shelves, and all kinds of rocks and shells and little eggs. But it was locked up and Grampa said he had lost the key.

There was a big brown sofa to bounce on.

"*Stop* it Rufus you'll break the *springs!*"

"*Rufus!* You're not in your own home."

In another picture it was dark too and there was a big stone lion with a smooth face kind of like Uncle Hugh. Not a lion face but a man. He was lying down in the sand and in between his paws there were people sleeping. A man and a lady and a baby and a donkey. They had a little fire.

"That was Jesus when he was just a tiny baby and his mama and his fos. Foss."

"*Foss*-tur-father Rufus."

"Fossturfather. They had to run away and hide in eejip because bad men were after them."

Eejip.

"Dark as eejip," Grampa said, and it was dark in the picture.

Eejip was a place. A country far far away. Very old. He could see it was always dark there, all sand, with stone lions lying down with smooth strange faces, and lonesome people resting, and smoke circling up from their little fires.

Dok-tur Foss-tur went-ter Gloss-tur.

Different.

The piano was tall and dark brown. It had narrow black things three at a time, then skip, then two at a time, then skip, then three at a time again, all the way up and down, and wide white things all the way with no skips. At one end it made a noise that tickled inside his ear. At the other end it made a noise higher than anybody could sing or even whistle. In the middle it made nice noises together. If he made noises they would say Rufus have you washed your hands? Always wash your hands before you play the piano. So Granma and Aunt Paula would wash his hands. Then after while Grampa would say "for God's sake stop *banging,*" and Granma would say "Why Joel, he's doing very *nicely.*" And Grampa would say, not loud enough for her to hear, "Sounds like all hell broken loose" or "you're lucky you're deaf." And Granma would say, "Granma thinks you play *beautifully* Rufus but perhaps we'd better not just now."

When he was just a little older, Granma said, she would give him lessons. That meant she would show him how to really play, the way she did and Aunt Paula.

When Granma played she bent way over to hear. Grampa always put one hand behind his ear because he couldn't hear very well either, though better than Granma. She loved to play, he could see that by the way she smiled and the way she used her hands and arms in clawings and pouncings and rapid tinklings and great sweeps. But after a while the whole piano would begin to roar and it would roar louder and louder so that all the noise was a great roaring blur with just the new notes sticking out on top. Then she always looked happiest but it was then that Grampa always began to say, not very loud, *good—God,* Emmah! or, have a little mercy, and before long he would take his hand down from his ear and just sit there looking serious, or reading. But he never told her to stop banging.

He found out how to make it roar. By keeping his foot down on the pettle. Mama said "you mustn't use the loud pettle like that." "But Granma does," he said. "Granma does because she's trying to hear, poor thing, and sometimes she forgets to take her foot off. But don't *you.*"

"That's right," Aunt Paula said.

Pettle was on a flower and on a piano too, but they were different.

Aunt Paula wore her hair in braids. She was nice with white teeth and she had a nice clear voice. She sang had a snake in silver lake, sing song kitty katchy kye-mee-o.

Bout five times as long as a rake.

There was a picture Grampa liked. It had colors. Deep dark brown. It was a dark picture too. Great big rocks came up on both sides from the bottom to the top. There were trees on top of the rocks and a long thin ladder down and in between the rocks at the bottom there was a river.

It was Oh Sable Cazzum.

Grampa and Aunt Jessie lived there when they were little.

Right *there?*

Of course not Rufus. *Near* there. But they used to play there. They used to come down the ladder and play.

Cazzum was a great deep place in the rocks. It sounded dark and scary and grand.

Oh Sable meant dark. Black. It wasn't black but it was awfully dark.

Oh Sable Cazzum. And that was the Oh Sable River.

There was another lion but he was little and white. He lay on the mantle. He had a round thing on with a cross on it. He had something sticking out of his side and it looked as if it hurt him.

Arrow.

Aunt Jessie was lots older than Aunt Paula. She was mama's Aunt too. Grampa's sister and older than he was. She had the thickest glasses of all.

She was ever so nice except when she got mad. She got mixed up with names. She would say Hu—Rufus, and Ja—Hugh I mean. When he said Aunt Jessie to her she said whatty.

Uncle Hugh had yellow hair and was nearly as tall as daddy. He painted pictures. Grampa had a little brown picture he liked, of a wet lady lying by the water very still. She was drowned. That meant there was too much water and it got inside her so she couldn't breathe. Uncle Hugh painted a big one in colors for a surprise for Grampa and Grampa liked it very much indeed. Her hair was brown like Mama's but her striped dress was blue and so was the sea. That was the water she got.

He liked to watch Uncle Hugh paint. There were thick smells and a wonderful sweet smell like new skin. That was banana oil.

Uncle Hugh said things that made people laugh but when he got mad it was as scary as daddy. When he knew Uncle Hugh was around he bounced on the sofa very quietly or not at all. Because once when he was bouncing, not very hard either, he got the hardest spank on his seat he had ever had and when he turned around there was Uncle Hugh, and his eyes and his voice were even scarier than the spank.

Once even Aunt Paula got mad.

He was looking at the white things on the piano. Keys. And he wondered what it would be like if he took a match and burned them. He got matches in the kitchen and burned one and it made a brown spot. The second match made a bigger spot because he held it longer. Before he could pull it away Aunt Paula came in from the Green Room and saw and said *don't do that!* in a bare fierce voice which scared him deeply. *What did you do that for,* she said, walking over to him fast. *I don't know,* he said. *You come with me,* she said, and he came with her and she got a cloth and Bon Ami and she said *now you clean that up.* He rubbed and rubbed but the spots stayed just the same. Then she rubbed, but they stayed just the same. *You see,* she said. *Now those will always be there. They'll never come off.*

When she said *don't do that* he was very much afraid, for the instant he saw her in the door he knew that what he was doing was wrong. Not just something they said not to do, but really wrong.

When she said *what did you do that for* she said it just as fiercely and was walking quickly towards him besides, yet he felt very sorry he had done it. He realized he had no idea why he had done it.

While he was trying to clean it up he very much hoped the spots would come off and he no longer felt quite so sorry.

While she was trying he only watched her try and was sure they would stay. He hardly felt sorry any more, only ashamed and interested.

When she said *now those will always be there. They'll never come off.,* he felt sorry all over again. Not as sorry as at first but still sorry. He wanted to say so. He knew only the feeling, not the word, so after trying hard to think how to say it he said, *I didn't mean to.* She turned suddenly on him with her voice even more bare and fierce than before and said *What do you mean you didn't mean to! You were doing it weren't you?*

After that he felt much less sorry, but still sorry, and it was the first time he had felt this in his life.

The Surprise
1912

Chapter 6

Rufus' house was on the way to school for a considerable neighborhood, and within a few minutes after his father had waved for the last time and disappeared, the walks were filled with another exciting thing to look at as the boys and girls who were old enough for school came by. At first he was content to watch them through the front window; they were creatures of an all but unimaginable world; he personally knew nobody who was big enough even for kindergarten. Later he felt more kinship with them, more curiosity, great envy, and considerable awe. It did not yet occur to him that he could ever grow up to be one of them, but he began to feel that in any case they were somehow of the same race. He wandered out into the yard, even to the sidewalk, even, at length, to the corner, where he could see them coming from three ways at once. He was fascinated by the way they looked, the boys so powerfully dressed and the girls almost as prettily as if they were going to a party. Nearly all of them walked in two's and three's, and members of these groups often called to others of other groups. You could see how well they all knew each other; any number of people; a whole world. And they all carried books of different colors and thicknesses, and lunches done up in packages or boxes, and pencils in still other boxes; or carried all these things together in a satchel. He loved the way they carried these things, it seemed to give them wonderful dignity and purpose. He particularly admired and envied the way the boys who carried their books in brown canvas straps could swing them, except when they swung them at his head. Then he was at the same time frightened and very much surprised, and the boy who had pretended he meant to hit him, and anyone else who saw, would laugh to see that look of fear and surprise on his face, and he felt puzzled and unhappy because they laughed.

But this did not happen often enough to discourage him, and going to the corner at the time they went to school, and at the time they could be expected back again, became quite a habit with him, almost as happy and exciting, in its way, as watching for the first glimpse of his father, late in the afternoon. Sometimes when he caught an eye he would even say hello, as much out of embarrassment as eagerness to communicate. Of course he was very seldom answered; the boys would merely stare at him for a second or so, with the stare turning hot or more often cold, and the girls, depending on age or disposition, either giggled in a way that made him look quickly away, or pretended that they had not even seen or heard him. But since he did not, after all, expect any answer, it was wonderfully pleasant when, occasionally, a much older boy would smile and say, "Hello there"; a few times they even reached out and mussed up his hair. Once, too, when he had said hello to some much older girls, one of them cried out in the strange, sticky voice he had heard grown women use, "Ooh, just *look* at the *dar*lin little *boy!*" He had felt embarrassed but pleasantly flattered for a moment; then he heard several boys squealing the same words, but insincerely, in fact with a hatred and scorn which appalled him, and he had wished that he could not be seen.

He never learned the names of more than two or three of these boys, for most of them lived several blocks away; but quite a few of them, in time, knew him very well. They would come up, nearly always, with the same question: "What's your name?" It seemed strange to him that they could not remember his name from one day to the next, for he always told it to them perfectly clearly, but he felt that if they forgot, and asked again, he ought to tell them again, and when he told them, politely, they all laughed. After a while he began to realize that they only asked him, day after day, not because they had really forgotten, but only to tease him. Then he became more careful. When they asked, "What's your name?" he would feel embarrassed and say, "Oh, you know my name, you're only trying to tease me."

And some of them would snicker, but invariably the boy who had asked it this time would say very seriously and politely, "No, *I* don't know your name, you never told *me* your name," and he would begin to wonder; had he or hadn't he.

"Yes I did, too," he would say, "I remember. It was only day before yesterday."

And again there would be snickering, but the questioner looked even more serious and kind, and one or two of the boys next him looked equally serious, and he would say, "No, honest. Honest, it couldn't have been me. *I* don't know your name."

And one of the other boys would say, very reasonably, "Gee, he wouldn't ast you if he knowed it already, would he?"

And Rufus would say, "Aw, you're just trying to tease me. *You* all know my name."

And one of the other boys would say, "I've forgot it. I knew it but I've plumb forgot it. I'd tell him if I could but I just can't remember it." And he too would look very sincere.

And the first questioner would say, almost pleading, and very kind looking, "*Come* on, *tell* us your name. Maybe you told it to *him* but *he* don't remember. If he could remember he'd tell me, now wouldn't he? *Would*n't you tell me?"

"Sure I'd tell you if I could remember it. Wisht you'd tell it to *me* again."

And two or three other boys, in similar tones of kindness, respect and concern, would chime in, "Aw *come* on, *tell* us your name."

And he was taken aback by all this kindness and concern, for they did not seem to act in that way towards him at any other time, and yet it did seem real. And after thinking a moment he would say, looking cautiously and earnestly, at the boy who had forgotten: "Do you promise you really honestly forgot?"

And looking back just as earnestly the boy said, "Cross my heart n body," and did so.

Then there was a snicker again from somebody, and Rufus realized that some of them were undoubtedly teasing, but he felt that he did not much mind, if these central boys were not. So he paid no attention to the snickering and said to every one of the kind-looking, serious boys, "You promise you *honestly* aren't teasing this time?" and they promised. Then he said, "If I tell you this time will you promise to do your very best to remember, and not ask me again?" and they said that they sure would, they crossed their hearts and bodies. At the last moment, just as he was beginning to tell them, he always felt such sudden, profound doubt of their sincerity that he did not want to go ahead, but he always felt, too, "*Maybe* they mean it. If they do, it would be mean not to tell them." So he always told them. "Well," he always said rather doubtfully, and brought out his name in a peculiarly muffled and shy way (he had come almost to feel that the name itself was being physically hurt, and he did not want it to be hurt again); "Well; it's Rufus."

And the instant it was out of his mouth he knew that he had been mistaken once again, that not a single one of them had meant one thing that he had said, for with that instant every one of them screamed as loudly as he could with a ferocious kind of joy, and it was as if the whole knot exploded and sent its fragments tearing all over the neighborhood, screaming his name with amusement and apparently with some kind of contempt; and many of them screamed, as well, a verse which they seemed to think very funny, though Rufus could not understand why.

Uh-Rufus, Uh-Rastus, Uh-Johnson, Uh-Brown,
uh-What ya gonna do when the rent comes roun?

and others yelled, "Nigger's name, Nigger's name," and chanted a verse that he had often heard them yell after the backs of colored children and even grown-up colored people,

Nigger, nigger, black as tar,
Tried to ride a lectric car,
Car broke down an broke his back
Poor nigger wanted his nickel back.

Three or four, instead of running, stood screaming his name and these verses at him, and the word, "Nigger," jumping up and down and shoving their fingers at his chest and stomach and face while he stood in abashment, and followed by these, he would walk unhappily home.

It puzzled him very deeply. If they knew his name all the time, as apparently they did, then why did they keep on asking as if they had never heard it, or as if they couldn't remember it? It was just to tease. But why did they want to tease? Why did they get such fun out of it? Why was it so much fun, to pretend to be so nice and so really interested, to pretend it so well that somebody else believed you in spite of himself, just so that he would show that he was deceived once again, because if you honestly *did* mean it, this time, he didn't want to not tell you when you honestly seemed to want so much to know. Why was it that when some of them were asking him, and others were backing them up or just looking on, there was some kind of a strange, tight force in the air all around them that made them all seem very much together and that made him feel very much alone and very eager to be liked by them, together with them? Why did he keep on believing them? It happened over and over and he could not think of a single time that they had looked so interested, and friendly, and kind, but what it had turned out that they didn't really mean one bit of it.

The ones who were really nice, the ones who never deceived him or teased him, were a few of the much bigger boys, who were never so attentive or kind as this, but just said, "hello, there," and smiled as they went by or maybe mussed up his hair or gave him a little punch, not to hurt or scare him, but only in play. They were very different from these, they never paid him such close attention or looked so affectionate, but they were the nice ones and these were mean to him, every time. But every time, it was the same. When they started he was always absolutely sure they were teasing, and he was always absolutely sure that this time, he would not give in to them; but every time, as they kept talking, he became less sure. At the same time that he became less sure, he became more sure, but that confused and troubled him, and the more sure he was that all this apparent kindness was merely deception and meanness, the more eagerly he studied their faces in the hope that this time they really meant it. The less he believed them, the more he wanted to believe them, and the easier it was for him to believe them. The more alone he felt, the more he wanted to feel that he was not alone, but one of them. And every time he finally gave in, he became a little more sure, just before he gave in, that he would not take this chance again. And every time he finally spoke his name, he spoke it a little more shyly, a little more in shame, until he began to feel some kind of shame about the name itself. The way they all screamed it at him, and screamed that rhyme they all laughed at, the more he came to feel that there must be something wrong with the name itself, so that even at home sometimes, even when Mama said it, if he heard it without expecting it, he felt some kind of obscure, wincing shock and shame. But when he asked her if Rufus was really a Nigger's name, and why that made everybody laugh at it, she turned on him sharply and said in a sharp voice, as if she were accusing him of something, "Who told you that?" and he had answered, in fear, that he did not know who, and she had said, "Don't you just pay any attention to them. It's a very fine old name. Some colored people take it too but that's perfectly all right and nothing for them to be ashamed of or for white people to be ashamed of who take it. You were given that name because it was your great-grandfather Tyler's name, and it's a name to be proud of. And Rufus: don't *ever* speak that word 'Nigger'!"

But he had felt that although maybe she was proud of the name, he was not. How could you be proud of a name that everybody laughed at? Once when they were less noisy and one of them said to him, quietly, "that's a nigger's name," he had tried to feel proud and had said, "It is not either, it's a very fine old name and I got it from my great-granpa Tyler," they yelled, "then your Granpa's a nigger too," and ran off down the street yelling, "Rufus is a Nigger, Rufus' granpa's a nigger, he's a niiig-ger, he's a niii-ger," and he had yelled after them, "He is *not, either,* it's my *great*-granpa and he is *not!*"; but after that they sometimes opened a conversation by asking, "How's your nigger Granpaw?" and he had to try to explain all over again that it was his *great* grandpa and he was *not* colored, but they never seemed to pay any attention.

He could not understand what amused them so much about this game, or why they should pretend to be all kindness and interest for the sake of deceiving him into doing something still again that he honestly knew better than to do, but it gradually became clear to him that no matter how much they pretended good, they always meant meanness, and that the only way to guard against this was never to believe them, and never to do what they asked him to. And so in time he found that no matter how nice they acted, he was not deceived by them and would not tell them his name, and this made him feel much better, except that now they seemed to have much less interest in him. He did not want them to go by without even looking at him, or just saying something mean or sneering as they passed, or pretending so successfully that they meant to hit him with their books, that he had to duck; he only wanted them not to tease and fool him; he only wanted them to be nice to him and like him. And so he remained very ready to do whatever seemed necessary to be liked, except that one thing, telling his name, which was clearly not ever a good thing to do. And so, as long as they didn't ask him his name (and they soon knew that this joke was no good any more), he continued to hope against hope that in every other way, they were not trying to tease or fool him. Now they would come up to him looking quite serious, the older boys, and say, as if it were a very serious question,

Rufus Rastus Johnson Brown
What you gonna do when the *rent* comes roun?

He always felt that they were still teasing him about his name, when they said this; there was something about the *Rastus* that they said in such a tone that he knew they disliked both names and held both in contempt, and he could not understand why they gave him so many names when only one was really his and his last name was really Agee. But at least they knew what his name was now, even if most of them pronounced it Roofeass; at least they weren't pretending they didn't know; it wasn't as bad as that. Besides, what they were really doing was asking him a question, "What you gonna do when the rent comes roun?" Though they asked it every time and it seemed a nonsensical question, they seemed to really want to know, and if he could answer them, then he could really tell them something they really didn't know and then maybe they would really like him and not tease him. Yet he realized that this too must be teasing. They did not really want to know. How could they, when the question had no meaning? What was The Rent? What did it look like when it came Roun? It probably looked very mean or maybe it looked nice but was mean when you got to know it. And what *would* you do when it came roun? What could you do if you didn't even know what it was? Or if it was just something they made up, that wasn't really alive, just a story? He wanted to ask what The Rent was, but he suspected that that was exactly what they wanted him to ask, and that if or when he asked it, it would turn out that the whole thing was a trap of some kind, a joke, and that he had done something shameful or ridiculous in asking.

So that was one thing he was now wise enough never to do; he never asked what The Rent was, and this was one of the things he felt sure that somehow he had better not ask his mother or his father, either. So when they came up to him now, he always knew they were going to ask this foolish question, and when they asked it he felt stubborn and shy, determined not to ask what The Rent was; and once they had asked it, and stood looking at him with a curious, cold look as if they were hungry, he looked back at them until he felt too embarrassed, and saw them start to smile in a way that might be mean or might possibly be friendly, and on the possibility that they were friendly, smiled unsurely too, and looked down at the pavement, and muttered, "I don't know"; which seemed to amuse them almost as much as when he had told what his name was, though not so loudly; and then sometimes he would walk away from them, and after a while he learned that he should not answer this question any more than he should answer the question about his name.

When he walked away, or when he refused to answer, he always realized that in some way he had defeated them, but he also always felt disconsolate and lonely, and sometimes, because of this, he would turn around after he had gone a little way, and look and they would come up and surround him again, and other times, when he kept on walking away, he felt even more lonely and unhappy, so much so that he went down between the houses into the backyard and stayed for a while because he felt uneasy about being seen, yet, by his mother. He began to anticipate going out to the corner with as much unhappiness as hope, and sometimes he did not go at all; but when he went again, after not going at all, he was asked where he had been and why he had not been there the day before, and he had not known what to answer, and had been much encouraged because they spoke in such a way that they really seemed to care where he had been.

And within the next days things did seem to change. The older and more perceptive of the boys realized that the shape of the game had shifted and that if they were to count on him to be there, and to be such a fool as always before, they had to act much more friendly; and the more stupid boys, seeing how well this worked, imitated them as well as they could. Rufus quickly came to suspect the more flagrant exaggerations of friendliness but the subtler boys found, to their intense delight, that if only they varied the surface, the bait, from time to time, they could almost always deceive him. He was ever so ready to oblige. How it got started none of them remembered or cared, but they all knew that if they kept at him enough he would sing them his song, and be fool enough to think they actually liked it. They would say, "Sing us a song, Roofeass," and he would look as if he knew they were teasing him and say, "Oh, you don't want to hear it." And they would say that they sure did want to hear it, it was a real pretty song, better than *they* could sing, and they liked the way he danced when he sang it, too. And since they had very early learned to take pains to listen to the song with apparent respect and friendliness, he was very soon and easily persuaded. And so, feeling odd and foolish not because he felt they were really deceiving him or laughing at him, but only because with each public repetition of it he felt more silly, and less sure that it was really as pretty and enjoyable as he liked to think it was, he would give them one last anxious look, which always particularly tickled them, and would then raise his arms and turn round and round, singing,

I'm a little busy bee, busy bee, busy bee,
I'm a little busy bee, singing *in,* the clover.

As he sang and danced he could hear through his own verses a few obscure, incredulous cackles, but nearly all of the faces which whirled past him, those of the older boys, were restrained, attentive and smiling, and this made up for the contempt he saw on the faces of the middle-sized boys; and when he had finished, and was catching his breath, these older boys would clap their hands in real approval, and say, "That's an awful pretty song, Rufus, where'd you learn that song?" And again he would suspect some meanness behind it and so would refuse to say until they had coaxed him sufficiently, and then out it came, "My Mama"; and at that point some of the smaller boys were liable to spoil everything by yelling and laughing, but often even if they did, the older boys could save it all by sternly crying, "You shut up! Don't you know a pretty song when you hear it?" and by turning to him, with faces which shut out those boys and included him among the big boys, and saying, "Don't you care about them, Rufus, they're just ignernt and don't know nothing. You sing your song." And another would chime in, "Yeah Rufus, sing it again. Gee, that's a pretty song;" and a third would say, "And don't forget to dance;" and for this reduced but select audience he would do the whole thing over again.

At that point someone usually said, abruptly, "Come on, we got to go," and as suddenly as if a chair had been pulled from under him, he would be left by himself; they hardly even clapped their hands before they walked away. But some of the boys with the nicest faces always took care, before they left, to tell him, "Gee, thanks, Rufus, that was *mighty* pretty," and to say, "Don't you forget, you be here tomorrow"; and this more than made up for the thing which never failed to perplex him. Why did they walk off so suddenly as all that? Why did they all keep looking back and laughing in that queer way; subdued talk, their heads close together, and then those sudden whoops of laughter? It almost seemed as if they were laughing at him. And once when one of the bigger boys suddenly flung up his arms and whirled into the street, piping in a high, squeaky voice, "*I'm a little busy bee,*" he was quite sure that they had not really liked the song, or him for singing it. But if they didn't, then why did they ask him to sing it? And then once he heard one of them, far down the block, squeak, "My Mama," and he felt as if something went straight through his stomach, and they all laughed, and he was practically certain that to those boys at least, the whole thing was just some kind of mean joke. But then he remembered how nice the boys he liked best and trusted most had been, and he knew that anyway the boys he liked best were not in any way trying to tease him.

After a while, however, he began to wonder even about them. Maybe their being so extra nice was just their way of getting him to do things he would never do if they were only nice part of the time and then laughed at him. Yet if they were nice all the time, it must be because they honestly meant it. And yet the way some of the others laughed, what he was doing must be wrong or silly somehow. He would be much more careful. He would be careful not to do anything or say anything anybody asked him to, unless he was sure they were really nice and really meant it. He now watched even the boys he liked best with very particular caution, and they saw that unless they were much more shrewd the game was likely to be spoiled again. They began to promise him rewards, a stick of chewing gum, the stub of a pencil, chalk, a piece of candy, and this seemed to convince him. The less shrewd of the boys often did not give him the promised reward, and this of course was more fun, but the smarter ones were always consistent, so that he never refused them. It was all so easy, in fact, that it began to bore them. They began to appreciate the tricks the more stupid boys played, one getting down behind him while he danced and another pushing him over backwards, but they were intelligent enough never to take part in this, always to pretend thorough disapproval, always to help him to his feet and brush him off and console him if he had struck his head hard and was crying, and always to conceal their astonished delight at his utter bewilderment and gullibility, and their astonished contempt at his complete lack of spirit to strike out against his tormentors, his lack of ability, even, for real solid anger. And because they were always there, and always seemed to be on his side, they could always keep him sufficiently deceived to come back for more than anyone in his right senses would come back for.

The oldest of them began to be obscurely ashamed, as well as bored. They were all much older and smarter than he was; even the youngest of the boys who went to school were enough older than he was that it seemed no wonder that he was continually fooled, and that he never fought back. They felt that this little song, for instance, was too sissy to be fun for much longer. They felt that more violent things should be done. But they themselves could not do such things. If they showed him they were not on his side, the fun would all be over. And even if it were not, they knew that it would be unfair of them to do the really violent things, which absolutely required violence in return, to anyone so much younger and smaller, no matter how big a fool he was. Besides, they had received more than enough hints that even if he were driven to fight, he would not have the nerve to, probably wouldn't even know he had to. They were curious to see what would happen. They left the game wider and wider open to the smaller, crueler and more simple boys. But it was no good. He would just look at them with surprise, pain and reproach, and get up and walk away; and if any of these older, normally friendly boys consoled him too closely, he would burst into sobs which disgusted as well as delighted them.

At length they found the right formula. They would put some boys as small as he was, up to some trick which nobody bigger would have any right to do.

Chapter 7

For some time now his mother had seemed different. Almost always when she spoke to him it was as if she had something else very much on her mind, and so, was making a special effort to be gentle and attentive to him. And it was as if whatever it was that was on her mind was very momentous. Sometimes she looked at him in such a way that he felt that she was very much amused about something. He did not know how to ask her what she was amused by and as he watched her, wondering what it was, and she watched his puzzlement, she sometimes looked more amused than ever, and once when she looked particularly amused, and he looked particularly bewildered, her smile became shaky and turned into laughter and, quickly taking his face between her hands, she exclaimed, "I'm not laughing at *you,* darling!"; and for the first time he felt that perhaps she was.

There were other times when she seemed to have almost no interest in him, but only to be doing things for him because they had to be done. He felt subtly lonely and watched her carefully. He saw that his father's manner had changed towards her ever so little; he treated her as if she were very valuable and he seemed to be conscious of the tones of his voice. Sometimes in the mornings Grandma would come in and if he was around he was told to go away for a little while. Grandma did not hear well and carried a black ear trumpet which was sticky and sour on the end that she put in her ear; but try as he would they talked so quietly that he could hear very little, and none of it enlightened him. There were special words which were said with a special kind of hesitancy or shyness, such as "pregnancy" and "kicking" and "discharge," but others, which seemed fully as strange, such as "layette" and "basinette" and "bellyband," seemed to inspire no such fear. Grandma also treated him as if something strange was going on, but whatever it was, it was evidently not dangerous, for she was always quite merry with him. His father and his Uncle Hugh and Grandpa seemed to treat him as they always had, though there seemed to be some hidden kind of strain in Uncle Hugh's feeling for his mother. And Aunt Jessie was the same as ever with him, except that she paid more attention to his mother, now. Aunt Paula looked at his mother a good deal when she thought nobody else was watching, and once when she saw him watching her she looked quickly away and turned red.

Everyone seemed either to look at his mother with ill-concealed curiosity or to be taking special pains not to look anywhere except, rather fixedly and cheerfully, into her eyes. For now she was swollen up like a vase, and there was a peculiar lethargic lightness in her face and in her voice. He had a distinct feeling that he should not ask what was happening to her. At last he asked Uncle Hugh: "Uncle Hugh; why is Mama so fat?" and his Uncle replied, with such apparent anger or alarm that he was frightened, "Why, don't you *know?*"; and abruptly walked out of the room.

Next day his mother told him that soon he was going to have a very wonderful surprise. When he asked what a surprise was she said it was like being given things for Christmas only ever so much nicer. When he asked what he was going to be given she said that she did not mean it was a present, specially for him, or for him to have, or keep, but something for everybody, and especially for them. When he asked what it was she said that if she told him it wouldn't be a surprise any more, would it? When he said that he wanted to know anyway she said that she would tell him, only it would be so hard for him to imagine what it was before it came that she thought it was better for him to see it first. When he asked when it was coming she said that she didn't know exactly but very soon now, in only a week or two, perhaps sooner, and she promised him that he would know right away when it did come.

He was aflame with curiosity. He had been too young, the Christmas before, to think of looking for hidden presents, but now he looked everywhere that he could imagine to look, until his mother understood what he was doing and told him there was no use looking for it because the surprise wouldn't be here until exactly when it came. He asked where was it, then, and heard his father's sudden laugh; his mother looked panicky and cried, "Jay!" all at once, and quickly informed him, "In heaven; still up in heaven." He looked quickly to his father for corroboration and his father, who appeared to be embarrassed, did not look at him. He knew about Heaven because that was where Our Father was, but that was all he knew about it, and he was not satisfied. Again, however, he had a feeling that he would be unwise to ask more.

"Why don't you tell him, Laura?" his father said.

"*Oh*, Jay," she said in alarm; then said, by moving her lips, "Don't talk of it in *front* of him!"

"Oh I'm sorry," and he, too, said with his lips—only a whisper leaked around the silence, "But what's the good? Why not get it over with?"

She decided that it was best to speak openly. "As you know, Jay, I've told Rufus about our surprise that's coming. I told him I'd be glad to tell him what it was, except that it would be so very hard for him to imagine it and *such* a lovely surprise when he first sees it. Besides, I just have a feeling he might m—make see oh en en ee see tee eye oh en ess, between—between one thing and another."

"Going to make them, going to make em anyhow," his father said.

"But Jay there's no use simply forcing it on his att—eigh ten ten, his attention, now is there? Is there, Jay!"

She seemed really quite agitated; he could not understand why.

"You're right Laura and don't you get excited about it. I was all wrong about it. Of course I was." And he got up and came over to her and took her in his arms, and patted her on the back.

"I'm probably just silly about it," she said.

"No you're not one *bit* silly. Besides, if you're silly about that, so am I, same way. That just sort of caught me off my guard, that about Heaven, that's all."

"Well what *can* you say?"

"I'm God d—I can't imagine sweetheart, and I better just keep my mouth shut."

She frowned, smiled, laughed through her nose and urgently shook her head at him, all at once.

And then one day without warning the biggest woman he had ever seen, shining deep black and all in magnificent white with bright gold spectacles and a strong smile like that of his Aunt Jessie, entered the house and embraced his mother and swept down on him crying with delight, "Lawd, chile, how mah baby *has growed!*" and for a moment he thought that this must be the surprise and looked enquiringly at his mother past the onslaught of embraces, and his mother said, "Victoria; *Victoria*, Rufus!"; and Victoria cried, "now bless his little heart, how would *he* remembuh," and all of a sudden as he looked into the vast shining planes of her smiling face and at the gold spectacles which perched there as gaily as a dragonfly, there was something that he did remember, a glisten of gold and a warm movement of affection, and before he knew it he had flung his arms around her neck and she whooped with astonished joy, "Why God bless him, why chile, chile," and she held him away from her and her face was the happiest thing he had ever seen, "Ah believe you *do* remembuh! Ah sweah ah believe you *do!* Do you?" She shook him in her happiness. "Do you remembuh y'old Victoria?" She shook him again. "*Do* you, honey?" And realizing at last that he was specifically being asked, he nodded shyly, and again she embraced him. She smelled so good that he could almost have leaned his head against her and gone to sleep then and there.

"Mama," he said later, when she was out shopping, "Victoria smells awful good."

"*Hush,* Rufus," his mother said. "Now you listen *very carefully* to me, do you hear? Say yes if you hear."

"Yes."

"Now you be *very careful* that you never say anything about how she smells where Victoria can hear you. Will you? Say yes if you will."

"Yes."

"Because even though you *like* the way she smells, you might hurt her feelings terribly if you said any such thing, and you wouldn't want to hurt dear old Victoria's feelings, I know. Would you. *Would* you, Rufus."

"No."

"Because Victoria is—is colored, Rufus. That's why her skin is so dark, and colored people are very sensitive about the way they smell. Do you know what sensitive means?"

He nodded cautiously.

"It means there are things that hurt your feelings so badly, things you can't help, that you feel like crying, and nice colored people feel that way about the way they smell. So you be very careful. Will you? Say yes if you will?"

"Yes."

"Now tell me what I've asked you to be careful about, Rufus."

"Don't tell Victoria she smells."

"Or say anything about it where she can hear."

"Or say anything about it where she can hear."

"Why not?"

"Because she might cry."

"That's right. And Rufus, Victoria is very, *very clean.* Absolutely spic and span."

Spic an span.

Victoria would not allow his mother to get dinner and after they had eaten she also took entire charge of packing some of his clothes into a box, asking advice, however, on each thing that she took out of the drawer. Then Victoria bathed him and dressed him in clean clothes from the skin out, much to his mystification, and once he was ready, his mother called him to her and told him that Victoria was going to take him on a little visit to stay a few days with Granpa and Granma and Uncle Hugh and Aunt Paula, and he must be a very good boy and do his *very* best not to wet the bed because when he came back, very soon now, in only a few more days, the surprise would be there and he would know what it was. He said that if the surprise was coming so soon he wanted to stay and see it, and she replied that that was just why he was going away to Granma's, so the surprise could come all by itself. He asked why it couldn't come if he was there and she said because he might frighten it away because it would still be very tiny and very much afraid, so if he really wanted the surprise to come, he could help more than anything else by being a good boy and going right along to Granma's. Victoria would come and bring him home again just as soon as the surprise was ready for him; "won't you, Victoria?" And Victoria, who throughout this conversation had appeared to be tremendously amused about something, giving tight little cackles of swallowed laughter and murmuring, "Bless his heart," whenever he spoke, said that indeed she most certainly would.

"And say your prayers," his mother said, looking at him suddenly with so much love that he was bewildered. "You're a big boy now, and you can say them by yourself; can't you?" He nodded. She took him by the shoulders and looked at him almost as if she were threading a needle. As she looked at him, some kind of astonishment and some kind of fear grew in her face. Her face began to shine; she smiled; her mouth twitched and trembled. She took him close to her and her cheek was wet. "God bless my dear little boy," she whispered, "for *ever* and *ever!* Amen," and again she held him away; her face looked as if she were moving through space at extraordinary speed. "Goodbye, my darling; oh, goodbye!"

"Now you keep aholt a my hand," Victoria told him, the sun flashing her lenses as she looked both ways from the curb. Arching his neck and his forelegs, a bright brown horse drew a buggy smartly but sedately past; in the washed black spokes, sunlight twittered. Far down the sunlight, like a bumblebee, a yellow streetcar buzzed. The trees moved. They did not wait.

"Victoria," he said.

"Wait, chile," said Victoria, breathing hard. "You wait till we're safe across."

"Now what is it, honey?" she asked, once they had attained the other curb.

"Why is your skin so dark?"

He saw her bright little eyes thrust into him through the little lenses and he felt a strong current of pain or danger. He knew that something was wrong. She did not answer him immediately but peered down at him sharply. Then the current passed and she looked away from him, readjusting her fingers so that she took his hand. Her face looked very far away, and resolute. "Just because, chile," she said in a stern and gentle voice. "Just because that was the way God made me."

"Is that why you're colored, Victoria?"

He felt a change in her hand when he said the word "colored." Again she did not answer immediately, nor would she look at him. "Yes," she said at length; "That's why I'm colored."

He felt deeply sad as they walked along, but he did not know why. She seemed to have no more to say, and he had a feeling that it was not proper for him to say anything either. He watched her great sad face beneath its brilliant cap, but she did not seem to know that he was watching her or even that he was there. But then he felt the pressure of her hand, and squeezed her hand, and he felt that whatever had been wrong was all right again.

After quite a little while Victoria said: "Chile, I want to tell you sumpn." He waited; they walked. "Victoria don't pay it no mind, because she knows you. She knows you wouldn't say a mean thing to nobody, not for this world. But dey is lots of other colored folks dat don't know you, honey. And if you say that, you know, about their skins, about their coloh, they goan think you're trine to be mean to um. They goan to feel awful bad and maybe they be mad at you too, when Victoria knows you doan mean nuthin by it, cause they don't know you like Victoria do. Do you understand me, chile?" He looked earnestly up at her. "Don't say nuthin bout skins, or coloh, wheah colored people can heah you. Cause they goana think you're mean toom. So you be careful." And again she squeezed his hand.

He thought about Victoria while they walked and he wished that she was happy, and he felt that it was because of him that she was not happy. "Victoria," he said.

"What is it, honey?"

"I didn't want to be mean to you."

She stopped abruptly and with creaking and difficulty squatted down in the middle of the sidewalk so that a man who was passing stepped suddenly aside and looked coldly down as he went by. She put both hands on his shoulders and her large kind face and her kind smell were close to him. "Lord bless you baby, *Victoria* knows you didn't! Victoria knows you is de goodest little boy in all dis world! She just had to tell you, you see. Cause colored folks has a hard time in dis world and she knows you wouldn't want to make um feel bad, not even if you didn't mean to."

"I didn't want to make you feel bad."

"Bless your little heart. I *don't* feel bad, not one bit. You make me feel happy, and your Mama makes me feel happy, and there's not one thing in dis world I wouldn't do for de bofe a you, honey, and dat you know. Dat you know," she said again, rocking her head and smiling and patting both his shoulders. "I missed you terrible, honey," she said, but somehow he felt that she was not talking exactly to him. "I couldn't hardly love you more if you was my own baby." A silence opened around them in which he felt at once great space, the space almost of darkness itself, and great peace and comfort; and the whole of this immensity was pervaded by her vague face and by the waving light of leaves. "Now let's git along," she said, creaking upright and smoothing her starched garments. "We don't want to keep your Granmaw waitn."

And there was the dusty ivy on the wall, the small glass house in front, and on the porch, Aunt Paula and his Grandma. Even when they were still across the street he saw his Aunt Paula wave and Victoria waved gaily back, chuckling and croaking "Hello," and he waved too;

and Paula leaned towards his grandmother who sought out and tilted her little trumpet and Paula leaned close to it and then they both turned to look and Grandma got up and he could hear her high "Hello," and they were at the front steps, and Grandma came cautiously down the steps from the porch, and they all met on the brick walk in the shade of the magnolia, while Aunt Paula came up smiling from behind her mother. And soon Victoria left; she disappeared around a corner, a few blocks up the street, handsomely and gradually as a sailboat.

Chapter 8

When he heard that it was still a secret Grampa grunted and said "the fait accompli," and then he made that noise with his lips that Mama didn't like. "Personally," he said, "I think it's a lot of damn nonsense. But if Poll wants it that way, that's all there is to it." He ate a few bites. "Ours not to reason why," he said. He ate a few bites more. "Betcha dollars to doughnuts she'll tell him it came from heaven," he said. "*God* did it, not us: God." And again he made the noise.

"Well what would *you* say, Papa?" Hugh asked.

"Fair question," Grampa said. He ate some more. "Well I wouldn't take him on a tour of the interior," he said.

Uncle Hugh laughed.

"*Papa,*" Aunt Paula said, and laughed and blushed.

"None of his business," Grampa went on. "But at least I'd let him know what's up. And I'd leave *God* where he belongs."

Grandma was looking polite with her trumpet stuck out and now Uncle Hugh told her what they were talking about.

"Yes," Granma said. "So Paula told me." And she laughed merrily and politely, all by herself. "I think perhaps we'd better not discuss it, before him," she said.

"So do I," Uncle Hugh said.

"Consider me squelched," Grampa said. "Let your vittles stop your mouth." And he said no more about it.

The next day his father didn't come to see him, though he had promised to.

"He has other fish to fry," Grampa said.

"He means he's so busy he can't come," Uncle Hugh explained.

But the next afternoon he did come, looking very tired and cheerful and somehow sheepish, and he brought candy for Rufus and ice cream for Rufus to give everybody else. "That surprise is home now," he said, "and tomorrow you'll come home and see it."

And instantly his curiosity, which had been uncomfortable but hopeless, became almost more than he could stand. "O goody goody," he hollered, "What *is* it! What *is* it daddy what *is* it!"

His father looked annoyed for a moment and then shook his head and smiled kindly, still looking annoyed. "I oughtn't even told you it's come," he said. "Dog *gone* it." And for a moment Rufus was sure he was going to tell. But he shook his head again and said, "Son if I told you she'd snatch me baldheaded." Rufus looked at his father very seriously, imagining his mother grabbing him by the hair and yanking it off so he had just a shining bald head like Grampa. It would be awful. His father looked into his worried eyes and laughed. "*Honey* I don't mean she *really* would," he said. "That's just a way of talking. Just a joke. I just mean mama'd be awful sorry, and mad. She'd feel just *awful* bad if she didn't get to tell you herself. She'd cry. Now you don't want to make mommer *cry, do* you."

"Oh *no!*"

"Then you just be a good boy and wait just one more day. Huh?"

"He's been just simply *swell* about it Jay," Hugh said. "If he could control his bladder the way he does his curiosity he'd be a champion, take it from me."

"Sure he's a champion," his father said. "He's my *boy.*" And he roughed his head against his thigh, and although Rufus was blushing about the wet bed, he felt wonderful. "All right then Rufus?" his father asked. He nodded. "All right then," he said. "Now kiss me goodbye and I'll see you tomorrow." And he stooped and Rufus came to him and suddenly he was swept up next the ceiling and looked down into his father's dark, exhausted, happy face, and his father shook him so hard that he screamed with pleasure. Then he set him down and said "Well I gotta make tracks—fast," and hurried out the back door while they all called "Love to Laura," and he called back, grinning, "I sure will," and he hurried with long strides up the hill; and as he watched him get smaller along the hill Rufus realized that he wanted so much to be home with the surprise that he hadn't even waited for the ice cream which just now, even though it wasn't long till supper, Granma brought in on a shining silver tray, in special dishes, with cookies, and iced tea, and little lace napkins. She was beaming and looking mischievous, and Rufus could see that she was surprised and disappointed that his father had already gone away, but she pretended that she wasn't and said gaily, "Well even if our guest of honor can't be with us I think it's a very suitable occasion to spoil our appetites." And a little later, after seeming to wait for Grampa to do something, she raised her frosty glass and said "To Jay and dear Laura and the darling little. . . ." She seemed to catch herself and she looked at Rufus and laughed mischievously. "The little *surprise!*" she said. "And little *Rufus too!*" Then they all drank iced tea. Grampa grunted, but he drank too. And she kept saying to Rufus, "is there still room in that little breadbasket for one more cookie?" So he ate all the cookies and ice cream he wanted, and even in spite of the bed she gave him a second glass of iced cambric tea.

"Afloat in the forest," Grampa said as Rufus shyly accepted it, and Uncle Hugh and Aunt Paula burst out laughing, though Rufus couldn't imagine why; and the more puzzled he looked, the harder they laughed.

"*In the forest* is good," Uncle Hugh said, looking at his bewilderment. "Me retrroveye donze oona selve oscoorrrah" [I found myself in a dark forest]. And they kept laughing. "Aww *pore* little Roofis," Uncle Hugh finally said. "He looks *soo* hacked."

"We're not laughing at *you,*" Aunt Paula said gaily, and that made him feel less uneasy, though they certainly did seem to be laughing at him; so he began to grin shyly himself, and at that they all laughed more, but he could see they were laughing kindly.

"Something amusing?" Granma asked; and suddenly they all realized that all this time she had been smiling courteously, with her trumpet ready.

"Oh poor Mama," Uncle Hugh said, and Grampa leaned close to her trumpet and said: "Nothing much, Emmah. It's just—too—com-pli-cated—to repeat." She nodded, smiling, with each word. "Sorry," he said.

"Thank you," Granma said, smiling; "no matter." And she laid her trumpet down and sat smiling, with her scarred hands in her lap: but now they all took care to talk to her.

Now say Now I lamey.

She said it with him in her soft voice.

Now I lamey down to sleep I pray the Lord my soul to keep If I should die before I wake I pray the Lord my soul to take amen.

Lame meant you hurt. Sometimes Granma had a lame back. What was lamey?

God bless daddy and mamma and Grampa and Granma and Granma and Grampa Agee and keep us safe till morning light amen.

Now *hop* into bed.

Good night. Sweet sleep.

That night he wet the bed so hard it even went off the oilcloth, and soaked his pillow, too, but Granma was just as nice about it as ever. "Some people simply learn more slowly than others," she said. "But you'll learn, and how nice that will be. *Won't* it."

"Yes, Granma," he shouted earnestly, and he could almost imagine how nice that would be. But not that he would ever learn.

Chapter 9

Next day right after his nap Granma said, "And now little Rufus is going home." She washed him all over and helped him into his white peekay [piqué]. To Aunt Paula she said, "Give dear Laura all my love and ask her, if she feels up to it, say we'd all like to pay a little call, late this afternoon." To Rufus she said, "Granma has been so happy to have you for this lovely little visit and she hopes that Rufus has enjoyed it too." She waited a moment. "Has he?" She said sweetly.

"O yes Granma," he called, and they kissed.

"Strong little back," Granma croaked, and she rubbed and patted it hard. "Tell Mama that Granma says you've been very *very good* and it was a joy to have you," she said.

"Yes Granma."

Now every step he took brought him nearer and nearer and nearer knowing what the surprise was, and he could not imagine what it was going to be. "Is it ice cream?" he asked Aunt Paula; but even before she smiled and said "no" he was sure it was something even nicer. "Is it chocolate candy?" But he knew it was better than that.

"No."

"Is it a vuh, a vuh, vuhl—"

"Velocipede?" Aunt Paula asked.

"*Is it?*" It must be, for she had said it, and that *would* be a wonderful surprise.

"No Rufus," she said. "You'll have to be a little bit bigger for that. But you just wait and see. It's a nice surprise."

It couldn't be as nice as a vuh, vuhl, he thought. Unless—He turned and looked up at her with his eyes shining, "Oh Aunt *Paula*," he said, almost breathless with joy. "Is it *pants that flap open in front?*"

"*Awww,*" she said. "No it *isn't* Roofis. But I know it's something you're going to like, just *ever* so much. I promise you."

By now he could not think of anything else that could be good enough; and soon they turned a corner and down the bright street in the twinkling shade he could see home. "*Run* Aunt Paula," he gasped, and he started running as fast as he could, and she trotted laughing beside him.

When he turned in from the sidewalk and ran straight for the front porch it was even more exciting, for the porch and the front door looked strangely still, as if nobody was inside, and they got big as he ran towards them, and when he heard his feet on the front steps and hollow on the porch floor his scalp began to prickle and he knew that in almost no time now he would know. And as he came, he could see through the screen door how something large and white came rushing through the dark hall getting bigger and bigger, and the screen door burst open and Victoria, in blazing white, with such black skin, ran out to him, stooping while she ran, and swept him into her arms. She was droning and groaning happily, words he could not quite hear, and now she took him by the shoulders and held him away, but she continued to look at him, through her little gold glasses, and as he looked back into the huge shining face and at the little glasses which perched on it like a butterfly, he liked her again so much that he asked Aunt Paula, "is she the surprise?"

She got up grunting. "Come on in chile and see yo lil—" she laughed and moaned inside. "You come an find out about dat lil suprise, honey." And she stood aside for him. "Ain't he a *dahlin,*" she said to Aunt Paula as they followed through the door. "Ain't he jist the *spittn image* of his *mama?*" "No, in heah, chile," she said, and turned ahead of him. "Mama's *down*stairs now;" and she led them back to the door of his room and rapped softly on the door. "Miss Laura?" she said in a low voice. "Mist Agee? He's done heah."

"Come in," he heard his mother's voice, and Victoria opened the door.

And there she was. She was propped up on pillows in bed, smiling, and she looked weak and gray and pretty. "Come here darling," she said in a weak voice, and smiled even more. And there was daddy. He was standing on the other side of the bed where it was almost dark and he looked shyly at his son, looking even more sheepish, and then he grinned and Rufus could see his white teeth in the shadow. "Come here," his mother said again, but he still hardly heard her. The shade was drawn more than halfway down so that the room was faint and hot and there was a stifling power and stillness all through the air and a delicate stifling smell, so that he stopped at the threshold without knowing he had stopped. Then he realized that she had said "come here," twice, and he walked shyly over to her, looking into her smiling eyes. "Oh be *careful,* dear," she gasped; and he was startled, and then realized that he had knocked against a sort of basket by her bed. He stepped away from it and she took him in her arms. "Mother's little boy," she said. The delicate smell was much heavier now. It came from her and he wished he could put his head out the window but he suspected that she would not like it if he pulled away. "Mother's so happy to see him again," she said. "Paula?"

"Hello Laura," and he felt her close behind him and stood aside, and Aunt Paula and his mother kissed.

"Hello daddy," Rufus said.

"Hello there," his father whispered, and he grinned again. He was wearing his best suit, coat and all, and a white shirt, and he was sweating.

"Rufus," he heard. It was his mother again. "See what's here."

"Huh?" he said before he thought, and expected her to say, "Don't say *huh* Rufus, say what *is* it?" But instead she said, "in the little basket, darling. Be very *quiet,*" and she pointed, and it was quite a big basket, the one he had knocked against; and standing on tiptoe to look in, he saw a baby there, smaller and redder than he had ever seen before. It was asleep and there were round bulges under the big eyelids. It smelled just like his mother did. He was very much interested and looked to his mother and then to his father to explain. They were watching him very closely and they were smiling. His father looked bashful and amused, but his mother said: "That's your little sister, Rufus. Little Emma. She's come to live with us and make us all happy."

Behind him he could hear Victoria, laughing hard but inaudibly inside herself and murmuring, almost inaudibly, "Bless his lil hot; hee hee hee! Whoooooeee! Bless his lil hot!"

So that was who. He looked back at the baby. That was where the air was so strong and still. The netted shadow of the curtain lay on her round cheek. It scarcely moved, but it moved more than she did. There was a little hand, almost lost in its sleeve. The way the long eyelid closed its lashes across the bulge it looked like a baseball.

He reached in with one stiff finger to see if he could make the eye open and heard his mother gasp "*O Rufus Jay Victoria!*" and when, startled, he looked up at her, she looked scared to death and looked at him with such hard sharp eyes that he was scared too, and his mother said "*He's trying* to put out her *eyes!*" And just as she said it a great black hand swept over his hand and pulled it gently away and he heard three people say "O *no*" and then his father laughing and saying "He just wanted her to open em up. Just wants to see what they look like, don't you Rufus?" and he nodded uncertainly, and Victoria said "He jes curious Miss Laura like his Daddy say, he ain't nevah seed his lil sistuh befo, dat's all. He wouldn't hurt her, *would* he?" She said to Rufus, "He wouldn't hahm a haih of her haid a purpose." That puzzled him a little because she had scarcely any hair *on* her head, but he knew he didn't want to hurt her, so he nodded.

"Of *course* he wouldn't," his mother said, "He just scared me to death for a minute that was all. I guess I must be just sort of nerved up."

"Sure, darling," his father said.

"But Rufus dear," his mother said, "You pay close attention now because there's something mother must tell you right now. Do you hear me?"

"Yesm."

"Tiny babies are very *very delicate* Rufus. They're very easy to hurt unless you know just how to take care of them. Do you see?"

"Yesm."

"So Rufus, you *look* at little Emma, all you *like.* We *know* you love her and want to see her. But don't *ever touch* her, dear, unless we say you can. Because Rufus." She made her voice very serious. "You might hurt her perfectly terribly Rufus, without meaning to. You see?"

"Yesm."

"Will you be sure and do that?"

"Yesm."

"Promise?"

"Yesm."

"Because if you don't Rufus, we might have to send little Emma away where you *couldn't* touch her, or even *see* her. You wouldn't want us to do that, would you darling."

"No mam."

"Of course you wouldn't."

"He thinks you're scoldin im Laura," his father said; and now that she took care she could see that he did look at least awfully unsure.

"Why *darling!*" she exclaimed. "Come here to mother!" And he came and she took both his hands in hers. "Mother's not scolding," she said. "Not one bit in this world. Mother just wants you to know how *very careful* you must be with little Emma because she loves you *both so much.* See Rufus?" He nodded.

"Yesm," he said.

"Sit down by me a minute," his mother said. "*O now be careful,*" she gasped, for he almost sat on her. "There." She put her hand over his knees and then lifted it and smoothed back his hair. "Is my little Rufus glad to be home again?" she asked.

"Mm-hm," he said. "Granma told me to tell you it was a joy to have me." He heard a kind of snicker from his father.

"Well now isn't that *nice* of Granma! Was he a good boy Paula? Why Paula! Why you haven't even seen the *baby* yet."

"Why that's all right," Aunt Paula said, stepping over towards the basket. "I just didn't want to interrupt." She stood shyly in her summer dress and looked down at the baby with her hands folded. "My she's just darling," she said.

"*Isn't* she," his mother said.

"Just perfectly darling," Aunt Paula said. "What I can't get over," she said after a while, "is those tiny hands."

"I know," his mother said. "They're so, well so *complete.* To be so tiny."

"I know."

"Even little fingernails."

"I know: It seems just incredible, doesn't it."

"Yes it does."

Aunt Paula looked a little while longer without saying anything, then she said "Just darling," and stepped back. "Mama's *so* happy about her *name,*" Aunt Paula said.

"*Is* she," his mother said. "Well I'm glad. I hoped she would be of course. I only hope *little* Emma'll like it."

"Why of course she will," Aunt Paula said. "Why wouldn't she?"

"Well you never know," his mother said. "I've never liked my name you know."

"Don't you," Aunt Paula said somewhat eagerly.

"Not that I care much anymore but I used to simply hate it. Hugh doesn't like his either."

"I like yours all right," Aunt Paula said, "but I can't *stand* mine."

"Why Paula! *Why!* It's a *nice* name!"

"I just don't, that's all. But don't ever tell them."

"Why Paula what a shame. I always assumed you *liked* your name."

Aunt Paula laughed. "Always thought both of you did, too." His mother laughed.

"Well as I said you just never *know,* do you. You *mean* so *well,* but the child may turn out to just hate it."

"How do you feel about your name, Jay?" Aunt Paula asked.

"Suits me all right," his father said.

"What about your other name. Hugh I mean."

"Well I don't use it but I ain't g—I haven't got anything against it. Seems to me it suits Hugh fine."

"It's a *nice* name *I* think," his mother said. "I like *both* your names Jay." He grinned.

"Well you're pretty *used* to both of them," he said.

"Well that's true of course," she said, "But I think I like them just on their *own merits,* too." She looked back and forth between his father and his aunt. "The only thing I feel a *little* sorry about," she said, "is not to have one of the Agee names in it. Like Lamar or Margroves at least. No not Margroves, for a girl, but Lamar. Jay's mother's maiden name, you know."

"O yes," Aunt Paula said. "That'd be a *very* pretty middle name, why didn't you use it?"

"Well once we'd settled on Emma, we just—well anyhow *I* just felt like doing all I could for Mama. Besides it just sounds better, Emma Farrand. Emma Lamar. Just too many ems don't you think?"

"Why I don't know," Aunt Paula said. "Emma Lamar. Emma Farrand. Emma Lamar Agee. No Laura I kinda like it."

"Me too," his father said.

"I know dear. But then people'd be so apt to call her *both* names. I know it's done a lot dear, you don't mind it at all."

"I kinda like it," he said.

"But I guess it's just too 'Southern' for me to get used to. I'm sorry. Emmer Lamaar. Immer Lamaarr," she called. "Don't you see?" she asked him.

"Sounds all right to me," he said, "but why I don't want it is, *you* don't like it."

"Aw, dear," she said, and took his hand. "I've been awfully selfish about it I'm afraid," she said. "And Jay's been just his own generous self." She squeezed his hand. "Jay wouldn't tell me which he hoped for," she told her sister, while his face darkened with a blush, "not till it was all over. Then he told me he'd *hoped* it would be a girl and he wanted to name it after his mother." She looked up at him. "Oh Jay, I'm embarrassing you!"

"Naw that's all right."

"I'm awfully sorry. I'll just shut my trap, as Papa would say."

"Honey you started, you might's well go on ahead."

"Dear," she said, and squeezed his hand again. "Well I spose you're right," she said, "Only I shouldn't ever have started." Nobody spoke. "Well I—just *couldn't,*" she said. "Much as I wanted to. I just couldn't give the name Jay wanted. Isn't that a shame Paula."

"What *is* the name," her sister asked.

"Actually it's a perfectly nice name I guess and certainly as Jay's *mother's* name I like it because I do think the *world* of *her.* But it did seem too—well, *odd* a name, to give a tiny baby girl to grow up with. I jus—"

His father broke in, smiling. "Laura's not goana get around to saying it if she talks all night," he said. "It's Moss," he said, bashfully.

"What?"

"Just Moss. Like on a rock. Em Oh Ess Ess."

"Moss," Aunt Paula said, carefully, "Moss. Why Laura I think that's a *nice* name. I like that. Moss. Moss Agee."

"And then people'd call her, Mossy," his mother said, "and that I just couldn't stand for. Do you *really!*"

"Why yes I do. Not Mossy but Moss. No I think that's nice."

"Well for goodness sakes well I'm glad you do. I'm glad you like it. It must just be something in *me* that I ought to—"

"Laura dear,"

"I ought"

"Laura, you know darn well you just don't like it and wouldn't ever feel easy with it so honey please don't backtrack like that. Besides it's too late now. Think how your mother'd feel if you went and changed now. Besides it's bad luck to change a name. So let's not keep bothern our heads about it."

"Well," Laura said. "You certainly make me ashamed of myself to be so selfish but I guess you're right. It *is,* it would be a shame now that Mama knows. And they ought to be names we *both* like, not just one of us. You *do* like Emma, Jay? You weren't just pretending?"

"Any name you like Laura, I told you. Cep maybe Gweldolyn. I'd bring my foot down on that." They laughed.

"Dear," she said, and she squeezed his hand and they smiled at each other.

"I don't want to stay too long," Aunt Paula said.

"Why, you're not Paula."

"You need to rest. Besides, Mama—"

"Yes?"

"Mama wanted me to tell you that if you feel up to it she'd like to come up a little while later this afternoon. Papa and Hugh too, probably."

"Why of *course* I feel up to it."

"So maybe you ought to get a breathing spell, hmm?"

"Well actually I feel pretty fine considering, Paula, but I pretty soon do have to nurse her and it's true I guess I ought to lie quiet a little bef—"

"Sure you ought." They kissed. "Mama sends you ever so much love," she said. "So do everybody. Clifford too. He wondered about later in the week, he'd—"

"That would be fine,"

"—he wanted to wait and give everybody plenty of time."

"Later in the week. That would be fine. And my love to everybody."

Victoria was no longer in the room, Rufus now realized, and now that Aunt Paula pulled the door softly to behind her the room became breathlessly still, and they all just stayed in a quietness so deep that they could hear the baby breathing. His mother drew his father down by the hand and he sat on the edge of the bed, and Rufus looked from one of them to the other and back, and again, and the two older people looked at each other and at him, smiling, and with very bright eyes, yet somehow very seriously, and the room seemed to lift quietly as a ship does when it is quietly lifted upon a long slow wave; and he saw how his father and mother now kept looking at each other, so gaily and yet so seriously, almost sadly, longer and longer, and how while they looked their smiles became so broad they tried to quiet them, and couldn't, and tried again, and just grinned, and how a tear ran out of his mother's eye and down across her smile, and she sniffed and smiled and looked at him and whispered, "Well, little Rufus," and, after a moment, "here we are." And his father nodded slowly, smiling, and stroked her wrist, and after a moment she whispered "Here's our family."

And then for quite a while nobody said anything, and Rufus watched the light and shadow freckle on the barely breathing curtain. And as he watched he began to remember what in the confusion and all the talk he had forgotten, and turned with joy to his mother and asked: "Where's the surprise?"

"Enter the Ford"
Travel, 1913–1916

Chapter 10

He saw his father, barefooted and naked to the waist, stealthily lifting his clothes from the chair, and with instant joy and anticipation he remembered. He shot up in bed so fast that the springs creaked and said, "Daddy!"

"*Whhssssht!*" his father warned, so sharply that he was alarmed; Emma groaned in her crib. He frowned, beckoned, and laid his finger on his mouth. Rufus followed him into the hallway.

"Ssh," he warned again, less sharply, and tiptoed towards the back stairs. A board creaked. "*Anhh,*" he grunted.

"Jay?" His mother's voice was muffled and bewildered.

His father spoke close to the door. "It's all right Laura," he said very low. "It's just us."

"See that Rufus wears his sweater," she said more clearly. "It's chilly still."

Rufus felt by the quality of his father's silence that he was annoyed.

"All right," he said. "Where's it at?"

"In the lower lefthand bureau drawer," his mother said.

"All right," he said, and started back along the hall.

"And Jay!"

He stopped. "Yeah?"

"When it gets warm, be sure he takes it off."

"Yeah." He started again.

"And make sure that Emma's covered, will you?"

"Sure. I will." He motioned Rufus to wait and hurried back along the hall. Rufus waited. He heard a drawer jam, and his father's grunt of annoyance; the sound of careful adjustment; the loud noise as it pulled open. "God damn it the hell," his father said tightly, under his voice. Emma wailed. There was intense silence. She whimpered. The silence was still more intense. His father emerged with a red sweater. He avoided the creaking board but his wife called, "Is she all right?"

"Yeah, she's all right."

"Thank you, Jay; goodbye. Goodbye, Rufus."

"Goodbye Laura," he said. "We'll be back by middle of the morning."

"All right."

"Goodbye, Mama."

"*Good*bye dear, have a good time."

"We will," his father said; and they went down the back stairs into the kitchen.

The coffee was already boiling strongly; it shuffled noisily onto the hot stovelid, smelling like heroism and profanity. His father rushed to it with a rag and shifted it to the back of the stove, wagging his scalded hand. He lifted the lid and put in bright yellow kindling. It made brilliant, splitting sounds. He put the skillet where the coffee had been. "Better get into your clothes," he said. He got out the bacon.

Rufus took off his nightgown and stood watching a network of blue form on his skin. His teeth rattled. His father looked up from the bacon.

"Get over by the fire," he said. "Hurry up and get your clothes on."

He stood by the pleasantly stinging stove and got into his drawers, watching his father. His father laid thick slices of bacon in the hot skillet and immediately they made a violent noise.

"Stand away," his father said. "That grease can burn the daylights out of you."

He stood away and slowly pulled one stocking on while he watched his father get into his shirt. He stood with his back turned partly towards his son, unbuttoned his pants, and took the galluses from both shoulders, spreading his knees to keep the pants from falling. He looked ludicrous with his knees spread, slightly squatted, the galluses down his back, and Rufus giggled.

"What *you* laughin' at," his father said in a good humor, tucking in the shirttails.

"Nothing," he said, starting the other stocking. Froggy would a wooin go, he thought to himself.

His father squatted still deeper, reaching inside his pants to straighten the tails, then straightened abruptly, resettled the galluses, and turned, buttoning his fly. "Christ's *sake* boy," he said fiercely. Don't stand on one leg like that next a stove! You could fall over and kill yourself!" He yanked a chair from the kitchen table. "Here! Sit down! And don't ever let me catch you doing *that* again!"

He sat down. He was startled, hurt and humiliated but this soon passed as he watched his father, and went on with his dressing. His father picked up the skillet and gave it a stiff shake and the bacon made a louder noise than ever. He turned it with a fork and took eggs from the icebox. Rufus was having considerable difficulty with his underwaist and normally, at this stage of dressing, he would have asked to be buttoned up, but his father had assumed that he was capable of the whole operation and he was determined not to disappoint him. Besides, his father was busy, and might still be mad at him for standing on one leg. He tried to take great care to get the right buttons in the right holes, but it was so hard to get them in any holes at all that when he had finished he was one button long at one place and one hole long at another. His father took the bacon from the skillet and broke in the eggs; they instantly turned into hard lace at the edges and shuddered all over, making a louder noise even than the bacon. His father salted the eggs and peppered them nearly black. Now if he was to match the extra buttons and the extra hole he would have to undo all the buttons between. His father laid out two plates and two cups, two knives, forks and spoons. He decided to say nothing about it. He pulled up one stocking and laid the suspender-button under it, and tried to slip the hook over it properly. He looked up to watch his father turn the eggs and the whole thing slipped. He tried again.

His father looked at him. "Having trouble?" he said.

He shook his head, and carefully laid the hook over the button, and pulled. Somehow it went wrong again. He wondered why. When he could see the button, doing it without the stocking in the way, he could do it practically every time, and very much enjoyed the way he could slide the button up and down inside the hook, or the hook up and down inside the button, whichever he chose. But with the stocking in the way, he never could count on getting it caught.

"Here, let me try," his father said. He set the skillet back on the stove, where the eggs quieted, and knelt down. It worked perfectly easily for his father. His father undid it and said, "Look here." He looked at him. His father said, impatiently, "No, *here* I mean," and he realized he was supposed to look at his stocking. "Trouble is, you don't pull up on it right. See? Look here." And he put the button under and pressed strongly up, so that the button showed sharply through the stocking. "Now what you do, you get the button way on down and then you try to get the hook over where it's too narrow to go. Like this. See?" He did it as he described and the whole thing flew apart. They both laughed. "You can't ever get it that way," his father said. "You got to pull up on it. *Up* on the button, *down* on the hook. Like this. See?" He put the button under, and pulled up with it sharply, and pulled strongly down on the hook. "See? You bring it *way up* from underneath, and *way down* from on top, so that the wide part of the hook fits over the button. And then you hold them *close together.* You got to keep 'um just as close together as you can. See?" He showed him how close together they were. "And then—now you hold them just as close together as you can while you do this—now you slide it into place, so the narrow part comes right *round* the button. See? Like this." He slid it very slowly, and Rufus watched how adroitly the narrow part slid round the button. His father undid it.

"All right now you try it," he said. Rufus put the button under. "Now way up on the button from below," his father said. He pressed up hard. "Now pull way down with the hook, so you get the wide part over the button." He did so. "Now what do you do?"

"Close together," said Rufus.

"That's right. And then what?"

"Now slide it."

"And what else?"

"Close together," said Rufus.

"That's right. Now let's see you do it."

He held them close together and slid them very slowly until the button was as far down as it would go. "Is that right?" he asked.

"Sure it's right," his father said. "Now hurry up and lets eat this while it's hot and you can finish with that later. Wait a minute," he said. "Got these buttons a little mixed up." He quickly unbuttoned and rebuttoned the underwaist. Always start at the bottom where you can see, he thought; tell him now? No, one thing at a time. "You're gettn pretty good, buttoning yourself," he said.

Rufus said nothing.

His father thought: damn fool thing to tell a child; dumb as a fish.

Chapter 11

It was a long way out to Chilhowee Park but even the ride out there was fun because the streetcar was all open. You didn't get in a door at the front, daddy just swung him up along the side wherever he liked, because there was a long step along each side and no walls on the car. The seats went right straight across. The conductor came right along the outside, and he could make change out of the little silver tubes while he hung on with one hand. They went all the way along Gay Street and out across the viaduct by the Southern Depot and then made a big curve to the right and then went straight again, out Magnolia Avenue. For a while there were big houses with big trees on the lawn, then there were smaller houses closer together, and smaller trees, then there were fewer houses, some big and some small, but farther apart, and more trees, and empty fields, and big signboards. Then there was always the place where Mama said "That's where we first lived when we came down from Kalamazoo," but there was nothing there except bushes and trees and lumps of clay and he remembered it had burned down, when Aunt Paula was still just a tiny baby. And not long after that they could see the first of the Park.

The first that he could see of the Park was in some ways almost the most exciting because there it was coming to him, or him to it, and soon he could be going right into it. High up beyond the green treetops he could see curves of white painted wood and he knew that one was the rolly coaster and the other was the fairy's wheel. For the first little while there was only the very top of them; the top of the popcorn white wheel, moving up from the treetops and down into them again, with dark little cars hanging just under the curve; and the top curve and then after a little the very lowest curve of the rolly coaster, and sometimes you could see a little dark car creeping up one of these curves or streaking down the other side, and the little dark heads of people sticking up from the car. Then while the streetcar came nearer, the trees began to come flakily apart and through them he could see the high white fence that kept people out who wouldn't pay and beyond it almost the whole wheel and nearly all of the rolly coaster, looping way up and way down and in and out and round and round itself like an enormous frozen white worm, and when a car was coming down why even when the streetcar was still moving you could hear the wonderful black roaring of the little car and even the yells of boys and the screams of ladies; and then the streetcar stopped and everybody got out and hurried across the gravel to the gate.

Inside the fence there were lots of things you could see that you couldn't see at all from outside. There was more than you could even see all at once, and even what you could see, it would take more than all day to do all of it. It was the most wonderful and beautiful place in the world except maybe the circus.

There were wide gravel walks full of people; and shade trees; and lawns with signs that told you to keep off but nobody did.

There were two lakes that really joined together, with a little gate in between which could be opened or shut. There were boats tied up side by side with their noses all pointing one way like minnows, and you could get in one of these boats, being very careful to step in the middle or it would turn over, and it always pressed down springily when you stepped in it, and then daddy would take off his coat and roll up his sleeves and pull at the oars and you could go right out in the middle of the water. If you looked over the side of the boat when it sat still, sometimes you could see fish hanging in the water, dark and wet and slowly wavy and if you put popcorn on the water there would soon be a quick *snap* and it was gone: a fish got it. Sometimes you could even see the fish come up and take it, and the minute he took it he *bent* back down in the water as fast as a ball bouncing off a wall. There were great white swans on the water with swelling chests and snarly necks; they carried their black faces way back against their chests with their necks arching above and they always looked very proud of themselves and a little bit mad at everybody else, even other swans. It was clear they did not like the people in the boats. They mostly stayed in shallow, narrow, shady places where the boats didn't go much or couldn't at all, and when a boat came near they swam away and you could see their dark wide feet kicking behind them in the water. Sometimes if people threw popcorn or pieces of sandwich they wouldn't even pay any attention. Sometimes they would, and then the strange neck moved just like a snake, daddy said, and they would take the food and swim away. Sometimes you saw one with his whole head and neck buried in the water, right up to the shoulders. He was eating something off the bottom of the lake, daddy said. And then the long limber neck and the head would come up dripping and the swan would shake, and there would be a little rainbow around him. Sometimes they snarled up their necks and jabbed and nibbled at their own necks with their own bills.

"Reckon he's got lice," daddy said. "Just like a chicken."

"O how awful," Mama said.

"What's awful about it," daddy said.

"They *look* so wonderful," she said.

Sometimes they got out on the bank, or got mad at each other or at people, and then they spread their wings and they were the biggest, grandest wings in the world.

"Why on earth don't they just fly away," she said.

"Clipped, I reckon."

"They don't *look* clipped goodness knows. They've got wings enough for an Angel."

The merry-go-round was all gold and red and flashing mirrors and paintings of mountains and fast rivers in orange and blue and white and while it was whirling it made such loud and happy music you could hardly hear the rush of the roller coaster cars. There were horses on it with gentle expressions and others rearing up with arched necks and red nostrils, and lions and tigers with yellow glass eyes and fierce faces, all in the brightest colors. Some of them went up and down wavily while the merry-go-round whirled and some of them stayed still except that they whirled by very fast too. If it was going when you came there you had to wait till it stopped. You had to wait your turn. It was nearly always crowded with children and you saw the same faces and the same fixed, excited eyes swing past over and over and over. The older children had all kinds of tricks on the animals; sometimes they were so brave that the man in the braided coat hollered at them to quit it or even swung aboard if it was still slow enough and made them stop. There were nearly always older people with the littler children, and other older people hung around looking, and waiting. There were even seats for the littlest children and sometimes ladies sat in these seats with their babies on their laps and sometimes a baby cried because it didn't know what was up, poor little child, it didn't know this was sposed to be fun. When you heard the music and came over it was always an awfully long time before the merry-go-round slowed down and stopped, and if he asked when it would stop or why it wouldn't stop or is it going to stop now, they were impatient with him and said for Heaven sakes have a little *patience* can't you. But after a while it would really go slower, and the music would begin to get wheezy and out of tune, and now the faces of the horses and lions and tigers were very clear and you could begin to pick out the one you wanted to ride on, and finally it would really stop all the way, and the music would stop too, and then you could begin to get on. You couldn't be sure if you could get the animal you wanted because lots of people stayed on and lots of others that weren't let stay on were very loud and mad if they were big or even crying if they were little. But you could always get something.

When they first came there mama wouldn't let him ride an animal, even one that stood still, even if daddy said but I'll *hold* him on; he had to sit in one of the seats with her or with daddy. They were pretty, all bright red with gold leaves wandering on them, but they were sissy. But by now he never had to sit in one of the seats, he could always go on one of the animals. Sometimes he liked the lions or tigers or even the one huge white swan, bigger than any in the lake, and sometimes he liked the horses better because they were the ones you could really ride, daddy said, a real lion or tiger would never let you and he wouldn't ride you any good even if he was willing to try, but he didn't really much care which. What he cared about was to ride the ones that went up and down, instead of the ones that stayed still, and that was what his mama and daddy argued about now—that, and whether he could ride all by himself without *anybody* looking out for him. His daddy would say but daw *gone* it Laura they're every bit as safe as the ones that stand *still.* And she would say Well they don't *look* as safe. They don't look safe *one bit.* And he would say Look dear. He's strapped on. He hangs on to the rod. All that happens is, it goes up and down. Now how in the world can *that* hurt anybody! And she would say, But Jay it *looks* so dangerous. I spose I'm just silly about it but it *does look more dangerous,* that's *all.* And why can't he *wait* for some things till he's a little *bigger?* she would say. They'll be all the more fun if he has to *wait* for them a *little* while. All right, he would say. You're the boss. Don't *say* that Jay, she would say. You *know* how that provokes me. And he would say All right then *I'm* the boss, and stand up big and bossy and pat her shoulder and grin if some man was looking and the man would grin back, and she would look flustered. But when she was there they always did what she wanted.

It was the same with whether he could go on by himself. Finally she said he could go by himself if he rode an animal that stayed still, and he could ride one that went up and down if daddy went with him and stayed right there holding him, but he positively couldn't do both at once, she just wouldn't stand for it, and so that was how it would be worked out. Daddy would pick him up by the armpits and say now get your foot in the stirrup, and help him get it in, and then he would say now swing yourself over, and he would let down some of his weight into the stirrup and with daddy's help swing himself over; and daddy would put the strap around his waist and buckle it, and he would say, now grab aholt of the rod and hang on tight. There was a silver rod that came right up through the animal's neck. So he would grab aholt of it and hang on tight. And then if daddy was getting off he would say now no cowboy stuff. Just set up straight. Promise? And he would promise and daddy would drop off even after it began to start. Or if the animal went up and down and he stayed, Rufus could feel his hand now and then between his shoulders and if he looked around there he was and they grinned, and he looked to the front again because then you could really see it rising up so noble and high, and then sinking, and then rising up again, and the animals ahead, rising or sinking too or just standing still, and he could always feel the rising and sinking more if he was watching it at the same time.

Riding all by himself was even better, and one of the best things of all was at the very beginning, when daddy had strapped him on and he had grabbed aholt of the silver rod and they just waited for everything to begin. Because for a little while, that seemed like a long time, everything stood very still and it seemed as if it would never get moving and yet you knew it would, so that you held your breath almost, waiting; and then all of a sudden things weren't quite standing still any more. Instead there was a kind of buckling lurch like two freight cars joining together and every car down the line budging a little too, and with this lurch the first slow whistlings and foofings of the music began and a few tight strings were plucked or hammered with a sound like very slowly breaking glass, and a second later you could feel that everything under you was beginning to move forward, and the people standing at the side began very slowly to drift, and if you looked at the round edge of the floor of the merry-go-round you could see how still it seemed to stand while the gravel slid past it, just a smooth quiet pouring like slow water, every gravel sharp from every other, and a kind of quiet happy *ahh* rising up from the children on the animals, and the animals which went up and down began some very slowly to rise and others very slowly to sink, and the foofing and whistling began to become faster and firmer and brighter, and the jangling strings and the drums and trepans began to really bang and glitter and sound like something, rising and getting faster and brighter all the time, and the gravel began to get blurry and long and the faces standing along the side swung to look as you swung by, and then everything outside the merry-go-round began to streak and stream, and the music was quick and loud and wild, and all the animals which could were rising up and sinking down as grandly as waves of the sea, and if you kept looking outside the merry-go-round everything streaked by in such a whirl it almost made you dizzy, so that what he would do instead was mainly just hold on, and look straight ahead, and look out only when he thought it was swinging around once more to where he could see daddy and mama. Things all went so fast that sometimes he missed them, or looked just in time to lose them again, but after a little while he knew just about when to look, and how long to wait, and when to look again, and there they were, nearly always looking right at him, and smiling, and sometimes waving: he had to learn to whirl his eyes very quickly to pick them out so they would be clear and not streak.

Sometimes I'm up sometimes I'm down
But still my soul seems heavenward bound

And finally, best of all, there was a time when he and daddy came out by themselves and daddy let him ride one of the ones that went up and down, and didn't stay on with him but got off and stood by the side and there he was, doing it all by himself; and the rising and sinking felt even better than ever before, and sometimes when he came past daddy he was up and sometimes he was down, so that he had to calculate for this, and he was so proud he screamed for him to look, and daddy looked and broke into a grin, and he yelled again the next time around, and daddy was still smiling from last time and grinned again and looked after him, and by next time around he felt so proud he wanted to show off, and took his hands off the rod and leaned far back and screamed *look daddy, no hands!* and the grin that was starting stopped and broke into frowning so that before he came round next time he knew he had better be holding on, and sure enough, even though he was holding on now, daddy was smiling and frowning and shaking his head all at the same time.

Sometimes right in the middle of the ride there would all of a sudden be no more music, and everything whirled along almost in silence, and with a hush over it besides, and seemed to go even faster and to be mysterious and frightening and happy, like silent falling in a dream when somehow you know you will land without hurting, and all you could hear was the oily clashing and elbowing and the occasional squeaking of parts of the great machine; and then all of a sudden a bran new tune would start and everything would be bright again, and with bran new cheerfulness it would seem to go even faster than in the silence or before it.

The only trouble with these rides was that though they seemed so long when you were waiting your turn, when you were on, they were really over awfully soon. It always kind of sneaked up on you that all of a sudden, when things still seemed to be careening along so beautifully, and the music was so loud and fine you couldn't hear anything else in the world, a kind of weakening would begin to sneak into the speed. Things began to be a little less streaky and before long they were hardly streaking at all, and the music began to sound a little the way mama did when she wasn't really thinking what she was saying, what she called thinking out loud, and a kind of queer sadness began to get under everything like sometimes late in the afternoon, as if something was beginning to be over with that you couldn't make last longer, and couldn't ever have again; this was so even when you were practically sure you would be let stay on for another ride but of course it was much more so when you knew that it was absolutely the last ride and that no amount of begging or arguing would make any difference. Everything and everybody outside began to be much too clear, and the moving animals moved all the time more tired and lazy, and the music gradually fell apart into unhappy-sounding foofs and bangs and grunts and gurgles, and the slowing strings sounded like a lot of springs on screen doors snapping, and all of a sudden everything would be over right in the middle of the tune, and the edge of the floor would stop right next the steady gravel and a certain piece of popcorn, and all the people and their faces outside would be still and ordinary, and you knew you were just as still and ordinary as they were. If you were staying on for another ride it was all right because right away you were waiting again for everything to start up, and seeing the ones get off who couldn't have another ride and feeling glad you weren't them. But if it was the last ride for you, then you saw mostly the other people who were staying on and weren't even budging but just looking at you, proud and easy, while daddy unstrapped things and helped you down, and when you were down on your own feet, it always felt queer and unsure for a minute or so, to be walking.

But there was something even more wonderful than the merry-go-round and that was the little train, and he always had at least one ride on that. If you got on the little train it took you way out along the side of the lake and around a little circle and back again to where you started. The cars of the train were not closed like the cars on a big train, they were open, but the engine was just exactly like a big engine, all over. It had a headlight and a little smokestack and a little bell, and a whistle, and smoke and steam came out of it and it burned real coal, and a shaft went up and down along the side pushing the wheels just like a real engine, and the whole thing was so little it was hardly any taller than he was. He liked to watch the engine start up almost as much as he liked to ride in the train, because when you were riding in the train you couldn't see it nearly as well. It ran on a little track so narrow he could step across it with one step. When it was ready to go, the engineer stepped aboard and sat down and rang the high little bell and made the steam puff, and he was so big he sat right back on a board across the coal car and his knees came right up to the top of the engine, and he reached in between his knees to run it. Then it would start up with the bell whanging and the hot, happy whistle blowing *wheeee, wheeee, whee-wheee-eeee,* and smoke and steam coming out, and one car after another would rattle smoothly past full of people, with the wheels making the same kind of clickety-clack-tee clickety clack, faster and faster, that a real train makes.

Of course it *was* a real train, like daddy said, not a make believe but a real one. The only difference was it was so little but someday, daddy said, maybe it would grow up and run on the big line. That was why its whistle was so high, it was still little, and its bell too, just like when people are little their voices are high, but it was a real train sure enough, all the same, and some ways even nicer. It wouldn't go as fast as a big train but it went plenty fast enough for its size, a lot faster than he could run, and it was bright red like a fire engine and the little bell was gold and the whistle was silver, and when you sat in it you could see so much more than in a big train. In a big train you could only see out the side through the window and a little bit out the other side through the windows over there, but when you rode the little train you could see out both sides and behind and up and down and straight ahead—wherever you wanted to look. Way up ahead you could always see the engineer's back, higher than anybody else, and when the back began to turn you knew a curve was coming and if you looked out along the side you could see the whole engine stretch out sideways and then the engineer and then the first two or three cars, just like on a real, on a big train, and then you began curving yourself and looking back you could see the other cars. Or if you stood up with daddy holding you, you could see all the cars ahead and all the cars behind, right in a line, each waggling a little different from the next one, and all the heads of all the people, and the engineer and the smoke up ahead, but you weren't supposed to stand up, it was against the rules on this line, daddy said. And you could see the whole park swimming past. The train ran between white fences, but they were not as high as the train, and two places it blew its whistle loudly and a gate came down and it went straight across a walk, and everybody who was walking had to stop and wait for it, and another place it went so near along the lake you could hardly see any ground on that side, only the water, moving very fast, as if you were riding a fast little boat, and if you looked out further you could see the water and everything on it, boats and swans and people and the little island in the middle and the trees on the island, turning slowly round, and the fairy's wheel and the rolly coaster and even the big fair buildings were winding slowly too.

There was a whole line of little places where you could do all kinds of things. One place you could get ice cream cones, and weenies, and popcorn, and peanuts, and sandwiches, and root beer. The other places were for grown-up people and there was always a crowd of them there. One place they turned a big rattling wheel and if it stopped right you could get prizes like an Indian blanket all in bright colors or a golden lady without arms, with a sheet around her waist and a clock right in the middle of her stomach. There was a place where you could get little flags, and little whips all in bright colors. Another place you tried to throw rings over things and if the ring went all the way over, not just the thing you were throwing at but the square block it stood on, too, you could take that home with you. Only, the things people wanted most, like the seventeen jewel watch or the genuine imitation diamond ring, why even if you tried and tried, you couldn't ever seem to get the ring quite over the square block, and daddy said it was a sell [a hoax] and he wouldn't even fool with it. There was a noisy place where they shot guns. You didn't get a prize there, you just shot for fun, daddy said. Shooting gallery. He liked the shooting gallery. There was another place where there was a darky with his head through a hole, only the man at the counter called him nigger, "hit the nigger in the head and you get a cigar" and the ladies got a kewpie doll. They threw baseballs at him, right at his head, and he dodged. Mama just hated it, she said it was an outrage and it ought to be stopped, there ought to be a law.

Daddy didn't like it either but he wasn't mad about it like Mama was. "He's got to make his living," he said. "That's one way he can do it."

"But what an unspeakable way to make a living, Jay."

"Wouldn't catch me doing it," daddy said. "I'd starve first."

"But the *principle* of it, Jay!" mama said.

"I said *I* wouldn't stand for it," Jay said, "or throw at him either, case you don't know it."

"Of *course* you wouldn't Jay, I know that. But *other* people do."

"That's none a my business," daddy said. "If he wants that job that's none of my business either. He's a pretty good dodger," he said. "I bet he don't get hit more'n one time in a hundred. Them balls look soft to me," he said. "They're lopsided like they're soft." Once he picked one up and held it out to Mama. "See they're soft," he said. "Couldn't even hurt if they did hit you."

"I don't even want to *touch* the horrid things," mama said.

"You buying that ball mister," the man at the counter said. "Three for a dime. Hit the nig—"

"Naw," daddy said, and he put the ball back on the counter.

"Don't handle nothing, Mac, if you ain't paying for it," the man said.

"It's back where it belongs, Buster," daddy said, "so look out who you try to boss around."

"*Jay!*" mama said desperately, and dragged him by the elbow. "*Your temper.*"

"Soon bust his jaw's not," daddy said.

"He was in the right Jay. He wasn't trying to *boss* you."

"Don't worry," daddy said, "I won't do nothing with you around"; and he came away, though Rufus could see the man and other men still watching after him.

"Not even if I *wasn't* around," mama said. "He was in the *right* you know."

"Not the way he talked to me he wasn't."

"But Jay he's just a, a *low boor,*" Mama said. "He doesn't *know* any better."

"I'll *boor him,*" daddy said, "if he ever talks like that to *me* again."

"What's a boor," he asked her later.

"Just someone without the beginning of courtesy," mama said.

Next time mama stayed home he went right to that counter first thing and just kept looking at the man, who was busy, until the man looked back at him, and then they kept looking straight into each other's eyes in a very exciting, unpleasant way, until finally the man at the counter said, "Whyn't you move along, Mac, I don't want no trouble."

"That's all I wanted to know," daddy said, and he smiled, but not nicely.

"If yer *lookin'* for trouble" the man said, "just say the word, cause there's plenty here that's paid just to find it."

"Just if you want it," daddy said. "If you want it I'll give you all I got. You and them too. Way you talked tother Satdy you was looking for it. Now I'm here without my wife you ain't looking so sharp."

"You picked up a ball," the man said.

"Yeah and I put it back," daddy said.

"You didn't have no business picking it up," the man said, "lessen you was aiming to buy."

"That's right," daddy said, "and you didn't have no call to talk bossy, not when I done already put it back, and what's more you only done it hiding behind my wife's skirts."

"I didn't even know you *had* no wife," the man said. "I can't keep track a everybody front a this stand, I'm a busy man. Now whyn't you move along Mac, they's people waitin here."

"All I want to know is, do you want to talk bossy now," daddy said. "Looky here." And he picked up one of the balls and held it out to the man. "Now I'm not stealing your damn ball," he said. "In a minute I'm putting it back where I got it. Now you got anything bossy to say about it?"

"You ain't got no right to touch nothing you don't pay for," the man said.

"I know that," daddy said. "And I'm putting it back. All I want to know is, do you want to get bossy about it cause if you do, Buster, hurry up and start bossing." The man looked at him and all the people looked eagerly at the man and at daddy, and the man didn't say anything. "All right," daddy said. "Now I'm putting it down." And he put it down gently where he had taken it from. "How about now," he said. "Other time you got bossy *after* I put it down." The man just kept looking at him, and his face got red all over. "All right," daddy said. "Just watch out who you try to boss around, next time." And he turned around and Rufus took his hand and people stood back and they walked through.

Rufus could hear the man shouting "all right now, three for a nickel, hit the nigger and you win a cigar," and he wanted to look around, but daddy never turned his head so he didn't either.

Chapter 12

Late one afternoon Uncle Ted and Aunt Kate came, all the way from Michigan. Aunt Kate had red hair. Uncle Ted had glasses and he could make faces. They brought him a book and what he liked best was a picture of a fat man with a cloth around his head, sitting on a tasseled cushion with a long snakey tube in his mouth, and it said:

> There was a fat man of Bombay
> Who was smoking his pipe one fine day
> When a bird called a snipe
> Flew away with his pipe,
> Which vexed that fat man of Bombay.

But there wasn't any bird in the picture. His father said he reckoned it was still out snipe-hunting.

They weren't really his uncle and aunt, it was like Aunt Hazel. Just a friend. But Aunt Kate was a kind of cousin. She was Aunt Carrie's daughter and Aunt Carrie was Granma's half-sister. You were a half-sister if you had the same father or mother but not the same other one, and they had the same mother.

They slept on the bran new davenport in the sitting-room.

Next morning before daylight they all got up and went to the L&N depot. A man came for them in an auto because there was no streetcar to the L&N. They had so much to carry that even he was given a box to carry. They sat in the big room and it was full of people. His mother told his Uncle Ted she liked it better than the Southern Depot because there were so many country folks and his father said he did too. It smelled like chewing tobacco and pee, and like a barn. Some of the ladies wore sunbonnets and lots of the men wore old straw hats, not the flat kind. One lady was nursing her baby.

They had a long time to wait for their train; his father said, "Count on Laura and you won't never miss a train but you may get the one the day before you aimed to," and his mother said "Jay" and Uncle Ted laughed; so he heard the man call several trains in his fine echoing voice, and finally he started calling out a string of stations and his father got up saying "that's us," and they got everything together and as soon as the man called the track they hurried fast, so they got two seats and turned them to face each other, and after while the train pulled out and it was already broad daylight. The older people were all kind of sleepy and didn't talk much, though they pretended to, and after while Aunt Kate dropped off to sleep and leaned her head against his mother's shoulder and the men laughed and his mother smiled and said, "*Let* her, the dear."

The news butcher came through and in spite of his mother, Uncle Ted bought him a glass locomotive with little bright-colored pieces of candy inside and Emma a glass telephone with the same kind of candy inside, which his father had never done. His father and Uncle Ted spent a good deal of time in the smoking car, to smoke, and to make more room. It got hot and dull. But after quite a while his father came hurrying back down the aisle and told his mother to look out the window and she did and said, "Well *what?*" and he said, "no, up ahead," and they all three looked up ahead and there on the sky above the scrubby hills, there was a grand great lift of grayish blue that looked as if you could see the light through it, and then the train took a long curve and those liftings of gray blue opened out like a fan and filled the whole country ahead, shouldering above each other high and calm and full of shadowy light, so that he heard his mother say, "*ohhh!* How perfectly *glorious!*" and his father say shyly, a little as if he owned them and was giving them to her, "That's them. That's the Smokies all right," and sure enough they did look Smoky, and as they came nearer, smoke and great shadows seemed to be sailing around on them, but he knew that must be clouds. After a while he could begin to see the shapes of them clearly, great bronzy bulges that looked as if they were blown up tight like balloons, and solemn deep scoops of shady blue that ran from the tops on down below the tops of the near hills, deeper than he could see; "they're just like huge *waves* Jay," his mother said with awe; "that's right," he said; "you remember?"; "sure I do," he said; "just like seeing sunlight striking through waves, just before they topple."

"Yeah," his father said.

"Kate mustn't miss this," his mother said; "Kate!" and she took Aunt Kate by the shoulder.

"*Sssh!*" his father hissed, and he frowned. "Let her alone!"

But Aunt Kate was already waked up, though she was still very sleepy, wondering what it was all about.

"Just *look,* Kate," his mother said. "Out *there!*" Aunt Kate looked. "See?" his mother said.

"Yes," Aunt Kate said.

"That's where we're going," his mother said.

"Yes," Aunt Kate said.

"Aren't they *grand?*" his mother said.

"Yes," Aunt Kate said.

"Well *I* think they're absolutely *breath*taking," his mother said.

"So do I," Aunt Kate said, and went back to sleep.

His mother made one of the funniest faces he had ever seen, looking at his father all bewildered and surprised and holding in her laughter, and his father laughed out loud but Aunt Kate didn't wake up. "Just like Emma," his mother whispered, laughing, and they all looked at Emma, who was staring out at the mountains and looking very heavy and earnest; and they laughed and Emma looked at them and began to realize they were laughing at her, and that made her face get red and that made them laugh some more, and even Rufus joined in, and they only stopped when Emma began to stick out her lower lip and her mother said, "*Mercy,* child, you've got to learn to take a *joke.*"

But her father said, "Doesn't anybody like to be laughed at," and took her on his lap, and she pulled her lip in and looked out the window again. Now they could even see the separate trees all over the sides of the mountains like rice, all shades of green and some almost black, and before much longer they were climbing more slowly past the feathery tops of trees and the high shoulders of the mountains and the great deep scoops were turning past them and beneath them as if they were very slowly and seriously dancing in sunlight and in cloud and in shadows almost of night, and now and then they could see a tiny cabin and a corn patch far off on the side of a mountain, and twice they even saw a tinier mule and a man with it, one of the men waved; and high above them in the changing sunlight, slowest of all, the tops of the mountains twisted and changed places. And after quite a while his father said he reckoned they better start getting their stuff together, and before much longer they got off.

That night at supper when Rufus asked for more cheese Uncle Ted said, "whistle to it and it'll jump off the table into your lap."

"Ted!" his mother said.

But Rufus was delighted. He did not know very well how to whistle yet, but he did his best, watching the cheese very carefully: it didn't jump off the table into his lap; it didn't even move.

"Try some more," Uncle Ted said. "Try harder."

"Ted Henwrich!" his mother said.

He tried his very best and several times he managed to make a real whistle, but the cheese didn't even move, and he began to realize that Uncle Ted and Aunt Kate were shaking with laughter they were trying to hold in, though he couldn't see what there was to laugh about in a cheese that wouldn't even move when you whistled even when Uncle Ted said it would and he was really whistling, not just trying to whistle.

"Why won't it jump to me daddy?" he asked, almost crying with embarrassment and impatience, and at that Uncle Ted and Aunt Kate burst out laughing out loud but his father didn't laugh, he looked all mixed up, and mad, and embarrassed, and his mother was very mad and she said, "That's just about *enough* of that, Ted Henwrich. I think it's just a perfect *shame,* deceiving a little child like that who's been brought up to *trust* people, and laughing right in his face!"

"Laura," his father said, and Uncle Ted looked very much surprised and Aunt Kate looked worried, though they were still laughing a little, as if they couldn't stop yet.

"Now, Laura," his father said again, and she turned on him and said angrily, "I don't *care* Jay! I just don't care a *hoot,* and if you won't stand up for him *I will,* I can *promise you that!*"

"Ted didn't mean any harm," his father said.

"Course I didn't Laura," Uncle Ted said.

"Of course not," Aunt Kate said.

"It was just a joke," his father said.

"That's all it was Laura," Uncle Ted said.

"He just meant it for a joke," his father and Aunt Kate said together.

"Well it's a pretty poor kind of a joke, if you ask me," his mother said, "violating a little boy's trust."

"Why Laura, he's got to learn what to believe and what not to," Uncle Ted said, and Aunt Kate nodded and put her hand on Uncle Ted's knee. "Gotta learn common sense."

"He's got *plenty* of common sense," his mother flashed. "He's a very bright child *indeed* if you must know. But he's been brought up to *trust* older people when they tell him something, not be *suspicious* of everybody. And so he trusted *you.* Because he *likes* you, Ted. Doesn't that make you ashamed?"

"Come on Laura, cut it out," his father said.

"But Laura, you wouldn't think *anybody'd* believe what I said about the *cheese,*" Uncle Ted said.

"Well you certainly *expected* him to believe it," she said, with fury, "otherwise why'd you ever *say* it?"

Uncle Ted looked puzzled, and his father said, trying to laugh, "Reckon she cornered you there, Ted," and Uncle Ted smiled uncomfortably and said, "I guess that's so."

"Of *course* it's so," his mother blazed, though his father frowned at her and said "*Ssh!*"

Chapter 13

"Thing is," Jay said. "They're not getting any younger."

"I know, Jay."

"Course Mother's strongern she looks, strong as a horse; may be, she'll bury the lot of us, but . . ."

"I know she isn't well, Jay, so crippled up so much of the time. Besides, you ought to see her more often. I know she misses you."

He said, shyly but with conviction, "Miss her, matter of that."

Laura put her hand over his. "Of course you do, Jay; why shouldn't you. She's a very fine, wonderful woman and I know you think the world of her."

He looked at her carefully, with particular love. "You two really do take to one another, don't you."

"I certainly take to her, Jay, and . . ."

"Well, I can promise you she likes you. Don't you ever doubt that."

"Thank you, Jay. No, I don't doubt it. Not one bit."

He thought for a minute.

"It's Paw I mean," he said.

"Yes?"

"I mean his heart. One of these days one of those attacks is goana take him off—like that;" and he flicked an ash from his cigaret so sharply that he frayed the damp end. "Damn it," he said.

"I know, Jay. And even if they were both *very well,* I'd still see your point."

"How do you mean?"

"I mean of course you ought to get it. Let them talk. It won't be easy but we can afford it perfectly well. You're perfectly right. They can't get over thinking of it as a luxury but I think of it as very close to a necessity. People lose touch with each other. And it's so hard by train. Besides, I want the children to know your mother and—well mainly your mother and father, and to know the country too, but all your people." Her voice was rising and becoming girlish, as it always did when she was excited. She put her face close to his and looked eagerly into his eyes. "Let's just go right ahead and get it, Jay, and think no more about it. I'm just—angry that discussion ever came up!" And her eyes were very excited and angry.

"Now wait a minute sweetheart," he said, smiling. "*Wait* a *minute!*" He kissed her cheek, and she made a movement like that of a bird settling its feathers. "Don't go and get sore at *them. They're* not to blame. Don't forget, Laura, they've got some right on their side. It's bound to seem extravagant to them. Besides, you know, if I didn't have any more to go on than they do I'd probably feel the same way. After all, I didn't really make any point of *why* we want it. I hate to argue and besides I just didn't want to. They weren't so bad about it. They didn't really get nosey, you know."

"I know they didn't. I just resent the way they kept so quiet about it. All that 'it's your business' attitude. Of *course* it's your business, Jay!" And again her eyes flashed.

"Well frankly," he said, deeply pleased. "I didn't much like it either. But how else were they to act. They wouldn't lie about it you know. They were probably just as sorry as we were, the whole thing came up."

"I'd never have brought it up if I'd known it was going to turn into a discussion!"

"Sure, sure, but it's all right. It was bound to come up sooner or later."

"Yes I suppose it would, it would have had to. But I don't like it all the same."

"We don't have to like it, sweetheart. We just have to go on about our business."

"Then it's settled," she said, with apprehension as well as exhilaration, for the idea that it really was settled took her a little by surprise.

He saw the look.

"Not one thing is settled, my darling," he said, "so long as you feel any doubts about it."

"Oh no Jay . . ."

"I mean that," he interrupted; "I mean that very seriously, Laura. So don't go making up your mind till it's good and ready to make up. And if you think we'd better not, why that absolutely settles it, and no regrets or disagreements from me. . . . You know I mean that, don't you Laura? You know I'm not just trying to push you into something."

"Yes I do, Jay, bless you. You never have tried and I know you never will. I better think a minute."

"That's hurrying, dear. Take your time. Think all night. Think a year if you need to."

"A minute'll do," she snapped out absently, concentrated on her thinking.

He watched with tenderness how her pretty face knotted up and frowned over the thinking; then it occurred to him that to be watched might of itself be a kind of forcing, and he looked away.

"Jay," she said.

"Yeah?"

"Aren't they—I don't mean to be silly but aren't they rather—dangerous?"

"Autos?"

"Well yes."

"I guess they can be, Laura," he said, trying to take the question really seriously. "People do get hurt; killed even. Run over. Accidents. Go too fast and blow a tire; don't drive carefully; don't keep a lookout for some fool, even if you're careful yourself. Yes, I spose there's a certain element of danger in it, that you can't get around. But after all, there's a certain amount of danger in living, whatever you do. You don't ever take a train trip but what the train might wreck. You never go on an ocean voyage but what the boat might sink. People on the Titanic certainly weren't expecting any trouble, Lord knows.

"But Laura, there's danger of a sort, not a very big sort but still some danger, if you do no more than just stay in the house, there too for that matter!" He laughed a little. "People have been known to break their necks in a bath tub, you know." She smiled at him uneasily. "Anyone's a fool that goes out *looking* for danger. But he's worse than a fool if he spends all his time worrying about how to avoid it. Then he's a fool and a coward besides.

"Not that I mean you," he said suddenly. "I wasn't even thinking of you. You've got a real point there that has to be taken seriously. Only I feel there are just certain things it's much better for a person not to dodge or fear too much if he wants to be really alive. I reckon I feel about it the way I do about money. You know I'm no spendthrift and I believe in being moderate but I *mean* moderate—not miserly. You see how I mean, don't you Laura?"

"Of course I do, Jay, and in principle I feel you're right. I just . . . really wonder whether we ought to think of a thing that involves any such risk, with the children and all."

"I know Laura, and don't think they haven't been on my mind too, because they have. But at the bottom of it, you see, the same thing applies to the children. Either they grow up healthy and normal, with a good healthy respect for danger but no terror of it, or they don't. Besides, one of the main things I mean is, the children are a kind of guarantee of safety."

"Guarantee? What do you mean?"

"Well of course I don't mean quite guarantee, but I do mean near it. As I figure it ninety-nine per cent of the accidents must come from people who are careless, and ninety-nine per cent of them must be careless simply because they haven't anything to give them a strong sense of responsibility. Now people with a strong sense of responsibility are going to be very specially careful. They're going to be on their guard against every contingency, even against the fools. So having children, and a wife," he smiled at her, "and feeling about them the way I do, I calculate that I reduce our margin of danger down to just about as small as it can possibly be reduced; and the rest—well, the rest you have to leave up to Fate, Laura.

"Same Fate that breaks your neck in the bath tub, even if you never dare go out of the house. Only even then, I bet a hundred to one it's carelessness.

"Besides we're talking out of all proportion, as if it were some sort of a death-machine or something.

"But Lord God I'm talking too much."

He started rolling another cigarette. He said, with shame, "And I guess I *was* trying to talk you into it."

"No you weren't Jay. You might have been, but you weren't. Because I think you're right. I think that's the way to feel about it. Let's just get it, dear. Let's."

"Now you're all excited. You cool off and tell me what you think in a day or so."

"No maybe I am but if I am it's a kind of excitement I believe in." Unexpected even to herself she said: "You don't think I married you because I was cautious do you?"

They were both transfixed by shock. Their eyes were extremely charged and complex.

He said, very gently: "Are you ever sorry you did, Laura? I know for awhile you had good reason to be. But are you ever sorry any more?"

She said, very fiercely: "*You know* I'm not!" and burst into tears.

He took her in his arms. "Laura, sweetheart, my darling wife, God bless your heart! Look at me Laura. No, forgive me, I know it. God yes I know it. Just for a minute, what you said, or something in how you said it, I wondered, that's all. I had to know. I could brain myself for asking but I had to know, everything just seemed to fall out from under. Forgive me Laura."

She looked up at him. "I love you with all my heart for asking," she said. "And don't you dare ever to doubt it again."

Late in the night they both lay awake and looked up into the dark. They had neither moved nor said anything for a long while and, although there had been no change in their breathing, each believed it possible that the other was asleep. She said, very quietly:

"Jay."

"What is it, Laura?"

"Do you remember writing me once, from Panama, 'I have a terrible premonition of impending disaster'?"

"Nope, can't say that I—yes, I do, too."

"You do remember?"

"Yes."

"Jay, I've been lying here awake—" her voice went dry; "I feel that now." She caught at his hand and her breath shook.

He quickly turned to her and stroked her forehead. "Oh Laura," he said. "Laura. No."

"Yes I do. I don't know when. Or which of us. Maybe all of us. But something dreadful is going to happen, Jay. Something irreparable. To our family. In that auto."

"Bless your heart my Laura, bless your heart. You're just a lot more scared about that daggoned auto than you thought you were. That's all. And that settles it. We just won't get it, dear, we just won't get it."

"Something terrible; terrible."

"Nothing is going to happen sweetheart, not in that auto anyhow, because we aren't going to have it, don't you see, we just aren't going to have it."

"Oh, Jay."

"That's all right. That's *all right.* We just won't have it. That's all. That's all."

"You must think I'm awfully foolish Jay, I'm ashamed of myself."

"I just think you're awfully scared and if you're so scared you'd be awfully foolish to walk right on into what scares you."

"It isn't like scare, Jay. It's something very different. Like a cold breath going all the way through me; *freezing* cold. It's knowledge, Jay."

"It can't be knowledge because we aren't going to get that car."

She said nothing. He stroked her forehead. She said: "Could you ever forgive me, if we didn't?"

He said: "I couldn't forgive myself if we did, if you feel this way."

"I don't *want* to feel this way. It just—seems to force itself on me. Believe me I don't want to."

"Of course you don't dear. We can't any of us help how we feel."

"Jay: if it *is*—knowledge—it's going to happen and nothing we can do will prevent it."

He felt impatience, but such love and sympathy that it was easy to subdue it. "There's one dern sure way to prevent it. And that's what we're going to do."

"You mind, don't you?"

"I mind a little, but nothing like I'd mind getting it when you feel so terrible about it."

"You're so good to me, Jay."

"Shucks."

"So kind and good."

"Sweetheart."

"Not to laugh at me."

"It's nothing to laugh *at.*"

"You do forgive me?"

"Course I forgive you. There's nothing to forgive."

"Thank you Jay. Oh I can't ever thank you enough."

"Nothing to thank for."

"Oh yes there is. Yes there is!"

Later, when they had lain silent and awake for a long while, she said again: "Jay?"

"Yes Laura."

"That was all very foolish of me. That—illusion I had, that premonition. I'm over it now."

He was deeply tired. "Are you sure?"

"Yes I really am. Those are terrible things while they last Jay, as you must have known when you wrote me from Panama, but when you're over them you know right away how foolish it would be to take them seriously."

"They're bad, all right, while they last." He felt generous. "I suppose sometimes they really come to pass."

"I guess they do. But yours didn't."

He smiled in the dark, and patted her. "None of mine ever did, dear."

She said nothing for a while. She was doing her best to prepare herself to say what she was going to say, with complete sincerity. Finally she was able to say it: "Jay, I really am over it now. Thoroughly and permanently. I feel just the way I did when we talked just tonight. Only more so. Let's get it, Jay, and I'll promise you I won't be silly again."

He leaned over her. "You're really sure you want it?"

"I'm really sure."

"You're not going to worry?"

"Not more than a sane woman ought to."

"Then it's all right?"

"Yes it's absolutely all right." She embraced him. "Abso*lute*ly posit*ivv*ly."

Before long, he was asleep. But Laura still lay awake. The force of her premonition was gone, and both her love and her common sense fortified her, but its coldness still echoed in her heart. Those things are very strange, she told herself; they *very* seldom come to pass. And she told herself: when sinister things come at us out of the outer darkness, we just have to put our trust in God. And for a considerable time she prayed, earnestly and humbly, receiving thorough comfort therefrom, before she fell asleep, with her hands still folded in prayer.

Chapter 14

So all of a sudden late one afternoon, when Rufus was already keeping an eye on the corner where he usually first saw his father coming, he heard a noise and turned to look, and there along the street came his father, sitting up high and proud in the most beautiful auto with his straw hat way on the back of his head; and when he could get back his breath he screamed "*Daddy!*" and his father lifted one hand to him grandly and shyly, and pulled in towards the curb, slowing down. "*Mama!*" he shrieked. "Daddy's got an *auto!*" and he ran out to the curb. His father overshot their front walk and stopped the auto, and made it tremble all over with a wonderful loud noise, and then he looked around and grinned at Rufus and quieted the engine and then slowly, to the child's ecstasy, he made the auto go backwards, exactly to where he wanted it; and reached down and pulled up on something that made a crackling of springs, and stepped out onto the sidewalk just as Rufus' mother hustled out the front door, wiping her hands on her apron.

"Why Jay!" she cried above the happy throes of the auto; and she ran down the steps and joined them. "You didn't *tell* me it was *today!*"

He smiled down at her. "Surprised?"

"Why I'm surprised out of my *life!*"

"*He's* sure surprised," his father said, for Rufus was jumping up and down as high and fast as he could and yelling with joy.

"Rufus," his mother said. He didn't even hear her. "*Rufus!*" she called much more loudly. He looked at her happily, out of breath. "Quiet *down* a little dear I can't even hear myself *think.*"

"Aw let him holler."

"Jay he's on the verge of *hysterics,*" she said confidentially.

"Oh pshaw he's nothing of the kind he's just tickled. Let him steam it off."

"Welll," his mother said uncertainly; and now he was somewhat quieter. Suddenly she realized something. "Why gracious goodness Jay," she exclaimed. "Where's the *man!*"

"What man?" he asked, amused.

"You know perf—you mean to tell me you drove here all by your*self?*"

"Sure I did," he said casually. "Don't take but one."

"But *how* on *earth!* I mean where in the world d—"

"Been sneakin some practice on you, that's all."

"Not *alone* Jay," she said with alarm.

"Course not. Till today."

"He says it's all right? You're sure?"

"Sure he does. Sides, he says come on back if I got any more questions."

"But you had to come why right through the middle of *town!*"

"Why sure."

"But Jay how could you *dare!*"

He laughed while she looked at him with doubt and admiration. "Good Lord Laura if other people can do it why so can I. Nothn to it when you get the hang of it."

"But all that traffic. I can see it—"

"I didn't get into much traffic till I got the hang of it."

"Welll."

"Well honey there's always got to be a first time."

"I spose so," she said rather vaguely. "Jay can't you turn it off?"

"Sure I can. Just like to hear it run. Sides we're gonna take a joy-ride and I hate to crank it up. Hurry up and get Emma."

"But supper's almost ready."

"Put it on the back of the stove."

"Couldn't we go *after?*"

"Aw come on Laura. Just a little spin. We'll go for a real ride, after."

"Well I'd—just a minute then." She hurried into the house.

Rufus and his father turned and looked at the auto. It was vibrating like jelly and glittering like patent leather, and it made such a strong pleased noise.

"How you like it?" his father said.

"*Oh!*" Rufus breathed. "*Oh* I *like* it. I *like* it daddy." He could see Arthur and Alvin standing in their yard looking. "Hello," he said.

"Hello," they said.

His father smiled and tipped his hat and he saw Mrs. Tripp standing by the vine on their porch.

"Look what my daddy got," Rufus said.

Arthur and Alvin nodded.

"It's a new auto."

Arthur and Alvin walked to the edge of their yard and stood looking again.

Across the street he could see Greta and Culin Biddle standing in their yard. Mr. Biddle was sitting in the hammock on the porch smoking. He walked around in front of the auto. It had round wide lights like eyes and they were edged with wide bands of yellow brass, and on a broad piece of brass at the top the name was stamped in writing. Ford. Up beyond that, the glass windshield was shining in the sun. "So you got you a gas buggy," he heard; Mr. Tripp had walked up. Alvin and Arthur were with him.

"Yeap," his father said.

"How much it set you back?"

"Not so much," his father said.

"Nice little machine," Mr. Tripp said.

"Yeah," his father said.

"No style, a course," Mr. Tripp said. "Got to put up with an awful lot a cheap Ford jokes. Tin Lizzie. But by all I hear they're the best things on the market, dollar for dollar."

"That's right," his father said.

"Course they got an awful name for breaking down," Mr. Tripp said. "But where Ford's ahead, he supplies you the parts. Have a breakdown, you can always count on getting a new part pronto."

"Uhuh," his father said.

"I'll be just a *minute* more Jay," his mother called from the door.

"Well get a wiggle on," his father called, but she was already gone.

Mr. King came up. "So that's your new machine," he said.

"Howdy," his father said. "Yeap. That's it."

"Evenin," Mr. King said.

"Evenin," Mr. Tripp said.

"Looks like a stout little buggy," Mr. King said. He leaned over and looked into the front seat. "How's it run?"

"Runs fine," his father said.

"Course they make a heck of a racket," Mr. Tripp said. "Hear one comin, mile off. But by what I hear it's a topnotch engine. Ford puts all his dollar value in the engine, don't care about style."

"Dollar for dollar," Mr. King said with dignity, "there ain't a thing on the market can come near it."

"That's right," his father said.

"What I was telling him," Mr. Tripp said.

"All ready," his mother called, and she hurried Emma through the door and hooked it. "Hello, Mr. Tripp, oh *hello,*" she nodded to Mrs. Tripp, who smiled beside her vine. "Why good afternoon Mr. King, how's Mrs. King. I've meant to run over these—"

"About the same, thanks," Mr. King said.

"You please give her my *very* best regards won't you and tell her I want to come over *very* soon? I've just been so awfull—"

"Thank you I'll tell her that. That's a dandy little auto you got there."

"*We* think so."

"It's a humdinger."

"Why thank you. You tell Mrs. King won't you, any time she feels up to an airing, we'd be deligh—"

"Why now she sure will appreciate that I *know,* and so do I. Thank you loads."

"That's right," his father said. "Let's do that now."

"And you too Mr. Tripp of course," his mother said.

His father said nothing.

"Thanks," Mr. Tripp said.

"Well spose we get goin," his father said. And he opened the door to the back seat, and helped her in, and lifted Emma by the armpits and swung her onto her mother's lap.

"Isn't it going to be awfully breezy, Jay," she asked, "with the top down?"

"Naw," he said, "it's just for a minute. Well, sir," he said to Rufus, and heisted him right over the shut door in to the front seat. It was quilted like a horsehair sofa, and it smelled like oilcloth, and now he could see iron pedals and rods sprouting complicatedly through the floor and the bran new ribbed rubber mat which also wore the name Ford. And now his father jackknifed himself in under the wheel with his knees sharp and high, and pulled the door to on his side with a light clear bang, and turned around to smile at his wife and his little girl.

"Hang on tight," he said; "Here we go!"

"Jay," she said to him low, not to embarrass him before the men, "do go *slowly* dear, remember it's our first time."

Rufus saw darkness flinch in his face but it vanished quickly and he said "Why sure dear I was aimin to."

"So long," Mr. King called.

His father lifted his hand in a half-salute at Mr. King and Mr. Tripp, who lifted their own hands in saluting waves; then he planted his feet masterfully among the cryptic pedals, and released the long brake with a pwong, and adjusted the little levers just under the wheel, and the whole auto lurched gently as if a hiccup had caught it, and the engine made a loud splendid noise which his father immediately subdued, and they drew grandly and smoothly away from the curb in a long clean line to straighten out just to the right of the middle of the street: and looking back, Rufus could see his mother's intensely excited face with hair blowing around it, and his sister's pink, interested face, and his home already shrinking a little among the moving trees, and the two men and two boys who watched after them; and even while he looked, they broke apart, and Mr. King started for his home and Mr. Tripp and his sons started for theirs; and looking sidewise from the auto, he could see the front porches and far shoulders of the road flow past like a quick silent river, and looking straight ahead, the lined houses and trees on both sides of the avenue swelled and opened up like arms to embrace, and slipped on by, and he knew that everybody on every porch and along the sidewalks was looking at them and wishing they had an auto too. Another auto was coming the other way and as it came nearer and Rufus could see the man who was driving it he felt as if they were special friends and waved and called out "hello" jubilantly, and the man smiled and lifted his hand; but Rufus' father did not wave; he only smiled with dignity, and drew over a couple of feet to the right so they would both have lots of room to pass; then brought it back towards the middle and glanced around.

"How you like it?" he said.

"Don't look back *please* Jay," his mother said.

His father looked quickly front and said out of the end of his mouth, over his shoulder, "*I* know what I'm doin Laura."

"I know dear I'm sorry. But *I don't*."

"I asked you how you like it," he said after a moment.

"Why I just simply *love* it of *course*," she called.

"Too breezy?"

"Little bit," she said. "I should have taken a scarf."

"I'll slow down," he said generously, and did so.

"Now that's lovely," she cried. "That's *just* right. Thank you dear."

He nodded.

"*Thank* you," she said more loudly.

"Sure," he said, and nodded vigorously; and then he slowed still more, for a horse and buggy was turning into the street at the corner nearly a block ahead. "Got to be real careful about horses," he called back over his shoulder. "Never know which one's agonna shy, at a machine"; and with his left hand he squeezed a rubber bulb discreetly, and a horn gave two short charming blasts. The buggy was already straightening out and now, instantly, it drew far in towards the curb. At the same moment a streetcar came round the quirk [a right-angled "S" bend] in Highland Avenue and headed towards them, swelling. It was clear to the grown people that if all the vehicles continued at the pace now established they would be passing each other at about the same time, with leeway, but not much. Rufus' father slowed down still more, and the swelling streetcar came even with the buggy and then, in another few seconds, passed them in a glorious yellow clanging. The driver of the buggy leaned out and nodded to Rufus' father, who somewhat increased his speed and swung far out to the middle of the street to pass, making his engine as smooth and quiet as he could; the beautiful black horse showed no extreme signs of fear but he was reined far back with a white edge at the corner of his mouth and he took prim little slantwise steps on tight legs, almost crossing his hoofs; the driver saluted his father thankfully, and his father politely returned the salute and, after a little, resumed his speed and his lane a little to the right of the car track.

"*My!*" Rufus' mother said, and he saw his father smile proudly. "I think you did that splendidly, Jay."

"Poor old nag," he said.

"Yes poor thing," she called, "just scared out of his wits but *much* too well-behaved to show it."

"They'll get used to it," his father said. "Like they are to streetcars. Lots of um're broke to it already. Broken."

"Some people think it's the end of em."

"Yeah I know. I doubt it though. Nothing like a horse for bum roads. Style either."

"If all the people who drive autos were as polite and careful as you Jay it'd be *all right.* But some of them are just simply *demons. No* consideration for *any*thing but just to *burn up the road.*"

"That's a fact," he said; and almost as if she had ordered it, a sound of wild threatening hurry grew behind them and a continuous and mercilessly loudening squeak squeak squeak of a horn, and glancing back they saw a big gray auto blaring straight up the middle of the street with its glass flashing the low sunlight and the horse was struggling in his harness like a dancer, and the ruthless horn grew even louder, and his father wrenched his auto to the right so violently they were all toppled, and the next instant the auto rocketed past them in a sneering streak, its driver grinning back cruelly under his goggles, and his mother yelled "*Mercy!*" and Emma began to cry, and his father stopped so abruptly they were thrown again, and he looked after the auto, as it wriggled past the quirk in the Avenue, and said in a low hard voice, "Why you crazy God damn son of a bitch I like to bust yer f—God damn jaw!" And his door was already wrenched open and one foot was out before he realized the uselessness. "I swear to God I could kill a man like that," he said. "I mean it. I could kill him and it'd be a pleasure to."

"It's just an absolute *out*rage," his wife said. "He ought to be jailed. Ought never to be allowed to *drive* an auto!"

"Oughta be murdered, that's what."

"You all right?"

"Yes."

He looked back along the street; the driver was out beside his horse's head now and the horse was almost calm. "How do you *like* that," he yelled. The driver shook his head very gravely. "You all right now?"

"Yeah; much obliged," the other voice came faintly.

His father and the driver waved, and his father got back under the wheel. He twisted, and patted Emma on the head. "Now now honey," he said. "There there there. It's all right now. Don't cry. Don't you cry."

"Awful sorry I shook you up so," he said to his wife.

"Why it wasn't your fault Jay. There was nothing on earth you could *do* but get out of the *way.*"

"I ought to pulled over quicker. Sooner I mean. I was worried for that horse."

"I think you did just right. And Jay. Dear." She touched his shoulder and he looked around. "Darling I want to thank you for stopping. Not chasing him. I know how much you must've wanted to just—chase him and beat him to a pulp but you stopped. For our sakes. I preciate that dear." She looked warmly into his eyes. "The thoughtfulness and self-*control* dear. *Very much!*"

He turned dark red and said, "Couldn't a caught him anyhow, he was agoin like a bat—This auto wouldn't go that fast even if I tried."

"Well it goes plenty fast enough I'm sure for all *decent purposes.*"

"Sure it does."

"Of *course* it does."

"How's little Emmer now," he asked Emma, and he put a finger under her chin. "Goana smile for Daddy? Huh? Goana give Daddy a big smile?" He lifted her chin and Emma looked at him lovingly, with her lower lip stuck out. "*Aww,*" he said. "Smile?" And he prodded her ribs gently.

"*No* dear," her mother said; but Emma began to smile bleakly, then warmly, and then she began to giggle.

"That's my brave little girl," her father said. "*That's* how we like to see her. Well," he said, "Reckon our joy-ride's about ruined."

"O *no* it isn't; don't *say* such a thing. It was just *awful* a minute that's all."

"You all right now?"

"Perfectly all right though I do think, Jay, I do have supper on my mind sort of."

"Sure you do, me too. Less just spin around a couple blocks and we'll take a *real* ride *after* supper."

"That's just what I was thinking."

"Sorry I cussed like that," he told her in a low voice.

"I don't blame you *one bit,*" she said stoutly, "only (she lowered her voice), I do wish you'd be more careful dear, in front—" she nodded, not mentioning them by name. "That's what I mean," he said.

"I know dear," she said. "But you had great provocation."

"I sure did have that," he said, and started driving again. At the quirk he went downhill towards the knitting mill and turned east on Forest Avenue; when they came to the corner just beyond and behind their house he turned to the right and then to the right again, onto Highland, and coasted in to their curb and shut off the engine. They sat for a few seconds, just enjoying themselves, and heard the cooling auto tick like a clock. "*I* don't think they're so noisy," his father said quietly.

"*What* are?"

"Fords," he said. He lowered his voice still more. "Tripp said sompn smart aleck about you can hear one a mile off, Ford."

"Why what—perfect nonsense Jay *did* he! *When* did he say that!"

"When you were still in the house."

"Well I certainly do like his *nerve!*" she said, and looked angrily at the Tripp's porch, but nobody was there. "Of *course* it isn't noisy!" A gleam came into her eye and she leaned forward and touched his shoulder. "You know what Jay?"

"Yeah?"

"*I* think he's *jealous,* that's all. Just *plain jealous!* Just like a silly little *boy!*"

His father began to smile.

"The *eye dea!*" she drawled contemptuously. "I'd like to catch him saying any such thing to *me,*" she said. "*I* think it runs just *beautifully,*" she said. "That's what *I* think."

"Sure it does," he said. "Runs fine."

"What did you say to him Jay?"

"Who?"

"Why Mr. Tripp of course."

"Nothing much."

"Well *I'd* certainly give him a piece of my mind, *believe me.*"

"No you wouldn't either," he said.

"Why what do you mean I wouldn't!"

"You don't want trouble with neighbors, no more'n I do."

"Well no. No. Certainly I don't but I do have my own opinion of Mr. Tee are eye pea pea from now on regardless. I think he's just a jealous little *pill,* that's what."

"*Sshh.*"

"What are you shushing me for. *They* can't hear."

"Little pitchers."

"Oh *my. Rufus. Look* at me. Don't you *ever repeat any* of this about," she whispered "Mister Tripp. Dyou hear? Cause if you did and it came to their ears it would be *just simply awful.* You understand?"

"Yesm."

"Promise Mother. You promise?"

"Yesm."

"Word of honor?"

"Yesm."

"*My,*" she gasped, and coughed softly. "I'm glad you stopped me Jay."

He laughed. "Can't be too careful," he said.

"You certainly *can not! Heavens!*" She giggled again, and he laughed, and Rufus giggled, wondering why.

"Well let's get some supper," he said.

"Yes indeed."

They all got out and stood looking at their auto, standing there so shining and pretty and ready to go. Rufus reached up and laid his hand on the hood; it was warm as toast.

"Don't do that son you'll spoil the finish," his father said. "See?" and he showed him the dark, dull print of his whole hand.

"Oh gee," Rufus said.

"Tsall right we can fix it," his father said, taking out a handkerchief and shaking it, "but let's all try and keep it good as new. Hah?"

"*Oh yes,*" Rufus said, and watched with respect and relief while his father gently polished every trace of his hand from the hood.

There it stood shining darkly, a little smaller, when they looked at it through the screen door. And there it was waiting, all through supper. Rufus and Emma both got up from the table several times during supper and went to the window, just to look at it standing there so beautiful, and they were not often told very urgently to stay in their places. Their father and mother looked out several times too from where they sat, their father even twisting around in his chair to really look, and they all had big appetites, though it was very ordinary food and twice Laura exclaimed that she wished she had known, she'd have fixed something special. When supper was nearly over she left the table suddenly and they heard her prowling around not in the kitchen and after a few minutes she came back with a dark bottle and two delicate glasses.

"Why *Sweetheart,*" their father said.

"Surprised?" she asked, looking roguish.

"Surprised and dee lighted," he said, and he poured out a glass for each of them. They lifted the glasses up to the level of their eyes and smiled at each other shyly.

"Well," he said.

"To many happy trips," she said, and they each sipped a little.

"*Mmm,*" he said.

"*Is* good isn't it," she said, her voice a little gurgly with it.

"How bout—" he said, and nodded towards the children.

"*Heavens* Jay *no!*" Her forehead puckered.

"Just a little bitty sip I mean," he whispered. "Just enough to wet their whistles."

"Well, Rufus maybe," she said, looking anxious. "A *really* tiny one."

"Here you are Rufus," his father said, and there was the fine glass close in front of him, small in his father's hand.

"What is it?" he asked.

"That's wine," his father said. "We're drinkin that to give the machine good luck."

"Just a teeny sip now. Just wet your lips."

It was a glowing red-brown like wood and it tasted rich and wise.

"Mmm," he said. "Yum yum."

His father laughed and his mother exclaimed "Why Rufus!" and laughed too.

"I can see that's a plenty for *you,*" he said.

"I want some too," Emma said.

"No Emma," her mother said. "Huh *uh!* Make you sick."

"Rufus got some and I want some too," Emma said, and she began to scowl.

"Mercy child don't *frown* so!"

"I want some too!" she said more firmly, and her lower lip began to stick out. Before her mother could stop him her father moistened his finger and rubbed it on her stuck-out lip.

"Now pull that little shovel in honey and taste it," he said, and she was already doing so.

"Like it?"

"Yes."

"That's wine. Sherry wine."

"I want more."

"Nope, that's all that's good for a little girl."

"Finish Jay, I better put it away before we're all simply reeling," his wife said, and they both laughed, and he drank what was left in his glass.

After supper that evening they drove down to 1115 and took Uncle Hugh and Aunt Paula for a joy-ride while his mother and Emma waited on the front porch, and then they took Granma and Grampa for another one while he and his mother waited and Uncle Hugh went along again to hold Emma in his lap. The first time they only went over as far as the U.T. [University of Tennessee] and drove up through the Campus, and Uncle Hugh and Aunt Paula said it was perfectly wonderful. The second time they were away so long that Rufus' mother began to worry and Rufus began to get restless and envious, but then finally, quite a while after dark, they heard a noise they thought they recognized and sure enough there they came, from a completely unexpected direction. They hadn't had a bit of trouble, and Rufus' father seemed to be slightly annoyed at the very idea they might have.

"Bran new machine," he said. "Good *night.*"

But it was *no wonder* they'd been gone so long, as his mother said (Rufus repeated it, "*No wonder!*"), for they had gone almost all the way out to Bearden and back.

Out of some kind of hidden uncomfortableness in the air, even Rufus began to suspect that in his effort to please older people and win them over to joy-riding, his father had driven them a lot farther than they had really expected to go or felt like going. Though nobody said anything of the kind. His grandmother was very pleased and polite as always, and even his grandfather said pleasantly that he had to admit it had its points on a hot evening. Though nobody would ever catch him buying one.

But mostly they talked about Emma instead of the ride. The minute his mother was sure it was they who were returning and that no harm had come to them, the thing she was really worried and angry about was that Emma had been kept out so awfully late; "she'll be just too exhausted to sleep all night," she said, "just crying her eyes out." But as it turned out, Emma had fallen asleep before they'd gone two blocks and had slept like a log right through the ride, only waking up and whimpering a little whenever they had to stop, and going right bang back to sleep the minute they got moving again.

Her father was tickled pink. "She takes to it like a duck to water," he said.

"She wasn't one bit of trouble," her Uncle Hugh said.

"Any time she's hard to get to sleep," her father said, "just let me take her for a spin. That'll fix her, I'll guarantee it."

Of course, as they all agreed, Emma nearly always slept the sleep of the just under almost any circumstances; still, it was certainly funny how she always woke up whenever they stopped, and always conked right off again the minute they got moving.

"She just plain likes to travel," her father said.

But then her mother said she had a bright idea. "You know how jiggling a baby will quiet it sometimes," she said, "and if you stop it just opens its little mouth and yells bloody murder till you jiggle it again. Like Rufus always did," she said.

"*Little* mouth!" Grampa said: "hah."

"O stop it papa," she said.

"Sure I bet that's it," Jay said, and Hugh said "why of course."

"Well: yes that's exactly," she said. "Just what I meant. It must be the vibration."

"Hmm," Granpa said. "Some use frm [for them] after all. Install one in every crib, live happily ever after."

"You know there might be real money in that Papa?" Laura said eagerly; she was quite flustered when they all laughed at her. "I don't care," she said earnestly, though she was beginning to laugh too; "I *mean* it. I bet you that's just the way *lots* of inventions happen and people make *scads* of money out of taking them *seriously* and putting them *through, not* just sitting around *laughing.*" All the same, they just kept sitting around laughing.

When they got home that night his father came around pretending to be a chauffeur and opened the door and bowed before he helped Laura and her sleeping child out of the back seat.

"Thank you James," she said.

"The pleasure's all mine Mam," he said: "No, that's not what they say is it? Very good Mam." He bowed again. "Well," he said. "Reckon Rufus and me better put the machine to bed."

"All right Jay take him along but don't go whirling off on your own."

"Course not."

"Hop back in son. Be back fore you get her to bed," he said, and without wasting any more time they started up the street. The minute they were over the little hump and couldn't see the house any more he began gradually to speed up so that the houses no longer just floated by, they streaked, and when they came to the quirk he didn't turn downhill to Forest Avenue but just slowed up enough to take the wriggling turn smoothly, and then pulled down on the little thing under the steering wheel as far as it would go and really tore up the empty street, so fast that the dark stretches of pavement which raced between the round pools of light at the corners seemed very short and it seemed as if they moved from pool to pool almost as fast as you could walk step by step. He leaned forward over the wheel and glanced at his son, smiling.

"Scared?" he asked.

"Huh uh," Rufus said.

"Like it?" his father asked, eyes on the road again.

"O *yes!*"

He saw his father smile. "Just wanted to open her up and see what she'll really do," he said, and they both watched the sleeping pavement stream towards them and under them in their yellow light while the air made a beautiful fluffing roar past both edges of the windshield and the branches of trees sailed swishing overhead like whips. All of a sudden a high weedy bank soared into their light and his father said "*Gahd dam*" under his breath and plunged his foot down hard on one brake and grabbed up hard on the other, and they careened, making a terrible noise, and stopped like hitting a stone wall, with the bank up high and glaring right in front of them and a tremendous noise from the engine until he remembered the engine and shut it down quiet.

"You all right?" he asked with terrible anxiousness.

"Mm hm," Rufus said, very much excited.

"Didn bump yer head, scare yourself."

"Huhuh."

His father just sat for a minute, breathing hard. "*Wow!*" he said finally. "That was a close call sure enough." He shook his head back and forth. "Lucky thing we got new brakes," he said. He got out of the car and walked slowly around to the front and Rufus could see him in the snubbed light, examining very seriously. He shook his head again. "Boy!" he exclaimed. "Come on out and looky here," he called quietly, and Rufus slid under the wheel and came to his side. "Lookit that." A big sharp rock jutted out bluish among burdocks, not two inches from the left headlight.

"Golly," his father said.

"Golly," Rufus said.

"That's last time I'll play I'm Barney Oldfield," his father said. "Less I got me a good clear piece a pike."

Rufus didn't understand the reference so he said *Golly* again, and shook his head slowly. Just to keep in touch. He felt a hand wad up his shoulder and looked up; his father's eyes were very blue and his face was ashamed and worried. He looked as if he wanted help and Rufus loved him and felt very proud to be looked at like that.

"Sure you're all right?" his father asked.

"Yeah," he said.

"That's good," his father said solemnly. He kept looking at him. "Don't say a word about this son," he said, and one hand gestured uneasily towards the auto. "Scare mama to death. She asks where we were all this time, we just tell her we took a little longern we aimed to, but we didn go fast. All right?"

"Sure," he said, using the manliest word he could think of.

"But don't tell her about this. Or goin so fast. Huh?"

"Huh *uh,*" he replied proudly.

"Hate to tell a lie," his father said. "But we don't want to skeer her do we."

"Huh *uh.*"

Chapter 15

After dinner the babies and all the children except Rufus were laid out on the beds to take their naps, and his mother thought he ought to lie down too, but his father said no, why did he need to, so he was allowed to stay up. He stayed out on the porch with the men. They were so full up and sleepy they hardly even tried to talk, and he was so full up and sleepy that he could hardly see or hear, but half dozing between his father's knees in the thin shade, trying to keep his eyes open, he could just hear the mild, lazy rumbling of their voices, and the more talkative voices of the women back in the kitchen, talking more easily, but keeping their voices low, not to wake the children, and the rattling of the dishes they were doing, and now and then their walking here or there along the floor; and mused with half-closed eyes which went in and out of focus with sleepiness, upon the slow twinkling of the millions of heavy leaves on the trees and the slow flashing of the blades of the corn, and nearer at hand, the hens dabbing in the packed dirt yard and the ragged edge of the porch floor, and everything hung dreaming in a shining silver haze, and a long, low hill of blue silver shut off everything against a blue-white sky, and he leaned back against his father's chest and he could hear his heart pumping and his stomach growling and he could feel the hard knees against his sides, and the next thing he knew his eyes opened and he was looking up into his mother's face and he was lying on a bed and she was saying it was time to wake up because they were going on a call and see his great-great-grandmother and she would most specially want to see him because he was her oldest great-great-grandchild.

And he and his father and mother and Emma got in the front seat and his Granpa Agee and Aunt Mossie and her baby and Joe Wheeler and Mary Elizabeth and Aunt Paralee and her baby got in the back seat and Uncle Frank stood on the running board because he was sure he could remember the way, and that was all there was room for, and they started off very carefully down the lane, so nobody would be jolted, and even before they got out to the road his mother asked his father to stop a minute, and she insisted on taking Mary Elizabeth in with them in front, to make a little more room in back, and after she insisted for a while they gave in, and then they all got started again, and his father guided the auto so very carefully across the deep ruts into the road, the other way from Jacksboro as Frank told him to ("Yeah, I know," his father said, "I remember that much anyhow."), that they were hardly joggled at all, and his mother commented on how *very* nicely and carefully his father always drove when he didn't just forget and go too fast, and his father blushed, and after a few minutes his mother began to look uneasy as if she had to go to the bathroom but didn't want to say anything about it and after a few minutes more she said, "Jay I'm awfully sorry but now I really think you *are* forgetting."

"Forgetting what?" he said.

"I mean a little too fast, dear," she said.

"Good road along here," he said. "Gotta make time while the road's good." He slowed down a little. "Way I remember it," he said, "there's some stretches you can't hardly even get a mule through, we're coming to, ain't they Frank?"

"Oh Mercy," his mother said.

"I'm just teasin you," he said. "They're not all *that* bad. But all the same we better make time while we can." And he sped up a little.

After another two or three miles Uncle Frank said, "Now around this bend you run through a branch and you turn up sharp to the right," and they ran through the branch and turned into a sandy woods road and his father went a little slower and a cool breeze flowed through them and his mother said how lovely this shade was after that terrible hot sun, wasn't it, and all the older people murmured that it sure was, and almost immediately they broke out of the woods and ran through two miles of burned country with stumps and sometimes whole tree trunks sticking up out of it sharp and cruel, and blackberry and honeysuckle all over the place, and a hill and its shadow ahead. And when they came within the shadow of the hill Uncle Frank said in a low voice, "Now you get to the hill, start along the base of it to your left till your second right and then you take that," but when they got there, there was only the road to the left and none to the right and his father took it and nobody said anything, and after a minute Uncle Frank said, "Reckon they wasn't much to choose from there, was they?" and laughed unhappily.

"That's right," his father said, and smiled.

"Reckon my memory ain't so sharp as I bragged," Frank said.

"You're doin fine," his father said, and his mother said so too.

"I could a swore they was a road both ways there," Frank said, "but it's been nigh on twenty years sin'ct I was out here."

Why for goodness sake, his mother said, then she *certainly* thought he had a wonderful memory.

"How long since *you* were here Jay?" He did not say anything. "Jay?"

"I'm a-studyin it," he said.

"There's your turn," Frank said suddenly, and they had to back the auto to turn into it.

They began a long, slow, winding climb, and Rufus half heard and scarcely understood their disjointed talking. His father had not been there in nearly thirteen years; the last time was just before he came to Knoxville.

He was always her favorite, Frank said.

Yes, his grandfather said, he reckoned that was a fact, she always seemed to take a shine to Jim.

His father said quietly that he always did take a shine to her. It turned out he was the last of those in the auto who had seen her. They asked how she was, as if it had been within a month or two. He said she was failing lots of ways, specially getting around, her rheumatism was pretty bad, but in the mind she was bright as a dollar, course that wasn't saying how they might find her by now, poor old soul; no *use* saying.

"Nope," Uncle Frank said, "*that* was a fact; time sure did fly, didn't it; seemed like before you knew it, this year was last year. She had never yet seen Jim's children, or Frank's, or Mossie's or Paralee's, it was sure going to be a treat for her. A treat *and* a surprise."

"Yes it sure would be that," his father said, always supposing she could still recognize them.

"Mightn't she even have died?" his mother wanted to know.

"*Oh* no," all the Agees said, they'd have heard for sure if she'd died. Matter of fact they *had* heard she had failed a good bit. Sometimes her memory slipped up and she got confused, poor old soul.

His mother said well she should *think* so, poor old lady. She asked, carefully, if she was taken good care of.

"Oh, yes," they said. That she was. "Paralee's practically given up her life to her." That was Grandpa Agee's oldest sister and young Paralee was named for her. Lived right with her tending to her wants, day and night.

"Well, isn't that just wonderful," his mother said.

"Wasn't anybody else could do it," they agreed with each other. All married and gone, and she wouldn't come live with any of them, they all offered, over and over, but she wouldn't leave her home.

"I raised my family here," she said, "I lived here all my life from fourteen years on and I aim to die here." That must be a good thirty-five—no it—a good—near forty year ago, Grampaw died."

"Goodness sake," his mother said, "and she was an old *old* woman *then!*"

His father said soberly: "She's a hundred and three years old. Hundred and three or hundred and four. She never could remember for sure which. But she knows she wasn't born later than eighteen twelve. And she always reckoned it might of been eighteen eleven."

"*Great—heavens,* Jay! Do you really *mean* that?" He just nodded, and kept his eyes on the road. "Just *imagine that* Rufus," she said. "Just *think* of *that!*"

"She's an old old lady," his father said gravely; and Frank gravely and proudly concurred.

"The things she must have *seen!*" Laura said quietly. "Indians. Wild animals." Jay laughed. "I mean *man*eaters, Jay. Bears, and wildcats—*terrible* things."

"There were cats back in these mountains, Laura—we called um painters, that's the same as a panther—they were around here still when *I* was a boy. And there is still bear, they claim."

"Gracious Jay did you ever see one? A panther?"

"Saw one'd been shot."

"Goodness," Laura said.

"A mean-lookin varmint."

"I know," she said. "I mean, I *bet* he was. I just can't get over—why she's almost as old as the country, Jay."

"*Oh,* no," he laughed. "Ain't nobody *that* old. Why I read somewhere, that just these mountains here are the oldest . . ."

"Dear I meant the nation," she said. "The United States, I mean. Why let me see, why it was hardly as old as I am when she was born." They all calculated for a moment. "*Not* even as old," she said triumphantly.

"By golly," his father said. "I never thought of it like that." He shook his head. "By golly," he said. "That's a fact."

"Abraham Lincoln was just two years old," she murmured. "Maybe three," she said, grudgingly. "Just try to *imagine* that Rufus," she said after a moment. "Over a hundred years." But she could see that he couldn't comprehend it. "You know what she is?" she said; "she's Grampa Agee's *grandmother!*"

"That's a fact Rufus," his grandfather said from the back seat, and Rufus looked around, able to believe it but not to imagine it, and the old man smiled and winked. "Woulda never believed you'd hear *me* call nobody Granmaw, now would you?"

"No sir," Rufus said.

"Well yer goana," his grandfather said, "quick's I see her."

Frank was beginning to mutter and to look worried and finally his brother said, "What's eaten ye, Frank? Lost the way?" And Frank said he didn't know for sure as he had lost it exactly, no, he wouldn't swear to that yet, but by golly he was damned if he was sure this was *hit* anymore, all the same.

"O *dear* Frank how *too bad,*" Laura said, "but don't you mind. Maybe we'll find it. I mean maybe soon you'll recognize a landmark and set us all straight again."

But his father, looking dark and painfully patient, just slowed the auto down and then came to a stop in a shady place. "Maybe we better figure it out right now," he said.

"Nothin roun hyer I know," Frank said, miserably.

"What I mean, maybe we ought to start back while we still know the way back. Try it another Sunday."

"O Jay."

"I hate to but we got to get back in town tonight don't forget. We could try it another Sunday. Make an early start."

But the upshot of it was that they decided to keep on ahead awhile, anyway. They descended into a long narrow valley through the woods of which they could only occasionally see the dark ridges and the road kept bearing in a direction Frank was almost sure was wrong, and they found a cabin, barely even cut out of the woods, they commented later, hardly even a corn patch, big as an ordinary barnyard; but the people there, very glum and watchful, said they had never even heard of her; and after a long while the valley opened out a little and Frank began to think that perhaps he recognized it only it sure didn't look like itself if it *was* it, and all of a sudden a curve opened into half-forested meadow and there were glimpses of a gray house through swinging vistas of saplings and Frank cried, "By golly," and again "By golly, thatn'z *hit.* That's hit all right. Only we come on it from behind!"

And his father began to be sure too, and the house grew larger, and they swung around where they could see the front of it, and his father and his Uncle Frank and his Grandfather all said "why sure enough," and sure enough it was; and, "there she is," and there she was: it was a great square-logged gray cabin cloven by a breezeway, with a frame second floor, and an enormous oak plunging from the packed dirt in front of it, and a great iron ring, the rim of a wagon wheel, hung by a chain from a branch of the oak which had drunk the chain into itself, and in the shade of the oak, which was as big as the whole corn patch they had seen, an old woman was standing up from a kitchen chair as they swung slowly in onto the dirt and under the edge of the shade, and another old woman continued to sit very still in her chair.

The younger of the two old women was Great Aunt Paralee, and she knew them the minute she laid eyes on them and came right on up to the side of the auto before they could even get out. "Lord God," she said in a low hard voice, and she put her hands on the edge of the auto and just looked from one to the other of them. Her hands were long and narrow and as big as a man's and every knuckle was swollen and split. She had hard black eyes, and there was a dim purple splash all over the left side of her face. She looked at them so sharply and silently from one to another that Rufus thought she must be mad at them, and then she began to shake her head back and forth. "Lord God," she said again. "Howdy John Henry," she said.

"Howdy Paralee," his Grandfather said.

"Howdy Aunt Paralee," his father and his Aunt Paralee said.

"Howdy Jim," she said, looking sternly at his father, "howdy Frank," and she looked sternly at Frank. "Reckon you must be Moss, and yore Paralee. Howdy Paralee."

"This is Laura Aunt Paralee," his father said. "Laura this is Aunt Paralee."

"I'm proud to know you," the old woman said, looking very hard at his mother. "I figured it must be you," she said, just as his mother said "I'm awfully glad to know you too."

"And this is Rufus and Emma and Frank's Joe Wheeler and Mary Elizabeth and Mossie's Charlie after his daddy and Paralee's Mossie after her Granmaw and her Aunt Mossie," his father said.

"Well Lord God," the old woman said. "Well pile on out."

"How's Granmaw?" his father asked, in a low voice, without moving yet to get out.

"Good as we got any right to expect," she said, "but don't feel put-out if she don't know none-a-yews. She mought and she mought not. Half the time she don't even know me."

Frank shook his head and clucked his tongue. "Pore old soul," he said, looking at the ground. His father let out a slow breath, puffing his cheeks.

"So if I was you-all I'd come up on her kind of easy," the old woman said. "Bin a coon's age since she seen so many folks at onct. Me either. Mought skeer her if ye all come a whoopin up at her in a flock."

"Sure," his father said.

"*Myy*," his mother whispered.

His father turned and looked back. "Whyn't you go see her the first Paw?" he said very low. "Yore the eldest."

"Tain't me she wants to see," Grandfather Agee said. "Hit's the younguns ud tickle her most."

"Reckon that's the truth, if she can take notice," the old woman said. "She shore like to cracked her heels when she heared *yore* boy was born," she said to Jay, "lame or no lame. Proud as Lucifer. Cause that was the first," she told Laura.

"Yes, I know," Laura said.

"Fift[h] gineration, that made. Did ye get her postcard Jim?"

"What postcard?"

"Why no," Laura said.

"She tole me what to write on one a them postcards and put hit in the mail to both a yews so I done it. Didn't ye never get it?"

Jay shook his head. "First I ever heard tell of it," he said. "Well I shore done give hit to the mail. Ought to remember. Cause I went all the way into Polly to buy it and all the way in again to put it in the mail."

"We never did get it," Jay said.

"What street did you send it, Aunt Paralee?" Laura asked. "Because we moved not long be—"

"Never sent it to no street," the old woman said. "Never knowed I needed to, Jim working for the Post Office."

"Why, I quit working for the Post Office a long time back Aunt Paralee. Even before that."

"Well I reckon that's how come then. Cause I just sent hit to Post Office, Cristobal, Canal Zone, Panamaw, and I spelt hit right, too. C-r-i—"

"Oh," Laura said.

"Aw," Jay said. "Why, Aunt Paralee, I thought you'd a known. We been living in Knoxvul since pert near two years before Rufus was born."

She looked at him keenly and angrily, raising her hands slowly from the edge of the auto, and brought them down so hard that Rufus jumped. Then she nodded, several times, and still she did not say anything. At last she spoke, coldly: "Well, they might as well just put me out to grass," she said. "Lay me down and give me both barls threw the head."

"Why Aunt Paralee," Laura said gently, but nobody paid any attention.

After a moment the old woman went on solemnly, staring hard into Jay's eyes: "I knowed that like I know my own name and it plumb slipped my mind."

"Oh what a shame," Laura said sympathetically.

"Hit ain't shame I feel," the old woman said, "hit's sick in the stummick."

"Oh I didn't m—"

"Right hyer!" and she slapped her hand hard against her stomach and laid her hand back on the edge of the auto. "If I git like that too," she said to Jay, "*then* who's agonna look out fer her?"

"Aw, tain't so bad, Aunt Paralee," Jay said. "Everybody slips up nown then. Do it myself an I ain't half yer age. And you just ought see Laura."

"Gracious yes," Laura said. "I'm just a perfect scatterbrain."

The old woman looked briefly at Laura and then looked back at Jay. "Hit ain't the only time," she said, "not by a long chalk. Twarn't three days ago I . . ." she stopped. "Talkin on about yer troubles ain't never holp nobody," she said. "You just set hyer a minute."

She turned away and walked slowly over to the older woman, keeping her feet flat to the ground because she was wearing men's work shoes without laces. She laid her hand on the old woman's wrist and leaned towards her and said, not loudly but very plainly, "Granmaw: ye got compny." And they watched the old woman's eyes, pale in the light shadow of the sunbonnet, which had not once looked at them all this while, and had rarely even blinked, to see whether she would look now, but she did not look, or seem even to know that she had been spoken to. "Ye hyer me Granmaw?" The old woman opened and shut her caved-in mouth but they could not hear any words and it was not as if she were saying anything, it was just the way sometimes a sunning turtle opens and closes its mouth for no apparent reason. "Hit's Jim and his wife an younguns, come up from Knoxvul in a bran new Ford to see you," Paralee called quietly, and they saw the hands crawl in her lap and lie still again and the head turned a little towards Paralee and they could hear a light dry croaking, but no words.

"She can't talk any more," Jay said almost in a whisper.

"O *no,*" Laura said.

But Paralee turned and came towards them and her hard eyes were bright. "She knows ye," she said quietly. "Come on over and tell her haowdy." And they climbed slowly and shyly out onto the swept ground. "I'll tell her about the rest a yuns in a minute," Paralee said.

"Don't want to mix her up," Frank explained, and they all nodded.

"Don't holler," Paralee said. "Hit don't only skeer her. Just talk real plain."

"I know," Laura said. "My mother is very deaf too."

"She hant deef," Paralee said. "Hyers a rat quickern I kin. Hit's jest to git her to pay notice but not skeer her."

"Yeah," Jay said.

Then they were all silent, and, they began to realize with embarrassment that they were still standing there by the auto, delaying out of some kind of deep shyness or even reluctance.

"Well—" Jay said; and the moment they started walking towards her slowly and bashfully through the mild wavering oakshade it was as if they had crossed a boundary into a world very different from theirs and into a silence which must not be violated.

Just below the shattered hem of her skirt her bare feet were crossed on the cool ground and she was slowly rubbing the lower foot with the upper foot with a sound like dry leaves.

"Jest talk plain," Paralee said.

His father came close to the old woman and bent deep towards her, smiling, and laid his hand on her wrist and said "Howdy Granmaw."

He drew back a little, where she might see him better, while his wife and his children, each holding one of their mother's hands, looked on from where, without being told, they had slipped few feet away. The shadow played quietly on his bowed head and his white shirt and he kept looking at her and smiling. She looked straight into his eyes with serene and in curious intensity, and her eyes didn't change in any way. In their shadow beneath the bonnet and beneath the great ledge of brow-bone, they were a smooth shining gray.

"She doesn't know him," Laura whispered.

His father leaned forward again and gently kissed her on the mouth, and drew back again where she could see him well, smiling somewhat anxiously; and drawing a sudden deep breath, Laura realized more frankly than in a long while, how deeply she loved him. The old woman's face restored itself from the kiss like grass after a light step; her eyes did not alter. Her skin looked like creased brown-marbled stone over which water had worked for so long that it has become as mild and sleek as soap.

"I'm Jim," his father said, touching his breastbone with his middle finger. "John Henry's boy."

Her hands crawled, and it looked as if she meant to take his hand but she did not take it and after a moment her hands lay still again on the blinded gingham, between her sharp little knees. Every white bone and black vein glowed through the varnishlike skin; the flesh at the knuckles was like wrinkled pouches; she wore a red rubber guard ahead of her broad wedding ring. Her feet were quiet now. Her mouth opened and shut and they could just hear the dry croaking, but there were no words, and there was no change in her eyes. It was clear that they were alive in their shadow, not blind, but there was no imagining whether she was using them, or what she saw or did notice, or what, if anything, it meant to her.

"I figger she knows ye," they heard Paralee's quiet voice.

His father stroked the old woman's hand and wrist. "She can't talk, can she," he said.

"Times she can," Paralee said. "Times she don't." He continued to stroke the hand and the wrist. "Reckon they hain't only so seldom call fer talk," Paralee said, "she loses the hang of it." His father shook his head and looked sad. "But I figger she knows ye," Paralee said, "cause she kinda worked her hands and tried to say sumpn. And I'm shore tickled if she does."

His father took his hand away, straightening up, and looked all around him in the shade, sad and unsure. On the ground beside the chair were several old-looking newspapers and magazines, and noticing them with relief he said, in a more cheerful voice, "Don't tell me she's done learnt how to read!" and he looked at Paralee, wrinkling his forehead.

"Naw," Paralee said. "Hit's pitcher's that pleasure her. Them with the colors, an the ads and the funny papers."

"Well I be dogged," Jay chuckled, and now that they were no longer looking at the old woman it was as if they were talking across a stump. "Hunderd n three years old and still takes an interest." He looked over at his wife. "Granmaw never did learn to read or write," he explained. "But she was always just as smart as a whip."

"Isn't that wonderful," Laura said.

"Never has wore glasses neither," Paralee said proudly. "She can see most as good as ever, when she puts her mind to it. Hit wasn't only the yuther morning I was out back gittin us some okry and I heared her acallin, I come to her, 'Sumpn died,' she says, but I couldn't smell nothing and I tole her, 'Naw,' she says, 'A way *over* yonder. Yonder behind the ridge,'" and Paralee lifted a long broken hand to point. "And shore enough I looked and I seen a turkey buzzard a-sailin round that warn't no biggern a speck. I says to her, 'Now I see him,' and she says, 'they's a couple on um,' an I looked again and shore enough thar he was, anothern; and *he* was so little I couldn't hardly see him myself."

"Well isn't that just wonderful," Laura said, and they all looked at the old woman and smiled, but she did not appear to notice; she only sat quiet and gazing, waist-high to them, and she was softly rasping her feet together again.

"Only thing is," Paralee said, "she don't all ways put her mind to thangs. Times, she knows what's agoan on as good as you or me, but other times they hain't nobody in this world could guess what's agoan on inside her head. Likely she hain't even a thinkin a nothin. Jest settn."

"She's tarred," Jay said after a moment.

"Yes," Laura sighed.

"Old and tarred," Jay said. "Pore old soul."

"That's a fact," Paralee said, and they were all quiet. "But like as not after ye done gone," Paralee said, "or tomorra maybe or even a week from now, she'll up and say sumpn another'll show she knowed ye was all hyer. Member ye jest clair as a bell."

"Is that a fact," Jay said.

"She'll say 'Whar's Jim at?' jest like she thought ye'd come back, time for yer dinner. Oh she done that the longest time, last time you come to see her."

"That a fact," Jay said very quietly, and he looked all around him on the dappled ground.

"You all ways was the one she set the most store by," Paralee said. "Cepn her own boy, the eldest. Got kilt when he warn't but only twelve yeir old," she explained to Laura.

"Mercy," Laura said.

"Mule kicked him, right sping [smack] in the forehead. Way she talks about him, it must a like to broke her heart, and she never did quite get over hit."

"Oh Lordy yes," Jay said. "I member how she'd talk about him." They were all silent for quite a while under the working shadow, but not uneasy in their silence. At length his father looked at him and said, "Come here, Rufus."

"Go to him," his mother whispered for some reason, and she gave his hand a little shove as she let it go.

"Just call her Granmaw," his father instructed quietly. "Stand close up by her ear like she was your Granmaw Tyler and say 'Granmaw I'm Rufus.' But don't holler. Just say it real plain."

He walked over to her as quietly as if she were asleep, feeling strange to be by himself, and stood on tiptoe beside her and looked down into her sunbonnet towards her ear. Her temple was deeply sunken as if a hammer had struck it and frail as a fledgling's belly. Her skin was crosshatched with the razor-fine slashes of innumerable square wrinkles and yet every slash was like smoothed stone; her ear was just a fallen intricate flap with a small gold ring in it; her smell was faint yet very powerful, and she smelled like new mushrooms and old spices and sweat, like his fingernail when it was coming off. "Granmaw I'm Rufus," he said carefully, and yellow-white hair stirred beside her ear. He could feel coldness breathing from her cheek.

"Come out where she can see you," his father said, and he drew back and stood still farther on tiptoe and leaned across her, where she could see.

"I'm Rufus," he said smiling, and suddenly her eyes darted a little and looked straight into his, but they did not in any way change their expression. They were just color: seen close as this, there was color through the blind gray shining: a dot at the middle, dim as blue-black oil, and then a circle of blue so pale it was almost white, that looked like glass, smashed into a thousand dimly sparkling pieces, smashed and infinitely old and patient, and then a ring of dark blue, so fine and sharp no needle could have drawn it, and then a clotted yellow full of tiny squiggles of blood, and then a wrongside furl of red-brown, and little black lashes. Vague light sparkled in the cracked blue of the eye like some kind of remote uncertain anger, and the sadness of time dwelt in the blue-breathing, oily center, lost and alone and far away, deeper than the deepest well.

His father was saying something but he did not hear and now he spoke again, careful to be patient, and Rufus heard, "Tell her I'm Jim's boy. Say 'I'm Jim's boy Rufus.'"

And again he leaned into the cold fragrant cavern next her ear and said, "I'm Jim's boy Rufus," and he could feel her face turn towards him.

"Now kiss her," his father said, and he drew out of the shadow of her bonnet and leaned far over and again entered the shadow and kissed her paper mouth, and the mouth opened, and the cold sweet breath of rotting and of spice broke from her with the dry croaking, and he felt the hands take him by the shoulders like knives and forks of ice through his clothes. She drew him closer and looked at him almost glaring, she was so filled with grave intensity. She seemed to be sucking her lower lip and her eyes filled with light, and then, as abruptly as if the two different faces had been joined without transition in a strip of moving picture film, she was not serious any more but smiling so hard that her chin and her nose almost touched and her deep little eyes giggled for joy. And again the croaking gurgle came, making shapes which were surely words but incomprehensible words, and she held him even more tightly by the shoulders, and looked at him even more keenly and incredulously with her giggling, all but hidden eyes, and smiled and smiled, and cocked her head to one side, and with sudden love he kissed her again. And he could hear his mother's voice say "Jay," almost whispering, and his father say "Let her be" in a quick soft angry voice, and when at length they gently disengaged her hands, and he was at a little distance, he could see that there was water crawling along the dust from under her chair, and his father and his Aunt Paralee looked gentle and sad and dignified, and his mother was trying not to show that she was crying, and the old lady sat there aware only that something had been taken from her, but growing quickly calm, and nobody said anything about it.

May 17, 1916
The Day Before

Chapter 16

At breakfast they never said much of anything, they just ate. Once they had sparrows with lots of pepper and his mother said she didn't care, she just plain didn't like the idea and that was all there was to it. Once he said he had to admit it, he liked the coffee even if it wasn't as strong as he really liked; twasn't dishwater, anyhow; and she looked at him in a funny way as if she might laugh and said "Jay I think I'm going to tell you something. Maybe I'm rushing in where angels fear to tread but I think I will. Do you know what that coffee really is?" she said.

"Well what is it?" he said.

"It's—Postum, Jay. It's been Postum for weeks now." He just looked at her and she was waiting for him to laugh, but he didn't laugh, he just looked at her, and he looked very mad. All of a sudden he stood up and raked back his chair and walked out of the room fast. "Jay," she called. "Jay!" She looked scared and mad at the same time. He didn't answer, though they could hear him in the front hall. "What on earth are you doing, Jay," she called, and he came in with his hat on looking madder than ever. "Jay!", she exclaimed, looking at him and laughing and frowning at the same time. But he paid no attention.

"Goin to the shop," he told her. "Whern helld ya think?"

"Don't speak to me like that," she said in a sharp cool voice. But again he paid no attention.

"I just want to tell you this," he told her in a quiet but frightening voice. "That's the last cup of any God damn slop they claim is coffee I'll ever drink in this house lessen you make me a promise and keep it. You hear me?"

She said in an even cooler voice, "I can promise you I don't hear one single word you say, when you talk to me like that."

"All right," he said, "I'll be polite about it. You promise me you'll never try to fool me in my own house again or I'll never drink another drop of coffee here or anything you claim is coffee. Now I want you to hear that cause I sure do mean it. You hear me now?"

"Yes Jay I hear you," she said. "I shouldn't have fooled you. There's no doubt about that."

"How about the promise?"

"You needn't ask a promise of me Jay, I've learned my lesson. More than learned it *I* would say."

"What you mean by that?"

"I mean you shouldn't deceive anybody, even for their own good, and you specially shouldn't deceive anybody who can't see any humor in it."

"I'God I'd love to know what's so funny about it. Fool a man in his own house."

"You *liked* that coffee, Jay," she said, and though she looked so much in earnest, her eyes were dancing.

"Told you how I *really* like my coffee," he said. "Serve me some 't's even halfway decent, try to be nice about it."

"Don't wiggle around it darling," she said. "You said you liked it and you meant it. And you know that good and well."

"I didn know what I was drinkin when I said that or I wouldn never a said it you can bet your sweet life."

She burst out laughing. "That's exactly what's so ridiculous about it," she said. "You've sworn to me up and down it would—make a dog throw up you said"

"I said puke . . ."

"stop it Jay, and all I have to do is make it a little bit strong and you don't even know the difference." And she kept on looking at him and laughing, and though he kept on looking mad, he began to smile too and then grudgingly to laugh; and after a little he did not look as mad as he looked sheepish.

"Well all I can say," he said, "you got a heck of an idea what a joke is."

"I'm sorry Dear," she said. "But really it *was* kind a funny."

"All right," he said, "go on and laugh. Ha ha. Laugh your head off if you like but just one thing." He stuck out his finger at her and she snapped her teeth at it and he laughed in spite of himself and stuck his hands in his pockets. "All the same," he said. "You throw out what's left of that dog gone burnt-up wheat and don't you ever give me coffee again that isn't coffee."

"All right Jay that's settled. Minutes ago. Now for heaven sake take off your hat and finish your breakfast."

She turned on them suddenly. "*Eat,*" she said, for they had been turning their heads as if they were watching a tennis match. They quickly attended to their food, but they could see that he had forgotten all about his hat, which he now surprisedly remembered and took off; then he sat down and finished breakfast.

Chapter 17

At supper that night, as many times before, his father said, "Well, spose we go to the picture show."

"Oh, Jay!" his mother said. "That horrid little man!"

"What's wrong with him?" his father asked, not because he didn't know what she would say, but so she would say it.

"He's so *nasty!*" she said, as she always did. "So *vulgar!* With his nasty little cane; hooking up skirts and things, and that nasty little walk!"

His father laughed, as he always did, and Rufus felt that it had become rather an empty joke; but as always the laughter also cheered him; he felt that the laughter enclosed him with his father.

They walked downtown in the light of mother-of-pearl, to the Majestic, and found their way to seats by the light of the screen, in the exhilarating smell of stale tobacco, rank sweat, perfume and dirty drawers, while the piano played fast music and galloping horses raised a grandiose flag of dust. And there was William S. Hart with both guns blazing and his long horse face and his long hard lip, and the great country rode away behind him as wide as the world. Then he made a bashful face at a girl and his horse raised its upper lip and everybody laughed, and then the screen was filled with a city and with the sidewalk of a side street of a city, a long line of palms, and there was Charlie; everyone laughed the minute they saw him, squattily walking with his toes out and his knees wide apart, as if he were chafed; Rufus' father laughed, and Rufus laughed too. This time Charlie stole a whole bag of eggs and when a cop came along he hid them in the seat of his pants. Then he caught sight of a pretty woman and he began to squat and twirl his cane and make silly faces. She tossed her head and walked away with her chin up high and her dark mouth as small as she could make it and he followed her very busily, doing all sorts of things with his cane that made everybody laugh, but she paid no attention. Finally she stopped at a corner to wait for a streetcar, turning her back to him, and pretending he wasn't even there, and after trying to get her attention for a while, and not succeeding, he looked out at the audience, shrugged his shoulders, and acted as if *she* wasn't there. But after tapping his foot for a little, pretending he didn't care, he became interested again, and with a charming smile, tipped his derby; but she only stiffened, and tossed her head again, and everybody laughed. Then he walked back and forth behind her, looking at her and squatting a little while he walked very quietly, and everybody laughed again; then he flicked hold of the straight end of his cane and, with the crooked end, hooked up her skirt to the knee, in exactly the way that disgusted Mama, looking very eagerly at her legs, and everybody laughed very loudly; but she pretended she had not noticed. Then he twirled his cane and suddenly squatted, bending the cane and hitching up his pants, and again hooked up her skirt so that you could see the panties she wore, ruffled almost like the edges of curtains, and everybody whooped with laughter, and she suddenly turned in rage and gave him a shove in the chest, and he sat down straight-legged, hard enough to hurt, and everybody whooped again; and she walked haughtily away up the street, forgetting about the streetcar, and "mad as a hornet!" as his father exclaimed in delight; and there was Charlie, flat on his bottom on the sidewalk, and the way he looked, kind of sickly and disgusted, you could see that he suddenly remembered those eggs, and suddenly you remembered them too. The way his face looked, with the lip wrinkled off the teeth and the sickly little smile, it made you feel just the way those broken eggs must feel against your seat, as queer and awful as that time in the white peekay [piqué] suit, when it ran down out of the pants-legs and showed all over your stockings and you had to walk home that way with people looking; and Rufus' father nearly tore his head off laughing and so did everybody else, and Rufus was sorry for Charlie, having been so recently in a similar predicament, but the contagion of laughter was too much for him, and he laughed too. And then it was even funnier when Charlie very carefully got himself up from the sidewalk, with that sickly look even worse on his face, and put his cane under one arm, and began to pick at his pants, front and back, very carefully, with his little fingers crooked, as if it were too dirty to touch, picking the sticky cloth away from his skin. Then he reached behind him and took out the wet bag of broken eggs and opened it and peered in; and took out a broken egg and pulled the shell disgustedly apart, letting the elastic yolk slump from one shell into the other, and dropped it, shuddering. Then he peered in again and fished out a whole egg, all slimy with broken yolk, and polished it off carefully on his sleeve, and looked at it, and wrapped it in his dirty handkerchief, and put it carefully into the vest pocket of his little coat. Then he whipped out his cane from under his armpit and took command of it again, and with a final look at everybody, still sickly but at the same time cheerful, shrugged his shoulders and turned his back and scraped backward with his big shoes at the broken shells and the slimy bag, just like a dog, and looked back at the mess (everybody laughed again at that) and started to walk away, bending his cane deep with every shuffle, and squatting deeper, with his knees wider apart, than ever before, constantly picking at the seat of his pants with his left hand, and shaking one foot, then the other, and once gouging deep into his seat and then pausing and shaking his whole body, like a wet dog, and then walking on; while the screen shut over his small image a sudden circle of darkness: then the player-piano changed its tune, and the ads came on in motionless color. They sat on into the William S. Hart picture to make sure why he had killed the man with the fancy vest—it was as they had expected by her frightened, pleased face after the killing; he had insulted a girl and cheated her father as well—and Rufus' father said, "Well, reckon this is where we came in," but they watched him kill the man all over again; then they walked out.

It was full dark now, but still early; Gay Street was full of striking and absorbed faces; many of the store windows were still alight. Plaster people, in ennobled postures, stiffly wore untouchably new clothes; there was even a little boy, with short straight pants, bare knees and high socks, obviously a sissy: but he wore a cap, all the same, not a hat like a baby. Rufus' whole insides lifted and sank as he looked at the cap and he looked up at his father; but his father did not notice; his face was wrapped in good humor, the memory of Charlie. Remembering his rebuff of a year ago, even though it had been his mother, Rufus was afraid to speak of it. His father wouldn't mind, but she wouldn't want him to have a cap, yet. If he asked his father now, his father would say no, Charlie Chaplin was enough. He watched the absorbed faces pushing past each other and the great bright letters of the signs: "Sterchi's." "George's." I can read them now, he reflected. I even know how to say "Sturkeys." But he thought it best not to say so; he remembered how his father had said, "Don't you brag," and he had been puzzled and rather stupid in school for several days, because of the stern tone in his voice.

What was bragging? It was bad.

They turned aside into a darker street, where the fewer faces looked more secret, and came into the odd, fluttering light of Market Square. It was almost empty at this hour, but here and there, along the pavement streaked with horse urine, a wagon stayed still, and lantern light shone through the white cloth shell stretched tightly on its hickory hoops. A dark-faced man leaned against the white brick wall, gnashing a turnip; he looked at them low, with sad, pale eyes. When Rufus' father raised his hand in silent greeting, he raised his hand, but less, and Rufus, turning, saw how he looked sorrowfully, somehow dangerously, after them. They passed a wagon in which a lantern burned low orange; there lay a whole family, large and small, silent, asleep. In the tail of one wagon a woman sat, her face narrow beneath her flare of sunbonnet, her dark eyes in its shade, like smudges of soot. Rufus' father averted his eyes and touched his straw hat lightly; and Rufus, looking back, saw how her dead eyes kept looking gently ahead of her.

"Well," his father said, "Reckon I'll hoist me a couple."

They turned in through the swinging doors into a blast of odor and sound. There was no music: only the density of bodies and of the smell of a market bar, of beer, whiskey and country bodies, salt and leather; no clamor; only the thick quietude of crumpled talk. Rufus stood looking at the light on a damp spittoon and he heard his father ask for whiskey, and knew he was looking up and down the bar for men he might know. But they seldom came from so far away as the Powell River Valley; and Rufus soon realized that his father had found, tonight, no one he knew. He looked up his father's length and watched him bend backwards tossing one off in one jolt in a grand manner, and a moment later heard him say to the man next him, "that's my boy"; and felt a warmth of love. Next moment he felt his father's hands under his armpits, and he was lifted, high, and seated on the bar, looking into a long row of huge bristling and bearded red faces. The eyes of the men nearest him were interested, and kind; some of them smiled; further away, the eyes were impersonal and questioning, but now even some of these eyes began to smile. Somewhat timidly, but feeling assured that his father was proud of him and that he was liked, and liked these men, he smiled back; and suddenly many of the men laughed. He was disconcerted by their laughter and lost his smile a moment; then, realizing it was friendly, smiled again; and again they laughed. His father smiled at him. "That's my boy," he said warmly. "Six years old, and he can already read like I couldn't read when I was twict his age."

Rufus felt a sudden hollowness in his voice, and all along the bar, and in his own heart. But how does he fight, he thought. You don't brag about smartness if your son is brave. He felt the anguish of shame, but his father did not seem to notice, except that as suddenly as he had lifted him up to the bar, he gently lifted him down again. "Reckon I'll have another," he said, and drank it more slowly; then, with a few good-nights, they went out.

His father proffered a Life-Saver, courteously, man to man; he took it with a special sense of courtesy. It sealed their contract. Only once had his father felt it necessary to say to him, "I wouldn't tell your mama, if I were you"; he had known, from then on, that he could trust Rufus; and Rufus had felt gratitude in this silent trust. They walked away from Market Square, along a dark and nearly empty street, sucking their Life-Savers; and Rufus' father reflected, without particular concern, that Life-Savers were not quite life-saver enough; he had better play very tired tonight, and turn away the minute they got in bed.

The deaf and dumb asylum was deaf and dumb, his father observed very quietly, as if he were careful not to wake it, as he always did on these evenings; its windows showed black in its pale brick, as the nursing woman's eyes, and it stood deep and silent within the light shadows of its trees. Ahead, Asylum Avenue lay bleak beneath its lamps. Latticed in pawnshop iron, an old sabre caught the glint of a street lamp, a mandolin's belly glowed. In a closed drug store stood Venus de Milo, her golden body laced in elastic straps. The stained glass of the L&N Depot smoldered like an exhausted butterfly, and at the middle of the viaduct they paused to inhale the acrid burst of smoke from a switch-engine which passed under; Rufus, lifted, the cinders stinging his face, was grateful no longer to feel fear at this suspension over the tracks and the powerful locomotives. Far down the yard, a red light flinched to green; a moment later, they heard the thrilling click. It was ten-seven by the depot clock. They went on, more idly than before.

If I could fight, thought Rufus. If I were brave; he would never brag how I could read: Brag. Of course. "Don't you brag." That was it. What it meant. Don't brag you're smart if you're not brave. You've got nothing to brag about. Don't you brag.

The young leaves of Forest Avenue wavered against street lamps and they approached their corner.

It was a vacant lot, part rubbed slick clay, part overgrown with weeds, rising a little from the sidewalk. A few feet in from the sidewalk there was a medium sized tree and, near enough to be within its shade in daytime, a high outcrop of limestone like a great bundle of dirty laundry. It was not wise to sit too near the tree, for it smelled bad there ("ornery sons a bitches," his father had once said; "Reckon they got dog blood"); but the rock was a very good place to sit and if you sat on a certain part of it the trunk of the tree shut off the weak street lamp a block away, and it seemed very dark. Whenever they walked downtown and walked back home, in the evenings, they always began to walk more slowly, from about the middle of the viaduct, and as they came near this corner they walked more slowly still, but with purpose; and paused a moment, at the edge of the sidewalk; then, without speaking, stepped into the dark lot and sat down on the rock, looking out over the steep fall of the hill and at the lights of North Knoxville. Deep in the valley an engine coughed and browsed; couplings settled their long chains, and the empty cars sounded like broken drums. A man came up the far side of the street, walking neither slow nor fast, and neither turning his head, as he passed, nor quite surely not noticing them; and they watched him until he was out of sight, and Rufus felt, and was sure that his father felt, that though there was no harm in the man and he had as good a right as they did to be there, minding his own business, their privacy was interrupted from the moment they first saw him until they saw him out of sight. Once he was out of sight they realized more pleasure in their privacy than before; they really relaxed in it. They looked across the darkness at the lights of North Knoxville. They were aware of the quiet leaves above them, and looked into them and through them. They looked between the leaves into the stars. Usually on these evening waits, for a few minutes before going on home, Rufus' father smoked a cigarette through, and when it was finished, it was time to get up and go on home. But this time he did not smoke. Up to recently, he had always said something about Rufus' being tired, when they were still about a block away from the corner; but lately he had not done so, and Rufus realized that his father stopped as much because he wanted to, as on Rufus' account. He was just not in a hurry to get home, Rufus realized; and, far more important, it was clear that he liked to spend these few minutes with Rufus. Rufus had come recently to feel a quiet kind of anticipation of the corner, from the moment they finished crossing the viaduct; and, during the ten to twenty minutes they sat on the rock, a particular kind of contentment, unlike any other that he knew. He did not know what this was, in words or ideas, or what the reason was; it was simply all that he saw and felt. It was, mainly, knowing that his father, too, felt a particular kind of contentment, here, unlike any other, and that their kinds of contentment were much alike, and depended on each other. Rufus seldom had at all sharply the feeling that he and his father were estranged, yet they must have been, and he must have felt it, for always during these quiet moments on the rock a part of his sense of complete contentment lay in the feeling that they were reconciled, that there was really no division, no estrangement, or none so strong, anyhow, that it could mean much, by comparison with the unity that was so firm and assured, here. He felt that although his father loved their home and loved all of them, he was more lonely than the contentment of this family love could help; that it even increased his loneliness, or made it hard for him not to be lonely. He felt that sitting out here, he was not lonely; or if he was, that he felt on good terms with the loneliness; that he was a homesick man, and that here on the rock, though he might be more homesick than ever, he was well. He knew that a very important part of his well-being came of staying a few minutes away from home, very quietly, in the dark, listening to the leaves if they moved, and looking at the stars; and that his own, Rufus' own presence, was fully as indispensable to this well-being. He knew that each of them knew of the other's well-being, and of the reasons for it, and knew how each depended on the other, how each meant more to the other, in this most important of all ways, than anyone or anything else in the world; and that the best of this well-being lay in this mutual knowledge, which was neither concealed nor revealed. He knew these things very distinctly, but not, of course, in any such way as we have of suggesting them in words. There were no words, or even ideas, or formed emotions, of the kind that have been suggested here, no more in the man than in the boy child: these realizations moved clearly through the senses, the memory, the feelings, the mere feeling of the place they paused at, about a quarter of a mile from home, on a rock under a stray tree that had grown in the city, their feet on undomesticated clay, facing north through the night over the Southern railway tracks and over North Knoxville, towards the deeply folded small mountains and the Powell River Valley; and above them, the trembling lanterns of the universe, seeming so near, so intimate, that when air stirred the leaves and their hair, it seemed to be the breathing, the whispering of the stars. Sometimes on these evenings his father would hum a little and the humming would break open into a word or two, but he never finished even a part of a tune, for silence was even more pleasurable, and sometimes he would say a few words, of very little consequence, but would never seek to say much, or to finish what he was saying, or to listen for a reply; for silence again was even more pleasurable. Sometimes, Rufus had noticed, he would stroke the wrinkled rock and press his hand firmly against it; and sometimes he would put out his cigarette and tear and scatter it before it was half finished. But this time he was much quieter than ordinarily. They slackened their walking a little sooner than usual and walked a little more slowly, without a word, to the corner; and hesitated, before stepping off the sidewalk into the clay, purely for the luxury of hesitation; and took their place on the rock without breaking silence. As always, Rufus' father took off his hat and put it over the point of his bent knee, and as always, Rufus imitated him, but this time his father did not roll a cigarette. They waited while the man came by, intruding on their privacy, and disappeared, as someone nearly always did, and then relaxed sharply into the pleasure of their privacy; but this time Rufus' father did not hum, nor did he say anything, nor even touch the rock with his hand, but sat with his hands hung between his knees and looked out over North Knoxville, hearing the restive assemblage of the train; and after there had been silence for a while, raised his head and looked up into the leaves and between the leaves into the broad stars, not smiling, but with his eyes more calm and grave and his mouth strong, and more quiet, than Rufus had ever seen his eyes and his mouth; and as he watched his father's face, Rufus felt his father's hand settle, without groping or clumsiness, on the top of his bare head: it took his forehead and smoothed it, and pushed his hair backward from his forehead, and held the back of his head while Rufus pressed his head backward against the firm hand, and, in reply to that pressure, clasped over his right ear and cheek, over the whole side of the head, and drew Rufus' head quietly and strongly against the sharp cloth that covered his father's body, through which Rufus could feel the breathing ribs; then relinquished him, and Rufus sat upright, while the hand lay strongly on his shoulder, and he saw that his father's eyes had become still more clear and grave and that the deep lines around his mouth were satisfied; and looked up at what his father was so steadily looking at, at the leaves which silently breathed and at the stars which beat like hearts. He heard a long, deep sigh break from his father, and then his father's abrupt voice: "*Well* . . ." and the hand lifted from him and they both stood up. The rest of the way home they did not speak, or put on their hats. When he was nearly asleep Rufus heard once more the crumpling of freight cars, and deep in the night he heard the crumpling of subdued voices and the words, "Naw: I'll probly be back before they're asleep"; then quick feet creaking quietly downstairs. But by the time he heard the cranking and departure of the Ford, he was already so deeply asleep that it seemed only a part of a dream, and by next morning, when his mother explained to them why his father was not at breakfast, he had so forgotten the words and the noises that years later, when he remembered them, he could never be sure that he was not making them up.

Chapter 18

Deep in the night they experienced the sensation, in their sleep, of being prodded at, as if by some persistent insect. Their souls turned and flicked out impatient hands, but the tormentor would not be driven off. They both awoke at the same instant. In the dark and empty hall, by itself, the telephone was shrilling fiercely, forlorn as an abandoned baby and even more peremptory to be stilled. They heard it ring once and did not stir, crystallizing their senses into annoyance, defiance, and acceptance of defeat. It rang again: at the same moment she exclaimed, "Jay! The children!" and he, grunting "Lie still," swung his feet thumping to the floor. The phone rang again. He hurried out in the dark, barefooted on tiptoe, cursing under his breath. Hard as he tried to beat it, it rang again just as he got to it. He cut it off in the middle of its cry and listened with savage satisfaction to its death rattle. Then he put the receiver to his ear.

"Yeah?" he said, forbiddingly: "*Hello.*"

"Is this the res-dence of, uh . . ."

"Hello, who is it?"

"Is this the res-dence of James Agee?"

Another voice said, "That's him, Central, let me talk to um, that's . . ." It was Frank.

"Hello," he said. "Frank?"

"One moment please, your party is not connec . . ."

"Hello, Jim?"

"Frank? Yeah. Hello. What's trouble?" For there was something wrong with his voice. Drunk, I reckon, he thought.

"Jim? Can you hear me all right? I said, Can you hear me all right, Jim?"

Crying too, sounds like. "Sure, I can hear you. What's the matter?" Paw, he thought suddenly. I bet it's Paw; and he thought of his father and his mother and was filled with cold sad darkness.

"Hit's Paw, Jim," said Frank, his voice going so rotten with tears that his brother pulled the receiver a little away, his mouth contracting with disgust. "I know I got no business aringin y'up this hour night but I know too you'd never a forgive me if . . ."

"Quit it, Frank," he said sharply. "Cut that out and tell me about it."

"Hit's only my duty, Jim, God Almighty I . . ."

"All right, Frank," he said, "I preciate your callin. Now tell me about Paw."

"I just got back frm thur, Jim, this minute, hurried home specially to ring you up . . . Course I'm agoan right back, you . . ."

"Listen, Frank. Listen here. Can you hear me?" Frank was silent. "Is he dead or alive?"

"Paw?"

Jay started to say, "Yeah, Paw," in tight rage, but he heard Frank begin again. He can't help it, he thought, and waited.

"Why, naw, he ain't dead," Frank said, deflated. The darkness lifted considerably from Jay: coldly, he listened to Frank whickering up his feelings again. Finally, his voice shaking satisfactorily, he said, "But O, Lord, God, hit looks like The End, Jim!"

"I should come up, huh?" He began to wonder whether Frank was sober enough to be trusted; Frank heard, and misunderstood, the doubt in his voice.

His own voice became dignified. "Course that's entirely up to you, Jim. I know Paw n all of us would feel it was mighty strange if his oldest boy, the one he always thought the most of . . ."

This new voice and this new tack bewildered Jay for a moment. Then he understood what Frank was driving at, and had misunderstood, and assumed about him, and was glad that he was not where he could hit him. He cut in:

"Hold on, Frank, you hold on there. If Paw's that bad you know damn well I'm comin so don't give me none a that . . ." But he realized, with self-dislike, how unimportant it was to argue this matter with Frank and said: "Listen here, Frank, now don't think I'm jumping on you just listen. Do you hear me?" His feet and legs were getting chilly. He warmed one foot beneath the other. "Hear me?"

"I can hear you, Jim."

"Frank, get it straight I'm not trying to jump on you, but sounds to me like you've had a few. Now . . ."

"I . . ."

"Now hold on. I don't give a damn if you're drunk or sober, far's you're concerned: point is this Frank. Anyone that's drunk, I know it myself, they're likely to exaggerate, do . . ."

"You think I'm a lyin to you? You . . ."

"Shut up, Frank. Course you're not. But if you're drunk you can get an exaggerated idea how serious a thing is. Now you think a minute. Just think it over. And remember nobody's goin to think bad of you if you change your mind, or for calling either. Just how sick is he really, Frank?"

"Course if you don't want to take my word for . . ."

"Think, Goddamn it!"

Frank was silent.

Jay changed his feet around. He suddenly realized how foolish he had been to try to get anything level-headed out of Frank. "Listen, Frank," he said. "I know you wouldn't a phoned if you didn't think it was serious. Is Vesta there?"

"Why yeah, she . . ."

"Let me talk to her a minute, will you?"

"Why I just told you she's out home."

"Course Mother's out there."

"Why, Jim, she wouldn't never leave his side. Mother . . ."

"Doctor's been out, of course."

"He's with him still. Was when I left."

"What's he say?"

Frank hesitated. He did not want to spoil his story. "He says he has a chance, Jim."

By the way Frank said it, Jay suspected the doctor had said, a good chance.

He was at the edge of asking whether it was a good chance or just a chance when he was suddenly overcome by even more disgust for himself, for haggling about it, than for Frank. Besides, his feet were so chilly they were beginning to itch.

"Look here, Frank," he said, in a different voice. "I'm talking too much. I . . ."

"Yeah, reckon our time must be about up, but what's a few . . ."

"Listen here. I'm starting right on up. I ought to be there by—what time is it, do you know?"

"Hit's two-thirty-seven, Jim. I *knowed* you'd . . ."

"I ought to be there by daylight, Frank, you tell Mother I'm coming right on up just quick's I can get there. Frank. Is he conscious?"

"Awfn own, Jim. He's been speakin yore name, Jim, hit like to broke muh heart. He'll sure thank his stars that his oldest boy, the one he always thought the most of, that you thought it was worth yer while to . . ."

"Cut it out, Frank. What the hell you think I am? If he gets conscious just let him know I'm comin'. And Frank . . ."

"Yeah?"

But now he did not want to say it. He said it anyway: "I know I got no room to talk, but—try not to drink so much that Mother will notice it. Drink some coffee fore you go back. Huh? Drink it black."

"Sure, Jim, and don't think I take offense so easy. I wouldn't add a mite to her troubles, not at this Time, not for this world, Jim. You know that. So Jim, I *thank* you. I *thank* you for calling it to my tention. I don't take offense. I *thank* you, Jim. I *thank* you."

"That's all right Frank. Don't mention it," he added, feeling hypocritical and a little disgusted again. "Now I'll be right along. So goodbye."

"You tell Laura how it is, Jim. Don't want her thinking bad of me, ringing . . ."

"That's all right. She'll understand. Good-bye, Frank."

"I wouldn't a rung you up, Jim, if . . ."

"That's all right. Thanks for calling. Goodbye."

Frank's voice was unsatisfied. "Well, goodbye," he said.

Wants babying, Jay realized. Not appreciated enough. He listened. The line was still open. The hell I will, he thought, and hung up. Of all the crybabies, he thought, and went on back to the bedroom.

Chapter 19

"Gracious *sake*," said Laura, under her breath. "I thought he'd talk for *ever!*"

"Oh, well," Jay said; "Reckon he can't help it." He sat on the bed and felt for his socks.

"It is your father, Jay?"

"Yup," he said, pulling on one sock.

"Oh, you're going up," she said, suddenly realizing what he was doing. She put her hand on him. "Then it's very grave, Jay," she said very gravely.

He fastened his garter and put his hand over hers. "Lord knows," he said. "I can't be sure enough of anything with Frank, but I can't afford to take the risk."

"Of course not." Her hand moved to pat him; his hand moved on hers. "Has the doctor seen him?" she asked cautiously.

"He says he has a chance, Frank says."

"That could mean so many things. It might be all right if you waited till morning. You might hear he was better, then. Not that I mean to . . ."

Because, to his shame, he had done the same kinds of wondering himself, he was now exasperated afresh. The thought even flashed across his mind, "that's easy for *you* to say. He's not *your* father, and besides you've always looked down on him." But he drove this thought so well away that he thought ill of himself for having believed it, and said:

"Sweetheart, I'd rather wait and see what we hear in the morning, just as much as you would. It may all be a false alarm. I know Frank goes off his trolley easy. But we just can't afford to take that chance."

"Of course not, Jay." There was a loud stirring as she got from bed.

"What *you* up to?"

"Why, your breakfast," she said, switching on the light. "Sakes *alive!*" she said, seeing the clock.

"Oh, Laura. Get on back to bed. I can pick up something downtown."

"Don't be ridiculous," she said, hurrying into her bathrobe.

"Honest, it would be just as easy," he said. He liked night lunchrooms, and had not been in one since Rufus was born. He was very faintly disappointed. But still more, he was warmed by the simplicity with which she got up for him, thoroughly awake.

"Why, Jay, that's out of the question!" she said, knotting the bathrobe girdle. She got into her slippers and shuffled quietly to the door. She looked back and said, in a stage whisper, "Bring your *shoes*—to the *kitchen*."

He watched her disappear, wondering what in hell she meant by that, and was suddenly taken with a snort of silent amusement. She had looked so deadly serious, about the shoes. God, the ten thousand little things every day, that a woman kept thinking of, on account of children. Hardly even thinking, he thought to himself, as he pulled on his other sock. Practically automatic. Like breathing.

And most of the time, he thought, as he stripped, they're dead right. Course they're so much in the habit of it (he stepped into his drawers) that sometimes they overdo it. But most of the time if you think even a second before you get annoyed (he buttoned his undershirt), there is good common sense behind it.

He shook out his trousers. His moment of reflection and lightheartedness was overtaken by shadow, and he felt a little foolish, for he couldn't be sure there was anything to worry about yet, much less feel solemn about. That Frank, he thought, hoisting the trousers and buttoning the top button. And he stood a moment looking at the window, polished with light, a deep blue-black beyond. The hour and the beauty of the night moved in him; he heard the flickering of the clock, and it sounded alien and mysterious as a rat in a wall. He felt a deep sense of solemn adventure, whether or not there was anything to feel solemn about. He sighed, and thought of his father as he could first remember him: beak-nosed, handsome, with a great, proud scowl of black mustache. He had known from away back that his father was sort of useless without ever meaning to be; the amount of burden he left to Jay's mother used to drive him to fury, even when he was a boy. And yet he couldn't get around it: he was so naturally gay and so deeply kindhearted, that you couldn't help loving him. And he never meant her any harm. He meant so well. That thought used particularly to enrage

Jay, and even now it occurred to him with a certain sourness. But now he reflected also: well, but damn it, he did. He may have traded on it, but he never tried to, never knew it gained him anything. He meant the best in the world. And for a moment as he looked at the window he had no mental image of his father nor any thought of him, nor did he hear the clock. He only saw the window, tenderly alight within, and the infinite dark leaning like water against its outer surface, and even the window was not a window, but only something extraordinarily vivid and senseless which for the moment occupied the universe. A sense of enormous distance stole over him, and changed, into a moment of insupportable wonder and sadness.

Well, he thought: we've all got to go sometime.

Then life came back into focus.

Clean shirt, he thought.

He unbuttoned the top buttons of his trousers and spread his knees, squatting slightly, to hold them up. Fool thing to do, he reflected. Do it every time. (He tucked in the deep tails and settled them; the tails of this shirt were particularly long, and always, for some reason, this still made him feel particularly masculine.) If I put on the shirt first, wouldn't have to do that fool squat. (He finished buttoning his fly.) Well (he braced his right shoulder) there's habit for you (he braced his left shoulder and slightly squatted again, readjusting).

He sat on the bed and reached for one shoe.

Oh.

Yup.

He took his shoes, a tie, a collar and collar buttons, and started from the room. He saw the rumpled bed. Well, he thought, I can do *something* for her. He put his things on the floor, smoothed the sheets, and punched the pillows. The sheets were still warm on her side. He drew the covers up, to keep the warmth, then laid them open a few inches, so it would look inviting to get into. She'll be glad of that, he thought, very well pleased with the looks of it. He gathered up his shoes, collar, tie and buttons, and made for the kitchen, taking special care as he passed the children's door, which was slightly ajar.

Chapter 20

She was just turning the eggs. "Ready in a second," he told her, and dodged into the bathroom. Ought to get this upstairs, he reflected for perhaps the five hundredth time.

He thrust his chin at the mirror. Not so bad, he thought, and decided just to wash. Then he reflected: after all, why had he worn a clean shirt? He could hope to God not, all he liked, but the chances were this was going to be a very solemn occasion. I'd do it for a funeral, wouldn't I? he reflected, annoyed at his laziness. He got out his razor and stropped it rapidly.

Laura heard this lavish noise of leather, and with a small spasm of impatience, shoved the eggs to the back of the stove.

Ordinarily he took a good deal of time shaving, not because he enjoyed it (he loathed it) but because if it had to be done he wanted to do it well, and because he hated to cut himself. This time, because he was in a hurry, he gave a special cold glance at the lump of alum [used to stop bleeding] before he leaned forward and got to work. But to his surprise, everything worked like a charm; he even had less trouble than usual at the roots of his nostrils, and with his chin, and there were no patches left. He felt so well gratified that he dabbed each cheekbone with lather and took off the little half-moons of fuzz. Still no complaints. He cleaned up the basin and flushed the lathery, hairy bits of toilet paper down the water-closet. Do I? he wondered, as the water-closet gargled. Nope. He reached for the collar buttons.

When Laura came to the door he was flinging over and noosing the four-in-hand, his chin stretched and tilted, as it always was during this operation, with the look of an impatient horse.

"Jay," she said softly, a little quelled by this impatient look, "I don't mean to hurry you, but things'll get cold."

"I'll be right out." He set the knot carefully above the button, glaring into his reflected eyes, made an unusually scrupulous part in his hair, and hurried to the kitchen table.

"Aw, *darling!*" There were the bacon and eggs and the coffee, all ready, and she was making pancakes as well.

"Well you got to *eat,* Jay. It'll still be chilly for hours." She spoke as if in a church or library, because of the sleeping children, and, unconsciously, because of the time of night.

"Sweetheart." He caught her shoulders where she stood at the stove. She turned, her eyes hard with wakefulness, and smiled. He kissed her.

"Eat your eggs," she said. "They're getting cold."

He sat down and started eating. She turned the pancake. "How many can you eat?" she asked.

"Gee, I don't know," he said, getting the egg down (don't talk with your mouth full) before he answered. He was not yet quite awake enough to be very hungry, but he was touched, and determined to eat a big breakfast. "Better hold it after the first two, three."

She covered the pancake to keep it hot and poured another.

He noticed that she had peppered the eggs more heavily than usual. "Good eggs," he said.

She was pleased. Not more than half consciously, she had done this because within a few hours he would doubtless eat again, at home. For the same reason she had made the coffee unusually strong. And for the same reason she felt pleasure in standing at the stove while he ate, as mountain women did.

"Good *coffee,*" he said. "Now that's more *like* it." She turned the pancake. She supposed she really ought to make two pots always, one that she could stand to drink and one the way he liked it, new water and a few fresh grounds put in, without ever throwing out the old ones until the pot was choked full of old grounds. But she couldn't stand it; she would as soon watch him drink so much sulfuric acid.

"Don't you worry," she smiled at him. "You won't get any from me that's *all* the way like it!"

He frowned at her.

"Come on sit down, sweetheart," he said.

"In a minute . . ."

"Come on. I imagine two's gonna be enough."

"You think so?"

"If it isn't I'll make the third one." He took her hand and drew her towards her chair. "You'll *sit* here." She sat down. "How about you?"

"I couldn't sleep."

"I know what." He got up and went to the icebox.

"What are you . . . Oh. No, Jay. Well. Thanks."

For before she could prevent him he had poured milk into a saucepan, and now that he put it on the stove she knew she would like it.

"Want some toast?"

"No, thank you darling. The milk, just by itself, will be just perfect."

He finished off the eggs. She got half out of her chair. He pressed down on her shoulder as he got up. He brought back the pancakes.

"They'll be soggy by now. Let me . . ." She started up again; again he put a hand on her shoulder.

"You stay *put,*" he said in a mockery of sternness. "They're fine. Couldn't be better."

He plastered on butter, poured on molasses, sliced the pancakes in parallels, gave them a twist with knife and fork and sliced them crosswise.

"There's plenty more butter," she said.

"Got a plenty," he said, spearing four fragments of pancake and putting them in his mouth. "Thanks." He chewed them up, swallowed them, and speared four more. "I bet your milk's warm," he said, putting down his fork.

But this time she was up before he could prevent her. "You eat," she said. She poured the white, softly steaming milk into a thick white cup and sat down with it, warming both hands on the cup, and watching him eat. Because of the strangeness of the hour, and the abrupt destruction of sleep, the necessity for action and its interruptive minutiae, the gravity of his errand, and a kind of weary exhilaration, both of them found it peculiarly hard to talk, though both particularly wanted to. He realized that she was watching him, and watched back, his eyes serious yet smiling, his jaws busy. He was glutted, but he thought to himself, I'll finish up those pancakes if it's the last thing I do.

"Don't stuff, Jay," she said after a silence.

"Hm?"

"Don't eat more than you've appetite for."

He had thought his imitation of good appetite was successful. "Don't worry," he said, spearing some more.

There wasn't much to finish. She looked at him tenderly when he glanced down to see, and said nothing more about it.

"*Mnh,*" he said, leaning back.

Now there was nothing to take their eyes from each other; and still, for some reason, they had nothing to say. They were not disturbed by this, but both felt almost the shyness of courtship. Each continued to look into the other's tired eyes, and their tired eyes sparkled, but not with realizations which reached their hearts very distinctly.

"What would you like to do for your birthday?" he asked.

"Why, Jay." She was taken very much by surprise. "Why you nice thing! Why . . . why . . ."

"You think it over," he said. "Whatever you'd like best—within reason, of course," he joked. "I'll see we manage it. The children, I mean." They both remembered at the same time. He said: "That is, of course, if everything goes the way we hope it will, up home."

"Of course, Jay." Her eyes lost focus for a moment. "Let's hope it will," she said, in a peculiarly abstracted voice.

He watched her. That occasional loss of focus always mystified him and faintly disturbed him. Women, he guessed.

She came back into this world and again they looked at each other. Of course, in a way, they both reflected, there isn't anything to say, or need for us to say it, anyhow.

He took a slow, deep breath and let it out as slowly.

"Well. Laura," he said in his gentlest voice. He took her hand. They smiled very seriously, thinking of his father and of each other, and both knew in their hearts, as they had known in their minds, that there was no need to say anything.

They got up.

"Now wher—*Ahh,*" he said in deep annoyance.

"Coat n vest," he said, starting for the stairs.

"You wait," she said, passing him swiftly. "Fraid you'd wake the children," she whispered over her shoulder.

While she was gone he went into the sitting-room, turned on one light, and picked up his pipe and tobacco. In the single quiet light in the enormous quietude of the night, all the little objects in the room looked golden warm brown and gentle. He was touched, without knowing why.

Home.

He snapped off the light.

She was a little slow coming down; seeing if they're covered, he thought. He stood by the stove, idly watching the flexions of the dark and light squares in the linoleum. He was glad he'd gotten it done, at last. And Laura had been right. The plain black and white did look better than colors, and fancy patterns.

He heard her on the stairs. Sure enough, first thing she said when she came in was: "You know, I was almost tempted to wake them. I suppose I'm silly but they're so used to—I'm afraid they're going to be very disappointed you didn't tell them goodbye."

"Good night! Really?" He hardly knew whether he was pleased or displeased. Were they getting spoilt maybe?

"I may be mistaken, of course."

"Be silly to wake em up. You might not get to sleep rest of the night." He buttoned his vest.

"I wouldn't think of it, except: well," (she was reluctant to remind him), "if worst comes to worst, Jay, you might be gone longer than we hope."

"That's perfectly true," he said, gravely. This whole sudden errand was so uncertain, so ambiguous, that it was hard for either of them to hold a focused state of mind about it. He thought again of his father.

"You think praps I should?"

"Let me think."

"N-no," he said slowly; "I don't reckon. No. You see, even, well even at the worst I'd be coming back to take you all up. Funeral I mean. And these heart things, they're generally decided pretty fast. Chances are very good, either way, I'll be back tomorrow night. That's tonight I mean."

"Yes, I see. Yes."

"Tell you what. Tell them, don't promise them or anything of course, but tell them I'm practicly sure to be back before they're asleep. Tell them I'll do my best." He got into his coat.

"All right, Jay."

"Yes. That's sensible." She reached so suddenly at his heart that by reflex he backed away; the eyes of both were startled and disturbed. With a frowning smile she teased him: "Don't be *frightened,* little Timid Soul; it's only a clean handkerchief and couldn't possibly hurt you."

"I'm sorry," he laughed, "I just didn't know what you were up to." He pulled in his chin, frowning slightly, as he watched her take out the crumpled handkerchief and arrange the fresh one. Being fussed over embarrassed him; he was still more sharply embarrassed by the discreet white corner his wife took care to leave peeping from the pocket. His hand moved instinctively; he caught himself in time and put his hand in his pocket.

"There. You look very nice," she said, studying him rather earnestly, as if he were her son. He felt rather foolish, tender towards her innocence of this motherliness, and quite flattered. He felt for a moment rather vainly sure that he did indeed look very nice, to her, anyhow, and that was all he cared about.

"Well," he said, taking out his watch. "Good! Lord a mercy!" He showed her. Three forty-one. "I didn't think it was hardly three."

"Oh yes. It's very late."

"Well: no more dawdling." He put an arm around her shoulder and they walked to the back door. "All right, Laura. I hate to go, but: can't be avoided."

She opened the door and led him through, to the back porch. "You'll catch cold," he said. She shook her head. "No. It feels milder outside than in."

They walked to the edge of the porch. The moistures of May drowned all save the most ardent stars, and gave back to the earth the subsumed light of the prostrate city. Deep in the end of the back yard, the blossoming peach tree shone like a blesséd spirit. The fecund air lavished upon their faces the tenderness of lovers' adoring hands, the dissolving fragrance of the opened world, which slept against the sky.

"What a heavenly night, Jay," she said in the voice which was dearest to him. "I almost wish I could come with you": (she remembered more clearly) " . . . whatever happens."

"I wish you could, dear," he said, though his mind had not been on such a possibility; frankly, he had suddenly looked forward to the solitary drive. But now the peculiar quality of her voice reached him and he said, with love, "I wish you could."

They stood bemused by the darkness.

"Well, Jay," she said abruptly: "I mustn't keep you."

He was silent a moment. "Nope," he said, a curious, weary sadness in his voice: "Time to go."

He took her in his arms, leaning back to look at her. It was not really anything of a separation, yet he was surprised to find that it seemed to him a grave one, perhaps because his business was grave, or because of the solemn hour. He saw this in her face as well, and almost wished they had waked the children after all.

"Goodbye, Laura," he said.

"Goodbye, Jay."

They kissed, and her head settled for a moment against him. He stroked her hair. "I'll let you know," he said, "quick as I can, if it's serious."

"I pray it won't be, Jay."

"Well: we can only hope." The moment of full tenderness between them was dissolved in their thought, but he continued gently to stroke the round back of her head.

"Give all my love to your mother. Tell her they're both in my thoughts and wishes—constantly. And your father of course, if he's—well enough to talk to."

"Sure dear."

"And take care of yourself."

"Sure."

He patted her back and they parted.

"Then I'll hear from you—see you—very soon."

"That's right."

"All right, Jay." She squeezed his arm. He kissed her, just beneath the eye, and realized her disappointed lips; they smiled, and he kissed her heartily on the mouth. In a glimmer of gaiety, both were on the verge of parting with their customary morning farewell, she singing, "Good-bye John, don't stay long," he singing back, "I'll be back in a week or two," but both thought better of it.

"All right, dear. Goodbye."

"Goodbye, my dear."

He turned abruptly at the bottom of the steps. "Hey," he whispered. "How's your money?"

She thought rapidly. "All right; thank you."

"Tell the children goodbye for me. Tell them I'll see them tonight."

"I better not promise that, had I?"

"No, but probably. And Laura: I hope I can make supper, but don't wait it."

"All right."

"Good night."

"Good night." He walked back towards the barn. In the middle of the yard he tuned and whispered loudly: "And you think it over about your birthday."

"Thank you, Jay. All right. Thank you."

She could hear him walking as quietly as possible on the cinders. He silently lifted and set aside the bar of the door, and opened the door, taking care to be quiet. The first leaf squealed; the second, which was usually worse, was perfectly still. Stepping to the left of the car, and assuming the serious position of stealth which the narrowness of the garage made necessary, he disappeared into the absolute darkness.

She knew he would try not to wake the neighbors and the children; and that it was impossible to start the auto quietly. She waited with sympathy and amusement, and with habituated dread of his fury and of the profanity she was sure would ensue, spoken or unspoken.

Uhgh—hyuh yuhyuhyuhyuh: wheek-uh-wheek-uh:

Ughh—hyuh yuh: wheek:

(now the nearly noiseless, desperate adjustments of spark and throttle and choke)

Ughgh—hyuhyuhyuhwheekyuhyuhwheekwheekwheekyuhyuhyuh: wheek:

(which she never understood and, from where she stayed now, could predict so well):

Ughgh—*Ughgh*—yuhyuh*Ugh* wheek yuh yuh *Ughgh* yuh wheek wheek yuhyuh: wheek wheek: uh:

(Like a hideous, horribly constipated great brute of a beast: like a lunatic sobbing: like a mouse being tortured):

Ughgh—*Ughgh*—*Ughgh* (Poor thing, he must be simply furious) *Ughgh*—wheek—*Whughugh*yuh—*Ughwhee*kyuh*uughgyugh*yuhyuhy a a a a a a a h h h h h h R h R h R H R H R H (o, *stop* it!) R H R H (a window went up) R H R H R H R H R H R yuhyuhRRHRHRHR HRHRHRHRHRHRH RH (the door smacked to in rage and triumph) RhRhRh————————- (the window went down) RHRHRHRHRH (the machine backed out, crackling on the cinders). RHRH——————— (he wrenched it rudely but adroitly in a backward curve, almost to the chicken wire; from between the houses, light from the street caught its black side) rhrh————- (and swung as rudely round the corner of the barn and, by opposite turn, into the alley, facing eastward, where it stood) rhrh————————- (smug, obedient, conquered, malicious as a mule, while he briefly reappeared, faced towards the house, saw her, waved one hand—she waved, but he did not see her—and drew the gate shut, disappearing beyond it) rhrhrhrhrhrhrh RHRHRHRHRHRHR

H
R
H
R
H
rh
rh
rh
rh
rh
rh
rh
rh
rh
rh
rh
rh

Cutta wawwwwk:
Craaawwrk?
Chiquawkwawh.
Wrrawkuhkuhkuh.
Craarrawwk.
rrrrrwrk?
qrk.
rk:

She released a long breath, very slowly, and went into the house.

There was her milk, untouched, forgotten, barely tepid. She drank it down, without pleasure; all its whiteness, draining from the stringing wet whiteness of the empty cup, was singularly repugnant. She decided to leave things until morning, ran water over the dishes, and left them in the sink.

If the children had heard so much as a sound, they didn't show it now. Emma, as always, was absolutely drowned in sleep, and both of them, as always, were absolutely drowned.

Really, they are too big for that, she thought. Rufus certainly. She carefully readjusted their covers, against catching cold. They scarcely stirred.

I ought to ask a doctor.

She saw the freshened bed. Why, the *dear,* she thought, smiling, and got in. She was never to realize his intention of holding the warmth in for her; for that had somewhile since departed from the bed.

Chapter 21

He imagined that by about now, she would about be getting back and finding the bed. He smiled to think of her, finding it.

He drove down Forest, across the viaduct, past the smoldering depot, and cut sharply left beneath the Asylum and steeply downhill. The L&N yards lay along his left, faint skeins of steel, blocked shadows, little spumes of steam; he saw and heard the flickering shift of a signal, but he could no longer remember what that one meant. Along his right were dark vacant lots, pale billboards, the darker blocks of small sleeping buildings, an occasional light. He would have eaten in one of these places, small, weakly lighted holes-in-the-wall, opaque with the smoke of overheated lard, some for Negroes, some for whites, which served railroad men and the unexplainable night-hawks you found in any fair sized town. You never saw a woman there, except sometimes behind a counter or sweating over a stove. He never used to talk when he went to them, but he enjoyed the feeling of conspiracy, and the sound of voices. If you went to the right ones, and if you were known, or looked like you could be trusted, you could get a shot or two of liquor, any hour of the night.

He ran his tongue over his teeth, tasting the last of the molasses, and coffee, and bacon, and eggs.

Before long the city thinned out into the darkened evidences of that kind of flea-bitten semi-rurality which always peculiarly depressed him: mean little homes, and others inexplicably new and substantial, set too close together for any satisfying rural privacy or use, too far, too shapelessly apart to have coherence as any kind of community; mean little pieces of ill-cultivated land behind them, and alongside the road, between them, trash and slash and broken sheds and rained-out billboards: he passed a late, late streetcar, no passengers aboard, far out near the end of its run.

Within two more minutes he had seen the last of this sort of thing. The darkness became at once more intimate and more hollow; the engine sounded different, a smooth, easy drone; budding limbs swelled up and swept with sudden speed through the last of the vivid light; the auto bored through the center of the darkness of the universe; its poring shafts of light, like an insect's antennae, feeling into distinctness every relevant small obstacle and ease of passage, and very little else. He unbuttoned his vest and the top button of his trousers and settled back. After a few moments he wondered about taking off his coat; but the rhythm and momentum of night driving were too strongly persuasive to wish to break. He settled still more deeply, his eyes shifting gear constantly between the farthest reaching of his lights and the nearest, and gave himself over entirely to the pleasures of the journey, and to its still undetermined but essentially grave significance.

It was just nearing daybreak when he came to the river; he had to rap several times on the window of the little shanty before the ferryman awoke.

"Have to double the charge, mister, cross at night," he said, intent on lighting his lantern.

"That's all right."

At the voice, he looked up, well awake for the first time. "Oh, howdy thur," he said.

"Howdy."

"You genally all ways come o' Sundays, yer womurn, couple o' young-uns."

"Yeahp."

He walked away, to the edge of the water, and holding his lantern low, examined the fit of his flatboat against the shore. Then he raised the lantern and swung it, as a railroad man would; Jay, who had left his engine running, braked it carefully down the steep, thickly tracked clay, and carefully aboard. He shut off his engine; the sudden silence was magical. He got out and helped the man block the wheels. "All ready here," he said, straightening; but the man said nothing; he was already casting off. They both watched the brown water widen under the lantern light, apparently with equal appreciation. Must be a nice job, Jay reflected, as he nearly always did; except of course winter.

"Run all winter?"

"Eah," said the man, warping his line.

"Tain't so bad," he added after a moment, "only for sleet. I do mislike them sleety nights."

Both were silent. Jay filled his pipe. As he struck a match he felt a difference in motion, a kind of dilation; the ferry was now warped into the bias of the current which carried it, and the ferryman worked no more; he merely kept one hand on his line. The flat craft rode against the water like a hand on a breast. The water mumbled a little; during this part of the crossing, that was always the only sound. And by now, the surface of the river gave back light which could not as yet be as clearly discerned in the sky, and along both banks the trees which crowded the water like drinking cattle, began to take on distinctness one from another. Far back through the country along both sides of the river, roosters screamed. The violet sky shone gray; and now for the first time both men saw, on the opposite shore, a covered wagon, and a little figure motionless beside it.

"I'God," said the ferryman. "Reckon how long *they* ben awaitn!" Suddenly he became very busy with his line; he had to build sufficient momentum in cross-power to carry it past the middle of the stream, where the broadside current, at full strength, could lock both line and craft. Jay hurried to help. "Tsah right," the man called him off, too busy for courtesy. Jay quit. After a moment the man's hauling became more casual. He turned, enough to meet Jay's eye. "F'warn't man enough to hanl that alone, wouldn't be man enough to hanl the job," he explained.

Jay nodded, and watched the expanding light.

"Hope tain't no trouble, brung ya up hyer sich an hour," the ferryman said.

Jay had realized his curiosity, and respected his silence, at the first, and so, although the question slightly altered this respect, he answered, somehow pleased to be able to communicate it to an agent at once so near his sympathies, and so impersonal: "My Paw. Took at the heart. Don't know yet how bad tis."

The man clucked his tongue like an old woman, shaking his head, and looking into the water. "That's a mean way," he said. Suddenly he looked Jay in the eyes: his own were strangely shy. Then he looked again into the brown water, and continued to haul at the line.

"Well, good luck," he said.

"Much obliged," said Jay.

The wagon grew larger and larger, and now the dark, deeply lined faces of the man and woman became distinct: the sad, deeply lined faces of the profound country which seemed ancient even in early maturity and which always gave Jay a sense of peace. The woman sat high above the mule; the flare of her deep bonnet had the shape of the flare of the wagon's canopy. The man stood beside his wagon, one clayed boot cocked on the clayed hub. They gazed gravely into the eyes of the men on the ferry, and neither of them moved, or made any sign of salutation, until the craft was made fast.

"Ben here long?" the ferryman asked.

The woman looked at him; after a moment the man, without moving his eyes, nodded.

"Didn't hear yer holler."

After a moment the man said, "I hollered."

The ferryman put out his lantern. He turned to Jay. "Twarnt rightly a dark crossing mister. I can't charge ye but the daytime toll."

"All right," Jay said, giving him fifteen cents. "And much obliged to you." He put out his headlights and stooped to crank the car.

"Hold awn, bud," the wagoner called. Jay looked up as he took two quick strides and took control of the mule's head. The man nodded.

The engine was warm, and started easily; and though with every wrench of the crank a spasm of anguish wrenched the mule, once the engine leveled out the mule stood quietly, merely trembling. Jay put it violently into low to get up the steep mudbank, giving the mule and wagon as wide a berth as possible, nodding his regret of the racket and his friendliness as he passed; their heads turned, the eyes which followed him could not forgive him his noise. At the top he filled his pipe and watched while the mule and wagon descended, the mule held at the head, his hocks sprung uneasily, hoofs prodding and finding base in the treacherous clay, rump bunched high, the wagon tilting, the block-brakes screeching on the broad iron rim.

Poor damn devils, he thought. He was sure they were bound for the Knoxville market. They had probably waited for the ferry as much as a couple of hours. They would be hopelessly late.

He waited out the lovely sight of the water gaping. The ferry took on its peculiar squareness, its look of exquisite silence. He looked at his watch. Five forty-five. Not so bad. He lighted his pipe and settled down to drive. He always felt different once he was across the river.

This was the real, old, deep country, now. Home country. The cabins looked different to him, a little older and poorer and simpler, a little more homelike; the trees and rocks seemed to come differently out of the ground; the air smelled different. Before long now, he would know the worst; if it was the worst. Quite unconsciously he felt much more deeply at leisure as he watched the flowing freshly lighted country; and quite unconsciously he drove a little faster than before.

Chapter 22

During the rest of the night, Laura lay in a "white" sleep. She felt as odd, alone in the bed, as if a jaw-tooth had just been pulled, and the whole house seemed larger than it really was, hollow and resonant. The coming of daylight did not bring things back to normal, as she had hoped; the bed and the house, in this silence and pallor, seemed even emptier. She would doze a little, wake and listen to the dry silence, doze, wake again, sharply, to the thing that troubled her. She thought of her husband, driving alone on one of the most solemn errands of his life, and of his father, lying fatally sick, perhaps dying, perhaps dead at this moment (she crossed herself), and she could not bring herself to feel as deeply about it as she felt that she should, for her husband's sake. She realized that if the situation were reversed, and it was her own father who was dying, Jay would feel much as she felt now, and that she could not blame either him or herself, but that did her no good. For she knew that at the bottom of it the trouble was, simply, that she had never really liked the old man.

She was sure that she didn't look down on him, as many of Jay's relatives all but said to her face and as she feared that Jay himself occasionally believed; certainly not; but she could not like him, as almost everyone else liked him. She knew that if it was Jay's mother who lay dying, there would be no question of her grief, or inadequacy to her husband; and that was a fair measure how little she really cared for his father. She wondered why she liked him so little (for to say that she actually disliked him, she earnestly assured herself, would be putting it falsely). She realized that it was mainly because everyone forgave him so much, and liked him so well in spite of his shortcomings, and because he accepted their forgiveness and liking so casually, as if this were his natural due or, worse, as if he didn't even realize anything about it. And the worst of this, the thing she resented with enduring anger and distaste, was the burden he had constantly imposed on his wife, and her perfect patience with him, as if she didn't even know it was a burden or that he was taking advantage. It was this unconsciousness in both of them that she could not abide, and if only once Jay's mother had shown one spark of anger, of realization, Laura felt she might have begun to be able to like him. But this brought her into a resentment, almost a dislike, of Jay's mother, which she knew was both unjust, and untrue to her actual feelings, and which made her uncomfortable; she was shocked also to realize that she was lying awake in the hour which might well be his last, to think ill of him. *Shame on* you, she said to herself, and thought earnestly of all that she knew was good about him.

He was generous, for one thing. Generous to a fault. And she remembered how, time and again, he had given away, "loaned," to the first person who asked him the favor, money or food or things which were desperately needed home to keep body and soul together. Fault, indeed. Yet it was a good fault. It was no wonder people loved him—or pretended to—and took every possible advantage of him. And he was very genuinely kind hearted. A wonderful virtue. And tolerant. She had never heard him say an unkind or a bitter word of anybody, not even of people who had outrageously abused his generosity—he could not, she realized, bear to believe that they really meant to; and he had never once, of that she was sure, joined with most of the others in their envious, hostile, contemptuous talking about her.

On the other hand she could be equally sure that he had never really stood up for her strongly and bravely, and angrily, against everyone, as his wife had, for he disliked arguments as much as he did unkindness; but she put that out of her mind. He had never, so far as she knew, complained, about his sickness or pain, or his poverty, and chronically, insanely, as he made excuses for others, he had never made excuses for himself. And certainly he had precious little right to complain, or make excuses; but that too she hastened to put out of her mind. She reproached herself by remembering how thoroughly nice and friendly he had always been to her; and if she had to realize that that was not at all for herself, but purely because she was "Jim's woman," as he'd probably say, she certainly couldn't hold that against him; her own best feelings towards him came out of her recognition of him as Jay's father. You couldn't like anyone more than you happened to like them; you simply couldn't. And you couldn't feel more about them than that amount of liking made possible to you. There was a special kind of basic weakness about him; that was what she couldn't like, or respect, or even forgive, or resign herself to accepting, for it was a kind of weakness which took advantages, and heaped disadvantage and burden on others, and it was not even ashamed for itself, not even aware. And worse, at the bottom of it all, maybe, Jay's father was the one barrier between them, the one stubborn, unresolved, avoided thing, in their complete mutual understanding of Jay's people, his "background." Even now she could not really like him much, or feel deep concern. Her thoughts for him were grave and sad, but only as they would be for any old, tired, suffering human being who had lived long and whose end, it appeared, had come. And even while she thought of him her real mind was on his son's grief and her inadequacy to it. She had not even until this moment, she realized with dismay, given Jay's mother a thought; she had been absorbed wholly in Jay. I must write her, she thought. But of course, perhaps, I'll see her soon.

And yet, clearly as she felt that she realized what the bereavement would mean to Jay's mother, and wrong as she was even to entertain such an idea, she could not help feeling that even more, his death would mean great relief, and release. And, it occurred to her, he'll no longer stand between me and Jay.

At this, her soul stopped in utter coldness. God forgive me, she thought, amazed; I almost *wished* for his death!

She clasped her hands and stared at a stain on the ceiling.

O Lord, she prayed; forgive me my unspeakable sinful thought. Lord, cleanse my soul of such abominations. Lord, if it be Thy Will, spare him long that I may learn to understand and care for him more, with Thy merciful help. Spare him not for me but for himself, Lord.

She closed her eyes.

Lord, open my heart that I may be worthy in realization of this sorrowful thing, if it must happen, and worthy and of use and comfort to others in their sorrow. Lord God, Lord Jesus, melt away my coldness and apathy of heart, descend and fill my emptiness of heart. And Lord, if it be Thy Will, preserve him yet a while, and let me learn to bear my burden more lightly, or to know this burden is a blessing. And if he must be taken, if he is already with Thee now (she crossed herself), may he rest in Thy Peace (again she crossed herself).

And Lord, if it be Thy Will, that this sorrow must come upon my husband, then I most humbly beseech Thee in Thy Mercy that through this tribulation Thou openest my husband's heart, and awake his dear soul, that he may find comfort in Thee that the world cannot give, and see Thee more clearly, and come to Thee. For there, Lord, as Thou knowest, and not in his poor father or my unworthy feelings, is the true, widening gulf between us.

Lord, in Thy Mercy, Who can do all things, close this gulf. Make us one in Thee as we are one in earthly wedlock. For Jesus' sake, Amen.

She lay somewhat comforted, but more profoundly disturbed than comforted. For she had never before so clearly put into words, into visible recognition, their religious difference, or the importance of the difference to her. And how important is it to him, she wondered. And haven't I terribly exaggerated my feeling of it? A "gulf"? And "widening"? Was it really? Certainly he never said anything that justified her in such a feeling; nor did she feel anything of that largeness. It really was only that both of them said so very little, as if both took care to say very little. But that was just it. That a thing which meant so much to her, so much more, all the time, should be a thing that they could not share, or could not be open about. Where her only close, true intimate was Aunt Jessie, and her chief love and hope had to rest in the children. That was it. That was the way it seemed bound to widen (she folded her hands, and shook her head, frowning): it was the children. She felt sure that he felt none of Hugh's anger and contempt, and none of her father's irony, but it was very clear by his special quietness, when any instances of it came up, that he was very far away from it and from her, that he did not like it. He kept his distance, that was it. His distance, and some kind of dignity which she respected in him, much as it hurt her, by this silence and withdrawal. And it would widen, oh, inevitably, because quiet and gentle as she would certainly try to be about it, they were going to be brought up as she knew she must bring them up, as Christian, Catholic children. And this was bound to come into the home, quite as much as in Church. It was bound in some ways, unless he changed; it was bound in some important ways, try as hard and be as good about it as she was sure they both would, to set his children apart from him, to set his own wife apart from him. And not by any action or wish of his, but by her own deliberate will. Lord God, she prayed, in anguish. Am I wrong? Show me if I am wrong, I beseech Thee. Show me what I am to do.

But God showed her only what she knew already: that come what might she must, as a Christian woman, as a Catholic, bring up her children thoroughly and devoutly in The Faith, and that it was also her task, more than her husband's, that the family remain one, that the gulf be closed.

But if I do this, nothing else that I can do will close it, she reflected. Nothing. Nothing will avail.

But I must.

I must just: trust in God, she said, almost aloud. Just: do His Will, and put all my trust in Him.

A streetcar passed; Emma cried.

Daytime
May 18, 1916

Chapter 23

The children were as prompt as she had expected, to ask where their father was, but once she had explained where he had gone, and why, and that he counted on seeing them that night before they went to sleep, they apparently lost interest in anything but their breakfasts. They were not in the least disappointed, as she had thought they might be; it never of course occurred to them that there had been any question of waking them up. They were not nearly so aware of his absence, once it was explained to them, as she was herself; and it was obvious that they had no feeling whatever about their grandfather's illness. Even though she had said, in a special tone, that he "might not get well," it apparently made no impression on them; she began to wonder even, whether they had understood her, or heard her at all. They just ate calmly ahead without a mention of their father or their grandfather, without a word except to ask for food, without so much as looking up. As she watched them eat, so stolid and untouched, and looked ahead into the early evening, imagining their father, very possibly in deep grief and at great inconvenience, doing his level best to get home in time not to disappoint these children who did not even seem to care that he was away, far less for what sad purpose, Laura began in her weariness to feel angry. Surely they were old enough, she told herself, to *realize,* that— But even while she watched them she realized that of course they were not by any means old enough, and she realized how mistaken her anger was. She had experienced an almost violent impulse, watching them, to shake them out of that stolidity, to make them at least a little aware of all that old age and sickness, sorrow and death and bereavement, can mean, to work upon their sympathies and their emotions until they were as she wished they were, and she need not sit unable to say a word, lonely, at her own table. But now she held these emotions up to shame, and gazed at Emma with particular tenderness, so little she still had to give her food her whole attention, to manage it without too much mess. Goodness sake! she thought, what in the world was I thinking of! How could they understand, no matter how much I said. And how *should* they! And then she remembered, as well, that her own realization was deficient. She did not quite become aware that it was this in fact which had angered her, and tempted her to misuse them, but she said to herself, suddenly bowing her head: God be merciful unto me, a sinner!

"Huh?"

She must have whispered, or spoken aloud. Had he heard?

"Nothing, Rufus." By his look, he must have. "Nothing meant for you. And don't say *huh,* dear. Say 'What is it, Mother?'"

"O all right."

"And not that either, Rufus, that's horribly impolite. Say 'Yes, Mother.'"

"Yes, Mother."

"*Finish,* Emma. You too, Rufus. First thing you know you'll be late for School." They finished the meal in silence.

Chapter 24

When Jay found how things were at the farm, he was angry at having been so grieved and alarmed; before long, he felt it had all happened very much as he had suspected. Frank had just lost his head, as usual. Now he was very much ashamed of himself, though still very defensive, and everyone, including Jay, tried to assure him that he had done the right thing. Jay could imagine how much Frank had needed to feel useful, to take charge. He couldn't think very well of him, but he was sorry for him. He felt he understood very well how it had happened.

Actually, he understood only a little about it, and Frank understood very little more.

Late in the evening before, their father had suffered a much more severe and painful attack than any up to then. After no more than a few minutes, his wife had realized its terrible gravity, and had woken Thomas Oaks. Thomas had hurried across the hill and roused up Maussie and Charley Hodges and, without waiting for them, had hurried back, saddled the horse, and whipped it as fast as it would go, into LaFollette. The doctor was out on a call; he left a message, and hurried on to Frank's. Frank was in a virtual panic of aroused responsibility, the instant he heard the news. He asked if the doctor was there yet. Thomas told him; Frank realized that his mother had told Thomas to hunt out the doctor even before he called her son to her side. He put it aside as an ungenerous and mean-spirited thought, yet it stayed, hurting him like a burr. He felt it was no time for resentments, though; not only he, but Vesta as well, must come to their help, must be there (Vesta'd never forgive me if she wasn't) if Paw was to die (she'd be the only wife there, of the only son; his mother would never forget that). He rushed back and told her what was happening as he hurried into his clothes, hurried two doors away, banged loudly on the Felts' door, and apologized for the banging by explaining (his voice was already damp) that his Paw was at death's door if not already passed on, and he wouldn't have roused them only he knew they would be only too willing to help out so Vesta could go too. They were very kind to him; Mrs. Felts arrived before Vesta had finished fixing her hair. While she was doing so, Frank sped across the street to his office, unlocked his desk, and took two choking swallows of whiskey in the dark. He rammed the bottle in his pocket and hurried down to start his car. They had been so quick that they overtook Thomas on his horse when he had scarcely passed the edge of town, going, as Frank said to himself, his eyes low and cold above the steering wheel, "like sixty," or anyhow as fast as it was safe to travel on these awful roads, perhaps a little faster, thinking of Barney Oldfield, in the Chalmers he had chosen because it was a better class of auto and a more expensive one than his brother's, a machine people made no smart jokes about. His first impulse, when he saw the horse and rider ahead, was to honk, both in self-advertisement, warning and greeting, but he remembered in time the seriousness of the occasion and did not do so, reflecting, after it was too late, that Thomas might feel he was snubbed, as if he had passed him in the street without speaking, and he was angry with Thomas for possibly having any such feeling about such petty matters, at such a time.

There were nearly two hours of helpless anguish and fright before the doctor arrived. During that time it is possible that Frank suffered more acutely than anyone else. For besides suffering, or believing that he suffered, all the pain that his father must be experiencing, and all of his mother's grief and anxiety, and all of the smaller emotions of all the smaller people who were present, he suffered terrible humiliation. When he rushed in and swept his mother into his arms he felt that his voice and his whole manner were all that they ought to be; that he showed himself to be a man who, despite his own boundless grief, was capable also of boundless strength to sustain others in their grief, and to take complete charge of all that needed to be done. But even in that first embrace he could see that his mother was only by an effort concealing her desire to draw away from him. He came near her over and over again, hugging her, sobbing over her, fondling her, telling her that she must be brave, telling her she need not try to be brave, to lean on him, and cry her heart out, for naturally at such a time she would want to feel her sons close around her; but every time, he felt that same patient stiffening and her voice perplexed him. Everyone in the room, even Frank in the long run, knew that he was only making things harder for her; only his mother realized that he was beseeching comfort rather than bringing it. She was not in the least angry with him; she was sorry for him and wished that she could be of more help to him, but her mind was not on him, her heart was not with him, and his sobs and the stench of his breath made her a little sick at her stomach. What perplexed him in her voice was its remoteness. He began to realize that he was bringing her no comfort, that she was not leaning on him, that just as he had always feared, she did not really love him. He redoubled his efforts to soothe her and to be strong for her. The harder he tried, the more remote her voice became. At the end of a half hour her face was no less desperate than it had been when he first saw her. And he began to feel that everyone else was watching him, and knew he was no use, and that his mother did not love him. The women watched him one way, the men watched him another. He felt that his wife was thinking ill of him, that she was not even sorry for him; he felt slobbering and fat, the way she looked at him and suddenly with terrible hatred was sure that she would prefer to sleep with flat-bellied men—what man? *Any* man, so long as his belly don't get in the way. As for Maussie, he knew she had always hated him, as much as he hated her. And Charley Hodges just sitting there looking serious and barrel-chested and always being careful to look away when their eyes met: Charley thought he was twice the man that Frank was and twice the good right at this time, better with his in-laws than Frank could be with his own flesh and blood; and they all knew that Charley was twice the man and were just trying not to say it or think it even, or let Frank know they thought it. And even Thomas Oaks, an ignorant hand, who couldn't even read or write, just setting there with his ropy hands hung between his knees, staring down at a knot in the floor with those washed-out blue eyes, even Tom was more of a man and more good use too. When Tom got up and said if there wasn't nothing he could do he reckoned he would get on up to the loft, but if there was anything, they would just let him know, Frank understood it. He knew Tom might be ignorant but he wasn't so ignorant but he knew when it was best to leave a family to itself; and when Frank's mother said, "all right, Tom," Frank heard more life and kindness, and more gratefulness in her voice, than in every word she'd said to him, the whole night; and as he watched Tom climb the ladder, heavily and quietly, rung by rung, he thought: there goes more of a man than I am, he knows how to take himself out of the way, and he thought: he's doing a power more good by going than I can by staying, and he thought: every soul in this room wishes it was me that was going, instead of him, and he called, in a voice which sounded unfriendly, though he had meant to make it sound friendly to everyone except Tom, "That's right, Tom, get ye some sleep"; and Tom pulled his head back through the ceiling and looked down at him with those empty blue eyes and said, "That's all right, Mr. Frank," and suddenly Frank realized that he had no intention of sleeping and would be there alone, not sleeping a wink, just ready in case he was needed; and that Tom had seen his malice, his desire to belittle him, and had belittled him instead, before his mother and his wife and his dying father. "That's all right, Mr. Frank." What's all right? What's all right? He wanted to yell it at him, "What's all right, you poor-white-trash son-of-a-bitch?" but he restrained himself.

Every time he felt their eyes on him especially strongly he went over to his mother again and hugged her, and held her head tightly against him, and tried to say things that would make her cry, and every time, her voice was a little bit farther away from him and her face looked a little older and dryer, and every time, he was still more acutely aware of their eyes on him and of the thoughts behind their eyes, and every time, he would swing away from his mother as if he could bear to leave her uncomforted for a moment only because there were still more important things to do, matters of life and death, which he and only he, the son, the man of the family, now that poor Paw lay there so near to death, could handle. And every time, there was nothing whatever to do except wait for the doctor. They had already given the medicine the doctor had given them to give, and they had already given him so much of the ginseng tea the doctor had said wouldn't anyhow do any harm, that Frank's mother decided they shouldn't give any more of it. His head was low; his feet were braced against hot stones wrapped in flannel, and Mother kept everyone except herself at the far, lighted end of the room, except for short visits. There was nothing to do, nothing to take charge of, and every time Frank swung about from his mother with an air of heroic authority and rediscovered this fact, he felt as if a chair had been pulled out from under him, in front of everybody, and he began to think that he would burn up and die if he didn't have another drink. He said, "scuse me," once in the choked and modest tone which should signify to the women that he had to empty his bladder, and he got a good, hard swig that time, and found when he came back in that he didn't care whether they were looking at him or not, or guessed what he really went out for; for two cents he'd take out the bottle and wave it at them. Sooner than it was possible to use that excuse again, he became even more thirsty than before. At the same time he first realized that he was drunk. He was bitterly ashamed of himself, drunk at this time, at his father's very deathbed, when his mother needed him so bad as never before, and when he knew, for he had learned by now to take people's word for it, that he was really good for nothing when he was drunk. And then to feel so thirsty on top of that. He braced himself with all the sternness and strength he was capable of. By God, he told himself, you'll pull yourself together, By God, or—By God, you will. You will. And he got up abruptly and walked straight through them into the dark, and splashed his face and neck with water. He realized then, that he could take another, now. Just a little one. To brace him. He cursed himself and splashed his face again, and dried carefully with his handkerchief before he came back in. He realized that to everyone else in the room, those two silences meant two more drinks. He made a cynical grimace. By God, *he* knew better! He felt as if he had great physical strength, and in this feeling of strength his thirst was merely like the bite under a punch-bar [a metal punch; a tool], a pleasure to feel and to brace against. But within a short while the thirst returned, even more fiercely as irresistible pain. No, by God, he said again to himself. But he began to wonder. If they thought he'd had one anyhow—two in fact—why in a way he owed himself a couple. Three, for that matter: a third, because he knew they mistook that cynical face he had made for a drunken shamelessness. After all, it wasn't *he* who didn't want to be drunk. He was being careful for *their* sake. And by God, if he was going to get blamed for it anyhow, what was the good of that. Besides, when he really took care he knew he could hold his liquor, good as the next man. He'd show them. But it wasn't so easy, figuring how to get out. Can't go out to pee so soon. Nor dipper of water. He felt a sudden terrible ocean of shame. No, *by God* he wouldn't sit there scheming himself a shot over his own dying father, and his mother looking on at him, knowing his mind, not saying a word. By *God* he wouldn't! He set himself to put everything out of his mind except his father, not as he had ever feared him, or wished he approved of him, or wished he was dead, but as he lay there now, old and broken, cast aside, near the end of the trail, yes sir, the embers fading; and within a short while he was sobbing, and talking of his father through his sobs, and within a short while more he began to realize that he had found his way out. His struggles against this temptation, his iterations of "*I'm* no good," and, "I'm the son he set least store by but I'm the one that cares for him the most," and the voices of the women, soothing him, trying to quiet him, only added to his tears, the richness of his emotions, and his verbosity, and before long he had realized that this too was useful, and was using it. Toward the end all genuine emotion left him and he had to scrape, tickle and torture himself into sufficient feeling and sufficient evidence of an impending breakdown he would inflict on nobody, but at length he felt he had achieved the proper moment, and rushed headlong from the room, all but upsetting his wife in her rocking chair. The instant he was outside he felt nothing in the world except the ferocity of his thirst. He leaned against the cabin wall, uncorked the bottle, wrapped his mouth over its mouth as ravenously as a famished baby takes the nipple, and tilted it straight up.

NNNhhh; with a sobbing groan he struck his temple against the side of the house so violently that he could scarcely keep his feet, flung the bottle as far from him as he was able. "*Oh, God! God! God! God! God!*" he moaned, the tears itching on his cheeks. *Fool! Fool! Fool! Why* hadn't he made sure before he left the office! There couldn't have been more than a half a dram left.

He dabbed at his head with his handkerchief and stole leaning into the path of the lamplight. Blood, all right. He felt sick at his stomach. He dabbed again. Not much. He dabbed again; again. Not running, anyhow. He took a deep breath and went back into the room.

"Stumbled," he said. "Taint nothin."

But even so, Vesta came over, and his mother came over, and they both looked carefully, pretending that it was perfectly natural to stumble in a flat clay dooryard, and when they agreed that it was a mean lump but needed no further attention he felt, suddenly, sad, and as little as a child, and he wished he were.

His rage and despair, and the shock of the blow had so quieted and sobered him that now he was beyond even self-hatred. He felt gentle and clear. The sadness grew and became all but insupportable, and for the first time that evening, one of the few times in his life, he began to see things more or less as they were. Yes, over on that bed beyond the carefully shaded lamp, moaning occasionally, his breathing so shaken and irregular that it was as if sorrow disordered it rather than death, his father, his own father, was indeed coming near his last hour; and his mother, his own mother, sat there so quiet and patient, and so strong. There was not likely anyone in the world enough stronger that she could find comfort in him. And he? Yes, he was here, for what little good that was, and he was the only son who was here. But there was no special virtue in that; he was the only son who lived near enough at hand. And he lived so near at hand because he had no courage, no intelligence, no energy, no independence. That was really it: no independence. He always needed to be near. He always needed to feel their support, their company, very near him. He always lived almost from day to day in the hope that by staying near, by always being on hand if he was needed, by always showing how much he loved them, he might at last be sure he had won their approval, their respect. He did not believe, he could not remember, one sober breath he had ever drawn, that he had drawn as if in his own right, feeling, I don't care what anybody thinks of me, this is myself and this is how *I* do it. Everything he did, every tone his voice took, was controlled by his idea of what would make the best impression on others. He was worse a slave to that, to his dread for other people's opinion of him, than any nigger had ever been a slave. And his meanness and recklessness when he was drunk enough, he knew that was no good, no good at all. It wasn't even real. It was just the way he wished he was, and it wasn't even that, for what he wished was not to be reckless, but brave, a very different thing, and not to be mean but proud, a different thing too. And what was the worst of it? Why, the worst of it was, that once in a great while he could see himself for what he really was, and almost believe that now that he saw himself so clearly, he could change, all it took was clearness of head, and patience, and courage; and at the same time he had to know that nothing that was in him to do about it could ever be done; that he would never change, except for the worse; that he had no kind of clearness of head, or patience, or courage, that would last beyond the little it took (and even that was enough to make him shrivel all over), to just be able, once in ever so long a time, to sit and look at himself for what he really was. He was just weak: he saw that, clear enough. Just no good. He saw that. Just incomplete some way, like a chicken that comes out of the shell with a wry neck and grows on up like that. Like his own poor little Joe Wheeler, that already showed the weakness, with his poor little washed out eyes, his clinging to Vesta, his terror of his father when his father was drunk or even teased him, his readiness to cry. I ought not ever to have fathered children, Frank thought. I ought not ever to have been born.

And looking at himself now, he neither despised himself nor felt pity for himself, nor blamed others for whatever they might feel about him. He knew that they probably didn't think the incredibly mean, contemptuous things of him that he was apt to imagine they did. He knew that he couldn't ever really know what they thought, that his extreme quickness to think that he knew, was just another of his dreams. He was sure, though, that whatever they might think, it couldn't be very good, because there wasn't any very good thing to think of. But he felt that whatever they thought, they were just, as he was almost never just. He knew he was wrong about his mother. He had no doubt whatever, just now, that she really did love him, had never stopped loving him, and never would. He knew even that she was especially gentle to him, that she loved him in a way she loved nobody else. And he knew why he so often felt that she did not really love him. It was because she was so sorry for him, and because she had never had and never possibly could have, any respect for him. And it was respect he needed, infinitely more than love. Just not to have to worry about whether people respect you. Not ever to have to feel that people are being nice to you because they are sorry for you, or afraid of you. He looked at Vesta. Poor girl. Afraid of me. That's Vesta. And it's all my own fault. Every bit mine. And I hate her for wanting other men when I know that unfaithfulness never once came into her head, and when I'm the worst tail-chaser in LaFollette and half of the town knows it, and Vesta knows it too, and is too gentle-hearted and too scared ever to reproach me with it. And sure I ought to be able to do something about that, at least about that. Any *man* could. Only I'm no man. So how can I expect that people can ever look up to me, or at least not look down on me. People are fair to me and more than fair. More than fair, if ever they knew me for what I really am.

And here tonight it comes like a test, like a trial, one of the times in a man's life when he is needed, and can be some good, just by being a man. But I'm not a man. I'm a baby. Frank's the baby. Frank's the baby.

Chapter 25

"Daddy had to go up to see Grandfather Agee," their mother explained. "He says to kiss both of you for him and he'll probably see you before you're asleep tonight."

"When?" Rufus asked.

"Way, early this morning, before it was light."

"Why?"

"Grampa Agee is very sick. Uncle Frank phoned up way late last night, when all of us were asleep. Grampa has had one of his attacks."

"What's attack?"

"Eat your cereal, Emma. Rufus, eat yours. His heart. Like the one he had that time last Fall. Only worse, Uncle Frank says. He wanted very much to see Daddy, just as quick as Daddy could come."

"Why?"

"Because he loves Daddy and if . . . *Eat,* wicker, or it'll all be nasty and cold, and *then* you know how you hate to eat it. Because if Daddy didn't see him soon, Grampa might not get to see Daddy again."

"Why not?"

"Because Grampa is getting old, and when you get old, you can be sick and not get well again. And if you can't get well again, then God lets you go to sleep and you can't see people any more."

"Don't you ever wake up again?"

"You wake up right away, in heaven, but people on earth can't see you any more, and you can't see them."

"Oh."

"*Eat,*" their mother whispered, making a big, nodding mouth and chewing vigorously on air. They ate.

"Mama," Rufus said. "When Oliver went to sleep did he wake up in heaven too?"

"I don't know; I imagine he woke up in a part of heaven God keeps specially for cats."

"Did the rabbits wake up?"

"I'm sure they did if Oliver did."

"All bloody like they were?"

"No, Rufus, that was only their poor little bodies. God wouldn't let them wake up all hurt and bloody, poor things."

"Why did God let the dogs get in?"

"We don't know, Rufus, but it must be a part of His Plan we will understand someday."

"What good would it do *Him?*"

"Children, don't dawdle. It's almost school time."

"What good would it do *Him,* Mama, to let the dogs in?"

"I don't know but someday we'll understand, Rufus, if we're very patient. We mustn't trouble ourselves with these things we can't understand. We just have to be sure, that, God knows best."

"I bet they sneaked in when He wasn't looking," Rufus said eagerly. "Cause He sure wouldn't have let them if He'd been there. Didn't they, Mama? Didn't they?"

Their mother hesitated and then said carefully: "No, Rufus, we believe that God is everywhere and knows everything, and nothing can happen without His knowing. But the Devil is everywhere too—everywhere except heaven, that is—and he is always tempting us. When we do what he tempts us to do, then God lets us do it."

"What's tempt?"

"Tempt is, well—, the Devil tempts us when there is something we want to do, but we know it is bad."

"Why does God let us do bad things?"

"Because He wants us to make up our own minds."

"Even to do bad things, right under His nose?"

"He doesn't *want* us to do bad things, but to know good from bad and do good of our own free choice."

"Why?"

"Because He loves us, and wants us to love Him, but if He just *made* us be good, we couldn't really love Him enough. You can't love to do what you are *made* to do, and you couldn't love God if He *made* you."

"But if God can do *any*thing, why can't He do that?"

"Because He doesn't *want* to," their mother said, rather impatiently.

"Why *doesn't* He want to?" Rufus said. "It would be so much easier for Him."

"*God—doesn't—believe*—in—the—*easy—way,*" she said with a certain triumph, spacing the words and giving them full emphasis. "Not for us, not for anything or anybody, not even for Himself. God wants us to *come* to Him, to *find* Him, the best we can."

"Like hide-and-go-seek," said Emma.

"What was that?" their mother asked rather anxiously.

"Like hide . . ."

"Aw, it isn't a *bit* like hide-and-seek, *is* it Mama?" Rufus cut in. "Hidenseek's just a *game,* just a *game.* God doesn't fool around playing *games, does* He, Mama! *Does* He! *Does* He!"

"*Shame on* you, Rufus," his mother said warmly, and not without relief. "Why, *shame on* you!" For Emma's face had swollen and her mouth had bunched tight, and she glared from her brother to her mother and back again with scalding hot eyes.

"Well He *does*n't," Rufus insisted, angry and bewildered at the turn the discussion had taken.

"That's *enough,* Rufus," his mother whipped out sternly, and leaned across and patted Emma's hand, which made Emma's chin tremble and her tears overflow. "That's *all right* little wicker! That's *all right!* He doesn't play games. Rufus is right about that, but it *is,* someways it *is* like hide and seek. You're ab so lootly *right!*"

But with this, Emma was dissolved, and Rufus sat aghast, less at her crying, which made him angry and jealous, than at his sudden solitude. But her crying was so miserable that angry and jealous as he was he became ashamed, then sorry for her, and was trying, helplessly, to find a way of showing that he was sorry when his mother glanced up at him fiercely and said, "*Now you march* and get ready for school. I ought to tell Daddy. You're a *bad boy!*"

At the door, a few minutes later, when she leaned to kiss him goodbye and saw his face, she mistook the cause of its sadness and said more gently but very earnestly: "Rufus, I can see you're sorry, but you mustn't be mean to Emma. She's just a little, *little* girl, your *little sister,* and you mustn't ever be unkind to her and hurt her feelings. Do you understand? *Do* you, Rufus?"

He nodded, and felt terribly sorry for his sister and for himself because of the gentleness in his mother's voice.

"Now you come back in and tell her how sorry you are, and *hurry,* or you'll be late for school."

He came in shyly with his mother and came up to Emma; her face was swollen and red and she looked at him bleakly.

"Rufus wants to tell you how sorry he is, Emma, he hurt your feelings," their mother said.

Emma looked at him, brutally, and doubtfully.

"I *am* sorry, Emma," he said. "Honest to goodness I am. Because you're just a little, *little girl,* and . . ."

But with this Emma exploded into a roar of angry tears, and brought both fists down into her plate, and Rufus, dumfounded, was hustled brusquely off to school.

Chapter 26

Jessie Tyler decided, that day, that she would go shopping and that if Rufus wanted to go, she would like to take him with her. She telephoned Rufus' mother to ask whether she had other plans for Rufus, that would interfere, and Laura said no; she asked whether, so far as Laura knew, Rufus had planned to do anything else, and Laura, a little surprised, said no, not as far as she knew, and whether he had or not, she was sure he would be glad to go shopping with her. Jessie, in a flicker of anger, was tempted to tell her not to make up children's minds for them, but held onto herself and said, instead, "well, we'll see," and that she would be up by the time he came back from school. Laura urgently replied that she mustn't come up—much as she would like to see her, of course—but that Rufus would make the trip instead to eleven fifteen [1115 Highland Avenue]. Jessie, deciding not to make an issue of it, said very well, she would be waiting, but he wasn't to come unless he really wanted to. Laura said warmly that of course he would want to and Jessie again replied, more coolly, "We'll see; it's no matter"; and, getting off the subject, asked: "Have you had any message from Jay?"

For Laura had telephoned her father, that morning, to explain why Jay could not be at the office. "No," Laura said, with slight defensiveness, for she felt somehow that criticism might be involved; and hadn't expected to unless, of course . . .

"Of course," Jessie replied quickly (for she had intended no criticism) "so no doubt we needn't worry."

"No, I'm sure he would have called if his father had—even if there was any grave *danger,*" Laura said.

"Of course he would," Jessie replied. Was there anything she could bring Laura?

"Let's see," Laura said a little vaguely: "why; aah"; and she realized that Emma could well use a new underwaist and that—and—; but suddenly recalled, also, that it was sometimes difficult to persuade her aunt to accept money, or even to render account, for things she bought this way; and lied, with some embarrassment, "why, no, thank you so much, it's very stupid of me but I just can't think of a thing."

"All right," Jessie said, honoring her embarrassment, and resolved to take care to embarrass her less often (but after all, *little gifts* should be possible from time to time without this silly pride); "all right; I'll be waiting, till three, and if Rufus has other things to do, just let me know."

"All right, Aunt Jessie, and it's so nice of you to think of him."

"Not a bit of it, I *like* to take him shopping."

"Well that's very nice and I'm sure *he* likes it."

"Perhaps so."

"Why *certainly* so, Aunt Jessie."

"All right. All right; *good*-bye. You'll let us know if you *do* hear from Jay?"

"Of course. Right away. But by now I don't really expect to. He'll very likely be back by supper-time, or a little after. He was sure he could, if, everything was, well, relatively all right."

"All right. All right; *good*bye."

"Goodbye. Goodbye," Laura's voice trailed, gently.

"Jay?" Hugh called over the banisters.

"No, just talking to Laura," Jessie said. "I guess it can't be so very serious, after all."

"Let's hope not," said Hugh, and went back to his painting.

Jessie made herself ready for town. When Rufus arrived, all out of breath, he found her on a hard little couch in the living-room, sitting carefully, not to rumple her long white-speckled black dress, and poring gravely through an issue of *The Nation* which she held a finger length before her thick glasses.

"Well," she smiled, putting the magazine immediately aside. "You're very prompt" (he was not; his mother had required him to wash and change his clothes) "and" (peering at him closely as he hurried up) "you look very nice. But you're all out of breath. Would you really like to come?"

"Oh, yes," he said, with a trace of falseness, for he had been warned to convince her; "I'm *very glad* to come, Aunt Jessie, and thank you very much for thinking of me."

"Huh . . ." she said, for she knew direct quotation when she heard it, but she was also convinced that in spite of the false words, he really meant it. "That's very nice," she said. "Very well; let's be on our way." She took her hard, plain black straw hat from its place on the sofa beside her and Rufus followed her to the mirror in the dark hallway and watched her careful planting of the hat pin. "Dark as the inside of a cow," she muttered, almost nosing the somber mirror, "as your Grandfather would say." Rufus tried to imagine what it would be like, inside a cow. It would certainly be dark, but then it would be dark inside anybody or anything, so why a cow? Grandma came prowling dim-sightedly up the hallway from the dining-room, smiling fixedly, even though she fancied she was alone, and the little boy and his great-aunt drew quickly aside, but even so, she collided, and gasped.

"Hello, Grandma, it's me," Rufus shrilled, and his Aunt Jessie leaned close across her to her good ear at the same moment and said loudly, "Emma, hello; it's only Rufus and I"; and as they spoke each laid a reassuring hand on her; and upstairs Rufus heard Hugh bite out, *"oh, Good Ggodd"*; but his grandmother, used to such frights and quickly recovered, laughed her tinkling ladylike laugh (which was beginning faintly to crack) very sportingly and cried, "Goodness gracious, how you startled me!" and laughed again. "And there's little *Rufus!*" she smiled, leaning deeply towards him with damaged, merry eyes and playfully patting his cheek.

"So you're ready to go!" she said brightly to Jessie.

Jessie nodded conspicuously and, leaning again close across her to get at her good ear, cried, "Yes; all ready!"

"Have a nice time," Grandma said, "and give Grandma a good hug," and she hugged him close, saying "Mm-*mmm;* nice little boy," and vigorously slapping his back.

"Goodbye," they shouted.

"*Good*bye," she beamed, following them to the door.

They took the streetcar and got out at Gay Street. There was no flurry and no dawdling as there would have been with any other woman Rufus knew; none of the ceremony that held his grandmother's shopping habits in a kind of stiff embroidery; none of the hurrying, sheepish refusal to be judicious, in which men shopped. Jessie steered her way through the vigorous sidewalk traffic and along the dense, numerous aisles of the stores with quiet exhilaration. Shopping had never lost its charm for her. She prepared her mind and her disposition for it as carefully as she dressed for it, and Rufus had seldom seen her forced to consult a shopping-list, even if she were doing intricate errands for others. Her personal tastes were almost as frugal as her needs; hooks-and-eyes, lengths of black tape and white tape, snappers so tiny it was difficult to handle them, narrow lace, a few yards, sometimes, of black or white cotton cloth, and now and then two pairs of black cotton stockings. But she loved to do more luxurious errands for others, and even when there were no such errands, she would examine a rich variety of merchandise she had no intention of buying, always skillful, in these examinations, never to disturb a clerk, and never to leave disturbed anything that she touched, imposing her weak eyes as intently as a jeweler with his glass and emitting little expletives of irony or admiration. Whenever she did have a purchase to make, she got hold of a clerk and conducted the whole transaction with a graceful efficiency which had already inspired in Rufus a certain contempt for every other woman he had seen shopping. Rufus, meanwhile, paid relatively little attention to what she was saying or buying; words passed above him, merely decorating the world he stared at with as much fascination as his aunt's; and best of all were the clashing, banging wire baskets which hastened along on little trolleys, high over them all, bearing to and fro wrapped and unwrapped merchandise, and hard leather cylinders full of money. Taken shopping with anyone else, Rufus suffered extreme boredom, but Jessie shopped much as a real lover of painting visits a gallery, and her pleasure clarified Rufus' eyes and held the whole merchant world in a clean focus of delight. If his mother or his grandmother was shopping, the tape which hung around the saleswoman's neck and the carbon pad in which she recorded purchases seemed twitchy and clumsy to Rufus; but in his aunt's company, the tape and pad were instruments of fascination and skill; and the housewives who ordinarily made the air of the stores heavy with fret and foolishness were like a challenging sea, instead, which his aunt navigated most deftly. She did not talk to him too much, nor did she worry over him, nor was Rufus disposed to wander beyond the range of her weak sight, for he enjoyed her company, and of all grown people she was the most considerate. She would remember, every ten minutes or so, to inquire courteously whether he was tired, but he was seldom tired in her company; with her, he never felt embarrassment in saying if he had to go to the bathroom, for she never seemed annoyed, but in consequence he seldom found it necessary to go when they came together on these downtown trips. Today Jessie bought a few of the simplest of things for herself and several more elaborate things for her sister-in-law and a beautifully transparent, flowered scarf for Laura's birthday, taking Rufus into this surprise; then, in the Art Store, she inquired whether the *Grammar of Ornament* had arrived. But when they showed her the enormous and magnificently colored volume, she exclaimed with laughter, "Mercy, that's no grammar; it's a whole encyclopedia," and the clerk laughed politely, and she said she was afraid it was larger than she could carry; she would like to have it delivered. She must be sure, though, that it was delivered personally to her, "no later than May twenty-first, that's three days, can I be sure of that? No," she interrupted herself, in one of her rare confusions or changes of decision, "that won't do." She explained to Rufus, parenthetically, "Suppose there was an accident, and your Uncle Hugh saw it too soon!" She paused. "Do you think you can help me with a few more of these bundles?" she asked him. He replied proudly that of course he could. "Then we'll take it now," his aunt told the clerk, and after careful testing and distribution of the various bundles, they came back into the street. And there his Aunt Jessie made a proposal which astounded Rufus with gratitude. She turned to him and said: "And now if you'd like it I'd like to give you a cap."

He was tongue-tied; he felt himself blush. His aunt could not quite see the blush but his silence disconcerted her, for she had believed that this would make him really happy. Annoyed with herself, she nevertheless could not help feeling a little hurt.

"Or is there something else you'd rather have?" she asked, her voice a little too gentle.

He felt a great dilation in his chest. "*Oh, no!*" he exclaimed with passion. "*Oh, no!*"

"Very well then, let's see what we can do about it," she said, more than reassured; and suddenly she suspected in something like its full magnitude the long, careless denial, and the importance of the cap to the child. She wondered whether he would speak of it—would try, in any cowardly or goody goody way, to be "truthful" about his mother's distaste for the idea (though she supposed he *ought* to be—truthful, that is); or, better, whether he could imagine, and try to warn her, that in buying it for him, she risked displeasing his mother; and realized, then, that she must take care not to set him against his mother. She waited with some curiosity for what he might say, and when he found no words, said: "Don't worry about Laur—about your mother. I'm sure if she knew you *really* wanted it, you would have had it long ago."

He just made a polite, embarrassed little noise and she realized, with regret, that she did not know how to manage it properly. But she was certainly not going, on that account, to deny what she had offered; she compressed her lips and, by unaccountable brilliance of intuition, went straight past Miller's, a profoundly matronly store in which Rufus' mother always bought the best clothes which were always, at best, his own second choice, and steered round to Market Street and into Harbison's, which sold clothing exclusively for men and boys, and was regarded by his mother, Rufus had overheard, as "tough" and "sporty" and "vulgar."

And it was indeed a world most alien to women; not very pleasant men turned to stare at this spinster with the radiant, appalled little boy in tow; but she was too blind to understand their glances and, sailing up to the nearest man who seemed to be a clerk (he wore no hat) asked briskly, without embarrassment, "where do I go, please, to find a cap for my nephew?" And the man, abashed into courtesy, found a clerk for her, and the clerk conducted them to the dark rear of the store. "Well, just see what you like," said Aunt Jessie; and still again, the child was astonished. He submitted so painfully conservative a choice, the first time, that she smelled the fear and hypocrisy behind it, and said carefully, "That's very nice, but suppose we look at some more, first." She saw the genteel dark serge, with the all but invisible visor, which she was sure would please Laura most, but she doubted whether she would speak of it; and once Rufus felt that she really meant not to interfere, his tastes surprised her. He tried still to be careful, more out of courtesy, she felt, than meeching [stealth], but it was clear to her that his heart was set on a thunderous fleecy check in jade green, canary yellow, black and white, which stuck out inches to either side above his ears and had a great scoop of visor beneath which his face was all but lost. It was a cap, she reflected, which even a colored sport might think a little loud, and she was painfully tempted to interfere. Laura would have conniption fits; Jay wouldn't mind, but she was afraid for Rufus' sake that he would laugh; even the boys in the block, she was afraid, might easily sneer at it rather than admiring it—all the more, she realized sourly, if they *did* admire it. It was going to cause no end of trouble, and the poor child might soon be sorry about it himself. But she was switched if she was going to boss him! "That's very nice," she said, as little drily as she could manage. "But think about it, Rufus. You'll be wearing it a long time, you know, with all sorts of clothes." But it was impossible for him to think about anything except the cap; he could even imagine how tough it was going to look after it had been kicked around a little. "You're very sure you like it," Aunt Jessie said.

"Oh, yes," said Rufus.

"Better than this one?" Jessie indicated the discreet serge.

"Oh, yes," said Rufus, scarcely hearing her.

"Or this one?" she said, holding up a sharp little checkerboard.

"I think I like it best of all," Rufus said.

"Very well, you shall have it," said Aunt Jessie, turning to the cool clerk.

Evening
May 18, 1916

Chapter 27

A few minutes before ten, the phone rang. Laura hurried to quiet it. "Hello?"

The voice was a man's, wiry and faint, a country voice. It was asking a question but she could not hear it clearly.

"Hello?" she asked again. "Will you please talk a little louder? I can't hear. . . . I said I can't hear you! Will you talk a little louder please! Thank you."

Now, straining and impatient, she could hear, though the voice seemed still to come from a great distance.

"Is this Miz James Agee?"

"Yes; what is it?" (for there was a silence); "yes, this is she."

After further silence the voice said, "There's been a slight—your husband has been in a accident."

His head!, she told herself.

"Yes," she said, in a caved-in voice. At the same moment the voice said, "A serious accident."

"Yes," Laura said more clearly.

"What I wanted to ask, is there a man in his family, some kin, could come out? We'd appreciate if you could send a man out here, right away."

"Yes; yes, there's my brother. Where should he come to?"

"I'm out at Powell Station, at Brannick's Blacksmith Shop, bout twelve miles out the Ball Camp Pike."

"Brannick's bl—"

"B-r-a-n-n-i-c-k. It's right on the left of the Pike comin out just a little way this side, Knoxvul side of Bell's Bridge." She heard muttering, and another muttering voice. "Tell him he can't miss it. We'll keep the light on and a lantern out in front."

"Do you have a doctor?"

"How's that again, mam?"

"A doctor, do you have one? Should I send a doctor?"

"That's all right, mam. Just some man that's kin."

"He'll come right out just as fast as he can." Arthur's auto, she thought. "Thank you very much for calling."

"That's all right, mam. I sure do hate to give you bad news."

"Good-night."

"Goodbye, mam."

She found she was scarcely standing, all but hanging from the telephone. She stiffened her knees, leaned against the wall, and rang 1115.

"Hugh?"

"Laura?"

She drew a deep breath.

"Laura."

She drew another deep breath; she felt as if her lungs were not large enough.

"Laura?"

Dizzy, seeing gray, trying to control her shifting voice, she said, "Hugh, there's been an—a man just phoned, from Powell's Station, about twelve miles out towards Jacksboro, and he says—he says Jay—has met with a very serious accident. He wants . . ."

"Oh, my God, Laura!"

"He said they want some man of his family to come out just as soon as possible and, help bring him in I guess."

"I'll call Arthur, he'll take me out."

"Yes do, will you, Hugh?"

"Of course I will. Just a minute."

"What?"

"Aunt Jessie."

"May I speak to her when you're through?"

"Certainly. Where is he hurt, Laura?"

"He didn't say."

"Well, didn't you—no matter."

"No I didn't," she said, now realizing with surprise that she had not, "I guess because I was so sure. Sure it's his head, that is."

"Do they—shall I get Dr. Delfrench?"

"He says no; just you."

"I guess there's already a doctor there."

"I guess."

"I'll call Ar—wait, here's Aunt Jessie."

"Laura."

"Aunt Jessie, Jay is in a serious accident, Hugh has to go out. Would you come up and wait with me and get things ready just in case? Just in case he's well enough to be brought home and not the hospital?"

"Certainly, Laura. Of course I will."

"And will you tell Mama and Papa not to worry, not to come out, give them my love. We might as well just be calm as we can, till we know."

"Of course we must. I'll be right up."

"Thank you, Aunt Jessie."

She went into the kitchen and built a quick fire and put on a large kettle of water and a small kettle, for tea. The phone rang.

"Laura! Where do I go!"

"Why, Powell's Station, out the Pike towards . . ."

"I know, but exactly where? Didn't he say?"

"He said Brannick's blacksmith shop. B-r-a-n-n-i-c-k. Do you hear?"

"Yes. Brannick."

"He said they'll keep the lights on and you can't miss it. It's just to the left of the Pike just this side of Bell's Bridge. Just a little way this side."

"All right. Laura, Arthur will come by here and we'll bring Aunt Jessie on our way."

"All right. Thank you, Hugh."

She put on more kindling and hurried into the downstairs bedroom. How do I know, she thought; he didn't even say; I didn't even ask. By the way he talks he may be—she whipped off the coverlet, folded it, and smoothed the pad. I'm just simply not going to think about it until I know more, she told herself. She hurried to the linen closet and brought clean sheets and pillowcases. He didn't say whether there was a doctor there or not. She spread a sheet, folded it under the foot of the mattress, pulled it smooth, and folded it under all around. Then she spread her palms along it; it was cold and smooth beneath her hands and it brought her great hope. O God, let him be well enough to come home where I can take care of him, where I can take *good* care of him. How good to rest! That's all right, mam. Just some man that's kin. She spread the top sheet. That's all right, mam. That can mean anything. It can mean there's a doctor there and although it's serious he has it in hand, under control, it isn't so dreadfully bad, although he did say it's serious or it can . . . A light blanket, this weather, Two, in case it turns cool. She hurried and got them, unaware whether she was making such noise as might wake the children and unaware that even in this swiftness she was moving, by force of habit, almost silently. Just some man that's kin. That means it's bad, or he'd ask for me. No, I'd have to stay with the children. But *he* doesn't know there are children. My place'd be home anyhow, getting things ready, he knows that. He didn't suggest getting anything ready. He knew I'd know. He's a man, wouldn't occur to him. She took the end of a pillow between her teeth and pulled the slip on and plumped it and put it in place. She took the end of the second pillow between her teeth and bit it so hard the roots of her teeth ached, and pulled the slip on and plumped it. Then she set the first pillow up on edge and set the second pillow on edge against it and plumped them both and smoothed them and stood away and looked at them with her head on one side, and for a moment she saw him sitting up in bed with a tray on his knees as he had sat when he strained his back, and he looked at her, almost but not quite smiling, and she could hear his voice, grouchy, pretending to be for the fun of it. If it's his head, she remembered, perhaps he'll have to lie very flat.

How do I know? How do I know?

She left the pillows as they were, and turned down the bed on that side, next the window, and smoothed it. She carefully refolded the second blanket and laid it on the lower foot of the bed, no, it'd bother his poor feet. She hung it over the footboard. She stood looking at the carefully made bed, and for a few seconds she was not sure where she was or why she was doing this. Then she remembered and said, "oh," in a small, soft voice. She opened the window, top and bottom, and when the curtains billowed she tied them back more tightly. She went to the hall closet and brought out the bedpan and rinsed and dried it and put it under the bed. She went to the medicine chest and took out the thermometer, shook it, washed it in cool water, dried it, and put it beside the bed in a tumbler of water. She saw that the hand-towel which covered this table was dusty, and threw it into the dirty-clothes hamper, and replaced it with a fresh one, and replaced that with a dainty linen guest-towel upon the border of which pansies and violets were embroidered. She saw that the front pillow had sagged a little, and set it right. She pulled down the shade. She turned out the light and dropped to her knees, facing the bed and closed her eyes. She touched her forehead, her breastbone, her left shoulder and her right shoulder, and clasped her hands.

"O God, if it be Thy Will," she whispered. She could not think of anything more. She made the sign of the Cross again, slowly, deeply, and widely upon herself, and she felt something of the shape of the Cross; strength and quiet.

Thy Will be done. And again she could think of nothing more. She got from her knees and without turning on the light or glancing towards the bed, went into the kitchen. The water for tea had almost boiled away. The water in the large kettle was scarcely tepid. The fire was almost out. While she was putting in more kindling, she heard them on the porch.

Jessie came in with her hands stretched out and Laura extended her own hands and took them and kissed her cheek while at the same instant they said "Laura" and "my dear"; then Jessie hurried to put her hat on the rack. Hugh stayed at the open door and did not speak but merely kept looking into her eyes; his own eyes were as hard and bright as those of a bird and they spoke to her of a cold and bitter sardonic incredulity, as if he were saying, "and you can still believe in that idiotic God of yours?" Arthur Savage stayed back in the darkness; Laura could just see his [eyeglasses'] large lenses, and the darkness of his mustache and of his heavy shoulders.

"Come in, Arthur," she said, and her voice was as over-warm as if she were coaxing a shy child.

"We can't stop," Hugh said sharply.

Arthur came forward and took her hand, and gently touched her wrist with his other hand. "We shan't be long," he said.

"Bless you," Laura murmured, and so pressed his hand that her arm trembled.

He patted her trembling wrist four times rapidly, turned away saying, "Better be off, Hugh," and went towards his automobile. And now, hearing how he had left the engine running, she realized all the more clearly how grave matters were.

"Everything's ready here in case—you know—he's—well enough to be brought home," Laura told Hugh.

"Good. I'll phone, the minute I know. Anything."

"Yes, dear."

His eyes changed, and abruptly his hand reached out and caught her shoulder. "Laura I'm so sorry," he said, almost crying.

"Yes, dear," she said again, and felt that it was a vacuous reply; but by the time this occurred to her, Hugh was getting into the automobile. She stood and watched until it had vanished and, turning to go in, found that Jessie was at her elbow.

"Let's have some tea," she said. "I've hot water all ready," she said over her shoulder as she hurried down the hall.

Let her, Jessie thought, following. By all means.

"Goodness no, it's boiled away! Sit down, Aunt Jessie, it'll be ready in a jiff." She hustled to the sink.

"Let me . . ." Jessie began; then knew better, and hoped that Laura had not heard.

"What?" She was drawing the water.

"Just let me know, if there's anything I can help with."

"Not a thing, thank you." She put the water on the stove. "Goodness, sit down." Jessie took a chair by the table. "Everything is ready that I can think of," Laura said. "That we can know about, yet." She sat at the opposite side of the table. "I've made up the downstairs bedroom" (she waved vaguely towards it), "where he stayed when his poor back was sprained, you remember. It's better than upstairs. Near the kitchen and bathroom both and no stairs to climb and of course if need be, that is, if he needs a nurse, night nursing, we can put her in the dining-room and eat in the kitchen, or even set up a cot right in the room with him; put up a screen; or if she minds that, why she can just sleep on the living-room davenport and keep the door open between. Don't you think?"

"Certainly," Jessie said.

"I think I'll see if I can possibly get Hazel, if she's available, or if she's on a case she can possibly leave, it'll be so much nicer for everyone to have someone around who is an old friend, really one of the family, rather than just a complete stranger, don't you think?"

Jessie nodded.

"Even though of course Jay doesn't specially, of course she's really an old friend of mine, rather than Jay's, still, I think it would be more, well, harmonious. Don't you think?"

"Yes indeed."

"But I guess it's just as well to wait till we hear from Hugh, not create any needless disturbance I guess. After all, it's very possible he'll have to be taken straight to a hospital. The man *did* say it was serious, after all."

"I think you're wise to wait," Jessie said.

"How's that water?" Laura twisted in her chair to see. "Sakes alive, the watched pot." She got up and stuffed in more kindling, and brought down the box of tea. "I don't know's I really want any tea anyway but I think it's a good idea to drink something warm while we're waiting, don't you?"

"I'd like some," said Jessie, who wanted nothing.

"Good, then we'll have some. Just as soon as the water's ready." She sat down again. "I thought one light blanket would be enough on a night like this but I've another over the foot of the bed in case it should turn cool."

"That should be sufficient."

"Goodness knows," Laura said, vaguely, and became silent. She looked at her hands, which lay loosely clasped on the table. Jessie found that she was watching Laura closely. In shame, she focused her sad eyes a little away from her. She wondered. It was probably better for her not to face it if she could help until it had to be faced. If it had to be. Just quiet, she said to herself. Just be quiet.

"You know," Laura said slowly, "the queerest thing." She began slowly to turn and rub her clasped fingers among each other. Jessie waited. "When the man phoned," she said, gazing quietly upon her moving fingers, "and said Jay had been in a—serious accident"; and now Jessie realized that Laura was looking at her, and met her brilliant gray eyes; "I felt it just as certainly as I'm sitting here now, 'It's his head.' What do you think of that?" she asked, almost proudly.

Jessie looked away. What's one to say, she wondered. Yet Laura had spoken with such conviction that she herself was half convinced. She looked into an image of still water, clear and very deep, and even though it was dark, and she had not seen so clearly since her girlhood, she could see sand, and twigs, and dead leaves, at the bottom of the water. She drew a deep breath, and let it out in a long slow sigh and clucked her tongue once. "We never know," she murmured.

"Of course we just have to wait," Laura said, after a long silence.

"Hyesss," Jessie said softly, sharply inhaling the first of the word, and trailing the sibilant to a hair.

Through their deep silence, at length, they began to be aware of the stumbling crackle of the water. When Laura got up for it, it had boiled half away.

"There's still plenty for two cups," she said, and prepared the strainer and poured them, and put on more water. She lifted the lid of the large kettle. Its sides, below the water line, were richly beaded; from the bottom sprang a leisured spiral of bubbles so small they resembled white sand; the surface of the water slowly circled. She wondered what the water might possibly be good for.

"Just in case," she murmured.

Jessie decided not to ask her what she had said.

"There's ZuZu's," Laura said, and got them from the cupboard. "Or would you like bread and butter? Or toast. I could toast some."

"Just tea, thank you."

"Help yourself to sugar and milk. Or lemon? Let's see, do I have le—"

"Milk, thank you."

"Me too." Laura sat down again. "My, it's frightfully *hot* in here!" She got up and opened the door to the porch, and sat down again.

"I wonder what ti—" She glanced over her shoulder at the kitchen clock. "What time did they leave, do you know?"

"Arthur came for us at quarter after ten. About twenty-five after, I should think."

"Let's see, Arthur drives pretty fast, though not so fast as Jay, but he'd be driving faster than usual tonight, and it's just over twelve miles. That would be, supposing he goes thirty miles an hour, that's twelve miles in, let's see, six times four is twenty-four, six times five's thirty, twice twelve is twenty-four, sake's alive, I was always dreadful at arithmetic . . ."

"Say about half an hour, allowing for darkness, and Arthur isn't familiar with those roads."

"Then we ought to be hearing pretty soon now. Ten minutes. Fifteen at the outside."

"Yes, I should think."

"Maybe twenty, allowing for the roads, but that's a good road out that far as roads go."

"Maybe."

"Why didn't he *tell* me!" Laura burst out.

"What is it?"

"Why didn't I *ask?*" She looked at her aunt in furious bewilderment. "I didn't even *ask! How* serious! *Where* is he hurt! Is he living or *dead!*"

There it is, Jessie said to herself. She looked back steadily into Laura's eyes.

"That, we simply have to wait to find out," she said.

"Of *course* we have," Laura cried angrily. "That's what's so *unbearable!*" She drank half her tea at a gulp; it burned her painfully but she scarcely noticed. She continued to glare at her aunt.

Jessie could think of nothing to say.

"I'm sorry," Laura said. "You're perfectly right. I've just got to hold myself together. That's all."

"Never mind," Jessie said; and they fell silent.

Jessie knew that silence must itself be virtually unbearable for Laura, and that it would bring her face to face with likelihoods still harder to endure. But she has to, she told herself; and the sooner the better. But she found that she herself could not bear to be present, and say nothing which might in some degree protect, and postpone. She was about to speak when Laura burst out: "In Heaven's *Name,* why didn't I ask him! *Why* didn't I? Didn't I *care?*"

"It was so sudden," Jessie said. "It was such a shock."

"You *would* think I'd *ask,* though! Wouldn't you?"

"You thought you knew. You told me you were sure it was his—in the head."

"But how *bad? What!*"

We both know, Jessie said to herself. But it's better if you bring yourself to say it. "It certainly wasn't because you didn't care, anyway," she said.

"No. No it certainly wasn't that, but I think I do know what it was. I think, I think I must have been too afraid of what he would have to say."

Jessie looked into her eyes. Nod, she told herself. Say yes I imagine so. Just say nothing and it'll be just as terrible for her. She heard herself saying what she had intended to venture a while before, when Laura had interrupted her: "Do you understand why J—your father stayed home, and your mother?"

"Because I asked them not to come."

"Why did you?"

"Because if all of you came up here in a troop like that, it would be like assuming that—like assuming the very worst before we even know."

"That's why they stayed home. Your father said he knew you'd understand."

"Of course I do."

"We just must try to keep from making any assumptions—*good* or bad."

"I know. I know we must. It's just, this waiting in the dark like this, it's just more than I can stand."

"We ought to hear very soon."

Laura glanced at the clock. "Almost any minute," she said.

She took a little tea.

"I just can't help wondering," she said, "why he didn't say *more.* 'A serious accident,' he said. Not a *very* serious one. Just *serious.* Though goodness knows that's serious enough. But why couldn't he *say?*"

"As your father says, it's ten to one he's just a plain damned fool," Jessie said.

"But it's such an *important* thing to say, and so *simple* to say, at least to give some general idea about. At least whether he could come home, or go to a hospital, or. . . . He didn't say anything about an ambulance. An ambulance would mean hospital, almost for sure. And surely if he meant the—the *very* worst, he'd have just said so straight out and not leave us all on tenterhooks. I know it's just what we have no earthly business guessing about, good *or* bad, but really it does seem to me there's every good reason for hope, Aunt Jessie. It seems to me that if . . ."

The telephone rang; its sound frightened each of them as deeply as either had experienced in her lifetime. They looked at each other and got up and turned towards the hall. "I . . ." Laura said, waving her right hand at Jessie as if she would wave her out of existence.

Jessie stopped where she stood, bowed her head, closed her eyes, and made the sign of the Cross.

Laura lifted the receiver from its hook before the second ring, but for a moment she could neither put it to her ear, nor speak. God *help me, help me;* she whispered "Hugh?"

"Poll?"

"Papa!" Relief and fear were equal in her. "Have you heard anything?"

"You've heard?"

"No. I said: '*Have you heard from Hugh?*'"

"No. Thought you might have by now."

"No. Not yet. Not yet."

"I must have frightened you."

"Never mind, Papa. It's all right."

"Sorry as hell, Poll, I shouldn't have phoned."

"Never mind."

"Let us know, quick's you hear anything."

"Of course I will, Papa. I promise. Of course I will."

"Shall we come up?"

"No, bless you, Papa, it's better not, yet. No use getting all worked up till we *know,* is there?"

"That's my girl!"

"My love to Mama."

"Hers to you. Mine, too, needless to say. You let us know."

"Certainly. Goodbye."

"Poll."

"Yes?"

"You know how I feel about this."

"I do, Papa, and thank you. There's no need to say it."

"Couldn't if I tried. Ever. And for Jay as much as you, and your mother too. You understand."

"I do understand, Papa. Goodbye."

"It's only Papa," she said, and sat down, heavily.

"Thought Hugh had phoned."

"Yes . . ." She drank tea. "He scared me half out of my wits."

"He had no business phoning."

"I don't blame him. I think it's even worse for them, sitting down there, than for us here."

"I've no doubt it's hard."

"Papa feels things a lot more than he shows."

"I know. I'm glad you realize it."

"I realize how very much he really does think of Jay."

"Great—heavens, I should hope you do!"

"Well for a long time there was no reason to be sure," Laura retorted with spirit. "Or Mama either." She waited a moment. "You and her Aunt Jessie," she said. "You know that. You tried not to show it, but I knew and you knew I did. It's all right, it has been for a long time, but you do know that."

Jessie continued to meet her eyes. "It's true, Laura. There were all kinds of—terrible misgivings; and not without good reason, as you both came to know."

"Plenty of good reasons," Laura said. "But that didn't make it any easier for us."

"Not for any of us," Jessie said, "Particularly you and Jay, but your mother and father too, you know. Anyone who loved you."

"I know. I *do* know, Aunt Jessie. I don't know how I got onto this tack. There's nothing there to resent any more, or worry over, or be grieved by, for any of us, and hasn't been for a long time, thank God. Why on earth did I get *off* on such a tangent! Let's not say another word about it!"

"Just one word more, because I'm not sure you've ever quite known it. Have you ever realized how very highly your father *always* thought of Jay, right from the very beginning?"

Laura looked at her, sensitively and suspiciously. She thought carefully before she spoke. "I know he's *told* me so. But every time he told me he was warning me, too. I know that, as time passed, he came to think a great deal of Jay."

"He thinks the world of him," Jessie rapped out.

"But, no, I never quite believed he really liked or respected him from the first and I never will. I think it was just some kind of soft soap."

"Is Joel a man for soft soap?"

"No," she smiled a little, "he certainly isn't, ordinarily. But what *am* I to make of it? Here he was praising Jay to the skies on the one hand and on the other, why practically in the same breath, telling me one reason after another why it would be plain foolhardiness to marry him. What would *you* think!"

"Can't you see that both things might be so—or that he might very sincerely have felt that both things were so, rather?"

Laura thought a moment. "I don't know Aunt Jessie. No I don't see quite how."

"You learned how yourself, Laura."

"Did I!"

"You learned there was a lot in what your father—in all our misgivings, but learning it never changed your essential opinion of him, did it? You found you could realize both things at once."

"That's true. Yes. I did."

"We had to learn more and more that was good. You had to learn more and more that wasn't so good."

Laura looked at her with smiling defiance. "All the same, blind as I began it," she said, "I was more right than Papa, wasn't I? It *wasn't* a mistake. Papa was right there'd be trouble—more than he'll ever know or any of you—but it *wasn't* a mistake. Was it!"

Don't *ask* me, child, *tell* me, Jessie thought. "Obviously not," she said.

Laura was quiet a few moments. Then she said, shyly and proudly: "In these past few months Aunt Jessie, we've come to a—kind of harmoniousness that—that," she began to shake her head. "I've no business talking about it." Her voice trembled. "*Least* of all *right now!*" She bit her lips together, shook her head again, and swallowed some tea, noisily. "The way we've been talking," she blurted, her voice full of tea, "it's just like a post-mortem!" She struck her face into her hands and was shaken by tearless sobbing. Jessie subdued an impulse to go to her side. God help her, she whispered. God keep her. After a little while Laura looked up at her; her eyes were quiet and amazed. "If he dies," she said, "if he's dead, Aunt Jessie, I don't know what I'll do. I just don't know what I'll do."

"God help you," Jessie said; she reached across and took her hand. "God keep you." Laura's face was working. "You'll do well. Whatever it is, you'll do well. Don't you doubt it. Don't you fear." Laura subdued her crying. "It's well to be ready for the worst," Jessie continued. "But we mustn't forget, we don't know yet."

At the same instant, both looked at the clock.

"Certainly by very soon now, he should phone," Laura said. "Unless *he's* had an accident!" she laughed sharply.

"O soon, I'm sure," Jessie said. Long before now, she said to herself, if it were anything but the worst. She squeezed Laura's clasped hands, patted them, and withdrew her own hand, feeling, there's so little comfort anyone can give, it'd better be saved for when it's needed most.

Laura did not speak, and Jessie could not think of a word to say. It was absurd, she realized, but along with everything else, she felt almost a kind of social embarrassment about her speechlessness.

But after all, she thought, what *is* there to say! What earthly help am I, or anyone else.

She felt so heavy, all of a sudden, and so deeply tired, that she wished she might lean her forehead against the edge of the table.

"We've simply got to wait," Laura said.

"Yes," Jessie sighed.

I'd better drink some tea, she thought, and did so. Luke-warm and rather bitter, somehow it made her feel even more tired.

They sat without speaking for fully two minutes.

"At least we're given the mercy of a little time," Laura said slowly, "awful as it is to have to wait. To try to prepare ourselves for whatever it may be." She was gazing studiously into her empty cup.

Jessie felt unable to say anything.

"Whatever is," Laura went on, "it's already over and done with." She was speaking virtually without emotion; she was absorbed beyond feeling, Jessie became sure, in what she was beginning to find out and to face. Now she looked up at Jessie and they looked steadily into each other's eyes.

"One of three things," Laura said slowly. "Either he's badly hurt but he'll live, and at best even get thoroughly well, and at worst be a helpless cripple or an invalid or, his mind impaired." Jessie wished that she might look away but she knew that she must not. "Or he is so terribly hurt that he will die of it, maybe quite soon, maybe after a long, terrible struggle, maybe breathing his last at this very minute and wondering where I am, why I'm not beside him." She set her teeth for a moment and tightened her lips, and spoke again, evenly: "Or he was gone already when the man called and he couldn't bear to be the one to tell me, poor thing.

"One, or the other, or the other. And no matter what, there's not one thing in this world *or* the next that we can do or hope or guess at or wish or pray that can change it or help it one iota. Because whatever is, is. That's all. And all there is now is to be ready for it, strong enough for it, whatever it may be. That's all. That's all that matters. It's all that matters because it's all that's possible.

"Isn't that so?"

While she was speaking, she was with her voice, her eyes and with each word opening in Jessie those all but forgotten hours, almost thirty years past, during which the iron of living had first nakedly borne in upon her being, and she had made the first beginnings of learning how to endure and accept it. *Your turn now, poor child,* she thought; she felt as if a prodigious page were being silently turned, and the breath of its turning touched her heart with cold and tender awe. Her soul is beginning to come of age, she thought; and within those moments she herself became much older, much nearer her own death, and was content to be. Her heart lifted up in a kind of pride in Laura, in every sorrow she could remember, her own or that of others; (and the remembrances rushed upon her); in all existence and endurance. She wanted to cry out *Yes! Exactly! Yes. Yes. Begin to see. Your turn now.* She wanted to hold her niece at arms' length and to turn and admire this blossoming. She wanted to take her in her arms and groan unto God for what it meant to be alive. But chiefly she wanted to keep stillness and to hear the young woman's voice and to watch her eyes and her round forehead while she spoke, and to accept and experience this repetition of her own younger experience, which bore her high and pierced like music.

"Isn't that so," Laura repeated.

"That and much more," she said.

"You mean God's mercy?" Laura asked softly.

"Nothing of the kind," Jessie replied sharply. "What I mean, I'd best not try to say." (I've begun, though, she reflected; and I startled her, I hurt her, almost as if I'd spoken against God.) "Only because it's better if you learn it for yourself. *By* yourself."

"What do you mean?"

"Whatever we hear, learn, Laura, it's almost certain to be hard. Tragically hard. You're beginning to know that and to face it: very bravely. What I mean is that this is only the beginning. You'll learn much more. Beginning very soon now."

"Whatever it is, I want so much to be *worthy* of it," Laura said, her eyes shining.

"Don't try too hard to be worthy of it, Laura. Don't think of it that way. Just do your best to endure it and let any question of worthiness take care of itself. That's more than enough."

"I feel so utterly unprepared. So little time to prepare *in.*"

"I don't think it's a kind of thing that can be prepared for; it just has to be lived through."

There was a kind of ambition there, Jessie felt, a kind of pride or poetry, which was very mistaken and very dangerous. But she was not yet quite sure what she meant; and of all the times to become beguiled by such a matter, to try to argue it, or warn about it! She's so young, she told herself. She'll learn; poor soul, she'll learn.

Even while Jessie watched her, Laura's face became diffuse and humble. *O, not yet,* Jessie whispered desperately to herself. *Not yet.* But Laura said, shyly, "Aunt Jessie, can we kneel down for a minute?"

Not yet, she wanted to say. For the first time in her life she suspected how mistakenly prayer can be used, but she was unsure why. *What can I say,* she thought, almost in panic. *How can I judge?* She was waiting too long; Laura smiled at her, timidly, and in a beginning of bewilderment; and in compassion and self-doubt Jessie came around the table and they knelt side by side. We can be seen, Jessie realized; for the shades were up. *Let us,* she told herself angrily.

"In the name of the Father and of the Son and of the Holy Ghost, Amen," Laura said in a low voice.

"Amen," Jessie trailed.

They were silent and they could hear the ticking of the clock, the shuffling of flame, and the yammering of the big kettle.

God is not here, Jessie said to herself; and made a small cross upon her breastbone, against her blasphemy.

"O God," Laura whispered. "Strengthen me to accept Thy Will, whatever it may be." Then she stayed silent.

God hear her, Jessie said to herself. God forgive me. God forgive me.

What can I know of the proper time for her, she said to herself. God forgive me.

Yet she could not rid herself: something mistaken, unbearably piteous, infinitely malign was at large within that faithfulness; she was helpless to forfend it or even to know its nature.

Suddenly there opened within her a chasm of infinite depth and from it flowed the freezing breath of eternal darkness.

I believe nothing. Nothing whatever.

"Our Father," she heard herself say, in a strange voice; and Laura, innocent of her terror, joined in the prayer. And as they continued, and Jessie heard more and more clearly than her own the young, warm, earnest, faithful, heartsick voice, her moment of terrifying unbelief became a remembrance, a temptation successfully resisted through God's grace.

Deliver us from evil, she repeated silently, several times after their prayer was finished. But the malign was still there, as well as the mercifulness.

They got to their feet.

Chapter 28

She was watching for him anxiously as he came back into the living-room; he bent to her ear and said: "Nothing."

"No word yet?"

"No." He sat down. He leaned towards her. "Probably too soon to expect to hear," he said.

"Perhaps." She did not resume her mending.

Joel tried again to read *The New Republic.*

"Does she seem well?"

Good God, Joel said to himself. He leaned towards her: "Well's can be expected."

She nodded.

He went back to *The New Republic.*

"Shouldn't we go up?"

That's about all it would need, Joel thought; to have to bellow at us. He leaned towards her and put his hand on her arm. "Better not," he said, "Till we know what's what. Too much to-do."

"Too much what?"

"*To-do.* Fuss. Too many people."

"Oh. Perhaps. It does seem our place to, Joel."

Rot! he said to himself. "Our place," he said rather more loudly, "is to stay where she prefers us to be." He began to realize that she had not meant *our place* in mere propriety. Goddamn it all, he thought, why *can't* she be there! He touched her shoulder. "Try not to mind it, Emma," he said. "I asked Poll, and she said, better not. She said, there's no use our getting all worked up until we know."

"Very sensible," she said, dubiously.

"*Damned* sensible," he said with conviction. "She's just trying her best to hold herself together," he explained.

Emma turned her head in courteous inquiry.

"Trying—to hold—herself—together!"

She winced. "Don't—shout at me, Joel. Just speak distinctly and I can hear you."

"I'm sorry," he said; he knew she had not heard. He leaned close to her ear. "I'm sorry," he said again, carefully and not too loudly. "Jumpy, that's all."

"No matter," she said in that level of her voice which was already old.

He watched her a moment, and sighed with sorrow for her, and said: "We'll know before long."

"Yes," she said. "I presume." She relaxed her hands in her sewing and gazed out across the shadowy room.

It became mere useless torment to watch her; he went back to *The New Republic.*

"I wonder how it happened," she said after a while.

He leaned towards her: "So do I."

"There must have been others, injured, as well."

Again he leaned towards her. "Maybe. We don't know."

"Even killed, perhaps."

"We don't—know, Emma."

"No."

Jay drives like hell broken loose, Joel thought to himself; he decided not to say it. Whatever's happened, he thought, one thing he doesn't need is that kind of talk about him. Or even thinking.

He began to realize, with a kind of sardonic amusement, that he was being superstitious as well as merely courteous. Why I don't want to go up till we hear, too, he said to himself. Hands off. Lap of the gods. Don't rock the boat.

Particularly not a wrecked boat.

"Of course, it does seem to me, Jay drives rather recklessly," Emma said, carefully.

And she's trying to work magic by the opposite method. Act as if nothing much is wrong.

"*Everybody* does," he told her. *Rather,* indeed!

Good a way as mine. Worthless, both ways.

"I remember I was *most uneasy* when they decided to purchase it."

Well, you're vindicated.

"Progress," he told her.

"Beg pardon?"

"*Progress.* We mustn't—stand—in the way—of Progress."

"No," she said uneasily, "I suppose not."

Good—God, woman!

"That's a joke, Emma, a very—poor—joke."

"Oh. I don't think it's a time for levity, Joel."

"Nor do I."

She tilted her head courteously. Taking care not to yell, he said, "You're right. Neither—do—I."

She nodded.

Working his way through another editorial as through barbed wire, Joel thought: I had no business calling her. Why couldn't I trust her to let me know, quick's she heard. Jessie, anyhow.

He pushed ahead with his reading.

A heaviness had begun in him from the moment he had heard of the accident; he had said to himself, *uh-huh,* and without expecting to, had nodded sharply. It had been as if he had known that this or something like it was bound to happen, sooner or later; and he was hardly more moved than surprised. This heaviness had steadily increased while he sat and waited and by now the air felt like iron and it was almost as if he could taste in his mouth the sour and cold, taciturn taste of iron. Well what else are we to expect, he said to himself. What life is. He braced against it quietly to accept, endure it, relishing not only his exertion but the sullen, obdurate cruelty of the iron, for it was the cruelty which proved and measured his courage. Funny I feel so little about it, he thought. He thought of his son-in-law. He felt respect, affection, deep general sadness. No personal grief whatever. After all that struggle, he thought, all that courage and ambition, he was getting nowhere. Jude the Obscure, he suddenly thought; and then of the steady thirty years' destruction of all of his own hopes. If it has to be a choice between crippling, invalidism, death, he thought, let's hope he's out of it. Even just a choice between that and living on another thirty or forty years; he's well out of it. In my opinion, damn it: not his. He thought of his daughter: all her spirit, which had resisted them so admirably to marry him, then only to be broken and dissolved on her damned piety; all her intelligence, hardly even born, came to nothing in the marriage and brats and making ends meet and again, above all, the God damned piety; all her innocent eagerness, which it looked as if nothing could ever kill, still sticking its chin out for more. And again he could feel very little personal involvement. She made her bed, he thought, and she's done a damned creditable job of lying in it; not one whine. And if he's—if that's—finished now, there's hell to pay for her, and little if anything I can do. Now he remembered vividly, with enthusiasm and with sadness, the few years in which they had been such good friends, and for a moment he thought *perhaps again,* and caught himself up in a snort of self-contempt. Bargaining on his death, he thought, as if I were the rejected suitor, primping up for one more try: *once more unto the breach.* Besides, that had never been the real estrangement; it was the whole stinking morass of Churchiness that really separated them, and now that was apt to get worse rather than better. Apt? Dead certain to.

And his wife, while she mended, was thinking: such a tragedy. Such a burden for her. Poor dear Laura. How on earth is she to manage. Of course, it's still entirely possible that he isn't—passed away. But that could make matters even more—tragic, for both of them. Such an active man, unable to support his family. How dreadful, in any event. Of course, we can help. But not with the hardest of the burden. Poor dear child. And the poor children. And beneath such unspoken words, while with her weak eyes she bent deeply to her mending, her generous and unreflective spirit was more deeply grieved than she could find thought for, and more resolute than any thought for resoluteness could have made it. How very swiftly life goes! she thought. It seems only yesterday that she was my little Laura, or that Jay first came to call. She looked up from her mending into the silent light and shadow, and the kind of long and profound sighing of the heart flowed out of her which, excepting music, was her only way of yielding to sadness.

"We must be very good to them, Joel," she said.

He was startled, almost frightened, by her sudden voice, and he wanted, in some vengeful reflex of exasperation, to ask her what she had said. But he knew he had heard her and, leaning towards her, replied, "Of course we must."

"Whatever has happened."

"Certainly."

He began to realize the emotion, and the loneliness, behind the banality of what she had said; he was ashamed of himself to have answered as if it were merely banal. He wished he could think what to say, which would make up for it, but he could not think of what to say.

He knew of his wife, with tender amusement, that she almost certainly had not realized his unkindness, and that she would be hopelessly puzzled if he tried to explain, and apologize. Let it be, he thought.

He feels much more than he says, she comforted herself; but she wished that he might ever say what he felt. She felt his hand on her wrist and his head close to hers. She leaned towards him.

"I understand, Emma," he said.

What does he mean that he understands, Emma wondered. Something I failed to hear, no doubt, she thought, though their words had been so few that she could not imagine what. But she quickly decided not to exasperate him by a question; she was sure of his kind intention, and deeply touched by it.

"Thank you, Joel," she said, and putting her other hand over his, patted it rapidly, several times. Such endearments, except in their proper place, embarrassed her and, she had always feared, were still more embarrassing to him; and now, though she had been unable to resist caressing him, and took even greater solace from his gentle pressing of her wrist, she took care soon to remove her hand, and soon after, he took his own away. She felt a moment of solemn and angry gratitude, to have spent so many years, in such harmony, with a man so good, but that was beyond utterance; and then once more she thought of her daughter and of what she was facing.

Joel, meanwhile, was thinking: *she needs that* (pressing her wrist), and, as she shyly took her hand away, *I wish I could do more;* and suddenly, not for her sake but by an impulse of his own, he wanted to take her in his arms. Out of the question. Instead, he watched her dim-sighted, enduring face as she gazed out once more across the room, and felt a moment of incredulous and amused pride in her immense and unbreakable courage, and of proud gratitude, regardless of and including all regret, to have had so many years beside such a woman; but that was beyond utterance; and then once more he thought of his daughter and of what she had been through and now must face.

"Sometimes life seems more—cruel—than can be borne," she said. "Theirs, I'm thinking of. Poor Jay's, and poor dear Laura's."

She felt his hand and waited, but he did not speak. She looked toward him, apprehensively polite, her beg-pardon smile, by habit, on her face; and saw his bearded head, unexpectedly close and huge in the light, nodding deeply and slowly, five times.

Chapter 29

As it became with every minute and then with every flickering of the clock more and more clear that Hugh had had far more than enough time to get out there, and to telephone, Laura and her aunt talked less and less. For a little while after their prayer, in relief, Laura had talked quite volubly of matters largely irrelevant to the event; she had even made little jokes and had even laughed at them, without more than a small undertone of hysteria; and in all this, Jessie had thought it best (and, for that matter, the only thing possible), to follow suit; but that soon faded away; nor was it to return; now they merely sat in quietness, each on her side of the kitchen table, their eyes cast away from each other, drinking tea for which they had no desire. Laura made a full fresh pot of tea, and they conversed a little about that, and the heated water with which to dilute it, and they discussed that briefly; but such little exchanges wore quickly down into silence. Laura, whispering, *excuse me,* retired to the bathroom, affronted and humbled that one should have to obey such a call at such a time; she felt for a few moments as stupid and enslaved as a baby on its potty, and far more ungainly and vulgar; then, with her wet hands planted in the basin of cold water she stared incredulously into her numb, reflected face, which seemed hardly real to her, until, with shame, she realized that at this of all moments she was mirror-gazing. Jessie, left alone, was grateful that we are animals; it was this silly, strenuous, good, humble cluttering of animal needs which saw us through sane, fully as much as prayer; and towards the end of these moments of solitude, with her mind free from the subtle enslavements of concern, she indulged herself in whispering, aloud, "He's dead. There's no longer the slightest doubt of it"; and began to sign herself with the Cross in prayer for the dead, but sharply remembering *we do not know,* and feeling as if she had been on the verge of exercising malign power against him, deflected the intention of the gesture towards God's mercy upon him, in whatsoever condition he might now be. When Laura returned, she put more wood on the fire, looked into the big kettle, saw that a third of the water had boiled away, and refilled it. Neither of them said anything about this, but each knew what the other was thinking, and after they had sat again in silence for well over ten minutes, Laura looked at her aunt who, feeling the eyes upon her, looked into them; then Laura said, very quietly: "I only wish we'd hear now, because I am ready."

Jessie nodded, and felt: you really are. How good it is that you don't even want to touch my hand. And she felt something shining and majestic stand up within her darkness as if to say before God: Here she is and she is adequate to the worst and she has done it for herself, not through my help or even, particularly, through Yours. See to it that You appreciate her.

Laura went on: "It's just barely conceivable that the news is so much less bad than we'd expected that Hugh is simply too overjoyed with relief to bother to phone, and is bringing him straight home instead, for a wonderful surprise. That would be like him. If things were that way. And like Jay, *if* they were, *if* he were, conscious enough, to go right along with the surprise and enjoy it, and just *laugh* at how scared we've been." By her shining eyes, and her almost smiling face, she seemed almost to be believing this while she said it; almost to be sure that within another few minutes it would happen in just that way. But now she went on: "That's just barely conceivable. Just about one chance in a million, and so long as there *is* that chance, so long as we don't absolutely know to the contrary, I'm not going to dismiss the possibility entirely from my mind. I'm not going to say he's dead, Aunt Jessie, till I know he is," she said as if defiantly.

"Certainly *not!*"

"But I'm all but certain he is, all the same," Laura said; and saying so, and meeting Jessie's eyes, she could not for a few moments remember what more she had intended to say. Then she remembered, and it seemed too paltry to speak of, and she waited until all that she saw in her mind was again clear and full of its own weight; then again she spoke: "I think what's very much more likely is, that he was already dead when the man just phoned, and that he couldn't bear to tell me, and I don't blame him, I'm grateful he didn't. It ought to come from a man in the family, somebody—close to Jay, and to me. I think Hugh was pretty sure—what was up—when he went out, and had every intention not to leave us in mid-air this way. He meant to phone. But all the time he was hoping against hope, as we all were, and when—when he *saw* Jay—it was more than he could do to phone, and he knew it was more than I could stand to *hear* over a phone, even from him, and so he didn't, and I'm infinitely grateful he didn't. He must have known that as time kept—wearing on in this terrible way, we'd draw our own conclusions and have time to—time. And that's best. He wanted to be with me when I heard. And that's right. So do I. Straight from his lips. I think what he did—what he's doing, it's . . ."

Jessie saw that she was now nearer to breaking than at any time before, and she could scarcely resist her impulse to reach for her hand; she managed, with anguish, to forbid herself.

After a moment Laura continued, quietly and in control: "What he's doing is to come in with Jay's poor body to the undertaker's, and soon now he'll come home to us and tell us."

Jessie continued to look into her gentle and ever more incredulous and shining eyes; she found that she could not speak and that she was nodding, as curtly and rapidly, almost as if she were palsied. She made herself stop nodding.

"That's what I think," Laura said, "and that's what I'm ready for. But I'm not going to say it, or accept it, or do my husband any such dishonor or danger—not until I know beyond recall that it's so."

They continued to gaze into the other's eyes; Jessie's eyes were burning because she felt she must not blink; and after some moments a long, crying groan broke from the younger woman and in a low and shaken voice she said, "Oh I do beseech my God that it not be so," and Jessie whispered, "So do I"; and again they became still, knowing little and seeing nothing except each other's suffering eyes; and it was thus that they were when they heard footsteps on the front porch. Jessie looked aside and downward; a long, breaking breath came from Laura; they drew back their chairs and started for the door.

Hugh did not bother to knock, but opened the door and closed it quietly behind him and, seeing their moving shadows near the kitchen threshold, walked quickly down the hall. They could not see his face in the dark hallway but by his tight, set way of walking, they were virtually sure. They were all but blocking his way. Instead of going into the hall to meet him, they drew aside to let him into the kitchen. He did not hesitate with their own moment's hesitation but came straight on, his mouth a straight line and his eyes like splintered glass, and without saying a word he put his arms around his aunt so tightly that she gasped, and lifted her from the floor. "*Laura,*" Jessie whispered, close to his ear; he looked; there she stood waiting, her eyes, her face, like that of an astounded child which might be pleading, *O, don't hit me;* and before he could speak he heard her say, thinly and gently, "He's dead, Hugh, isn't he"; and he could not speak, but nodded, and he became aware that he was holding his aunt a foot off the floor and virtually breaking her bones, and his sister said, in the same small and unearthly voice, "He was dead when you got there"; and again he nodded; and then he set Jessie down carefully on her feet and, turning to his sister, took her by her shoulders and said, more loudly than he had expected, "He was instantly killed"; and he kissed her upon the mouth and they embraced, and without tears but with great violence he sobbed twice, his cheek against hers, while he stared downwards through her loose hair at her humbled back and at the changeful blinking of the linoleum; then, feeling her become heavy against him, said "*Here Laura,*" catching her across the shoulders and helping her to a chair, just as she, losing strength in her knees, gasped "I've got to sit down" and looked timidly towards her aunt, who at the same moment saying, in a broken voice, "Sit down, Laura," was at her other side, her arm around her waist and her face as bleached and shocking as a skull. She put an arm tightly around each of them and felt gratitude and pleasure, in the firmness and warmth of their moving bodies, and they walked three abreast (like bosom friends, it occurred to her, the three Musketeers) to the nearest chair; and she could see Hugh twist it towards her with his outstretched left hand, and between them, slowly, they let her down into it, and then she could see only her aunt's face, leaning deep above her, very large and very close, the eyes at once intense and tearful behind their heavy lenses, the strong mouth loose and soft, the whole face terrible in love and grief, naked and undisciplined as she had never seen it before.

"Let Papa know and Mama," she whispered. "I promised."

"I will," Jessie said, starting for the hall.

"Arthur's bringing them straight up," Hugh said. "They know by now." He brought another chair. "Sit down, Aunt Jessie." She sat and took both Laura's hands in her own, on Laura's knees, and realized that Laura was squeezing her hands with all her strength, and as strongly as she was able. She replied in kind to this constantly shifting, almost writhing pressure.

"Sit with us, Hugh," Laura said, a little more loudly; he was already bringing a third chair and now he sat, and put his hands upon theirs, and, feeling the convulsing of her hands, thought, Christ, it's as if she *were in labor. And she is.* Thus they sat in silence a few moments while he thought: now I've got to tell them how it happened. In God's name, how can I begin!

"I want whiskey," Laura said, in a small, cold voice, and tried to get up.

"I'll get it," Hugh said, standing.

"You don't know where it is," she said, continuing to put aside their hands even after they were withdrawn. She got up and they stood as if respectfully aside and she walked between them and went into the hall; they heard her rummaging in the closet, and looked at each other.

"She needs it," Jessie said.

He nodded. He had been surprised, because of Jay, that there was whiskey in the house; and he was sick with self-disgust to have thought of it. "We all do," he said.

Without looking at them Laura went to the kitchen closet and brought a thick tumbler to the table. The bottle was almost full. She poured the tumbler full while they watched her, feeling they must not interfere, and took a deep gulp, and choked on it, and swallowed most of it.

"Dilute it," Jessie said, slapping her hard between the shoulders and drying her lips and her chin with a dish towel. "It's much too strong, that way."

"I will," Laura croaked, and cleared her throat. "I will," she said more clearly.

"Just sit down Laura," Hugh and Jessie said at the same moment, and Hugh brought her a glass of water and Jessie helped her to her chair.

"I'm going to have some, too," Hugh said.

"Goodness, do!" said Laura.

"Let me fix us a good strong toddy," Jessie said. "It'll help you to sleep."

"I don't want to sleep," Laura said; she sipped continuously at her whiskey and took plenty of the water. "I've got to learn how it happened."

"Aunt Jessie," Hugh asked quietly, motioning towards the bottle.

"Please."

While he broke ice and brought glasses and a pitcher of water, none of them spoke; Laura sat in a distorted kind of helplessness at once meek and curiously sullen, waiting. Months later, seeing a horse which had fallen in the street, Hugh was to remember her; and he was to remember it wasn't drunkenness, either. It was just the flat of the hand of Death.

"Let me pour my own," Laura said. "Because," she added with deliberation while she poured, "I want it just as strong as I can stand it." She tasted the dark drink, added a little more whiskey, tasted again, and put the bottle aside. Jessie watched her with acute concern, thinking, *if she gets drunk tonight, and if her mother sees her drunk, she'll half die of shame,* and thinking, *nonsense. It's the most sensible thing she could do.*

"Drink it very slowly, Laura," Hugh said gently. "You aren't used to it."

"I'll take care," Laura said.

"It's just the thing for shock," Jessie said.

Hugh poured two small straight drinks and gave one to his aunt; they drank them off quickly and took water, and he prepared two pale highballs.

"Now, Hugh, I want to hear all about it," Laura said.

He looked at Jessie.

"Laura," he said. "Mama and Papa'll be here any minute. You'd just have to hear it all over again. I'll tell you of course if you prefer, right away but—could you wait?"

But even as he was speaking she was nodding, and Jessie was saying, "Yes, child," as all three thought of the confusions and repetitions which were, at best, inevitable.

Now after a moment Laura said: "Anyway, you say he didn't have to suffer. *Instantly,* you said."

He nodded, and said, "Laura, I saw him—at Roberts'. There was just one mark on his body."

She looked at him. "His head."

"Right at the exact point of the chin, a small bruise. A cut so small—they can close it with one stitch. And a little blue bruise on his lower lip. It wasn't even swollen."

"That's all," she said.

"All," Jessie said.

"That's all," Hugh said. "The doctor said it was concussion of the brain. It was instantaneous."

She was silent; he felt that she must be doubting it. Christ, he thought furiously, at least she could be spared *that!*

"He can't have suffered, Laura, not even for a fraction of a second. Laura, I saw his face. There wasn't a glimmer of pain in it. Only—a kind of surprise. Startled."

Still she said nothing. I've got to make her sure of it, he thought. How in heaven's name can I make it clearer? If necessary, I'll get hold of the doctor and make him tell her hims—

"He never knew he was dying," she said. "Not a minute, not one moment, to know, 'my life is ending.'"

Jessie put a quick hand to her shoulder; Hugh dropped to his knees before her, took her hands and said, most earnestly, "Laura, in God's name be thankful if he didn't! That's a hideous thing for a man in the prime of life to have to know. He wasn't a *Christian,* you know," he blurted out fiercely. "He didn't have to make his peace with God. He was a man, with a wife and two children, and I'd say that sparing him *that* horrible knowledge was the one thing we can thank God for!" And he added in a desperate voice, "I'm so terribly sorry I said that, Laura!"

But Jessie, who had been gently saying, "He's right, Laura, he's right, be thankful for that," now told him quietly, "It's all right, Hugh"; and Laura, whose eyes, fixed upon his, had shown increasing shock and terror, now said tenderly, "Don't mind, dear. Don't be sorry. I understand. You're right."

"That venomous thing I said about Christians," Hugh said after a moment. "I can never forgive myself Laura."

"Don't grieve over it Hugh. Don't. Please. Look at me please." He looked at her. "It's true I was thinking as I was bound to as a Christian, but I was forgetting we're human, and you set me right and I'm thankful. You're right. Jay wasn't—a religious man, in that sense, and to realize could have only been—as you said for him. Probably as much so, even if he were religious." She looked at him quietly. "So just please know I'm not hurt or angry. I needed to realize what you told me and I thank God for it."

There was a noise on the porch; Hugh got from his knees and kissed his sister on the forehead. "Don't be sorry," she said. He looked at her, tightened his lips, and hurried to the door.

"Papa," he said, and stood aside to let him past. His mother fumbled for his arm, and gripped it hard. He put his hand gently across her shoulders and said, next her ear, "They're back in the kitchen"; she followed her husband. "Come in, Arthur."

"Oh no. Thank you," Arthur Savage said. "These are family matters. But if there's . . ."

Hugh took him by the arm. "Come in a minute, anyway," he said. "I know Laura'll want to thank you."

"Well now . . ." Hugh led him in.

"Papa," Laura said, and got up and kissed him. He turned with her towards her mother. "Mama?" she said in a pinched, almost crying voice, and they embraced. "There there there," her mother said in a somewhat cracked voice, clapping her loudly on the back. "Laura, dear. There there there!"

She saw Arthur Savage, looking as if he were sure he was unwelcome. "Why Arthur!" she whispered, and hurried to meet him. He put out his hand, looking frightened, and said, "Mrs. Agee, I just couldn't ever . . ."

She threw her arms around him and kissed him on the cheek. "Bless you," she whispered, crying softly.

"There now," he said, blushing deeply and trying to embrace and to sustain her without touching her too closely. "There now," he said again.

"I must stop this," she said, drawing away from him and looking about wildly for something.

"Here," said Hugh and her father and Arthur Savage, each offering a handkerchief. She took her brother's, blew her nose, dried her eyes, and sat down. "Sit down, Arthur."

"Oh thank you, no. I don't think," Arthur said. "Only dropped in a moment; really must be off."

"Why Arthur, what nonsense, you're one of the family," Laura said, and those who could hear nodded and murmured "of course," although they knew this was embarrassing for him, and hoped he would go home.

"Now that's ever so kind," Arthur said, "but I can't stay. Really must be off. Now if . . ."

"Arthur I want to thank you," she said; for now she too had reconsidered.

"So do we all," Hugh said.

"More than I can say," Laura finished.

He shook his head. "Nothing. Nothing," he said. "Now I just want you to know, if there's anything in the world I can do, be of help in any way, let me please, don't hesitate to tell me."

"Thank you Arthur. And if there is, we certainly will. Gratefully."

"Goodnight then."

Hugh walked with him to the front door. "Just let me know, Hugh. *Anything,*" Arthur said.

"I will and thank you," Hugh replied. Their eyes met, and for a moment both were caught in astonishment. *He wishes it was me!* Hugh thought. *He wishes it was himself,* Arthur thought. *Perhaps I do too,* Hugh thought, and once again, as he had felt when he first saw the dead body, he felt absurd, ashamed, guilty almost of cheating, even of murder, in being alive.

"Why Jay, of all people?" Hugh said, in a low voice.

Still watching his splintered eyes, Arthur heavily shook his head.

"Goodnight, Hugh."

"Goodnight Arthur."

He shut the door.

Laura's father caught her eye; with his chin he beckoned her to a corner of the kitchen. "I want to talk to you alone a minute," he said in a low voice.

She looked at him thoughtfully, then took her glass from the table, said "excuse us a minute" over her shoulder, and ushered him into the room she had prepared for her husband. She turned on the bedside lamp, quietly closed both doors, and stood looking at him, waiting.

"Sit down, Poll," he said.

She looked about. One of them would have to sit on the bed. It was neatly laid open, cool and pleasant below the plumped pillows.

"I had it all ready," she said, "but he never came back."

"What's that?"

"Nothing, Papa."

"Don't stay on your feet," he said. "Let's sit down."

"I don't care to."

He came over to her and took her hand and looked at her searchingly. Why he's just my height, she realized again. She saw how much his eyes, in sympathy and pain, were like his sister's, tired, tender and resolute beneath the tired, frail eyelids. He could not speak at first.

You're a *good* man, she said to herself, and her lips moved. A good, good man. My father. In an instant she experienced afresh the whole of their friendship and estrangement. Her eyes filled with tears and her mouth began to tremble. "Papa," she said. He took her close to him and she cried quietly.

"It's hell, Poll," she heard him say. "Just hell. It's just plain hell." For a few moments she sobbed so deeply that he said nothing more, but only stroked the edge of her back, over and over, from her shoulder to her waist, and cried out within himself in fury and disgust, God *damn* it! God *damn* such a life! She's too young for this. And thinking of that it occurred to him that it was at just her age that his own life had had its throat twisted, and not by death, but by her own birth and her brother's.

"But you gotta go through with it," he said.

Against his shoulder he could feel her vigorous nodding. You will, he thought; you've got spunk.

"No way out of it," he said.

"I think I *will* sit down." She broke from him and with an almost vindictive sense of violation sat heavily at the edge of the bed, just where it was turned down, next the plumped pillows. He turned the chair and sat with her knee to knee.

"Something I've got to tell you," he said.

She looked at him and waited.

"You remember what Patty was like? When she lost George?"

"Not very well. I wasn't more than five or six."

"Well, I do. She ran around like a chicken with its head off. 'Oh, why does it have to be *me?* What did *I* ever do that it happened to *me?*' Banging her head against the furniture, trying to stab herself with her scissors, yelling like a stuck pig: you could hear her in the next block."

Her eyes became cold. "You needn't worry," she said.

"I don't, because you're not a fool. But *you'd* better, and that's what I want to warn you about."

She kept looking at him.

"See here, Poll," he said. "It's bad enough right now, but it's going to take a while to sink in. When it really sinks in it's going to be any amount worse. It'll be so much worse you'll think it's more than you can bear. Or any other human being. And worse than that, you'll have to go through it alone, because there isn't a thing on earth any of us can do to help, beyond blind animal sympathy."

She was gazing slantwise towards the floor in some kind of coldly patient irony; he felt sick to death of himself.

"Look at me, Poll," he said.

She looked at him.

"That's when you're going to need every ounce of common sense you've got," he said. "Just spunk won't be enough; you've got to have gumption. You've got to bear it in mind that nobody that ever lived is specially privileged; the axe can fall at any moment, on any neck, without any warning or any regard for justice. You've got to keep your mind off pitying your own rotten luck and setting up any kind of a howl about it. You've got to remember that things as bad as this and a hell of a lot worse have happened to millions of people before and that they've come through it and that you will too. You'll bear it because there isn't any choice—except to go to pieces. You've got two children to take care of. And regardless of that you owe it to yourself and you owe it to him. You understand me."

"Of course."

"I know it's just unmitigated tommyrot to try to say a word about it. To say nothing of brass. All I want is to warn you, that a lot worse is yet to come than you can imagine yet, so for God's sake brace yourself for it and try to hold yourself together." He said, with sudden eagerness: "It's a kind of test, Laura, and it's the only kind that amounts to anything. When something rotten like this happens. Then you have your choice. You start to really be alive, or you start to die. That's all."

Watching her eyes, he felt fear for her and said, "I imagine you're thinking about your religion."

"I am," she said, with a certain cool pride.

"Well, more power to you," he said. "I know you've got a kind of help I could never have. Only one thing: take the greatest kind of care you don't just—crawl into it like a hole and hide in it."

"I'll take care," she said.

She means there's nothing I can tell her about that, he thought; and she's right.

"Talk to Jessie about it," he said.

"I will, Papa."

"One other thing."

"Yes?"

"There are going to be financial difficulties. We'll see just what, and just how to settle them, course of time. I just want to take *that* worry off your hands. Don't worry. We'll work that out."

"Bless you, Papa."

"Rats. Drink your drink."

She drank deeply and shuddered.

"Take all you can without getting drunk," he said. "I wouldn't give a whoop if you got blind drunk, best thing you could do. But you've got tomorrow to reckon with." And tomorrow and tomorrow.

"It doesn't seem to have any effect," she said, her voice still liquid. "The only times I drank before I had a terribly weak head, just one drink was enough to make me absolutely squiffy. But now it doesn't seem to have any effect in the slightest." She drank some more.

"Good," he said. "That can happen. Shock, or strain. I know once when your Mother was very sick I . . ." They both remembered her sickness. "No matter. Take all you want and I've more if you want it, but keep an eye on yourself. It can hit you like a ton of bricks."

"I'll be careful."

"Time we went back to the others." He helped her to her feet, and put a hand on her shoulder. "Just bear in mind what I said. It's just a test, and it's one that good people come through."

"I will, Papa, and thank you."

"I've got absolute confidence in you," he said, wishing that this was entirely true, and that she could entirely care.

"Thank you, Papa," she said. "That's going to be a great help to know."

Her hand on the doorknob, she turned off the light and preceded him into the kitchen.

Chapter 30

"Why where . . ." Laura began, for there was nobody in the kitchen.

"Must be in the living-room," her father said, and took her arm.

"There's more room here," Hugh told her, as they came in. Although the night was warm, he was nursing a small fire. All the shades, Laura noticed, were drawn to their sills.

"Laura," her mother said loudly, patting a place beside her on the sofa. Laura sat beside her and took her hand. Her mother took Laura's left hand in both of her hands, drew it into her lap, and pressed it against her thin thighs with all her strength.

Her aunt sat to one side of the fireplace and now her father took a chair at the other side. The morris-chair just stood there empty beside its reading lamp. Even after the fire was going nicely, Hugh squatted before it, making small adjustments. Nobody spoke, and nobody looked at the morris-chair or at another person. The footsteps of a man, walking slowly, became gradually louder along the sidewalk, and passed the house, and diminished into silence; and in the silence of the universe they listened to their little fire.

Finally Hugh stood up straight from the fire and they all looked at his despairing face, and tried not to demand too much of him with their eyes. He looked at each of them in turn, and went over and bent deeply towards his mother.

"Let me tell you, Mama," he said. "That way, we can all hear. I'm sorry, Laura."

"Dear," his mother said gratefully, and fumbled for his hand and patted it.

"Of course," Laura said, and gave him her place beside the "good" ear. They shifted to make room, and she sat at her mother's deaf side. Again her mother caught her hand into her lap; with the other, she tilted her ear-trumpet. Joel leaned toward them, his hand behind his ear; Jessie stared into the wavering hearth.

"He was all alone," Hugh said, not very loudly but with the most scrupulous distinctness. "Nobody else was hurt, or even in the accident."

"That's a mercy," his mother said. It was, they all realized; yet each of them was shocked. Hugh nodded sharply to silence her.

"So we'll never know exactly how it happened," he went on. "But we know *enough,*" he said, speaking the last word with a terrible and brutal bitterness.

"*Mmh,*" his father grunted, nodding sharply; Jessie drew in and let out a long breath.

"I talked with the man who found him. He was the man who phoned you, Laura. He waited there for me all that time because he thought it would help if—if the man who first saw Jay, was there to tell one of us all he could. He told me all he knew of course," he said, remembering, with the feeling that he would never forget it, the awed, calm, kind, rural face and the slow, careful, half-literate voice. "He was just as fine as a human being can be." He felt a kind of angry gratitude that such a man had been there, and had been there first. Jay couldn't have asked for anyone better, he said to himself. Nobody could.

"He said he was on his way home, about nine o'clock, coming in towards town, and he heard an auto coming up from behind, terrifically fast, and coming nearer and nearer, and he thought, 'There's somebody that's sure got to get some place in a bad hurry'" ("He was hurrying home," Laura said) "or else he's crazy" (he had said "crazy drunk").

"He wasn't crazy," Laura said. "He was just trying to get home, bless his heart, he was so much later than he'd said."

Hugh looked at her with dry, brilliant eyes and nodded.

"He'd told me not to wait supper," she said, "but he wanted to get home before the children were asleep."

"What is it?" her mother asked, with nervous politeness.

"Nothing important, Mama," Hugh said gently. "I'll explain later." He drew a deep breath in very sharply, and felt less close to tears.

"All of a sudden, he said, he heard a perfectly terrifying noise, just a second or two, and then dead silence. He knew it must be whoever was in that auto and that they must be in bad trouble, so he turned around and drove back, about a quarter of a mile, he thinks, just the other side of Bell's Bridge. He told me he almost missed it altogether because there was nothing on the road and even though he'd kind of been expecting that and driving pretty slowly, looking off both sides of the road, he almost missed it because just next the bridge on that side, the side of the road is quite a steep bank."

"I know," Laura whispered.

"But just as he came off the far end of the bridge—you come down at a sort of angle, you know . . ."

"I know," Laura whispered.

"Something caught in his lights and it was one of the wheels of the automobile." He looked across his mother and said: "Laura, it was still turning."

"Beg pardon?" his mother said.

"It was still, turning," he told her. "The wheel he saw."

"Mercy, Hugh," she whispered.

"*Hahh!*" her husband exclaimed, almost inaudibly.

"He got out right away and hurried down there. The auto was upside down and Jay . . ."

Although he did not feel that he was near weeping he found that for a moment he could not speak. Finally he said: "He was just lying there on the ground beside it, on his back, about a foot away from it. His clothes were hardly even rumpled."

Again he found that he could not speak. After a moment he managed to force himself to.

"The man said somehow he was sure he was—dead—the minute he saw him. He doesn't know how. Just some special kind of stillness. He lighted matches though of course, to try and make sure. Listened for his heartbeat and tried to feel for his pulse. He moved his auto around so he could see by the headlights, He couldn't find anything wrong except a little cut, exactly on the point of his chin. The windshield of Jay's car was broken and he even took a piece of it and used it like a mirror, to see if there was any breath. After that he just waited a few minutes until he heard an auto coming and stopped them and told them to get help as soon as possible."

"Did they get a doctor?" Laura asked.

"Laura says did they get a doctor," Hugh said to his mother. "Yes, he told them to and they did. And other people. Including—Brannick, Papa," he said; "that blacksmith you know. It turns out he lives quite near there."

"*Huh!*" said Joel.

"The doctor said the man was right," Hugh said. "He said he must have been killed instantly. They found who he was, by papers in his pocket, and that was when he phoned you, Laura.

"He asked me if I'd please tell you how dreadful he felt to give you such a message, leaving you uncertain all this time. He just couldn't stand to be the one to tell you the whole thing—least of all just bang like that, over a phone. He thought it ought to be somebody in the family."

"That's what I came to imagine," Laura said.

"He was right," Jessie said; and Joel and Laura nodded and said "yes."

"By the time Arthur and I got there, they'd moved him," Hugh said. "He was at the blacksmith shop. They'd even brought in the auto. You know, they say it ran perfectly. Except for the top, and the windshield, it was hardly even damaged."

Joel asked, "Do they have any idea what happened?"

Hugh said to his mother: "Papa says, do they have any idea how it happened." She nodded, and smiled her thanks, and tilted her trumpet nearer his mouth.

"Yes, some idea," Hugh said. "They showed me. They found that a cotter pin had worked loose—that is, it had fallen all the way out—this cotter pin had fallen out, that held the steering mechanism together."

"Hahh?"

"Like this, Mama—*look,*" he said sharply, thrusting his hands under her nose.

"Oh *excuse* me," she said.

"See here?" he said: he had locked a bent knuckle between two bent knuckles of the other hand. "As if it were to hold these knuckles together—See?"

"Yes?"

"There would be a hole right through the knuckles and that's where the cotter pin goes. It's sort of like a very heavy hairpin. When you have it all the way through, you open the two ends flat—spread them—like this. . . ." He showed her his thumb and forefinger, together, then spread them as wide and flat as he could. "You understand?"

"No matter."

"Let it go, Hugh," his father said.

"It's all right, Mama," Hugh said. "It's just something that holds two parts together—in this case, his steering gear—what he guided the auto with. Th—"

"*I understand,*" she said impatiently.

"*Good,* Mama. Well this cotter pin, that held the steering mechanism together down underneath the auto, where there was no chance of seeing it, had fallen out. They couldn't find it anywhere, though they looked all over the place where it happened and went over the road for a couple of hundred yards with a fine-tooth comb. So they think it may have worked loose and fallen out quite a distance back—it could be, even miles, though probably not so far. Because they showed me," again he put his knuckles where she could see, "even without the pin, those two parts might hang together," he twisted them, "you might even steer with them, and not have the slightest suspicion there was anything wrong, if you were on fairly smooth road, or didn't have to wrench the wheel, but if you hit a sharp bump or a rut or a loose rock, or had to twist the wheel very hard very suddenly, they'd come apart, and you'd have no control over anything."

Laura put her hands over her face.

"What they think is that he must have hit a loose rock with one of the front wheels, and that gave everything a jolt and a terrific wrench at the same time. Because they found a rock, oh, half the size of my head, down in the ditch, very badly scraped and with tire marks on it. They showed me. They think it must have wrenched the wheel right out of his hands and thrown him forward very hard so that he struck his chin, just one sharp blow against the steering wheel. And that must have killed him on the spot. Because he was thrown absolutely clear of the car as it ran off the road—They showed me. I never saw anything to equal it. Do you know what happened? That auto threw him out on the ground as it careened down into that sort of flat, wide, ditch, about five feet down from the road; then it went straight on up an eight-foot embankment—they showed me the marks where it went—almost to the top, and then toppled backward and fell bottom side up right beside him, without even grazing him!"

"Gracious," Emma whispered; "*Tst,*" Jessie clucked.

"How are they so sure it was—instant, Hugh?" Jessie asked.

"Because if he'd been conscious they're sure he wouldn't have been thrown out of the auto, for one thing. He'd have grabbed the wheel, or the emergency brake, still trying to control it. There wasn't time for that. There wasn't any time at all. At the most there must have been just the tiniest fraction of a second when he felt the jolt and the wheel was twisted out of his hands and he was thrown forward. The doctor says he probably never even knew what hit him—hardly even felt the impact, it was so hard and quick."

"He may have just been unconscious," Laura groaned through her hands. "Or conscious and—p-paralyzed; unable to speak or even seem to breathe. If only there'd been a doctor, right there, mayb—"

Hugh reached across his mother and touched her knees.

"No, Laura," he said. "I have the doctor's word for that. He says the only thing that could have caused death was concussion of the brain. He says that when that—happens to kill, it—does so instantly, or else takes days or weeks. I asked him about it very particularly because—I knew you'd want to be sure just how it was. He said it couldn't have been even a few seconds of unconsciousness, and then death, because nothing more happened, after that one blow, that could have added to what it did. He said it's even more sudden than electrocution. Just an enormous shock to the brain. The quickest death there is." He returned to his mother. "I'm sorry, Mama," he said. "Laura was saying, perhaps he was only unconscious. That maybe if the doctor had been there right on the spot, he could have been saved. I was telling her, no. Because I asked the doctor everything I could think to, about that. And he said no. He says that when a concussion of the brain—is fatal—it's the quickest death there is."

He looked at each of them in turn. In a light, vindictive voice he told them: "He says it was just a chance in a million."

"Good God, Hugh," his father said.

"Just that one tiny area, at just a certain angle, and just a certain sharpness of impact. If it had been even a half an inch to one side, he'd be alive this minute."

"Shut up, Hugh," his father said harshly; for with the last few words that Hugh spoke, a sort of dilation had seized Laura, so that she had almost risen from her place, seeming larger than herself, and then had collapsed into a shattering of tears.

"Oh Laura," Hugh groaned, and hurried to her, while her mother took her head against her breast. "I'm so sorry. God, what possessed me! I must be out of my mind!" And Jessie and Joel had gotten from their chairs and stood nearby, unable to speak.

"Just—have a little *mercy,*" she sobbed. "A little *mercy.*"

Hugh could say only, "I'm so sorry. I'm *so* sorry, Laura," and then he could say nothing.

"Let her cry," Joel said quietly to his sister, and she nodded. As if anything on earth could stop her, he said to himself.

"O God, *forgive* me," Laura moaned. "*Forgive* me! *Forgive* me! It's just more than I can bear! Just more than I can bear! *Forgive* me!" And Joel, with his mouth fallen open, wheeled upon his sister and stared at her; and she avoided his eyes, saying to herself, *no, no,* and *protect her, O God, protect Thy poor child and give her strength;* and Hugh, his face locked in a murderer's grimace, contained the furious and annihilating words which were bursting within him to be spoken, groaned within himself, *God, if you exist, come here and let me spit in your face. Forgive her, indeed!*

Then Jessie moved him aside and stooped before Laura, taking her wrists and talking earnestly into her streaming hands: "Laura, listen to me. Laura. There's nothing to ask forgiveness for. There's nothing to ask forgiveness for, Laura. Do you hear me? Do you hear me, Laura?" Laura nodded within her hands. "God would never ask of you not to grieve, not to cry. Do you hear? What you're doing is absolutely natural, absolutely right. Do you hear! You wouldn't be human if you did otherwise. Do you hear me Laura? You're not human to ask His forgiveness. You're wrong. You're terribly mistaken. Do you hear me my dear? Do you hear me?"

While she was speaking, Laura, within her hands, now nodded and now shook her head, always in contradiction of what her aunt was saying, and now she said: "It isn't what you think. I spoke to Him as if He had no mercy!"

"Hugh? Hugh was ju—"

"No: to God. As if He were trying to rub it in. Torment me. That's what I asked forgiveness for."

"There, Laura," her mother said; she could hear virtually nothing of what was said, but she could feel that the extremity of the crying had passed.

"Listen, Laura," Jessie said, and she bent so close to her that she could have whispered. "Our Lord on the Cross," she said, in a voice so low that only Laura and Hugh could hear, "do you remember?"

"My God, my God, why hast Thou forsaken me."

"Yes. And then did He ask forgiveness?"

"He was God. He didn't have to."

"He was human, too. And he didn't ask it. Nor was it asked of him to ask it, no more are you. And no more *should* you. What was it he said, instead? The very next thing he said."

"Father, into Thy hands I commend my spirit," she said, taking her hands from her face and looking meekly at her aunt.

"Into Thy hands I commend my spirit," her aunt said.

"There, dear," her mother said, and Laura sat upright and looked straight ahead.

"Please don't feel sorry, Hugh," she said. "You're right to tell me, every last bit you know. I want to know—all of it. It was just—it just overwhelmed me for a minute."

"I shouldn't tell you so much all in a heap."

"No that's better. Than to keep hearing—horrible little new things, just when you think you've heard the worst and are beginning to get used to it."

"That's right, Poll," her father said.

"Now just go straight on telling me. Everything there is to tell. And if I do break down why don't reproach yourself. Remember I *asked* you. But I'll try to not. I think I'll be all right."

"All right, Laura."

"Good, Poll," her father said. They all sat down again.

"And Hugh, if you'll get it for me, I think I'd like some more whiskey."

"Of course I will." He had brought the bottle in; he took her glass to the table.

"Not quite so strong as last time, please. Pretty strong, but not so strong as that."

"This all right?"

"A little more whiskey, please."

"Certainly."

"That looks all right."

"You all right, Poll?" her father asked. "Isn't going to your head too much?"

"It isn't going anywhere so far as I can tell."

"Good enough."

"I think perhaps it would be best if we didn't—prolong the discussion any further tonight," Emma said, in her most genteel manner; and she patted Laura's knee.

They looked at her with astonishment and suddenly Laura and then Hugh began to laugh, and then Jessie began to laugh, and Joel said, "What's up? What's all the hee-hawing about?"

"It's Mama," Hugh shouted joyfully, and he and Jessie explained how she had suggested, in her most ladylike way, that they adjourn the discussion for the evening when all they were discussing was how much whiskey Laura could stand, and it was as if she meant that Laura was much too thirsty to wait out any more of it; and Joel gave a snort of amusement and then was caught into the contagion of this somewhat hysterical laughter, and they all roared, laughing their heads off, while Emma sat there watching them, disapproving such levity at such a time, and unhappily suspecting that for some reason they were laughing at her; but in courtesy and reproof, and in expectation of hearing the joke, smiling, and lifting her trumpet. But they paid no attention to her; they scarcely seemed to know she was there. They would quiet down now and then and moan and breathe deeply, and dry their eyes; then Laura would remember, and mimic, precisely the way her mother had patted her knee with her ringed hand, or Hugh would mimic her precise intonation as she said "*prolong*," or any of the four of them would roll over silently upon the tongue of the mind some particularly ticklish blend of the absurdity and horror and cruelty and relief, or would merely glance at Emma with her smile and her trumpet, and would suddenly begin to bubble and then to spout with laughter, and another would be caught into the machinery, and then they would start all over again. Some of the time they deliberately strained for more laughter, or to prolong it, or to revive it if it had died; some of the time they tried just as hard to stop laughing or, having stopped, not to laugh any more. They found that on the whole they laughed even harder if they tried hard not to, so they came to favor that technique. They laughed until they were weak and their bellies ached. Then they were able to realize a little more clearly what a poor joke they had all been laughing at and the very feebleness of the material, and outrageous disproportion of their laughter started them whooping again; but finally they quieted down, because they had no strength for any more, and into this nervous and somewhat aborted silence Emma spoke: "Well, I have never in my life been so thoroughly shocked and astonished," and it began all over again.

But by now they were really worn out with laughter; moreover, images of the dead body beside the capsized automobile began to dart in their minds, and then to become cold, immense, and immovable; and they began fully to realize, as well, how shamefully they had treated the deaf woman.

"Oh, *Mama,*" Hugh and Laura cried out together, and Laura embraced her and Hugh kissed her on the forehead and on the mouth. "It was awful of us," he said. "You've just got to try to forgive us. We're all just a little bit hysterical, that's all."

"Better tell her, Hugh," his father said.

"Yes, poor thing," Jessie said; and he tried as gently as he could to explain it to her, and that they weren't really laughing at her expense, or even really at the joke, such as it was, because it wasn't really very funny he must admit, but it had simply been a Godsend to have something to laugh about.

"I see," she said ("'I see,' said the blindman," Hugh said), and gave her polite, tinkling, baffled little laugh. "But of course it wasn't the—question of Spirits that I meant. I just felt that perhaps for poor dear Laura's sake we'd better . . ."

"Of course," Hugh shouted. "We understand, Mama. But Laura'd rather hear now. She'd already said so."

"Yes, Mama," Laura screamed, leaning across towards her "good" ear.

"Well in that case," Emma said primly, "I think it would have been kind so to inform me."

"I'm awfully sorry Mama," Hugh said. "We would have. We really would have. In about another minute."

"Well," Emma said; "no matter."

"Really we would, Mama," Laura said.

"Very well," Emma said. "It was just a misfortune, that's all. I know I make it—very difficult, I try not to."

"Oh, Mama, no."

"No I'm not hurt. I just suggest that you ignore me now, for everybody's convenience. Joel will tell me, later."

"She means it," Joel said. "She's not hurt any more."

"I know she does," Hugh said. "That's why I'm *God* damned if I'll leave her out. Honestly, Mama," he told her, "Just let me tell you. Then we can all hear. Don't you see?"

"Well, if you're sure; of course I'd be most grateful. Thank you." She bowed, smiled, and tilted her trumpet.

It required immediate speech. That trumpet's like a pelican's mouth, he thought. Toss in a fish. "I'm sorry, Mama," he said. "I've got to try to collect my wits."

"That's perfectly all right," his mother said.

What was I—oh. Doctor. Yes.

"I was telling you what the Doctor said."

Laura drank.

"Yes," Emma replied in her clear voice. "You were saying that it was only by merest chance, where the blow was struck, a chance in a million, that . . ."

"Yes, Mama. It's just unbelievable. But there it is."

"Hyesss," Jessie sighed.

Laura drank.

"It does—beat—all—hell," Joel said. He thought of Thomas Hardy. There's a man, he thought, who knows what it's about. (And *she* asks God to forgive *her!*) He snorted.

"What is it, Papa?" Laura asked quietly.

"Nothing," he said, "just the way things go. As flies to wanton boys. That's all."

"What do you mean?"

"As flies to wanton boys are we to the gods; they kill us for their sport."

"No," Laura said; she shook her head. "No, Papa. It's not that way."

He felt within him a surge of boiling acid; he contained himself. If she tries to tell me it's God's inscrutable mercy, he said to himself, I'll have to leave the room. "Ignore it, Poll," he said. "None of us knows one damned thing about it. Myself least of all. So I'll keep my trap shut."

"But I can't bear to have you even *think* such things, Papa."

Hugh tightened his lips and looked away.

"Laura," Jessie said.

"I'm afraid that's something none of us can ask—or change," her father said.

"Yes Laura," Jessie said.

"But I can assure you of this, Poll. I have very few thoughts indeed and none of 'em are worth your minding about."

"Is there something perhaps I should be hearing?" Emma asked.

They were silent a moment. "Nothing, Mama," Hugh said. "Just a digression. I'd tell you if it was important."

"You were about to continue, with what the Doctor told you."

"Yes I was. I will. He told me a number of other things and I can—assure—everybody—that such as they are, at least they're some kind of cold comfort."

Laura met his eyes.

"He said that if there had to be such an accident, this was pretty certainly the best way. That with such a thing, a concussion, he might quite possibly have been left a hopeless imbecile"—"*Oh, Hugh!*" Laura burst out—"the rest of his life, and that could have been another forty years as easily as not. Or maybe only a semi-invalid, laid up just now and then, with terrific recurrent headaches, or spells of amnesia. Those are the things that *didn't* happen, Laura," he told her desperately. "I think I'd just better get them over and done with right now."

"Yes," she said through her hands. "Yes you had. Go on Hugh. Get it over."

"He pointed out what would have happened if he'd stayed conscious, if he hadn't been thrown clear of the auto. Going fast, hopelessly out of control, up that eight-foot embankment and then down. He'd have been crushed, Laura. Horribly mangled. If he'd died it would have been slowly, and agonizingly. If he'd lived, he'd have probably been a hopeless cripple."

"Dreadful," Emma cried loudly.

"An idiot, or a cripple, or a paralytic," Hugh said. "Because another thing a concussion can do Laura is paralyze. Incurably. Those aren't fates you can prefer for anyone, to dying. Least of all a man like Jay, with all his vigor, of body and mind too, his independence, his loathing for being laid up even one day. You remember how impossible it was to keep him quiet enough when his back was strained."

"Yes," she said. "Yes, I do." Her hands were still to her face and she was pressing her fingers tightly against her eyeballs.

"Instead . . ." Hugh began; and he remembered his face in death and he remembered him as he lay on the table under the glare.

"Instead of that, Laura, he died the quickest and most painless death there is. One instant he was fully alive. Maybe more alive than ever before for that matter, for something had suddenly gone wrong and everything in him was roused up and mad at it and ready to beat it—because you know that of Jay, Laura, probably better than anyone else on earth. He didn't know what fear was. Danger only made him furious—and tremendously alert. It made him every inch of the man he was. And the next instant it was all over. Not even time to know it was hopeless, Laura. Not even one instant of pain, because that kind of blow is much too violent to give pain. Immediate pain. Just an instant of surprise and every faculty at its absolute height, and then just a tremendous blinding shock, and then nothing. You see, Laura?"

She nodded.

"I saw his face, Laura. It just looked startled, and resolute, and mad as hell. Not one trace of fear or pain."

"There wouldn't have been any fear, anyway," she said.

"I saw him—stripped—at the undertaker's," Hugh said. "Laura there wasn't a mark on his body. Just that little cut on the chin. One little bruise on his lower lip. Not another mark on his body. He had the most magnificent physique I've ever seen in a human being."

Nobody spoke for a long while; then Hugh said, "All I can say is, when my time comes, I only hope I die half as well."

His father nodded; Jessie closed her eyes and bowed her head. Emma waited, patiently.

"In his strength," Laura said; and took her hands from her face. Her eyes were still closed. "That's how he was taken," she said very tenderly; "in his strength. Singing, probably"—her voice broke on the word—"happy, all alone, racing home because he loved so to go fast and couldn't except when he was alone and because he didn't want to disappoint his children. And then just as you said, Hugh. Just one moment of trouble, of something that might be danger—and was; it was death itself—and everything in his nature springing to its full height to fight it, to get it under control, not in fear. Just in bravery and nobility and anger and perfect confidence he could. It's how he'd look Death itself in the face. It's how he did! In his strength. Those are the words that are going to be on his gravestone, Hugh."

That's what they're for, epitaphs, Joel suddenly realized. So you can feel you've got some control over the death. You *own* it. You choose a name for it. The same with wanting to know all you can about how it happened. And trying to imagine it as Laura was. Hugh, too. Any poor subterfuge'll do; and welcome to 'em.

"Don't you think?" Laura asked shyly; for Hugh had not replied.

"Yes I do," he said, and Jessie said, "Yes, Laura," and Joel nodded.

Jessie: I want to *know* when I die, and not just for religious reasons—

"Mama," Laura called, drawing at her arm. Her mother turned eagerly, thankfully, with her trumpet. "I was telling Hugh," Laura told her, "I think I know the words, the epitaph, that ought to go on Jay's—on the headstone." Her mother tilted her head politely. "In his strength," Laura said. Her mother looked still more polite. "In—his—*strength,*" Laura said, more loudly. Christ I don't think I can stand this, Hugh thought. "Because that was the way it happened. Mama. Just so suddenly, without any warning, or suffering, or weakness, or illness. Just—instantly. In the very prime of his life. Do you see?"

Her mother patted her knee and took her hand. "Very appropriate, dear," she said.

"*I* think so," Laura said; she wished she had not spoken of it.

"It is, Laura," Hugh assured her.

"Why didn't you answer when I asked you?"

"I was just thinking about him."

There was a silence; Emma who had still held her trumpet hopefully extended, turned away.

"He was thirty-six," Laura said. "Just exactly a month and a day ago."

Nobody spoke.

"And last night—great, *goodness* it was only last night! Just think of that. Less than twenty-four hours ago, that awful phone ringing and we sat in the kitchen together—thinking of *his father!* We both thought it was his *father* who was at death's door. That's why he went up there. That's why it happened! And that miserable Frank was so drunk he couldn't even be sure of the need. He just had to go *in case.* Oh it's just beyond words!"

She finished her drink and stood up to get more.

"I'll get it," Hugh said quickly, and took her glass.

"Not quite so strong," she said. "Thank you."

"It's like a checkerboard," her father said.

"*What* is?"

"What you were saying. You think everything bears on one person's dying, and b'God it's another who does. One instant you see the black squares against the red and the next you see the red against the black."

"Yes," Laura said, somewhat in her mother's uncertain tone.

"None of us know what we're doing, any given moment."

How you manage not to have religious faith, Jessie wanted to tell him, is beyond me. She held her tongue.

"A tale told by an idiot: signifying nothing."

"Signifying something," Hugh said, "but we don't know what."

"Just as likely. Choice between rattlesnake and skunk."

"Jay knows what; now," Laura said.

"I certainly won't swear he doesn't," her father said.

"He does, Laura," her aunt said.

"Of course he does," Laura said.

Child, you'd better believe it, her aunt thought, disturbed by the "of course."

"I wonder," Emma said; everyone turned towards her. "Laura's suggestion—for—an epitaph—is very lovely and appropriate: but I *wonder*—whether people will quite—*understand* it."

"*Agh,*" Joel growled.

"What if they don't?" Hugh said.

Laura leaned across her. "Yes, Mama! What if they *don't! We* understand it. *Jay* understands it. What do *we* care if they *don't!*"

She was surprised and somewhat hurt by the violence of this attack. "It was merely something to be considered," she said with dignity. "After all, it will be in a *public place.* Many people will see it besides ourselves. I've always—*supposed*—it was the business of *words*—to *communicate—clearly.*"

"Oh Mama, don't be mad," Laura cried. "I understand. I appreciate the suggestion. I just can't see that in a—that in this particular case, it's anything to be seriously concerned about. It's Jay we're thinking of. Not other people."

"I see; perhaps you're right. Praps I shouldn't have ment—"

"We're very glad you mentioned it Mama. We appreciate you mentioning it. It hadn't even occurred to me and it ought to of. Only now that it does, now that you've told me—why—well, I just still think it's all right as it is. That's all."

"*Let it go, Emmah, for God's sake let it go!*" Joel was saying in a low voice; but now she nodded and became quiet.

"I hate to hurt Mama's feelings," Laura said, "but *really!*"

"It's all right Laura," Hugh said.

"Let it go Poll," her father said.

"I am," Laura said; she took a drink.

"We've got to let them know," she said. "His mother. We'll have to phone Frank. Hugh, will you do that?"

"Of course I will." He got up.

"Just tell them I'm sorry, I couldn't come to the phone. Will you Hugh? I'm sure they'll understand."

"Of course they will."

"Just tell them—how it happened. Tell Frank I send his mother all my love." He nodded. "And Hugh. Be sure and ask how Jay's father is." He nodded. "And let them know when—why; why we don't even *know,* do we. When the—what day he'll, h—the *funeral,* Hugh!"

"Not for sure. I told them I'd see them in the morning about all that."

"Well you'll just have to tell them we'll let them know as soon as we do. In plenty of time. To get here I mean."

"What's the number, Laura?"

"Number?"

"What is Frank's telephone number?"

"I—can't remember. I guess I don't know for sure. You'll have to ask Central. It's always Jay who called."

"All right."

"It's LaFollette," she called, as he went into the hall.

"All right Laura." He went out.

"And Hugh."

"Yes Laura?" He put his head in.

"Talk as quietly as you can. We don't want to wake the children."

"Yes Laura."

"It's queer I don't know," she told the others. "But it was always Jay who called."

"Tell your mother what's up," her father advised, for she was looking inquiring.

Laura leaned across her.

"Bathroom?" her mother whispered discreetly.

"No, Mama. He's gone to telephone Jay's brother."

Her mother nodded, and still extended her trumpet, but Laura had nothing to say.

"I hope he will extend all our most—heartfelt—sympathies," her mother said.

Laura nodded conspicuously. "I specially asked him to," she lied.

After a few moments Emma gave up, and relaxed her trumpet between her withered hands into her lap.

Chapter 31

Hugh had shut the door but they could hear him, trying to talk quietly. He was talking, indeed, very quietly, close to the mouthpiece with his hand around it; even so, Laura and Jessie could hear most of what he said. They did not want to listen, but they couldn't help it.

He said, "I want to make a long distance call, please," and the quietness of his voice made them listen the more carefully. It was full of covered danger.

"Hello? Hello, is this long distance? Long distance I want to call Frank Agee, Frank, Agee, A, g, e, e, no Central not H. A. The first letter in the—A, g, Have you got that, e, e. Agee. At LaFollette, Tennessee. No I haven't. Thank you. I said thank you."

"I don't see how his mother's going to bear it," Laura said, in a subdued voice. "I said I just don't see how Jay's mother is going to bear it," she told her mother.

"Her own husband right at death's door," she said to Jessie, "and now this. He was just the apple of her eye, that's all."

"Hello?"

"She has a world of grit," Jessie said.

"Frank? Is this Frank Agee?"

"If she hadn't she wouldn't be alive today," Laura said.

"Frank, this is Hugh Tyler." They sat very still and made no pretense of not listening.

"Yes. Hugh. Frank I have to tell you about Jay." Jessie and Laura looked at each other. With everything that Hugh said, from then on, they realized in a sense which they had failed to before, that it had really happened and that it was final.

"Jay—died tonight, Frank.

"He's dead.

"He died in an auto accident, on the way home, out near Powell's Station. He was instantly killed."

Laura looked down into the whiskey and began to tremble.

"Instantly. I have a doctor's word for it. He couldn't even have known what hit him.

"It was concussion of the brain, Frank. Concussion—of the brain. Just so hard a shock to the brain that it killed him instantly."

"They mustn't tell his father," Laura said suddenly. "It'll just kill his father."

"I don't see how they can avoid it," Jessie said. "Laura says they mustn't tell his, Jay's father," Jessie told her brother. "In his condition the news might kill him. I told her I simply don't see how they can avoid it. They'll have to account for coming away to the funeral, after all."

"Just tell him he's hurt," Joel said.

Laura hurried into the hall. "*Hugh,*" she whispered loudly. With a contortion of the face which terrified her he slapped his hand through the air at her as if she had been a mosquito. "Just that one place, on the point of the chin," he was saying. He turned to Laura but the voice held him and he turned away. "He may have driven for miles that way. They don't know. They looked all around and quite a distance up the road—yes, of course with flashlights—and they couldn't find it." Again she heard the voice, squirming like a wire. "No they haven't any idea. Except that there are some very rough stretches in those roads and Jay was driving very fast. Just a minute Frank." He covered the mouthpiece. "What is it Laura?"

She could hear the distraught and squirming voice. Like a worm on a hook, she thought. Poor nasty fat thing! "Tell Frank not to tell his father," she whispered. "In his condition it might kill him. If they have to say anything, about—coming down—tell him he's hurt." Hugh nodded.

"Frank," he said. "Go away," he whispered, for she was lingering. "We just want to remind you, it might be very dangerous to your father" (by now Laura heard him through the door; she took her seat) "if he heard this now. Of course you and your mother'll know best but in case you have to explain, when you come away to the funeral, it might be better just to say that Jay's been hurt; not in danger. Don't you think?

"What did you say?

"Why no, we . . .

"He's at Roberts'. I came in with him tonight.

"Why I'd suppose that . . ."

"Oh *heavens!*" Laura said, loudly enough that her father jumped. "Frank's an undertaker!"

"Of course, I see your point, Frank.

"No. Not yet.

"Well the saving of money is not a question in this.

"Look here Frank will you just . . .

"Will you just hold the phone a minute, please? I really think we should leave this up to Laura, don't you?

"Of course she does. You too, I . . .

"I don't doubt it at all.

"No, I appreciate it very deeply Frank and I know Laura will but just let me consult her wishes on it please. Just wait."

They heard his rapid walk and he thrust his infuriated face into the room.

"Frank," he announced, "is an undertaker. I imagine you know what he wants. I told him it was up to you to decide."

"Good—God!" Joel exclaimed.

"Hugh, you'll have to tell him—I—just simply can't."

"He's blaming himself for Jay's . . . He wants to try to make up for it."

"How on earth can he blame himself!"

"For phoning Jay in the first place."

"What nonsense," Jessie said.

"But Jay's already at Ro—"

"Frank says that's easily arranged. He can come down first thing tomorrow."

"Well then we just can't. We just won't, no matter what. Tell him how very *very* much I appreciate it and thank him, but I just can't. Tell him I'm prostrated. I don't care what you tell him, you handle it Hugh."

"I'll handle it." He went back to the phone.

"Seems downright incestuous," Joel said.

His sister laughed harshly.

"Nothing important, Mama," Laura said. "Just—arrangements about the funeral."

Nothing important! Joel thought. People can only get through these things by being blind at least half the time. No: she was just cutting a corner for Emma.

"When will the ceremony be held?"

Jessie stifled a laugh and Joel did not. Laura's face worked curiously with a smile as she told her mother, "We don't know yet. This was a question of where. Here or his parents' farm in Jacksboro?"

"I would have supposed that his home was Knoxville."

"We think so too. That's how it's settled."

"That seems as it should be."

Hugh came in. "Well," he said, "it was either Frank or you and I chose you."

"Oh Hugh, you must have hurt him."

"There wasn't any way out. He just wouldn't take no for an answer."

"He's going to make an awful case of it to his mother."

"Well he'll just have to then."

"She's got sense Laura," Jessie said.

"I'm going to have a drink," Hugh said. "*God!*" he groaned. "Talking to that fool is like trying to put socks on an octopus!"

"Why, *Hugh,*" Laura laughed; she had never heard the expression. "I'm very grateful to you, dear," she said. "You must be worn to a frazzle."

"We all are," Jessie said. "You most of all, Laura. We better think about getting some sleep."

"I suppose we must but I really don't feel as if I *could* sleep. *You*-all better though."

"We're all right," Hugh said. "Except maybe Mama. And Papa, you'd b—"

"Never sleep before two in the morning," Joel said. "You know that."

"Let me fix you a good stiff hot toddy," Jessie said. "It'll help you sleep."

"It all just seems to wake me up."

"Hot."

"Maybe just some hot milk. *No I won't, either,*" she cried out, with sudden tears; they looked at her and looked away; she soon had control of herself.

"One of the last things Jay did for me," she explained, "way early in the morning before he—went away. He fixed me some hot milk to help me sleep." She began to cry again. "Bless his heart," she said. "Bless his dear heart!

"You know almost the last thing he said to me?

"He asked me to think what I wanted for my birthday.

"'Within reason,' he said. He was just joking.

"And he said not to wait supper, but he'd—he'd try to be back before the children were asleep, for sure."

She'd feel better later on if she'd kept a few of these things to herself, Joel thought.

Or would she. I would. But I'm not Poll.

"Rufus just—*wouldn't* give up. He just *wouldn't* go to sleep. He was so proud of that cap, Aunt Jessie. He wanted *so much* to show it to his father."

Jessie came over to her and leaned to her, an arm around her shoulder.

"Talk if you want to Laura," she said. "If you think it does you good. But try not to harp on these things."

"And I was so mad at him, only a few hours ago, for not phoning all day, and because of Rufus. I had such a good supper ready, and I *did* wait it, and . . ."

"It wasn't *his* fault it was good," Jessie said.

"Of *course* it isn't his fault and I had no *business* waiting it but I *did*, and I was so angry with him—why I even—I even . . ."

But this she found she would not tell them. I even thought he was drunk, she said to herself. And if he was why what in the world of it. Let's hope if he was he really loved being. God bless him always. *Always.*

And then a terrifying thought occurred to her, and she looked at Hugh. No, she thought, he wouldn't lie to me if it were so. No, I won't even ask it. I won't even imagine it. I just don't see how I could bear to live if that were so.

But there he was, all that day, with Frank. He *must* have. Well he probably did. That was no part of the promise. But not really *drunk.* Not so he couldn't—navigate. Drive well.

No.

O no.

No I won't even dishonor his dear memory by asking. Not even Hugh in secret. No I won't.

And she thought with such exactness and with such love of her husband's face, and of his voice, and of his hands, and of his way of smiling so warmly even though his eyes almost never lost their sadness, that she succeeded in driving the other thought from her mind.

"Hark!" Jessie whispered.

"What *is* it?"

"*Ssh!* Listen."

"What's up?" Joel asked.

"Be quiet, Joel, *please.* There's something."

They listened most intently.

"I can't hear anything," Hugh whispered.

"Well *I* do," Jessie said, in a low voice. "Hear it or feel it. There's *something.*"

And again in silence they listened.

It began to seem to Laura, as to Jessie, that there was someone in the house other than themselves. She thought of the children; they might have waked up. Yet listening as intently as she could, she was not at all sure that there was any sound; and whoever or whatever it might be, she became sure that it was no child, for she felt in it a terrible forcefulness, and concern, and restiveness, which were no part of any child.

"There *is* something," Hugh whispered.

Whatever it might be, it was never for an instant at rest in one place. It was in the next room; it was in the kitchen; it was in the dining-room.

"I'm going out to see," Hugh said; he got up.

"Wait, Hugh, don't, not yet," Laura whispered. "No; no"; now it's going upstairs, she thought; it's along the—it's in the children's room. It's in *our* room.

"Has somebody come into the house?" Emma enquired in her clear voice.

Hugh felt the flesh go cold along his spine. He bent near her. "What made you think so, Mama?" he asked quietly.

"It's right here in the room with us," Laura said in a cold voice.

"Why, how very stupid of me, I *thought* I *heard.* Footsteps." She gave her short, tinkling laugh. "I must be getting old and dippy." She laughed again.

"*Sshh!*"

"It's Jay," Laura whispered. "I know it now. I was so wrapped up in wondering *what* on earth . . . Jay. Darling. Dear heart, can you hear me?

"Can you tell me if you hear me, dearest?

"Can you?

"Can't you?

"O try your best, my dear. Try your *very* hardest to let me know.

"You can't, can you? You can't, no matter *how* hard.

"But O, do hear me, Jay. I do pray God with all my heart you can hear me, I want so to assure you.

"Don't be troubled dear one. Don't you worry. Stay near us if you can. *All* you can. But let not your heart be troubled. They're all right my sweetheart, my husband. I'm going to be all right. Don't you worry. We'll make out. Rest, my dear. Just rest. Just rest my heart. Don't ever be troubled again. Never again darling. Never, never again."

"May the souls of the faithful through the mercy of God rest in peace," Jessie whispered. "Blessed are the dead."

"Laura!" her brother whispered. He was crying.

"He's not here any more now," she said. "We can talk."

"Laura in God's name what was it?"

"It was Jay, Hugh."

"It was *something.* I haven't any doubt of that, but—good God, Laura."

"It was Jay, all right. I *know!* Who else would be coming here tonight, so terribly worried, so terribly concerned for us and restless! Besides Hugh it—it simply *felt* like Jay."

"You mean . . ."

"I just mean it felt like his *presence.*"

"To me, too," Jessie said.

"I don't like to interrupt," Joel said, "but would you mind telling me please what's going on here?"

"You felt it too, Papa?" Laura asked eagerly.

"Felt what?"

"You remember when Aunt Jessie said there was something around, someone or something in the house?"

"Yes, and she told me to shut up so I did."

"I simply asked you please to be quiet, Joel, because we were trying to hear."

"Well, what did you hear?"

"I don't know's I *heard* anything, Joel. I'm not a bit sure. I don't think I did. But I *felt* something, very distinctly. So did Hugh."

"Yes I did, Papa."

"And Laura."

"Oh, very much so."

"What do you mean you *felt* something?"

"Then you didn't, Papa?"

"I got a feeling there was some kind of a strain in the room, something or other was up among you; Laura looking as if she'd seen a ghost; *all* of you . . ."

"She did," Hugh said. "That is, she didn't actually see anything but she felt it. She knew something was there. She says it was Jay."

"*Hahh?*"

"Jay. Aunt Jessie thinks so too."

"Jessie?"

"Yes I do Joel. I'm not as sure as Laura but it did seem like him."

"What's '*it*'?"

"The thing, Papa, whatever it was. The thing we all felt."

"What did it feel like?"

"Just a . . ."

"You think it was Jay?"

"No, I had no idea *what* it was. But I know it was *something.* Mama felt it too."

"Emma?"

"Yes. And it couldn't have been through us because she didn't even know what we were doing. All of a sudden she said, 'has somebody come into the house?' and when I asked her why she thought so she said she thought she'd heard footsteps."

"Could be thought transference."

"None of the rest of us thought we heard footsteps."

"All the same. It can't be what you think."

"I don't know what it was, Papa, but there are four of us here independently who are sure there was something."

"Joel I know that God in a wheelbarrow wouldn't convince you," his sister said. "We aren't even trying to convince you. But while you're being so rational why at least please be rational enough to realize that we experienced what we experienced."

"The least I can do is accept the fact that three people had a hallucination, and honor their belief in it. Most I can do, too, I guess. I believe you, for yourself Jessie. All of you. I'd have to have the same hallucination myself to be convinced. And even then I'd have my doubts."

"What on earth do you mean, *doubts,* Papa, if you had it yourself?"

"I'd suspect it was just a hallucination."

"O good Lord! You've got it going and coming, haven't you!"

"Is this a dagger that I see before me? Wasn't, you know. But you could never convince Macbeth it wasn't."

"Hugh," Laura broke in; "Tell Mama. She's just dying to know what we're . . ." she trailed off. I must be out of my mind, she said to herself. *Dying!* And she began to think with astonishment and disgust of the way they had all been talking—herself worst of all. How can we bear to chatter along in normal tones of voice!, she thought; how can we even use ordinary words, or any words at all! And now, picking his poor troubled soul to pieces, like so many hens squabbling over. . . . She thought of a worm, and covered her face in sickness. She heard her mother say, "Why Hugh how perfectly *extraordinary!*" and then she heard Hugh question her, had she had any special *feeling* about what *kind* of a person or thing it was, that is, was it quiet or active, or young or old, or disturbed or calm, or was it anything: and her mother answered that she had had no particular impression except that there was someone in the house besides themselves, not the children either, somebody mature, some sort of intruder; but that when nobody had troubled to investigate, she had decided that it must be an hallucination—all the more so because, as she'd said, she thought she'd actually *heard* someone, whereas with her poor old ears (she laughed gracefully), that was simply out of the question, of course. O I do wish they'd leave him in peace, she said to herself. A thing so wonderful. Such a *proof!* Why can't we just keep a reverent silence! But Hugh was asking his mother, had she, a little later than that, still felt even so that there was somebody? or not. And she said that indeed she had had such an *impression.* Where? Why she couldn't say where, except that the *impression* was even stronger than before, but, of course, by then she realized it was an hallucination. But they felt it too! Why how perfectly uncanny!

"Laura thinks it was Jay," Hugh told her.

"Why, I . . ."

"So does Aunt Jessie."

"Why how—how perfectly extraordinary, Hugh!"

"She thinks he was worried about . . ."

"O Hugh!" Laura cried. "Hugh! *Please* let's don't *talk* about it any more! Do you mind?"

He looked at her as if he had been slapped. "Why Laura of course not!" He explained to his mother: "Laura'd rather we didn't discuss it any more."

"O it's not that Hugh. It just—means so much more than anything we can *say* about it or even think about it. I'd give anything just to sit quiet and think about it a little while! Don't you see? It's as if we were driving him away when he wants so much to be here among us, with us, and can't."

"I'm *awfully* sorry Laura. Just *awfully* sorry. Yes of *course* I *do* see. It's a kind of sacrilege."

So they sat quietly and in the silence they began to listen again. At first there was nothing but after a few minutes Jessie whispered, "he's there," and Hugh whispered, "where?" and Laura said quietly, "with the children," and quietly and quickly left the room.

When she came through the door of the children's room she could feel his presence as strongly throughout the room as if she had opened a furnace door: the presence of his strength, of virility, of helplessness, and of pure calm. She fell down on her knees in the middle of the floor and whispered, "Jay. My dear. My dear one. You're all right now darling. You're not troubled any more are you my darling? Not any more. Not ever any more, dearest. I can feel how it is with you. I know, my dearest. It's terrible to go. You don't want to. Of *course* you don't. But you've got to. And you know they're going to be all right. Everything is going to be all right my darling. God take you. God keep you my own beloved. God make his Light to shine upon you." And even while she whispered his presence became faint, and in a moment of terrible dread she cried out "Jay!" and hurried to her daughter's crib. "Stay with me just one minute," she whispered, "just one minute my dearest"; and in some force he did return; she felt him with her, watching his child. Emma was sleeping with all her might and her thumb was deep in her mouth; she was scowling fiercely. "Mercy, child," Laura whispered, smiling, and touched her hot forehead to smooth it, and she growled. "God bless you, God keep you," her mother whispered, and came silently to her son's bed. There was the cap in its tissue-paper, beside him on the floor; he slept less deeply than his sister, with his chin lifted, and his forehead flung back; he looked grave, serene and expectant.

"Be with us all you can," she whispered: "This is goodbye"; and again she went to her knees. Goodbye, she said again, within herself; but she was unable to feel much of anything. "God help me to *realize* it," she whispered, and clasped her hands before her face: but she could realize only that he was fading, and that it was indeed goodbye, and that she was at that moment unable to be particularly sensitive to the fact.

And now he was gone entirely from the room, from the house, and from this world.

"Soon, Jay. Soon, dear," she whispered; but she knew that it would not be soon. She knew that a long life lay ahead of her, for the children were to be brought up, and God alone could know what change and chance might work upon them all, before they met once more. She felt at once a calm and annihilating emptiness, and a cold and overwhelming fulness.

"God help us all," she whispered. "May God in his loving mercy keep us all."

She signed herself with the Cross and left the room.

Chapter 32

She looks as she does when she has just received [Holy Communion], Jessie thought as she came in and took her old place on the sofa; for Laura was trying, successfully, to hide her desolation; and as she sat among them in their quietness it was somewhat diminished. After all, she told herself, he *was there.* More strongly even than when he was here in the room with me. Anyhow. And she was grateful for their silence.

Finally Hugh said: "Aunt Jessie has an idea about it, Laura."

"Maybe you'd prefer not to talk about it," Jessie said.

"No; it's all right; I guess I'd rather." And with mild surprise she found that this was true.

"Well, it's simply that I thought of all the old tales and beliefs about the souls of people who die sudden deaths, or violent deaths. Or as Joel would prefer it, not souls. Just their life force. Their consciousness. Their life itself."

"Can't get around that," Joel said. "Jessie was saying that everything of any importance leaves the body then. I certainly have to agree with that."

"And that even whether you believe or not in life after death," Laura said, "in the Soul, as a living, immortal thing, creature, why it's certainly very believable that for a little while afterwards, this force, this life, stays on. Hovers around."

"Sounds highly unlikely to me but I suppose it's conceivable."

"Like looking at a light and then shutting your eyes. No, not like that but—but it does stay on. Specially when it's someone very strong, very vital, who hasn't been worn down by old age, or a long illness or something."

"That's exactly it," Hugh said. "Something that comes out whole, because it's so quick."

"Why they're as old as the hills, those old beliefs."

"I should imagine they're as old as life and death," Hugh said.

"The thing I mean is, they aren't taken straight to God," Jessie said. "They've had such violence done them, such a shock, it takes a while to get their wits together."

"That's why it took him so long to come," Laura said. "As if his very *soul* had been struck unconscious."

"I should think maybe."

"And above all with someone like Jay, young, and with children and a wife, and not even dreaming of such a thing coming on him, no time to adjust his mind and feelings, or prepare for it"—

"That's just it," Hugh said; Jessie nodded.

—"why he'd feel, 'I'm worried. This came too fast without warning. There are all kinds of things I've got to tend to. I can't just leave them like this.' *Wouldn't* he! And that's just how he was, how we felt he was. So anxious. So awfully concerned, and disturbed. Why yes, it's just exactly the way it was!

"And only when they feel convinced you know they care, and everything's going to be taken good care of, just the very best possible, it's only then they can stop being anxious and begin to rest."

They nodded and for a minute they were all quiet.

Then Laura said tenderly: "How awful, pitiful, beyond words it must be, to be so terribly anxious for others, for others' good, and not be able to do anything, even to say so. Not even to help. Poor things.

"O they *do* need reassuring. They *do* need rest. I'm *so grateful* I could assure him. It's so good he can rest at last. I'm *so glad.*" And her heart was restored from its desolation into warmth and love and almost into wholeness.

Again they were all thoughtfully silent, and into this silence Joel spoke quietly and slowly: "I *don't—know.* I *just—don't—know.* Every bit of gumption I've got tells me it's impossible but if this kind of thing is so, it isn't with gumption that you see it is. I *just—don't—know.*

"If you're right, and I'm wrong, then chances are you're right about the whole business. God, and the whole crew. And in that case I'm just a plain damned fool.

"But if I can't trust my common sense—I know it's nothing much Poll but it's all I've got. If I can't trust that, what in hell *can* I trust!

"God, you'n Jessie'd say. Far's I'm concerned, it's out of the question."

"Why, Joel?"

"It doesn't seem to embarrass your idea of common sense, or Poll's, and for that matter I'm making no reflections. You've got plenty of gumption. But how you can reconcile the two, I can't see."

"It takes faith, Papa," Laura said gently.

"That's the word. That's the one makes a mess of everything, far's I'm concerned. Bounces up like a jack-in-the-box. Solves everything.

"Well it doesn't solve anything for me, for I haven't got any.

"Wouldn't hurt it if I had. Don't believe in it.

"Not for me.

"For you, for anyone that can manage it, all right. More power to you. Might be glad if I could myself. But I can't.

"I'm not exactly an atheist, you know. Least I don't suppose I am. Seems as unfounded to me to say there isn't a God, as to say there is. You can't prove it either way. But that's it: I've got to have proof. And on anything can't be proved, be damned if I'll jump either way. All I can say is, I hope you're wrong but I just don't know."

"I don't, either," Hugh said. "But I hope it's so."

He saw Laura and Jessie look at him hopefully.

"I don't mean the whole business," he said. "I don't know anything about that. I just mean tonight."

Can't eat your cake and have it, his father thought.

Like slapping a child in the face, Hugh thought; he had been rougher than he had intended.

"But Hugh dear," Laura was about to say, but she caught herself. What a thing to argue about, she thought; and what a time to be wrangling about it!

Each of them realized that the others felt something of this; for a little while none of them had anything to say.

Finally Hugh said, "I'm sorry."

"Never mind," his sister said. "It's all right, Hugh."

"We just each believe what we're able," Jessie said after a moment.

"Even you, Joel. You have faith in your mind. Your reason."

"Not very much: all I've got, that's all. All I can be sure of."

"That's all I mean."

"Let's not talk about it any more," Laura said. "Tonight," she added, trying to make her request seem less peremptory.

The word was a reproach upon them all, so much more grave, they were sure, than Laura had intended, that to spare her regret they all hastened to say, kindly and as if somewhat callously, "No let's not."

In the embarrassment of having spoken all at once they sat helpless and sad, sure only that silence, however painful to them all and to Laura, was less mistaken than trying to speak. Laura wished that she might ease them; her continued silence, she was sure, intensified their self-reproach; but she felt, as they did, that an attempt to speak would be worse than quietness.

In this quietness their mother sat, and smiled nervously and politely, and tilted her trumpet in a generalized way towards all of them. She realized that nobody was speaking and it was at such times, ordinarily, that she felt sure that she could speak without interrupting anyone, but she feared that anything that she might say might brutally or even absurdly disrupt a weaving of thought and feeling whose motions within the room she could most faintly apprehend.

After a little while it occurred to her that even to hold out her trumpet might seem to require something of them; she held it in her lap. But lest any of them should feel that this was in any sense a reproach, or should in the least feel sorry for her, she kept her little smile, thinking, how foolish, how very foolish, to smile.

Smiling at grief, Joel thought. He wondered whether his sister and his son and his daughter, if they were thinking of it at all, understood the smile as he was sure he did. He wished that he could pat her hand. By God they'd better, he thought.

Hugh could not get out of his mind the image of his brother-in-law as he had just seen him. By the mere shy, inactive way the men stood who, as he and Arthur just came up, stood between them and Jay, he had realized, instantly, before anyone spoke, "he's dead." Somebody had murmured something embarrassed about identification and he had answered, sharply, that they'd managed to phone the family, hadn't they? and again they had murmured embarrassedly, and ashamed of his sharpness he had assented, and there in the light of the one bulb one of the men had gently turned down the sheet (for he gathered a little later that the blacksmith's wife, finding him covered with a reeking horse blanket, had hurried to bring this sheet); and there he was; and Hugh nodded, and made himself say, "yes," and he heard Arthur's deep, quiet breathing at his shoulder and heard him say "yes," and he stood a little aside in order that Arthur might have room, and together they stood silent and looked at the uncovered head. The strong frown was still in the forehead but even as they watched it seemed to be fading very slowly; already the flesh had settled somewhat along the bones of the prostrate skull; the temples, the forehead, and the sockets of the eyes were more subtly molded than they had been in life and the nose was more finely arched; the chin was thrust upward as if proudly and impatiently, and the small cut at its point was as neat and bloodless as if it had been made by a chisel in soft wood. They watched him with the wonder which is felt in the presence of anything which is great and new, and, for a little while, in any place where violence has recently occurred; they were aware, as they gazed at the still head, of a prodigious kind of energy in the air. Without turning his head, Hugh became aware that tears were running down Arthur's cheeks; he himself was cold, awed, embittered beyond tears. After perhaps a half minute he said coldly, "yes that's he," and covered the face himself and turned quickly away; Arthur was drying his face and his glasses; aware of some obstacle Hugh glanced quickly down upon a horned, bruised anvil; and laid his hand flat against the cold, whelmed iron; and it was as if its forehead gave his hand the stunning shadow of every blow it had ever received.

Now these images manifolded upon each other with great rapidity, at their constant center the proud, cut chin, and could be driven from his mind's eye only by two others, Jay as he felt he had seen him, the instant after the accident, lying, they had told him, so straight and unblemished beside the car, the dead eyes shining with starlight and the hands still as if ready to seize and wrestle; and as he had last actually seen him, naked on the naked table, a block beneath his nape.

Somebody sighed, from the heart; he looked up; it was Jessie. They were all looking downward and sidelong. His sister's face had altered strangely during this silence; it had become thin, shy, and somehow almost bridal. He remembered her wedding in Panama; yes, it was much the same face. He looked away.

"Aunt Jessie will you please stay with me here tonight?" Laura asked.

Mama, Hugh thought, and his heart went out to her as he looked at her deaf, set smile.

"Why certainly Laura."

Joel decided not to look at his watch. Hugh covertly glanced at the mantel clock. It was. . . .

"I hope Mama won't mind too much. I hope she'll understand. Poor thing. Mama," she suddenly called, and put her hand on her mother's hand and on the trumpet. Her mother eagerly tilted it. "I think it's about time we all tried to get some sleep." Her mother nodded, and seemed to be about to speak; Laura pressed her hand for silence and continued: "Mama I've asked Aunt Jessie if she'll stay here the night with me." Her mother nodded and again seemed to be about to speak. Again Laura pressed her hand: "I'd love it if you could but I just know how it would disrupt things at eleven-fifteen,"—"*Hahh,*" her father exclaimed—"and I just . . ."

"*Tell* her, Poll!"

"Also, Mama. Also it's just—I hope you'll understand and not mind, Mama dear—it's just it would be so very hard for us to *talk, quietly,* and with the children and all, why I just sort of think . . ."

"Why certainly Laura," her mother interrupted, in her somewhat ringing voice. "I absolutely agree with you. I think it's so nice that Jessie can stay!" she added, almost as if Laura and Jessie were little girls.

"I hope you know, Mama, how *very much!*—I hope you don't mind. I just appreciate it so much, I . . ."

Her mother patted her hand rapidly. "It's perfectly all right Laura. It's very, *sensible.*" She smiled.

Laura put an arm around her and hugged her; she turned her aging face and smiled very brightly and Laura could see the tears in her eyes. She was speechless and her head was shaking in her effort to convey her love and the entirety of her feeling. "*Anything* I can do dear child," she said after a few moments. "*Anything!*"

"Bless you, Mama!"

"Beg pardon?"

"I said *bless* you, dear!"

Emma patted her hand on the back and smiled even more tightly.

I love you so much! Laura exclaimed within herself.

"Praps the children," Emma said. "I could take care, if, if it would be more, *convenient* . . ."

"O I don't think we should wake them up!" Laura said.

"She doesn't mean . . ." Hugh began.

"Tomorrow," her mother said. "Just perhaps during the—interim . . ."

"That's wonderful Mama, that may turn out to be just the thing and if it is I most certainly will. *Most gratefully.* It's just, I'm in such a spin it's just too early to quite know yet, make any plans. Anything. Tomorrow."

"Tomorrow then."

"Thank you Mama."

"Not at all."

"Thank you all the same."

Her mother smiled and shook her head.

Joel and his sister stood up.

"Laura, before we go," Hugh said.

"?"

"It's much too late, Laura, you're much too tired."

"Not if it's important, Hugh."

"Let's let it go till morning."

"What is it, Hugh?"

"Just—various things we'll have to discuss pretty soon."

He took a deep breath and said in a hard voice: "Getting a plot; making arrangements about the funeral; seeing about a headstone. Let's wait till morning."

Earth, stone, a coffin. The ugly craft of undertakers became real and tangible to her, but as if she touched them with frozen hands. She looked at him with glazed eyes.

"That'll be plenty of time, Laura," she heard her aunt say.

"Of course it will," Hugh said. "It was foolish of me to even speak of it tonight."

"Well *if* there's time," she said vaguely. "Yes *if* there's time, Hugh," she said more distinctly. "Yes then I'd rather if you don't mind. Tomorrow in the morning." She glanced at the clock. "Goodness *this* morning," she exclaimed.

"Of course not," Hugh said. He turned to his aunt and said in a low voice, as one speaks before an invalid, "Let her sleep if she can. You phone me."

Jessie nodded.

"Must've . . ." Joel said, and went into the hall.

"What's . . ." Jessie began.

"Hat I guess. Mine too." Hugh left the room; in the hall he met his father, carrying his own hat, his wife's, and Hugh's.

"Left them in the kitchen," his father said.

"Thank you, Papa." Hugh took his hat.

Emma was standing uneasily in the middle of the room, holding her trumpet and her purse and looking towards the hall door. "Thank you, Joel," she said. She settled and pinned her hat by touch, a little crooked, and looked at Jessie inquiringly.

"It's all right, Emma," her husband said.

Hugh was watching his sister. It seemed to him that these preparations for departure put her into some kind of silent panic. Maybe we should stay, he thought. All night. I could. But Laura was chiefly watching her mother's difficulties with the hat. No it's the slowness, he corrected himself. Sooner the better.

"Well Laura," he said, and stepped to her and put his arms around her. He saw that her eyes were speckled; it was as if the irises had been cracked into many small fragments; and in her eyes and her presence he felt something of the shock and energy which had been so strong about the dead body. She was new; changed. Nothing I can do, he thought.

"Thank you for everything," she said. "I'm so sorry you had it to do."

He could not answer or continue to look into her eyes; he embraced her more closely. "Laura," he said finally.

"I'm all right Hugh," she said quietly. "I've got to be."

He nodded sharply.

"You come up in the morning. We'll—make our plans."

"Sleep if you can."

"Just come up first thing cause I know there's an awful lot to do and not much time."

"All right."

"Goodnight, Hugh."

"Goodnight, Laura."

"*Bless you,*" her mother exploded, almost as if she were cursing; deaf, near-sighted, she caught her daughter in her arms with all her strength and patted her back with both hands, thinking: how young and good she smells!

She wants so to help, Laura realized. To stay! Under her caress she felt the hard round shoulders, sharp backbone, already hunching with age. Leaning back in her mother's embrace, she straightened the hat, looked into the trembling face, and kissed her hard on the mouth. Her mother twice returned the kiss, then stood aside, gathering her long skirt for the porch steps.

"Poll," her father said; she felt the beard against her cheek and heard his whisper: "Good girl. Keep it up."

She nodded.

"Good-night," Jessie said.

"Goodnight, Aunt Jessie," Hugh replied.

"Night Jessie," her brother said. Joel steered Emma by one elbow, Hugh by the other; they went onto the porch.

"Light!" Laura exclaimed.

"What?" Hugh and Jessie asked, startled.

Laura switched on the porch light. "Tsall right," her father said in mild annoyance; "Thank you," her mother chimed, politely. Laura and Jessie stood at the door while they carefully descended the porch steps, and they watched them until they reached the corner and then until they had safely crossed the street. Under the corner lamp, Hugh turned his head and lifted and let fall his hand in something less than a wave. The others did not turn; and now Hugh also had turned away, and they went carefully away along the sidewalk, and Laura switched off the light, and still watched. Jessie could no longer see them now, and after a few moments gave up pretending to watch them and watched Laura as she looked after them, as intently, Jessie felt, as if it were of more importance than anything else, to see them until the last possible instant. And still Laura could see them, somewhat darker against the darkness and of uneven heights, growing smaller, so that it was not finally the darkness which made them impossible to see, but the corner of the Biddles' house.

When they were gone she continued to look up and down the street as far as she could see. There was the strong carbon light at the corner, and there was the glow of an unseen light at a more distant corner to the west; and of another, still more distant, to the east. There was no sound, and there were no lights on in any of the houses. The air moved mildly on her forehead. She turned, and saw that her aunt was watching her, and looked into her eyes.

"Time to sleep," she said.

She closed the door; they continued to look at each other.

"It was just about this time last night," she said.

Jessie sighed, very low; after a moment she touched Laura's hand. Still they stood and looked at each other.

"Yes just about," Laura whispered strangely.

Through the silence they began to hear the kitchen clock.

"Let's not even *try* to talk now," Laura said. "We're both worn out."

"Let me fix you a good hot toddy," Jessie said, as they turned towards the living-room. "Help you sleep."

"I honestly don't think I'll *need* it Aunt Jessie."

I'll make one and you take it or not as you like, Jessie wanted to say; suddenly she realized: I'm only trying to think I'm useful. She said nothing.

There was an odd kind of shyness or constraint between them, which neither could understand. They stood still again, just inside the living-room; the silence was somewhat painful for both of them, each on the other's account. Does she really *want* me to stay, Jessie wondered; what earthly use am I! Does she think I don't *want* her to stay, Laura wondered, just because I can't talk? No, she's no talker.

"I just can't talk just now," she said.

"Of course you can't, child."

Jessie felt that she probably ought to take charge of everything, but she felt still more acutely that she should be at the service of Laura's wishes,—or lack of them for that matter, she told herself.

I can't stand to *send* her to bed, Laura thought.

"It's all ready," she said abruptly and, she feared, rather ruthlessly, and walked quickly across to the downstairs bedroom door and opened it. "See?" She walked in and turned on the light and faced her aunt. "I got it ready in case Jay," she said, and absently smoothed the pillow. "Just as well I did."

"You go straight to bed Laura," Jessie said. "Let me help if I . . ."

Laura went into the kitchen; then Jessie could hear her in the hall; after a moment she came back. "Here's a clean nightgown," she said, "and a wrapper," putting them across her aunt's embarrassed hands. "It'll be big, I'm afraid, the wrapper, it's—was—it's Jay's, but if you'll turn up the sleeves it'll do in a pinch I guess." She went past Jessie into the living-room.

"I'll see to that Laura," Jessie hurried after her; she was already gathering tumblers towards the tray.

"Great—goodness!" Laura exclaimed. She lifted the bottle. "Do you mean to say *I* drank all *that?*" It was three-quarters empty.

"No. Hugh had some, so did I, so did J—your father."

"But—just one apiece Aunt Jessie. I *must* have. Nearly all of it."

"It hasn't had any effect."

"How on earth!" She held the low whiskey close to her eyes and looked at it as if she were threading a needle. "Well I most *certainly* don't need a *hot toddy,*" she said.

"I never *heard* of such a thing!" she exclaimed quietly.

"Aspirin, perhaps."

"Aspirin?"

"You might wake up with a headache."

"It must just, Papa, Papa says, he said it sometimes doesn't, in a state of shock or things . . .

"Aunt Jessie?" She called more loudly: "Aunt Jessie?" Mustn't wake them, she remembered. She waited. Her aunt came in from the hall with a glass of water and two aspirins.

"Here," she said, "you take these."

"But I . . ."

"Just swallow them. You don't want to wake up with a headache and they'll help you sleep, too."

She took them docilely; Jessie loaded and lifted the tray.

Chapter 33

Along Laurel, it was much darker; heavy leaves obscured the one near street lamp. Hugh could hear only their footsteps; his father and mother, he realized, could hear nothing even of that. How still we see thee lie. Yes, and between the treetops; the pale scrolls and porches and dark windows of the homes drifting past their slow walking, and not a light in any home, and so for miles, in every street of home and of business; above thy deep and dreamless sleep, the silent stars go by.

He helped his mother from the curb; this slow and irregular rattling of their little feet.

The stars are tired by now. Night's nearly over.

He helped her to the opposite curb.

Upon their faces the air was so marvelously pure, aloof and tender; and the silence of the late night in the city, and the stars, were secret and majestic beyond the wonder of the deepest country. Little houses, bigger ones, scrolled and capacious porches, dark windows, leaves of trees already rich with May, homes of rooms which chambered sleep as honey is cherished, drifted past their slow walking and were left behind, and not a light in any home. Along Laurel Avenue it was still darker. The lamp behind them no longer cast their shadows; in the light of the lamp ahead, a small and distant bit of pavement looked scalded with emptiness, a few leaves were touched to acid flame, the spindles and turned posts of one porch were rigidly white. Helping his mother along through the darkness, Hugh was walking much more slowly than he was used to walking, and all these things entered him calmly and thoroughly. Full as his heart was, he found that he was involved at least as deeply in the loveliness and unconcern of the spring night, as in the death. It's as if I didn't even care, he reflected, but he didn't mind. He knew he cared; he felt gratitude towards the night and towards the city he ordinarily cared little for. *How still we see thee lie,* he heard his mind say. He said the words over, dryly within himself, and heard the melody; a child's voice, his own, sang it in his mind.

Hm.

He tried to remember when he had last walked in the open night at such an hour. He wasn't sure he even—God. Years. Seve—about sixteen, when he still thought he was Shelley. Watching the river. Leaning on the bridge rail and literally praying with gratitude for being alive.

Instinctively, he turned his head so that his parents could not see his face.

I don't want to see it either, he thought.

By that time, Jay was trying to teach himself law.

Above thy deep and dreamless sleep, the silent stars go by.

The words had always touched him; every year they still brought back Christmas to him, for some reason, as nothing else could. Now they seemed to him as beautiful as any poetry he had ever known.

He said them over to himself very slowly and calmly: just a statement.

They do indeed, he thought, looking up. They do indeed. And God, how tired they look!

It's the time of night.

The silent stars go by, he said aloud, not whispering, but so quietly he was sure they would not hear.

His eyes sprang full of tears; his throat, his chest knotted into a deep sob which he subdued, and the tears itched on his cheeks.

Yet in thy dark streets shineth, he sang loudly, almost in fury, within himself: *The Everlasting Light!* and upon these words a sob leapt up through him which he could not subdue but could only hope to conceal.

They did not notice.

This is crazy, he told himself incredulously. *No sense in this at all!*

Everlasting Light!

The hopes and fears, a calm and implacable voice continued within him; he spoke quietly: *Of all the years.*

Are met in thee tonight, he whispered: and in the middle of a wide plain, the middle of the dark and silent city, slabbed beneath shadowless light, he saw the dead man, and struck his thigh with his fist with all his strength.

All he could hear in this world was only their footsteps; his father and mother, he realized, could hear nothing even of that.

He helped her from the curb; this slow and irregular rattling of their little feet; and across the space of bitter light.

He helped her to the opposite curb; they followed their absurd shadows until all was once more one shadow.

None of the three of them spoke, throughout their walk; when they came to the corner at which they would turn for home, it was as if all three spoke, accepting the fact: for each man tightened his hand gently at the woman's elbows and, bowing her head, she pressed their hands against her sides. They turned down the steep hill, walking still more slowly and tightening their knees, and saw the one light which had been left burning, and entered their home, quietly as burglars, by the back way.

Chapter 34

They stopped at the foot of the stairs.

"Laura," Jessie asked, "is there anything I can do?"

You want to come up with me, Laura realized. "I think I just better be alone," she said. "But thank you. Thank you Aunt Jessie."

"Just call if you want me. You know how lightly I sleep."

"I'll be all right, I really will."

"You rest in the morning. I'll take care of the children."

Laura looked at her with brightened eyes, and said, "Aunt Jessie I'll have to tell them."

Jessie nodded, and sighed: "Yesss. Good night then," she said, and kissed her niece. "God bless you," she said, in a broken voice.

Laura looked at her carefully and said, "God help us all."

She turned and went up the stairs, and leaned, smiling, just before she disappeared, and whispered, "Goodnight."

"Good night, Laura," Jessie whispered.

Jessie turned off the hall light and the light in the living-room and went into the lighted bedroom and pulled down the shade and shut the doors to the kitchen and the living-room. She took off her dress and laid it over the back of a chair and sat on the edge of the bed to unlace her shoes, and hesitated, until she was certain that she remembered, clearly, putting out the lights in the kitchen and bathroom. She put on the nightgown except for the sleeves and finished undressing under the nightgown; it was rather large for her and she gathered and lifted it about her. She knelt beside the bed and said an Our Father and a Hail Mary, and found that her heart and mind were empty of further prayer or even of feeling. May the souls of the faithful, she tried; she clamped her teeth and, after a moment, prayed angrily: May the souls of everyone who has ever had to live and die, in the Faith or outside it or defiant of it, rest in peace. And especially his!

Strike me down, she thought. Visit upon me Thy lightnings. I don't care. I can't care.

Forgive me if I'm wrong, she thought. If you can. If you will. But that's how I feel, and that's all there is to it.

Again her heart and mind were empty; even now, feeling the breath of the abyss, she could not feel otherwise, or even care or fear.

Lord, I believe. Help thou mine unbelief.

But I don't really know's I do.

I can't pray, God. Not now. Try to forgive me. I'm just too tired and too appalled.

Thirty-six years old.

Thirty-six.

Well why not. Why one time worse than another. God knows it's no picnic or ever was intended as such.

Into Thy hands I commend my spirit.

She made the sign of the Cross, raised the shade, opened the window, and got into bed. As her bare feet slid along the cold clean linen and she felt its cold clean blandness beneath her and above her, she was taken briefly by trembling and by loneliness, and remembered touching her dead mother's cheek.

O why am I alive!

She took off her glasses and laid them carefully in reach at the foot of the lamp, and turned out the light. She straightened formally on her back, folded her hands upon her breast, and shut her eyes.

I can't worry any more about anything, tonight, she said to herself. He'll just have to take care of it.

Till morning.

Laura did not bother to turn on the light; she could see well enough by the windows. She put on her nightgown and undressed beneath it, and saw to it that the door was left ajar for the children, and climbed into bed before she realized that these were the same sheets and before it occurred to her that she had not said her prayers: and for such a while now she had felt that if only she could be alone, only for that!

It's all right, she whispered to herself; it's all right, she whispered aloud. She had meant that she was sure that God would understand and forgive her inability to pray, but she found that she meant too that it really was all right, everything, the whole thing, really all right. Thy will be done. All right. Truly all right. She lay straight on her back with her hands open, upward at her sides and could just make out, in the subtly diminished darkness, a familiar stain which at various times had seemed to resemble a crag, a galleon, a fish, a brooding head. Tonight it was just itself, with one meaningless eye. It seemed to her that she was falling backward and downward, prostrate, through eternity; she felt no concern. Without concern she heard a voice speak within her: Out of the deep have I called unto Thee, O Lord: Lord, hear my voice, she joined in. O let thine ear consider well: the voice of my complaint. And now the first voice said no more and, aware of its silent presence, Laura continued, whispering aloud: If Thou, Lord, wilt be extreme to mark what is done amiss: Lord, who may abide it? And with these last words she began to cry freely and quietly, her hands turned downward and moved wide on the bed.

O Jay! Jay!

Under the lid of the large kettle the low water was luke-warm: one by one, along the curved firmament, the last of the bubbles broke and vanished.

Jessie lay straight on her back with her hands folded: in their deep sockets, beneath lids as frail as membranes, her eyeballs were true spheres. No lines were left in her face; she might have been a young woman. Her lips were parted, and each breath was a light sigh.

Laura lay watching the ceiling: Who may abide it, she whispered.

Silently.

One by one, million by million, in the prescience of dawn, every leaf in that part of the world was moved.

Morning
May 19, 1916

Chapter 35

When he woke it was already clear daylight and the sparrows were making a great racket and his first disappointed thought was that he was too late, though he could not yet think what it was he was too late for. But something special was on his mind which made him eager and happy almost as if this were Christmas morning and within a second after waking he remembered what it was and, sitting up, his lungs stretching full with anticipation and pride, put his hand into the crisp tissue paper with a small smashing noise and took out the cap. There was plenty of light to see the colors well; he quickly turned it around and over, and smelled of the new cloth and of the new leather band. He put it on and yanked the bill down firmly and pelted down the hallway calling "*Daddy! Daddy!*" and burst through the open door into their bedroom; then brought up short in dismay, for his father was not there. But his mother lay there, propped up on two pillows as if she were sick. She looked sick, or very tired, and in her eyes she seemed to be afraid of him. Her face was full of little lines he had never seen before; they were as small as the lines in her mended best teacup. She put out her arms towards him and made an odd, kind noise. "Where's Daddy?" he shouted, ignoring her arms.

"Daddy—isn't here yet," she told him, in a voice like hot ashes, and her arms sank down along the sheet.

"Where *is* he, then!" he demanded, in angry disappointment, but she thrust through these words with her own: "Go wake—little Emma and bring her straight here," she said, in a voice which puzzled him; "there's something I must tell you both together."

He was darting his eyes everywhere for clues of his father: clothes? watch? tobacco? nightshirt? "*Right away,*" she said, in a desperate voice.

Startled by its mysterious rebuke, and uneasy in his stomach because she had said "little" Emma, he hurried out—and all but collided with his Aunt Jessie. Her mouth was strong and tightly pressed together beneath her glittering spectacles as she stooped peering forward.

"Hello Aunt Jessie," he called with astonishment, as he sped round and past her; he saw her go into the bedroom, her hair sticking out from her thin neck in two gray twiggy braids; he hurried to Emma's crib.

"Wake *up* Emma!" he yelled. "Mama says wake *up!* Right *away!*" He shook her.

"*Stob*bit," she bawled, her round red face glaring.

"Well mama *said* so, mama *said* so, wake *up!*"

And a few moments later he hurried back ahead of her and hollered breathlessly, "She's coming!" and she trailed in, two-thirds asleep, snuffling with anger, her lower lip stuck out.

"*Take off that cap!*" his Aunt Jessie snapped with frightening sternness, and his hands only just caught it against her snatching. He was appalled by this betrayal, and the hardness of her mouth as she struggled with self-astonishment and repentance was even more ominous.

"Oh, Jessie no, let him," his mother said in her strange voice, "he was so crazy for Jay to see it," and even as she said it he was surprised all over again for his Aunt, whispering something inaudible, touched his cheek very gently. And now as she had done before, his mother lifted forward her hands and her kind arms; "Children come close," she said.

Aunt Jessie went silently out of the room.

"Come close"; and she touched each of them. "I want to tell you about Daddy." But upon his name her voice shook and her whole dry-looking mouth trembled like the ash of burned paper in a draft. "Can you hear me Emma?" she asked, when she had recovered her voice. Emma peered at her earnestly as if through a thick fog. "Are you waked up enough yet, my darling?" And because of her voice, in sympathy and for her protection, they both came now much nearer, and she put her arms around both of them, and they could smell her breath, a little like sauerkraut but more like a dried-up mouse. And now even more small lines like cracked china, branched all over her face. "Daddy," she said, "your father, children": and this time she caught control of her mouth more quickly, and a single tear spilled out of her left eye and slid crookedly across all the crooked lines: "Daddy didn't come home. He isn't going to come home ever any more. He's—gone away to Heaven and he isn't ever coming home again. Do you hear me Emma? Are you awake?" Emma stared at her mother. "Do *you* understand, Rufus?"

He stared at his mother. “Why not?” he asked.

She looked at him with extraordinary closeness and despair and said, “Because God wanted him.” They continued to stare at her severely and she went on: “Daddy was on his way home last night and he was—he—got hurt and—so God let him go to sleep and took him straight away with Him to Heaven.” She sank her fingers in Emma’s springy hair and looked intently from one to the other. “Do you see, children? Do you understand?”

They stared at her, and now Emma was sharply awake.

“Is Daddy *dead?*” Rufus asked.

Her glance at him was as startled as if he had slapped her, and again her mouth and then her whole face began to work, uncontrollably this time, and she did not speak, but only nodded her head once, and then again, and then several times rapidly, while one small, squeaky “*yes*” came out of her as if it had been squeezed out; then suddenly sweeping both of them close against her breasts, she tucked her chin down tightly between the crowns of their heads and they felt her whole body shaken as if by a violent wind, but she did not cry.

Emma began to sniffle quietly because everything seemed very serious and very sad.

Rufus listened to his mother’s shattered breathing and gazed sidelong past her fair shoulder at the sheet, rumpled, and at a rubbed place in the rose-patterned carpet and then at something queer, that he had never seen before, on the bedside table, a tangle of brown beads and a little cross; through her breathing he began once more to hear the quarreling sparrows; he said to himself: *dead, dead,* but all he could do was see and hear; the streetcar raised and quieted its grim iron cry; he became aware that his cap was pushed crooked against her and he felt that he ought to take it off but that he ought not to move just now to take it off, and he knew why his Aunt Jessie had been so mad at him. He could no longer hear even a rumor of the streetcar, and his mother’s breathing had become quiet again. With one hand she held Emma still more closely against her, and Emma sniffled a little more comfortably; with the other hand she put Rufus quietly away, so that she could look clearly into his eyes; tenderly she took off his cap and laid it beside her, and pushed the hair back from his forehead.

“Neither of you will quite understand for a while,” she said. “It’s—very *hard* to understand. But you will,” she said (I do, he said to himself;

he's dead. That's what.) and she repeated rather dreamily, as if to herself, though she continued to look into his eyes, "you will." Then she was silent; and some kind of energy intensified in her eyes and she said: "When you want to know more—*about* it" (and her eyes became still more vibrant) "just, just ask me and I'll tell you because you ought to know." *How did he get hurt,* Rufus wanted to ask, but he knew by her eyes that she did not mean at all what she said, not now anyway, not this minute, he must not ask: and now he did not want to ask because he too was afraid; he nodded to let her know he understood her. "Just ask," she said again, and he nodded again; a strange, cold excitement was rising in him; and in a cold intuition that it would be kind, and gratefully received, he kissed her. "God *bless* you," she groaned, and held them passionately against herself; "*both* of you!" She loosened her arms. "And now you be a good boy," she said in almost her ordinary voice, wiping Emma's nose. "Get little Emma dressed, can you do that?" (he nodded proudly) "and wash and dress yourself, and by then Aunt Jessie will have breakfast ready."

"Aren't you getting up Mama?" he asked, much impressed that he had been deputized to dress his sister.

"Not for a while," she said, and by her way of saying it he knew that she wanted them to go out of the room right away.

"Come on Emma," he said and found, with surprise, that he had taken her hand. Emma looked up at him, equally surprised, and shook her head.

"Go with Rufus dear," her mother said, "he's going to help you get dressed, and eat your breakfast. Mother will see you soon."

And Emma, feeling that for some reason to do with her father, who was not where he ought to be, and her mother too, she must try to be a very good girl, came away with him without further protest. As they turned through the door to go down, Rufus saw that his mother had taken the beads and cross from the bedside table (they were like a regular necklace) and the beads ran among her fingers and twined and drooped from her hands and one wrist while she looked so intently at the upright cross that she did not realize that she had been seen. *She'd be mad if she knew,* he was sure.

Before he did anything about Emma he put his cap back in the tissue-paper. Then he got her clothes. "Take off your nightie," he said. "Sopping wet," he added, as nearly like his mother as possible.

"You're sopping wet too," she retorted.

"No I didn't either" he said, "not last night."

He found that she could do a certain amount of the dressing herself; she got on the panties and she nearly got her underwaist on right too, except that it was backwards. "That's all right," he told her, again as much like his mother as he was able, "you do it fine. Just a *little bit* crooked"; and he fixed it right.

He buttoned her panties to her underwaist. It was much less easy, he found, than buttoning his own clothes. "Stand still," he said, because to tell her so seemed only a proper part of carrying out his duty.

"I am," Emma replied, with such firmness that he said no more.

That was all that either of them said before they went down to breakfast.

Chapter 36

Emma did not like being buttoned up by Rufus or bossed around by him, and breakfast wasn't like breakfast either. Aunt Jessie didn't say anything and neither did Rufus and neither did she, and she felt that even if she wanted to say anything she oughtn't. Everything was queer; it was so still and it was so still it seemed dark. Aunt Jessie sliced the banana so thin on the Post Toasties it looked cold and limp and slimy. She gave each of them a little bit of coffee in their milk and she made Rufus' a little bit darker than hers. She didn't say, "eat"; "eat your breakfast, Emma"; "don't dawdle"; like Emma's mother; she didn't say anything. Emma did not feel hungry, but she felt mildly curious because things tasted so different, and she ate slowly ahead, tasting each mouthful.

Everything was so still that it made Emma feel uneasy and sad. There were little noises when a fork or spoon touched a dish; the only other noise was the very thin dry toast Aunt Jessie kept slowly crunching and the fluttering sipping of the steamy coffee with which she wet each mouthful of dry crumbs enough to swallow it. When Emma tried to make a similar noise sipping her milk, her Aunt Jessie glanced at her sharply as if she wondered if Emma was trying to be a smart-aleck but she did not say anything. Emma was not trying to be a smart-aleck but she felt she had better not make that noise again. The fried eggs had hardly any pepper and they were so soft the yellow ran out over the white and the white plate and looked so nasty she didn't want to eat it but she ate it because she didn't want to be told to and because she felt there was some special reason, still, why she ought to be a good girl. She felt very uneasy but there was nothing to do but eat, so she always took care to get a good hold on her tumbler and did not take too much on her spoon, and hardly spilled at all, and when she became aware of how little she was spilling it made her feel proud like a big girl and yet she did not feel any less uneasy, because she knew there was something wrong. She was not as much interested in eating as she was in the way things were, and listening carefully, looking mostly at her plate, every sound she heard and the whole quietness which was so much stronger than the sounds, meant that things were not good.

What it was was that he wasn't here. Her mother wasn't either but she was upstairs. He wasn't even upstairs. He was coming home last night but he didn't come home and he wasn't coming home now either, and her mother felt so awful she cried, and maybe that was why, and Aunt Jessie wasn't saying anything, just making all that noise with the toast and big loud sips with the coffee and swallowing, *grrmmp,* and then the same thing over again and over again, and every time these noises meant, you be quiet, and every time she made the noise with the toast it was almost scary, as if she was talking about some awful thing, and every time she sipped it was like crying or like when Granma sucked in air between her teeth when she hurt herself, and every time she swallowed, *crrmmp,* it meant it was all over and there was nothing to do about it or say or even ask, and then she would take another bite of toast, as hard and shivery as gritting your teeth, and start the whole thing all over again. Her mother said he wasn't coming home ever any more. That was what she said, but why wasn't he home eating breakfast right this minute? Because he was not with them eating breakfast it wasn't fun and everything was so queer. Now maybe in just a minute he would walk right in and grin at her and say *good morning merry sunshine* because her lip was sticking out, and even bend down and rub her cheek with his whiskers and then sit down and eat a big breakfast and then it would be all fun again and she would watch from the window when he went to work and just before he went out of sight he would turn around and wave and she would wave but why wasn't he here right now where she wanted him to be and why didn't he come home? Ever any more. What's ever any more. He won't come home again ever any more. Won't come home again ever. But he will though because it's home. But why's he not here. He's up seeing Grampa Agee. Grampa Agee is very very sick. But Mama didn't feel awful then, she feels awful now. But why didn't he come back when she said he would. He went to Heaven and now Emma could remember about Heaven, that's where God lives, way up in the sky. Why'd he do that. God took him there. But why'd he go there and not come home like Mama said. Last night Mama said he was coming home last night. We could even wait up a while and when he didn't and we had to go to bed she *promised* he would come if we went to sleep and she promised he'd be here at breakfast-time and now it's breakfast-time and she says he won't come home ever any more.

Now her Aunt Jessie folded her napkin, and folded it again more narrowly, and again still more narrowly, and pressed the butt-end of it against her mouth, and laid it beside her plate, where it slowly and slightly unfolded, and, looking first at Rufus and then at Emma and then back at Rufus, said quietly: "I think you ought to know about your father" she said. "Whatever I can tell you. Because your mother's not feeling well."

Now I'll know when he *is* coming home, Emma thought.

All through breakfast, Rufus had wanted to ask questions, but now he felt so shy and uneasy that he could hardly speak. "Who hurt him?" he finally asked.

"Why *nobody* hurt him, Rufus," she said, and she looked shocked. "What on earth made you think so!"

Mama said so, Emma thought.

"Mama said he got hurt so bad God put him to sleep," Rufus said.

Like the kitties, Emma thought; she saw a dim gigantic old man in white take her tiny father by the skin of the neck and put him in a huge slop jar full of water and sit on the lid, and she heard the tiny scratching and the stifled mewing.

"That's true he was hurt but nobody hurt him," her Aunt Jessie was saying. How could that be, Emma wondered. "He was driving home by himself. That's all, all by himself, in the auto last night, and he had an accident."

Rufus felt his face get warm and he looked warningly at his sister. He knew it could not be that, not with his father, a grown man, besides, God wouldn't put you to sleep for *that,* and it didn't hurt, anyhow. But Emma might think so. Sure enough, she was looking at her aunt with astonishment and disbelief that she could say such a thing about her father. Not in his *pants,* you dern fool, Rufus wanted to tell her, but his Aunt Jessie continued: "A *fatal* accident"; and by her voice as she spoke the strange word, "fatal," they knew she meant something very bad. "That means that, it's just as your mother told you, that he was hurt so badly that God put him to sleep right away."

Like the rabbits, Rufus remembered, all torn white bloody fur and red insides. He could not imagine his father like that. Poor little things, he remembered his mother's voice comforting his crying, hurt so terribly that God just let them go to sleep.

If it was in the auto, Emma thought, then he wouldn't be in the slop jar.

They couldn't be happy any more if He hadn't, his mother had said. They could never get well.

Jessie wondered whether they could comprehend it at all and whether she should try to tell them. She doubted it. Deeply uncertain, she tried again.

"He was driving home last night," she said, "about nine, and apparently something was already wrong with the steering mech—with the wheel you guide the machine with. But your father didn't know it. Because there wasn't any way he *could* know until something went wrong and then it was too late. But one of the wheels struck a loose stone in the road and the wheel turned aside very suddenly, and when . . ." She paused and went on more quietly and slowly: "You see, when your father tried to make the auto go where it should, stay on the road, he found he couldn't, he didn't have any control. Because something was wrong with the steering gear. So instead of doing as he tried to make it, the auto twisted aside because of the loose stone and ran off the road into a deep ditch." She paused again. "Do you understand?"

They kept looking at her.

"Your father was thrown from the auto," she said. "Then the auto went on without him up the other side of the ditch. It went up an eight-foot embankment and then it fell down backward, turned over, and landed just beside him.

"They're pretty sure he was dead even before he was thrown out. Because the only mark on his whole body," and now they began to hear in her voice a troubling intensity and resentment, "was right—here!" She pressed the front of her forefinger to the point of her chin, and looked at them almost as if she were accusing them.

They said nothing.

I suppose I've got to finish, Jessie thought; I've gone this far.

"They're pretty sure how it happened," she said. "The auto gave such a sudden terrible *jerk*"—she jerked so violently that both children jumped, and startled her; she demonstrated what she said next more gently: "That your father was thrown forward and struck his chin, very hard, against the wheel, the steering wheel, and from that instant he never knew anything more."

She looked at Rufus, at Emma, and again at Rufus. "Do you understand?" They looked at her.

After a while Emma said, "he hurt his chin."

"Yes Emma. He did," she replied. "They believe he was *instantly killed,* with that one single blow, because it happened to strike just exactly where it did. Because if you're struck very hard in just that place, it jars your whole head, your brain so hard that—sometimes people die in that very instant." She drew a deep breath and let it out long and shaky. "Concussion of the brain, that is called," she said with most careful distinctness, and bowed her head for a moment; they saw her thumb make a small cross on her chest.

She looked up. "Now do you understand, children?" she asked earnestly. "I know it's very hard to understand. You please tell me if there's anything you want to know and I'll do my best to expl—tell you better."

Rufus and Emma looked at each other and looked away. After a while Rufus said: "Did it hurt him bad?"

"He could never have felt it. That's the one great mercy" (or *is* it, she wondered); "the doctor is sure of that."

Emma wondered whether she could ask one question. She thought she'd better not.

"What's an eight-foot embackmut?" Rufus asked.

"Em-bank-ment," she replied. "Just a bank. A steep little hill, eight feet high. Bout's high's the ceiling."

He and Emma saw the auto climb it and fall backward rolling and come to rest beside their father. Umbackmut, Emma thought; em-*bank*-ment, Rufus said to himself.

"What's instintly?"

"Instantly is—quick's that"; she snapped her fingers, more loudly than she had expected to; Emma flinched and kept her eyes on the fingers. "Like snapping off an electric light." Rufus nodded. "So you can be very sure, both of you, he never felt a moment's pain. Not one moment."

"When's . . ." Emma began.

"What's . . ." Rufus began at the same moment; they glared at each other.

"What is it Emma?"

"When's Daddy coming home?"

"Why *good golly* Emma," Rufus began; "Hold your Tongue!" his Aunt Jessie said fiercely, and he listened, scared, and ashamed of himself.

"Emma he *can't* come home," she said very kindly. "That's just what all this means, child." She put her hand over Emma's hand and Rufus could see that her chin was trembling. "He died, Emma," she said. "That's what your mother means. God put him to sleep and took him, took his soul away with Him. So he can't come hom—" She stopped, and began again. "We'll see him once more," she said, "tomorrow or day after; that I promise you," she said, wishing she was sure of Laura's views about this. "But he'll be asleep then. And after that we won't see him any more in this world. Not until God takes us away too.

"Do you see, child?" Emma was looking at her very seriously. "Of course you don't, God bless you"; she squeezed her hand. "Don't even try too hard to understand child. Just try to understand it's so. He'd come if he could but he simply can't because God wants him with Him. That's all." She kept her hand over Emma's a long while more, while Rufus realized much more clearly than before that he really could not and would not come home again: because of God.

"He would if he could but he can't," Emma finally said, remembering a joking phrase of her mother's.

Jessie, who knew the joking phrase too, was startled, but quickly realized that the child meant it in earnest. "That's it," she said gratefully.

But he'll come once more, anyway, Rufus realized, looking forward to it. Even if he *is* asleep.

"What was it you wanted to ask, Rufus," he heard his aunt say.

He tried to remember and remembered. "What's kuh, kuhkush, kuh, . . . ?"

"Con-*cus*-sion, Rufus. Concus-sion of the brain. That's the doctor's name for what happened. It means, it's as if the brain were hit very hard and suddenly, and joggled loose. The instant that happened, your father was—he . . ."

"Instintly killed."

She nodded.

"Then it was that, that put him to sleep."

"Hyess."

"*Not* God."

Emma looked at him, bewildered.

Chapter 37

When breakfast was over he wandered listlessly into the sitting-room and looked all around, but he did not see any place where he would like to sit down. He felt deeply idle and empty and at the same time gravely exhilarated, as if this were the morning of his birthday, except that this day seemed even more particularly his own day. There was nothing in the way it looked which was not ordinary, but it was filled with a noiseless and invisible kind of energy. He could see his mother's face while she told them about it and hear her voice, over and over, and silently, over and over, while he looked around the sitting-room and through the window into the street, words repeated themselves: He's dead. He died last night while I was asleep and now it is already morning. He has already been dead since way last night and I didn't even know until I woke up. He has been dead all night while I was asleep and now it is morning and I am awake but he is still dead and he will stay right on being dead all afternoon and all night and all tomorrow while I am asleep again and wake up again and go to sleep again and he can't come back home again ever any more but I will see him once more before he is taken away. Dead now. He died last night while I was asleep and now it is already morning.

A boy went by with his books in a strap.

Two girls went by with their satchels.

He went to the hat rack and took his satchel and his hat and started back down the hall to the kitchen to get his lunch; then he remembered his new cap. But it was upstairs. It would be in Mama's and Daddy's room, he could remember when she took it off his head. He did not want to go in for it where she was lying down and now he realized, too, that he did not want to wear it. He would like to tell her goodbye before he went to school but he did not want to go in and see her lying down and looking like that. He kept on towards the kitchen. He would tell Aunt Jessie goodbye instead.

She was at the sink washing the dishes and Emma sat on a kitchen chair watching her. He looked all around but he could not see any lunch. I guess she doesn't know about lunch, he reflected. She did not seem to realize that he was there so, after a moment, he said, "Goodbye."

"What-*is*-it?" she said and turned her lowered head, peering. "Why, Rufus!" she exclaimed, in such a tone that he wondered what he had done. "You're not going to *school,*" she said, and now he realized that she was not mad at him.

"I can stay out of school?"

"Of course you can. You must. Today and tomorrow as well and—for a sufficient time. A few days. Now put up your things, and stay right in this house, child."

He looked at her and said to himself: but then they can't see me; but he knew there was no use begging her; already she was busy with the dishes again.

He went back along the hall towards the hat rack. In the first moment he had been only surprised and exhilarated, not to have to go to school, and something of this sense of privilege remained, but almost immediately he was also disappointed. He could now see vividly how they would all look up when he came into the schoolroom and how the teacher would say something nice about his father and about him, and he knew that on this day everybody would treat him well, and even look up to him, for something had happened to him today which had not happened to any other boy in school, any other boy in town. They might even give him part of their lunches.

He felt even more profoundly empty and idle than before.

He laid down his satchel on the seat of the hat rack, but he kept his hat on. She'll spank me, he thought. Even worse, he could foresee her particular, crackling kind of anger. I won't let her find out, he told himself. Taking great care to be silent, he let himself out the front door.

The air was cool and gray and, here and there along the street, shapeless and watery sunlight strayed and vanished. Now that he was in this outdoor air he felt even more listless and powerful; he was alone, and the silent, invisible energy was everywhere. He stood on the porch and supposed that everyone he saw passing knew of an event so famous. A man was walking quickly up the street and as Rufus watched him, and waited for the man to meet his eyes, he felt a great quiet lifting within him of pride and of shyness, and he felt his face break into a smile, and then an uncontrollable grin, which he knew he must try to make sober again; but the man walked past without looking at him, and so did the next man who walked past in the other direction. Two schoolboys passed whose faces he knew, so he knew that they must know his, but they did not even seem to see him. Arthur and Alvin Tripp came down their front steps and along the far sidewalk and now he was sure, and came down his own front steps and halfway out to the sidewalk, but there he stopped, for now, although both of them looked across into his eyes, and he into theirs, they did not cross the street to him or even say hello, but kept on their way, still looking into his eyes with a kind of shy curiosity, even when their heads were turned almost backwards on their necks, and he turned his own head slowly, watching them go by, but when he saw that they were not going to speak, he took care not to speak either.

What's the matter with them, he wondered, and still watched them; and even now, far down the street, Arthur kept turning his head, and for several steps Alvin walked backwards.

What are they mad about?

Now they no longer looked around, and now he watched them vanish under the hill.

Maybe they don't know, he thought. Maybe the others don't know either.

He came out to the sidewalk.

Maybe everybody knew. Or maybe he knew something of great importance which nobody else knew. The alternatives were not at all distinct in his mind; he was puzzled, but no less proud and expectant than before. My daddy's dead, he said to himself slowly, and then, shyly, he said it aloud: "My daddy's dead." Nobody in sight seemed to have heard; he had said it to nobody in particular. "My daddy's dead," he said again, chiefly for his own benefit. It sounded powerful, solid, and entirely creditable, and he knew that if need be he would tell people. He watched a large, slow man come towards him and waited for the man to look at him and acknowledge the fact first, but when the man was just ahead of him, and still did not appear even to have seen him, he told him, "My daddy's dead," but the man did not seem to hear him, he just swung on by. He took care to tell the next man sooner and the man's face looked almost as if he were dodging a blow but he went on by, looking back a few steps later with a worried face; and after a few steps more he turned and came slowly back.

"What was that you said, sonny?" he asked; he was frowning slightly.

"My daddy's dead," Rufus said, expectantly.

"You mean that sure enough?" the man asked.

"He died last night when I was asleep and now he can't come home ever any more."

The man looked at him as if something hurt him.

"Where do you live, sonny?"

"Right here"; he showed with his eyes.

"Do your folks know you out here wandern round?"

He felt his stomach go empty. He looked frankly into his eyes and nodded quickly.

The man just looked at him and Rufus realized: He doesn't believe me. How do they always know.

"You better just go on back in the house, son," he said. "They won't like you being out here on the street." He kept looking at him, hard.

Rufus looked into his eyes with reproach and apprehension, and turned in at his walk. The man still stood there. Rufus went on slowly up his steps, and looked around. The man was on his way again but at the moment Rufus looked around, he did too, and now he stopped again.

He shook his head and said, in a friendly voice which made Rufus feel ashamed: "How would your daddy like it? You out here telling strangers how he's dead?"

Rufus opened the door, taking care not to make a sound, and stepped in and silently closed it, and hurried into the sitting-room. Through the curtains he watched the man. He still stood there, lighting a cigarette, but now he started walking again. He looked back once and Rufus felt, with a quailing of shame and fear, he sees me; but the man immediately looked away again and Rufus watched him until he was out of sight.

How would your daddy like it.

He thought of the way they teased him and did things to him, and how mad his father got when he just came home. He thought how different it would be today if he only didn't have to stay home from school.

He let himself out again and stole back between the houses to the alley, and walked along the alley, listening to the cinders cracking under each step, until he came near the sidewalk. He was not in front of his own home now, or even on Highland Avenue; he was coming into the side street down from his home, and he felt that here, nobody would identify him with his home and send him back to it. What he could see from the mouth of the alley was much less familiar to him, and he took the last few steps which brought him out onto the sidewalk with deliberation and shyness. He was doing something he had been told not to do.

He looked up the street and he could see the corner he knew so well, where he always met the others so unhappily, and, farther away, the corner around which his father always disappeared on the way to work, and first appeared on his way home from work. He felt it would be good luck that he would not be meeting them at that corner. Slowly, uneasily, he turned his head, and looked down the side street in the other direction; and there they were: three together, and two along the far side of the street, and one alone, farther off, and another alone, farther off, and, without importance to him, some girls here and there, as well. He knew the faces of all of these boys well, though he was not sure of any of their names. The moment he saw them all he was sure they saw him, and sure that they knew. He stood still and waited for them, looking from one to another of them, into their eyes, and step by step at their several distances, each of them at all times looking into his eyes and knowing, they came silently nearer. Waiting, in silence, during those many seconds before the first of them came really near him, he felt that it was so long to wait, and to be watched so closely and silently, and to watch back, that he wanted to go back into the alley and not be seen by any of them or by anybody else, and yet at the same time he knew that they were all approaching him with the realization that something had happened to him which had not happened to any other boy in town, and that something had happened to his father which had not happened to the father of any other boy in town, and that now at last they were bound to think well of him; and the nearer they came but were yet at a distance, the more the gray, sober air was charged with the great energy and with a sense of glory and of danger, and the deeper and more exciting the silence became, and the more tall, proud, shy and exposed he felt; so that as they came still nearer he once again felt his face break into a wide smile, with which he had nothing to do and, feeling that there was something deeply wrong in such a smile, tried his best to quiet his face and told them, shyly and proudly, "My daddy's dead."

Of the first three who came up, two merely looked at him with suspicion and the third said, "Huh! Betcha he ain't"; and Rufus, astounded that they did not know and that they should disbelieve him, said, "why he is so!"

"Where's your satchel at?" said the boy who had spoken. "You're just making up a lie so you can lay out of school."

"I am not laying out," Rufus replied. "I was going to school and my Aunt Jessie told me I didn't have to go to school today or tomorrow or not till—not for a few days. She said I mustn't. So I am not laying out. I'm just staying out."

And another of the boys said, "That's right. If his daddy is dead he don't have to go back to school till after the funerl."

While Rufus had been speaking two other boys had crossed over to join them and now one of them said, "He don't have to. He can lay out cause his daddy got killed," and Rufus looked at the boy gratefully and the boy looked back at him, it seemed to Rufus, with deference.

But the first boy who had spoken said, resentfully, "How do *you* know?"

And the second boy, while his companion nodded, said, "Cause my daddy seen it in the paper. Can't your daddy read the paper?"

The paper, Rufus thought: it's even in the paper! And he looked wisely at the first boy. And the first boy, interested enough to ignore the remark against his father, said, "well how did he get killed, then?" and Rufus, realizing with respect that it was even more creditable to get killed than just to die, took a deep breath and said, "Why, he was . . ."; but the boy whose father had seen it in the paper was already talking, so he listened, instead, feeling as if all this were being spoken for him, and on his behalf, and in his praise, and feeling it all the more as he looked from one silent boy to the next and saw that their eyes were constantly on him. And Rufus listened, too, with as much interest as they did, while the boy said with relish: "In his ole Tin Lizzie, that's how. He was driving along in his ole Tin Lizzie and it hit a rock and throwed him out in the ditch and run up a eight-foot bank and then fell back and turned over and over and landed right on top of him *whomph* and mashed every bone in his body, that's all. And somebody come and found him and he was dead already time they got there, that's how."

"He was instantly killed," Rufus began, and expected to go ahead and correct some of the details of the account, but nobody seemed to hear him, for two other boys had come up and just as he began to speak one of them said, "Your daddy got his name in the paper didn he, and you too," and he saw that now all the boys looked at him with new respect.

"He's dead," he told them. "He got killed."

"That's what my daddy says," one of them said, and the other said, "What you get for driving a auto when you're drunk, that's what my dad says," and the two of them looked gravely at the other boys, nodding, and at Rufus.

"What's drunk?" Rufus asked.

"What's drunk?" one of the boys mocked incredulously: "Drunk is fulla good ole whiskey"; and he began to stagger about in circles with his knees weak and his head lolling. "At's what drunk is."

"Then he wasn't," Rufus said.

"How do *you* know?"

"He wasn't drunk because that wasn't how he died. The wheel hit a rock and the other wheel, the one you steer with, just hit him on the chin, but it hit him so hard it killed him. He was instantly killed."

"What's instantly killed?" one of them asked.

"What do *you* care?" another said.

"Right off like that," an older boy explained, snapping his fingers. Another boy joined the group. So that was what instantly meant. Right off like that. He had thought it meant not feeling anything. Thinking of what instantly meant, and how his father's name was in the paper and his own too, and how he had got killed, not just died, he was not listening to them very clearly for a few moments and then, all of a sudden, he began to realize that he was the center of everything and that they all knew it and that they waited to hear him tell the true account of it.

"I don't know nothing about no chin," the boy whose father saw it in the paper was saying. "Way I heard it he was a-drivin along in his ole Tin Lizzie and he hit a rock and ole Tin Lizzie run off the road and thowed him out and run up a eight-foot bank and turned over and over and fell back down on top of him *whomp.*"

"How do *you* know?" an older boy was saying. "*You* wasn't there. Anybody here knows, it's *him.*" And he pointed at Rufus and Rufus was startled from his revery.

"Why?" asked the boy who had just come up.

"Cause it's his daddy," one of them explained.

"It's my daddy," Rufus said.

"What happened?" asked still another boy, at the fringe of the group.

"My daddy got killed," Rufus said.

"His daddy got killed," several of the others explained.

"My daddy says he bets he was drunk."

"Good ole whiskey!"

"Shut up, what's *your* daddy know about it."

"Was he drunk?"

"No," Rufus said.

"No," two others said.

"Let *him* tell it."

"Yeah, *you* tell it."

"Anybody here ought to know, it's him."

"Come on and tell us."

"Good ole whiskey."

"Shut your mouth."

"Well come on and tell us, then."

They became silent and all of them looked at him. Rufus looked back into their eyes in the sudden deep stillness. A man walked by, stepping into the gutter to skirt them.

Rufus said, quietly: "He was coming home from Grampa's last night, Grampa Agee. He's very sick and Daddy had to go up way in the middle of the night to see him, and he was hurrying as fast as he could to get back home because he was so late. And there was a cotter pin worked loose."

"What's a cotter pin?"

"Shut up."

"A cotter pin is what holds things together underneath, that you steer with. It worked loose and fell out so that when one of the front wheels hit a loose rock it wrenched the wheel and he couldn't steer and the auto ran down off the road with an awful bump and they saw where the wheel you steer with hit him right on the chin and he was instantly killed. He was thrown all the way out of the auto and it ran up an eight-foot emb—embackment and then it rolled back down and it was upside down beside him when they found him. There wasn't another mark on his body my Uncle Hugh says. Only a little tiny blue mark right on the end of the chin and another on his lip."

In the silence he could see the auto upside down with its wheels in the air and his father lying beside it with the little blue marks on his chin and on his lip.

"Heck," one of them said, "how can *that* kill anybody?"

He felt a kind of sullen stirring among the others, and he felt that he was not believed, or that they did not think very well of his father for being killed so easily.

"It was just exactly the way it just happened to hit him, Uncle Hugh says. He says it was just a chance in a million. It gave him a concush, con, concush—it did something to his brain that killed him."

"Just a chance in a million," one of the older boys said gravely, and another gravely nodded.

"A million trillion," another said.

"Knocked him crazy as a loon," another cried, and with a waggling forefinger he made a rapid blubbery noise against his loose lower lip.

"Shut yer God damn mouth," an older boy said coldly. "Ain't you got no sense at all?"

"Way I heard it, ole Tin Lizzie just rolled right back on top of him *whomp.*"

This account of it was false, Rufus was sure, but it seemed to him more exciting than his own, and more creditable to his father and to him, and nobody could question, scornfully, whether that could kill, as they could of just a blow on the chin; so he didn't try to contradict. He felt that he was lying, and in some way being disloyal as well, but he said only: "He was instantly killed. He didn't have to feel any pain."

"Never even knowed what hit him," a boy said quietly, "That's what my dad says."

"No," Rufus said. It had not occurred to him that way. "I guess he didn't." Never even knowed what hit him. Knew.

"Reckon that ole Tin Lizzie is done for now. Huh?"

He wondered if there was some meanness behind calling it an old Tin Lizzie. "I guess so," he said.

"Good ole waggin, but she done broke down."

His father sang that.

"No more joy-rides in that ole Tin Lizzie, huh Rufus?"

"I guess not," Rufus replied shyly.

He began to realize that for some moments now a bell, the school bell, had been weltering on the dark gray air; he realized it because at this moment the last of its reverberations were fading.

"Last Bell," one of the boys said in sudden alarm.

"Come on, we're goana git hell," another said; and within another second Rufus was watching them all run dwindling away up the street, and around the corner into Highland Avenue, as fast as they could go, and all round him the morning was empty and still. He stood still and watched the corner for almost half a minute after the fattest of them, and then the smallest, had disappeared; then he walked slowly back along the alley, hearing once more the sober crumbling of the cinders under each step, and up through the narrow side yard between the houses, and up the steps of the front porch.

In the paper! He looked for it beside the door, but it was not there. He listened carefully but he could not hear anything. He let himself quietly through the front door, at the moment his Aunt Jessie came from the sitting-room into the front hall. She wore a cloth over her hair and in her hands she was carrying the smoking stand and the ash tray with two weighted straps, and two pipes. She did not see him at first and he saw how fierce and lonely her face looked. He tried to make himself small but just then she wheeled on him, her lenses flashing, and exclaimed, "Rufus Agee, where on earth have you been!" His stomach quailed, for her voice was so angry it was as if it were crackling with sparks.

"Outdoors."

"Where, outdoors! I've been looking for you all over the place."

"Just out. Back in the alley."

"Didn't you hear me calling you?"

He shook his head.

"I shouted until my voice was hoarse."

He kept shaking his head. "Honest," he said.

"Now listen to me carefully. You mustn't go outdoors today. Stay right here inside this house, do you understand?"

He nodded. He felt suddenly that he had done an awful thing.

"I know it's hard to," she said more gently, "but you've got to. Help Emma with her coloring. Read a book. You promise?"

"Yes'm."

"And don't do anything to disturb your mother."

"No'm."

She went on down the hall and he watched her. What was she doing with the pipes and the ash tray, he wondered. He considered sneaking behind her, for he knew that she could not see at all well, yet he would be sure to get caught, for her hearing was very sharp. All the same, he sneaked along to the back of the hall and watched her empty the ashes into the garbage pail and rap out the pipes against its rim. Then she stood with the pipes in her hand, looking around uncertainly; finally she put the pipes and the ash tray on the cupboard shelf, and set the smoking stand in the corner of the kitchen behind the stove. He went back along the hall on tiptoe and into the sitting-room.

Emma sat in the little chair by the side window with a picture book on her knees. Her crayons were all over the windowsill and she was working intently with an orange crayon. She looked up when he came in and looked down again and kept on working.

He did not want to help her, he wanted to be by himself and see if he could find the paper with the names in it, but he felt that he ought to try to be good, for by now he felt a dark uneasiness about something, he was not quite sure what, that he had done. He walked over to her. "I'll help you," he said.

"No," Emma said, without even looking up. It was the Mother Goose book and with her orange crayon she was scrawling all over the cow which jumped over the moon, inside and outside the lines of the cow.

"Aunt Jessie says to," he said, disgusted to see what she was doing to the cow.

"No," Emma said, and again she did not look up or stop scrawling for a second.

"That ain't no color for a cow," he said. "Whoever saw an orange cow!" She made no reply, but he could see that her face was getting red. "Besides, you're not even coloring inside the cow," he said. "Just look at that. You're just running that crayon around all over the place and it isn't even the right color." She bore down harder and harder with the crayon and pushed it in a wider and wider tangle of lines and all of a sudden it snapped and the long part rolled to the floor. "See now, even you busted it," Rufus said.

"Leave me lone!" She tried to draw with the stub of the crayon but it was too short, and the paper got in the way. She looked along the windowsill and selected a brown crayon.

"What you goana do with that brown one?" Rufus said. "You already got all that orange all over everything, what you goana do with that brown one?" Emma took the brown crayon and made a brutal tangle of dark lines all over the orange lines. "Now all you did is just spoil it," Rufus said. "*You* don't know how to draw!"

"*Quit* it!" Emma yelled, and all of a sudden she was crying. He heard his Aunt Jessie's sharp voice from the kitchen: "Rufus?"

He was furious with Emma. "Crybaby," he whispered with cold hatred: "Tattletale!"

And there was Aunt Jessie at the door, just as mad as a hornet. "Now, what's the matter! What have you done to her!" She walked straight at him.

It wasn't fair. How did she know he was doing anything? With a feeling of real righteousness he talked back: "I didn't do one single thing to her. She was just messing everything up on her picture and I tried to help her like you told me to and all of a sudden she started to cry."

"What did he do, Emma?"

"He wouldn't let me alone."

"Why good night, I never even touched you and you're a liar if you say I did!"

All of a sudden he felt himself gripped by the shoulders and shaken and he turned his rattling head from his sister to look into his Aunt Jessie's furious eyes.

"Now you just listen to *me*," she said. "Are you listening?" She squatted. "*Are you listening?*" she said still more intensely.

"Yes," he managed to get out, though the word was all shaken up.

"I don't want to spank you on this day of all days but if I hear you say one more rough thing like that to your sister I'll give you a spanking you'll remember to your dying day, do you hear me? *Do you hear me?*"

"Yes."

"And if you tease her or make her cry just one more time I'll—I'll turn the whole matter over to your Uncle Hugh and we'll see what *he'll* do about it. Do you want me to call him? He's upstairs this minute! Shall I call him?" She stopped shaking him and looked at him. "Shall I?" He shook his head; he was terrified. "All right, but this is my last warning. Do you understand?"

"Yes'm."

"Now if you can't play with Emma in peace like a decent boy just—stay by yourself. Look at some pictures. Read a book. But you be quiet. And good. Do you hear me?"

"Yes'm."

"Very well." She stood up and her joints snapped. "Come with me, Emma," she said. "Let's bring your crayons." And she helped Emma gather up the crayons and the stubs from the windowsill and from the carpet. Emma's face was still red but she was not crying anymore. As she passed Rufus she gave him a glance filled with satisfaction, and he answered it with a glance of helpless malevolence.

He listened towards upstairs. If his Uncle Hugh had overheard this, there would really be trouble. But there was no evidence that he had. Rufus felt weak in the knees and in the stomach. He went over to the chair beside the fireplace and sat down.

It was mean to pester Emma like that but he hadn't wanted to do anything for her anyway. And why did she have to holler like that and bring Aunt Jessie running. He remembered the way her face got red and he knew that he had really been mean to her and he was sorry. But what did she holler for, like a regular crybaby? He would be very careful today, but sooner or later he sure would get back on her. Darn crybaby. Tattletale.

The others really did pay him some attention, though. Anybody here ought to know, it's him. His daddy got killed. Yeah *you* tell it. Come on and tell us. Just a chance in a million. A million trillion. Never even knowed, knew, what hit him. Shut yer god damn mouth. Ain't you got no sense at all?

Instantly killed.

Concussion, that was it. Concussion of the brain.

Knocked him crazy as a loon, bibblibblebbble.

Shut yer God damn mouth.

But there was something that made him feel wrong.

Ole Tin Lizzie.

What you get for driving a auto when you're drunk, that's what my dad says.

Good ole whiskey.

Something he did.

Ole Tin Lizzie just rolled back down on top of him *whomp.*

Didn't either.

He didn't say it didn't. Not clear enough.

Heck, how can *that* kill anybody?

Did, though. Just a chance in a million. Million trillion.

Instantly killed.

Worse than that, he did.

What.

How would your daddy like it?

He would like me to be with them without them teasing; looking up to me.

How would your daddy like it?

Like what?

Going out in the street like that when he is dead.

Out in the street like what?

Showing off to people because he is dead.

He wants me to get along with them.

So I tell them he is dead and they look up to me, they don't tease me.

Showing off because he's dead, that's all you can show off about. Any other thing they'd tease me and I wouldn't fight back.

How would your daddy like it?

But he likes me to get along with them. That's why I—went out—showed off.

He felt so uneasy, deep inside his stomach, that he could not think about it any more. He wished he hadn't done it. He wished he could go back and not do anything of the kind. He wished his father could know about it and tell him that yes he was bad but it was all right he didn't mean to be bad. He was glad his father didn't know because if his father knew he would think even worse of him than ever. But if his father's soul was around, always, watching over them, like his mother said, then he knew. And that was worst of anything because there was no way to hide from a soul, and no way to talk to it, either. He just knows, and it couldn't say anything to him, and he couldn't say anything to it. It couldn't whip him either, but it could sit and look at him and be ashamed of him.

"I didn't mean it," he said aloud. "I didn't mean to do bad."

I wanted to show you my cap, he added, silently.

He looked at his father's morsechair [morris-chair].

Down at Mr. Roberts', he thought. Not another mark on his body.

He still looked at the chair.

Why did she put away his things?

He went over to the chair and touched it on the right arm and where the head rested. The cloth was rough and cool. He leaned close and smelled of the cloth, along the arms, and the back, and in the hollowed seat of the chair. It smelled only of cold tobacco except where his father had leaned his head back. There it smelled faintly of hair, as well, and for a moment it was as if his father were sitting there; he could feel how rough his clothes and his cheek were, and he could see how he smiled and how he let the smoke ooze slowly out of his nostrils. At that part of the chair he smelled for a good while, until the smell of hair seemed as cold and shut away as the smell of stale tobacco. He went back and sat down on the stool beside the fireplace and kept on looking at his father's chair.

"all the way home"
The Last Day

Chapter 38

They were told they could eat, that morning, in their nightgowns and wrappers. Their mother still wasn't there, and Aunt Jessie talked even less than at any meal before. They too were very quiet. They felt that this was an even more special day than day before yesterday. All the noises of their eating and from the street were especially clear, but seemed to come from a distance. They looked steadily at their plates and ate very carefully.

First thing after breakfast Aunt Jessie said "Now come with me, children," and they followed her into the bathroom. There she washed their faces and hands and arms, and behind the ears, and their necks, and up each nostril, carefully and gently with soap and warm water; she did not get soap in the eyes of either of them, or hurt their skins with the washcloth. Then she took them into the bedroom and opened the bureaus and took out everything bran clean, from the skin out, and told Rufus to get his clothes on and to ask for help if he wanted it, and started dressing Emma. Rufus began to see the connection between all this and the bath, the night before. When he had on his underclothes she brought out new black stockings and his Sunday serge. While she was helping Emma on with her stockings, which were also new but white, the phone rang and she said, "now sit still and be good. I'll be straight back," and hustled from the room. They heard her say rather loudly and distinctly, up the hall, "I'm getting it, Laura," then her feet, fast on the stairs. They sat very still, looking at the open door, and tried to hear. They found they could hear quite distinctly, for Jessie spoke to the telephone as she did to her deaf brother and sister-in-law. They heard: "Hello . . . Hello . . . yes . . . *Father?*" and when they heard the word "Father" they looked at each other with curiosity and with an uneasy premonition. They heard "Yes . . . yes . . . yes . . . yes . . . yes . . . yes Father . . . yes . . . yes, as well as could be expected . . . yes . . . yes . . . thank you.

I'll tell her . . . yes . . . yes . . . very well . . . yes . . . the *Highland* Avenue . . . yes . . . yes . . . *any* . . . yes . . . *any* car to the corner of Clinch and Gay, then transfer to the Highland—yes—very well . . . yes . . . thank you . . . we'll be waiting . . . yes . . . no . . . yes, Father . . . yes F— . . . goodb . . . yes, Father . . . thank you . . . goo(d)— . . . yes . . . thank you . . . goodbye . . . goodbye."

They heard her let out a long tired angry breath and they could hear her joints snapping as she sprinted up the stairs. They were sitting exactly where she had left them. Rufus thought, Maybe she will say we were good children, but without a word she finished with Emma's stockings. She gave Rufus a new white shirt from which he slowly and with fascination drew the pins, running them between his teeth as he watched Aunt Jessie help Emma into her new dress, which was white, speckled with small dark blue flowers. Emma stood holding the hem and looking at the skirt and at her white-stockinged feet, which she could see through the skirt. "And now your necktie," Aunt Jessie said. She took his dark blue tie and made expert motions beneath his chin while alternately he tried to watch her hands and looked into her intent eyes behind their heavy lenses. Her eyes looked stern and sad and exhausted.

Then she cleaned their nails and combed and brushed their hair, and put a clean handkerchief in Rufus' breast-pocket and blacked their shoes. "Now wait a moment," she said, leaving the room. They heard her rap softly on their mother's door.

"Laura?" she said.

"Yes," they heard, dimly.

"The children are ready. Shall I bring them in?"

"Yes do, Jessie; thank you."

"Come in now and see your mother," she told them from the door.

They followed her in.

"Oh, they look *very nice,*" she exclaimed, in a voice so odd that it seemed to the children that she must be sorry that they did. Yet by her face they could see that she was not sorry. "Jessie, thank you so much, I don't know what I'd have . . ."

But Jessie had left the room and closed the door.

They stood and looked at her with curiosity. Her eyes seemed larger and brighter than usual; her hair was done up as carefully as if she were going to a party. She wore her wrapper and where it opened in front they could see that she had on something dull and black underneath. Her face was like folded gray cloths.

She watched them look at her; they did not move. Her face altered as if a very low light had gone on, behind it.

"Come here, my darlings," she said, and smiled, and squatted with her hands out towards them.

Rufus came shyly; Emma ran. She took one of them in each arm.

"There, my darlings," she said above them; "there, there, my dear ones. Mother's here. Mother's here. Mother has wanted to see you more, these last days; a *lot* more: she just—couldn't, Rufus and Emma. Just couldn't do it." When she said "couldn't" she held them very tightly and they knew they were loved. "Little Emma"—and she held Emma's head still more tightly to her—"bless her soul! and Rufus"—she held him away and looked into his eyes—"You both know how much Mother loves you, with all her heart and soul, all her life—You know, don't you? Don't you?" Rufus, puzzled but moved, nodded politely, and again she took him to her. "Of course you do," she said, as if she were not speaking to them. "Of course you do.

"Now," she said, after a moment. She stood up and drew them by their hands to the bed. They sat down and she sat in a chair and looked at them for a few seconds without speaking.

"Now," she said again. "I want to tell you about Daddy, because this morning, soon now, we're all going down to Grampa's and Grandma's, and see him once more, and tell him goodbye." Emma's face brightened; her mother shook her head and placed a quieting hand on Emma's knees, saying, "No, Emma, it won't be like you think, that's what I must tell you about him. So listen very carefully, you too, Rufus."

She waited until she was sure they were listening carefully.

"You both understand what has happened to Daddy, don't you. That something happened in the auto, and God took him from us, very quickly, without any pain, and took him away to Heaven. You understand that, don't you?"

They nodded.

"And you understand, that when God takes you away to Heaven you can never come back?"

"*Never* come back?" Emma asked.

She stroked Emma's hair away from her face. "No, Emma, not ever, in any way we can see and talk to. Daddy's soul will always be thinking of us, just as we will always think of him, but we will never see him again, after today." Emma looked at her very intently; her face began to redden. "You must learn to believe that and know it, darling Emma. It's so."

She seemed to be about to cry; she swallowed; and Emma seemed to accept it as true.

"We'll always remember him," she told both of them; "*Always.* And he'll be thinking of us. Every day. He's waiting for us in Heaven. And someday, if we're good, when God comes for us, He'll take us to Heaven too and we'll see Daddy there, and all be together again, forever and ever."

Amen, Rufus almost said; then realized that this was not a prayer.

"But when we see Daddy today, children, his soul won't be there. It'll just be Daddy's body. Very much as you've always seen him. But because his soul has been taken away, he will be lying down, and he will lie very still. It will be just as if he were asleep, so you must both be just as quiet as if he were asleep and you didn't want to wake him. Quieter."

"But I do," said Emma.

"But Emma you can't, dear, you mustn't even think of trying. Because Daddy is dead now, and when you are dead that means you go to sleep and you never wake up—until God wakes you."

"Well when *will* He?" Rufus asked.

"We don't know, Rufus, but probably a long, long time from now. Long after we are all dead."

Rufus wondered what was the good of that, then, but he was sure he should not ask.

"Now we'll all just go in, and look at Daddy together a few minutes and tell him goodbye, and then you're both going down to Mr. and Mrs. Savage's and have dinner. Then right after dinner Mr. Savage will bring you back for just a few minutes, to see Granma Agee, who's coming down to tell Daddy goodbye too, and you'll look at Daddy once more.

"So I don't want you to wonder about it, children. Daddy may seem very queer to you, because he's so still, but that's—just simply the way he's got to look."

Suddenly she pressed her lips tightly together and they trembled violently. She clenched her cheekbone against her left shoulder, squeezing their hands with her trembling hands, and tears slipped from her tightly shut eyes. Rufus watched her with awe, Emma with forlorn worry. She suddenly hissed out, "Just-a-minute," with her eyes still closed, startling and shocking Emma, so that she looked as if she were ready to cry.

But before Emma could commit herself to crying, her hands relaxed, pressing them gently, and she raised her head and opened her clear eyes, saying: "Now Mother must get dressed, and I want you to take Emma downstairs, Rufus, and both of you be very quiet and good till I come down. And don't make any bother for Aunt Jessie, because she's been wonderful to all of us and she's worn out.

"You be good," she said, smiling and looking at them in turn. "I'll be down in a little while."

"Come on, Emma," Rufus said.

"I'm coming," Emma replied, looking at him as if he had spoken of her unjustly.

"Mama"; Rufus stopped near the door. Emma hesitated, bewildered.

"Yes, Rufus?"

"Are we orphans, now?"

"*Orphans?*"

"Like the Belgians," he informed her. "French. When you haven't got any daddy or mama because they're killed in the war you're an orphan and other children send you things and write you letters."

She must have been unfamiliar with the word, for she seemed to have to think very hard before she answered. Then she said: "Of *course* you're not orphans Rufus and I don't want you going around saying that you are. Do you hear me? Because it isn't so. Orphans haven't got *either* a father *or* a mother, you see, and nobody to take care of them or love them. You see? That's why other children send things. But you both have your mother. So you aren't orphans. Do you see? Do you?" He nodded; Emma nodded because he did. "And Rufus." She looked at him very searchingly; without quite knowing why, he felt he had been discovered in a discreditable secret. "Don't be sorry you're not an orphan. *You be thankful.* Orphans sound lucky to you because they're far away and everyone talks about them now. But they're very, very unhappy little children. Because *nobody* loves them. Do you understand?"

He nodded, ashamed of himself and secretly disappointed.

"Now run along," she said. They left the room.

Aunt Jessie met them on the stairs. "Go into the liv—sitting-room for a while like good children," she said. "I'll be right down." And as they reached the bottom of the stairs they heard their mother's door open and close. They sat, looking at their father's chair, thinking.

Emma felt more virtuous and less troubled than she had for some time, for she had watched Rufus being scolded, all to himself, and it more than wiped out her unhappiness at his telling her to come along when of course she was coming and he had no right even if she wasn't. But she couldn't see how anyone could look as if they were asleep and not wake up, and something else her mother had said—she tried hard to remember what it was—troubled her much more deeply than that. And what was a norphan?

Rufus felt that his mother was seriously displeased with him. It was the wrong time to ask her. Maybe he ought not to have asked her at all. But he did want to know. He had not been sure whether or not he was an orphan, or the right kind of orphan. If he claimed he was an orphan in school and it turned out that he was not, people would all laugh at him. But if he really was an orphan he wanted to know, so he would be able to say he was, and get the benefit. What was the good of being an orphan if nobody else knew it. Well, so he was not an orphan. Yet his father was dead. Not his mother, too, though. Only his father. But one was dead. One and one makes two. One-half of two equals one. He was half an orphan, no matter what his mother said. And he had a sister who was half an orphan too. Half and half equals a whole. Together they made a whole orphan. He felt that it was not worth mentioning, that he was half an orphan, although he privately considered it a good deal better than nothing; and that also, he would not volunteer the fact that he and his sister together made a whole orphan. But if anyone teased either of them about not being an orphan at all, then he would certainly speak of that. He decided that Emma should be warned of this, so that if they were teased, they could back each other up.

"Both of us together is a whole orphan," he said.

"Huh?"

"Don't say 'huh,' say, 'what is it, Rufus?'"

"I will not!"

"You will so. Mama says to."

"She does not."

"She does so. When I say 'huh' she says 'Don't say "huh," say "what is it, Mother?"' When you say 'huh' she tells you the same thing. So don't say 'huh.' Say 'What is it, Rufus?'"

"I won't say it to you."

"Yes you will."

"No I won't."

"Yes you will because Mama said for us to be good. If you don't I'll tell her on you."

"You tell her and I'll tell on you."

"Tell on me for what?"

"Listening at the door."

"No you won't."

"I will so."

"You will not."

"I will so."

He thought it over.

"All right, *don't* say it, and I *won't* tell on you if you won't tell on me."

"I will if you tell on me."

"I said I won't, didn't I? Not if you don't tell on me."

"I won't if you don't tell on me."

"All right."

They glared at each other.

They heard loud feet on the porch, and the doorbell rang. Upstairs they heard their mother cry "Oh, goodness!" They ran to the door. He blocked Emma away from the knob and opened it.

A man stood there, almost as tall as Daddy. He had a black glaring collar like Dr. Whittaker but wore a purple vest. He wore a long shallow hat and he had a long sharp bluish chin almost like a plow. He carried a small, shining black suitcase. He seemed to be as disconcerted and displeased as they were. He said, "Oh, good morning" in a voice that had echoes in it and, frowning, glanced once again at the number along the side of the door. "Of course," he said, with a smile they did not understand. "You're Rufus and Emma. May I come in?" And without waiting for their assent or withdrawal (for they were blocking the door) he strode forward, parting them with firm hands and saying "Isn't Miss T . . ."

They heard Aunt Jessie's voice behind them on the stairs, and turned. "Father?" she said, peering against the door's light. "Come right in." And she came up as he quickly removed his oddly shaped hat, and they shook hands. "This is Father Robertson, Rufus and Emma," she said. "He has come specially from Chattanooga. Father, this is Rufus, and this is Emma."

"Yes, we've already introduced ourselves," said Father Robertson, as if he thought it was funny. That's a lie, Rufus reflected. Father

Robertson left one hand at rest for a moment on Emma, then removed it as if he had forgotten her. "And where is Mrs. Agee?" he asked, almost whispering "Mrs. Agee."

"If you'll just wait a moment, Father, she isn't quite ready."

"Of course." He leaned towards Aunt Jessie and said, in a grinding, scarcely audible voice, "Is she—chuff-chuff-chuff?"

"Oh yes," Jessie replied.

"But does she whehf-wheff-whehf-whef-tized?"

"I'm afraid not, Father," said Jessie, gravely. "I wasn't quite sure enough, myself, to tell her. I'm sorry to burden you with it but I felt I should leave that to you."

"You were right, Miss Tyler. Absolutely." He looked around, his head gliding, his hat gliding in his hand. "Now little man," he said, "if you'll kindly relieve me of my hat."

"Rufus," said Jessie. "Take Father's hat to the hat rack."

Bewildered, he did so. The hat rack was in plain sight.

"Now Father, if you won't mind waiting just a moment," Jessie said, showing him in to the sitting-room. "Rufus: Emma: sit here with Father. Excuse me," she added, and she hastened upstairs.

Father Robertson strode efficiently across the room, sat in their father's chair, crossed his knees narrowly, and looked, frowning, at the carefully polished toe of his right shoe. They watched him, and Rufus wondered whether to tell him whose chair it was. Father Robertson held his long, heavily veined right hand palm outward, at arm's length, and, frowning, examined his nails. He certainly wouldn't have sat in it, Rufus felt, if he had known whose chair it was, so it would be mean not to tell him. Father Robertson, tilting his head, examined, frowning, the nails of his long, heavily veined left hand. But if he was told now, it would make him feel bad, Rufus thought. Emma noticed, with interest, that outside the purple vest he wore a thin gold chain; on the chain was a small gold crucifix. Father Robertson changed knees and, frowning, examined the carefully polished toe of his left shoe. Better not tell him, Rufus thought; it would be mean. How do you get such a blue face, Emma wondered; I wish my face was blue, not red. Father Robertson, frowning, looked all around the room and smiled, faintly, as his gaze came to rest on some point above and beyond the heads of the children. Both turned to see what he was smiling at, but there was nothing there except the picture of Jesus when Jesus was a little boy, staying up late in his nightgown and talking to all the wise men in the temple. "Oh," Rufus realized; "that's why."

When they turned Father Robertson was frowning again and looking at them just as he had looked at his nails. He quickly smiled, though not as nicely as he had smiled at Jesus, and changed his way of looking so that it did not seem that he was curious whether they were really clean. But he still looked as if he were displeased about something. They both looked back, wondering what he was displeased about. Was Emma wetting her panties, Rufus wondered; he looked at her but she looked all right to him. What was Rufus doing that the man looked so unpleasant, Emma wondered. She looked at him, but all he was doing was looking at the man. They both looked at him, wishing that if he was displeased with them he would tell them why instead of looking like that, and wishing that he would sit in some other chair. He looked at both of them, feeling that their rude staring was undermining his gaze and his silence, by which he had intended to impress them into a sufficiently solemn and receptive state for the things he intended to say to them; and wondering whether or no he should reprimand them. Surely, he decided, if they lack manners even at such a time as this, this is the time to speak of it.

"Children must not stare at their elders," he said. "That is ill-bred."

"Huh?" both of them asked. What's "stare," they wondered; "elders"; "ill-bred"?

"Say 'Sir,' or 'I beg your pardon, Father.'"

"Sir?" Rufus said.

"You," Father Robertson said to Emma.

"Sir?" Emma said.

"You must not stare at people—look at them, as you are looking at me."

"Oh," Rufus said. Emma's face turned red.

"Say, 'Excuse me, Father.'"

"Excuse me, Father."

"You," Father Robertson said to Emma.

Emma became still redder.

"Excuse me Father," Rufus whispered.

"No prompting, please," Father Robertson broke in, in a voice pitched for a large class. "Come now, little girl, it is never too soon to learn to be little ladies and little gentlemen, is it?"

Emma said nothing.

"Is it?" Father Robertson asked Rufus.

"I don't know," Rufus replied.

"I consider that a thoroughly uncivil answer to a civil question," said Father Robertson.

"Yes," Rufus said, beginning to turn cold in the pit of his stomach. What was "uncivil"?

"You agree," Father Robertson said. "Say, 'yes, Father.'"

"Yes, Father," Rufus said.

"Then you are aware of your incivility. It is deliberate and calculated," Father Robertson said.

"No," Rufus said. He could not understand the words but clearly he was being accused.

Father Robertson leaned back in their father's chair and closed his eyes and folded his hands. After a moment he opened his eyes and said: "Little boy, little sister" (he nudged his long blue chin towards Emma), "this is neither the time nor place for reprimands." His hands unfolded; he leaned forward, tapping his right kneecap with his right forefinger, and frowning fiercely, said in a voice which sounded very gentle but was not: "But I just want to tell"—they heard Jessie on the stairs—"Children," he said, rising, "This must wait another time." He pointed his jaw at Jessie, raising his eyebrows.

"Will you come up, Father?" she asked in a shut voice.

Without looking again at the children, he followed her upstairs.

They looked each other in the eyes; their mouths hung open; they listened. It was as they had begun to expect it would be: the steps of two along the upper hallway, the opening of their mother's door, their mother's strangely shrouded voice, the closing of the door: silence.

Taking great care not to creak they stole up to the middle of the stairs. They could hear no words, only the tilt and shape of voices. Their mother's, still so curiously shrouded, so submissive, so gentle; it seemed to ask questions and to accept answers. The man's voice was subdued and gentle but rang very strongly with the knowledge that it was right and that no other voice could be quite as right; it seemed to say unpleasant things as if it felt they were kind things to say, or again as if it did not care whether or not they were kind because in any case they were right; it seemed to make statements, to give information, to counter questions with replies which were beyond argument or even discussion, and to try to give comfort whether what it was saying could give comfort or not. Now and again their mother's way of questioning sounded to the children as if she wondered whether something could be fair, could possibly be true, could be so cruel, but whenever such tones came into their mother's voice the man's voice became still more ringing and overbearing, or still more desirous to comfort, or both; and their mother's next voice was always very soft.

Aunt Jessie's voice was almost as clear and light as always, but there was now in it also a kind of sweetness and of sorrow they had not heard in it before. Mainly she seemed only to agree with Father Robertson, to add her voice to his, though much more kindly, in this overpowering of their mother. But now and again it seemed to explain more fully, and more gently, something which he had just explained, and twice it questioned almost as their mother questioned, but with more spirit, with an edge almost of bitterness or temper. And on these two occasions Father Robertson's voice shifted and lost a bit of its vibrancy, and for a moment he talked as if rapidly in a circle, seeming to assure them that of course he did not at all mean what they had thought he meant, but only, that (and then the voice would begin to gather assurance); they must realize (and now it had almost its old drive); in fact, of course—and now he was back again, and seemed to be saying precisely what he had said before, only with still more authority and still less possibility of disagreement. And then their Aunt Jessie murmured agreement in an oddly cool, remote tone, and their mother's voice of acceptance was scarcely audible at all.

Once in a while when these voices came to crises in their subdued turmoil Rufus and Emma looked into each other's cold bright eyes which brightened and chilled the more with every intensification of the man's voice, and every softening and defeat of their mother's voice. But most of the time they only stared at the knob on their mother's door, shifting delicately on the stairs whenever they became cramped. They could not conceive of what was being done to their mother, but in his own way each was sure that it was something evil, to which she was submitting almost without a struggle, and by which she was deceived. Rufus repeatedly saw himself flinging open the door and striding in, a big stone in his hand, and saying, "You stop hurting my mother." Emma knew only that a tall stranger in black, with a frightening jaw and a queer hat, a man whom she hated and feared, and broken into their house, had been welcomed first by Aunt Jessie and then by her mother herself, had sat in her father's chair as if he thought he belonged there, talked meanly to her in words she could not understand, and was now doing secret and cruel things to her mother while Aunt Jessie looked on. If Daddy was here he would kill him. She wished Daddy would hurry up and come and kill him and she wanted to see it. But Rufus realized that his Aunt Jessie and even his mother were on Father Robertson's side and against him, and that they would just put him out of the room and punish him terribly and go right on with whatever awful thing it was they were doing. And Emma remembered, with a jolt, that Daddy would not come back because he was down at Grandma's and Grandpa's and soon they would see him again and then they would never see him any more until Heaven.

But suddenly there was a kind of creaking and soft thumping and the voices changed. Father Robertson's voice was even more strongly in charge, now, than before, although it did not seem that he was arguing, or informing, or trying to bring comfort, or even that he was speaking to either of the two women. Most of its theatrical resonance had left it, and all of its dominance. He seemed to be speaking as if to someone at least as much more assured and strong than he was, as he was more assured and strong than their mother was, and his voice had something of their mother's humbleness. Yet it was a very confident voice, as if it were sure that the person who was being addressed would entirely approve what was said and what was asked, and would not rebuff him as he had rebuffed their mother. And in some way the voice was even more authoritative than before, as if Father Robertson were speaking not for himself but for, as well as to, the person he addressed, and were speaking with the power of that person as well as in manly humility before that person. Clearly, also, the voice loved its own sound, inseparably from its love of the sound and contour of the words it spoke, as naturally as a fine singer delights inseparably in his voice and in the melody he is singing. And clearly, although not one word was audible to the children, the voice was not mistaken in this love. Not a word was distinct from where they stood, but the shapes and rhythms and the inflections were as lovely and as bemusing as any songs they had ever heard. In general rhythm, Rufus began to realize, it was not unlike the prayers that Dr. Whittaker said; and he realized, then, that Father Robertson also was praying. But where Dr. Whittaker gave his words and phrases special emphasis and personal coloring, as though they were matters which required argument and persuasion, Father Robertson spoke almost wholly without emphasis and with only the subtlest coloring, as if the personal emotion, the coloring, were cast against the words from a distance, like echoes. He spoke as if all that he said were in every idea and in every syllable final, finished, perfected beyond disquisition long before he was born; and truth and eternity dwelt like clearest water in the rhythms of his language and in the contours of his voice: his voice accepted and bore this language like the bed of a brook. They looked at each other once more; Rufus could see that Emma did not understand. "He's saying his prayers," he whispered.

She neither understood him nor believed him but she realized, with puzzlement, that now the man was being nice, though she did not even want him to be nice to her mother, she did not want him to be anything, to anybody, anywhere. But it was clear to both of them, that things were better now than they had been before; they could hear it in his voice, which at once enchanted and obscurely disturbed them, and they could hear it in the voices of the two women, which now and again, when he seemed to pause for breath, chimed in with a short word or two, a few times with whole sentences. Both their voices were more tender, more alive, and more inhuman, than they had ever heard them before; and this remoteness from humanity troubled them. They realized that there was something to which their mother and their great-aunt were devoted, something which gave their voices peculiar vitality and charm, which was beyond and outside any love that was felt for them; and they felt that this meant even more to their mother and their great-aunt than they did, or than anyone else in the world did. They realized, fairly clearly, that the object of this devotion was not this man whom they mistrusted, but they felt that he was altogether too deeply involved in it. And they felt that although everything was better for their mother than it had been a few minutes before, it was far worse in one way. For before, she had at least been questioning, however gently. But now she was wholly defeated and entranced, and the transition to prayer was the moment and mark of her surrender. They stared so long and so gloomily at the doorknob, turning over such unhappy and uncertain intuitions in their souls, that the staring, round white knob became all that they saw in the universe except a subtly beating haze pervaded with magnificent quiet sound; so that when the doorbell rang they were so frightened that their hearts contracted.

Then, with almost equal terror, they realized that they would be caught on the stairs. They started down, in haste as desperate as their efforts to be silent. The door burst open above them. She can't see, they realized (for it was Jessie who came out), and in the same instant they realized: but she can hear better than anybody. A stair creaked loudly; terror struck them; against it, they continued. "Yes," Jessie called sharply; she was already on the stairs. The doorbell rang again. On the last stair, they were hideously noisy; they wanted only to disappear in time. They ducked through the sitting-room door and watched her pass: they were as insane with excitement as if they could still dare hope they had not been discovered, and solemnly paralyzed in the inevitability of dreadful reprimand and of physical pain.

Jessie did not even glance back at them: she went straight to the door.

It was Mr. Savage. Usually he wore suits as brown and hairy as his mustache, but this morning he wore a dark blue suit and a black tie. In his hand he carried a black derby.

"Arthur," Aunt Jessie said, "you know what all you're doing means to us."

"Aw now," Arthur said.

"Come in," she said. "Laura'll be right down. Children, you know Mr. Sava . . ."

"Course we do," Mr. Savage said, smiling at them with his warm brown eyes through the lenses. He put the hand holding the derby on Rufus' shoulder and the other on Emma's cheek. "You come on in and sit with me, will you, till your mother's ready."

He walked straight for their father's chair, veered unhappily, and sat on a chair next the wall.

"Well, so you're coming down and visit us," he said.

"Huh?"

"Coming down," Arthur said. "Or ma—Did your mama say anything about maybe you were coming down sometime, and pay us a visit?"

"Huh-uh."

"Oh, well, there's lots of time. Did you ever hear a gramophone?"

"She can't hardly hear when she does."

"Eigh?" He seemed extremely puzzled.

"Uncle Hugh says she's crazy even to try."

"Who?"

"Why, Granma." Mr. Savage had never before seemed stupid, but now Rufus began to think his memory was as bad as those of the boys at the corner. Could he be teasing? It would be very queer if Mr. Savage would tease. He decided he should trust him. "You know, when she phones, like you said."

Mr. Savage thought that over for a moment and then he seemed to understand. But almost the moment he understood he started to laugh, so he must have been teasing, after all. Rufus was deeply hurt. Then almost immediately he stopped laughing as if he were shocked at himself.

"Well now," he said. "I begin to see how we both got a bit in a muddle. You'd never heard of the thing I was talking about, and it sounds mighty like grandma phone, did you ever hear grandmaphone. Of course. Naturally. But what I was talking about was a nice box that music comes out of. Did you ever hear music come out of a box?"

"Huh-uh."

"Well down home, believe it or not, we got a box that music comes out of. Would you like to hear it sometime?"

"Uh-huh."

"Good. We'll see if that can't be arranged. Soon. Now would you like to know what they call this box?"

"Uh-huh."

"A gram-a-phone. See? It sounds very much like grandma phone, but it's just a little different. Gram-a-phone. Can you say it?"

"Gram-uh-phone."

"That's right. Can Baby Sister say it I wonder?"

"Emma? He means you."

"Gran-muh-phone."

"Gra*mm*-uh-phone."

"Gra*mm*-mhuh-phone."

"That's fine. You're a mighty smart little girl to say a big word like that."

"I can say some ever so big words," Rufus said. "Want to hear? The Dominant Primordrial Beast."

"Well now, that's mighty smart. But of course I don't mean smarter than Sister. You're a lot bigger boy."

"Yes but I could say that when I was four years old. She's almost four and I bet she can't say it. Can you Emma? Can you?"

"Well, now, some people learn, little quicker than others. It's nice to learn fast but it's nice to take your time, too." He walked over and picked Emma up and sat down with her in his lap. He smelled almost as good as her father, although he was soft in front, and she looked happy. "Now what does that word 'primordrial' mean?"

"I dunno, but it's nice and scary."

"Is it scary? Yes? Yes, spose it does have a sort of a scary sound. Now you can say it, you ought to find out what it means, sometime."

"What *does* it mean?"

"Not sure myself, but then I don't say it. Don't have occasion." He opened out one arm and Rufus walked across to him without realizing he was doing so. The arm felt strong and kind around him. "You're a fine little boy," Mr. Savage said. "But it isn't nice of you to Lord it over your sister."

"What's 'Lord it'?"

"Brag about things you can do, that she can't do yet. That isn't nice."

"No, sir."

"So you watch, and don't do it."

"No siree."

"Because Emma's a fine little girl, too."

"Yes, sir."

"Aren't you, Emmer?" He smiled at her and she blushed with delight. Rufus liked Emma so well, all of a sudden, that he smiled at her, and when she smiled back they were both happy and suddenly he was very much ashamed to have treated her so.

"I want to tell you two something," they heard Mr. Savage's quieted voice. They looked up at him. "Not because you'll understand it now, but I have to, my heart's full, and it's you I want to tell. Maybe you'll remember it later on. It is about your Daddy. Because you never got a real chance to know him. Can I tell you?"

They nodded.

"Some people have a hard, hard time. No money, no good schooling, scarcely enough food. Nothing that you children have, but good people to love them. Your daddy started like that. He didn't have one thing. He had to work till it practicly killed him, for every little thing he ever got.

"Well, some of the greatest men start with nothing. Like Abraham Lincoln. You know who he was?"

"He was born in a log cabin," Rufus said.

"That's right, and he became the greatest man we've ever had."

He said nothing for a moment and they wondered what he was going to tell them about their father.

"Somehow I never got a chance to know Jay—your father—well as I wish. I don't think he ever could have dreamed how much I thought of him. Well I thought the world of him, Rufus and Emma. My own wife and son couldn't mean more to me I think." He waited again. "I'm a pretty ordinary man myself," he went on. "Not a bad one. Just ordinary. But I always thought your father was a lot like Lincoln. I don't mean getting ahead in the world. I mean a man. Some people get where they hope to in this world. Most of us don't. But there never was a man up against harder odds than your father. And there was never a man who tried harder, or hoped for more. I don't mean getting ahead. I mean the right things. He wanted a good life, and good understanding, for himself, for everybody. There never was a braver man than your father, or a man that was kinder, or more generous. They don't make them. All I wanted to tell you is, your father was one of the finest men that ever lived."

He suddenly closed his eyes tightly behind his glasses, and swallowed; a long sobbing sigh fell from him. Deeply and solemnly touched, they moved closer to him, whether to comfort him or themselves they did not know. "There there," he said, his eyes still closed. "There there now. There there."

Upstairs, they heard the door open.

Chapter 39

When grief and shock surpass endurance there occur phases of exhaustion, of anesthesia, in which relatively little is felt and one has the illusion of recognizing, and understanding, a good deal. Throughout these days Laura had, during these breathing spells, drawn a kind of solace from the recurrent thought: at least I am enduring it. I am aware of what has happened, I am meeting it face to face, I am living through it. There had been, even, a kind of pride, a desolate kind of pleasure, in the feeling: I am carrying a heavier weight than I could have dreamed it possible for a human being to carry, yet I am living through it. It had of course occurred to her that this happens to many people, that it is very common, and she humbled and comforted herself in this thought. She thought: this is simply what living is; I never realized before what it is. She thought: now I am more nearly a grown member of the human race; bearing children, which had seemed so much, was just so much apprenticeship. She thought that she had never before had a chance to realize the strength that human beings have, to endure: she loved and revered all those who had ever suffered, even those who had failed to endure. She thought that she had never before had a chance to realize the might, grimness and tenderness of God. She thought that now for the first time she began to know herself, and she gained extraordinary hope in this beginning of knowledge. She thought that she had grown up almost overnight. She thought that she had realized all that was in her soul to realize in the event, and when at length the time came to put on her veil, leave the bedroom she had shared with her husband, leave their home, and go down to see him for the first time since his death and to see the long day through, which would cover him out of sight for the duration of this world, she thought that she was firm and ready. She had refused to "try on" her veil; the mere thought of approving or disapproving it before a mirror was obscene; so now when she came to the mirror and drew it down across her face to go, she saw herself for the first time since her husband's death. Without either desiring to see her face, or caring how it looked, she saw that it had changed; through the deep, clear veil her gray eyes watched her gray eyes watch her through the deep, clear veil. I must have fever, she thought, startled by their brightness; and turned away. It was when she came to the door, to walk through it, to leave this room and to leave this shape of existence forever, that realizations poured upon and overwhelmed her through which, in retrospect, she would one day know that all that had gone before, all that she had thought she experienced and knew—True, more or less, though it all was—was nothing, to this. The realization came without shape or definability, save as it was focused in the pure physical act of leaving the room, but came with such force, such monstrous piercing weight, in all her heart and soul and mind and body but above all in the womb, where it arrived and dwelt like a cold and prodigious, spreading stone, that she groaned almost inaudibly, almost a mere silent breath, an *Ohhhhhhh,* and doubled deeply over, hands to her belly, and her knee-joints melted.

Jessie, smaller than she, caught her, and rapped out, "*Close that door!*" It would be a long time before either of the women realized their resentment of the priest and their contempt for him, and their compassion, for staying in the room. Now they did not even know that he was there. Jessie helped her to the edge of the bed and sat beside her exclaiming, over and over, in a heartbroken voice, "Laura, Laura. Laura, Laura. Oh Laura. Laura. Laura," resting one already translucent, spinster's hand lightly upon the back of her veiled head, and with the other, so clenching one of Laura's wrists that she left a bracelet of bruise.

Laura meanwhile rocked quietly backward and forward, and from side to side, groaning, quietly, from the depths of her body, not like a human creature but a fatally hurt animal; sounds low, almost crooned, not strident, but shapeless and orderless, the sisters, except in their quietude, to those transcendent idiot bellowing screams which deliver children. And as she rocked and groaned, the realization gradually lost its fullest, most impaling concentration: there took shape, from its utter darkness, like the slow emergence of the countryside into first daylight, all those separate realizations which could be resolved into images, emotions, thought, words, obligations: so that after not more than a couple of minutes, during which Jessie never ceased to say to her,

"Laura. Laura.", and Father Robertson, his eyes closed, prayed, she sat still for a moment, then got quietly onto her knees, was silent for not more than a moment more, made the sign of the Cross, stood up, and said "I'm ready now."

But she swayed; Jessie said, "Rest, Laura. There's no hurry," and Father Robertson said "Perhaps you should lie down a little while"; but she said, "No; thank you; I want to go now," and walked crookedly to the door, and opened it, and walked through.

Father Robertson took her arm, in the top hallway. Although she tried not to, she leaned on him very heavily.

Chapter 40

They heard feet on the front stairs, and knew it was their grandfather. They heard him turn to go down the hall and then they heard his subdued, surprised voice: "Hugh? Where's Poll?"

And their uncle's voice, cold, close to his ear: "In—there—with Father—Robertson"—

"Unh!" they heard their grandfather growl. Their Aunt Jessie hurried towards the door.

—"Praying."

"Unh!" he growled again.

Their Aunt Jessie quickly closed the door, and hurried back to her chair.

But much as she had hurried, all that she did after she got back to her chair was to sit with her hands in her lap and stare straight ahead of her through her heavy lenses, and all that they could do was to sit quietly too, and look at the clean lace curtains at the window, and at the magnolia tree and the locust tree in the yard, and at the wall of the next house, and at a heavy robin which fed along the lawn, until he flew away, and at the people who now and then moved past along the sunny sidewalk, and at the buggies and automobiles which now and then moved along the sunny street.

They felt mysteriously immaculate, strange and careful in their clean clothes, and it seemed as if the house were in shadow and were walking on tiptoe in the middle of an easy, sunny world. When they tired of looking at these things, they looked at their Aunt Jessie, but she did not appear to realize that they were looking at her; and when there was no response from their Aunt Jessie they looked at each other. But it had never given them any pleasure or interest to look at each other and it gave them none today. Each could see only that the other was much too clean, and each realized, through that the more acutely, that he himself was much too clean, and that something was wrong which required of each of them such careful conduct, and particularly good manners, that there was really nothing imaginable that might be proper to do except to sit still. But through sitting so still, with nothing to fix their attention upon except each other, they saw each other perhaps more clearly than at any time before; and each felt uneasiness and shyness over what he saw. Rufus saw a much littler child than he was, with a puzzled, round, red face which looked angry, and he was somewhat sorry for her in the bewilderment and loneliness he felt she was lost in, but more, he was annoyed by this look of shut-in anger and this look of incomprehension, and he thought over and over: "Dead. He's dead. That's what he is; he's dead"; and the room where his father lay felt like a boundless hollowness in the house and in his own being, as if he stood in the dark near the edge of an abyss and could feel that droop of space in the darkness; and watching his sister's face he could see his father's almost as clearly, as he had just seen it, and said to himself, over and over: "Dead. Dead"; and looked with uneasiness and displeasure at his sister's face, which was so different, so flushed and busy, so angry, and so uncomprehending.

And Emma saw him struck down there in the long box like a huge mute doll, who would not smile or stir, and smelled sweet and frightening, and because of whom she sat alone and stiffly and too clean, and nobody was kind or attentive, and everything went on tiptoe, and with her mother's willingness a man she feared and hated put his great hand on her head and spoke incomprehensibly. Something very wrong was being done, and nobody seemed to care or to tell her what or to help her or love her or protect her from it and there was her too-clean brother, who always thought he was so smart, looking at her with dislike and contempt.

So after gazing coldly at each other for a little while, they once more looked into the side yard and down into the street and tried to interest themselves in what they saw, and to forget the thing which so powerfully pervaded their thoughts, and to subdue their physical restiveness in order that they should not be disapproved; and, tiring of these, would look once more at their aunt, who was as aloof almost as their father; and, uneased by that, would look once more into each other's eyes; and so again to the yard and the street, upon which the sunlight moved slowly. And there they saw an automobile draw up and Mr. Savage got quickly out of it and walked slowly up towards the house.

Chapter 41

"Come, now," their mother whispered, and, taking them each by the hand, led them through the Green Room and into the living-room.

There it was, against the fireplace, and there seemed to be scarcely anything else in the room except the sunny light on the floor.

It was very long and dark; smooth like a boat; with bright handles. Half the top was open. There was a strange, sweet smell, so faint that it could scarcely be realized.

Rufus had never known such stillness. Their little sounds, as they approached his father, vanished upon it like the infinitesimal whisperings of snow, falling on open water.

There was his hand, his arm; suit: there he was.

Rufus had never seen him so indifferent; and the instant he saw him, he knew that he would never see him otherwise. He had his look of faint impatience, the chin strained a little upward, as if he were concealing his objection to a collar which was too tight and too formal. And in this slight urgency of the chin; in the small trending of a frown which stayed in the skin; in the arch of the nose; and in the still, strong mouth, there was a look of pride. But most of all, there was indifference; and through this indifference which held him in every particle of his being—an indifference which would have rejected them; have sent them away, except that it was too indifferent even to care whether they went or stayed; in this self-completeness which nothing could touch, there was something else, some other feeling which he gave, which there was no identifying even by feeling, for Rufus had never experienced this feeling before; there was perfected beauty. The head, the hand, dwelt in completion, immutable, indestructible: motionless. They moved upon existence quietly as stones which withdraw through water for which there is no floor.

The arm was bent. Out of the dark suit, the starched cuff, sprang the hairy wrist.

The wrist was angled; the hand was arched; none of the fingers touched each other.

The hand was so composed that it seemed at once casual and majestic. It stood exactly above the center of his body.

The fingers looked unusually clean and dry, as if they had been scrubbed with great care.

The hand looked very strong, and the veins were strong in it.

The nostrils were very dark, yet he thought he could see, in one of them, something which looked like cotton.

On the lower lip, a trifle to the left of its middle, there was a small blue line which ran also a little below the lip.

At the exact point of the chin, there was another small blue mark, as straight and neat as might be drawn with a pencil, and scarcely wider.

The lines which formed the wings of the nose and the mouth, were almost gone.

The hair was most carefully brushed.

The eyes were casually and quietly closed, the eyelids were like silk on the balls, and when Rufus glanced quickly from the eyes to the mouth it seemed as if his father were almost about to smile. Yet the mouth carried no suggestion either of smiling or of gravity; only strength, silence, manhood, and indifferent contentment.

He saw him much more clearly than he had ever seen him before; yet his face looked unreal, as if he had just been shaved by a barber. The whole head was waxen, and the hand too was as if perfectly made of wax.

The head was lifted on a small white satin pillow.

There was the subtle, curious odor, like fresh hay, and like a hospital, but not quite like either, and so faint that it was scarcely possible to be sure that it existed.

Rufus saw these things within a few seconds, and became aware that his mother was picking Emma up in order that she might see more clearly; he drew a little aside. Out of the end of his eye he was faintly aware of his sister's rosy face and he could hear her gentle breathing as he continued to stare at his father, at his stillness, and his power, and his beauty.

He could see the tiny dark point of every shaven hair of the beard.

He watched the way the flesh was chiseled in a widening trough from the root of the nose to the white edge of the lip.

He watched the still more delicate dent beneath the lower lip.

It became strange, and restive, that it was possible for anyone to lie so still for so long; yet he knew that his father would never move again; yet this knowledge made his motionlessness no less strange.

Within him, and outside him, everything except his father was dry, light, unreal, and touched with a kind of warmth and impulse and a kind of sweetness which felt like the beating of a heart. But borne within this strange and unreal sweetness, its center yet alien in nature from all the rest, and as nothing else was actual, his father lay graven, whose noble hand he longed, in shyness, to touch.

"Now, Rufus," his mother whispered; they knelt. He could just see over the edge of the coffin. He gazed at the perfect hand.

His mother's arm came round him; he felt her hand on the crest of his shoulder. He slid his arm around her and felt her hand become alive on his shoulder and felt his sister's arm. He touched her bare arm tenderly, and felt her hand grapple for and take his arm. He put his hand around her arm and felt how little it was. He could feel a vein beating against the bone, just below her armpit.

"Our Father," she said.

They joined her, Emma waiting for those words of which she was sure, Rufus lowering his voice almost to silence while she hesitated, trying to give her the words distinctly. Their mother spoke very gently.

"Our Father, who art in Heaven, hallowed be Thy Name; Thy Kingdom come, Thy—"

"Thy Will be d—", Rufus went on, alone; then waited, disconcerted.

"Thy Will be done," his mother said. "On Earth," she continued, with some strange shading of the word which touched him with awe and sadness; "As it is in Heaven."

"Give us this d—"

Rufus was more careful this time.

"Daily bread," Emma said confidently.

"Give us this day our daily bread," and in those words still more, he felt that his mother meant something quite otherwise, "And forgive us our trespasses as we forgive those who trespass against us.

"And lead us not into temptation; but deliver us from evil," and here their mother left her hands where they dwelt with her children, but bowed her head:

"For Thine is the Kingdom, and the Power, and the Glory," she said with almost vindictive certitude, "forever and ever. Amen."

She was silent for some moments, and still he stared at the hand.

"God bless us and help us all," she said. "God help us to understand Thee. God help us to know Thy will. God help us to put all our trust in Thee, whether we can understand or not.

"God help these little children to remember their father in all his goodness and strength and kindness and dearness, and in all of his tremendous love for them. God help them ever to be all that was good and fine and brave in him, all that he would most have loved to see them grow up to be, if Thou in Thy great wisdom had thought best to spare him. God let us be able to feel, to know, he can still see us as we grow, as we live, that he is still with us; that he is not deprived of his children and all he had hoped for them and loved them for; nor they of him. Nor they of him.

"God make us to know he is still with us, still loves us, cares what comes to us, what we do, what we are; *so much.* O God . . ."

She spoke these words sharply, and said no more; and Rufus felt that she was looking at his father, but he did not move his eyes, and felt that he should not know what he was sure of. After a few moments he heard the motions of her lips as softly again as that falling silence in which the whole world snowed, and he turned his eyes from the hand and looked towards his father's face and, seeing the blue-dented chin thrust upward, and the way the flesh was sunken behind the bones of the jaw, first recognized in its specific weight the word, *dead.* He looked quickly away, and solemn wonder tolled in him like the shouldering of a prodigious bell, and he heard his mother's snowy lips with wonder and with a desire that she should never suffer sorrow, and gazed once again at the hand, whose casual majesty was unaltered. He wished more sharply even than before that he might touch it; but whereas before he had wondered whether he might, if he could find a way to be alone, with no one to see or ever know, now he was sure that he must not. He therefore watched it all the more studiously, trying to bring all of his touch into all that he could see; but he could not bring much. He realized that his mother's hand was without feeling or meaning on his shoulder. He felt how sweaty his hand, and his sister's arm, had become, and changed his hand, and clasped her gently, but without sympathy, and felt her hand tighten, and felt gentle towards her because she was too little to understand. The hand became, for a few moments, a mere object, and he could just hear his mother's breath repeating: "Goodbye,

Jay, goodbye. Goodbye. Goodbye. Goodbye, my Jay, my husband. O, Goodbye. Goodbye." Then he heard nothing and was aware of nothing except the hand, which was an object; and felt a strong downward clasping pressure upon his skull, and heard a quiet but rich voice.

His mother was not—yes, he could see her skirts, out behind to the side; and Emma, and a great hand on her head too, and her silent and astounded face. And between them, a little behind them, black polished shoes and black, sharply pressed trouser legs, without cuffs.

"Hail Mary, full of grace," the voice said; and his mother joined; "The Lord is with Thee; blessed art thou among women, and blessed is the fruit of thy womb, Jesus.

"Holy Mary, Mother of God, pray for us sinners, now, and in the hour of *our* death. Amen."

"Our Father, Who art in Heaven," the voice said; and the children joined; "Hallowed be Thy Name," but in their mother's uncertainty, they stopped, and the voice went on: "Thy Kingdom Come, Thy Will be done," said the voice, with particular warmth, "on earth as it is in Heaven. Give us this day our daily bread and forgive us our trespasses as we forgive those who trespass against us." Everything had been taken off the mantelpiece. "And lead us not into temptation, but deliver us from evil," and with this his hand left Rufus' head and he crossed himself, immediately restoring the hand, "for Thine is the Kingdom, and the Power, and the Glory, for ever and ever, Amen."

He was silent for a moment. Twisting a little under the hard hand, Rufus glanced upward: the priest's jaw was hard, his face was earnest, his eyes were tightly shut.

"O Lord cherish and protect these innocent, orphaned children," he said, his eyes shut. *Then we are!* Rufus thought, and knew that he was very bad. "Guard them in all temptations which life may bring. Grant that when they come to understand this thing which in Thy inscrutable Wisdom Thou hast brought to pass, they may know and reverence Thy will. God we beseech Thee that they may ever be the children, the boy and girl, the man and woman, which this good man would have desired them to be. Let them never discredit his memory, O Lord. And Lord by thy Mercy may they come quickly and soon to know, the True and all-loving Father whom they have in Thee. Let them seek Thee out the more, in their troubles and in their joys, as they would have sought their good earthly father, had he been spared them. Let them ever be, by Thy Great Mercy, true Christian Catholic children. Amen."

Some of the tiles of the hearth which peeped from beneath the coffin-stand, those at the border, were a grayish blue. All the others were a streaked and angry reddish yellow.

The voice altered, and said delicately: "The Peace of God, which passeth all understanding, keep your hearts and minds in the knowledge and love of God." His hand again lifted from Rufus' head, and he drew a great cross above each of them as he said: "And the blessing of God Almighty, the Father, the Son, and the Holy Ghost, be upon you, and remain with you always."

"Amen," their mother said.

The priest touched his shoulder, and Rufus stood up. Emma stood up. Their father had not, of course not, Rufus thought, he had not moved, but he looked to have changed. Although he lay in such calm and beauty and grandeur, it looked to Rufus as if he had been flung down and left on the street, and as if he were a very successfully disguised stranger. He felt a pang of distress and of disbelief and was about to lean to look more closely, when he felt a light hand on his head, his mother's he knew, and heard her say, "Now, children"; and they were conveyed to the hall door.

The piano, he saw, was shut.

"Now Mother wants to stay just a minute or two," she told them. "She'll be with you directly. So you go straight into the East Room, with Aunt Jessie, and wait for me."

She touched their faces, and noiselessly closed the door.

Crossing to the East Room they became aware that they were not alone in the dark hall. Hugh stood by the hat rack, holding to the banister, and his rigid, weeping eyes, shining with fury, struck to the roots of their souls like ice, so that they hastened into the room where their great-aunt sat in an unmoving rocking chair with her hands in her lap, the sunless light glazing her lenses, frostlike upon her hair.

Chapter 42

As they drew near Rufus noticed that a man who went past along the sidewalk looked back at his grandfather's house, then quickly away, then back once more, and again quickly away. He saw that there were several buggies and automobiles, idle and empty, along the opposite side of the street, but that the space in front of his grandfather's house was empty. The house seemed at once especially bare, and changed, and silent, and its corners seemed particularly hard and distinct; and beside the front door there hung a great knotted bloom and streamer of black cloth. The front door was opened before it was touched and there stood their Uncle Hugh and their mother and behind them the dark hallway, and they were all but overwhelmed by a dizzying, sickening fragrance, and by a surging outward upon them likewise, of multitudinous and incomprehensible vitality. Almost immediately they were drawn within the darkness of the hallway and the fragrance became recognizable as the fragrance of flowers, and the vitality which poured upon them was that of the people with whom the house was crowded. Rufus experienced an intuition as of great force and possible danger on his right and, glancing quickly into the East Room, saw that every window shade was drawn except one and that against the cold light which came through that window the room was filled with dark figures which crouched disconsolately at the edges of chairs, heavy and primordial as bears in a pit; and even as he looked he heard the rising of a great, low groan, which was joined by a higher groan, which was surmounted by a low wailing and by a higher wailing, and he could see that a woman stood up suddenly and with a wailing and bellowing sob caught the hair at her temples and pulled, then flung her hands upward and outward: but upon this moment Hugh rushed and with desperate and brutal speed and silence, pulled the door shut, and Rufus was aware in the same instant that their own footsteps and the wailing had caused a commotion on his left and, glancing as sharply into the sunlit room where his father lay, saw an incredibly dense crowd of soberly dressed people on weak, complaining chairs, catching his eye, looking past him, looking quickly away, trying to look as if they had not looked around.

"It's all right, Hugh," his mother whispered. "Open the door. Tell them we'll be in, in just a minute." And she drew the children more deeply into the hallway, where they could not be seen through either door, and whispered to Arthur Savage: "Papa is in the Green Room, and Mama. Thank you, Arthur."

"Don't you think of it," Arthur said, as he passed her; and his hand hovered near her shoulder, and he went quietly through the door into the dining-room.

"Now children," their mother said, lowering her face above them. "We're all going in, to see Daddy, just once more. But we won't be able to stay, we can just look for a moment. And then you'll see your Grandma Agee, just for a moment. And then Mr. Savage will take you down again to his house and Mother will see you again later this afternoon."

Hugh came toward her and nodded sharply.

"All right, Hugh," she said. "All right children." Reaching suddenly behind the crest of her skull she lowered her veil and they saw her face and her eyes through its darkness. She took their hands. "Now come with Mother," she whispered.

There was Uncle Clifford in a dark suit; he was very clean and pink and his face was full of little lines. He looked quickly at them and quickly away. There was old Miss Knapp and there were Miss Lizzie Salmon and Miss Fanny Salmon and Doctor Delfrench and Mrs. Delfrench and Uncle Albert Delfrench and Aunt Hazel Goff and Mrs. Goff and Ben Goff and Aunt Marcia Perkins and Aunt Nell Wylie, and ever so many others, as well, whom the children were not sure they had seen before, and all of them looked as if they were trying not to look and as if they shared a secret they were offended to have been asked to tell; and there was the most enormous heap of flowers of all kinds that the children had ever seen, tall and extravagantly fresh and red and yellow, tall and starchy white, dark roses and white roses, ferns, carnations, great leaves of varnished-looking palm, all wreathed and wired and running with ribbons of black and silver and bright gold and dark gold, and almost suffocating in their fragrance; and there, almost hidden among these flowers, was the coffin, and beside it, two last strangers who, now that they entered the room, turned away and quickly took chairs: and now a strange man in a long, dark coat stepped towards their mother with silent alacrity, his eyes shining like dark jelly, and with a courtly gesture ushered her forward and stood proudly and humbly to one side: and there was Daddy again.

He had not stirred one inch; yet he had changed. His face looked much more remote than before and much more ordinary and it was as if he were tired, or bored. He did not look as big as he really was, and the fragrance of the flowers was so strong and the vitality of the mourners was so many-souled and so pervasive, and so perverted and compounded by propriety and restraint, and they felt so urgently the force of all the eyes upon them, that they saw their father almost as idly as if he had been a picture, or a substituted image, and felt little realization of his presence and little interest. And while they were still looking, bemused in this empty curiosity, they felt themselves drawn away, and walked with their mother past the closed piano into the Green Room. And there were Grandpa and Grandma and Uncle Hugh and Aunt Paula and Aunt Jessie; and Grandma got up quickly and took their mother in her arms and patted her several times emphatically across the shoulders, and Grandpa stood up too; and while Grandma stooped and embraced and kissed each of the children, saying "darlings, darlings" in a somewhat loud and ill-controlled voice, they could see their Grandfather's graceful and cynical head as he embraced their mother, and realized that he was not quite as tall as she was; and their Aunt Paula stood up shyly with her elbows out. As their mother led them from the room they looked back through the door and saw that the man in the long coat and another strange man had closed the coffin and were silently and quickly screwing it shut.

Chapter 43

Arthur Savage stood back in the middle of the hall, looking as if he did not know what to do. Their mother went straight up to him.

"Now we're all ready, Arthur," she said. He nodded very shyly and stepped a little to one side as she spoke to the children.

"Now it's time to go," she told them. "Back to Mr. Savage's, as I told you this morning. And have a nice time and be very good and quiet and Mr. Savage will bring you back to Mother later this afternoon." She straightened Emma's little collar, which was wilting. "Now goodbye," she said; "Mother will see you before long." She kissed them lightly.

Before long, now; before long:

They went so quietly past the living-room door and along the hushed porch and down the steps that Rufus felt that they were moving as stealthily as burglars.

When they had driven almost all the way to Mr. Savage's home Mr. Savage surprisingly turned a wrong corner, and then another, and then said to the children, "I think you'll want to see. Maybe not but I think you'll be glad later on I took you back." And he drove somewhat more rapidly up the silent, empty, back street, then once again turned a corner, moved very slowly and quietly, and came to a stop.

They were in the side street, just across from Dr. Delfrench's house, and across the street corner and the wide lawn they could see their grandfather's house and everything that went on, and they knew that they were not seen. Six men, their Uncle Hugh, their Uncle Frank, their Uncle Clifford Glenn, their Uncle Jim Hodges, and Mr. King, and a man whom they had never seen before, were carrying a long gray shining box by handles, very carefully and slowly down the curved brick walk from the house to the street, and they realized that this was the box in which their father lay, and that it must be very heavy. The men were of different heights so that Uncle Hugh, who was tall, and Uncle Jim Hodges, who was even taller, had to squat slightly at the knees, whereas Uncle Clifford, who was shortest, was leaning outward and lifting upward. Just behind, seeming to walk even more slowly, came their grandfather, and a tall woman all veiled in black whom by her tallness and humbled grace they knew was their mother; and just behind her, with Aunt Mossie on one side and Father Robertson on the other, came a second woman, all veiled in black, who by her shortness and lameness they knew was their Grandmother Agee. And just behind them came Granma and Aunt Jessie, and Aunt Vesta and Aunt Paula, and Aunt Hazel Goff and Mrs. Goff and Miss Bess Goff, and old Mr. Glenn, and Miss Lizzie Salmon and Miss Fanny Salmon, and Doctor Delfrench and Mrs. Delfrench and Uncle Albert Delfrench, and the porch and the porch steps were still full of darkly dressed people whose faces and bearing they could unsurely recognize but whose names they did not know, and of people whom they could not be sure whether they had ever seen before, and more were still shuffling slowly out through the front door onto the porch.

And up the hill alongside the house, behind it, stood a shining black automobile, and two small quick men dressed in black sped constantly between the house and the wagon, bringing from the house great armsful of bright flowers, and stowing them in the automobile. And down in front of the front steps the man in the long coat who had ushered them to the coffin now made an imperious gesture and, drawn by three shining black horses and one horse of a shining red-brown, a long, tall, narrow box of whorled and glittering black and of black glass was pulled forward a few feet, and then a foot more, so that its black and glittering rear end was just beyond the opening of the steps; and the men who carried their father's coffin now hesitated at the head of the steps, and the man in the long coat nodded courteously as he turned and opened the shining back doors of the tall, blind-looking wagon, so that they carefully and uneasily made their way down the narrow steps, squeezing gingerly together, and he stood aside from the open doors and seemed to speak and to instruct them with his hands; and while their mother and her father hesitated at the head of the steps and behind them, all the dark column of mourners hesitated likewise, the men who carried their heavy father lifted him as if he were hard to lift and they were careful but unwilling, and studiously, with reverent nudgings and hitchings, shoved the coffin so deeply into the dark wagon that only its hard end showed, and they could hear a streetcar coming. And the man in the long coat closed one of the doors, and they could see only a corner of the box, and then he closed the other door and they could not see it at all, and he tightened over the shining silver handle which held the doors locked, and one of the horses twitched his ears, and the streetcar, which had paused, was now louder. And the long, dark wagon was drawn forward a few paces, and paused again, and a closed and shining black buggy moved forward and took its place, and the streetcar moved past and they could see heads turning through its windows and a man took off his hat, and their mother and their Grandfather came down the steps and their Grandfather helped their mother to climb in, and their Grandmother Agee and their Aunt Maussie and Father Robertson came down the steps and their Grandfather and Father Robertson helped their Grandmother Agee to climb in, and they helped Aunt Maussie in, and the noise of the streetcar was fading, and Uncle Frank stood aside so that their Grandfather might get in, and then they both stood aside so that their Grandmother Tyler might get in, and after some hesitation, their Grandmother was helped in and then Uncle Frank stepped in after her, and the curtains of the windows were drawn and the long dark wagon and the dark buggy moved forward, and a second buggy took its place, and a long line of buggies and automobiles, after a moment's hesitancy, advanced a few feet, and now a man who had stood in the empty sidewalk across from the house walked westward and crossed the street in front of the children, putting on his hat as he reached the farther curb, and they heard the last of the streetcar, but now they heard the hard chipping of two sparrows, worrying a bit of debris in the street, and Mr. Savage said: "Better go now"; and they realized that he had never shut off his engine, for as soon as he said this he began to back the car as silently as he could and with great care; and he twisted it backward around the corner, and they slowly descended the same quiet back street up which he had brought them.

When he had stopped the car in front of his home he said, before he moved to get out: "Maybe you'd better not say anything about this." He still did not move to get out, so they too sat still. After a little he said, "No . . . you do as you think best." He did not look at them; he had not looked at them during all of this time. They watched the shadows work, and the leaves waving.

He got out of the car, and opened the door on their side, and held out his hands to Emma.

"Up she goes," he said.

Chapter 44

The house echoed, and there was still an extraordinary fragrance of carnations.

Their mother was in the East Room.

"My darlings," she said; she looked as if she had traveled a great distance, and now they knew that everything had changed. They put their heads against her, still knowing that nothing would ever be the same again, and she caught them so close they could smell her, and they loved her, but it made no difference.

She could not say anything, and neither could they; they began to realize that she was silently praying, and now instead of love for her they felt sadness, and politely waited for her to finish.

"Now we'll stay here at Granma's," she finally said; "Tonight, anyway." And again there was nothing further that she could say.

Her hands on them began to feel merely heavy. Rufus moved nearer, trying to recover the lost tenderness; at the same moment, Emma pulled away.

He understands, their mother thought; and tried not to feel hurt by Emma's restiveness. Emma, aware at this absolute moment that her brother was preferred, was hurt so bitterly that her mother felt it in her body, and lightened her hold, at just the moment when Emma most desired to be taken close in to her kindness. By the way she held him Rufus realized, *she thinks I'm better than I am;* he felt as if he had been believed in a lie, but this time it was not a good feeling.

"God bless my children," she whispered. "God bless and keep us all."

"Amen," Rufus whispered courteously; he tried to lose his uneasiness by holding her still more closely, and felt her still more passionate hand; while Emma, in an enchantment of pain and loneliness, stayed like a stone.

There they stayed quiet, the deceived mother, the false son, the fatally wounded daughter; it was thus that Hugh found them and, with a glimpse of the noble painting it could be, said to himself, crying within himself, “It beats the Holy Family.”

“Come for a walk with me [Rufus],” Hugh said; from the front porch Emma watched them until she could no longer see them. Then she pulled one of the chairs away from the wall and sat in it and rocked. She had a feeling that it would be all right to rock if she could rock without making any noise, and it interested her to try. But no matter how carefully and quietly she moved, the rockers gave out a cobbling noise on the boards of the porch, and the chair squeaked gently. Hearing these small noises, she felt that they were wrong, then that she did not want to be heard. She stopped rocking. She sat with her arms and hands high and straight along the arms of the chair and looked through the railing at the lawn and down into the street. A robin hopped heavily along the grass. He gave her a short, hard look, then a second, short and hard as the jab of a needle, then paid her no further attention, but hopped, heavily, and jabbed and jabbed in the short grass with jabs which were much like his short, hard way of looking.

Down across the street she saw Dr. Delfrench come along the sidewalk towards home; he was still in his dark clothes. Remembering how her father always saw her from a distance and waved, she waited for the moment when he would look over and wave, but he did not wave, or even look over; he went straight into his house.

Deep in the side yard among her flowers she saw Mrs. Delfrench in a long white dress and long white gloves, wearing a paper bag on her head. She bent deeply above the flowers, rather than squatting, and whenever she moved to another place she straightened, tall and very thin, and gathered her skirt in one hand and delicately lifted it, as Grandma did when she stepped up or down from a curb. Then she would bend deeply over again, as if she were leaning over a crib to say goodnight.

There were quite a few people along the sidewalks, and most of them were walking in one direction, away from downtown.

On the sage-orange tree beside the porch the leaves lay along the air as lazily as if they were almost asleep, and ever so quietly moved, and lay still again.

The robin had hold of a worm; he braced his heels, walked backward, and pulled hard. It stretched like a rubber band and snapped in two; Emma felt the snapping in her stomach. He quickly gobbled what he had, his head in a regular spasm and, darting his beak even more quickly, took hold of the rest and pulled again. It stretched but did not break, and then all came loose from the ground; she could see it twisting as he flew away with it. He flung himself in a great curve upward among the branches of a tree in the side yard, and Emma could just hear the thin hissing cries of the little robins.

Now Dr. Delfrench stood beside his wife and they were looking at each other and talking. She was taller than he was, but he was thicker through. He had taken off his coat and pale blue suspenders crossed on his back. Above his white shirt his neck was dark red.

All the way down the block where the next street crossed she could see that there were still other people along the walks, looking tired yet walking fast, tiny at this distance, and nearly all of these people, too, were walking away from downtown.

Uncle Albert Delfrench came towards his house. He was still wearing his dark suit and he carried his hat in one hand. His bottom was fat and he walked like a duck. Even from here Emma could see how choked-up and thick he looked in the face and neck, Uncle Hugh said, as if his mouth was stuffed full of hot mashed potato. He looked up and across at the house and Emma raised her hand, but he looked quickly away again, and cut across the lawn to join his father and mother. They all three talked.

A small, sudden noise frightened Emma; then she realized it came from the living-room. There was no more sound. She got from the chair in perfect silence and stole to the window in the angle of the porch. Grandma was sitting at the piano and she had opened it; Emma could see the keys. She sat for a long while without lifting her hands from her lap. Then she stood up and shut the piano and went into the Green Room; she was wearing her apron. But before Emma could move from the window she came in again (she can't see this far, Emma quickly reassured herself), looked carefully about with her near-sighted peering look, pursed her lips, and sat down again at the piano. Now she opened the keyboard once more and curved her hands powerfully above the keys and moved her fingers, but there was no sound. Grandma can't hear very well, Emma remembered; talk very loud. So she can't hear very well when she plays music, either. She was bent way over, with her good ear close to the keys, the way she always was when she played, and her feet were working the pedals, yet she couldn't hear a sound.

But why can't *I* hear? Emma suddenly thought. I always do. She watched and listened much more sharply: not one sound.

With sudden pleasure, Emma thought of listening through a large black ear trumpet; then she realized that she was still hearing the shuffling street and the murmurous city, and knew why she could hear no music. Grandma was just making the notes go down without making any noise.

Then, close beside Emma, her grandfather came through the door, and stopped abruptly. He was looking at Grandma. He couldn't hear very well either, but he could hear better than Grandma could; he always sat at this far end of the room when there was music. So he knew too. After he had stood a few moments he walked quickly down almost to where she sat with her back to him and both of his hands lifted above her as if he were going to touch her humped-over shoulders or her hair. Then after standing for a moment again, he turned away and walked even more quickly and quietly out by the way he had come in, and his face was so tucked down that Emma was sure she had not been seen.

Now Grandma finished and left her hands quiet among the keys, moving them only to stroke the black keys and the white ones between. Then she took her hands away and folded them in her lap. Then she stood up, closed the piano, and went into the Green Room.

Dr. Delfrench and Mrs. Delfrench and Uncle Albert were no longer in the garden.

Where's Daddy?

All of a sudden she felt that she could not bear to be alone. She went into the hall and into the East Room but her mother was no longer in the East Room. She went down the hall towards the dining-room and she could hear her Grandmother busy in the pantry, but she knew that she did not want to see her or be found by her. She hurried on tiptoe across the corner of the dining-room, hiding behind the table, and into the Green Room, but there was nobody there. She looked out and saw her Grandfather standing in the middle of the garden, gazing down into the strong spikes of the century plant. She hurried through the dizzying fragrance of the living-room and climbed the front stairs as quickly and quietly as she was able; Aunt Paula's door was closed.

By now her face felt very hot and she was crying. She hurried along the hallway; shut. Aunt Jessie's door was shut. Behind it there was a coldly tender waning of a voice; Aunt Jessie's voice; her mother's. She set her ear close to the door and listened.

O Almighty God, with whom do live the spirits of just men made perfect, after they are delivered from their earthly prisons; We humbly commend the soul of this thy servant, our dear brother, into thy hands, as into the hands of a faithful Creator and most merciful Saviour; most humbly beseeching thee that it may be precious in thy sight. Wash it, we pray thee, in the blood of that immaculate Lamb that was slain to take away the sins of the world; that whatsoever defilements it may have contracted in the midst of this miserable and naughty world, through the lusts of the flesh or the wiles of Satan, being purged and done away, it may be presented pure and without spot before thee; through the merits of Jesus Christ thine only Son our Lord, *Amen.*

O God, whose days are without end, and whose mercies cannot be numbered; Make us, we beseech thee, deeply sensible of the shortness and uncertainty of human life; and let thy Holy Spirit lead us through this vale of misery, in holiness and righteousness, all the days of our lives; that when we shall have served thee in our generation, we may be gathered unto our fathers, having the testimony of a good conscience; in the communion of the Catholic Church; in the confidence of a certain faith; in the comfort of a reasonable, religious, and holy hope; in favour with thee our God, and in perfect charity with the world. All which we ask through Jesus Christ our Lord. *Amen.*

Her mother's voice choked. Aunt Jessie, with great quietness, spoke what she had been speaking from the beginning, and continued it and brought it to a close. Then, even more quietly, she said, "Laura, my dear, let's stop."

And after a moment Emma could hear her mother's voice, shaken and almost squeaking: "no, no; no, no; I asked you to, Aunt Jessie. I . . . I . . ."

And again, Aunt Jessie's voice: "Let's just stop it."

And her mother's: "Without this I don't think I could bear it *at all.*"

And Aunt Jessie's: "There, dear. God bless and keep you. There. There."

And her mother's: "Just a minute and I'll be all right."

And a silence.

And then Aunt Jessie's voice, coldly tender: . . . and her mother's:. . . .

In intense quietness, Emma stole through the open door opposite Aunt Jessie's door, and hid herself beneath her grandparents' bed. She was no longer crying. She only wanted never to be seen by anybody again. She lay on her side and stared down into the grim grain of the carpet. When Aunt Jessie's door opened she felt such terror that she gasped, and drew her knees up tight against her chest. When the voices began calling her, downstairs, she made herself even smaller, and when she heard their feet on the stairs and the rising concern in their voices she began to tremble all over. But by the time she heard them along the hallway she was out from under the bed and sitting on its edge, her back to them as they came in, her heart knocking her breath to pieces.

"Why *there* you *are,*" her mother cried, and turning, Emma was frightened by the fright and the tears on her face. "Didn't you *hear* us?"

She shook her head, no.

"Why how could you *help* but . . . were you asleep?"

She nodded, yes.

"I thought she was with you, Paula."

"I thought she was with you or Mama."

"Why, where on earth *were* you, darling? Heavens and earth, have you been all *alone?*"

Emma nodded yes; her lower lip thrust out farther and farther and she felt her chin trembling and hated everybody.

"Why, bless your little heart, come to Mother"; her mother came toward her stooping with her arms stretched out and Emma ran to her as fast as she could run, and plunged her head into her, and cried as if she were made only of tears; and it was only when her mother said, just as kindly, "just look at your panties, why they're *sopping* wet," that she realized that indeed they were.

Chapter 45

Hugh had never invited him to take a walk with him before, and he felt honored, and worked hard to keep up with him. He realized that now, maybe, he would hear about it, but he knew it would not be a good thing to ask. When they got well into the next block beyond his grandfather's, and the houses and trees were unfamiliar, he took Hugh's hand and Hugh took his firmly, but did not press it or look down at him. Pretty soon maybe he'll tell me, Rufus thought. Or anyway say something. But his uncle did not say anything. Looking up at him, from a half step behind him, Rufus could see that he looked mad about something. He looked ahead so fixedly that Rufus suspected he was not really looking at anything; even when they stepped from the curb, and stepped up for the curb across from it, his eyes did not change. He was frowning, and the corners of his nose were curled as if he smelled something bad. Did I do something? Rufus wondered. No, he wouldn't ask me for a walk if I did. Yes, he would too if he was real mad and wanted to give me a talking-to and not raise a fuss about it there. But he won't say anything, so I guess he doesn't want to give me a talking-to. Maybe he's thinking. Maybe about Daddy. The funeral. (He saw the sunlight on the hearse as it began to move.) What all did they do out there? They put him down in the ground and then they put all the flowers on top. Then they say their prayers and then they all come home again. In Greenwood Cemetery. He saw in his mind a clear image of Greenwood Cemetery; it was on a low hill and among many white stones there were many green trees through which the wind blew in the sunlight, and in the middle there was a heap of flowers and beneath the flowers, in his closed coffin, looking exactly as he had looked this morning, lay his father. Only it was dark, so he could not be seen. It would always be dark there. Dark as the inside of a cow.

The sun's agonna shine, and the wind's agonna blow.

The charcoal scraping of the needle against the record was in his ears and he saw the many sharp grinning teeth in Buster Brown's dog.

"If anything ever makes me believe in God," his uncle said.

Rufus looked up at him quickly. He was still looking straight ahead, and he still looked angry but his voice was not angry.

"Or life after death," his uncle said.

They were working and breathing rather hard, for they were walking westward up the steep hill towards Fort Sanders. The sky ahead of them was bright and they walked among the bright, moving shadows of trees.

"It'll be what happened this afternoon."

Rufus looked up at him carefully.

"There were a lot of clouds," his uncle said, and continued to look straight before him, "but they were blowing fast so there was a lot of sunshine too. Right when they began to lower your father into the ground, into his grave, a cloud came over and there was a shadow just like iron, and a perfectly magnificent butterfly settled on the . . . coffin, just rested there, right over the breast, and stayed there, just barely making his wings breathe, like a heart." Hugh stopped and for the first time looked at Rufus. His eyes were desperate. "He stayed there all the way down, Rufus," he said. "He never stirred, except just to move his wings that way, until it grated against the bottom like a . . . rowboat. And just when it did the sun came out just dazzling bright and he flew up out of that—hole in the ground, straight up into the sky, so high I couldn't even see him any more." He began to climb the hill again, and Rufus worked hard again to stay abreast of him. "Don't you think that's wonderful, Rufus?" he said, again looking straight and despairingly before him.

"Yes," Rufus said, aware that his uncle really was asking him; "yes": he was sure was not enough, but it was all he could say.

"If there are any such things as miracles," his uncle said, as if someone were arguing with him, "then *that's* surely miraculous."

Miraculous. Magnificent. He was sure he had better not ask what they were. He saw a great butterfly clearly, and how he moved his wings so quietly and grandly, and the colors of the wings, and how he sprang straight up into the sky and how the colors all took fire in the sunshine, and he felt that he probably had a fair idea what magnificent meant.

But miraculous. He still saw the butterfly, which was resting there again, waving his great wings. Maybe miraculous was the way the colors were streaks and spots in patterns on the wings, or the bright flickering way they worked in the light when he flew fast, straight upwards. Miraculous. Magnificent.

He could see it very clearly, because his uncle saw it so clearly when he told about it, and what he saw made him feel that a special and good thing was happening. He felt that it was good for his father and that lying there in the darkness did not matter so much. He did not know what this good thing was, but because his uncle felt that it was good, and felt so strongly about it, it must be even more of a good thing than he himself could comprehend. His uncle even spoke of believing in God, or anyway, *if* anything could ever make him believe in God, and he had never before heard his uncle speak of God except as if he disliked Him, or anyway, disliked people who believed in Him. So it must be about as good a thing as a thing could be. And suddenly he began to realize that his uncle told it to him, out of everyone he might have told it to, and he breathed in a deep breath of pride and of love. He would not admit it to those who did believe in God, and he would not tell it to those who didn't, because he cared so much about it and they might sneer at it, but he had to tell somebody, so he told it to him. And it made it much better than it had been, about his father, and about his not being let to be there at just that time he most needed to be there; it was all right now almost. It was not all right about his father because his father could never come back again, but it was better than it had been anyway, and it was all right about his not being let be there, because now it was almost as if he had been there and seen it with his own eyes, and seen the butterfly, which showed that even for his father, it was all right. It was all right and he felt as his uncle did. There was nobody else, not even his mother, not even his father if he could, that he ever wanted to tell, or talk about it to. Not even his uncle, now that it was told.

"And *that* son of a bitch!" Hugh said.

He was not quite sure what it meant but he knew it was the worst thing you could call anybody; call anybody that, they had to fight, they had a right to kill you. He felt as if he had been hit in the stomach.

"That Robertson," Hugh said; and now he looked so really angry that Rufus realized that he had not been at all angry before. "'*Father*' Robertson," Hugh said, "as he insists on being called.

"Do you know what he did?"

He glared at him so, that Rufus was frightened. "What?" he asked.

"He said he couldn't read the complete, the complete burial service over your father because your father had never been baptized." He kept glaring at Rufus; he seemed to be waiting for him to answer. Rufus looked up at him, feeling scared and stupid. He was glad his uncle did not like Father Robertson but that did not seem exactly the point, and he could not think of anything to say.

"He said he was deeply sorry," Hugh savagely caricatured the inflection, "but it was simply a rule of the Church."

"Some Church," he snarled. "And they call themselves Christians. Bury a man who's a hundred times the man *he'll* ever be, in his stinking swishing black petticoats, and a hundred times as good a man too, and 'no, there are certain requests and recommendations I cannot make Almighty God for the repose of this soul, for he never stuck his head under a holy-water tap.' Genuflecting, and ducking and bowing and scraping, and basting themselves with signs of the Cross, and all that disgusting hocus-pocus, and you come to one simple single act of Christian charity and what happens? The rules of the Church forbid it. He's not a member of our little club.

"I tell you, Rufus, it's enough to make a man puke up his soul.

"That . . . that butterfly has got more of God in him than Robertson will ever see for the rest of eternity.

"Priggish, mealy-mouthed son of a bitch."

They were standing at the edge of Fort Sanders and looking out across the waste of briars and of embanked clay, and Rufus was trying to hold his feelings intact. Everything had seemed so nearly all right, up to a minute ago, and now it was changed and confused. It was still all right, everything which had been, still was, he did not see how it could stop being, yet it was hard to remember it clearly and to remember how he had felt and why it had seemed all right, for since then his uncle had said so much. He was glad he did not like Father Robertson and he wished his mother did not like him either, but that was not all. His uncle had talked about God, and Christians, and faith, with as much hatred as he had seemed, a minute before, to talk with reverence or even with love. But it was worse than that. It was when he was talking about everybody bowing and scraping and hocus-pocus and things like that, that Rufus began to realize that he was talking not just about

Father Robertson but about all of them and that he hated all of them. He hates mother, he said to himself. He really honestly does hate her. Aunt Jessie too. He hates them. They don't hate him at all, they love him, but he hates them. But he doesn't hate them, really, he thought. He could remember how many ways he had shown how fond he was of both of them, all kinds of ways, and most of all by how easy he was with them when nothing was wrong and everybody was having a good time, and by how he had been with them in this time too. He doesn't hate them, he thought, he loves them, just as much as they love him. But he hates them too. He talked about them as if he'd like to spit in their faces. When he's with them he's nice to them, he even likes them, loves them. When he's away from them and thinks about them saying their prayers and things, he hates them. When he's with them he just acts as if he likes them but this is how he really feels, all the time. He told me about the butterfly and he wouldn't tell them because he hates them but I don't hate them, I love them, and when he told me he told me a secret he wouldn't tell them as if I hated them too.

But they saw it too. They sure saw it too. So he didn't, he wouldn't tell them, there wouldn't be anything to tell. That's it. He told me because I wasn't there and he wanted to tell somebody and thought I would want to know and I do. But not if he hates them. And he does. He hates them just like opening a furnace door but he doesn't want them to know it. He doesn't want them to know it because he doesn't want to hurt their feelings. He doesn't want them to know it because he knows they love him and think he loves them. He doesn't want them to know it because he loves them. But how can he love them if he hates them so? How can he hate them if he loves them? Is he mad at them because they can say their prayers and he doesn't? He could if he wanted to, why doesn't he? Because he hates prayers. And them too for saying them.

He wished he could ask his uncle, "why do you hate Mama?" but he was afraid to. While he thought he looked now across the devastated Fort, and again into his uncle's face, and wished that he could ask. But he did not ask, and his uncle did not speak except to say, after a few minutes, "It's time to go home," and all the way home they walked in silence.

Textual Commentary and Notes

This section documents the step-by-step restoration of *A Death in the Family,* any significant editorial changes introduced (please see the "Preface" to this volume and "General Textual Method" for examples), and small variant sections of the manuscript under one hundred words in length that were not incorporated into the final text. Larger unincorporated variants are included in the section entitled "Major Manuscript Variants." This section also includes reference to the variants printed in error in the McDowell edition, but does not reproduce their texts. These printed McDowell variants are also noted in the section below in regard to the rationale for selecting the primary texts.

Each entry below begins with the page and line number of the present edition separated by a period. Thus, a note concerning something on page 4, line 24 of the text would be listed as 4.24. Chapter headings such as "*Chapter 1*" are included in this line count, but spaces included by Agee to separate sections of a chapter are not. Running heads and rules added by the printer to separate the running head from the text proper are also not included in this count. The text to the left of the square left-facing bracket is the matter that is under discussion. The material to the right of the bracket refers to Agee's original holograph manuscript and is a discussion of the manuscript (see 4.1) or the notation of an editorial change to the manuscript (see 4.24). Thus, 4.24 records that "too" in the restored text is a correction of "to" in Agee's manuscript. A solidus (/) within Agee's text to the left of the square bracket indicates a line break, usually in Agee's marginalia. Information provided by the editor in these notes is enclosed in parentheses (see 3.1–2). Occasionally this results in the double use of parentheses within a sentence or comment.

Please also refer to the "General Textual Method" section for other matters of editorial methodology.

Title Page   *A Death in the Family*]

The title is most likely one created by David McDowell. No evidence has yet been uncovered that would help determine Agee's intent regarding the title of the novel. He most often referred to it as "the book."

3.1–2 "towards the middle of the twentieth century"] (This and all other section headings—15.1–2, 49.1–2, 83.1–2, 141.1–2, 181.1–2, 203.1–2, 283.1–2, and 311.1–2—are supplied by the editor.)

Introduction

4.1 *Introduction*]

This and all other chapter headings from chapter 1 through chapter 45 are supplied by the editor. Only in a few isolated instances did Agee label or number his chapters or his manuscript pages.

The inclusion of this introductory chapter (TX 5.2, [45–53]) is certainly one of the more important decisions in restoring the novel. Victor A. Kramer has consistently argued in favor of it (most recently in 1996 in his *Agee: Selected Literary Documents,* 260–61), and David McDowell defended his original rejection of it as late as 1980 in an interview published in the *Western Humanities Review.* In that same interview McDowell notes that there were "two versions of that nightmare scene" (123), but any other complete version, if extant, has not been discovered. Two brief fragments that may possibly be part of the other version to which McDowell refers are recorded in "Major Manuscript Variants." See also the discussions in the "Preface" to this volume and "General Textual Method."

The external evidence that supports the nightmare introduction is twofold. It is a given that "Knoxville: Summer of 1915" was not part of Agee's plan for the novel, and no other section of Agee's known manuscripts can serve as an introduction. If an introduction was intended, the nightmare chapter, which features a severed head as its most powerful symbol, is the likeliest candidate. That it was intended as the introduction is also supported by two of his outlines for the novel in which Agee lists "head, as now" and "head as now" as the first subject treated (TX 5.1, [10, 11]). Since Agee normally described rather than numbered or entitled his chapters, his labeling the introduction in his outline with its most vivid image is a reasonable assumption. Likewise these notes record that his plan for the book was "Maximum simple: Just the story of my relation with my father and, through that, as thorough as possible an image of him: winding into other things on the way but never dwelling on them" (TX 5.1, [15]). This introduction to the restored novel admirably fulfills his purpose by moving the narrator in the present through a surreal adventure of intermingled self-analysis, guilt, religion, anger, doubt, and loneliness, then stripping him "as naked as the man he dragged" (10.2–3), and ultimately allowing him to find the meaning of his search in the quest itself—a return to his earliest years: "he could make the journey, as he had dreamed the dream, for its own sake, without trying to interpret; and if the journey was made with sufficient courage and care, very likely that of itself would be as near the answer as he could ever hope to get" (13.9–12).

Much of the compelling internal evidence that argues for this section's inclusion as the introduction occurs at its end, after the narrator awakes from his dream and identifies the corpse as his father: before, in the dream, it was "John the Baptist" (5.5); now, awake and with the link of a beheading in both instances, it was "his father [who] had come out of the wilderness . . ." (12.18). The narrator interprets the dream at some length (12.5–13.38) and provides direct connections between the nightmare introduction and the text of the novel, connections that begin to become completely evident in the following extract that ends with the previously noted hope of the "journey" bringing him "near the answer":

> *He thought of his father in his grave, over seven hundred miles away, and how many years. If he could only talk with him.* But he knew that even if they could talk, they could never come at it between them, what the betrayal was.
>
> *He thought of the dream. He had no doubt of the terrifying magnitude of the dream, or that its meaning was the meaning he sought, but he doubted so thoroughly that the true meaning of any dream could ever be known,* that he suspected that every effort to interpret a dream serves only to obscure and to distort what little of the true meaning may ultimately suggest itself.
>
> He thought of all he could remember about his father and about his own direct relations with him. He could see nothing which even faintly illuminated his darkness, nor did he expect ever to see anything; *yet if he could be sure of anything except betrayal and horror, he could be sure that that was where the dream indicated that he should go. He should go back into those years. As far as he could remember; and everything he could remember; nothing he had learned or done since; nothing except (so well as he could remember) what his father had been as he had known him, and what he had been as he had known himself, and what he had seen with his own eyes, and supposed with his own mind.*
>
> *The more he thought of it the surer he became that there was nothing he could hope to understand out of it which was not already obvious to him. All the same, he could make the journey, as he had dreamed the dream, for its own sake, without trying to interpret; and if the journey was made with sufficient courage and care, very likely that of itself would be as near the answer as he could ever hope to get.* (12.24–13.12; italics added for emphasis)

This introduction thus provides the rationale for the novel Agee intended, the literal reason for its being written: "All his life, as he had begun during recent years to realize, had been shaped above all else by his father and by his father's absence" (13.23–24). The introduction also brings the character of the father and the father-son relationship from a distant position in the wings of the McDowell edition and places both stage center in the retelling of their shared and remembered lives. As the narrator states, "that was where the dream indicated that he should go. He should go back into those years. As far as he could remember; and everything he could remember; nothing he had learned or done since; nothing except (so well as he could remember) what his father had been as he had known him, and what he had been as he had known himself, and what he had seen with his own eyes, and supposed with his own mind." Agee's draft letters to his father and to his mother echo these statements. (See appendices V and VI.)

Mute support for this decision comes as well in the "waking" part of the introduction from the immediate appearance of the comforting apparition of the father in the restored introduction. The vision presents the father

> not as the son could remember him, but was as he would have become by that time, by that morning of awakening from the dream: a strong, brave, sad old man, who also knew the dream, and no more knew or hoped ever to know its meaning, than the son. . . . And here he was, and all was well at last, and even though he was now rapidly fading, and most likely would never return, that was all right too. It might never be fully understood, but it would be all right from now on. From now on it was going to be all right. Thank you for coming, he said in silence. Goodbye. God keep you. Or whatever it is that keeps you.
>
> His father did not say goodbye, anymore than the other time, but he knew of his brief smile, much as it had always been, and then he was gone.
>
> He was alone again now, but that was no harm, for in a way in which he had been alone for so many years, he knew that he would never be alone again. (13.17–38)

Not only does the vision of the father help to end the effects of the nightmare and solidify the narrator's resolve to make the journey back to childhood, but it also makes clear reference to "the other time," the first apparition of his father's spirit immediately after his accidental death that likewise gave so much comfort to some of the distressed family (258.38–264.11) and provided a subject for debate over the existence of spirits and over the belief in reason versus faith for others in the novel proper (265.8–268.3). Rufus and his sister Emma were asleep during this first visit of their father's spirit and never received any closure, if such is possible for children aged six and four, through it. The introduction, moreover, is both a conclusion and a beginning. It is a conclusion since it allows Rufus to consummate the search for his father and join with him spiritually, but it is also the beginning, the dream and the waking analysis of the dream, that sets him off on his search back in time to his earliest memories. The journey is necessary because the first apparition of Jay's spirit in the body of the novel marks a union that is never brought to such a positive conclusion for Rufus' mother despite the prolonged and intimate contact with her husband's spirit. The parting of Laura from Jay's spirit is in fact quite different than that of the adult narrator's:

> "Be with us all you can," she whispered: "This is goodbye"; and again she went to her knees. Goodbye, she said again, within herself; but she was unable to feel much of anything. "God help me to *realize* it," she whispered, and clasped her hands before her face: but she could realize only that he was fading, and that it was indeed goodbye, and that she was at that moment unable to be particularly sensitive to the fact.
>
> And now he was gone entirely from the room, from the house, and from this world.
>
> "Soon, Jay. Soon, dear," she whispered; but she knew that it would not be soon. She knew that a long life lay ahead of her, for the children were to be brought up, and God alone could know what change and chance might work upon them all, before they met once more. She felt at once a calm and annihilating emptiness, and a cold and overwhelming fulness. (263.33–264.8)

Her union with her husband is postponed and the "calm and annihilating emptiness, and a cold overwhelming fulness" she feels is far less comforting than the narrator's realization in the restored introduction that "From now on it was going to be all right"; she receives none of the solace of his departing father's "brief smile" that declared "that he would never be alone again."

The use of the apparition clearly ties this introduction to the structure of the novel proper, and the simple acceptance and peace that mark its "waking" part are just as much the result of the spiritual and intellectual agonizing in the text over the father's death as of the narrator's nightmare. Both in a sense are rituals of purgation, but only through this introduction does the path to transcendence and acceptance become truly evident.

Similar foregrounding likewise links the nightmare portion of the introduction to the body of the novel through two powerful images—the emphasis upon the head of the body the narrator carries and upon the vacant lot with the rock and tree that is their final destination.

The image of the head is perhaps the more vivid of the two as it transforms from simply a "killed head" (6.28–29) to something like a severed "frightened animal" that then transforms into "one organ, so disfigured, that it was impossible to know whether it was a bloody glaring eye, or a mutely roaring mouth" (11.34, 12.2–4). An echo of this transformation in the novel also draws it together with the nightmare introduction. It occurs when Laura tries to go to sleep after the impact of her husband's death begins to register fully: "She lay straight on her back with her hands open, upward at her sides and could just make out, in the subtly diminished darkness, a familiar stain which at various times had seemed to resemble a crag, a galleon, a fish, a brooding head. Tonight it was just itself, with one meaningless eye" (281.1–5).

The image of the head is likewise tied directly to the body of the novel in that the very first mention of the father's accident through a telephone stimulates an immediate and prescient thought in Laura's mind:

> "Is this Miz James Agee?"
>
> "Yes; what is it?" (for there was a silence); "yes, this is she."
>
> After further silence the voice said, "There's been a slight—your husband has been in a accident."
>
> His head! she told herself.
>
> "Yes," she said, in a caved-in voice. At the same moment the voice said, "A serious accident." (204.11–17)

She later realizes that she never asked about where Jay was injured, saying, "I guess because I was so sure. Sure it's his head, that is" (205.35). Similarly, when confirmation comes from Hugh, her brother, that Jay is dead, he continues to say

> "Laura, I saw him—at Roberts'. There was just one mark on his body."
>
> She looked at him. "His head."
>
> "Right at the exact point of the chin, a small bruise. A cut so small—they can close it with one stitch. And a little blue bruise on his lower lip. It wasn't even swollen."
>
> "That's all," she said.
>
> "All," Jessie said.
>
> "That's all," Hugh said. "The doctor said it was concussion of the brain. It was instantaneous." (230.29–38)

A link between this scene and the introduction may well have been intended by Agee to emphasize the contrast established between the descriptions of the head. The fact that Rufus, his childhood companions, and many of the adults find it hard to believe that Jay could be killed by a blow to his head without profound disfigurement may provide the rationale for the inclusion of the overtly graphic description of the head in the nightmare part of the introduction. It finally makes the death real. It also makes it more sacred. When the narrator "slid both hands beneath it and lifted its cold and gritty weight as if it were a Grail" (11.36–38), the head becomes part of a sacramental communion, the vessel that held the blood of Christ, again providing a vivid contrast between this wake at the vacant lot where the dead man "wanted to lie for a while before burial" (6.34–35) and the formality of the actual wake in the novel where Rufus and his little sister Emma are shielded from the emotions of the event and essentially excluded from participating in it:

> "Now children," their mother said, lowering her face above them. "We're all going in, to see Daddy, just once more. But we won't be able to stay, we can just look for a moment. And then you'll see your Grandma Agee, just for a moment. And then Mr. Savage will take you down again to his house and Mother will see you again later this afternoon." (341.13–17)

A final connection is forged earlier in the novel when the narrator describes the moment when Hugh and Arthur Savage, a family friend, had to identify Jay's body near the site of the accident, a scene that naturally focuses upon the head but also emphasizes the powerful effect this viewing of the body had:

> They watched him with the wonder which is felt in the presence of anything which is great and new, and, for a little while, in any place where violence has recently occurred; they were aware, as they gazed at the still head, of a prodigious kind of energy in the air. (269.8–12)

The introduction and the novel proper are again thus remarkably linked, not simply by the predominant image of the head, but as well by the idea of a "great and new" event and the "prodigious kind of energy in the air" in a "place where violence has recently occurred."

The second major image of the nightmare sequence, the vacant lot with its rock and tree that is the final destination of the narrator and the body he carries, also clearly ties the introduction to the novel proper. The lot first surfaces in the introduction when the narrator picks up the dead man and says

> We're going to find you a better place to rest than this. We're going to find you a place where you can lie out in the open, but in honor and in state. Laid out decently as a dead man ought to be. Where everyone who goes by can know you for a dead man and a hero. He squatted down and put his arms under the shoulders and under the knees and picked him up and carried him like a baby, but with the killed head lolling deep and heavy. The place you want to be, he whispered, as he started walking; and instantly he knew where that place was, and how to get there, though it was so many years now since he had been in Knoxville. He was pleased that he could remember the way so well. It was a certain corner, a certain vacant lot; he could already see it vividly in his mind's eye. That was where John wanted to lie for a while before burial and that was where he would bring him. (6.23–35)

As they come near to the vacant lot as a place for this personal wake, in opposition to the formal wake Rufus barely experienced as a child, the narrator's comments make clear that the site of the lot holds great power for him and was, in fact, being *re*visited:

> He looked ahead to see how far they must still go, not far, he could remember, and sure enough he could see it, with a flinching deep within him of tenderness and joy and melancholy and great loneliness, he could see it, the very corner, the same outcrop of wrinkled limestone, like a lump of dirty laundry, the same tree even, and the tree had not even grown an inch. So shabby and sad; it had been waiting there all this time, and it had never changed, not a bit. So patient, and aloofly welcoming. Well. So you came back. His cold heart lifted in love and he walked more quickly. . . . (11.14–22)

While in the novel proper this "welcoming" corner occupies only one scene of slightly more than a thousand words, it immediately echoes the descriptions of the introduction:

> The young leaves of Forest Avenue wavered against street lamps and they approached their corner.
>
> It was a vacant lot, part rubbed slick clay, part overgrown with weeds, rising a little from the sidewalk. A few feet in from the sidewalk there was a medium sized tree and, near enough to be within its shade in daytime, a high outcrop of limestone like a great bundle of dirty laundry. It was not wise to sit too near the tree, for it smelled bad there ("ornery sons a bitches," his father had once said; "Reckon they got dog blood"); but the rock was a very good place to sit and if you sat on a certain part of it the trunk of the tree shut off the weak street lamp a block away, and it seemed very dark. (150.1–11; please see also the note for 150.6 in chapter 17 in this section)

This description by Rufus reaches back to the introduction even to the point of repeating the distinctive image of the "outcrop" of "limestone" looking like "dirty laundry" and sets before the reader the fact that the stop there was part of their past pattern of their behavior for it was "*their* corner" (emphasis mine). This particular time, however, the situation is somewhat different because young Rufus realizes that this lot provides the place and time where he and his father achieve a spiritual union. In the waking part of the nightmare, the narrator links the images of head and lot together to contrast their effect upon him: "the head had come off just short of the corner, and it was he who was responsible. The corner was where he used to sit with his father and it was there of all times and places that he had known best that his father loved him, and had known not only that he loved him but that he was glad of his existence and that he thought well of him" (12.13–18).

The lot casts the same spell in the novel proper:

> Up to recently, he had always said something about Rufus' being tired, when they were still about a block away from the corner; but lately he had not done so, and Rufus realized that his father stopped as much

> because he wanted to, as on Rufus' account. He was just not in a hurry to get home, Rufus realized; and, far more important, it was clear that he liked to spend these few minutes with Rufus. Rufus had come recently to feel a quiet kind of anticipation of the corner, from the moment they finished crossing the viaduct; and, during the ten to twenty minutes they sat on the rock, a particular kind of contentment, unlike any other that he knew. He did not know what this was, in words or ideas, or what the reason was; it was simply all that he saw and felt. It was, mainly, knowing that his father, too, felt a particular kind of contentment, here, unlike any other, and that their kinds of contentment were much alike, and depended on each other. Rufus seldom had at all sharply the feeling that he and his father were estranged, yet they must have been, and he must have felt it, for always during these quiet moments on the rock a part of his sense of complete contentment lay in the feeling that they were reconciled, that there was really no division, no estrangement, or none so strong, anyhow, that it could mean much, by comparison with the unity that was so firm and assured, here. (150.33–151.15)

It is no wonder that the narrator in the introduction refuses to rest until he brings the body to this same vacant lot, and that upon waking he eventually understands his dream and again achieves a spiritual union with his father that allows him to recapture the intimacy and contentment so emphasized in the scene noted above.

This union also contains the city versus country dichotomy that defines the father and fosters a shared dependence, just as the bonding of father and son links them both to a larger and far older heritage of the mountains of East Tennessee. Rufus

> knew that a very important part of his [father's] well-being came of staying a few minutes away from home, very quietly, in the dark, listening to the leaves if they moved, and looking at the stars; and that his own, Rufus' own presence, was fully as indispensable to this well-being. He knew that each of them knew of the other's well-being, and of the reasons for it, and knew how each depended on the other, how each meant more to the other, in this most important of all ways, than anyone or anything else in the world; and that the best of this well-being lay in this mutual knowledge, which was neither concealed nor revealed. He knew these things very distinctly, but not, of course, in any such way as we have of suggesting them in words. There were no words, or even ideas, or formed emotions, of the kind that have been suggested here, no more in the man than in the boy child: these realizations moved clearly through the senses, the memory, the feelings, the mere feeling of the place they paused at, about a quarter of a mile from home, on a rock under a stray tree that had grown in the city, their feet on undomesticated clay, facing north through the night over the Southern railway tracks and over North Knoxville, towards the deeply folded small mountains and

> the Powell River Valley; and above them, the trembling lanterns of the universe, seeming so near, so intimate, that when air stirred the leaves and their hair, it seemed to be the breathing, the whispering of the stars. Sometimes on these evenings his father would hum a little and the humming would break open into a word or two, but he never finished even a part of a tune, for silence was even more pleasurable, and sometimes he would say a few words, of very little consequence, but would never seek to say much, or to finish what he was saying, or to listen for a reply; for silence again was even more pleasurable. (151.21–152.10)

Despite his great love for his family and the consequent need to be in the city of Knoxville to provide well for them, Jay's yearning for his first home, the "deeply folded small mountains and the Powell River Valley," for the freedom and rejuvenation that that rugged life held out to him, is a constant part of his depiction in the novel. It likewise is a feeling and more than a feeling that is passed on to his son. The narrator's first self-descriptive comment in the introduction characterizes his walking as "the loose stride inherited from the mountains" (4.20–21). While of no great weight on its own, this comment adds to the sense of unity between father and son and to the vacant lot that effectively mediates between city and mountain life.

To my mind, these sections of substantial internal connections between the introduction and the body of the novel and the external evidence of Agee's "Maximum simple" plan for his book and his outlines for the novel all combine to form a convincing argument for the inclusion of this nightmare introduction. It both unifies the text and adds intensity to Rufus' subsequent childhood recollections by foregrounding them in his adult present. For additional evidence, see note 339.15–21 below. The importance of explaining the dream and using it as a tool for self-understanding may reflect as well Agee's ongoing interest in Freudian and Jungian psychoanalysis, especially in relationship to surrealism. On this topic, see Hugh Davis, "The Making of James Agee," Ph.D. dissertation, University of Tennessee, 2005, pp. 173–204, and Laurence Bergreen, *James Agee: A Life* (New York: E. P. Dutton, 1984), pp. 82–83, 152–53, 374.

4.24 too] to

8.16 plowlike] (The word "plowlike" is written above "the underside" without a caret by Agee and is included by the editor.)

8.28 on both sides] (This phrase is written interlinearly above "houses, an" in the manuscript and is inserted before the comma by the editor.)

9.4–11 But when he . . . with every second.] (An earlier version of this passage precedes Agee's final version in the manuscript. It reads: "But when he bent low to lift him again the smell had become so sickening that he had immediately to straighten up into the clean air. He stood there a few seconds and thought about it, with his stomach knocking and his mouth flooding saliva. He knew that it was going to be more than

	he could do, to carry him now. The whole body had softened and was streaked with brown, and it seemed that the stench became still worse with every second." Agee often redrafted sentences and paragraphs immediately after his first draft and, as in this case, sometimes forgot to mark them for deletion.)
10.10	cut] (This word is overwritten and difficult to make out with complete assurance, but seems very likely given the context.)
10.26	weird] wierd
12.24	over seven hundred miles away] (This distance may well place the narrator in New York City, one of Agee's major places of residence.)

Chapter 1

16.1 *Chapter 1*]

David McDowell chooses to print an earlier version (TX 5.3, [33–35]) of this chapter (TX 5.2, [22–24]. (Please see "Major Manuscript Variants" for corrections to his transcription.) He then combined it with other chapters and included it out of order as part of the first batch of italicized "flashback" materials in the published novel (80–83). It is clear that the present text is a separate chapter. The manuscript pages are numbered "1", "2", "3" by Agee (one of the few instances of page numbering in the work), and the text ends before the midpoint of manuscript page [24], with the rest of the page left blank.

The evidence also is quite strong that this edition's version is a later version of the earlier draft that McDowell printed. The chart below presents a sample of this evidence.

	Restored Edition	McDowell Edition/TX 5.3
16.25	The word "All" which begins the sentence is crossed out and the "t" of "The" is capitalized	"All the" begins the sentence
17.6	"Somewhere very" is struck out and "near" is changed to "Nearby"	"Somewhere very near" begins the sentence
17.15–16	Adds "breathing, without words," after "peace,"	"peace." ends the sentence
18.3	"astonished or bewildered" is struck out and "dismayed" is written over these words	The text reads "astonished or bewildered"
18.12	"Surely fear can never enter me:" is added to the sentence	No material added
18.28–29	"and who establish quiet and beauty for their gathering;" is added	No material added

There are other significant differences in the two manuscripts, but those above do the most to establish the priority of the restored text for inclusion in the novel.

The placement of TX 5.2, [22–24] as the first chapter in the restored edition is determined both by the need for a chronological sequence of events to meet Agee's plan for the novel as discussed in the "Introduction" to this edition and by his notes. TX 5.1 records "Open at night." and "Summer. (start)." and "Summer opening:" on pages [15], [7], and [5] respectively, and chapter 1 begins with "He woke in darkness" (16.2) and states "He heard the summer night" (16.24). Similarly, in a list of major events to include in the work, Agee begins with "*Waking*" [8]. While the notes in TX 5.1 alone cannot be considered conclusive evidence, they do support the present placement of the chapter as does an adherence to chronology.

It is also noteworthy that even though McDowell incorrectly combined chapters to make the flashback sections of the novel, his text has been further degraded in subsequent paperback editions (I use the Bantam 1969 edition for illustrative purposes) that substitute small spaces for breaks that were originally chapter separations (97 [four lines of space], 102 [no space at all, since the previous chapters text ended on the last line of a page], 213 [joined to McDowell's chapter 13 with only one line of space], 227 [one line of space], 241 [three lines of space]).

16.4	ceiling] cieling
16.28	Hoofs] Hooves
16.29	with] (Added for clarity by editor.)
18.7–8	I know my] (There are two indications as to the placement of this interlinear insertion. A caret places it after the word "laughter", and an arrow places it after the original phrase "is my best", which Agee simply did not cross out or mark for deletion. Either placement requires the deletion. Otherwise the first choice would read "in their laughter I know my is my best delight" and the second "in their laughter is my best I know my delight.")
18.24–25	(The space inserted between the sentence that ends with "to sleep" and the new paragraph that begins with "You come" reflects the space left at the bottom of TX 5.2, [23] before Agee resumed on the top of [24] and the switch to second-person narration.)
18.31	mountains] (No punctuation comes after this word in the manuscript, perhaps to encourage its linkage with the next line.)
18.35	(Agee often separates sections within a chapter and quotations by skipping a line, and these breaks occasionally occur at the bottom of a page in this edition, somewhat obscuring the separation. Such separations occur at the bottom of pages 18, 41, 43, 46, 55, 57, 122, and 352.)

Chapter 2

20.1 *Chapter 2*]

While the text of its opening clearly links this chapter in proper sequence as following chapter 1, chapter 2 is also a separate chapter (see note 16.1) as it begins on a separate, now unnumbered page. The pencil script is darker on these two manuscript pages (TX 5.2, [25–26]) than on the three previous pages. The paper itself is also somewhat darker and has matching corner smudges that do not appear on the manuscript pages for chapter 1.

The evidence in this chapter again is quite strong that this edition's version is a later version of the earlier draft that McDowell printed. TX 5.3, the source of McDowell's materials, has several versions of this chapter. McDowell rightly skips those pages [35 (partial), 36, 37, 38] and uses pages [41–42], the most finished of the TX 5.3 versions (pages 84–86 of the novel). (Please see "Major Manuscript Variants" for corrections to his transcription.)

The chart below presents samples of the evidence for using TX 5.2, [25–26]. While several of these changes are equivocal as to establishing the final version of the chapter, 20.25, 21.11, , and 22.3 show that 5.2 is a later version of 5.3.

	Restored Edition	McDowell Edition/TX 5.3
20.2–3	The sentence "He could feel . . . an iceberg." is added by Agee	Not present
20.3	"terrible" is an interlinear addition by Agee	Not present
20.5–6	Agee deletes a paragraph (by bracketing it) that was in rough essence reduced to the sentence added (20.2–3)	Page 84, paragraph 3. Paragraph 6 is similarly deleted
20.25	"You hear" is struck out and "Listen to" is added interlineally above it	"You hear" is present
21.11	"vex" is incorporated into the text and no alternative is noted	"vex" is written above "grieve" and no choice is made
21.16	"withdrew and watched, speechless and cold, and the other" is added by Agee	Not present
22.3	"Deadly," is incorporated into the text as the introduction to "the opposite"	"Deadly," is added to the left of the original start of the sentence "The opposite"

These revisions, particularly the paragraph deletions, also reinforce his philosophy of "Maximum simple" (always qualified by the fact that Agee's "Maximum simple" might not be all that simple) for which he was striving in the novel.

20.11 Know] (Agee's capitalization. Capitalizations for emphasis are generally not noted and are retained.)

Chapter 3

23.1 *Chapter 3*]

This chapter clearly follows the chronological sequence of the novel since it begins with Rufus' parents hearing his scream that was recorded on the final line of chapter 2 (22.8): "He screamed for his father." It also begins on a separate page that bears the number "2." centered at its head, likely indicating an early placement within the novel and that perhaps it was once its second chapter. Further support for this view comes from one of Agee's outlines for the book in which the first subject listed—"head, as now" (see note 4.1)—is followed on the next line by "(Long 2) Chapter on domestic pleasures. Advance time. Set up all characters etc. Bring car in this far back?" (TX 5.1, [10]). This chapter that Agee labeled "2." is quite long and does do most of what the outline lists. Agee ultimately chooses not to bring the car into the narrative "this far back" in the story. The restored version also omits the father and mother's discussion of her pregnancy that concludes this section of McDowell's flashback, delaying the introduction of "the surprise" that is later used so effectively to confound young Rufus.

Once again, the evidence in this chapter is quite strong that this edition's version is a later version of the earlier draft that McDowell printed. The corrections to the version printed by McDowell are recorded in the "Major Manuscript Variants" section of this book. TX 5.3, [43–48], the source of McDowell's materials, is clearly updated in TX 5.2, which has as well several working versions of various sections of this chapter. The 5.2 manuscript was in some disarray when examined, but Agee's final version is reconstructed as follows with my numbering again reflecting the original order of the manuscript leaves: [27–30, 32, 31, 36, 41]. The last three pages are coded with an encircled capital "A" in the upper right-hand corner by Agee and provide reasonable evidence that he wished to group them together.

The chart below presents samples of the evidence for using TX 5.2. While several of these changes are equivocal as to establishing the final version of the chapter, 25.5, 25.8–10, 25.13–14, 26.9, 28.29–30, and 31.37 show that 5.2 is a later version of 5.3 that was published on pages 87–96. Further support comes from the questions to himself that Agee records in the margins of 5.3. No marginal questions are present in 5.2. For other earlier versions of sections of this chapter, see the section entitled "Major Manuscript Variants."

	Restored Edition	McDowell Edition/TX 5.3
23.6–7	“, almost frightened and defending and reproving” is added interlinearly by Agee	Not present
23.21–22	“and squatted by the bed.” is added interlinearly by Agee	Not present
23.29	“whole” is added interlinearly by Agee	Not present
25.5	“firetipped” incorporated into the primary text with no alternative noted	“firetipped” is written above “lighted” and no choice is made
25.8–10	“while his father too remembered, how he . . . and how it was already too late.” is incorporated into the primary text	“His father too remembered, how he . . . and how it was now too late.” is an insertion
25.13–14	“He glanced anxiously at his father.” is incorporated into the primary text with no crossed-out section	“looked anxiously at his father” is crossed out and rewritten as “glanced anxiously at his father.”
26.9	“while he gazed” is incorporated into the primary text with no crossed-out words	“*the[?]* child” is crossed out between “while” and “he”
27.24	“*car*-wheells” is incorporated into the primary text	“train wheels” is the original phrase and “car” is written above “train” and “cars” above “wheels”
28.29–30	Agee deletes an expanded version of what McDowell prints between “Sugar-Babe” and “If he”. The deletion incorporates a change in the order of presenting the words “father” and “mother” in McDowell’s text and substitutes “daddy’s” for “her father’s”	Three paragraphs present from “A great cedar” to “break your heart.” (McD 94.8–95.5)
28.30–31.28	This section expands and replaces the two next paragraphs printed by McDowell	The two paragraphs are from “He felt thirsty” to “for these emotions.” (McD 95.6–21)
31.37	“tell you” is incorporated into the primary text	“tell you” is an interlinear addition to the text

Other evidence for the restored version comes from TX 5.4, [44]. That page of notes states:

> Shorten J’s recall & meditation. less soft.
> If argument is used she says: I’m not used to being talked to liked that.
> But probably: shorten that too, keep it in the one room. She asks him what he was doing, last, not first.
>
> She senses the anger, but not the self-reproach—as if an angry animal in a cave.
>
> J’s past life?

Both the restored and McDowell’s versions are shortened overall, but the restored version, and all the TX 5.2 variants for that matter, are much “less soft” than McDowell’s. Compare 31.5–30 to McD 95.6–22. Similarly the restored version mentions "self-reproach" (31.28), "fury . . . like an animal in a cave" (31.29), and the inner monolog "Jay I'm simply not going to stand for this any longer, she wanted to say" (32.12–13), all of which reflect Agee's notes for revision stated above.

The conformity to these notes, when added to the textual evidence given above, indicates clearly that McDowell chose to print an earlier version of the chapter, one that again presents a less complex characterization of Jay.

23.7	defending and] defending &
23.29	whole] (The word "whole" is written above "his chest" without a caret by Agee and is included by the editor.)
25.12	comfort,] comfort
26.9	sassafras] sassafrass
26.36	"I got a . . . my baby"] (Quotation marks added for this line and all subsequent lines or excerpts from lines of the songs.)
27.24	"*Ohhh,* I *hear* . . . a-*rum*blinn,"] (Quotation marks added for this line and all subsequent lines or excerpts from lines of the songs.)
27.34	*reckon* I see?] *reckon* I see,?
28.5	darky] Darky
28.5	Victoria] (Although not introduced fully until chapter 7 in the paragraph beginning on 63.31, Victoria is mentioned here and on 34.27 (see below). Victoria is an African American nurse-midwife who assists Laura in the birth of both Rufus and Emma and for a time immediately after their births.)
29.28	*Don't you fret.*] Don't you fret. (Italics are added to distinguish the interior monolog.)
29.32	*Don't you fret.*] Don't you fret. (Italics are added to distinguish the interior monolog.)
30.1	*Now don't you fret.*] Now don't you fret. (Italics are added to distinguish the interior monolog.)

Chapter 4

33.1	*Chapter 4*]

McDowell properly chooses the latest version of this section to print (TX 5.3, [49–51]. A previous editor, probably McDowell, has numbered the manuscript pages "1", "2", and "3" and has written "IV" at the beginning and conclusion of the chapter. Corrections to McDowell's version are incorporated silently into the restored chapter. The version present in TX 5.2 is incomplete and is a version of its last page (TX 5.3, [51]) and adds a bit to it before presenting an earlier version of parts of chapter 5. It is recorded in the "Major Manuscript Variants" section of this book.

This chapter of the restored edition clearly follows chapter 3 in the chronological sequence of the novel since much of chapter 3 involves Rufus' father singing to him and this chapter begins with “His mother sang to him too.” McDowell also follows the same immediate placement of this chapter in his flashback section (McD 97.1–101.29), even though he chose to use an earlier draft of chapter 3 to precede it.

The manuscript chapter opens with a deleted section of seven lines which Agee rewrites immediately below that section.

33.3–4 “Sleep baby sleep . . . the sheep”] (Quotation marks added for this line and all subsequent lines or excerpts from lines of the songs.)

34.2–4 (Quotation marks added.)

34.10 “care”] care

34.21–29 (Quotation marks added.)

34.27 , more like Victoria] (Omitted by McDowell since in his edition no reference to Victoria has yet been made due to his change in the order of the chapters and use of flashbacks.)

34.31 *l*] 1

35.19 his father] (The manuscript [page 50] reads “*and after a while* his father” (italics mine). Agee’s inadvertent repetition (the italicized words) have been deleted.)

36.4 Whiskey.] Whisky.

36.15–16 over the back of it] (In the manuscript [page 51], “over” is followed by “it” and then the “t” of “it” is crossed out. Agee’s inadvertent retention of the “i” of “it” has been deleted since his intended revision is clear.)

Chapter 5

37.1 *Chapter 5*]

This new chapter from manuscript TX 5.2, [8–16] follows the chronological sequence of the novel as Rufus moves from the perceptions of his parents to perceptions of members of his mother’s and father’s families. A short early outline of the novel (TX 5.1, [8]) does in fact list “*Tylers*” and “*Agees*” as sections. Other sections noted eventually become a single chapter (“*Park*” [Chilhowee Park] becomes chapter 11) or several chapters (“*Death*” occupies much of the latter one-third of the book). While no conclusive evidence can be drawn from Agee’s list, it does demonstrate that his intent to include substantial material on his immediate and extended family was established early in his thinking about the novel. The present chapter is a revised version of TX 5.2, [1–7]. Pages [1–4] and [7] are an earlier version of pages [8-16], and pages [5] and [6] form a version and extension of TX 5.3, [51] as previously noted and already transcribed in the “Major Manuscript Variants” for chapter 4. This overlap and intersection of TX 5.2, [1–7] (variant of chapter 5) with TX 5.2, [8–16] (chapter 5) and hence also with TX 5.3, [49–51] (chapter 4) also underscores the sequential link of these manuscripts.

38.15 Grampa] (Agee is not consistent in the novel in his spelling of "Grampa" whether he is referring to the same individual or to the maternal (Tyler) versus paternal (Agee) sides of the family. The same holds true for variations of "Granma" (38.17). No attempt to regularize these spellings is made, but any instance in which confusion might exist as to which branch of the family is referred is clarified in these notes. These grandparents are the Tylers.)

38.18–39.1 "Talk very loud . . . learn without trying"] (Quotation marks are added throughout this section and throughout the rest of this chapter, but only for what seems to be direct speech. Most of the chapter might best be described as a type of interior monolog, and in those instances no quotation marks are added by the editor.)

39.15–40.3 (Quotation marks added.)

39.26 mouth full] mouthful

40.25–44.18 (Quotation marks added.)

40.32 Sometimes daddy leaned] (These words begin page 5.2, [11]. The three previous manuscript pages have been numbered "1", "2", and "3" in the upper right-hand corner apparently by Agee, but are linked to the subsequent unnumbered pages by the revision of text. The sentence and two words that are crossed out at the end of page [10] (numbered "3") are rewritten as the start of page [11].)

41.8 front of . . ." her voice] front of : he voice

42.8 Grampa would say] Grampa would sat

42.21 Green Room] green room

43.1 a pillowcase] an ~~old~~ pillowcase

43.6 It's just . . .] It's just :

44.23 Dok-tur Foss-tur] (Given the age of the speaker, this is likely a nursery rhyme. One version from *http://ingeb.org/nurseryr.html* is:

> Doctor Foster went to Glo[uce]ster,
> In a shower of rain;
> He stepped in a puddle, up to the middle,
> And never went there again.

This line also opens a somewhat off-color limerick, but it is unlikely that Agee meant to refer to:

> Doctor Foster went to Gloucester
> His aim, to accost 'er
> He slipped on a banana
> And lost his bandana
> which stuffed up his roster
> [*http://www.bbc.co.uk/dna/h2g2/A163153*]

44.23 went] wentt

44.33–34 "for God's sake stop *banging*,"] (Quotation marks added.)

45.1 lucky you're deaf] lucky youre deaf

45.2	"Granma thinks you] Granma thinks you
45.26–28	had a snake . . . long as a rake.] (One title for this folk song is "Keemo Kyemo"; the lyrics exist in many variants.)
45.34	Oh Sable Cazzum] (Likely the famous Ausable Chasm located 1.3 miles north of Keeseville, NY, where U.S. Route 9 crosses the AuSable River. However, the Tylers come from Michigan where there is also an Au Sable River, but apparently no chasm. In Michigan, the Au Sable is a major tributary to Lake Huron. It drains a north-south basin that includes 1,932 square miles in north-central lower Michigan. The basin is approximately 90 miles long and 10 to 30 miles wide. The river basin is partially within the Huron National Forest and includes parts of Otsego, Montmorency, Crawford, Osco, Alcona, Roscommon, Ogemaw, and Iosco Counties.)
47.7–29	(Perhaps to underscore the anger Aunt Paula feels, Agee underlines her words that Rufus remembers. These underlinings are rendered in italics.)
47.29	*mean*] mean
47.31	(After skipping one line, Agee begins a paragraph on the entrance of Victoria, Rufus' former nanny, who has come to help with the birth of his parents' next child. He subsequently marks it for deletion. It is included below to serve as the basis of comparison to Victoria's actual entrance (63.31–64.13) and demonstrates how Agee shifted the focus of the meeting so that it came much more from Rufus' perspective. Agee's brackets are at the beginning and end of this paragraph.)

> [One day the doorbell rang and his mother hurried past him in the hall and there was a great big fat old lady with black skin and white hair under her black straw hat and a little shiny black suitcase. She put her head on one side and beamed at his mother and his mother stood still a moment and said in a loving voice "Well here you are!", and shoved open the screen door quickly and they flung their arms around each other while the old lady almost groaned in her deep voice] (TX 5.2, [16]).

The third of the four short fragments printed by Robert Fitzgerald in *The Collected Short Prose of James Agee* and given the title "A Birthday" ([124]–25) may fit between chapters 5 and 6 chronologically, but may also be a draft fragment whose ideas are later elaborated in other chapters. It is therefore not included in the restored text of the novel, but is recorded at the end of the "Major Manuscript Variants" of chapter 5.)

Chapter 6

50.1	*Chapter 6*]

McDowell properly chooses to print this section (TX 5.3, [124–30]) for which there are no apparent other versions (McD, 213–26). While there is no doubt about the need to include this chapter on Rufus' victimization by schoolboys of different ages since Agee refers to it in his notes and outlines five times (TX

5.1, [1, 8, 10, 12, 15]), there is no conclusive evidence as to the placement of this chapter. A previous editor, probably McDowell, has numbered the manuscript pages "7" through "13", and that pagination follows from the pages that comprise this edition's chapter 7, which are numbered "1" through "6" (TX 5.3, [52–57]; McD, 102–11). However, McDowell's initial editorial numbering (which he subsequently violates by splitting and putting the chapters into different flashback groupings) does not make chronological sense, as chapters 7, 8, and 9, as grouped together in this volume, are clearly meant to be together.

Some matters concerning placement are sure, however. All the outlines, notes, and chronology describe and place this section as an early chapter of the novel. The outline on TX 5.1, [8] has the "corner" occur immediately after "*Tylers*" and "*Agees*" (the present chapter 5). On TX 5.1, [10] "Me at the corner." follows the line "Chapter on domestic pleasures. Advance time. Set up all characters etc. Bring car in this far back?" "Domestic pleasures" are covered in chapters 3 and 4, the "characters" are the family members noted in chapter 5, and the chapter "Enter the Ford" (chapter 14), one of the few chapters to which Agee actually gave a title, is deferred since Emma, who is not yet born, is a character in that chapter. Likewise on TX 5.1, [1], "The chapter about me on the corner" comes before "mother's awful mistake of Talking to Tripp," an event that is a part of chapter 14. Agee's uncertainty about the chapter's placement is underscored in his note when he writes "when and where, the stuff at the corner?" (TX 5.1, [15]), but he also begins another page of notes with "straight plot line: I do badly at the corner." (TX 5.1, [12]). While no priority can be assigned to the notes, their general trend supports placing the chapter early in the novel.

Other contextual matters combine with these notes and the clear interlocking of chapters 7, 8, and 9 to argue for the present placement of this chapter. The chapter takes place at a time when Rufus is too young to attend school, but looking forward to becoming old enough to do so. There is also no mention of his mother's pregnancy or the general preparations for Emma's birth which are the focus of the three subsequent chapters. All this evidence supports the present position in the narrative as the best and far most likely choice.

Corrections to McDowell's version of the text are incorporated silently into the restored chapter.

50.2 Rufus'] (Agee's inconsistent use of the possessive—Rufus'/Rufus'—is standardized to his dominant use of Rufus' throughout the novel and the "Major Manuscript Variants.")

50.6–8 they were creatures . . . even for kindergarten.] (Very light brackets in faint pencil—not Agee's normal bold strokes for indicating deletion with brackets—surround this passage and part of the next sentence noted below on 50.8–9. Both sections are retained since the editing necessary to have the version with the deletions make grammatical sense were never completed.)

50.8–9 kinship with them . . . and considerable awe.] (Light brackets surround this passage. See note above.)

50.21–22 dignity and purpose.] (McDowell subsequently includes a section after "purpose" that is clearly bracketed for deletion. It reads "[to be the mark that set them apart in their privileged world.]")

51.16 appalled] (This word is bracketed for deletion, but since no alternative is provided, it is retained.)

51.26–27 "What's your name?"] "What's your name"

52.11 *Would*n't you tell me?] *Would*n't you tell me!

52.26 kind-looking] kind looking

52.33 they mean it.] (A question mark is inserted interlinearly above the deleted word that follows "it." but is linked to the interlinear insertion of "But what if" over "*Maybe.*" Agee indicates no choice between these options and, following this volume's general policy, the first choice is included in preference to the interlinear insertions.)

53.11 and others yelled] , and others yelled

53.14–17 *Nigger, nigger, black . . . his nickel back.*] (Agee is inconsistent in his underlining of these taunts. Hence "*Uh-Rufus, Uh-Rastus . . . rent comes roun?*" (53.9–10) is italicized, and these four lines originally are not.)

53.19 "Nigger,"] "Nigger"

53.28 again,] again

54.1 on believing them?] on believing them.

54.7 this, but just said, "hello, there,"] this but just said hello there

54.24 shyly] shily

55.9–10 niiig-ger] (Agee hyphenates this word.)

55.36–37 Rufus Rastus Johnson . . . *rent* comes roun?] (Space added before and after this verse. Agee does not italicize all the words to the verse as he did previously.)

56.9 "What you gonna . . . rent comes roun?"] (Quotation marks added.)

56.20 what The Rent] what the Rent

56.25 what The Rent] what the Rent

56.38 any more than] and more than

57.13 and had been] and and been

58.1–2 I'm a little . . . the clover.] (Agee does not italicize all the words to the verse as he did previously.)

58.3 As he sang] (Agee indents the opening of this paragraph approximately half the width of the manuscript page.)

59.10 the way] they way

Chapter 7

61.1 *Chapter 7*]

McDowell properly chooses to print this section (TX 5.3, [52–57]) for which there are no apparent other versions (McD, 102–11). He incorporates it as the last episode of the first section of flashbacks. Its placement in this edition is determined by its context and follows the chronological development of the novel. (See also note 50.1 above for the linkage of chapters 7, 8, and 9 and their relationship to chapter 6.) The present chapter deals with the changes brought about by his mother's pregnancy and the general preparations for Emma's impending birth, the meaning of which Rufus is unaware. Chapter 8 (TX 5.2, [54–56, with an insert of page 75 on page 56]) deals with the few days immediately before the birth when he is sent to visit with his maternal grandparents and chapter 9 (TX 5.2, [57–61]) with his going home to be told the nature of "the surprise." All are part of an obvious sequence dealing with an important event in the life of the family, and the inclusion of this birth (which McDowell does not incorporate) provides an excellent counterpoint to and balance for the death to come.

Corrections to McDowell's version are incorporated silently into the restored chapter.

61.9	looked] lookeed
61.22	(This reference to the ear trumpet repeats the statement in 38.20, but is likely an accurate reflection of a child's perception of and repetition of a key object associated with his grandmother and thus is here retained.)
63.4	Laura?] Laura,
63.27	sweetheart,] sweetheart
63.31–64.13	(See note for 47.31.)
64.6	him, why] him why
64.10	"*Do* you, honey?"] *Do* you, honey?"
64.11	shyly] shily
64.33–34	Say yes if] (The incorrect quotation marks at the beginning of this sentence are partially erased and are not included in the text.)
65.11	ready, his] ready, Then his (Agee forgot to delete "Then" after adding the interlinear insertion of "Then Victoria bathed . . . he was ready," before the original start to his sentence.)
66.12	honey?"] honey,"
67.17	bless you baby,] bless you baby

Chapter 8

69.1	*Chapter 8*]

Neither this chapter nor its storyline companion, chapter 9, are included in McDowell's text because of minor overlapping with parts of the flashback that now constitutes chapter 7. Both new chapters, however, fill out the portrait of the family that would otherwise be incomplete and, as previously noted (66.1 above), provide a counterpoint to and a balance for the death of the father. Necessary editorial excision to eliminate the overlap/repetition is described below, and omitted sections or parts of sections are recorded in these notes or in the section of "Major Manuscript Variants," depending on their length.

Another bit of evidence that argues for the inclusion of these chapters is the introduction of the image of the butterfly in chapter 9 as a description for Victoria's glasses (74.20), a feature which continues the link between Rufus' father and Victoria through his affinity for "darky" language when singing, and foregrounds the use of the butterfly as an image of resurrection and the afterlife when one perches upon the father's coffin during the burial service (353.4–354.31).

Victor A. Kramer transcribes both chapters as one under the title "The Surprise" in his *Agee: Selected Literary Documents,* pages [275]–85. Corrections to Kramer's version are incorporated silently into the restored chapters, notes, and variants.

See "Major Manuscript Variants" for the portion of TX 5.2, [54] omitted at the outset of the chapter to avoid overlap.

69.18	Granma] (See 38.15 in these notes.)
69.22	vittles] vittles:
70.7	it's] its
70.25	goodbye] goobye
70.27	next the ceiling] (Agee's idiomatic usage of "next" for "near")
71.5	. . . .] ___
71.7	they] They (Agee inserted "Then" interlinearly before "They" and forgot to make the second capital lowercase.)
71.12	shyly] shily
71.17	"Me . . . oscoorrrah"] (There are many variants of the translation of this, the second line of Canto I of Dante's *Inferno*—"mi ritrovai per una selva oscura." Agee here has Hugh sound out the line as Rufus would have heard it. In combination with Dante's next line in that stanza, it is clear that the speaker is lost and likely bewildered in that "dark forest," an apt description of Rufus' state having missed his grandfather's allusion to his bedwetting. Hugh's comment is all the more appropriate, since Dante's description makes clear that the narrator's bewilderment is due to his feeling that he has awakened in the midst of a dream or vision. See *Dante Alighieri's Divine Comedy,* trans. Mark Musa (Bloomington: Indiana University Press, 1996), Vol. 2, p. 4, note for line 2, and *The Divine Comedy of Dante Alighieri,* trans. Robert M. Durling and Ronald L. Martinez (New York: Oxford University Press, 1996), p. 34, note for line 2. Agee's use of "donze" in the line, instead of Dante's "per," is unclear. Perhaps he is trying to give the sound of the Italian "donde"—meaning "where" or "in which"—a choice that certainly works to reinforce the sense of location given in the line; or perhaps he is mixing languages and using the sound of the French "dans"—meaning "in" or "within"—a choice that again supports the idea of location.)
71.22	shyly] shily

71.34–72.6	Now say Now . . . Sweet sleep.] (This section, which comprises all of TX 5.2, [75], has been inserted at this point by the editor before the last paragraph of TX 5.2, [56]. This preference is based on the quality of the scene, a physical comparison of the paper and Agee's handwriting, and the fact that it reinforces the final scene with his grandmother, making it the most likely place for its inclusion. The editor has likewise inserted the space of a line before and after this material to indicate its separation from the text proper. Agee gives no information about the placement or inclusion of the page.)
71.36	If] (The original "i" is overwritten to form a capital letter. This gives a sense of the appropriate pause or partial breath in the prayer that Agee has Rufus run through quickly by eliminating any punctuation.)

Chapter 9

73.1 *Chapter 9*]

See 69.1 above. While clearly linked contextually to the preceding material of chapter 8, there is a definite chapter break between TX 5.2, [56] and TX 5.2, [57]. Agee leaves extra space at the bottom of [56] and begins [57] somewhat down from his normal starting point at the top of a continued page, a common indication for him of beginning a new chapter. This chapter also begins on the "Next day" (73.2).

74.11–22	(See "Major Manuscript Variants" for the portions of TX 5.2, [57–58] omitted from this section of the chapter to avoid overlap.)
74.22	yo lil—"] yo lil—
74.30	"Come in," . . . voice,] "Come in, . . . voice,"
74.36	shyly] shily
75.5	shyly] shily
75.25	It] She (Agee does not have Laura identify the baby as a female until three sentences later.)
76.5	put] but
77.18	shyly] shily
78.3	said] says
78.34	all.] all,
78.35–36	he said. [paragraph break] "But I guess] he said, "but I guess (The change is needed to correct Agee's mistake which has Jay unintentionally reverse his view. The dialog clearly switches from Jay to Laura at this point. She is the northerner.)
80.1	"Well," Laura said.] "Well," his mother said. (Agee mistakenly switches to Rufus' point of view when the conversation is between Laura and her husband, Jay.)
80.11	"Besides, Mama—"] "Besides, Mama."
80.25	"—he wanted] "he wanted
81.1	mother's] mothers

Chapter 10

84.1 *Chapter 10*]

The three manuscript pages that comprise this chapter were provided by The James Agee Trust. They were found in July 2003 in a folder on which was written by a hand other than Agee's "Draft fragments of a story or screen treatment about the Civil War—plus draft fragment for *A Death in the Family*" and are now on deposit in the Special Collections Library of the University of Tennessee.

This chapter is included for several reasons, not the least of which is that it is not a "fragment" per se; it is a complete scene or episode featuring Rufus and his father. The manuscript is a near fair copy with few corrections and revisions by Agee. It may well be the preceding chapter to an undiscovered or never written "fishing" episode that Agee refers to three times in his notes (twice in TX 5.1, [11] and once in TX 5.1A, [4], part of a second section of six manuscript pages located with Agee's other notes, that is entitled by him "Notes, 1909–16"). While the scene does not connect directly to another chapter, it does fit the stated pattern of complete recollection underscored in the introduction by the narrator: "He should go back to those years. As far as he could remember; and everything he could remember; nothing except (so well as he could remember) what his father had been as he had known him . . ." (13.1–5). It fits as well Agee's category in his notes of "Episodes to build up chiefly my relation to him & the reader's liking for him" (TX 5.1, [11]) and Agee draws a line to connect "Episodes" with the word "fishing?", which is written interlinearly above it to the right. The final reason for inclusion is that the chapter does present an intimate look at Jay and Rufus and their growing bond.

Agee's notes indicate that he was not completely sure of the placement of this scene. However, by focusing upon content and particularly upon the character of Emma within a chronological perspective, the placement of the chapter can be determined with reasonable certainty. In this chapter, Emma appears to be an infant or perhaps toddler (she is in a crib, the parents try extremely hard not to awaken her, and she is not included on whatever outing Jay and Rufus will take). Chapter 11, the trip to Chilhowee Park by streetcar, likewise excludes Emma, and Agee's notes state that "We will go to Chilhowee Park & Paula will stay with the baby?" (TX 5.1, [4]). Another note similarly lists "To the park. (Paula staying with Emma?)" (TX 5.1A, [4]), but in this outline the mention of "Early morning fishing" comes after the trip to the park. The chronology for the next chapters is clear. Chapter 11 is linked internally to the trip to the Great Smoky Mountains by train in chapter 12. Agee's marginal notes on TN 1A.19, [15] (see 88.1 below for full citation) mention "glass, / RR. Trains with candy" opposite what becomes 95.14–15 in chapter 11 of this text and one of the images of chapter 12 is just that: "the glass locomotive with little bright-colored pieces of candy inside" (101.15–16). Emma is also old enough to be taken on this train excursion, a much longer one well beyond the city limits of Knoxville. The next two chapters deal with the discussion and purchase of a new Model T Ford, which eliminates the need for public transportation, and in that second chapter, Emma is speaking for the first time and does so on a level of conversation with her father that marks her as older (122.20–33). (Jay does not need a car to go fishing with Rufus, since the river is an easy walk from their house.) Thus, the bulk of the textual and contextual evidence makes the most logical place for this episode after Emma's birth (chapter 9) and before the trip to the park (chapter 11). It also provides a scene that may parallel the process of getting Rufus ready for other trips at this age, such as the one to Chilhowee Park

84.14 sweater,] sweater
85.38 abruptly] apruptly
86.36 quieted] quietened (The British "quietened"—that is, to become quiet—is changed to its American counterpart by the editor.)
87.13 "And] And
87.16 Rufus] R.

Chapter 11

88.1 *Chapter 11*]

This new chapter is from MS 1500, the University of Tennessee's manuscript collection "The James Agee–David McDowell Papers, 1909–1985, Box 1A, Folder 19, pages [10–17]" and is designated in this edition as TN 1A.19, [10–17]. This chapter follows the chronological sequence of the novel as explained in note 84.1 above and those reasons likewise determine its placement and some of the rationale for its inclusion. Other reasons for its inclusion include the fact that Agee's notes list "Chilhowee Park" as an early episode in the novel twice (TX 5.1, [4, 15]) and "*Park*" is part of an outline-list that begins with "*Waking*" and ends with "*Death*" (TX 5.1, [8]).

88.25 popcorn white] pure white (Agee wrote "popcorn white" boldly in the left margin of TN 1A.19, [10], and the editor has adopted that reading.)
89.1 nearer,] nearer
89.30 ball] bill [*sic*]
89.32 black faces] *sleek sneering* heads narrow *black faces* (Agee draws a line to the underlined phrase in the margin to "black faces" to indicate his preference for inclusion. While the phrase might also be rendered as "narrow black faces" the lack of underlining and the repetition of "narrow" in 89.35 makes that alternative less likely.)
89.35 shallow, narrow, shady] (Agee circles these words and draws a line to his marginalia (see 89.34–38 in "Marginal Notes"), but his additional

	comments are not fully worked out, do not fit well with this particular section of his narrative, and are not incorporated into the text.)
90.21	merry-go-round] Merrygoround (All of Agee's variants are rendered as "merry-go-round".)
91.2	child] (Agee's word is indistinct. The most likely reading is "chid" ["child" with the omission of "1"]; "kid" is also possible, but is a word seldom used by Agee in the text. The other possibility of "dud" was rejected as eccentric.)
93.5	from every other,] from every other,, (Agee forgot to include one of these commas in his subsequent deletion signaled by bracketing "then every gravel getting blurred and long and the whole ground beginning to streak and stream, and a kind of *ahh* rising up from the children on the animals.")
93.8	foofing] foofling [*sic*]
93.26–27	Sometimes I'm up . . . heavenward bound] (This lyric is in the left margin of the manuscript just under and at roughly a right angle to the marked insertion from the margin that precedes it of "he had to . . . streak." While its insertion is not definitively indicated, the lyric follows the pattern of the use of lines from songs earlier established by Agee and is incorporated into the text.)
94.11	hurting,] hurting
94.14, 15	bran new] (Two of the many instances of Agee's re-creation of dialect.)
94.38–95.1	right next the] (Agee's dialect rendering)
95.11–12	walking. . . . But] (Agee deletes a paragraph at this point that he later revises and incorporates as the first part of the paragraph that begins at 96.30.)
97.25	more'n] moren
98.13–14	(Line break (space) inserted. Lines 98.12–13 are inserted interlinearly by Agee.)

Chapter 12

100.1	*Chapter 12*]

McDowell properly chooses to print this section (TX 5.3, [142–44]). He incorporates it as the last of his flashbacks (McD, 241–46). No typescript or variant manuscript versions of this material apparently survive. The chapter's placement is determined by three facts: the family takes the trip by train (Jay has evidently not purchased his car as yet); Emma is now old enough to come on the trip and to understand at least some of what the adults are saying; and, in his notes, Agee lists "Trip to Elkmont" under a section of episodes entitled "Holidays & Trips," and that "Holidays & Trips" comes immediately before a new section of episodes that begins with "The car" (TX 5.1, [15]). Elkmont was established as a logging camp in 1908, but the desire to protect its fine fishing and hunting and the beauty of the region (as noted on 101.19–103.2) made it a prime tourist destination and eventually led to the creation of the Great Smoky Mountains National Park.

100.7–11	There . . . Bombay] (A limerick that was incorporated into Edward Lear's *A Book of Nonsense* in 1846.)
100.16, 16–17	half-sister] half sister (Hyphen added in both instances.)
100.19	bran new] (One of many instances of Agee's re-creation of dialect.)
100.20–21	L&N depot] (The Louisville and Nashville train depot)
101.8, 10	after while] (Two of the many instances of Agee's re-creation of dialect.)
101.14	butcher] butch
101.15–16	glass locomotive . . . candy] (Agee here incorporates his marginal note of 95.10–11.)
101.28	shyly] shily
103.10	Henwrich] (In its two occurrences, here and 103.21, the spelling of this surname is questionable. Only "H. . . . rich" seems recoverable after comparing both examples. McDowell simply omits the name (McD 245.10, 23), but that wrongly reduces Laura's motherly anger.)

Chapter 13

105.1

This chapter, TX 5.2, [17–21], was not used by McDowell. It is likely the first of "The car" episodes mentioned in Agee's notes (TX 5.1, [15]; see also note 100.1 above) and provides a logical introduction to the subsequent chapter, "Enter the Ford." On TX 5.1, [15], this section of episodes is written in one line by Agee: "The car. dialogue as written. Enter the Ford. General writing on trips. Looking for a country place. Topside. Trip or trips to Grandparents." It seems likely, as Victor A. Kramer has suggested, that this chapter is the "dialogue as written" about the car. See Victor A. Kramer, "Premonition of Disaster: An Unpublished Section for Agee's *A Death in the Family*," *Costerus: Essays in English and American Language and Literature*, ed. James L. West III (Amsterdam: Rodopi, 1974), p. 85. Kramer gave the chapter the title "Premonition" and published its text in the same article (86–93). The chapter also exists in typescript (TX 4.5, x 1–11). The present version is edited from the original manuscript.

105.5	. . .] __
105.8	shyly] shily
105.10–11	and I know . . . of her.] (This phrase is written above the first part of the same sentence. The "and" indicates the possibility of its inclusion, even without one of Agee's normal indicators, and it is incorporated in the present text.)
105.14	. . .] __
106.4	Jay,] Jay

106.13 it. I] it, I
106.22 to turn into] to be (Agee marks a caret through "be" indicating the substitution of "turn into" which is written interlinearly above "be.")
106.35 . . ."] __
107.1 . . . .] ____
107.5 Take your time.] (This sentence is written interlinearly above the space between the first two sentences of the paragraph and is included by the editor.)
107.34 suddenly.] suddenly,
108.3 . . .] __
108.8 Either they] They either they
108.13, 14 ninety-nine] ninety nine
108.23–30 (Agee's paragraph breaks for Jay's dialog are retained even though they may be somewhat confusing, since he normally uses such breaks to indicate a shift in speaker.)
109.13–14 (Line break (space) seems called for, but cannot be completely determined since 109.13 ends manuscript page [19] near the bottom and 109.14 commences at the top of page [20] with a new paragraph. Space is included by editor.)
111.19 permanently] Permanently (Agee added "Thoroughly and" to his original one-word sentence of "Permanently" and did not convert the capital "P" to lowercase.)
111.27 positi*vv*ly] (Agee's spelling for dialect/emphasis is retained.)

Chapter 14

112.1 *Chapter 14*]

This new chapter is from MS 1500, the University of Tennessee's manuscript collection "The James Agee–David McDowell Papers, 1909–1985, Box 1, Folder 19, pages [1–9]" and is designated in this edition as TN 1A.19, [1–9]. This chapter follows the chronological sequence of the novel as explained in notes 84.1, 100.1, and 105.1 above, and those reasons likewise determine its placement and some of the rationale for its inclusion. It is logical that Jay's bringing home his new Model T in this chapter follows his decision with Laura to buy it in the previous chapter. This order likewise follows Agee's outline on TX 5.1, [15] quoted in note 105.1.

112.8 shyly] shily
112.15 Rufus'] Rufu's
113.30 *after*] *afte*
114.13 Ford] (The larger typeface replicates Agee's emphasis in his manuscript.)
114.20 Tripp said] Tripp
115.14 awfull—] (Agee has Mr. King interrupt Laura's statement in the midst of the word "awfully".)

115.35 bran new] (One of many instances of Agee's re-creation of dialect.)

116.21 and far shoulders of the road] and far shoulders ("far" is a conjectural reading of these three somewhat illegible characters on TN 1A.19, [3]; "of the road" is added by the editor for clarity. "and far shoulders" is positioned interlinearly over "porches flow past like"; its placement is normal for Agee's inclusions, but no line or caret to indicate inclusion is present.)

117.15 quirk] (Agee crossed out the word "bend" and inserted "quirk." Highland Avenue remains the same today with vehicles having to turn left and travel for a short distance on Seventeenth Street before turning right to get back onto Highland.)

119.21 isn't;] isn't

119.30–31 "only . . . , I] only . . ." I

120.27 more'n] moren

120.29 pea pea] pea pee

120.34 about,"] about"

121.22 And there] And There (Agee inserted "And" and forgot to make the "T" of "There" lower case.)

121.37 shyly] shily

123.17 Bearden] ("Bearden" is an area in Knoxville, Tennessee, located approximately five miles west of Agee's neighborhood of Fort Sanders.)

124.16 after."] after."" (The doubling of the quotation marks resulted from an insert by Agee.)

124.28 pleasure's] pleasures

Chapter 15

127.1 *Chapter 15*]

The text for this chapter is TX 5.3, [131–35 {excluding the material bracketed for deletion at the bottom of 135}, 136–38, 140 {bottom 17 mss. lines}, and 141 {top 4 mss. lines plus marked insertion of 18 lines at the bottom of the page}] and is not in as final a form as many of Agee's chapters. McDowell prints [131–35, 140, 141] as his italicized flashback section 13.2 (McD, 227–40), a choice supported by its eliminating the need to purge the top part of [140] to avoid repetition in the restored text. Please see "Major Manuscript Variants" for corrections to McDowell's transcription.

However, with this choice he fails to observe that the bottom of [135] is clearly marked for deletion with a large bracket and that [136] is a revised later version of this final part of [135], which then expands to new material [136–38]. Page [136] begins at 134.35; [138] concludes at 138.24.

That McDowell's inclusion of McD 237.6–22 (the material marked for deletion at the bottom of [135]) is in error is additionally supported by the revisions present on [136]. A sample is presented below.

	Restored Edition	McDowell Edition/TX 5.3
134.35	Agee starts a new paragraph	No new paragraph
135.1	"pale eyes" crossed out and replaced by "eyes"	"pale eyes" remains
135.1–2	"in the light shadow of the sunbonnet" is incorporated into the primary text	"in the light . . . sunbonnet" is added interlinearly
135.5	"hear" is crossed out and replaced by "hyer"	"hear" remains
135.9	"in a bran new Ford" is added to the sentence	No material added

Further important evidence for following the stated pattern of the new/expanded chapter comes from the marking of all the included sections from the bottom of [137] through [141] with a vertical line in the left margin of all those pages and a large arrow in the margin indicating that the proper starting point on [140] commences with the final eighteen lines of the manuscript page.

The evidence for this edition's version of the chapter is thus both Agee's habit of revising his work immediately after a previous draft and the marking of the included sections of [137–41] as a unit.

The placement of this chapter at this point in the restored text is supported by Agee's notes in which he states that "Trip or trips to Grandparents" comes after "Enter the Ford" (TX 5.1, [15]), the present chapter 14, and the fact that there was no feasible way to make the trip other than by car. Agee's outline mentions other trips as well under his heading of "The car," but these materials have not been found and may not have ever been written.)

127.16 packed] (The letter "a" is indistinct but likely, since Agee commonly refers to dirt yards as "packed" elsewhere in the manuscript.)

127.18–19 and a long, low hill of blue silver shut off everything against a blue-white sky,] (This addition is written centered above "silver haze, and he leaned" without a caret and is included by the editor.)

127.24 great-great-grandmother] great great grandmother

127.25 great-great-grandchild] great great grandchild

128.14 what?"] what,

129.14 years;] years,

129.37 Paralee's] Paralee'd

130.8–9 thirty-five—no it—a good—near] thirty-five, no it, a good, near

130.16 *Great—*] *Great:*

131.22–23 the auto] ~~his driv~~ing ("the auto" is written above this conjectural reading of an incomplete strike-out.)

131.29 hate to] hate too

132.3 were glimpses] was ~~a glimpse~~ (“were glimpses” is Agee’s correction written above an incomplete strike-out.)

132.4 thatn’z] thatn z

132.10 square-logged] squarelogged

132.33 Howdy Paralee.”] Howdy Paralee.””

133.37 be—] b—

134.15 threw] thew

134.33 Talkin] Takin

135.4 that] the

135.17 shyly] shily

135.26 they began] They began (Agee interlinearly adds in a new introductory phrase and forgets to revise “They” into “they”.)

135.33 her bare] Her bare (Agee interlinearly adds in a new introductory phrase and forgets to revise “Her” into “her”.)

137.18 died,’] died,”

137.19 ‘A] “A

137.23 ‘they’s . . . um,’] “they’s . . . um,”

137.34 She’s] She

138.13 sping [smack]] (“sping” is somewhat illegible)

138.13 forehead. Way] forehead.” “Way

138.23–24 ‘Granmaw I’m Rufus.’] Granmaw I’m Rufus.

139.3 seen] Seen

Chapter 16

142.1 *Chapter 16*]

This new chapter comes from The Agee Trust (UT MS 2730, 4.13, [8-9]) and is in near final copy. Its placement is determined contextually by two points. The “them” that Laura commands to “*Eat*” in the final paragraph are her children, Rufus and Emma, who have witnessed their parents’ fight and reconciliation over Laura’s covertly replacing Jay’s coffee with Postum, a coffee substitute. The scene thus takes place after Emma’s birth, the “surprise” that so disappointed Rufus, and it likewise takes place at home and does not involve the travel group of chapters begun by “Enter the Ford” that follows the “surprise.” This chapter thus seems to fit best as the first of those in the next section of “May 17, 1916: The Day Before” because its beginning (“At breakfast”) parallels the beginning of Chapter 17 (“At supper that night”), and chapters 18, 19, and 20 deal with Jay’s being awakened by the phone and having to get ready to visit his sick father, and Laura’s making him breakfast about which he states: “‘Good *coffee*,’ he said. ‘Now that’s more *like* it’” (162.26). Thus the emphasis Agee places on the present coffee seems a comment designed to mirror Laura’s previous switch of Postum for coffee. Since Jay dies before returning home, the present placement of chapter 16 seems most likely.

142.5 admit it,] admit it

142.9 really is?] really is,

142.11 Postum] (Postum is a powdered, non-caffeinated substitute for coffee created by C.W. Post in 1895. Post was also the creator of Post cereals such as Grape Nuts. Postum is currently marketed by Kraft foods.)

142.14 raked] (The word is somewhat unclear in the manuscript.)

143.12 I'God] I God (Agee leaves approximately two extra spaces between the words.)

143.25 puke . . ."] puke"

Chapter 17

145.1 *Chapter 17*]

McDowell properly chooses to print this section (TX 5.3, [1–7]), but places it well out of order, using it as his chapter 1. No typescript or variant manuscript versions of this material apparently survive. Commencing with this chapter, the order of Agee's manuscripts is much easier to determine. This edition generally concurs with McDowell's order of presentation after this point (exceptions are explained in the first note of the appropriate chapters below) since the bulk of the "new" material that McDowell chose not to incorporate and all the manuscript pages that he formed into the six flashback chapters (his sections 7.1, 7.2, 7.3, 13.1, 13.2, 13.3 that he placed out of chronological order) have already been incorporated into the previous chapters. The movement of the novel also quickens at this point to focus in depth upon several days rather than Rufus' available recollections of his first six years. Two of Agee's notes also convey the "now easy" sense of the ordering of material and are linked to the main events of this chapter—the movie and the vacant lot. TX 5.1, [15] records "then he takes me to the movies: and so on, to end of book." This part of Agee's outline occurs after the "Trip or trips to Grandparents." in these notes that appears as chapter 15. Two similarly brief lines of other notes that separate these episode descriptions mention an "Autumn trip" for which no manuscript apparently exists and Agee's query to himself about where to put the chapter on "the corner" (chapter 6; the final part of the present chapter also takes part on the corner, but it was never referred to by Agee in that way). TX 5.1A, [4], part of a second section of six manuscript pages located with Agee's other notes and entitled by him "Notes, 1909–16," has as its last two entries in a substantial list: "Movie evenings. Stopping in vacant lot. / Full narration of day before death, and of death, through funeral?" The chapter's general placement is also supported by the fact that the Ford is present in this chapter and seems a normal rather than new part of the family's life.

145.9 Rufus] (See 146.29 below.)

145.16 Hart] Hart was (Agee forgot to delete "was" after adding "And there was" to the beginning of his sentence. William S. Hart was the first cowboy star of silent films.)

145.20–21 city, . . . palms,] city . . . palms ("a long line of palms" is Agee's interlinear insertion.)

146.1 streetcar] street car

146.26 peekay] pekay

146.29 Rufus'] Rufus' (Here "Rufus'" is written above "Richard's" in the manuscript. "Richard" is the name used for "Rufus" three times before this interlinear insertion of "Rufus'" by Agee. In his next usage (146.30) "Richard" is partially crossed out ("~~Rich~~ard") and "Rufus" is written above it, but then "Richard' occurs thirty-six times after this point with no change. That the vast majority of the novel uses the name "Rufus" may mark this chapter as one that Agee created early in his project. The light brown coloration of the paper, which physically differentiates this chapter from much of the rest of the manuscript, may support this conjecture.)

146.33 sidewalk] side walk

147.1 shell] shells

147.18 on in] on,

147.20 frightened,] frightened

147.24–25 striking and] (Reading is conjectural. "striking" is indistinct and "and" may be part of the subsequent deletion of "of".)

147.34 now, his father would] now His father would (Capital letter not corrected after the interlinear insertion of "If he asked his father now".)

147.36–37 "Sterchi's." "George's."] Sterchi's. George's.

147.38 "Sturkeys."] Sturkeys.

148.3 bragging?] bragging.

148.9 white brick] (The words "white brick" are written above "the wall" without a caret by Agee and are included by the editor.)

148.33 kind;] kind,

148.35 now even some of these] (Agee wrote this phrase interlinearly above "even further away, the" and indicated its inclusion with a caret, but forgot to cross out his original phrase, which repeated the words "further away" in the same line.)

149.21 as if he were] ("he" is conjectural, but quite likely given the structure and context of the sentence.)

149.22–23 nursing woman's eyes] (This may be a reference to Victoria.)

149.24–25 Latticed in pawnshop iron] (Agee wrote this new introduction to the sentence over "Behind the iron lattice" which he forgot to delete after deleting the subsequent phrase "of a pawn shop" that originally followed it.)

150.2 (Another sentence follows this one, but is bracketed for deletion: "The corner was best, to Richard [*sic.* Rufus], of all these evenings." It is often impossible to determine the authorship of brackets, and the present deletion stands because bracketing is one of Agee's standard methods of indicating excision. However, see also 150.7–9 below.)

150.6 dirty laundry] (TX 5.3, [5] has "dirty laundry" written above "wrinkled cloth" with no choice made by Agee. The use of "dirty laundry" somewhat enhances the evidence for the use of the nightmare introduction by direct repetition, but the image Agee intends to convey is clearly the same and linked by the remaining direct repetition of the "vacant lot" with the "outcrop of limestone" and the "tree" as well as the other features previously discussed in the notes to the nightmare introduction. The likely early drafting of this chapter (see 146.29 above) may support this choice. McDowell also uses "dirty laundry" in his edition.)

150.7–9 It was not . . . place to sit and] (Although bracketed for deletion, the correction of the "i" in the word "if" that follows "and" is not in Agee's hand. Taken together with the nature of the material excised, this seems a deletion by a previous editor rather than Agee and is restored to the present text.)

150.18 chains] chain

150.34 tired] (The word may be "tarred" but is indistinct in the manuscript. "Tarred" is a phonetic spelling of "tired" and fits the dialect that Agee often reproduces.)

153.6 "*Well . . .*"] "*Well* ____:",

153.14 his father] he (An editorial change made for clarification.)

Chapter 18

154.1 *Chapter 18*]

McDowell properly chooses to print this section (TX 5.3, [11–13]), but combines this chapter and the two subsequent chapters 19 and 20 (TX 5.3, [13–15] and [15–21]) into one to form his chapter 2. Agee delineates the chapter breaks by additional space before and after three centered spaced asterisks on pages [13] and [15], a method that he uses regularly. For example, the same method is used on TX 5.3, [7] to separate chapters on the same page, which in this case are chapters 17 and 25. McDowell likewise observes this chapter break (between his chapters 1 and 5). In the present chapter, McDowell simply skips two lines to indicate the chapter divisions (McD 27, 31) Agee indicates, but prefers a longer chapter here and generally throughout the novel. A typescript of McDowell's edition that begins with this combined chapter exists (TX 4.1–4.2) as well as a copyedited typescript (TX 4.5). These will not be cited unless they have some significance for the present restored text. The manuscripts used by McDowell from this point on have notations by an editor in the left margin that correspond to the page number of the typescripts, likely for transcribing and proofreading purposes. These numbers will not be recorded in the present edition. No variant manuscript versions of these three chapters (18, 19, and 20) apparently survive.

The order of presentation of chapter 18 is clear and linked to chapter 17; it begins to fill in what happens after Rufus returns home with his father and goes to sleep. Rufus is partially awakened by the sound of his father leaving in the Ford at the end of chapter 17. All the chapters from 18 through and including chapter 23 cover the time from when Rufus goes to sleep through the start of the next morning's breakfast. Chapter 24, which switches to Jay's arrival at his parents' farm, likely occurs about the same time as the children's breakfast. Chapters 18 through and including chapter 21 are physically linked by shared manuscript pages, as are chapters 22 through 24. Chapter 25 returns to Rufus' mother explaining his father's trip over breakfast.

154.16	res-dence] res dence
154.18	res-dence] res dence
155.32	self-dislike] self dislike
155.33	said: "Listen] said: (Agee's paragraph break.) "Listen
156.28	Frank] F.
156.28	Jay] J
157.3	quick's] quicks
157.12	but—] but:

Chapter 19

158.1	*Chapter 19*] (Please see 154.1 above.)
159.32	beak-nosed] beak nosed
160.34	he] the

Chapter 20

161.1	*Chapter 20*] (Please see 154.1 above.)
161.23	water-closet.] water closet.
164.14	said: "That] said: (Agee's paragraph break.) "That
164.32	children," she] children," he
165.7	was: "You] was: (Agee's paragraph break.) "You
165.23	N-no] N no
165.28	Yes.] Yes,
166.12	forty-one] forty one
166.25	sky.] sky
167.24	gaiety] gayety
168.7	the second,] the second was (Agee forgot to cross out "was" after interlinearly adding the next phrase, likely because there is a page break between "was" and the phrase "which was usually worse, was".)
168.25	(Like] Like

168.26 tortured)] tortured
168.38 smug] (This word is conjectural; McDowell (41) simply omits it.)

Chapter 21

171.1 *Chapter 21*]

McDowell properly chooses to print this section (TX 5.3, [21–23]), which begins on the same manuscript page ([21]) on which chapter 20 ends; the context also makes clear that it follows in the correct order. It is his chapter 3. Agee again delineates the chapter break by inserting additional space before and after three centered spaced asterisks. No manuscript variants of this chapter have been discovered. Please also see 154.1 above.

171.4 Forest] Forrest
171.6 blocked] (The "o" of "blocked" is unclear, but "blocked" is a more logical reading because it continues the references to shape begun by "skeins" and because "blacked shadows" is redundant.)
171.10 places,] (The phrase which follows "places"—"he ran his tongue over his teeth"—is bracketed for deletion, either by Agee or a previous editor. The deletion stands since the phrase is repeated at the start of the following paragraph and was never well integrated into the original sentence.)
171.24 too far,] too far
172.24 womurn,] womurn
172.36 except] xcept
173.16 I'God] I God
174.19 up as he took] up: he took (Altered in the present text to correct the ambiguity of "he" in the manuscript.)
174.37 Five forty-five.] (Agee's note says only "(Time?)." The U. S. Naval Observatory Astronomical Applications Department notes that sunrise for Knoxville on Thursday 18 May 1916 occurred at 5:28 a.m. Daylight Saving Time did not yet exist. The actual time cited is an approximation based upon Agee's descriptions in the scene.)

Chapter 22

176.1 *Chapter 22*]

McDowell properly chooses to print this section (TX 5.3, [24–26]) next, which begins on the following manuscript page ([24]) after chapter 21 ends. It is his chapter 4. The bottom of [23] contains a draft fragment of the beginning of chapter 25 (McDowell's chapter 5), but the content and context makes clear that the present chronological order is correct. Agee delineates the chapter break by inserting additional space after three centered spaced asterisks. Please also see "Major Manuscript Variants" and 154.1 above.

176.2 During . . . sleep.] (The first sentence, which was bracketed for deletion by Agee, originally read: "Laura did not sleep very well, during the rest of the night." This may help to clarify the meaning of a "'white' sleep.")
176.18 (Paragraph break added. A previous editor has inserted a symbol for a new paragraph to begin at this point as well.)
177.12 (Paragraph break added. A previous editor has inserted a symbol for a new paragraph to begin at this point as well.)
177.18 kind hearted] kindhearted
178.2 couldn't] (A conjectural reading that may also be read as "could not" in the manuscript.)
179.8 Who] who
179.15 anything] anything,

Chapter 23

182.1 *Chapter 23*]

This short section is a new chapter that McDowell chooses not to print (TX 5.3, [26–27]) even though he, or another editor, originally numbered it in Agee's manuscripts as his next chapter ("Chap 5"). It is also next in the consecutive series of numbers given the manuscript pages by the previous editor and also in the consecutive series of different page numbers that records its conversion into typescript. The strongest evidence for inclusion is that chapter 23 begins in the middle of the manuscript page ([26]) immediately after Agee delineates the chapter break from chapter 22 by inserting additional space before and after three centered spaced asterisks. McDowell likely excised the chapter because its last line states that the children "finished the meal in silence." This one line of the chapter thus overlaps the time frame of chapter 25 (McDowell's actual chapter 5), a chapter which contains Laura's full explanation to the children over breakfast of Jay's absence. There is, however, no overlap of content between the two chapters. In fact, this chapter is mainly Laura's thinking about Jay's absence and his father's illness in relation to the children, and chapter 25 is her trying to explain the situation to them. For that reason and because the chapter is clearly next in Agee's manuscripts, it is incorporated into the restored edition.

For further evidence in favor of two distinct chapters, please see "Major Manuscript Variants." See also 154.1 above.

Chapter 24

184.1 *Chapter 24*]

McDowell properly chooses to print this section (TX 5.3, [27–32]), which begins midway on manuscript page ([27]) after chapter 23 ends. He does, however, break the manuscript and his typescript order by making it his chapter 6. Agee again delineates the chapter break by inserting additional space after three centered spaced asterisks. His order of the manuscript chapters thus supports the present placement of this chapter. No manuscript variants of this chapter have been discovered. Please also see 154.1 above.

184.23 thought,] thought
187.13 right?] right
187.13 right?] right
187.14 bitch?] bitch
189.21 *Fool! Fool! Fool!*] (The words "*Fool! Fool! Fool!*" are written above "cheeks" and "*Why*" without a caret by Agee and are included by the editor.)
190.26 too] to
191.20 respect he] respected he

Chapter 25

192.1 *Chapter 25*]

The choice of this particular breakfast scene (TX 5.3, [7–10]), a choice that agrees with McDowell's selection which he prints as his chapter 5, is complicated. The matter of Laura trying to explain Jay's absence to the children is a scene that is meant to be included, since general references to it appears three times in Agee's outline notes for the book (TX 5.1, [3, 4, and 6]). However, a viable alternative version exists—variant 1 as recorded in "Major Manuscript Variants"—as well as three other variants also recorded in that section, and with the possibility of variant 4 completing variant 2. These variants were likely written later, since they consistently use the name "Rufus" rather than "Richard" (TX 5.3 [7] uses "Rufus" once) and Agee reworked this scene many times in different ways. Please again see "Major Manuscript Variants" and do so for chapters 22, 23, and 25, since Agee produced versions which also overlapped or borrowed elements from each other. Most of these, however, are earlier versions.

The rationale for the present selection (TX 5.3, [7–10]) stems from its physical link to chapter 17, the chapter that records the Chaplin movie and father-son bonding at their special corner. This breakfast scene begins two-thirds of the way down the same manuscript page on which chapter 17 ends (TX 5.3, [7]), and Agee again delineates the chapter break by inserting additional space after three centered spaced asterisks. The rationale for chapter 17's inclusion thus may suggest the inclusion of this version of the breakfast scene. Stronger internal evidence for this choice is that this version is also the only one that contains a section on Oliver, the cat who died earlier in the book, a scene that introduces Rufus to death (42.19–43.4), and the only one that develops the brother-sister conflict that Agee cites repeatedly in his notes for the book (TX 5.1, [1, 2, 9, 10, 11, and 12]).

Please also see 182.1 and 154.1 above.

192.7	"Why?"] "Why."
192.11	Rufus] (This is Agee's one use of "Rufus" in the chapter. "Richard" is otherwise used throughout this manuscript chapter.)
192.15	if . . .] if.
192.15	wicker] (A term of endearment Laura uses for Emma.)
192.18	not?"] not."
193.1	know;] know,
193.12	dawdle. It's] dawdle, it's
193.15	mustn't] musn't
193.26	well—] we, (Agee's two or three characters before the comma cannot be discerned with certainty.)
193.29	He] he
193.30	His] his
193.34	He just] he just
193.37	He] he
194.4	in—the—*easy*—*way*] in the *easy way* (Dashes added for consistency because of Agee's subsequent description of Laura's statement.)
194.7	to Him, to *find* Him] to him, to *find* him
194.12	Hidenseek's] Hidenseeks
194.15	relief. "Why] relief, "why
194.33	said] said, said (Agee's inadvertent repetition due to an insertion.)
194.35	mustn't] musn't
195.5	shyly] shily

Chapter 26

196.1	*Chapter 26*]

TX 5.3, [58–61] is the only manuscript version of this chapter that apparently survives. Its placement is determined by its content—Rufus is hurried off to school at the end of chapter 25, and in this chapter Aunt Jessie gets permission and takes him shopping after school—and by Agee's notes: "Finally he gets the cap. But his father is away. On his way home he is killed." (TX 5.1, [9]). This description supports this chapter's present position in the narrative. "Enter, the cap" also appears as an episode in another outline (TX 5.1, [11]), but is between general descriptions, deletions with brackets, and episode or scene descriptions recorded with question marks. The outline then moves to Agee's critical notes to himself that these portions need "Clearing & tightening storyline in this, seems to make it thin and phony." The placement of the chapter is roughly the same, with "Enter, the cap" occurring before "start action towards school," but

inconclusive as to exact placement in the text. Its presence does, however, add support for the inclusion of the chapter. McDowell includes it as his chapter 7.

The light brown foxing of the paper for this section and the stain on the bottom of the pages seems to match the paper for chapters 17 and 25 and may provide partial evidence for the same approximate date of composition/revision. See the more detailed marginal notes on the first manuscript page of the chapter in the "Marginal Notes" section, which give insight into Agee's plan for the novel and may also mark this chapter as composed earlier in the process. See also 196.3 below.

196.3	Rufus] Richard (Agee refers to Rufus as Richard throughout this chapter, likely marking it as composed at an earlier date.)
196.10–197.20	"well, we'll see," . . ."Goodbye. Goodbye"] (Quotation marks added for all dialog.)
197.27	dress] gress
197.27	poring] pouring
198.8	dim-sightedly] dim sightedly
200.3	*Grammar of Ornament*] Grammar of Ornament (Owen Jones's *The Grammar of Ornament* [1856] was a popular book for design that went through many editions and was heavily illustrated. The volume likely purchased was the one published by Bernard Quaritch [London: 1910] and contained 112 illustrated plates.)
200.8–10	"no . . . won't do."] (Quotation marks added for all dialog.)
201.3	offered;] offered:
201.9	mother] Mother

Chapter 27

204.1	*Chapter 27*]

This chapter, TX 5.3, [62–76], shows heavy revision by Agee upon several of its pages, and it may not be in as final a form as many of his other chapters. Its placement in this edition is based upon chronology. McDowell includes it as the first part of his chapter 8. Please see "Major Manuscript Variants."

204.7	hear. . . . I] hear. (Agee's paragraph break) "I
204.13	slight—] slight,
204.14	a accident] (Agee's rendering of local dialect.)
204.19	is] Is (Agee added the previous phrase interlinearly and forgot to correct his initial capitalization of "Is".)
205.2	doctor?] doctor.
205.20	—he says Jay—] , he says Jay,
205.26	Hugh?] Hugh.
206.3	Laura.] Laura,

206.7	Laura. Of] Laura. (Agee's paragraph break) Of
206.8	tell] Tell (Agee added the previous phrase interlinearly and forgot to correct his initial capitalization of "Tell". No caret indicates the placement of the phrase, but it clearly begins the sentence and starts with "And".)
206.19–207.33	(This manuscript page, TX 5.3, [64], clearly is in its proper place here, but is skipped over in the numbering of the previous editor. It may have been located later.)
206.23	Laura, Arthur] Laura. Arthur
206.35–36	where I can take] (This phrase is circled in the manuscript, but with no other direction present, it is retained.)
207.3	in] (This word is circled in the manuscript, but with no other direction present, it is retained.)
208.12–13	(Agee skips a line here, before commencing his next section. This might indicate a chapter break, but since he does not record his normal three asterisks to signal such a division, the present text simply replicates his manuscript page, TX 5.3, [65].)
208.18–19	sardonic incredulity] (These words are bracketed for deletion, but are included since without them there is no object for "bitter" to modify.)
208.19	were saying] (McDowell includes the following material that was bracketed for deletion between these two words: "accusing something or someone (even perhaps his sister), which it was useless beyond words to accuse. (She felt he was".))
208.20	yours?" Arthur] (McDowell, however, then deletes the subsequent following material that was bracketed for deletion between these two words: "and she was not entirely wrong, except that he was also saying, 'and we think we enjoy being alive, in such a universe?[']"). Since this second deletion completes the first [note the position of the leading and closing parentheses], they should either both be retained or deleted. This edition deletes both, in keeping with the assumption that bracketed deletions are generally Agee's, even though it is difficult to ascertain the authorship of such brackets.)
208.32	hearing how he] (Agee writes "hearing how he" interlinearly over the original text and indicates its insertion, but forgets to cross out "she could hear that he" in the text.)
208.34	case—you know—he's—well] case, you know, he's, well
209.12	me . . .] m(e)____
209.21	It's] "It's (Agee's inadvertent repetition of quotation marks.)
209.25	why she can just] why just she can just (Agee's inadvertent repetition or omission of punctuation after the first "just".)
209.37	not] not,
209.38	possible] lpossible (Agee may have started to write "likely" and switched to "possible".)
210.10	Good,] Good
210.24	a—] a,

211.12 ZuZu's] (Popular packaged cookies made by Nabisco.)
211.22 twenty-five] twenty five
211.24 Jay,] Jay
211.27 twenty-four] twenty four
211.28 arithmetic . . .] arithmetic ___
211.34 twenty] (The word is either "twenty" or "thirty"; "twenty" seems most likely, given the previous sentences.)
212.5 "That,] "That
212.20 such] Such (Agee added the previous phrase "It was" interlinearly and forgot to correct his initial capitalization of "Such".)
212.21 Wouldn't] wouldn't
212.22 his—] his,
212.33 had] ("had" is written interlinearly in this position in the sentence without a caret.)
213.18 or. . . .] or ___
213.20 the—] the,
213.23 if . . .] if ___
213.26 I . . .] I ___
213.32 *me;* she whispered] *me,* she whispered (The original punctuation after "whispered" is crossed out and unclear, but the present editing separates Laura's thoughts from what she says in a whisper, since it is unlikely that Agee would have her whisper her thoughts. McDowell's choice of "whispered. 'Andrew [Hugh]?'" is not likely if Agee crossed out the punctuation. Further support for the present choice may come from Agee's frequent use of a comma to reflect longer than normal pauses and perhaps from his intent to have Laura gradually recover her ability to speak.)
213.37 I said:] (The words "I said:" are written above "No." and "*Have*" without a caret by Agee and are included by the editor.)
214.24 Yes . . .] Yes ___
215.15 very beginning?] (Agee writes "very beginning?" interlinearly over the original text and indicates its insertion with a caret, but forgets to cross out "first?" in the text.)
215.19–21 (The alternation of dialog by inserted paragraphing follows Agee's intent in the conversation between Laura and Jessie, but his text is somewhat confused in the manuscript. The following additional changes have been made:

215.19 Jay."] Jay,"
215.20 out.] out,
215.21 "But,] "but,

The final emendation is the most significant as it switches the speaker from Jessie to Laura, but given Agee's own subsequent paragraphing and the content of the conversation, this change is obviously required.)
215.30 so,] so
216.8 shyly] shily

216.9–10 a— . . . that—] a, . . . that,

217.13 eyes.] (TX 5.3, [73] ends at this point, about one-third down from the top of the manuscript page. However, the deleted top half of [74] (all but the first four lines) is a version of 216.34–217.13, and 217.14 immediately follows this section with no space, asterisks, or any standard indication of Agee's desiring a chapter break. These points and the continuing flow of the narrative argue for the present connection, one that McDowell incorporates as well.)

217.29 so?] so.

217.30 speaking,] speaking

218.5 arms'] arm's

218.14–30 (This section was marked for deletion and restoration, both likely by a previous editor rather than Agee.)

218.38 shyly] shily

219.7 angrily.] (TX 5.3, [75] ends at this point, at the bottom of the manuscript page. A bit more than the top one-third of [76] (all but the top two lines) is deleted as an earlier version of 217.14–219.7, and 219.8 immediately follows this section with no space, asterisks, or any standard indication of Agee's desiring a chapter break. These points and the continuing flow of the narrative argue for the present connection, one that McDowell incorporates as well. See also the second variant for this chapter recorded in "Major Manuscript Variants.")

219.12 big] (The word "big" is written above "the" and "kettle" without a caret by Agee and is included by the editor.)

219.30 faithful,] ("faithful," is written above "earnest," and "heartsick," without a caret by Agee and is included by the editor.)

Chapter 28

220.1 *Chapter 28*]

Agee indicates the start of a new chapter by the inclusion of three asterisks centered at the top of manuscript page TX 5.3, [79]. The placement of this chapter, TX 5.3, [79–82], is determined by its content, the chronology of the novel, and the necessary correction of McDowell's editorial manipulation of chapter 29. Chapter 28 (McDowell's chapter 9) deals with Laura's parents, Joel and Emma, after Joel's telephone call to Laura (which occurred just past the midpoint of chapter 27) to see if Hugh had called and told her any more about what had happened to Jay in the accident. The rest of chapter 27 focuses on Laura and Aunt Jessie talking first about how the family had felt about Laura marrying Jay and then on Jessie's retelling of Laura's gradual realization of the full impact that the accident would have. Chapter 28 begins with Joel returning from his telephone conversation with Laura to tell his wife that he had learned nothing. Since chapter 27 ends with

Laura and Jessie getting to their feet and the first section of chapter 29 (marked by Agee's inserted space) ends with "they drew back their chairs and started for the door" (227.31), it seems likely that Agee wished to insert the effect of the accident on Joel and Emma, then bring the narrative back to Laura and Jessie, and then to the same chronological point, the point just before Hugh enters at the start of the second and largest section of chapter 29 with the news of Jay's death.

Strong structural evidence supports these conclusions. The first section of chapter 29 (TX 5.3, [77–78, 83]) begins at the top of TX 5.3, [77] and is preceded by three centered asterisks with space above and below the line they occupied (Agee's standard designation for a new chapter), and the second section of chapter 29 (TX 5.3, [83–89]) begins on the same page [83] immediately after the first section ends, a break indicated by Agee's skipping a line. A previous editor had also numbered pages [77–78, 83–89] as 15 through 23 consecutively in the upper right-hand corner. McDowell chose to attach the first section of chapter 29 to chapter 27 and indicated the break with only a space rather than following Agee's markers for a new chapter. The color and type of the paper of the manuscript pages also lends support to the present order of the chapters: 27 and 28 are on inexpensive yellow paper while both sections of chapter 29 are on white paper that has age-toned to light brown. It is clear that the two sections of chapter 29 were never meant to be divided.

221.20 "No."] "No,"

221.31–32 And . . . wrong.] (These lines and line 34 were marked for deletion by McDowell or another previous editor.)

221.33–34 *Rather* . . . ways] (Lines 33 and 34 are rendered as Agee wrote them. However, the paragraph break may be extraneous, since all the material seems a part of Joel's interior monolog. "*Rather,* indeed!" may also be Emma's thought, but as the choice is equivocal, Agee's lines remain as written. Agee again splits Joel's comment and thought in lines 221.36–37, perhaps lending weight to Joel as the source of lines 33–34.)

222.5 "Oh. I] (A paragraph symbol is erroneously inserted at this point between "Oh." and "I", perhaps by a previous editor or perhaps by Agee.)

222.10 Working] (The space preceding this section, which commences TX 5.3, [81–82], is included by the editor because of the space left at the bottom of the previous manuscript page by Agee and his then starting a new page. The two halves of this chapter may have been composed or revised by Agee at different times. [79–80] is nearly a fair copy with, for Agee, broad and generous script. [81–82] bears more correction and in a far tighter and cramped script.)

223.4 he's—if that's—finished] he's, if that's, finished

223.15 isn't—] isn't:

223.31–32 replied, "Of] replied, (Agee's paragraph break.) "Of

224.24 shyly] shily

224.29–30 and including] & including (Agee added this phrase in the left margin just to the left of "all regret".)

224.33 more—cruel—than] more, cruel, than

Chapter 29

225.1 *Chapter 29*]

Please see note 220.1 above for the rationale for the placement of this chapter and for the unity of its two sections. Please also see "Major Manuscript Variants" for an earlier version of the part of the second section of this chapter. The first part of chapter 29 forms the final part of McDowell's chapter 8; its second part is McDowell's chapter 10.

225.6 volubly] (The bracketed phrase "and, on the whole, with considerable practicality," which follows "volubly" is not included in the text on the assumption that it is Agee's deletion.)

225.19 stared] stared with (Agee crossed out the phrase that "with" introduced, but inadvertently forgot to delete "with".)

226.12 Yours] yours

226.12 You] you

227.9 it's . . .] it's ___

227.13 control: "What] control: (Agee's paragraph break) "What

228.26 three] 3

232.4 there's . . .] there's ___

232.7 now . . .] now ___

232.15 ever . . .] ever ___

232.27 nonsense,] nonsense

232.31 if . . .] if ___

236.10 I . . .] I ___

Chapter 30

237.1 *Chapter 30*]

This chapter (TX 5.3, [91–101]) follows its predecessor in chronological order. Chapter 29 ends with Laura and her father walking into the kitchen after their talk, and chapter 30 begins with their arrival there. The chapter break is determined by spacing. Agee ends chapter 29 halfway down the page (TX 5.3, [89]) and begins chapter 30 at the top of a new manuscript page (TX 5.3, [91]). Chapter 30 is McDowell's chapter 11.

237.2 where . . .] where ___

238.25 (he had . . . drunk")] (The parentheses are square brackets in the manuscript. Rather than a deletion, however, these brackets may indicate an aside containing Hugh's mental editing of the text he relates to protect Laura from the idea that Jay might have been drinking. This view gains support from the later introduction of that possibility. The present treatment concurs with that of the McDowell edition.)

238.26 said.] said,

238.26–27 bless his heart] (The words "bless his heart," are written above "get home," and "he" without a caret by Agee and are inserted by the editor.)

239.7 know . . .] know ___

239.14 "Mercy,] "Mercy

239.17 Jay . . .] Jay ___

239.31 breath.] (The sentence "There wasn't." follows this word in the manuscript, but is bracketed for deletion.)

240.23 Hahh?"] Hahh!" (The editorial change in punctuation better suits Hugh's subsequent demonstration.)

240.34 this. . . ." He] this ___" he

240.37 Hugh] Tom (Agee apparently toyed with changing Hugh's name to Tom. Hugh appears as "Tom" in several places in the manuscript for the novel. See, for example, note 242.31 below, page [5.2.7] in "Major Manuscript Variants" for chapter 5, and 242.27 in "Word Choice Where No Preference Is Indicated." McDowell chooses to replace "Tom" with "son".)

241.31–32 eight-foot embankment—] eight foot embankment,

241.32 went—] went,

242.8 p-paralyzed] pparalyzed

242.26 them: "He] them: (Agee's paragraph break) "He

242.31 Hugh] Tom (See 240.37 above.)

243.22 His] his

243.25 speaking,] speaking

244.6 Thy] thy

245.20 mimic] mimick

245.24 absurdity and horror and] (Both uses of "and" are lightly bracketed in the manuscript, but are included by the editor since no other alternative is offered.)

245.33 and their] and until their (The second use of "until" in the sentence is lightly bracketed in the manuscript and deleted by the editor. These lightly bracketed deletions are noted since many of the brackets indicating deletions are composed of strokes of approximately the same pressure as the text they enclose.)

245.38 spoke: "Well] spoke: (Agee's paragraph break) "Well

246.12 Hugh] Tom (See 240.37 above.)

246.18 "'I see,'] "I see,

246.18 "'I see,' said the blindman,"] (Hugh quotes the first half of a Wellerism, an old proverb of unknown origin, to underscore the irony of his mother's supposed understanding of what occurred despite her deafness. The entire

	Wellerism is "'I see,' said the blindman, as he picked up his hammer and saw.")
246.21	better . . .] better ___
247.15	that . . .] that ___
247.19	does—beat—all—hell] does, beat, all, hell
247.22	Papa?] Papa,
247.27	sport."] sport.
248.7–8	can—assure—everybody—that] can, assure, everybody, that
248.13–14	imbecile"—"Oh, . . . out—"the rest] imbecile" "Oh, . . . out, "the rest
248.16	amnesia.] amnesia, or feeble-mindedness (", or feeble-mindedness" is enclosed in light brackets and deleted by the present editor.)
248.36	Instead . . .] Instead ___
249.7	furious—and] (The manuscript has a dash inserted interlinearly over a comma with no choice made by Agee.)
249.27	—her . . . word—] , her . . . word,
249.37	epitaphs] (The word "epitaphs," is written above "for," and "Joel" without a caret by Agee and is included by the editor.)
250.2	Hugh] Tom (See 240.37 above.)
250.4	shyly] shily
250.6	and] &
250.11	In—his—*strength*] In, his, *strength*
250.29	his *father*] ("his" was originally lightly underlined, but the underlining was lightly marked for deletion.)
251.15–16	"of course."] 'of course.'
251.18–19	(Dashes replace Agee's commas.)
251.27	(Dashes replace Agee's commas.)
251.30	a—] a,
251.33	ment—"] me"
251.36	me—why—well] me, why, well
253.4	most—heartfelt—sympathies] most, heartfelt, sympathies

Chapter 31

254.1 *Chapter 31*]

This chapter (TX 5.3, [102–10]) follows its predecessor in chronological order. Chapter 30 ends with Hugh going into the hall to make the telephone call to notify Jay's parents of his death and chapter 31 opens with Hugh making that call. Page [101] ends with a deleted paragraph at the bottom of the page also dealing with Hugh's making the call. This material is revised by Agee and serves as the first paragraph of page [102], with the text commencing after Agee skips down one line to begin. This space and his beginning of a new manuscript page likely indicate Agee's intent to start a new chapter at this point. Chapter 31 is the first part of McDowell's chapter 12.

254.28 Jay—] Jay,
255.6 Concussion—] Concussion,
255.11 his,] his
255.29 about—coming down—tell] about, coming down, tell
255.38 we . . .] we ___
256.2 that . . ."] that ___
256.4 "Frank's an undertaker!"] (This sentence is bracketed for deletion, but needs to be included to make sense of Laura's previous exclamation.)
256.8 just . . .] just
256.11 I . . .] I ___
256.21 Jay's . . .] Jay's ___
256.36–38 Nothing . . . Emma.] (This section was bracketed for deletion, but is retained by the editor to add to the development of Joel's character and for a better introduction to his wife Emma's subsequent question. Other deletions on this page of manuscript are boldly crossed out.)
257.4 his parents' farm in] (Added by editor to clarify that Jay's parents lived closest to the town of Jacksboro, five or six miles south of LaFollette, a larger community where Frank lived.)
257.23 Except] Excep
258.16 and . . ."] and ___
258.19 even . . ."] even ___
259.18 dining-room.] dining-room,
259.21 the—it's] the; it's
259.33 earth . . .] earth ___
260.19 mean . . .] mean ___
261.3 you . . .] you ___
261.13 a . . .] a ___
261.20 house?] house,
261.22 thought] though
262.4 we're . . .] we're ___
262.9 over. . . . She] over ___ She
262.30 I . . .] I ___
262.33 about . . .] about ___
262.35 Do] D
263.17 darling?] darling.
263.37 goodbye] good-bye

Chapter 32

265.1 *Chapter 32*]

This chapter (TX 5.3, [110–17]) follows its predecessor in chronological order and is the second part of McDowell's chapter 12. Chapter 31 ends with Laura finishing her conversation with Jay's spirit and her prayers in the children's room, and chapter 32 begins with her return to her family in the living room.

Chapter 32 begins on the same manuscript page [110] on which chapter 31 ends, with Agee separating the two chapters by a space and the use of three centered asterisks, a frequent indicator of his beginning a new chapter. McDowell ignores this indicator and presents chapters 31 and 32 as his chapter 12, skipping two lines to note the separation in the manuscript text.

266.10	it"—] it," (This change and that of 266.12 were made by the editor to clarify that Hugh is interrupting Laura's explanation.)
266.12	—"why] "why
266.29	slowly: "I *don't*] slowly: (Agee's paragraph break) "I *don't*
266.37	Jessie'd] Jessied
267.21–22	(Between these two lines, Agee has written "[Thanksgiving Day]" near the right margin on a separate line. The significance of the bracketed comment is unknown, and the text has been continued without leaving any space since Joel's thoughts respond immediately to his son, Hugh's, previous statement.)
268.7	them;] them,
269.4	forehead,] forehead
269.38	was. . . .] was ___.
270.3	it.] it:
270.10	just . . ."] just ___"
270.14	think . . ."] think ___"
270.19	I . . ."] I ___"
270.32	if, if it] if, [if] it (The inclusion of the second "if" by the present editor although bracketed in the manuscript, seems better to support Agee's style. These brackets may be a previous editor's and not Agee's, since two subsequent bracketed lines on this page [see 271.3 and 271.5 below] are marked marginally with question marks that are not in Agee's hand. McDowell does not include the second "if"; he does include both lines marked with question marks.)
270.33	*convenient . . ."*] *convenient* ___"
270.35	mean . . ."] mean ___"
270.36	"Just perhaps during the—interim . . ."] "Just perhaps during the, interim, ___" (Agee or a previous editor bracketed "perhaps" and indicated that it should be moved from after "interim" to after "Just" with a line and arrow, but never changed the original punctuation. The sentence appears in the manuscript, without the line and arrow being noted, as follows: "Just during the, interim, [perhaps] ___.")
271.3	"Tomorrow then."] ? ["Tomorrow then."] (Question mark is in a previous editor's hand.)
271.5	"Not at all."] ? ["Not at all."] (Question mark is in a previous editor's hand.)
271.16	voice:] voice.
271.16	plot;] plot,

271.33 Must've . . .] Must've ___
271.34 What's . . .] What's ___
272.22 We'll—] We'll;
272.34 shoulders,] shoulders
272.34 backbone] back-bone
273.6 Joel] He (The sentence immediately preceding this one was deleted by Agee and began with "Joel"; "He" was meant to refer to Joel, but after the deletion would mistakenly refer to Hugh, as the subsequent text makes clear.)
274.5 Jessie."] Jessie.
274.26 I . . .] I ___
274.30 It's—was—] it's, was,
275.2 close] closed
275.10 things . . .] things,
275.11 loudly:] loudly.
275.15 I . . .] I ___

Chapter 33

276.1 *Chapter 33*]

This chapter (TX 5.3, [117–19]) follows its predecessor in chronological order. Chapter 32 ends with Laura and Jessie cleaning up and discussing the amount of whiskey Laura had drunk and getting ready for bed. All this occurs immediately after Laura watches Hugh and Joel guide Emma home until she can no longer see them. Chapter 33 commences Hugh's interior monolog as the three walk home. Chapter 33 begins near the bottom of the same manuscript page [117] on which chapter 32 ends, with Agee separating the two chapters by a space of two or three skipped lines. McDowell concurs with this chapter separation, but—perhaps judging the section too short to stand on its own, even though the entire section is solely Hugh's—mistakenly combines it with chapter 34 to form his chapter 13. See also 279.1 below.

Please see the "Marginal Notes" section for 276.1 for information on previous editors' mark-ups. The McDowell edition treats this section of text correctly by not including the first five lines of page [118], which Agee rewrote immediately below on the same page after skipping a line and perhaps drawing the line across the page. The five lines were likely crossed out by a previous editor rather than Agee, given the sine wave marking used through that text, but it is clear that they were not meant for inclusion.

277.2 dryly] drily
277.13 *sleep*] *streets* (Agee inadvertently has Hugh say "*streets*" instead of "*sleep*" in the manuscript.)

Chapter 34

279.1 *Chapter 34*]

This chapter (TX 5.3, [120–21]) follows its predecessor in chronological order. Chapter 33 ends with Hugh, Joel, and Emma entering the Tyler house, and chapter 34 returns to the scene with Laura and Jessie back at the Agee house, the scene that was interrupted by the Tylers' walk home. McDowell joins the chapters together as his chapter 13 undoubtedly because of their short length, and denotes the break by skipping two lines in his text, but chapter 33 ends a little below midway down manuscript page [119] and chapter 34 begins a new page [120] one or two lines down from the top of that page, a normal indication of Agee's beginning a new chapter. Thus, the present edition presents this material as a separate chapter. See also 276.1 above.

279.3 is] Is

279.11 "Yesss. Good] "Yesss. (Agee's paragraph break) "Good (Agee's paragraph break has been eliminated to avoid the initial ambiguity of the "her" that follows.)

279.17 Jessie] She (Another editorial change to avoid ambiguity. This sentence commences Jessie's internal monolog, a rumination that continues until the first section break. Then Laura's internal monolog occupies that second section, and both are joined together in the third short and final section of the chapter.)

279.19 living-room] living room

281.8 O Lord] o Lord

281.23 ceiling] cieling

Chapter 35

284.1 *Chapter 35*]

This chapter (TX 5.3, [145–47]) follows its predecessor in chronological order. Chapter 34 ends with Laura and Jessie in bed and trying to go to sleep, and chapter 35 begins the next morning with Rufus waking up. Chapter 35 begins a new page [145] approximately three lines down from the top of that page, a normal indication of Agee's beginning a new chapter, and ends a little more than three-quarters of the way down page [147]. McDowell prints this chapter as his chapter 14.

284.11 the new cloth] ("new" is written above the space between the other two words without a caret and is included by the editor.)

284.11 the new leather] ("new" is written above the space between the other two words without a caret and is included by the editor.)

284.18 best teacup] best-teacup

284.20 shouted,] (The word "imperiously" appears in brackets, and hence marked for deletion, after "shouted"; it is deleted from this edition as a poor match for Rufus' character, whereas McDowell includes it.)

285.15 betrayal] (The word "inexplicable" appears in brackets, and hence marked for deletion, before "betrayal"; it is deleted from this edition as a poor match for Rufus' character, whereas McDowell includes it.)

285.26 Emma?] Emma,

286.26 *dead, dead*] *dead. dead*

287.2 will."] will"; (Agee ends his page [146] with a semicolon, but begins a new sentence with "Then" on the next manuscript page.)

287.15–16 (he nodded proudly)] he nodded proudly

287.30 down,] down

Chapter 36

289.1 *Chapter 36*]

This chapter (TX 5.3, [148–52]) follows its predecessor in chronological order. Chapter 35 ends with Rufus and little Emma going downstairs to breakfast, and chapter 36 begins with their breakfast with Aunt Jessie. Chapter 36 begins a new page [148] approximately two lines down from the top of that page, a normal indication of Agee's beginning a new chapter, and ends just a few lines from the bottom of page [152]. As previously noted, chapter 35 ends a little more than three-quarters of the way down page [147] and reinforces the integrity of this unit as a chapter. McDowell prints this chapter as his chapter 15.

289.5 queer;] queer

289.5–6 it was so still and it was so still it seemed dark] it was so still and it was so still it seemed dark > so sort of dark (While Agee indicates the inclusion of the longer, and repetitive for emphasis, interlinear conclusion to the sentence with a caret, he does not mark "so sort of dark" for deletion.)

289.7 Post Toasties] postoasties

289.10 Emma";] Emma,"

289.10 dawdle";] dawdle",

289.18 milk,] milk

289.29 proud] (The word is encircled in the manuscript and omitted by McDowell. There is no consistency in omission or retention of words and phrases that are circled. Sometimes it also seems to indicate that the word or phrase cannot be deciphered.)

290.8 and maybe that was why,] (The phrase is encircled in the manuscript and omitted by McDowell. See 289.29 above.)

290.11–12 these noises meant, you be quiet, and every time] (The phrase is encircled in the manuscript and omitted by McDowell. See 289.29 above.)

290.19 said,] said

290.20	minute?] minute.
290.23	*good morning merry sunshine*] good morning merry sunshine
290.29	Ever any more. What's ever any more.] (An editor has bracketed the first sentence for deletion, then bracketed "what's" for deletion, and then overwritten the "e" of "ever" to make it a capital. That "e" is not in Agee's hand, and therefore this edition restores the bracketed material that the McDowell edition omits.)
290.37	We] , we
291.7	quietly: "I think] quietly: (Agee's paragraph break) "I think
291.11	him?] him,
291.31	continued: "A *fatal*] continued: (Agee's paragraph break) "A *fatal*
291.32	"fatal,"] fatal,
292.13	when . . .] when ___
292.17	make it,] make it
292.19	again. "Do you] again. (Agee's paragraph break) "Do you
292.22–23	eight-foot] eight foot
292.23	backward,] backward
292.32	They're] Theyre
293.10–11	they . . . chest.] (This clause is enclosed in brackets, possibly by a previous editor rather than Agee, and is retained for its content and the fact that no correction of the previous punctuation was made to render a complete the sentence after the indicated deletion.)
293.12	children?] children,
293.22	eight-foot] eight foot
293.24	ceiling] cieling
293.31	Rufus] Richard
293.33	moment."] moment.
293.34	When's . . .] When's ___
293.35	What's . . .] What's ___
294.32	he . . .] he ___

Chapter 37

295.1	*Chapter 37*]

This chapter (TX 5.3, [153–64]) follows its predecessor in chronological order. Chapter 36 ends with Rufus' and little Emma's questions being answered by Aunt Jessie after breakfast, and chapter 37 begins with Rufus leaving the room after breakfast is over. Chapter 37 begins a new page [153] approximately two or three lines down from the top of that page, a normal indication of Agee's beginning a new chapter, and ends after recording nine lines on [164]. McDowell prints this chapter as his chapter 16, but alters its conclusion by substituting an earlier draft version from a different manuscript (see 308.38 below).

Since this edition agrees with McDowell's choice of manuscript (with the exception of his altering the conclusion), no thorough-going evaluation of manuscripts TX 5.3, [153–64] and the earlier TX 5.2, [87–90] seems necessary. Selected evidence, in addition to its greater elaboration, includes two instances on 5.2, [89] in which two interlinear additions ("it was just a chance in a million" and "as a loon,") and a marginal insertion ("and more creditable to him and to his father;") are incorporated into the normal text of 5.3, [159]. See the text of this edition for the context of the incorporated materials (303.11, 16, 23) and note that Agee further revises the last insertion by reversing the order of "him" and "his father"). See also "Major Manuscript Variants" for the entire 5.2, [87–90] text.

295.11	themselves:] themselves,
296.18	hat rack] hatrack
296.29	hat rack] hatrack
297.28	proud] proud. (Agee inadvertently forgets to delete this period when editing and adding to the sentence.)
297.29	shyly] shily
298.5	sonny?] sonny,
300.1	quiet] quieten (The British "quieten"—that is, to make quiet—is changed to its American counterpart by the editor.)
300.2	shyly] shily
300.4	ain't] aint
300.11	till—] till,
300.27	was . . .] was ___
300.35	eight-foot] eight foot
301.13	incredulously:] incredulously;
301.34	eight-foot] eight foot
302.4	happened?] happened,
302.25	Agee. He's] Agee, he's
302.36–37	eight-foot] eight foot
302.37	emb—] emb,
303.38	shyly] shily
304.37	Yes'm] Yesm
305.3	tray] trays
306.19	night,] night
306.29	day, do] day do
306.37	Yes'm] Yesm
307.4	Yes'm] Yesm
308.8	it?] it.
308.11	it?] it.
308.12	what?] what.
308.14	what?] what.
308.20	it?] it.
308.21–22	I—went out—showed] I: went out: showed
308.38	(At this point, McDowell substitutes the conclusion of an earlier draft of the chapter. He uses the final part of Agee's last paragraph from 5.2,

[90] in place of part of page 5.3, [164]. See "Major Manuscript Variants" for the entire earlier version (5.2, [87–90]).

The conclusion used by McDowell is the last eight manuscript lines of 5.2, [90] extracted from Agee's eighteen-line concluding paragraph of the 5.2, [87–90] draft and could in no way be connected to the rest of the 5.3, [153–64] manuscript that McDowell uses for his chapter 17. McDowell in fact uses two of Agee's first three sentences on 5.3, [164]. See also "Marginal Notes," for 308.37. McDowell's conclusion is rendered below for the convenience of the reader.

McDowell deletes the first sentence ("Down at Mr. Roberts', he thought.") from line 308.38, uses the remainder of that line and line 309.1 ("Not another mark on his body. / He still looked at the chair."), and then adds the following from 5.2, [90]:

> With a sense of deep stealth and secrecy he finally went over and stood beside it. After a few moments, and after listening most intently, to be sure that nobody was near, he smelled of the chair, its deeply hollowed seat, the arms, the back. There was only a cold smell of tobacco and, high along the back, a faint smell of hair. He thought of the ash tray on its weighted strap on the arm; it was empty. He ran his finger inside it; there was only a dim smudge of ash. There was nothing like enough to keep in his pocket or wrap up in a paper. He looked at his finger for a moment and licked it; his tongue tasted of darkness.)

Chapter 38

312.1 *Chapter 38*]

This chapter (TX 5.3, [165–75]) follows its predecessor in chronological order in that no other chapter that survives intervenes. There is a small gap in time, certainly not uncommon in the novel, between the chapters. The break may comprise the latter part of day of chapter 37 and at least one additional day as well, since chapter 38 begins with breakfast and in the first paragraph Agee mentions that Rufus and Emma "felt like this was an even more special day than day before yesterday." (312.4–5), and later, Laura says to her children that "'Mother has wanted to see you more, these last days;'" (314.9–10).

Interestingly, after skipping a line of space on page [164], the last page of chapter 37, Agee records two two-line beginnings (all subsequently crossed out) of a section (chapter?) that may have featured Hugh. No other version of this material apparently survives. It is likely that Agee instead chose to continue the Rufus–Emma–Aunt Jessie material as a transition between the chapters. Thus, chapter 37 concludes with Rufus' scene with Emma and Aunt Jessie and his contemplations of his actions that day (all of which occur after the last bell rings for school, the only previous referent before "day before yesterday" to determine how much time after that has passed) and Rufus' and Emma's breakfast with Aunt Jessie, the scene that begins chapter 38. McDowell prints this section as his chapter 17.

312.21	good.] good
312.28	"Father"] Father
313.4	yes F—] yes F __
313.19	and sad] + sad (The first part of Agee's interlinear addition of this phrase is unclear. The symbol is quite small. The "+" could be "&" or even a comma written above the level of the word "sad.")
313.34	have . . .] have ___
314.7	shyly] shily
314.10	just—couldn't,] just—couldn't
314.11	said "couldn't"] said couldn't
314.36	back?] back,
315.20	Rufus asked.] (These words, which appear to be bracketed for deletion by a previous editor, are included for clarity.)
315.25–29	"Now . . . more.] (This paragraph appears to have been bracketed for deletion by a previous editor and is restored for several reasons. It completes Laura's explanation of the wake to her children, likely a necessary part of her talk, and the brackets are heavier and larger than Agee's normal deletion marks. The word "dinner" is also encircled in the paragraph as a word that could not at one point be made out by the editor or the typist.)
315.27	Savage's] Savages
315.34	violently. She] violently, She
316.3	saying: "Now] saying: (Agee's paragraph break) "Now
316.20	said: "Of] said: (Agee's paragraph break) "Of
317.12	orphan, or] (Agee marks three lines of narrative between these words for deletion by bracketing them in the paragraph. He apparently indicates the reason for his choice with another bracket that runs the length of the three lines in the left margin of the manuscript and writing the word "*earlier*" just to the left of that bracket. The gist of the omitted material is, in fact, treated earlier in the chapter. McDowell does not incorporate these lines, but they are included in the recent Library of America edition of the novel. See its page 814, note 698.22–27.)
317.30	'huh,' say 'what is it, Rufus?'"] huh, say what is it, Rufus?"
317.34–36	"She . . . Rufus?'"] (All internal quotation marks added as necessary for dialog.)
318.21	black] blank
318.23	and he] and he and he (The placement of Agee's marginal insertion of "He wore a long shallow hat and he" is problematic, but the present choice is likely and agrees with McDowell.)
318.30	T . . .] T ___
318.34	and Emma] & Emma

318.34–35 she said.] she said:
319.2 her.] her—
319.2 Agee?] Agee,
320.22–23 "stare," they wondered; "elders"; "ill-bred"?] stare, they wondered; elders; ill-bred?
320.24 'Sir,' or 'I beg your pardon, Father.'"] Sir, or I beg your pardon, Father."
320.31 'Excuse me, Father.'"] excuse me, father."
320.32 Father] father
321.7 "uncivil"?] uncivil
321.8 'yes, Father.'"] yes, Father."
321.16 sister] Sister
321.20–21 tell"—they heard Jessie on the stairs—"Children] tell—" they heard Jessie on the stairs "—Children
321.24 children,] children
323.1 first by Aunt] first Aunt
323.7 were on] were no
323.27 in manly] in manly in
323.30 singer] singe
325.4 realized (for] realized, (for
325.9 sitting-room] sitting room
325.22 Sava . . .] Sava ___
326.34 Primordrial] (Agee humorously has Rufus mispronounce one of his "big words" of which he is proud and has Arthur Savage, who does not know the word, subsequently echo the mistake when he asks Rufus the meaning of the word.)
327.15 'Lord it'] Lord it
328.9 I always thought] I always thought &c / I always thought (At this point the manuscript has multiple marginal insertions. The repetition of "I always thought" followed by "&c" directs the text from one insertion back to the previous insertion in which the remainder of the sentence—"'your father was a lot like Lincoln,' he said."—had been crossed out. The "&c" requires the restoration of Mr. Savage's dialog, but one of the "I always thought" statements needs to be deleted. Similarly, the "he said" needs to remain deleted to prevent the interruption of Savage's continuing monolog. McDowell's edition concurs in this treatment of the text.)

Chapter 39

329.1 *Chapter 39*]

This chapter (TX 5.3, [175–76]) follows its predecessor in chronological order. Chapter 39 begins on the same manuscript page [175] on which chapter 38 ends, with Agee separating the two chapters by a space and the use of three centered asterisks, a frequent indicator of his beginning a new chapter. Chapter 39 brings the reader inside Laura's mind and bedroom to provide her perspective on her ordeal and on the conversations which the children had partially overheard in chapter 38. It forms the first part of McDowell's chapter 18. However, his edition prints chapters 39, 41 (TX 5.3, [177–80], and 40 (TX 5.3, [181–82]) as one, and prints them in improper order (as indicated by the numbering of this edition's chapters).

Both editors agree that chapter 39 comes first, and this placement is supported by its beginning on the same manuscript page on which chapter 38 ends, as noted above. The order of presentation of chapters 40 and 41 is resolved in this edition using the chronology of the events in the chapters. The order of this edition allows for the arrival of Joel Tyler, the children's grandfather, at the beginning of chapter 40, before the main viewing of Jay's body (chapter 41) and gives Hugh the chance to explain to his father, Joel, that Laura (nicknamed Poll) is praying with Father Robertson, providing a direct link to and some overlap with the end of chapter 39. This order also allows Joel, Hugh, and Walter Savage, who enters at the end of the chapter, to all be present before Laura takes her children to see their father's body for the first time. Most importantly, chapter 40 has the children sitting (likely in the "East Room" of the house) with their Aunt Jessie, waiting for their mother, and chapter 41 begins with Laura then bringing them from "through the Green Room and into the living-room" to view their father. This order is further supported by the continuity from chapter 41 to 42 (the latter contains the second and last viewing of the body). At the end of chapter 41, the children are crossing back and going into the "East Room" to be with Aunt Jessie as their mother has asked, see Aunt Jessie motionless, and chapter 42 begins with "As they drew near. . . ." They are thus returned to the room where they likely first sat to wait for their mother, and then they wait again to see their father's body until the other mourners have paid their respects. Chapter 42 ends with the coffin being screwed shut. With chapters 41 and 42 and also 38 and 39 thus linked together, the placement of chapter 40 between them because of its content is a relatively confident one.

This edition's order also eliminates the need for McDowell's altering of the first words of chapter 42 (his chapter 19). McDowell changes the manuscript's text of "As they drew near" to "As they came back with Mr. Starr", evidently to affect a transition with the out-of-order chapter 40 which ends with Savage's entrance. ("Starr" is the name McDowell substituted for "Savage.")

It is fairly likely that McDowell's placement of the material contained in chapter 40 was determined by the interpretation that the children had already seen their father. But the text upon which one could base that belief (333.16–24) is more logically either the relation of their thoughts about soon going to see him or their seeing the casket from the room in which they were sitting and waiting for their mother. No matter what the interpretation of this particular section, the substantial weight of textual evidence points to the correctness of the order of the chapters as incorporated in this edition.

In regard to the presentation of each of these chapters as distinct units, chapter 39 is treated above. It also ends leaving several lines of space at the bottom of page [176]. Chapter 40 begins after skipping approximately three lines of space down from the top of page [181], a normal indication of Agee's beginning a new chapter, and ends one-third of the way down page [182]. Chapter 40 appears to be of earlier composition in that Hugh is referred to as Tom. The toning and condition of its paper is also distinctly different from that of chapters 39 and 41. Chapter 41 begins after skipping a space of two or three lines down from the top of page [177] and ends three-quarters of the way down page [180]. These separations are common indications of Agee's desire to have them as separate chapters.

In his chapter 18, McDowell does separate chapter 39 from 41 by skipping a space of two lines, but simply appends chapter 40 to chapter 41 as a continuation with no indication of its separate nature. As noted above, differences in pagination and paper strongly argue against such a union, as do other physical indicators such as paper clip marks that appear only on the pages of chapter 40. Thus McDowell combines chapters 39, 41, and 40 to form his chapter 18.

329.4–10	Throughout . . . carry] (This section originally began the chapter, was then marked for deletion within brackets, and then marked for inclusion by Agee after a new first sentence was recorded.)
329.18	suffered,] suffered;
330.10	knew—] knew,
330.11	was—] was,
331.3	Cross] cross

Chapter 40

332.1	*Chapter 40*]

This chapter (TX 5.3, [181–82]) follows its predecessor in chronological order. See 329.1 above for an overview of the rationale for chapter order. Chapter 40 begins after skipping approximately three lines of space down from the top of page [181], a normal indication of Agee's beginning a new chapter, and ends one-third of the way down page [182]. Chapter 40 appears to be of earlier composition in that Hugh is referred to as Tom. The toning and condition of its paper is also distinctly different from that of chapters 39 and 41. This chapter forms the final part of McDowell's chapter 18.

332.2	on] in
332.4	voice: "Hugh] voice: (Agee's paragraph break) "Hugh
332.4	Hugh] Tom (See also 240.37.)

332.5–6 “In—there—with Father—Robertson”—] “In: there: with Father: Robertson:”
332.9 —“Praying] “Praying

Chapter 41

334.1 *Chapter 41*]

This chapter (TX 5.3, [177–80]) follows its predecessor in chronological order. See 329.1 above for an overview of the rationale for chapter order. Chapter 41 begins after skipping a space of two or three lines down from the top of page [177], a normal indication of Agee’s beginning a new chapter, and ends three-quarters of the way down page [180]. These manuscript pages have also been folded twice, perhaps to fit inside a business envelope. Chapter 41 is the second part of McDowell’s chapter 18.

334.3 Green Room] green room
335.4 center] centre
336.38 “forever] forever
337.15 God . . .] God:
339.8 God.” His] (McDowell changes the text at this point to read “‘God, and of his Son Jesus Christ our Lord’: His”.)
339.11 always.”] always.
339.15–21 it looked to Rufus . . . to the hall door.] (Within these lines is additional support for the nightmare introduction of this edition: “it looked to Rufus as if he [his father] had been flung down and left on the street, and as if he were a very successfully disguised stranger.” Compare these words to the introduction in which a man has been killed and left on the street, a man that the narrator eventually recognizes as his father. Rufus is about to draw closer to his father’s coffin to determine what has happened, but is prevented as his mother guides him away. Agee uses this important unresolved episode in Rufus’ life to plant the seeds that grow into the nightmare introduction of the adult narrator. It is perhaps noteworthy that Agee added “he [his father] had been flung down and left on the street, and as if” interlinearly to reinforce the connection between the text proper and the nightmare introduction.)

Chapter 42

340.1 *Chapter 42*]

This chapter (TX 5.3, [183–85]) follows its predecessor in chronological order. Like the pages of chapter 41, these manuscript pages have also been folded twice, perhaps to fit inside a business envelope, and perhaps provide additional evidence for the linkage of chapters 41 and 42. See 329.1 above for an overview of the rationale for chapter order. Chapter 42 begins two-thirds of the way down page [183] after four sections of Agee's notes and drafts of the opening and ends one-quarter of the way down page [185], a structure that commonly indicates Agee's desire for the material to stand as a separate chapter. McDowell, however, combines chapter 42 with chapter 43 to form his chapter 19 and indicates the division only by skipping two lines of space between them.

The items that constitute the first section of Agee's notes are all bracketed, and none of the concepts receive significant development in the novel. The second section has two ideas cast as alternatives: the adults not telling the children too much about the wake and Laura's worrying about the appearance of Jay's family. Both were superseded. The third and fourth sections are short, alternative starts of the present chapter that were in part revised and incorporated into the final version. They are given below.

[Section Three]

> As they drew near it seemed to Rufus that the house was especially silent and that all its corners were especially distinct; and each of the bushes on the lawn seemed to stand particularly apart. This was because a number of automobiles and buggies were drawn up along the street across from the house, whereas the the [*sic*] spacious porch of the house itself was bare, and because by intuition he was aware that indoors, the big empty-looking house was crowded with silent people.

[Section Four]

> The house seemed especially silent and bare and its corners were especially distinct, and each of the bushes on the lawn seemed to stand particularly apart.

340.2 As they drew near Rufus noticed] (As noted in 329.1 above, McDowell changes this text to "As they came back with Mr. Starr, Rufus noticed" evidently to affect a transition with the out-of-order chapter 40 which ends with Savage's entrance. "Starr" is the name McDowell substituted for "Savage.")

340.14 multitudinous and] multitudinous &

342.17 Green Room] green room

342.25 shyly] shily

Chapter 43

343.1 *Chapter 43*]

This chapter (TX 5.3, [186–88]) follows its predecessor in chronological order. In chapter 42, Laura tells the children that they will go with Mr. Savage back again to his house after seeing their father's body for the second and last time. Chapter 42 ends with the sealing of the coffin and the family's exit from the room, and chapter 43 begins with Laura delivering the children to Arthur Savage. Chapter 43 is a separate chapter. Agee ends chapter 42 one-quarter of the way down page [185], a structure that commonly indicates his desire to begin a new chapter, and chapter 43 begins with Agee skipping the space of two lines down from the top of page [186], again a common signal on his part of the start of a new chapter. As previously noted, McDowell, however, combines chapter 42 with chapter 43 to form his chapter 19 and indicates the division only by skipping two lines of space between them. Like the pages of chapters 41 and 42, these manuscript pages have also been folded twice, perhaps to fit inside a business envelope, and perhaps provide additional evidence for the linkage of chapters 41, 42, and 43.

343.4 shyly] shily
343.12 living-room] living room
343.25 Uncle Jim] uncle Jim
344.5 Mossie] Maussie
345.33 No . . . you] No you

Chapter 44

346.1 *Chapter 44*]

This chapter (TX 5.3, [189–92]) follows its predecessor in general chronological order, but one manuscript page ([189]) is somewhat problematic in terms of its placement. (The reasons for the page's inclusion are given below.) Page [189] seems to have been properly placed by McDowell at the start of this chapter (the first part of his chapter 20, which combines chapters 44 and 45). The page, however, does not bear any of Agee's indicators that mark the start of a new chapter (no asterisks; no skipped space), but it does begin a new page. However, its text also ends three or four lines from the bottom of the page, perhaps marking a break or even the end of a chapter. The page might also be placed after the end of chapter 45 (TX 5.3, [193–96]), and hence the novel, as its conclusion, but the handwriting of page [189] differs substantially from that of the pages of chapter 45. Pages [190–92] and [193–96] are each properly grouped together and present evidence for their integrity as separate chapters and their order of presentation. The text of pages [190] and [193] both begin two lines down from the top of their pages. Each ends at the bottom of their final manuscript pages [192] and [196], respectively. The narrative flow connects the pages of the two chapters internally, with [193], [194], and [195] connected as well by carry-over sentences. Both chapters occur after the burial and have parallel beginnings with Rufus going for a walk with Hugh, but with chapter 44 moving the focus to Emma and 45 bringing the focus back to Rufus.

While it is perhaps possible that page [189] is the conclusion to chapter 45, Agee's handwriting on that page is somewhat closer, though by no means a match, to that of the pages of chapter 44. Agreeing with McDowell's placement also helps bridge chapters 43 and 44, since the narrative of page [189] brings the children back to their mother, as per her previous instructions to Walter Savage in chapter 43, even though Savage and the actual return of the children by him receive no mention. This very brief section might also refer to Hugh's returning to the house with Rufus after their walk, except that both children enter to meet their mother simultaneously—they are greeted by Laura as "'My darlings,'" (346.5). Also, Rufus needs to be brought back to the house before Hugh can ask him to leave to go on a walk, and it is unlikely that Hugh would do so before Rufus had had the chance to see his mother after the funeral. Another transition that page [189] provides between chapter 43 and 44 is that in the house "there was *still* [editor's emphasis] an extraordinary fragrance of carnations"; this statement in the second part of the first sentence of the chapter, plus the preceding echoing of the house, indicates that the mourners had left and the flowers had been brought to the burial site. Placing page [189] at the start of chapter 44 helps to bring the focus of the novel to the immediate and just reunited family, before featuring the children's separate attempts to try to understand what had happened as fully as they can. Importantly, it also allows for the reconciliation of Emma with her mother in a logical progression. Emma is described as emotionally "fatally wounded" in the last paragraph of page [189], and chapter 44 records her attempts to deal with her emotions alone, her eventual hiding under her grandparents' bed while her mother searches for her, and ends with their reunion in a loving embrace. It would make no sense for Emma to be in "an enchantment of pain and loneliness" ([189]) after purging her emotional wounds with a cascade of tears in her mother's arms in the last paragraph of chapter 44.

The chronologies of events and other textual evidence thus strongly support the placement of page [189] at the beginning of chapter 44 rather than at the conclusion of the novel. Readers, however, may wish to read the text using both placements. Page [189] is separated from page [190] in this edition at 347.4–5 to indicate the space left or skipped at the bottom of page [189] and the beginning of page [190]. McDowell combines the two pages seamlessly with no indication of Agee's spacing.

Chapter 44 forms the first part of McDowell's chapter 20.

346.6	now they knew that everything] (Agee's original line reads "suddenly they knew that now everything"; "suddenly" and "now" are very lightly crossed out and "now" is written interlinearly above "suddenly" by Agee.)
346.23	*she . . . am*] "she . . . am" (Italics replace direct quotation to denote Rufus' thoughts.)
347.5	[Rufus]] (Rufus' name is added to the text by the editor for clarification.)
347.25	Mrs.] Mrs

348.4 had, his] had his

348.7 in a great curve upward] ("in a great curve" is written interlinearly over "himself upward among" and begins over the "self" of "himself" with no caret to indicate the correct place for insertion. Since Agee often, but not always, begins his interlinear insertions a bit before the place where the caret appears, this order is chosen. McDowell chooses the alternative. Both choices of placement have essentially equal validity.)

348.13 Above] Above above (Agee forgot to delete the second above after an interlinear insertion was added.)

348.31–32 Green Room] green room

349.4 hear?] hear,

349.18 again,] again

349.24 Green Room] green-room

349.30 dining-room] dining room

349.33 dining-room] dining room

349.34 Green Room] Green room

350.5–25 O Almighty God . . . our Lord. *Amen.*] (At this point in the manuscript, at the top part of a blank space of approximately three lines, Agee records: "(Quote the last half of vespers)." According to correspondence in the Tennessee archives, McDowell had asked Father Flye to provide the prayers—the obvious person whom Agee himself might likely have asked—but apparently, given the statements in Flye's subsequent letters, McDowell had not given Flye sufficient information regarding the context into which the prayers would be inserted. Flye wrote to McDowell on January 10, 1958, July 9, 1958, and July 28, 1959, stating that the prayers that were printed were not the correct ones and urged that they be replaced as soon as possible in subsequent reprintings of the novel (TN 1A.2.23, TN 1A.2.23, and TN 1A.2.24, respectively). Flye's first letter includes his typed version of the correct prayers, and all the letters cite the pages in the Episcopal prayer book where the proper prayers can be found. Flye introduces the prayers with the note "from the Book of Common Prayer." Flye uses the 1928 version of the *Book of Common Prayer* which makes the prayers differ slightly from the prayers that would actually have been said in 1916 when the 1892 version was still in effect. This restored edition is the first to print the prayers that Flye said were appropriate, and they certainly do bear more on the situation of the loss of a loved one than the prayers which he mistakenly first supplied. The prayers printed by McDowell can be found in "Major Manuscript Variants" for chapter 44.

Agee's mother was a member of St. John's Episcopal Church in Knoxville, but gravitated toward the Anglo-Catholic movement within that church (often termed "high church"), likely under the influence of her Aunt Jessie. The situation is reflected in the novel with the presence of both Father Robertson, an Anglo-Catholic priest from Chattanooga, and Dr. Walter C. Whitaker, the rector of St. John's Episcopal Church. Laura subsequently married an Anglo-Catholic priest from St. Andrew's, Father Erskine Wright, marriage being permitted in that church; it is in the Roman Catholic faith that priests must remain celibate.)

350.31–32 I . . . I . . .] I, I,

351.3 tender: . . . and her mother's:. . . .] (Each ellipsis represents a line of approximately one inch in length in the manuscript.)

351.18 but . . .] but ___

351.21 Mama] Mamma

Chapter 45

352.1 *Chapter 45*]

This chapter (TX 5.3, [193–96]) follows its predecessor in chronological order. For the evidence for this material as a new chapter and the possible alternative, though less likely, reading of the repositioning of page [189] to the end of this chapter, please see note 346.1 above. Chapter 45 forms the second part of McDowell's chapter 20.

352.17 talking-to] talking to

352.19 talking-to] talking to

353.1 The sun's . . . blow.] (The space on either side of this line from a song that Rufus hears on his walk with Hugh is added by the editor. That it is from a record is evident from the next line, but the exact song itself could not be ascertained. The line is a common one and appears in slightly modified versions in present-day songs as well.)

353.3 Buster Brown's dog] (Agee is likely conflating two of the most famous dogs in advertising in the early twentieth century—Buster Brown's Tige, and Nipper, "His Master's Voice." Originally a cartoon character, Tige, Buster Brown's dog, did indeed have a pronounced row of "grinning" teeth, but the name and image was purchased by the Brown Shoe Company in 1904 and used to introduce Buster Brown shoes at the St. Louis World's Fair that year. Marketing history was also made that year when the company hired a series of midgets who, dressed as Buster, would tour the country with various Tiges selling the shoes. The tours were so successful they were continued until 1930. However, Tige had nothing to do with records. Nipper, the central feature of Francis Barraud's painting *Dog Looking at and Listening to a Phonograph* (1898), became the trademark of The Gramophone Company in Britain, which sold the American rights to it to the Victor Talking Machine Company. From 1900 on Victor marketed their records using the image, also now retitled as "His Master's Voice," and its successor RCA continued the tradition.)

353.8	for they were walking] for They were walking (Agee forgot to make the first letter of the original first word of his sentence lower case after inserting a new beginning to the sentence interlinearly.)
353.16	ground, into his grave,] ground; into his grave;
353.17	the . . . coffin] the, coffin
353.22	a . . . rowboat] a, rowboat
354.14	disliked Him] disliked him
354.15	in Him] in him
354.34	call anybody; call] call anybody, call
355.2	What?] What,
355.17	Cross] cross
355.18	hocus-pocus] hocus pocus
355.22	That . . .] That ___
355.24	mealy-mouthed] mealy mouthed
355.37	hocus-pocus] hocus pocus
356.30	Mama?] Mama,

Major Manuscript Variants

This section contains significant earlier drafts of chapters or parts of chapters. It does not present all versions, but does present the most finished of the variants that deal with the same material. Agee often worked through multiple drafts of his material. For clarity, distinct variants of the same chapter are separated by a centered line; multiple versions of the same material are not, but are numbered.

There are also three main types of variants: those manuscript variants that were incorrectly chosen by David McDowell for inclusion in the novel, those that survive only in typescript and printed form (in Robert Fitzgerald's *The Collected Short Prose of James Agee*), and those that remain in manuscript form and are used in neither the McDowell edition nor the present restored edition.

Those variants that were incorrectly chosen by David McDowell for inclusion in the novel are reproduced in the variants for chapters 1, 2, and 3 below, and the notes that follow those variants provide the corrections to McDowell's texts using a similar system to the "Textual Commentary and Notes." Also noted are any significant differences between the printed text and Agee's manuscript. Such differences are listed by citing the page and line number of variant text as printed below, followed by the necessary correction from the manuscript and then by McDowell's text. Each such entry thus begins with the page and line number separated by a period. Thus, a note concerning an item or issue on page 80, line 8 of the present transcription of McDowell's edition would be listed as McD 80.8. Space(s) included by Agee to separate sections of a chapter and bracketed page numbers are not included in this count. Thus the entry "McD 80.8 limpid] limp" indicates that the word on page 80, line 8 of the McDowell text should be "limpid," as in the manuscript, rather than "limp" which appears in the version printed by McDowell. Further explanation, if needed, appears in parentheses following the initial note.

There are also three instances of short variants that survive only in Robert Fitzgerald's *The Collected Short Prose of James Agee* and in his typescripts. These are treated in the same manner as the McDowell variants, but their textual notes are prefixed with "RF" rather than "McD." Headnotes also clearly label the McDowell and Fitzgerald variant texts.

By far the largest number of variants are those that remain in manuscript form and are used in neither the McDowell edition nor the present restored edition. These are cited by collection, folder, and page number. Notes on such variants have no prefix and are listed after their texts, again using the same page and line notation system as in the "Textual Commentary and Notes," and sometimes include additional explanations which are in parentheses. Headings, space(s) included by Agee to separate sections of a chapter, and bracketed page numbers are not included in the line number count. In some cases, the note is inserted within the text itself in square brackets for needed clarity. The major collections are abbreviated as "TX" for the Humanities Research Center at the University of Texas and "TN" for Special Collections, University of Tennessee Library, and "AT" for the Agee Trust materials on deposit in Special Collections, University of Tennessee Library. Those materials not in folders are given other appropriate descriptions. Page numbers are noted in brackets, because very few of the manuscript pages are numbered by Agee. The numbers provided thus indicate only the order in which I found the papers in a particular folder or location. The order may have been changed by subsequent readers. Some help may be provided by the editor's pencil numbers that sometimes appear on the pages, but these numbers do not necessarily reflect Agee's ordering of the pages and often clearly do not.

Introduction

There are no major manuscript variants for the introduction, but since it replaces "Knoxville: Summer of 1915," that work is reproduced in full in appendix III as it first appeared in the *Partisan Review* in 1938. Agee never intended that this separately published story be a part of the novel.

There are two short fragments that may be variants or earlier versions of the introduction. Both were printed by Robert Fitzgerald in *The Collected Short Prose of James Agee* (Boston: 1968; [121]–23). They are reproduced below from pages 287–90 of Fitzgerald's typescripts (TX 3, 7) since Agee's original manuscripts apparently do not survive. The typescripts for Fitzgerald's volume that survive (TX 3, 6–7) are mainly copyedited typescripts, except for a few original typescript pages at the end of folder 7. These fragments are part of that latter small group. (See "Major Manuscript Variants" below for chapter 5 and appendix VIII for the other two fragments printed by Fitzgerald.) Notes on the corrected text of these original typescripts are given after the fragments and cited by page and line number as RF 287.2, for example. These notes do not list Fitzgerald's alterations that were made to produce the copyedited typescript version (TX 3, 6–7), but do also list the final changes to the text that appear in print in Fitzgerald's edition.

Fragment 1

[287]

(A note, undated, among others handwritten.) [Fitzgerald's note]

I was rounding the corner into Asylum Avenue, ambling home in the middle of the afternoon, and there at the curb was a crowd and there in the middle of the crowd was a big thin black cat with wild red blood all over its face and its teeth like long thorns and its tongue curled like that of a heraldic lion. Right across the middle it was as flat as an ironed britches leg. Purple guts stained the pavement and a pale bloody turd stood out under its tail. Its head was split open like a melon; against the black fur, its crushed skull was like an egg. This cat was not lying still, nor keeping still: it was as lively as if it were on a gridiron and it was yelling and gasping satanically, the yells sounding like something through a horn whose reed is split: never getting to its feet but flailing this way and that, lying still and panting hardly five seconds at a time: people sidestepping the tatters of blood and slime and closing in again when he was off in another direction. The people were fairly quiet; talking in undertones and not saying much, but never looking away. Something respectful in every one of them. Someone said he had nine lives. It was the first I had ever heard of that, and I believed it. Other people were speculating how many of them he'd lost by now: nobody agreed on that, but they were mostly defending the cat as if against libel: he had plenty more left to go through yet.

Not that anyone there was fool enough to think he'd come out of this and get well, with two or three lives up his sleeve to spare for later contingencies, but he was putting up one whale of a fight, and though there was now and then a murmur about "putting him out his misery," which no voice was raised against, nobody ventured to in-

[288]

terfere with the wonderful processes of nature. (Things like this are happening somewhere on the earth every second.)

Fragment 2

[289]

(Handwritten note undated, datable to the late thirties.) [Fitzgerald's note]

I suppose I may have seen everything in detail, but I don't remember everything, and there's no use inventing it. All I remember is the long blueblack gash made in the asphalt by the dragged axle, which led forty feet right into the hind legs of the mob, and, after I had fought my way through the mob, the man they were looking at. I don't doubt other people were hurt; but I don't recall even seeing them: they couldn't have been hurt as this man was. He was propped up against the ivy on our wall. The right inner forearm and the palm of the right hand were laid open like an anatomical illustration, but less neatly, right to the bone, and the bone was broken, midway between wrist and elbow, like a stick, some pieces still holding. His whole [word omitted: face?] was snatched off as neatly as a wig off a head, and somebody was wiping the blood and glass away, mainly to give him a chance to breathe, but also apparently in some idiotic hope that he might be able to see; and care to if he could. So, just after the wiping, you saw his eyes, like a couple of pale marbles on strings, and you saw his flat nostrils, an inch behind where his nose had been, quite distinctly, and at any time you saw his lipless and broken grinning teeth, those of them that weren't scattered down his shirt. Then the eyes would submerge again, and be wiped off again. He was lying still, not doing anything at all except snoring monstrously, great, soulful, rhythmic, rattling snores that sucked the blood down till the holes were visible and blew it out like tobacco juice (I had forgotten the tobacco juice: it was all over his throat and a quid lay back among his teeth: no one had quite the courage to fish it out and save him the swallowing). There is nothing more

[290]

really to say about him; he just lay there snoring; I am sure you could have heard it a block: it was rather like the sharp, rasping flutter of a rubber farting-whistle, and this fact registered, I suspect, on one woman who was watching, who tried desperately to hide her feeling, and then broke into the craziest, gayest sort of laughter. I think it was this rather than hysterics because I noticed that as she was breaking down and that horrid farting continued, quite a number of men around her had a very hard time, and a very self-ashamed one, keeping their faces straight. Meanwhile traffic was piled up a block around, policemen were pushing people around and asking questions, a street car fought its way painfully up half the block, gave it up and disgorged its occupants, who ran up asking questions too (they weren't within a mile of being able to see anything) and all the time, of course, people were sincerely saying give him air, give him air, and sincerely trying to, and were totally unable to bring themselves, or a lot of others, to do any such thing.

An ambulance came to the outskirts, whining; people in white fought through and carried him off, still snoring like a comic-strip, and the newspapers said he never regained consciousness, and he died on the way to the hospital.

Notes to Fragments 1 and 2 [page and line number cited]

RF 287.1 (A . . . handwritten.)] (Fitzgerald italicizes the phrase and also gives the fragment the title *Run Over;* no title is present on the typescript.)

RF 287.2 Asylum Avenue] asylum avenue

RF 287.25–26 "putting . . . misery,"] (Fitzgerald deletes the quotation marks.)

RF 289.1 (Handwritten . . . thirties)] (Fitzgerald italicizes the phrase and also gives the fragment the title *Give Him Air;* no title is present on the typescript. He also changes "handwritten" to "*Hand-written*" in the opening phrase.)

RF 289.1 (Fitzgerald correctly omits the typist's typed comment on the top of this page: "note on mutilated man (2)" in his edition.)

RF 289.12–13 [word omitted: face?]] (word omitted: face?) (Fitzgerald also makes this change in his printed text. Perhaps "scalp" is a better choice.)

RF 289.26 swallowing).] swallowing.) (Fitzgerald's handwritten symbol on the typescript indicates the need for this transposition.)

Chapter 1

David McDowell chooses to print an earlier version (TX 5.3, [33–35]) of this chapter that appears on pages 80–83 of the first edition. 5.3, [39–40] is an earlier version of [34–35]. For further information on all the McDowell variants, please see the section "Textual Commentary and Notes."

Chapters 1, 2, and 3 of the restored edition are the final versions of the drafts that McDowell mistakenly selects and combines together as the first italicized flashback section of the novel. His italicization is reversed below for clarity.

McDowell's earlier version of chapter 1, printed as a flashback as his pages 80–83, is given below as a variant. Corrections to this variant using Agee's manuscripts follow the text as notes and are cited by page and line number.

[80]

Walking in darkness, he saw the window. Curtains, a tall, cloven wave, towered almost to the floor. Transparent, manifold, scalloped along their inward edges like the valves of a sea creature, they moved delectably on the air of the open window.

Where they were touched by the carbon light of the street lamp, they were as white as sugar. The extravagant foliage which had been wrought into them by machinery showed even more sharply white where the light touched, and elsewhere was black in the limp cloth.

The light put the shadows of moving leaves against the curtains, which moved with the moving curtains and upon the bare glass between the curtains.

Where the light touched the leaves they seemed to burn, a bitter green. Elsewhere they were darkest gray and darker. Beneath each of these thousands of closely assembled leaves dwelt either no natural light or richest darkness. Without

[81]

touching each other these leaves were stirred as, silently, the whole tree moved in its sleep.

Directly opposite his window was another. Behind this open window, too, were curtains which moved and against them moved the scattered shadows of other leaves. Beyond these curtains and beyond the bare glass between, the room was as dark as his own.

He heard the summer night.

All the air vibrated like a fading bell with the latest exhausted screaming of locusts. Couplings clashed and conjoined; a switch engine breathed heavily. An auto engine bore beyond the edge of audibility the furious expletives of its incompetence. Hooves broached, along the hollow street, the lackadaisical rhythms of the weariest of clog dancers, and endless in circles, narrow iron tires grinced continuously after. Along the sidewalks, with incisive heels and leathery shuffle, young men and women advanced, retreated.

A rocking chair betrayed reiterant strain, as of a defective lung; like a single note from a stupendous jew's-harp, the chain of a porch swing twanged.

Somewhere very near, intimate to some damp inch of the grass between these homes, a cricket peeped, and was answered as if by his echo.

Humbled beneath the triumphant cries of children, which tore the whole darkness like streams of fire, the voices of men and women on their porches rubbed cheerfully against each other, and in the room next his own, like the laboring upward of laden windlasses and the ildest pouring out of fresh water, he heard the voices of men and women who were familiar to him. They groaned, rewarded; lifted, and spilled out: and watching the windows, listening at the heart of the proud bell of darkness, he lay in perfect peace.

Gentle, gentle dark.

[82]

My darkness. Do you listen? Oh, are you hollowed, all one taking ear?

My darkness. Do you watch me? Oh, are you rounded, all one guardian eye?

Oh gentlest dark. Gentlest, gentlest night. My darkness. My dear darkness.

Under your shelter all things come and go.

Children are violent and valiant, they run and they shout like the winners of impossible victories, but before long now, even like me, they will be brought into their sleep.

Those who are grown great talk with confidence and are at all times skillful to serve and to protect, but before long now they too, before long, even like me, will be taken in and put to bed.

Soon come those hours when no one wakes. Even the locusts, even the crickets, silent shall be, as frozen brooks

In your great sheltering.

I hear my father; I need never fear.

I hear my mother; I shall never be lonely, or want for love.

When I am hungry it is they who provide for me; when I am in dismay, it is they who fill me with comfort.

When I am astonished or bewildered, it is they who make the weak ground firm beneath my soul: it is in them that I put my trust.

When I am sick it is they who send for the doctor; when I am well and happy, it is in their eyes that I know best that I am loved; and it is towards the shining of their smiles that I lift up my heart and in their laughter that I know my best delight.

I hear my father and my mother and they are my giants, my king and my queen, beside whom there are no others so wise or worthy or honorable or brave or beautiful in this world.

[83]

I need never fear: nor ever shalt I lack for lovingkindness.

And those also who talk with them in that room beneath whose door the light lies like a guardian slave, a bar of gold, my witty uncle, and my girlish aunt: I have yet to know them well, but they and my father and my mother are all fond of each other, and I like them, and I know that they like me.

I hear the easy chiming of their talk and their laughter.

But before long now they too will leave and the house will become almost silent and before long the darkness, for all its leniency, will take my father and my mother and will bring them, even as I have been brought, to bed and to sleep.

You come to us once each day and never a day rises into brightness but you stand behind it; you are upon us, you overwhelm us, all of each night. It is you who release from work, who bring parted families and friends together, and people for a little while are calm and free, and all at ease together; but before long, before long, all are brought down silent and motionless

Under your sheltering, your great sheltering, darkness.

And all through that silence you walk as if none but you had ever breathed, had ever dreamed, had ever been.

My darkness, are you lonely?

Only listen, and I will listen to you.

Only watch me, and I will watch into your eyes.

Only know that I am awake and aware of you, only be my friend, and I will be your friend.

You need not ever fear; or ever be lonely; or want for love.

Tell me your secrets; you can trust me.

Come near. Come very near.

Notes for McD 80–83 Variant (TX 5.3, [33–35])

McD 80.1 Walking] Waking (This error was corrected in subsequent printings of the first issue of the first edition.)
McD 80.8 limp] limpid
McD 81.3–4 window, too,] window too
McD 81.14 sidewalks,] sidewalks
McD 81.27 windows] window
McD 82.8 victories,] victories
McD 82.11 protect,] protect
McD 82.16 father;] father:
McD 82.17 mother;] mother:
McD 82.18 for me;] for me:
McD 82.23 loved;] loved:
McD 83.1 lovingkindness] loving kindness
McD 83.13 behind it;] behind it:
McD 83.15 families,] families
McD 83.15 together;] together:
McD 83.26 not ever] never

Chapter 2

TX 5.3, [41–42] is printed as pages 84–86 of McDowell's edition. TX 5.3 has several variants of this chapter. McDowell rightly omits those pages [35 (partial), 36, 37, and 38] to use [41–42], the most finished of the TX 5.3 versions, but it is still an earlier version than that of TX 5.2, [25–26] which is incorporated into this restored text. TX 5.3, [35, 36, 37] are all partial earlier drafts of [41–42] and begin with "Darkness" while [38] is composed only of two lines. For further information on all the McDowell variants, please see the section "Textual Commentary and Notes."

Chapters 1, 2, and 3 of the restored edition are the final versions of the drafts that McDowell mistakenly selects and combines together as the first italicized flashback section of the novel. His italicization is reversed below for clarity.

McDowell's earlier version of chapter 2, printed as a flashback as his pages 84–86, is given below as a variant. Corrections to this variant using Agee's manuscripts follow the text as notes and are cited by page and line number.

[84]

Darkness indeed came near. It buried its eye against the eye of the child's own soul, saying:

Had ever breathed, had ever dreamed, had ever been.

And somewhat as in blind night, on a mild sea, a sailor may be made aware of an iceberg, fanged and mortal, bearing invisibly near, by the unwarned charm of its breath, nothingness now revealed itself: that permanent night upon which the stars in their expiring generations are less than the glinting of gnats, and nebulae, more trivial than winter breath; that darkness in which eternity lies bent and pale, a dead snake in a jar, and infinity is the sparkling of a wren blown out to sea; that inconceivable chasm of invulnerable silence in which cataclysms of galaxies rave mute as amber.

Darkness said:

When is this meeting, child, where are we, who are you, child, who are you, do you know who you are, do you know who you are, child; are you?

He knew that he would never know, though memory, almost captured, unrecapturable, unbearably tormented him. That this little boy whom he inhabited was only the cruelest of deceits. That he was but the nothingness of nothingness, condemned by some betrayal, condemned to be aware of nothingness. That yet in that desolation, he was not without companions. For featureless on the abyss, invincible, moved monstrous intuitions. And from the depth and wide throat of eternity burned the cold, delirious chuckle of rare monsters beyond rare monsters, cruelty beyond cruelty.

Darkness said:

Under my sheltering: in my great sheltering.

In the corner, not quite possible to detach from the darkness, a creature increased, which watched him.

Darkness said:

You hear the man you call your father: how can you ever fear?

[85]

Under the washstand, carefully, something moved.

You hear the woman who thinks you are her child.

Beneath his prostrate head, eternity opened.

Hear how he laughs at you; in what amusement she agrees.

The curtain sighed as powers unspeakable passed through it.

Darkness purred with delight and said:

What is this change your eye betrays?

Only a moment ago, I was your friend, or so you claimed; why this sudden loss of love?

Only a moment ago you were all eagerness to know my secrets; where is your hunger now?

Only be steadfast: for now, my dear, my darling, the moment comes when hunger and love will be forever satisfied.

And darkness, smiling, leaned ever more intimately inward upon him, laid open the huge, ragged mouth—

Ahhhhh . . . !

Child, child, why do you betray me so?

Come near. Come very near.

Ohhhhhh . . . !

Must you be naughty? It would grieve me terribly to have to force you.

You know that you can never get away: you don't even want to get away.

But with that, the child was torn into two creatures, of whom one cried out for his father.

The shadows lay where they belonged, and he lay shaken in his tears. He saw the window; waited.

[86]

Still the cricket struck his chisel; the voices persisted, placid as bran.

But behind his head, in that tall shadow which his eyes could never reach, who could dare dream what abode its moment?

The voices chafed, untroubled: grumble and babble.

He cried out again more fiercely for his father.

There seemed a hollowing in the voices, as if they crossed a high trestle.

Serenely the curtain dilated, serenely failed.

The shadows lay where they belonged, but strain as he might, he could not descry what lay in the darkest of them.

The voices relaxed into their original heartlessness.

He swiftly turned his head and stared through the bars at the head of the crib. He could not see what stood there. He swiftly turned again. Whatever it might be had dodged, yet more swiftly: stood once more, still, forever, beyond and behind his hope of seeing.

He saw the basin and that it was only itself; but its eye was wicked ice.

Even the sugar curtains were evil, a senselessly fumbling mouth; and the leaves, wavering, stifled their tree like an
infestation.

Near the window, a stain on the wallpaper, pale brown, a serpent shape.

Deadly, the opposite window returned his staring.

The cricket cherished what avaricious secret: patiently sculptured what effigy of dread?

The voices buzzed, pleased and oblivious as locusts. They cared nothing for him.

He screamed for his father.

Notes for McD 84–86 Variant (TX 5.3, [41–42])

McD 84.5 armed > fanged (No choice indicated by Agee.)

McD 84.21 to unawareness > condemned to be aware of nothingness (No choice indicated by Agee.)

McD 84.24 burned] purred

McD 84.24–25 rare monsters beyond rare monsters] ravenousness beyond ravenousness

McD 85.7 change,] change

McD 85.8 ago,] ago

McD 85.16 *Ahhhhh . . .*] *Ahhhhh—*

McD 85.19 *Ohhhhhh . . .*] *Ohhhhhh—*

McD 85.20 vex > grieve (No choice indicated by Agee.)

McD 85.24–25 But with that . . . for his father.] (In the manuscript, Agee skips a line before and after this sentence.)

McD 86.23 Deadly, the] (McDowell properly corrects Agee's "Deadly, The".)

Chapter 3

TX 5.3, [43–48] is printed as pages 87–96 of McDowell's edition and is a complete, but earlier version of TX 5.2, [27–30, 32, 31, 36, 41].

Chapters 1, 2, and 3 of the restored edition are the final versions of the drafts that McDowell mistakenly selected and combined together as the first italicized flashback section of the novel. His italicization is reversed below for clarity.

McDowell's earlier version of chapter 3, printed as a flashback as his pages 87–96, is given below as a variant. He incorrectly joins it directly to the previous flashback with no separation, even though the previous manuscript page [42] ends a little below midway on that page, one of Agee's standard indications of beginning a new chapter. For further information on all the McDowell variants, please see the section "Textual Commentary and Notes." Corrections to this variant using Agee's manuscripts follow the text as notes and are cited by page and line number.

[87]

And now the voices changed. He heard his father draw a deep breath and lock it against his palate, then let it out harshly against the bones of his nose in a long snort of annoyance. He heard the Morris chair creak as his father stood up and he heard sounds from his mother which meant that she was disturbed by his annoyance and that she would see to him, Jay; his uncle and his aunt made quick, small, attendant noises and took no further part in the discussion and his father's voice, somewhat less unkind than the snort and the way he had gotten from his chair but still annoyed, saying, "No, he hollered for me, I'll see to him"; and heard his mastering, tired approach. He was afraid, for he was no longer deeply frightened; he was grateful for the evidence of tears.

The room opened full of gold, his father stooped through the door and closed it quietly; came quietly to the crib. His face was kind.

"Wuzza matter?" he asked, teasing gently, his voice at its deepest.

"Daddy," the child said thinly. He sucked the phlegm from his nose and swallowed it.

His voice raised a little. "*Why, what's* the *trouble* with my *little boy,*" he said, and fumbled and got out his handkerchief. "*What's* the *trouble! What's* he *crine* about!" The harsh cloth smelt of tobacco; with his fingertips, his father removed crumbs of tobacco from the child's damp face.

"Blow," he said. "You know your mamma don't like you to swallah that stuff." He felt the hand strong beneath his head and a sob overtook him as he blew.

"*Why, what's wrong?*" his father exclaimed; and now his voice was entirely kind. He lifted the child's head a little more, knelt and looked carefully into his eyes; the child felt the strength of the other hand, covering his chest, patting gently. He endeavored to make a little more of his sobbing than came out, but the moment had departed.

[**88**]

"Bad dream?"

He shook his head, no.

"Then what's the trouble?"

He looked at his father.

"Feared a—fraid of the dark?"

He nodded; he felt tears on his eyes.

"Noooooooo," his father said, pronouncing it like *do.* "You're a *big* boy now. *Big* boys don't get skeered of a little dark. *Big* boys don't cry. Where's the dark that skeered you? Is it over here?" With his head he indicated the darkest corner. The child nodded. He strode over, struck a match on the seat of his pants.

Nothing there.

"Nothing there that oughtn't to be. . . . Under here?" He indicated the bureau. The child nodded, and began to suck at his lower lip. He struck another match, and held it under the bureau, then under the washstand.

Nothing there. There either.

"Nothing there but an old piece a baby-soap. See?" He held the soap close where the child could smell it; it made him feel much younger. He nodded. "Any place else?"

The child turned and looked through the head of the crib; his father struck a match. "Why, there's poor ole Jackie," he said. And sure enough, there he was, deep in the corner.

He blew dust from the cloth dog and offered it to the child. "You want Jackie?"

He shook his head.

"You *don't* want poor little ole Jackie? So lonesome? Alayin back there in the corner all this time?"

He shook his head.

"Gettin too big for Jackie?"

He nodded, uncertain that his father would believe him.

"Then you're gettin too big to cry."

[89]

Poor ole Jackie.

"Pore ole Jackie."

"Pore little ole Jackie, so lonesome."

He reached up for him and took him, and faintly recalled, as he gave him comfort, a multitude of fire-tipped candles (and bristling needles) and a strong green smell, a dog more gaily colored and much larger, over which he puzzled, and his father's huge face, smiling, saying, "It's a dog." His father too remembered how he had picked out the dog with great pleasure and had given it too soon, and here it was now too late. Comforting gave him comfort and a deep yawn, taking him by surprise, was half out of him before he could try to hide it. He glanced anxiously at his father.

"Gettin sleepy, uh?" his father said; it was hardly even a question.

He shook his head.

"Time you did. Time we all got to sleep."

He shook his head.

"You're not skeered any more are you?'

He considered lying, and shook his head.

"Boogee man, all gone, scared away, huh?"

He nodded.

"Now go on to sleep then, son," his father said. He saw that the child very badly did not want him to go away, and realized suddenly that he might have lied about being scared, and he was touched, and put his hand on his son's forehead. "You just don't want to be lonesome," he said tenderly; "just like little ole Jackie. You just don't want to be left alone." The child lay still.

"Tell you what I'll do," his father said, "I'll sing you one song, and then you be a good boy and go on to sleep. Will you do that?" The child pressed his forehead upward against the strong warm hand and nodded.

"What'll we sing?" his father asked.

[90]

"Froggy would a wooin go," said the child; it was the longest.

"At's a long one," his father said, at's a *long old song*. You won't ever be awake that long, will you?"

He nodded.

"Ah *right,*" said his father; and the child took a fresh hold on Jackie and settled back looking up at him. He sang very low and very quietly: *Frog he would a wooin' go uh-hooooo!, Frog he would a wooin' go uh*-hooooo, uh-hoooooo, and all about the courting-clothes the frog wore, and about the difficulties and ultimate success of the courtship and what several of the neighbors said and who the preacher would be and what he said about the match, uh-hoooo, and finally, what will the weddin supper be uhooooo, catfish balls and sassafras tea uh-hoooo, while he gazed at the wall and the child gazed up into the eyes which did not look at him and into the singing face in the dark. Every couple of verses or so the father glanced down, but the child's eyes were as darkly and steadfastly open at the end of the long song as at the beginning, though it was beginning to be an effort for him.

He was amused and pleased. Once he got started singing, he always loved to sing. There were ever so many of the old songs that he knew, which he liked best, and also some of the popular songs; and although he would have been embarrassed if he had been made conscious of it, he also enjoyed the sound of his own voice. "Ain't you asleep *yet?*" he said, but even the child felt there was no danger of his leaving, and shook his head quite frankly.

"Sing gallon," he said, for he liked the amusement he knew would come into his father's face, though he did not understand it. It came, and he struck up the song, still more quietly because it was a fast, sassy tune that would be likely to wake up. He was amused because his son had always mistaken

[91]

the words "gal and" for "gallon," and because his wife and to a less extent her relatives were not entirely amused by his amusement. They felt, he knew, that he was not a man to take the word "gallon" so purely as a joke; not that the drinking had been any sort of problem, for a long time now. He sang:

I got a gallon an a sugarbabe too, my honey, my baby,
I got a gallon an a sugarbabe too, my honey, my sweet thing.
I got a gallon an a sugarbabe too,
Gal don't love me but my sugarbabe do
This mornin,
This evenin,
So soon.

When they kill a chicken, she saves me the wing, my honey, my baby,

When they kill a chicken, she saves me the wing, my honey, my sweet thing,

When they kill a chicken, she saves me the wing, my honey
Think I'm aworkin ain't adoin a thing
This mornin,
This evenin,
So soon.

Every night about a half past eight, my honey, my baby,
Every night about a half past eight, my honey, my sweet thing
Every night about a half past eight, my honey
Ya find me awaitin at the white folks' gate
This mornin,
This evenin,
So soon.

[92]

The child still stared up at him; because there was so little light or perhaps because he was so sleepy, his eyes seemed very dark, although the father knew they were nearly as light as his own. He took his hand away and blew the moisture dry on the child's forehead, smoothed his hair away, and put his hand back:

What in the world you doin, Google Eyes? he sang, very slowly, while he and the child looked at each other,
What in the world you doin, Google Eyes?
What in the world you doin, Google Eyes?
What in the world you doin, Google Eyes?

His eyes slowly closed, sprang open, almost in alarm, closed again.

Where did you get them great big Google Eyes?
Where did you get them great big Google Eyes?
You're the best there is and I need you in my biz,
Where in the world did you get them Google Eyes?

He waited. He took his hand away. The child's eyes opened and he felt as if he had been caught at something. He touched the forehead again, more lightly. "Go to sleep, honey," he said. "Go on to sleep now." The child continued to look up at him and a tune came unexpectedly into his head, and lifting his voice almost to tenor he sang, almost inaudibly:

Oh, I hear them train car wheels arumblin,
Ann, they're mighty near at hand,
I hear that train come arumblin,

Come arumblin through the land.
Git on board, little children,
Git on board, little children,

[93]

Git on board, little children,
There's room for many and more.

To the child it looked as if his father were gazing off into a great distance and, looking up into these eyes which looked so far away, he too looked far away:

Oh, I look a way down yonder,
Ann, uh what dyou reckon I see,
A band of shinin angels,
A comin' after me.
Git on board, little children,
Git on board, little children,
Git on board, little children,
There's room for many and more.

He did not look down but looked straight on into the wall in silence for a good while, and sang:

Oh, every time the sun goes down,
There's a dollar saved for Betsy Brown,
Sugar Babe.

He looked down. He was almost certain now that the child was asleep. So much more quietly that he could scarcely hear himself, and that the sound stole upon the child's near sleep like a band of shining angels, he went on:

There's a good old sayin, as you all know,
That you can't track a rabbit when there ain't no snow
Sugar Babe.

Here again he waited, his hand listening against the child, for he was so fond of the last verse that he always hated to

[94]

have to come to it and end it; but it came into his mind and became so desirable to sing that he could resist it no longer:

Oh, tain't agoin to rain on, tain't agoin to snow:

He felt a strange coldness on his spine, and saw the glistening as a great cedar moved and tears came into his eyes:

But the sun's agoin to shine, an the wind's agoin to blow

Sugar Babe.

A great cedar, and the colors of limestone and of clay; the smell of wood smoke and, in the deep orange light of the lamp, the silent logs of the walls, his mother's face, her ridged hand mild on his forehead: *Don't you fret, Jay, don't you fret.* And before his time, before even he was dreamed of in this world, she must have lain under the hand of her mother or her father and they in their childhood under other hands, away on back through the mountains, away on back through the years, it took you right on back as far as you could ever imagine, right on back to Adam, only no one did it for him; or maybe did God?

How far we all come. How far we all come away from ourselves. So far, so much between, you can never go home again. You can go home, it's good to go home, but you never really get all the way home again in your life. And what's it all for? All I tried to be, all I ever wanted and went away for, what's it all for?

Just one way, you do get back home. You have a boy or a girl of your own and now and then you remember, and you know how they feel, and it's almost the same as if you were your own self again, as young as you could remember.

And God knows he was lucky, so many ways, and God knows he was thankful. Everything was good and better than he could have hoped for, better than he ever deserved; only,

[95]

whatever it was and however good it was, it wasn't what you once had been, and had lost, and could never have again, and once in a while, once in a long time, you remembered, and knew how far you were away, and it hit you hard enough, that little while it lasted, to break your heart.

He felt thirsty, and images of stealthiness and deceit, of openness, anger and pride, immediately possessed him, and immediately he fought them off. If ever I get drunk again, he told himself proudly, I'll kill myself. And there are plenty good reasons why I won't kill myself. So I won't even get drunk again.

He felt consciously strong, competent both for himself and against himself, and this pleasurable sense of firmness contended against the perfect and limpid remembrance he had for a moment experienced, and he tried sadly, vainly, to recapture it. But now all that he remembered, clear as it was to him, and dear to him, no longer moved his heart, and he was in this sadness, almost without thought, staring at the wall, when the door opened softly behind him and he was caught by a spasm of rage and alarm, then of shame for these emotions.

"Jay," his wife called softly. "Isn't he asleep *yet?*"

"Yeah, he's asleep," he said, getting up and dusting his knees. "Reckon it's later than I knew."

"Andrew and Amelia had to go," she whispered, coming over. She leaned past him and straightened the sheet. "They said tell you good night." She lifted the child's head with one hand, while her husband, frowning, vigorously shook his head; "It's all right, Jay, he's *sound* asleep;" she smoothed the pillow, and drew away: "They were afraid if they disturbed you they might wake Rufus."

"Gee. I'm sorry not to see them. Is it so late?"

"You must have been in here nearly an *hour!* What was the matter with him?"

"Bad dream, I reckon; fraid of the dark."

[96]

"He's all right? Before he went to sleep, I mean?"

"Sure; *he's* all right." He pointed at the dog. "Look what I found."

"Goodness sake, where was it?'

"Back in the corner, under the crib."

"Well shame on *me!* But Jay, it must be awfully dirty!"

"Naww; I dusted it off."

She said, shyly, "I'll be glad when I can stoop again."

He put his hand on her shoulder. "So will I."

"Jay!" she drew away, really offended.

"*Honey!*" he said, amused and flabbergasted. He put his arm around her. "I only meant the baby! I'll be glad when the baby's here!"

She looked at him intently (she did not yet realize that she was near-sighted), understood him, and smiled and then laughed softly in her embarrassment. He put his finger to her lips, jerking his head towards the crib. They turned and looked down at their son.

"So will I, Jay darling," she whispered. "So will I."

Notes for McD 87–96 Variant (TX 5.3, [43–48])

McD 87.3	Morris chair] morris-chair
McD 88.13	be. . . .] be.
McD 88.13	Under here?] (This sentence begins a new paragraph.)
McD 88.19	close; the child smelled it (descr.?) > where the child could smell it; (No choice indicated by Agee. McDowell properly chose the finished version.)
McD 88.30	Gettin] Gettn (A marginal note on 5.3, [44] above this line gives the song title "Every Time the Sun Goes Down.")
McD 88.32	gettin] gettn

McD 89.5	fire-tipped > lighted (No choice indicated by Agee, and "fire tipped" does not have the hyphen that McDowell supplied.)
McD 89.5–6	+ bristling needles > candles (No indication of its inclusion by Agee is given, and McDowell renders it as "(and bristling needles)". A marginal note on 5.3, [44, line 8] lined in after the sentence "It's a dog." states "end, summer '47" and another note two lines later in the manuscript states "October '47" perhaps indicating the general dates of composition for sections of this variant and a pause in its composition).
McD 89.8	remembered] remembered,
McD 89.9	here] how
McD 89.22	realized] realized, (McDowell correctly removes Agee's comma.)
McD 89.25	Jackie] Jackie" (McDowell correctly removes Agee's inadvertent quotation marks.)
McD 90.9	uh-hoooooo] ? ? ? ? uh-hooooooo (Besides the additional "o", McDowell deletes the question marks which may refer to Agee's marginal note of "descr. tune?", a note that is apparently Agee's note to himself.)
McD 90.13	uh-hoooo] uh-hooooo
McD 90.17	steadfastly] stedfastly
McD 90.19	amused] amused,
McD 90.29	tune] tune,
McD 91.1	(McDowell has to use quotation marks around "gal and" and "gallon" rather than correctly italicizing them—they are underlined in the manuscript—because he has already incorrectly chosen to italicize the entire section when he changed it to a flashback.)
McD 91.3	"gallon"] gallon
McD 91.22, 23, 24	eight,] eight
McD 91.24	honey] honey,
McD 91.25	awaitin] awaitn
McD 92.6	slowly,] slowly
McD 92.7	other,] other;
McD 92.8, 9, 10	doin] doin' (There is also a line between 7 and 8 composed of underlinings and commas that McDowell omits that may indicate Agee's desire to insert another line or repeat the previous one.)
McD 92.11	His eyes . . . closed again.] (McDowell moves this sentence to this position. It should follow after the second verse of "Google Eyes" in his text. He also omits the next line which reads "3rd stanza". Agee evidently intended to include another verse of the song at this point and McDowell chooses not to do so.)
McD 92.22	Oh] Ohh
McD 92.22	train car wheels] (Agee's manuscript—TX 5.3, [46]—appears undecided on the phrase. The original was "train wheels" but then "car" is written over "train" and "cars" is written over "wheels" with a line

drawn that may indicate that he wished to choose between "train cars" and "car wheels" for the final phrase. It seems likely that Agee simply had not made a decision.)

McD 92.24 I] I,
McD 92.25 land.] land,
McD 92.26, 27 children,] children
McD 93.1 children,] children
McD 93.6 Oh] Ohh
McD 93.8, 9 A] A,
McD 93.12 little] little,
McD 93.21 sound] sounds
McD 93.24 snow] snow,
McD 94.3 on] an (And perhaps for the second "tain't" on this line, read "taint" instead.)
McD 94.6 blow] blow,
McD 94.6–7 (There should be no space between these lines.)
McD 94.10 ridged > edged (No choice indicated by Agee.)
McD 94.11 *Jay*] (McDowell regularizes "Jim" to "Jay".)
McD 95.10 even] ever
McD 95.26 frowning] frow[n]ing (Agee inadvertently omits the "n" from "frowning" and it is supplied by McDowell.)

TX 5.2, [33, 37, 38, 40, 42, 34, 43] is an earlier draft of part of chapter 3 of the restored manuscript. It is perhaps the earliest draft of this section of TX 5.2. The page grouping [33, 37, 38, 40, 42] parallels the restored text (28.30–32.25) and the grouping [42, 34, 43] contains a long argument and eventual reconciliation between Rufus' father and mother that Agee decided not to use. The bracketed page numbers mark the beginning of each manuscript page, and some necessary notes follow this variant.

[5.2.33]

The big old shaggy cedar was blowing in the sunshine. When the wind blew it looked as if it was covered with sparks. He could see how the blue limestone jutted out of the clay. If he was right there he couldn't have seen any clearer. He could even smell the woodsmoke. He could make out hickory and oak and pine. He could see how the square logs of the wall lay on top of each other side by side, still and quiet in the dark orange lamplight. And there was his mother's face. She leaned over close above him and her face was young and round. She had a quilt pinned round her shoulders and it smelled of woodsmoke. He could feel her ridgy hand on his forehead, stroking it and pushing back the hair, and she was saying, *Don't you fret Jim. Now don't you fret.* She was saying, *git on to sleep now. They ain't nothing to be afeared about.* She was saying, *Maw's right here son. Paw's right here. Git on back to sleep now. Don't you fret.*

Any house that wasn't full of that smoky smell just didn't smell like home.

He could see the chimney along the outside and the fireplace on the inside, both at the same time. Some of the chimney was stone, the rest of it was made of woven saplings and clay.

Her face was young and round but it was already full of lines. Her hand felt almost raspy but it was the gentlest hand there was.

He could see the low fire lazing in the fireplace and the sparks wisking along the soot at the back.

She was just sixteen when I was born.

He could see the humps of bread under the hot ashes. Blow off the ashes, they're browning good. That's how bread tastes the best. Just blow the ashes off of it and eat it so hot it burns you.

He could see strings of peppers hanging from a rafter, and strings of popcorn.

Just a girl.

Lord God and before his time, before he was even dreampt of in this world, she must have laid like that under her own mother's hand or her daddy's; *don't you fret;* and when they were young ones they looked up and saw faces he had never seen even a picture of, that were still young then and dead and gone now long ago. And so on back. A way on back through the mountains and a way on back through the years. It took you right on back as far as you could ever study, right on back to Adam. Only there wasn't nobod—anybody could lay their hand on his forehead when he had a bad dream or got scared of the dark. Unless maybe God like they claim.

But Adam wasn't ever a young one. The way they tell it, God just

[5.2.37]

took him a handful of dirt and he made him a man in full.

He looked around the room, and down at his son, and back at the wall.

Some places that clay was rust-color. Some places it looked like it was on fire. Some places it was pretty near purple. Some places it was pure gold.

A long deep sigh broke out of him.

What a long way we all come.

Such a lot grows up between, you can't ever get back.

Oh sure you can go back home. Good to go home and see the old folks. And all the places you knew, and the ones that stayed.

But if you ever leave it you can't ever really get all the way back home again in your lifetime.

Agee rewrites but does not delete the rest of this page [37] on the following page [38]. See the notes below for the transcription of the original text of this part of page [37].

[5.2.38]

And what's the good of it.

All I aimed to make of myself. Left my people and sweat blood to get it.

What's the good.

All that happens, you don't ever get what you started out after, and you can't ever get back where you started.

Thought I hated it. Couldn't get away soon enough to suit me.

I sure did find out different.

Just one way.

You make you a home of your own and you get you a youngun, boy of your own or even a girl. And ever so often there's something they do that makes you remember. Even just some way they look or you know they feel.

Then you know just exactly how it feels t be that young and ignorant. See the logs in a wall and not even know what they are. Because you can remember then. And how your folks felt to see you too, and you put them in mind of when they were younguns. Because now *you* feel like that.

You even begin to know what it's going to feel like to get old. Have grandchildren, and die.

You know what it feels like to be so little and puny you can't do for yourself and it's pretty near the same as if you were your own self again, as little and far back as you can remember.

He looked down again at his son.

What'll it be like to see *his.*

Grampaw.

He smiled.

Maybe he'll do better. Smart as a tack, and better chances.

He could feel himself blush.

He told himself, smiling with stern self-disgust: And I'm the one thought I was Abe Lincoln.

He could remember sickening daydreams of winning hopeless trials, and of great simple speeches, some funny and some noble. Sometimes he even had a beard. He could remember saving his country, and how his mother had the best room in the White House and smoked her pipe if she damn well had a mind to. Some of the high falutin society people wouldn't even come there any more but all the real people knew she was the salt of the earth and that was how he picked his Cabinet.

Good God Almighty!

All the same by God I worked.

And look at me now.

[5.2.40]

Lord knows I'm lucky. I ain't asking for better. Everything's a sight better than *I* ever had coming to me. But not what I aimed to be. What I used to be, neither.

Every once in a while you remember and it's enough to break your heart.

He could feel the breath of a dark coldness touching him. Sometimes it got all the way inside him and then sometimes for days on and he wasn't any good for anything. Just dark and ice cold plumb through, and heavy as lead. So heavy he couldn't hardly say a word, or pick up one foot after the other.

He was pretty sure it wouldn't get a hold on him like that, this time. He was feeling too good. He could stave it off.

But he sure could use a couple of slugs.

Images of stealth and deceit, and of brutal openness and anger and pride, immediately became clear to him, and he could taste in the lining of his mouth and feel it plumb down into his belly and right out his arms to the ends of the fingers, how good that would be. His jaws and then his whole body moved in a kind of flinching of thirst, anger and will.

Like hell I will, he said to himself. Like all hell.

In this good knowledge of competence and strength, trying to recapture the moment of perfect and limpid remembrance, he was staring into the wall almost without thought when the door opened cautiously behind him, and he was caught by a spasm of anger and by self-reproof for the anger.

"Jay," his wife called softly, "isn't he asleep *yet?*"

"*Oh* yeah," he said. As he got to his feet his joints hurt.

"What on earth *took* so long?"

Lie to her. Couldn't get him to sleep.

"I was just studyin."

"What about, Jay?" she asked too quickly. I shouldn't ask, she knew. Well and why in the world shouldn't I?

"Studyin, that's all." It was the cold, dark voice which warned her, and shut her out.

Jay I'm just simply not going to *stand* for this, she wanted to say. "Hugh and Paula had to go," she whispered, tiptoeing over. She leaned past him and smoothed the sheet. "They said tell you goodnight."

She put one hand under the child's head and lifted it while her husband, frowning, vigorously shook his head. "It's all right Jay, he *sound* asleep." With her other hand she smoothed the pillow.

[5.2.42]

"Why didn't they wait?"

"Jay you were in here for*ever.* They did. What was the matter with him?"

"'Fraid of the dark, I reckon."

"He's all right? Before he went to sleep I mean?"

"Sure, *he's* all right."

"Well let's get to bed. It's high time. Do you want anything to eat?"

"Huh uh."

"Well I'm going up then. Be sure and hook both doors."

"I'll be right up."

"Jay?"

"Yeah?"

"You awake?"

"Yeah."

"Jay I've been lying here wondering whether or not I ought to say it and I've decided I ought to. It isn't that I want to intrude on you, you ought to know that. It's simply that I just can't stand always to be shut out like that. I'm just simply not going to stand for it. It isn't right."

"Like what."

"You must know perfectly well what I mean. When I asked you what you were thinking about and you—just answered in a way that absolutely shut me out in the cold. That's all."

He lay silent remembering it and trying to figure out what to say.

"Do you hear me Jay?"

"Sure I hear you."

"Well *answer* me then. For goodness sake *say* something."

"Nothn to say."

"What do you mean there's nothing. This is *serious* Jay. I wouldn't bring it up if I didn't feel it was serious. How can you *say* that, there's nothing to say."

"I meant I was trying to study what to say if you'd give me a chance."

"Well then just please *say* so, so I'll know you *heard* me at least. Of *course* I want to give you a chance!"

"All right. Now I'm studyin."

"All *right.*"

They lay in stiff unhappy silence for several minutes. Finally he said: "I didn't aim to shut you out like you say."

[5.2.34]

"Well it certainly did *sound* like it."

"Hold on now. I say I didn't aim to. If it sounded like that, I reckon I was just out of sorts and I'm sorry. What it was, was just sometime you get to studyin and if somebody says what you studyin about you don't even know for sure, not good eno—well enough to tell about it anyhow. Didn't that ever happen to you?"

"Of course it has Jay but you were in there so *long.* And you seemed so *annoyed* when I came in."

I was, too, he thought. "I reckon I was a little bit," he said. "But I wasn't holding it against you. I was holding it against myself."

"*Why* were you, Jay? Please don't mind my asking but I really need to know. I don't like to *annoy* you, not if I can only know how not to."

Well quit asking so damn many questions then, he thought. "I reckon you just sort of happened to bust in on a train of thought," he said. "Wasn't no fault of yours. Just happened to."

"But Jay that happens all the *time,*" she said. "To *everybody.* That's just a thing people have to get *used* to. Not get *mad* about."

"Well I told you, I was holding it against myself."

She was silent for a few moments.

"I'm sorry," she said. "I was just trying to—I don't want things ever to get like Panama again Jay."

"Don't you worry."

"I didn't mean *that.* Not now I didn't. I just mean all the silence. Just not being able to reach you when I know you're troubled or there's trouble between us. That's all I mean, dear." She put her hand on his shoulder and he took the hand in his. "You probably don't have the faintest idea how often I just overlook it. But you can't overlook it *every* time. Don't you see?"

He was no longer quite clear what she was talking about, but he was filled with kind will towards her: if only she wouldn't get these streaks of pestering. "I don't know exactly what it is I do," he said, "but I do *something* wrong. But I can tell you one thing for sure anyhow. I wasn't in any kind of trouble. Nothing you used to worry about, dear."

"Well then what *was* it?" She spoke without thinking and instantly knew she had made a bad mistake. Before she could correct it he said fiercely:

"God damn it all if you must know, I was thinking what a lucky man I am to be married to you but now I'm not so sure!"

"Jay!"

"I didn't mean that Laura." He reared up on one elbow, feeling like hell.

"You said it though."

"I didn't mean it I tell you. I was just sore."

She did not answer.

"Laura."

[5.2.43]

She did not answer.

"Laura," he said again more gently.

She did not answer.

He spoke quietly and very much in earnest.

"I tell you I didn't mean that," he said, "and you know darn good and well I didn't mean it. I mean what I say Laura and you know I do. I didn't mean that about not being sure. Course to *hell* I'm sure."

"Don't swear, Jay."

"*Course* I'm sure. I was just getting sleepy, and tired, I reckon, and when you asked me again what it was I was studyin about it just made me sore as a boil, that's all. Probably it oughtn't to, but I was just so sore I said the first thing came in to my head to make you mad. That's all. I'm sorry. Doggoneit I'm sorry as all—I'm terribly sorry. But I didn't mean it and you know I didn't. Now don't you?"

He touched her hair.

"Don't you Laura?"

She wanted to take his hand but she was still too shaken.

"I was wrong Jay," she said. "The minute I asked you I knew I shouldn't have. But before I could say a word more you came out with *that* awful thing. But of *course* it got you mad. I don't blame you."

"You know I didn't mean it don't you?"

"Yes Jay. Yes I do. But please don't ever say such a thing to me again."

He thought a minute. "I can't promise that if I get sore, but I can promise you I won't mean it."

They lay uneasily becalmed. After a while she said, very shily: "You were thinking how lucky."

He nodded, and stroked her hair. "Yeah" he said.

She took his hand. So am I," she whispered. "Lucky too I mean."

Variant Notes for Manuscript 5.2 (page and line number cited)

33.5 hickory] hickory hickory (Inadvertent repetition by Agee.)

33.6–7 still and quiet] very sleepy-looking and still > still and quiet (No choice indicated by Agee.)

33.7 lamplight.] lamplight, (Agee forgot to alter the comma after a deletion.)

33.15 [in left margin] crawling

37.14–16 (The transcription of the text that was subsequently rewritten on page [38] is as follows.)

And what's the good of it.

All I thought I was going to be. All I ever went away for and sweat blood to get.

What's the good of it. What's it all for.

All that happens, you can't ever get back where you started.

Now he could remember a great deal of misery, and anger, and resoluteness, and hard work.

Thought I hated it.

I found out different.

Just one way. You make you a home of your own. You have you a youngun, a boy of your own or a girl. And ever so often there's something they do or some [3 or 4 illegible characters; possible insertion?] way they look or feel, that makes you remember.

You know just how it feels to be that young and ignorant. And just how your folks felt to see you, and remembered when they were younguns. You even begin to know how it'll feel to get old, and have grandchildren, and die.

You know how it feels to be so little and puny you can't take care of yourself and it's pretty near the same as if you were your own self again, as little and far back as you can remember.

He looked down at his son.

You'll have them too.

And I'm the one that thought I was Abe Lincoln.

He could remember, with stern disgust, daydreams of winning hopeless trials, and of great, simple speeches, some funny and some noble. He could remember saving his country, and how his mother had the best room in the White House and smoked her pipe if she damn well had a mind to.

Good God Almighty, look at me now!

The following manuscript page (TX 5.2, [35]) is a variant of 28.30–30.10 of the restored text (TX 5.2, [31, 36]) and is a later version of a part of the large early draft cited above.

The big old shaggy cedar was blowing in the sunshine. It looked as if it was full of sparks. He could see how the limestone jutted out of the clay. If he was right there he couldn't have seen any clearer. He could even smell the woodsmoke. He could see how the square logs of the walls lay on top of each other side by side, very sleepy looking and still in the light of the fire and the lamp. And there was his mother's face. It was young and round and it leaned over close above him.

He could feel her ridgy hand on his forehead, stroking it and pushing back the hair, and in a low voice she was saying, *don't you fret Jim, now don't you fret.* She was saying, *git on to sleep now. They ain't nothing to be afeared about.* She was saying, *Maw's right here son. Paw's right here. Now git on back to sleep now. Don't you fret.*

She had a quilt pinned around her shoulders and it smelled of smoke. Hickory, and oak, and pine.

Any house that wasn't full of that smoky smell, it just didn't smell like home.

He could see the chimney up against the end of the place and the fireplace on the inside, both at the same time. Some of the chimney was stone, the rest was made of woven saplings and clay.

Her face was young and round but it was already full of lines and gouges. Her hand felt raspy on his skin but it was the gentlest hand there was.

He could see the fire lazing in the stone fireplace and the sparks crawling along the soot at the back.

Fifteen when she got married, just sixteen when I was born.

He could see the humps of bread under the hot ashes. That's how bread tastes the best. Just blow the ashes off of it and eat it so hot it burns you.

He could see strings of peppers hanging from a rafter, and strings of corn. He could see the marks of the axe in the logs of the wall and a place where the clay chinking had fallen out and a towsack had been prodded in.

Just a girl.

Don't you fret.

Lord God and before his time, before he was ever dreamt of in this world, she must have laid like that under her own mother's hand or her daddy's. Don't you fret. And when they were younguns they looked up and saw faces that were still young then and dead and gone now long ago. And so on back with them too. A way on back through the mountains, and a way on back through the years. It took you back farther than you could ever study.

Now don't you fret.

He looked around the room, and down at his son, and back into the wall. He shook his head slowly from side to side.

Long way.

Such a lot grows up between, you can't ever get back.

Oh sure you can go back home. Good to go home and see the old folks. All the places you used to know. The ones that stayed.

But if you ever leave it you can't ever honestly get all the way back home in your life.

The following is a partial page (TX 5.2, [39]) that is an earlier version of part of the draft page TX 5.2, [40].

[5.2.39]

He could feel the breath of a dark coldness touching him. Sometimes it got all the way inside him and then sometimes for days on and he wasn't any good for anything. Just dark and ice cold straight through, and heavy as lead. So heavy he couldn't hardly say a word, or lift one foot after the other. He didn't think it would get him like that this time; he was feeling too good. He could keep it off. But he sure could use a drink.

Images of stealth and deception, and of brutal openness and anger and pride, immediately became clear to him, and he could taste in the lining of his mouth and feel it straight down into his belly and out his arms to the tips of the fingers, how good a couple of slugs of whiskey would be. Just a couple. What harm did they ever do a man. With hard cold self-contemptuous pride he began to fight it off before it could get any more of a hold on him. Sure it would help. Seem to anyhow. And he knew what it really did to him. It didn't really keep off a black time like that. It seemed like it did but as a matter of fact it helped bring it on, and the worse he felt the more he was apt to drink, and the more he drank the worse he felt. And worse than that, he always felt as if she was an enemy, then, and she always felt as if he was, too. And probably at those times they were, for the matter of that.

His jaws and then his whole body moved in a kind of flinching of appetite and strength and impatience. Maybe some time I'll know I can take a couple and let it go at that, he told himself. Not till. Just isn't worth it.

Chapter 4

TX 5.2, [5–6] is an unfinished version that expands upon TX 5.3, [51] (printed as pages 35.25–36.20 of this edition). As noted below, Agee breaks off this extension in mid-sentence. Part of the expanded material is incorporated near the beginning of chapter 5.

[5.2.5]

He came almost up to her hip bone. Not so high on his father. What a big boy, they said.

She wore dresses, his father wore pants. Pants were what he wore too, but they were short and soft. His father's were hard and rough and went right down to his shoes.

The cloth of his mother's clothes were soft like his.

His father wore hard coats and a hard collar and sometimes a vest with hard buttons. Mostly his clothes were scratchy except the shirts.

Some of the shirts were stripid [*sic.* striped], some had little dots or diamonds.

He had two deep lines between his eyes, right over his nose. They were there even when he wasn't mad but they were much deeper when he was.

There were two more deep lines from the corners of his nose on down past his mouth.

His eyes were very light and his hair was black.

It was always nice when he smiled and even better when he laughed, but when he got mad his eyes were almost white.

His cheeks were warm and cool at the same time and they were scratchy even when he had just shaved. It always tickled on his cheek and still more on his neck, or even hurt a little, but it was always fun because he was so strong and because when he rubbed his whiskers against him that always meant he liked him.

He smelled like tobacco, leather and dry grass.

For a while he had a big mustache. Then he took it off and mama said "O Jay you look just *worlds* nicer! You have such a *nice* mouth, it's a *shame* to hide it!" After while he grew the mustache again, bigger than ever. It made him look much older, taller and stronger. When he frowned the mustache frowned too and it was very scary. Then he made it smaller so that it just looked neat, and Mama said "if you must have one, Jay, please keep it like that. At least it looks *respectable.*" When she said *respectable* he looked annoyed but he did not say anything. Then after a while he took it all off again and then mama said all over again what a shame it was to hide such a nice mouth and how glad she was the horrible old thing was gone, and after that he kept it off.

She called it ms*tash.* He called it *mus*tache. And sometimes *mush*tash but then he was joking, talking like a darky.

He liked to talk darky talk and he liked darkies. The way he sang was like a darky too, only when he sang he wasn't joking.

His neck was dark tan and there were deep crisscross cracks all over the back of it.

They both had such big hands. Whenever the hands touched him he could see and feel how big they were and strong. But his were bigger and stronger than hers. There were big blue strings under the skin on the backs of them. Veins. Black hair even on the backs of his fingers and ever so much on his wrists. Big veins in his arms like ropes.

His fingernails had ridges. Hers were smooth. She had a bright ring. That's my wedding ring. Daddy gave it to me when we married.

His hands were stronger but hers were gentler. She knew how to dress him. Daddy didn't know how so well and if he had a hard time with a button he got mad.

[5.2.6]

She was the one who was so good to him. There there there, she would say when he cried.

The other one liked to laugh when he laughed but when he cried he didn't know what to do and sometimes he got mad.

She was soft and warm in front and so was her neck. He nearly always saw her very close, leaning over him. Her eyes were soft and bright and often she was smiling.

Their faces were as big as skies and their hands were almost as big as he was. Their voices were different from each other and they smelled different.

The one with the deep voice was daddy. He held him way up to the top of the room and laughed.

The one with the gentle voice was Mama.

Some of the time there was a clear light which came into the room through wide glass holes. Other times these holes were black and then they were covered and the light was in the room, warm and yellow.

Some of the time he was out in the clear light and he could feel it move on his face and hand and feet. Things waved in the air. People and other things went back and forth. Sometimes some of them stopped and put their faces close to his. They said things and smiled. They said ahh-*boo!* They said kitchy kitchy kitchy and poked fingers at him.

People would lean over and say things and poke fingers at him and then suddenly they would go away.

People would pick him up and bounce him up and down and laugh when he laughed and then suddenly they would put

[Here the manuscript breaks off.]

Variant Notes for Manuscript 5.2 (page and line number cited)

5.2 [in left margin] spoon to cheek

The following early (and perhaps earliest extant) version of chapter 4 was found in a folder of Agee's notes (TX 5.1A, [5–6]). All but the last paragraph parallels pages 33.2–35.24 of this edition and the last paragraph is reworked and used in chapter 7 (62.17–29).

[5.1A.5]

His mama sang to him, too. She sang sleep baby sleep, and the pale moon the shepherdess. Her voice was like her hair, her face, and her dear gray eyes. She sang Go tell Aunt Rhoda, and soon he could sing it too:

Go tell Aunt Rhoda,
Go tell Aunt Rhoda,
Go tell Aunt Rhoda,
The old gray goose is dead.

[large indent] Aunt Rhoda seemed to him a tall and very old figure in gray, standing at some distance away in a deep gray light, her face hidden in the deep shadow of her bonnet, and he was sad about the old gray goose.

She sang swing low sweet cherriot, and when she sang that and daddy could hear her, he could hear his voice joining in, even in the next room:

Swing low, sweet cherriut,
Comin for to carry me home;

and sometimes he would hear footsteps and daddy would come in too, and they would both go on,

Swing low, sweet chariot,
Coming for to carry me home.

He almost liked it best of all the songs, it was so loving and peaceful and full of shining darkness. He did not know what a cherriut was but it was large and bright and sweet, something like a cherry only much nicer, and it was coming for to carry him home. And not only him, but Mama and daddy too, for they sang me, just as he did. Jordan was just a grave, wide space of darkness, but when you looked over it, what did you see? A band of angels comin after me, a band of shinin angels, comin for to carry me home, and Mama and daddy too. Everyone. There's room for many an more.

And even better, when it sang,

If you get there before I do,
Comin for to carry me home,
Tell all my friends I'm comin too.
Comin for to carry me home.

When he heard their voices singing that with special gentleness, and saw their large heads close above him in the dim light, and tried to sing too and felt their hands on him and their kind smiles, solemn, a little, because they felt the way the music and the words made them feel, he felt at the same time solemn, and lonely, and loved, and happy, and he seemed to see deep silent starlight above him. For once when they had all sat in the backyard singing and the stars were especially low and bright, he had said, when they came to that part of the song, "Those are the angels. Aren't they the angels Mama",

[5.1A.6]

and she had said, "yes darling, those are the shining angels," and his father had touched his hair and had said, "That's what they are, all right", and they had sung the line again, and then gone on. And when they came to tell all my friends I'm comin too he had realized that the stars were also the friends. They got there before he did, and when they moved and worked the way they did they were telling each other that he was coming too; but he felt he would rather not tell about this, and whenever the words were sung after that, he saw the stars shining and talking.

Whenever they finished singing this song they were always quiet for a little while. Then sometimes Mama would say, "that's such a *lovely* song," and he would say, in a deeper voice than usual, "Yeah—they don't come any bettern that". Or sometimes they would just stay quiet where they were, and not say a word, until finally one or other of them would say, "Well—" in a strangely sad way, and that always seemed to mean that it was time to do something else.

One day his mother told him that soon now he was going to have a wonderful surprise. When he asked what a surprise was she said that this one was like getting things for Christmas only ever so much nicer. When he asked what this one was she said now if I told you, it wouldn't be a surprise any more, would it? When he said he would rather know now than wait and see she said that she would tell him, only even if she told him he wouldn't be able to imagine what it was, so she thought it would be nicer if he waited, because it was ever so much nicer than he could possibly imagine.

Variant Notes for Manuscript 5.1A, [5–6] (page and line number cited)

6.7 and] but > and (No choice indicated by Agee.)

Chapter 5

TX 5.2, [1–4, 7] is an earlier version of chapter 5 (TX 5.2, [8–16]) and pages [5] and [6] of TX 5.2 form a version and extension of TX 5.3, [51] as previously noted and already transcribed in the "Major Manuscript Variants" for chapter 4. Page [7] ends with an outline of how to continue the section, reinforcing its status as a draft.

[5.2, 1]

At first their faces and hands were so big he could hardly see anything else.

Mamma was all soft in front and her neck was soft and warm. He nearly always saw her very close, leaning over him, and her eyes were gentle and bright, and often she was smiling. She was the one that was so good to him.

Some of the time here was a clear colorless light that came into the room through wide glass holes in it. Some of the time these holes were covered and then the light was in the room. It was yellow.

Some of the time he was out in the clear light and he could feel it move on his face and hands and feet, and things moved in the air, many of them, and people and other things moved along. Sometimes some of them stopped and leaned over and said things to him and smiled.

People would lean over and say things and poke fingers at him and then they would go away. People would pick him up and bounce him up and down and laugh when he laughed and then they would put him down and go away.

He did not like them to go away.

Sometimes if he cried they would come back. Sometimes not.

It felt nice to be warm and wet. It felt bad to be cold and wet.

It felt good to kick but it felt best of all to eat until there wasn't any more to eat. Then it felt bad.

The one with the deep voice was daddy. Sometimes he smiled and then it was nice. Sometimes he was mad and then it wasn't. When he said god damn it mamma didn't like it.

Grampa had red and white hair all over his face.

Granma was deaf. Talk loud, Granma doesn't hear very well. Talk right into her trumpet Rufus.

Ear trumpet. It sounded funny. It tasted queer on the end she stuck to her ear.

"Rufus!"

Why?

The things that moved in the clear light were leaves. They were on trees.

On the ground it was grass.

And flowers.

Not by the heads, Rufus!

Not by the roots, Rufus!

Just leave them alone if you don't know how to pick them.

Eat, Rufus.

Eat your supper.

Mush. Soft and white and warm and sometimes molasses.

The white in the glass was milk.

Say please.

Say thank you.

[5.2, 2]

Don't talk with your mouth full.

Don't sing at the table.

After a while he could take the glass and suck it against his face so that it stuck there, under his chin and over his eyes, so he could look through it. Sometimes daddy laughed. Sometimes he was mad. Mama never laughed, she said it isn't one bit funny Jay. Jay was daddy. She never got so mad either.

He could put his spoon in his mouth and bend the handle up so the end touched his forehead and then take the spoon out of his mouth and make it all go straight up so that end was over his head.

They were the same about that.

If you can't eat decently Rufus you'll just have to eat by yourself.

Daddy went away in the morning. Then he came home at night.

He went to the shop.

Sometimes Uncle Hugh came up to supper. Sometimes Aunt Paula. Uncle Hugh was Mama's brother and Aunt Paula was her sister. Grampa was their daddy and Granma was their mama. They called him papa but they called her mama.

They lived in the other house, it had a piano.

Sometimes they all came up for Sunday dinner and sometimes he and his mama and daddy went to the other house for Sunday dinner.

It was full of things.

There was a bay window with ferns and chairs and a table. There were white cloths pinned on the chairs and when he took the pins out the cloths fell down.

Don't, Rufus!

Why do you do that!

I like to see the cloths fall down.

Well why on earth do you suppose Granma pins them up?

What could he answer to that.

There was a big brown sofa to bounce on.

Stop it Rufus you'll break the springs.

Rufus! You're not in your own home.

His Grampa called him Rambunctious. He liked to tickle. Sometimes he talked about brats. That meant him. He didn't like brats. I can just about stand children, he said, but I can't stand brats.

But he liked him. That's why he tickled.

Granma never said brats. She always smiled merrily when he tried to talk to her, even when she couldn't hear. She liked to rub her hand up and down his back and

[5.2, 3]

then slap it several times, but not like a spanking, and say "Strong little back!"

Aunt Paula wore her hair in braids. She was nice with white teeth and she had a nice clear voice. She sang had a snake in a silver lake, sing song kitty katchy kye mee o, and she smiled while she sang, showing her teeth.

Bout five times as long as a rake.

Uncle Hugh had yellow hair and was nearly as tall as daddy. He said things that made people laugh but when he got mad it was as scary as daddy was.

When he knew Uncle Hugh was around he bounced on the sofa very quietly or not at all, because once when he was bouncing he got the hardest spank on his seat he'd ever had and when he turned around there was Uncle Hugh and his eyes and his voice were even scarier than the spank.

Aunt Jessie was lots older than Aunt Paula. She was mama's Aunt too. Grampa's sister. She had the thickest glasses.

She was nice except when she got mad. When he said Aunt Jessie she always said whatty.

[Earlier.] [This is Agee's bracketed comment.]

When they said you they meant him. When they said me they meant themselves. And I. And we.

But if he said you, meaning himself, that wasn't it. And if he said me or I or we, meaning the others, that wasn't it either. They laughed sometimes but it was because he didn't say something right.

When he cried they said well well well *what's* the *matter!*

But then after while when he cried they said Rufus is a big boy now, *he* doesn't cry. (Though there he was crying.) They said don't be a cry-baby.

The piano was tall and brown.

Granma played the piano and so did Aunt Paula.

When Granma played she leaned far over so she could hear.

In the corner was a picture with lions. It was dark and the lions padded along in the moonbeams. There were big steps with weeds growing in them.

In another picture it was dark too and there was a big stone lion with a face kind of like Uncle Hugh, not a lion face but a man. In between his paws there were people sleeping. A man and a lady and a little baby and a donkey, and they had a little fire.

That was Jesus when he was a little baby and his mama and his foss. Foss.

Foss-tur-father Rufus.

Fossturfather. They had to run away and hide in Eejipt.

Dark as Eejipt, Grampa said, and it was dark in the picture.

Doctor Fosstur went to Glosstur.

That was different.

There was another picture Grampa liked, it had colors. Deep dark brown. It was a dark picture too. Great big rocks came up on both sides from the bottom to the top and in between the rocks, at the

[5.2, 4]

bottom, there was a dark little river. There were trees on top of the rocks:

O Sable Cazzum.

Grampa and Aunt Jessie lived there when they were little.

Right *there?*

Of course not Rufus, *near* there.

They used to come on picnics.

Cazzum.

Oh Sable Cazzum.

There was another lion but he was little and white and he lay on the mantle. He had something sticking out of his side and he looked as if it hurt.

Arrow.

Over the sideboard there was another picture. He had whiskers along the sides of his cheeks and little corners on his collar like Grampa.

That's who you're named after Rufus.

Your Great Grampa Tyler. He was a very nice man.

He didn't look very nice.

He was Grampa's and Aunt Jessie's father, and our Grandfather, Uncle Hugh's and Aunt Paula's and mine, and that makes him your Great-Grandfather.

(Why does it *make* him.)

Where is he?

Where *is* he? Oh. Why. Why after he got very old, much older than Grampa or Granma, he got very tired so God took him away where he could sleep.

Where did he take him?

To heaven we hope, Mamma said, and Uncle Hugh laughed.

Hugh!

We hope. Ha ha ha.

Where's heaven.

Far, far away up in the sky, where we see the stars.

Oh.

Oh, Hugh said. I see said the blind man.

Stop teasing, Hugh.

[5.2, 7]

[This page revises and expands the latter part of the previous page.]

Over the china closet there was another picture. He had gray whiskers along the edges of his cheeks and little corners on his collar like Grampa.

That's who you're named after Rufus.

The old man did not look at him. He just looked out across the room. He did not look very happy.

Your Great Grandfather Tyler. He was very good to Grampa and all of us. He was a very nice man.

He didn't look very nice.

He was Grampa's and Aunt Jessie's father, and our Grandfather. Uncle Hugh's and Aunt Paula's and mine, and that makes him your Great Grandfather. Your Great Grampa Rufus Tyler.

He wondered why it *made* him.

Where is he?

Is h—? Oh. Why. Why he got very *old* Rufus. Lots older than Grampa or Granma. And then he got very tired the way old people do and so God took him away where he could sleep a long long time.

Where did he take him?

To Heaven we hope, Mama said, and Uncle Hugh laughed.

Hugh! Just because *you* don't—

O Laura! It's just your caution. We hope. Hahaha.

Well it's not a laughing matter.

Where's Heaven?

Far away up in the sky Rufus dear where we see the stars.

Oh.

Oh, Hugh said. I see said the blind man.

Stop it Hugh!

Tom!, Grampa said at the same moment, though Rufus could see that he was amused.

Granma, noticing laughter, cocked her trumpet and smiled politely.

Nothing Mama, his mother and Uncle Hugh called at the same time.

They all went on eating Sunday dinner and after a while somebody changed the subject.

Names &c &c.

Birth of Emma.

Variant Notes for Manuscript 5.2 (page and line number cited)

1.1	so big] big as the sky > so big (No choice indicated by Agee.)
1.21	It felt nice to be warm and wet. It felt bad to be cold and wet.] Warm and wet felt good. Cold and wet felt bad. > It felt nice to be warm and wet. It felt bad to be cold and wet. (No choice indicated by Agee.)
1.34	moved] waved > moved (No choice indicated by Agee.)
2.25–28	[in right margin] Spit in fireplace.

The third of the four short fragments printed by Robert Fitzgerald in *The Collected Short Prose of James Agee* and given the title "A Birthday" ([124]–25) may fit between chapters 5 and 6 chronologically, but may also be a draft fragment whose ideas are later elaborated in other chapters. It is therefore not included in the restored text of the novel, but is reproduced below from pages 291–92 of Fitzgerald's original typescripts (TX 3, 7) since Agee's original manuscripts apparently do not survive. The typescripts for Fitzgerald's volume that survive (TX 3, 6–7) are mainly copyedited typescripts, except for a few original typescript pages at the end of folder 7. This fragment is part of that latter small group. (See "Major Manuscript Variants" above for the nightmare introduction to the novel and appendix VIII for the other three fragments printed by Fitzgerald.) Notes on the corrected text of these original typescripts are given after the fragments and cited by page and line number as RF 291.1, for example. These notes do not list Fitzgerald's alterations that were made to produce the copyedited typescript version (TX 3, 6–7), but do also list the final changes to the text that appear in print in Fitzgerald's edition.

[291]

(typescript page, for the autobiographical novel. No date) [Fitzgerald's note]

it is thanksgiving and I am four years old and this is my birthday, and we all dangle in from the living room through the greenroom into the dining room to the table and granma puts down the bell when she sees us. grampa says sherry. unc' hugh gets another big book and puts it on the big book on the chair and daddy hise me up, there you are, here i am. happy birthday. many happy returns of the day. huh? california sherry. say i beg your pardon? i beg your pardon? california. many happy returns of the day. say thank you granma. say the same to you and many of them, say it *loud.* same to you and many of them. thank you. thank you. thank you granma, seee,

tom? thank you seee, what rufus has got. seee, what, right on the napkin by the plate. granma puts down her glass and dabs her mouth with a fold of napkin. do you know what that is rufus? what is it rufus? a course he doesnt. Of course he does. Sure he does, heez seen um, seen um out at chilholly park, haven't you rufus. seen what. them those birds, on the pond. what birds. why the birds for god sake like the jay. like the big white birds with the long necks on the lake, dear. what is it. look like a sort of a sort of bird or something. sort of a bird. swan. swan. tadadadaah, ta tadadaa, ta tadaaah (dadadadadadidledydaddle) hhh? swan. swan. swan. swan? sure. swan. well I swan. mine leeeeebr sschhhwannnnn, here, eat your dinner, rufus. here, let it swim. give hima swim. hm? swim. not good to eat. daddys hand reached across him dragging stuffing at the cuff, took his fingers from around the swan and set the swan up in the tumblerful a water. It Floats. it stands right up on the water. there. see? just like chilholly park. not very much. eat your dinner dear, don't dawdle. there he is, standing

[292]

right up on top of the water, waving up and down.

[I omit a little at the end] [Typist's statement; previous editor's brackets.]

Notes

RF 291.1	(A . . . handwritten.)] (Fitzgerald italicizes the phrase and also gives the fragment the title *A Birthday;* no title is present on the typescript.)
RF 291.12	granma] (Fitzgerald changes the "g" to "G" in his final text.)
RF 291.14	a course] (Fitzgerald changes the "a" to "A" in his final text.)
RF 291.15	chilholly] (A dialect rendering of "Chilhowee.")
RF 291.15	them] Fitzgerald changes "them" to "then" in his final text.)
RF 292.1–2	down . . . end] (Fitzgerald omits the typist's note on line 2 and substitutes "down. . . ." as the conclusion to the fragment.)

Chapter 8

The first two paragraphs and the first sentence of the third paragraph of TX 5.2, [54] rendered below were omitted from the text proper to eliminate repetition with a section of chapter 7 (65.7–66.2) and with getting Rufus to his grandparents' house.

One day his mother gave him a bath all over right in the middle of the afternoon and put new white stockings on him and the shining, crackling thing she called his white peakay, and while she dressed him she told him that soon now Aunt Paula was going to come and take him down to Granma and Grampa's for a nice visit, two or three days maybe, and when he came home again there was going to be the most wonderful surprise. He thought he knew what a surprise was but to make sure he asked, and sure enough, she said it was like at Christmas when Santy brings us all presents, you remember don't you Rufus?, and he could vaguely remember; only, his mother said, this was going to be even more wonderful than

Christmas. When asked what is it she said, Now if I told you it wouldn't be a surprise anymore, now would it? And no matter how he begged, she wouldn't tell him. It'll be so much more fun, she said, if you *wait* and find out. I just want to see your little face, she said, when you *see* it.

Then Aunt Paula came and his mother told her that everyone must keep the surprise a deep-dark, ess ee see are—now isn't that silly of me: *secret!* And they both laughed. Before he left she took him to the bathroom for one last try, and even washed his hands for him though he knew how, and then she said come here a minute Rufus, and sat on the creaking dirty clothes hamper and took him between her knees. She looked into his eyes very closely and began to smile. "Little Rufus," she said, and her head tilted to one side and she still looked at him, still smiling. "Now be a good boy," she said. "And Rufus. Try your *very* best not to wet the bed. Will you?" He nodded. "Don't drink *any*thing for supper or from *then on.* And be sure you try one last time. *Just* before you go to bed. Will you?" He nodded. He knew all this by heart and he knew there was no use in it. "And the *minute* you feel you want to go in the night just *rush* out of bed and use the potty. Don't wait one *single minute!* Will you?" He nodded. She put her long warm hand along his cheek and he leaned his head against it. He could see the little orange freckles dancing in her eyes. She did not speak. Her face looked almost frightened. For a moment a strange feeling came over him as if they were both moving very fast. "Goodbye my darling," she whispered finally, and he wondered whether she was going to cry, though her eyes were dry and very bright. "Mother loves you *so dearly,*" she whispered, and hugged him hard.

But she didn't tell him what the surprise was, and during all the three days he stayed at Grandma and Grampa's, nobody else would tell him either.

The TX 5.2 manuscript shows how many combinations Agee tried in regard to this chapter about the surprise of a new baby sister. Four variant versions exist, but differ as to whether or not Rufus is told that the surprise is a new baby and to whether or not Victoria is present as a character. No priority is established among them, as they differ significantly from each other and from the chosen text.

Variant 1

TX 5.2, [70] (Secret is kept; Victoria is present [Although closest of the four variants to the chosen text in regard to these events, this variant is too short for meaningful comparison to the chosen text, but it is quite likely that it represents an earlier version].)

[70]

One day his mother told him that soon now she was going to get him all dressed up and he would go down for a nice visit at Granma and Grampa's for maybe two or three days and when he came home there would be wonderful surprise. When he asked what a saprise was she said it was like Christmas when Santy brings presents only this one was ever so much nicer. When he asked what the saprise was going to be she said now if I told you it wouldn't be a surprise any more, would it. But she could promise him it was something that would make him very happy, and daddy and mama too.

He could remember Christmas and Santy when she spoke of it but it did not mean very much to him. But about this new surprise he was aflame with curiosity. But she wouldn't say what it was.

Not long after that the doorbell rang and there was a great big fat lady with black skin and deep roaring voice and a beautiful happy smile. The old lady and his mother threw their arms around each other and then the old lady saw him back in the hall and drew back and looked and said "Don't tell me *dat's* mah baby!"

"Yes, that's little Rufus," his mother said, as if she didn't expect to be believed.

The old lady suddenly ran at him getting bigger and bigger as she came, so that he was almost scared, and calling "why bless his little heart." And she squatted down fast and put her arms around him and she smelled so comfortable and warm that he wasn't scared any more; he almost felt like leaning his head against her and going to sleep. The she said "Lemme git a *look* at you chile!"; and she took him by both shoulders and held him away and leaned her head back and looked at him, while he looked at her big smile and at her eyes through their little gold glasses. "Lawd God how mah baby *has growed!*" she called. "I wouldn know him, cepn he's the spittin image of you Miss Laura; cepn de eyes."

"Yes he has his father's eyes," his mother said. "His hands too I think."

Variant Notes for Manuscript 5.2 (page and line number cited)

70.18, 20, 31 (Paragraph breaks added)

Variant 2

TX 5.2, [71–73, 64] (Secret is kept; Victoria not present)

[71]

One day his mother gave him a bath all over right in the middle of the afternoon and put new white stockings on him and the stiff, careful thing she called his white peekay, and while she dressed him she told him that Aunt Paula was going to come and take him down to Granma n Grampa's for a nice visit, two three days maybe, and when he came home again there was going to be the most wonderful surprise for him. He thought he knew what saprise was but to make sure he asked, and sure enough, she said it was like at Christmas when Santy brings us all presents, you remember don't you Rufus?, and vaguely he could remember; only, his mother said, this was going to be even more wonderful. When he asked what is it, she said now if I told you it wouldn't be a surprise any more now would it? And no matter how he begged, she wouldn't tell him. It'll be so much more fun, she said, if you wait and find out. I just want to see your face, she said, when you *see* it.

He looked forward to asking Aunt Paula. But Aunt Paula was hardly in the door when his mother said to her, Paula, I've told Rufus what a wonderful surprise he's going to get when he comes home, it seems the correct way, don't you think? And they both looked amused about something, though Rufus couldn't imagine what. So up to then, his mother said, let's make sure it's a deep, dark, ess ee see are ee—now isn't that silly of me; and they both laughed: *secret.* She reached for the hat which she called peekay too and suddenly said oh Rufus, and got up and beckoned in such a silent way that he knew she must mean go to the bathroom. She went with him and helped him unbutton his pants, and buttoned them up again and even washed his hands for him though he knew how, and then she said come here a minute Rufus, and sat on the clothes hamper and took him between her knees. "Now be a good boy," she said. And Rufus. Try your *very* best not to wet your bed! Will you?" He nodded. "Don't drink *anything* after supper or from then on. And be sure you try, just before you go to bed. Will you?" He nodded. "And the *minute* you feel you want to go, just *rush* out of bed and use the potty. Don't wait *one minute!* Will you?" He nodded. She put her hand along his cheek and he could see the little orange freckles dancing in her eyes. She did not say anything. She looked as if she were moving very fast and he too began to feel as if he were moving fast. "Goodbye my darling," she whispered, and he was afraid she was going to cry. "Mother loves you *so much!*"

By the time they got to Granma n Grampa's it was almost supper time. Daddy came in with Grampa and stayed a few minutes, and he asked him what the surprise was going to be, but daddy said Well, if mama wants it to be a surprise, I reckon you better just wait. Twon't be long. And soon he kissed him goodbye and said I'll see you tomorrow and went away

[72]

up the hill towards home.

At supper he told everybody that there was going to be a surprise and Aunt Paula hurried to say that Laura wanted to keep it a secret still. "Hhm," Grampa said. Granma looked polite and put up her trumpet and Uncle Hugh explained what hey were talking about.

"Yes," Granma said, "Paula told me right away." And she laughed politely, all by herself. "The fait accompli," Grampa said. And he made that noise with his lips that mama did not like. "Personally," he said, "I think it's a lot of damn nonsense. But if Poll want it that way, that's all there is to it." He ate a few bites. "Ours is not to reason why," he said. He ate a few bites more. "Betcha dollars to doughnuts she'll tell him it came from heaven," he said. "*God* did it." And again he made the noise. Rufus began to feel uneasy but just then Grampa said "About time I shut up," and he said no more about it.

Putting him to bed that night Granma was very friendly and gay. Sweet sleep, she told him, and many pleasant dreams about the surprise. And she showed him exactly where the potty was.

[73]

He was there three nights and he wet the bed but Granma didn't scold. She just said it was good they had the oilcloth, and during the day, he could see his sheets out on the line. He didn't have to wear the white peekay, he wore rompers. He helped her make the beds, and watched her do her housework. He watched Aunt Paula do her practising, and he watched Uncle Hugh do his painting. Sometimes he played by himself in the yard or looked at the picture-books, which were mostly ladies without much clothes on or any at all. Sometimes one of them or another would not be busy and would sing him a few songs or play with him. Once at supper Uncle Hugh said "if you ask me, Rufus is being *darned good* about it. He hasn't asked me a single question," and Aunt Paula said, "So do I." He felt like a very good boy indeed, even if he did wet the bed. "Wouldn't be surprised if he has a pretty shrewd idea what it's all about," Grampa said. "Oh that's absurd, Papa," Uncle Hugh said. "Maybe," Grampa said, "but I wouldn't be surprised." Another time Grampa said at dinner, "Dellfruke got back this morning." "But is he well enough?" Uncle Hugh asked. "Wobbly," Grampa said. "Scared to death. But he says he'll do it if it kills him, long as Poll wants him so much." "He needn't be scared then," Uncle Hugh said. "He'll do it well." "Does everything well," Grampa said. "That's a *man*." Another time when Grampa was fixing to go back to the Shop Rufus found him alone and asked, "*What* did God do, Grampa?"

"Nothing whatever, far's I'm concerned," Grampa said. "What in hell you talking about?"

"You said God did something. It came from heaven. Something about the surprise."

"Goodd Godd," Grampa said. "Little pitchers!" He bent down and spoke much more kindly than ordinary. "Look here Rambunctious," he said. "I think it's a lot of tommyrot. But if your mother wants it to be a surprise why by God you're gonna be surprised. All right?" Rufus nodded. "All right," Grampa said. "Far's God's concerned," he added,

"*If* at all: just forget I said anything. Dunno a thing about it; care less. Whatever your mother says, that's her business."

[64]

And that was all he would say.

In spite of his promise daddy did not come late that afternoon.

"He's got other fish to fry," Grampa said.

"He means he's awfully busy," Uncle Hugh explained.

But the next afternoon he did come, looking very tired and cheerful and somehow sheepish, and he brought candy for Rufus and ice cream for Rufus to give everybody else. "That surprise has come," he said, "and tomorrow you'll come home and see it."

And suddenly his curiosity, which had been uncomfortable but hopeless, became almost more than he could stand. "O goody goody," he hollered. "What *is* it! What *is* it daddy what *is* it!"

And his father looked annoyed for a moment and shook his head and smiled kindly, still looking annoyed, and said "I oughtn't to told you even it's come. Dog *gone* it," he said. "No I ain—can't tell you son. She'd snatch me baldheaded."

But that would be awful, Rufus thought, and he looked at his father, imagining his mother grabbing him by his head and yanking it off so he had just a shiny bald head like Grampa.

His father looked at him and laughed. "I don't mean she really would," he said. "That was just a joke. I just mean your mama's be awful sorry, honey. I think she'd feel awful bad if she didn't get to tell you herself. Now you don't want mammer to feel bad, do you?"

"Oh *no.*"

"Then you just be a good boy and wait one more day. Huh?"

"He's been absolutely *fine* about it Jay," Hugh said. "He hasn't even asked us *once.*"

"*Sure* he has," his father said, "he's my *boy,*" and he roughed his head against his thigh, and in spite of his disappointment Rufus felt wonderful. "All right son?" He nodded. "All right then," daddy said. "Now kiss me goodbye and I'll see you tomorrow." And he stooped and Rufus came to him and suddenly he was swept up next the ceiling and looked down into his father's dark, happy face, and his father shook him so violently that he screamed with pleasure. Then he set him down and hurried out the back door while they all called "love to Laura" and he called back "I sure will", and he hurried with long strides up the hill, and Rufus realized he was in such a hurry to get home he hadn't even waited for the ice cream which just now, even though it was so soon before supper, Granma brought in, in special dishes, with little lace napkins.

Right after dinner next day Grandma cleaned him all up and dressed him in the white peekay

Variant Notes for Manuscript 5.2 (page and line number cited)

71.1	[in top left margin] *dressing* detail
71.6	the most] a the most (Agee inserted "the most" interlinearly and forgot to cross out "a".)
71.18	correct way] (Quirks in Agee's orthography make this a conjectural reading, but the context supports it.)
73.1	He was there] (Agee inserts a section break just before this text begins. He has deleted the bottom two-thirds of [72] and the top one-quarter of [73] and commences his revised version of this material at this point.)
73.16	Dellfruke] (The doctor in the novel who would have been called to tend to Jay after his accident was named Delfrench. This may be an earlier name for the same person.)
64.1	(This page was clearly out of order in manuscript folder 5.2 and does not follow [63] of variant 3 recorded below. [64] keeps the surprise, while variant 3 ([62–63]) reveals the surprise. The text of [63] also ends just below the midpoint of the page. Page [64] is mated to [71–73] in this version because it follows the narrative flow of [71–73], the text of [73] ends at the bottom of that page, and characteristics of Agee's handwriting provide significant similarities between [71–73] and [64].)
64.3–25	(Paragraph breaks added)
64.4	explained] explained"
64.20	"That was] (A conjectural but likely reading of Agee's script based also upon the use of "That's" in the final version in the present edition.)
64.41	white peekay] (The manuscript breaks off at this point with no final punctuation.)

Variant 3

TX 5.2, [62–63] (Laura tells Rufus the secret; Victoria not present.)

[62]

One day his mother got him all cleaned up and put on his white peekay and told him just sit to sit still and stay very clean because in a little while Aunt Paula was coming for him and she'd take him on a nice visit to Granma and Grampa's. He would stay at Granma and Grampa's all night and all next day, she said, and all night after that and the *next* day, and maybe a little longer but not *very* long. And then he would come back home. And when he came home there would be the most wonderful saprise. When he asked what a saprise was she said it was like Christmas when Santy brings presents only this one was ever so much nicer. When he asked what the saprise was going to be she said now if I told you it wouldn't be a saprise any more, would it. She said the whole fun in a saprise was waiting, and not knowing until you saw it, wasn't it.

He did not feel that way, and she said that anyway she could promise him it was something that would make him very happy, and daddy and mama too.

Soon Aunt Paula came and he didn't want to go away if a saprise was coming. So his mother said "Paula will you wait a few minutes," and Aunt Paula said, "Why of course." And they left Aunt Paula in the sitting room and went into his mother's room and his mother sat down on the edge of the bed and took him between her knees and looked into his eyes almost frowning, as if she were threading a needle. He could see the orange freckles sparkling in her eyes and he knew she was going to say something but she didn't. Then she said "Little Rufus," and laid her hand along the side of his head and smiled. The she said, "Mama's going to tell you what the saprise is because it would be so hard to wait."

"Oh goody," he said.

"When you come back from Granma and Grampa's," she said, "a tiny new baby will be here to live with us." He waited to see if she would say more but she only looked at him. "That's the saprise," she said. "Isn't that lovely?"

"Why?"

She looked as if she hurt. Then she looked kind and loving and said "Why what *what,* dear?"

"Why will a tiny new baby be here to live with us?"

"Because mama and daddy wanted a new baby so much that God is going to give us one. And because we thought Rufus would be so happy too. To have a little brother or sister. Isn't Rufus happy too dear?"

"Yes," he said. "Where is it?"

"God's taking care of it," she said, "until it's ready to come to us."

"When'll it be ready?"

"When God knows it's strong enough."

"What's the matter with it?"

"Nothing's the matter with it Rufus. It's just that new babies are very tiny and weak at first so God keeps them in Heaven until He knows they're strong enough to come into the world."

[63]

"Up with Great Grampa Tyler?"

"No in a different part of Heaven," she said. "you see Heaven's a very big place because there has to be room for everybody there ever was or ever will be. Grampa Tyler's in the part where the old people rest who got so tired, you remember?" He nodded.

"Like Oliver," he said.

"Yes like Oliver," she said uneasily, "only we're not sure whether animals go to Heaven. And the little new baby's in another part of Heaven where all the little babies are waiting to be born."

"What's born?"

"I mean till they're strong enough to come and live with us."

"When'll it come?"

"Very soon now. Tomorrow or in a day or two."

"I want to be here when it comes."

"No Rufus that's why we're sending you on a nice visit. Because new babies are very weak and tiny and the least thing might scare them so they'd go away and not come at all. You wouldn't want to scare the new baby away would you?"

"I wouldn't scare it[.] I'd be nice to it."

"Of course you would dear. Be nice. You wouldn't mean to scare the little thing for the world. But little children *do,* even when they don't mean to. That's why it's always good for them to be away when a new baby comes."

"How do they scare um?"

"They just *do* Rufus and that's all there is to it. Now don't ask to stay again dear because you simply can't, that's all."

He could see there was no use asking.

Variant Notes for Manuscript 5.2 (page and line number cited)

62.2	just to sit still] just sit to still (Agee inserted "to" one space too soon in the line.)
62.3	was coming] was coming coming (Agee's inadvertent repetition resulting from the insertion of "was coming" above the original word "coming".)
62.5	Grampa's] Grampas
62.28	"Oh goody,"] (Paragraph break added)
62.29	"When] (Paragraph break added)
62.35	"Why what] "Wy what
63.6	"Like Oliver] (Paragraph break added)
63.7	"Yes like] (Paragraph break added)

Variant 4

TX 5.2, [65–69] (Laura tells Rufus the secret; Victoria is present)

[65]

One day the doorbell rang and his mother hurried past him in the hall and opened the door and there was a great big old lady, very strong looking and fat, with gray hair under her black straw hat, and black skin, and a little shiny black suitcase. She looked at his mother just a moment smiling through her little gold glasses and his mother looked at her with her head on one side and said Victoria! and then his mother flung open the screen door and they threw their arms around each other while the big old lady almost groaned in a deep voice, *Bless you, bless you chile, ole Victoria's so happy to see you agin!* And then she caught sight of him in the hallway and took a step back as if she was surprised, and said "Don't tell me *dat's* my baby!", and his mother said "Yes that's Rufus," as if she realized it was hard to believe (he couldn't see why it was) and then she came running at him so fast along the hall and so much huger with every step that he was almost scared, and she squatted and flung her arms around him, and smiled so happily and kindly that he wasn't scared at all any more. She said *Law, chile, how you done growed!*, very loudly, and then she laughed and laughed.

Mama said "Don't you *remember* Rufus? Why it's *Victoria!*" And Victoria hugged him again, clapping him on the back with both hands, and said "Bless his little heart how *would* he, how *would* he remember his ole Victoria. He wasn't even out of *didies* when I seed him last!" And she hugged him again and put her head back and said "Stand back chile and lemme git a good *look* at you!", and held him away by the shoulders and looked at him closely through the little gold glasses while he looked at her big black shining face. And seeing her face so near, he began uncertainly to remember another big face with little gold glasses, smiling, and looking at him happily and with love, only that was an even bigger face and the clothes she had worn were all blazing white. And his mother was saying, "Yes Victoria took *care* of you when you were just a tiny baby. Took care of *both* of us." And Victoria was saying, "Why he's the spittin image of you, Miss Laura, cepn de eyes." And his mother said "Yes he's got his father's eyes. And his hands I think." "An his heighth too," Victoria said, "or I miss my guess. You goanna be a big tall man like Daddy ain't you!" she said and, after he realized she was talking to him, he replied "Yes'm." "Yes'm," Victoria said, and they both laughed though he could not see why, and his mother said "Come Victoria I'll show you your room." And Victoria in turn said "Yesm", and picked up her little suitcase. "It's your same old room," his mother said. "My same ole room", Victoria said, following her. "Now ain't that nice! I feel most like I was comn back home!"

When Victoria had shut the door to her room his mother whispered "Come Rufus" in a way which seemed important and mysterious, and he followed her into the bedroom. She sat down on the edge of the bed as if it was hard to sit down and took him between her knees and just looked at him very closely for a moment without saying anything. He could see the orange speckles dancing in her gray eyes and he knew she was about to say something; he wondered what she would say.

"Mother has a wonderful surprise for you," she said.

A surprise was like Christmas.

[66]

"What," he asked.

She smiled and her eyes danced even more.

"Very soon now a little baby is coming to live with us."

He had not known it but it did not seem like a wonderful surprise. He looked at her carefully to see if there was more to the surprise but she only looked as if she were disappointed about something.

"Why?" he asked.

His mother looked for a moment as if he had said something wrong but she quickly covered this look with a gentle and loving look and said, "Because Rufus, daddy and mama wanted another little baby very much and so God is giving us one." He still looked at her, feeling, why then it's all right, but wondering what it had to do with him, and she went on, "and because we were both sure you'd be so happy to have a little brother or sister."

"What's a little brother or sister?"

"It's a baby that's your very own brother or your very own sister, not anybody else's. Like Arthur and Alvin are brothers. Like Uncle Hugh is mama's brother and Aunt Paula is her sister don't you see? Only little. A tiny new baby. If it's a baby boy then it's your brother and if it's a baby girl then it's your sister. And when it's a little bit bigger you can both play together. See?"

It began to sound as if it might be nice. "How big?" he asked.

She looked a little annoyed. "Oh just—bigger, Rufus," she said. "This time next summer maybe," she added quickly. "But even long before then it'll be fun because it'll be so cunning. You say ah-*boo!* and it'll smile at you all over its little face. And before long it'll make the cunningest little crowing noises of its own, just like a little bird. Mamma knows you'll just love it the minute you see it. And it won't be like playing with other children because instead you can always tell them this is my very own brother. Or this is my very own little sister."

If he had a brother he would be even with Arthur and Alvin.

"Don't you see?"

"Where is it. I want to see it."

"It hasn't come yet Rufus but it'll come soon and then you can I promise."

"When?"

"Very very soon now, tomorrow or next day or very very soon."

"Where is it now?"

"God's still keeping it safe until it's ready to come."

"Where's he keeping it?"

"Up in Heaven, Rufus."

"With Great-Grampa Tyler?"

"Well in the same general place. You see, heaven's a very big place. Grampa Tyler's in the part of heaven where all the old people stay who are tired and weak to rest. The baby's in the part where all the tiny babies stay who aren't quite ready yet to come and live in this world."

[67]

"Why aren't they."

"Why aren't they what?"

"Ready yet."

"Because they're still so little and tiny and weak. Just as soon as they're strong enough God sends them. But even then we have to take ever so much care of them for a while, until they get stronger."

"Why are they so tiny and weak?"

"They're just made that way. All of us were teensy tinesy babies once Rufus. You were. So tiny I could just hold you in the crook of my arm, like this. I was. Daddy too. Even Grampa and Granma and Aunt Jessie were."

He tried to imagine Grampa very tiny, lying on her arm with his glasses and his hairy face.

"That's why Victoria has come back," his mother said. "Because when a baby first comes, it's very tiny and helpless. When you first came and were just a teensy tinesy baby, Victoria stayed with us and took care of us. And now as soon as you get cleaned up, Victoria's going to take you down to Granma and Grampa's to wait till the baby comes."

"Why?"

"Because when a baby first comes it's very tiny and weak, and Mother and Victoria will have their hands full just tending to the baby, without taking care of you too."

"Can't I stay till the baby comes and then go to Grampa and Granma's?"

"No dear. It's better not. Cause when the baby makes up its mind to come, it's likely to come just any minute, and then we'll need to give it all our attention."

"What makes the baby make up its mind?"

"I mean when *God* makes up *His* mind the baby's ready."

"When does He do that?"

"When He's sure the little baby is strong enough Rufus."

"Oh."

"So just as soon as Victoria's ready now, we're going to get *you* all ready and she'll take you down. Won't that be fun?"

[68]

"Why?"

"I mean to have a nice visit with Grampa and Granma."

"Yes."

"And then *just* as soon as baby can see you, Victoria'll bring you back to see the baby!"

There was a knock on the door. "Come right in, Victoria," his mother called, and there she was in a blazing white dress and a little white cap on her white hair, and now he was almost sure he could remember her. "*Now* you membuh me chile?", she grinned, putting her head on one side and smiling roguishly and he shyly said "Mm-hm," but his mother meanwhile was saying, "Victoria I've just been telling Rufus about the little new baby who's coming so soon, and how you're going to take him down to his Grampa and Granma for a nice little visit."

And so before she could hear him say "mm-hm," Victoria quickly stopped smiling and listened very respectfully while his mother said all she had to say, and then she smiled and said "Well bless his little heart. An when you come home, dare it'll be, yo lil brothuh or yo lil sistuh. Ain't dat *nice* now?"

"Yesm," he said, but already his mother was saying, "I thought of having him all ready to go."

And again Victoria stopped talking to him or waiting for a reply and listened to her earnestly, smiling just a little. "Yesum," she said, half in question, just while he was saying "yesm", and his mother went on, "and save you some bother", "Taint no bothuh to *me* Miss Laura," Victoria said; "some bother," his mother repeated; "but then it occurred to me it might just get him all mixed up if he had too long to wait, you know, in his best clothes all cleaned up, just waiting, before anything really started to *happen.* I mean waiting for *you* on top of waiting for everything else you know. I don't know. Perhaps it was just kind of silly but that's what I'd—"

"Bless you Miss Laura jist anyways you take a mind to do, hit's agoan be all right."

"So now if you'll just come with me I'll show you where his things are and . . . I've got his little suitcase all ready but. . . ."

Victoria hurried to her and took her elbow and put one arm around her waist. "Lawd chile," she said, "don't you git up without you git helped up. You just show me and lay back down and take it easy. You just leave everthang to me!" And she helped her stand up from the side of the bed.

"Thank you Victoria," his mother said. "That's what I was trying to say. I hate you to just have to take over *everything* your first minute but I think I better just stay on my back."

Victoria stopped them both dead in their tracks and looked at her sharply. "Hit ain't already—" She glanced at Rufus.

"*Oh* no," his mother said, "Only I just feel awfully heavy and I guess, well, just terribly *lazy.*"

She laughed a little, and Victoria patted her shoulder and said "An dat's just how you ought to feel, and not make no bones about it. Dat's what your ole Victoria's *heah* faw!", and he followed them into his own room.

"I thought he might wear the little white piqué," his mother said, "just because it's sort of an occasion." "Mm-*hmm,*" Victoria nodded, "and the little patten leather shoes and I've got those new stockings," ("O *my*", Victoria nodded), "and the little white hat. And here in his suitcase I've got two pairs of rompers and his sandals, and socks, and *four* nighties Victoria—he still, well, sometimes he still wets the bed Victoria," she said in a lowered voice while he winced "and I wouldn't want Mam—Mrs. Tyler to have to wash out for him; and for the same reason a piece of oilcloth.["]; "Aww," Victoria said; "and extra panties and shirtwaist, and I think that ought to do him. Don't you?"

"Mm-*hmm*," Victoria said. "Cose it will. *Cose* it will."

"Because it oughtn't to—be longer than that do you think?"

"I wouldn' reckon so Miss Laura. No I wouldn't. An' if he needs warshin done or fresh duds why I can do it in a jiffy."

"No Victoria you're going to have more than enough without that. You're

[69]

going to have your hands *full*." "Why taint nuffin, lil nightie, lil rawm-puhs, I fix em in a jiffy."

"Well as I say let's *hope*—I *think* they'll last him anyway."

"I reckon most likely so Miss Laura."

"Now I'll just go back and lie down a little. Rufus can wash himself can't you Rufus?"

He looked at her, a little startled, being spoken to again.

"Well now," Victoria exclaimed.

"So it . . . you'll just make sure he gets his *ears* clean," she lowered her voice for some reason, "and the back of his neck."

Victoria nodded and kept going *Mm-hmm*.

"And bring him into me when you're ready to go."

Variant Notes for Manuscript 5.2 (page and line number cited)

65.9	*happy*] proud > *happy*
65.32	And his hands] Hands too > And his hands (No choice indicated by Agee.)
66.33	it.] it
68.10	shyly] shily
68.14–69.12	(Paragraph breaks added)
68.34	are and . . .] are and.
68.34	ready but. . . .] ready but.
69.7	He] he
69.9	"So it . . . you'll] "So it you'll

Chapter 9

The following is the unedited transcription of part of TX 5.2, [57–58] that is only partially incorporated into the final text of this edition to avoid repetition. See 74.11–22 for comparison.

And as he came, he could see through the screen door how something large and white came rushing through the dark hall getting bigger and bigger, and the screen door burst open and a great big fat old lady in blazing white, with such black skin, ran out to him, stooping while she ran, and swept him into her arms, crying "Lord God how mah baby done *growed!*" She was so big and she came so fast that she frightened him but as soon as she took him in her arms she smelled so good that he wasn't frightened anymore; mystified as he was, he pushed his forehead against her warm neck and for a moment he felt almost sleepy. She was droning and groaning happily, words he could not quite hear, and now she took him by the shoulders and held him away, saying "Lemme git a good *look* at you chile; hello Miss Paula," she said over her shoulder, "You lookin *mighty* sweet," but she continued to look at him, through her little gold glasses, and as he looked back into the huge shining face and at the little glasses which perched on it like a butterfly, he liked her so much that he asked Aunt Paula, "is she the surprise?" "Why no Rufus," Aunt Paula said, "that's *Victoria.* Don't you remember *Victoria?* It's all a surprise to him," she explained to Victoria. "It's still a secret." "Bless his lil hot," Victoria said. "Victoria took care of you when you were just a tiny baby," Aunt Paula said. "Bless his lil hot how *would* he membuh," Victoria exclaimed. "He was still in didies when I seed him de las." She got up grunting.

Chapter 14

There are several alternate beginnings in the Tennessee manuscripts to the chapter that Agee called "Enter the Ford" in his notes. These variants are found in TN 1A.20, [18–21] and are transcribed together below as a set, rather than placing those that are under one hundred words in length in the "Textual Commentary and Notes."

[18; paper has been crumpled up]

So all of a sudden late one afternoon, when Rufus was already keeping an eye on the corner where he usually just saw his father coming, he turned to look for the source of an unfamiliar noise and there came his father sitting up high in the most beautiful new auto, and he screamed "*Daddy!*" and his father waved to him and pulled in towards the curb. "*Mama!*", he screamed. "Daddy's home and he's coming home in an *auto!*", and he ran out to the curb. His father overshot the walk to the steps and stopped the auto and made it tremble all over with a wonderful loud noise, and then looked around and grinned at Rufus and made the auto go backwards, right to where he wanted it, and then he reached down and pulled up on something that made a metal creaking and got out of the auto just as Rufus' mother hurried out the front door wiping her hands on her apron. "Why Jay!" she cried above the loud happy noise of the auto. "You didn't *tell* me it was *today!*" He smiled down at her. "Surprised?" "Why I'm surprised out of my *life!*"

"*He's* good and surprised all right," his father said, for Rufus was jumping up and down and yelling with excitement. "*Rufus!*" his mother said. He didn't even hear her. "*Rufus!*" she called much more loudly. He looked at her happily, out of breath. "Quiet *down* a little dear I can't even hear myself *think.*" "Aw let him holler." "Jay he's on the verge of *hysterics,*" she said confidentially, as if she didn't wish Rufus to hear. "Oh shaw he's nothing of the kind he's just excited. Let him steam it off." "Welll," his mother said uncertainly; and now he was somewhat quieter. "Why goodness gracious Jay where's the *man!*" "What man," he asked, amused. "Why you know perf—you mean you drove it here all by your*self?*" "Sure I did. Don't take but one." "But how on *earth!* I mean, when in the world did y—" "Been sneakin lessons on you, that's all." ["]But you had to come right through the middle of *town!*" "Why sure." "But Jay how could you *dare!*" He laughed, while she looked at him with doubt and admiration. "Good Lord Laura if other people can do it so can I. Tisn't so hard when you get the hang of it. Not hard a bit." "Jay can't you turn it off?" For the auto was still trembling all over. "Sure I can but I like to hear it running. Sides we're gonna take a joyride and I hate to crank it up. So hurry up and get Emma." "But I'm right in the middle of supper." "Aw put it on the back of the stove." She hesitated. "Come on Laura. We won't be long."

[**the following introduction is crossed-out on back of page 18**]
So all of a sudden late one afternoon, when Rufus was already watching the corner where he usually first saw his father, he heard a noise down the street and looked and it was an auto, and his father was in it and so was another man in a straw hat who was driving [end crossed-out introduction]

[19]

So all of a sudden late one afternoon, there it was, right in front of the house, and his father stepped out of it grinning from ear to ear and it stood there glittering like patent leather and trembling all over with a loud happy noise. And Rufus' mother hurried out wiping her hands on her apron and she was almost as surprised as Rufus was, for she hadn't expected it to arrive that day, much less that her husband had already learned to drive it.

[20]

So all of a sudden late one afternoon there it was right in front of the house, glittering like patent leather and trembling all over with a loud and happy noise. It had big front lights with yellow brass rims and in behind, a little light with red glass over it, and in front it had a shining yellow plate of brass with its name on it, Ford.

[21]

All of a sudden Daddy got a Ford. A Ford was a car. A car was an auto. An auto was an automobile. Fords were also called tin-lizzie, and

Henry, but Daddy said that was all right it was a darn good car and he was sick and tired of all the Ford jokes before even he owned one, and he called it The Ford. So they all called it The Ford.

Rufus had overheard a certain amount of talk about it before it arrived, before he even knew what they were talking about, so the name was not new to him; nor was the knowledge that Daddy had gone ahead and gotten it in spite of some people's feelings that it was an expensive thing to afford (Ford); but he had never had any idea it would be like this. It was wonderful. He could hardly take his eyes off it. It was mostly black and shining, but in front it was bright shining yellowlike gold in a great wide band of bare metal, and across that, like better handwriting than anybody could just write, it said what it was:

FORD.

It had two seats, front and back, that smelled like what Mama put under his sheet, and a top that would go up and down, when it rained, and curtains with limber smelly windows that snapped on when it was raining hard. Inside there were things he could not really see or understand with names like magneto, and carberator [*sic.* carburetor], and spark plugs, and valves, and on the body there was a gas tank full of gas, which turned out to be like thin water, only smelling very good, instead of the strange, dark-smelling air that came out of the gas-jets at granpas and granmas. You had to be very careful with the gas. You could look in but you absolutely must *not* strike a light to look in. When Daddy looked in, if he was smoking a cigarette he always first put it under his shoe and twisted his foot, before he even came near the tank, or if it was a long one he would say, "D'you mind holding this for me Laura," and she would say "of course, Jay", and he would look. He took a piece of wood with marks and numbers on it, not a ruler, a gauge, and put it [narrative breaks off here; in the left margin a line is drawn down the length of this paragraph and to the side is written "later"]

Chapter 14 also marks the introduction of Arthur and Alvin Tripp into the novel, if only to say hello to Rufus and look at the new Model T. In TN 1A.19 are two manuscript pages that expand their characters. The first [3.1] deals with a fight scene between the two brothers, and the second [3.2] with a brief encounter between Rufus and Alvin. Neither scene is incorporated into the novel, though Agee annotates the bracketed two paragraphs of the fight scene with the word "later".

[3.1]

The only other boy in the block who was his age was Alvin Tripp, but Alvin always seemed older because he was much less clumsy and because he was always accompanied by his older brother, Arthur, when Arthur was not in school, and Arthur always stood up for Alvin except when they themselves were quarreling. Because Arthur was around, Alvin often dared to say and do things to older boys than he was, that astonished Rufus. In fact some of the much older boys insisted that Alvin could whip Arthur any old time if he got mad enough, and Rufus was among those who had seen this almost prove itself. For Alvin was naturally skilful with his body and looked extremely dangerous when he got mad, and Arthur was soft-looking, with a rather girlish smile, and had curly hair. But others of the older boys argued that Alvin so nearly whipped Arthur only because Arthur wasn't half trying; he wouldn't want to whip his own brother, smaller than he was; and Rufus, remembering this fight and how alarmed Arthur had looked, backing away and guarding himself rather than hitting out, felt that that was the truth.

Generally, though, the Tripps backed each other up, and they did not have many serious fights. Once Johnny Breen got in a fight with Arthur. He was smaller than Arthur, hardly bigger than Alvin, but everyone knew he was the best fighter his size in the block. Arthur tried to back away from him too. Some of the older boys said it was because he was a coward, others said it was because he was bigger. But Johnny forced on him so hard that he had to hit back, as hard as he could, even to defend himself. And even that was not enough. Johnny bloodied his nose for him and that brought tears into Arthur's eyes and most of the boys began yelling *cry-baby cry,* and Arthur, still trying to keep Johnny off, insisted that he was not crying, but they yelled it all the more, and under this humiliation and injustice he really did start to cry. It was obvious that he wanted to quit fighting but did not know how to, and Johnny kept on punching him, and it was so unpleasant and uneven that some of the boys stopped yelling (though others yelled all the louder), when suddenly Alvin rushed in at Johnny from the back, stuttering with rage, beating him with his fists on the back of the head and neck and kicking him, and then grabbed him and threw him to the ground, and Arthur piled on top, and everybody started yelling at the tops of their lungs again, and the bigger boys started laughing as well.

[3.2]

Rufus was as big as most boys two years older; like most oversized children, he was also as clumsy as most boys two years younger: but this, naturally enough, occurred neither to him nor to anyone else. He knew simply that he wholly lacked confidence in his body in any actions which required particular combinations of skill and strength;

and equally, he was incapable of pleasure in such actions, of the focussed resoluteness, anger and self-confidence and of the incuriosity or unreflectiveness, which give them their essential vitality and shape. When Alvin Tripp had rung the doorbell once, when they were both three, and he had gone from the table and opened the door, and Alvin had said, "If you wear a bib, you're a baby," he had simply not known what to say; it had only left him with a distaste for bibs which it had never before occurred to him to have, and he had felt particularly pleased when, at last, he was allowed not to wear a bib, and could watch Emma wearing hers.

Chapter 15

As recorded in "Textual Commentary and Notes," McDowell uses TX 5.3, [131–35, 140–41], a somewhat different and shorter version of this chapter. His variant appears as section 13.2 (McD, 227–40) of his edition.

[227]

After dinner the babies and all the children except Rufus were laid out on the beds to take their naps, and his mother thought he ought to lie down too, but his father said no, why did he need to, so he was allowed to stay up. He stayed out on the porch with the men. They were so full up and sleepy they hardly even tried to talk, and he was so full up and sleepy that he could hardly see or hear, but half dozing between his father's knees in the thin shade, trying to keep his eyes open, he could just hear the mild, lazy rumbling of their voices, and the more talkative voices of the women back in the kitchen, talking more easily, but keeping their voices low, not to wake the children, and the rattling of the dishes they were doing, and now and then their walking here or there along the floor; and mused with half-closed eyes which went in and out of focus with sleepiness, upon the slow twinkling of the millions of heavy leaves on the trees and the slow flashing of the blades of the corn,

[228]

and nearer at hand, the hens dabbing in the pocked dirt yard and the ragged edge of the porch floor, and everything hung dreaming in a shining silver haze, and a long, low hill of blue silver shut off everything against a blue-white sky, and he leaned back against his father's chest and he could hear his heart pumping and his stomach growling and he could feel the hard knees against his sides, and the next thing he knew his eyes opened and he was looking up into his mother's face and he was lying on a bed and she was saying it was time to wake up because they were going on a call and see his great-great-grandmother and she would most specially want to see him because he was her oldest great-great-grand-child. And he and his father and mother and

Catherine got in the front seat and his Granpa Follet and Aunt Jessie and her baby and Jim-Wilson and Ettie Lou and Aunt Sadie and her baby got in the back seat and Uncle Ralph stood on the running board because he was sure he could remember the way, and that was all there was room for, and they started off very carefully down the lane, so nobody would be jolted, and even before they got out to the road his mother asked his father to stop a minute, and she insisted on taking Ettie Lou with them in front, to make a little more room in back, and after she insisted for a while, they gave in, and then they all got started again, and his father guided the auto so very carefully across the deep ruts into the road, the other way from LaFollette as Ralph told him to ("Yeah, I know," his father said, "I remember that much anyhow."), that they were hardly joggled at all, and his mother commented on how very nicely and carefully his father always drove when he didn't just forget and go too fast, and his father blushed, and after a few minutes his mother began to look uneasy, as if she had to go to the bathroom but didn't want to say anything about it, and after a few minutes more she said, "Jay, I'm awfully sorry but now I really think you are forgetting."

[229]

"Forgetting what?" he said.

"I mean a little too fast, dear," she said.

"Good road along here," he said. "Got to make time while the road's good." He slowed down a little. "Way I remember it," he said, "there's some stretches you can't hardly ever get a mule through, we're coming to, ain't they Ralph?"

"Oh mercy," his mother said.

"We are just raggin you," he said. "They're not all *that* bad. But all the same we better make time while we can." And he sped up a little.

After another two or three miles Uncle Ralph said, "Now around this bend you run through a branch and you turn up sharp to the right," and they ran through the branch and turned into a sandy woods road and his father went a little slower and a cool breeze flowed through them and his mother said how lovely this shade was after that terrible hot sun, wasn't it, and all the older people murmured that it sure was, and almost immediately they broke out of the woods and ran through two miles of burned country with stumps and sometimes whole tree trunks sticking up out of it sharp and cruel, and blackberry and honeysuckle all over the place, and a hill and its shadow ahead. And when they came within the shadow of the hill, Uncle Ralph said in a low voice, "Now you get to the hill, start along the base of it to your left till you see your second right and then you take that," but when they got there, there was only the road to the left and none to the right and his father took it and nobody said anything, and after a minute Uncle Ralph said, "Reckon they wasn't much to choose from there, was they?" and laughed unhappily.

"That's right," his father said, and smiled.

"Reckon my memory ain't so sharp as I bragged," Ralph said.

[230]

"You're doin fine," his father said, and his mother said so too.

"I could a swore they was a road both ways there," Ralph said, "but it was nigh on twenty years since I was out here." Why for goodness sake, his mother said, then she *certainly* thought he had a wonderful memory.

"How long since *you* were here, Jay?" He did not say anything. "Jay?"

"I'm a-studyin it," he said.

"There's your turn," Ralph said suddenly, and they had to back the auto to turn into it.

They began a long, slow, winding climb, and Rufus half heard and scarcely understood their disjointed talking. His father had not been there in nearly thirteen years; the last time was just before he came to Knoxville. He was always her favorite, Ralph said. Yes, his grandfather said, he reckoned that was a fact, she always seemed to take a shine to Jay. His father said quietly that he always did take a shine to her. It turned out he was the last of those in the auto who had seen her. They asked how she was, as if it had been within a month or two. He said she was failing lots of ways, specially getting around, her rheumatism was pretty bad, but in the mind she was bright as a dollar, course that wasn't saying how they might find her by now, poor old soul; no use saying. Nope, Uncle Ralph said, *that* was a fact; time sure did fly, didn't it; seemed like before you knew it, this year was last year. She had never yet seen Jay's children, or Ralph's, or Jessie's or Sadie's, it was sure going to be a treat for her. A treat *and* a surprise. Yes it sure would be that, his father said, always supposing she could still recognize them. Mightn't she even have died? his mother wanted to know. *Oh* no, all the Follets said, they'd have heard for sure if she'd died. Matter of fact they *had* heard she had failed a good bit. Sometimes her memory slipped up and she got

[231]

confused, poor old soul. His mother said well she should *think* so, poor old lady. She asked, carefully, if she was taken good care of. Oh, yes, they said. That she was. Sadie's practically giving her life to her. That was Grandpa Follet's oldest sister and young Sadie was named for her. Lived right with her tending to her wants, day and night. Well, isn't that just wonderful, his mother said. Wasn't anybody else could do it, they agreed with each other. All married and gone, and she wouldn't come live with any of them, they all offered, over and over, but she wouldn't leave her home. I raised my family here, she said, I lived here all my life from fourteen years on and I aim to die here, that must be a good thirty-five, most, a good near forty year ago, Grampaw died. Goodness sake, his mother said, and she was an old *old* woman *then!* His father said soberly, "She's a hundred and three years old. Hundred and three or hundred and four. She never could remember for sure which. But she knows she wasn't born later than eighteen-twelve. And she always reckoned it might of been eighteen-eleven."

"*Great heavens,* Jay! Do you *mean* that?" He just nodded, and kept his eyes on the road. "Just *imagine that,* Rufus," she said. "Just *think* of *that!*"

"She's an old, old lady,"' his father said gravely; and Ralph gravely and proudly concurred.

"The things she must have seen!" Mary said, quietly. "Indians. Wild animals." Jay laughed. "I mean *man*-eaters, Jay. Bears, and wild-cats—terrible things."

"There were cats back in these mountains, Mary—we called em painters, that's the same as a panther—they were around here still when *I* was a boy. And there is still bear, they claim."

"Gracious Jay, did you ever see one? A panther?"

"Saw one'd been shot."

"Goodness," Mary said.

[232]

"A mean-lookin varmint."

"I know," she said. "I mean, I *bet* he was. I just can't get over—why she's almost as old as the country, Jay."

"*Oh,* no," he laughed. "Ain't nobody *that* old. Why I read somewhere, that just these mountains here are the oldest . . ."

"Dear, I meant the nation," she said. "The United States, I mean. Why let me see, why it was hardly as old as I am when she was born." They all calculated for a moment. "*Not* even as old," she said triumphantly.

"By golly," his father said. " I never thought of it like that." He shook his head. "By golly," he said, "that's a fact."

"Abraham Lincoln was just two years old," she murmured. "Maybe three," she said grudgingly. "Just try to *imagine* that, Rufus," she said after a moment. "Over a hundred years." But she could see that he couldn't comprehend it. "You know what she is?" she said, "she's Granpa Follet's *grandmother!*"

"That's a fact, Rufus," his grandfather said from the back seat, and Rufus looked around, able to believe it but not to imagine it, and the old man smiled and winked. "Woulda never believed you'd hear *me* call nobody 'Granmaw,' now would you?"

"No sir," Rufus said.

"Well, yer goana," his grandfather said, "quick's I see her."

Ralph was beginning to mutter and to look worried and finally his brother said, "What's eaten ye, Ralph? Lost the way?" And Ralph said he didn't know for sure as he had lost it exactly, no, he wouldn't swear to that yet, but by golly he was damned if he was sure this was *hit* anymore, all the same.

"Oh *dear,* Ralph how *too bad,*" Mary said, "but don't you mind. Maybe we'll find it. I mean maybe soon you'll recognize landmarks and set us all straight again."

But his father, looking dark and painfully patient, just

[233]

slowed the auto down and then came to a stop in a shady place. "Maybe we better figure it out right now," he said.

"Nothin round hyer I know," Ralph said, miserably. "What I mean, maybe we ought to start back while we still know the way back. Try it another Sunday."

"Oh, Jay."

"I hate to but we got to get back in town tonight, don't forget. We could try it another Sunday. Make an early start." But the upshot of it was that they decided to keep on ahead awhile, anyway. They descended into a long, narrow valley through the woods of which they could only occasionally see the dark ridges and the road kept bearing in a direction Ralph was almost sure was wrong, and they found a cabin, barely even cut out of the woods, they commented later, hardly even a corn patch, big as an ordinary barnyard; but the people there, very glum and watchful, said they had never even heard of her; and after a long while the valley opened out a little and Ralph began to think that perhaps he recognized it, only it sure didn't look like itself if it *was* it, and all of a sudden a curve opened into half-forested meadow and there were glimpses of a gray house through swinging vistas of saplings and Ralph said, "By golly," and again, "By golly, that is *hit.* That's hit all right. Only we come on it from behind!" And his father began to be sure too, and the house grew larger, and they swung around where they could see the front of it, and his father and his Uncle Ralph and his Grandfather all said, "Why sure enough," and sure enough it was: and, "There she is," and there she was: it was a great, square-logged gray cabin closed by a breezeway, with a frame second floor, and an enormous oak plunging from the packed dirt in front of it, and a great iron ring, the rim of a wagon wheel, hung by a chain from a branch of the oak which had drunk the chains into itself, and in the shade of the oak, which was as big as the whole corn patch they had seen,

[234]

an old woman was standing up from a kitchen chair as they swung slowly in onto the dirt and under the edge of the shade, and another old woman continued to sit very still in her chair.

The younger of the two old women was Great Aunt Sadie, and she knew them the minute she laid eyes on them and came right on up to the side of the auto before they could even get out. "Lord God," she said in a low, hard voice, and she put her hands on the edge of the auto and just looked from one to the other of them. Her hands were long and narrow and as big as a man's and every knuckle was swollen and split. She had hard black eyes, and there was a dim purple splash all over the left side of her face. She looked at them so sharply and silently from one to another that Rufus thought she must be mad at them, and then she began to shake her head back and forth. "Lord God," she said again. "Howdy, John Henry," she said.

"Howdy, Sadie," his grandfather said.

"Howdy, Aunt Sadie," his father and his Aunt Sadie said.

"Howdy, Jay," she said, looking sternly at his father, "howdy, Ralph," and she looked sternly at Ralph. "Reckon you must be Jess, and yore Sadie. Howdy, Sadie."

"This is Mary, Aunt Sadie," his father said. '"Mary, this is Aunt Sadie."

"I'm proud to know you," the old woman said, looking very hard at his mother. "I figured it must be you," she said, just as his mother said, "I'm awfully glad to know you too." "And this is Rufus and Catherine and Ralph's Jim-Wilson and Ettie Lou and Jessie's Charlie after his daddy and Sadie's Jessie after her Granma and her Aunt Jessie," his father said.

"Well, Lord God," the old woman said. "Well, file on out."

"How's Granmaw?" his father asked, in a low voice, without moving yet to get out.

"Good as we got any right to expect," she said, "but don't

[235]

feel put out if she don't know none-a-yews. She mought and she mought not. Half the time she don't even know me."

Ralph shook his head and clucked his tongue. "Pore old soul," he said, looking at the ground. His father let out a slow breath, puffing his cheeks.

"So if I was you-all I'd come up on her kind of easy," the old woman said. "Bin a coon's age since she seen so many folks at onct. Me either. Mought skeer her if ye all come a whoopin up at her in a flock."

"Sure," his father said.

"*Ayy,*" his mother whispered.

His father turned and looked back. "Whyn't you go see her the first, Paw?" he said very low. "Yore the eldest."

"Tain't me she wants to see," Grandfather Follet said. "Hit's the younguns ud tickle her most."

"Reckon that's the truth, if she can take notice," the old woman said. "She shore like to cracked her heels when she heared yore boy was born," she said to Jay, "Mary or no Mary. Proud as Lucifer. Cause that was the first," she told Mary.

"Yes, I know," Mary said. "Fifth generation, that made."

"Did you get her postcard, Jay?"

"What postcard?"

"Why no," Mary said.

"She tole me what to write on one a them postcards and put hit in the mail to both a yews so I done it. Didn't ye never get it?"

Jay shook his head. "First I ever heard tell of it," he said.

"Well I shore done give hit to the mail. Ought to remember. Cause I went all the way into Polly to buy it and all the way in again to put it in the mail."

"We never did get it," Jay said.

"What street did you send it, Aunt Sadie?" Mary asked. "Because we moved not long be . . ."

[236]

"Never sent it to no street," the old woman said. "Never knowed I needed to, Jay working for the post office."

"Why, I quit working for the post office a long time back, Aunt Sadie. Even before that."

"Well I reckon that's how come then. Cause I just sent hit to 'Post Office, Cristobal, Canal Zone, Panama,' and I spelt hit right, too. C-r-i . . ."

"Oh," Mary said.

"Aw," Jay said. "Why, Aunt Sadie, I thought you'd a known. We been living in Knoxvul since pert near two years before Rufus was born."

She looked at him keenly and angrily, raising her hands slowly from the edge of the auto, and brought them down so hard that Rufus jumped. Then she nodded, several times, and still she did not say anything. At last she spoke, coldly, "Well, they might as well just put me out to grass," she said. "Lay me down and give me both barls threw the head."

"Why, Aunt Sadie," Mary said gently, but nobody paid any attention.

After a moment the old woman went on solemnly, staring hard into Jay's eyes: "I knowed that like I know my own name and it plumb slipped my mind."

"Oh what a shame," Mary said sympathetically.

"Hit ain't shame I feel," the old woman said, "hit's sick in the stummick."

"Oh I didn't m . . ."

"Right hyer!" and she slapped her hand hard against her stomach and laid her hand back on the edge of the auto. "If I git like that too," she said to Jay, "*then* who's agonna look out fer her?"

"Aw, tain't so bad, Aunt Sadie," Jay said. "Everybody slips up nown then. Do it myself an I ain't half yer age. And you just ought see Mary."

"Gracious, yes," Mary said. "I'm just a perfect scatterbrain."

[237]

The old woman looked briefly at Mary and then looked back at Jay. "Hit ain't the only time," she said, "not by a long chalk. Twarn't three days ago I . . ." she stopped. "Takin on about yer troubles ain't never holp nobody," she said. "You just set hyer a minute."

She turned and walked over to the older woman and leaned deep over against her ear and said, quite loudly, but not quite shouting, "Granmaw, ye got company." And they watched the old woman's pale eyes, which had been on them all this time in the light shadow of the sunbonnet, not changing, rarely ever blinking, to see whether they would change now, and they did not change at all, she didn't even move her head or her mouth. "Ye hear me, Granmaw?" The old woman opened and shut her sunken mouth, but not as if she were saying anything. "Hit's Jay and his wife and younguns, come up from Knoxvul to see you,"' she called, and they saw the hands crawl in her lap and the face turned towards the younger woman and they could hear a thin, dry crackling, no words.

"She can't talk any more," Jay said, almost in a whisper.

"Oh *no,*" Mary said.

But Sadie turned to them and her hard eyes were bright. "She knows ye," she said quietly. "Come on over." And they climbed slowly and shyly out onto the swept ground. "I'll tell her about the rest a yuns in a minute," Sadie said.

"Don't want to mix her up," Ralph explained, and they all nodded.

It seemed to Rufus like a long walk over to the old woman because they were all moving so carefully and shyly; it was almost like church. "Don't holler," Aunt Sadie was advising his parents, "hit only skeers her. Just talk loud and plain right up next her ear."

"I know," his mother said. "My mother is very deaf, too."

"Yeah," his father said. And he bent down close against her ear. "Granmaw?" he called, and he drew a little away,

[238]

where she could see him, while his wife and his children looked on, each holding one of the mother's hands. She looked straight into his eyes and her eyes and her face never changed, a look as if she were gazing at some small point at a great distance, with complete but idle intensity, as if what she was watching was no concern of hers. His father leaned forward again and gently kissed her on the mouth, and drew back again where she could see him well, and smiled a little, anxiously. Her face restored itself from his kiss like grass that has been lightly stepped on; her eyes did not alter. Her skin looked like brown-marbled stone over which water has worked for so long that it is as smooth and blind as soap. He leaned to her ear again. "I'm Jay," he said, "John Henry's boy." Her hands crawled in her skirt: every white bone and black vein showed through the brown-splotched skin; the wrinkled knuckles were like pouches; she wore a red rubber guard ahead of her wedding ring. Her mouth opened and shut and they heard her low, dry croaking, but her eyes did not change. They were bright in their thin shadow, but they were as impersonally bright as two perfectly shaped eyes of glass.

"I figure she knows you," Sadie said quietly.

"She can't talk, can she?" Jay said, and now that he was not looking at her, it was as if they were talking over a stump.

"Times she can," Sadie said. "Times she can't. Ain't only so seldom call for talk, reckon she loses the hang of it. But I figger she knows ye and I am tickled she does."

His father looked all around him in the shade and he looked sad, and unsure, and then he looked at him. "Come here, Rufus," he said.

"Go to him," his mother whispered for some reason, and she pushed his hand gently as she let it go.

"Just call her Granmaw," his father said quietly. "Get right

[239]

up by her ear like you do to Granmaw Lynch and say, 'Granmaw, I'm Rufus.'"

He walked over to her as quietly as if she were asleep, feeling strange to be by himself, and stood on tiptoe beside her and looked down into her sunbonnet towards her ear. Her temple was deeply sunken as if a hammer had struck it and frail as a fledgling's belly. Her skin was crosshatched with the razor-fine slashes of innumerable square wrinkles and yet every slash was like smooth stone; her ear was just a fallen intricate flap with a small gold ring in it; her smell was faint yet very powerful, and she smelled like new mushrooms and old spices and sweat, like his fingernail when it was coming off. "Granmaw, I'm Rufus," he said carefully, and yellow-white hair stirred beside her ear. He could feel coldness breathing from her cheek.

"Come out where she can see you," his father said, and he drew back and stood still further on tiptoe and leaned across her, where she could see. "I'm Rufus," he said, smiling, and suddenly her eyes darted a little and looked straight into his, but they did not in any way change their expression. They were just color: seen close as this, there was color through a dot at the middle, dim as blue-black oil, and then a circle of blue so pale it was almost white, that looked like glass, smashed into a thousand dimly sparkling pieces, smashed and infinitely old and patient, and then a ring of dark blue, so fine and sharp no needle could have drawn it, and then a clotted yellow full of tiny squiggles of blood, and then a wrongside furl of red-bronze, and little black lashes. Vague light sparkled in the crackled blue of the eye like some kind of remote ancestor's anger, and the sadness of time dwelt in the blue-breathing, oily center, lost and alone and far away, deeper than the deepest well. His father was saying something, but he did not hear and now he spoke again,

[240]

careful to be patient, and Rufus heard, "Tell her 'I'm Jay's boy.' Say, 'I'm Jay's boy Rufus.'"

And again he leaned into the cold fragrant cavern next her ear and said, "I'm Jay's boy Rufus," and he could feel her face turn towards him.

"Now kiss her," his father said, and he drew out of the shadow of her bonnet and leaned far over and again entered the shadow and kissed her paper mouth, and the mouth opened, and the cold sweet breath of rotting and of spice broke from her with the dry croaking, and he felt the hands take him by the shoulders like knives and forks of ice through his clothes. She drew him closer and looked at him almost glaring, she was so filled with grave intensity. She seemed to be sucking on her lower lip and her eyes filled with light, and then, as abruptly as if the two different faces had been joined without transition in a strip of moving-picture film, she was not serious any more but smiling so hard that her chin and her nose almost touched and her deep little eyes giggled for joy. And again the croaking gurgle came, making shapes which were surely words but incomprehensible words, and she held him even more tightly by the shoulders, and looked at him even more keenly and incredulously with her giggling, all but hidden eyes, and smiled and smiled, and cocked her head to one side, and with sudden love he kissed her again. And he could hear his mother's voice say, "Jay," almost whispering, and his father say, "Let her be," in a quick, soft, angry voice, and when at length they gently disengaged her hands, and he was at a little distance, he could see that there was water crawling along the dust from under her chair, and his father and his Aunt Sadie looked gentle and sad and dignified, and his mother was trying not to show that she was crying, and the old lady sat there aware only that something had been taken from her, but growing quickly calm, and nobody said anything about it.

Notes for McD 227–40 Variant (TX 5.3, [131–35, 140–41])

McD 228.1 pocked] packed
McD 228.19 with] in with
McD 228.20 while,] while
McD 228.22 LaFollette] Jacksboro (McDowell changes some of the place names in the novel as well as those of the characters.)
McD 228.25 very] *very*
McD 228.27 uneasy,] uneasy
McD 228.28 about it,] about it
McD 228.29 Jay,] Jay

McD 228.30 are] *are*

McD 229.3 Got to] Gotta

McD 229.5 ever] even

McD 229.7 mercy] Mercy

McD 229.8 We are] I'm (The words are indistinct in the manuscript.)

McD 229.8 raggin > teasin (No choice indicated by Agee.)

McD 229.14 among > through (No choice indicated by Agee.)

McD 229.20 hill,] hill

McD 229.22 till you see] till

McD 230.3 it was] it's been

McD 230.3 since] sin'ct

McD 230.6 here,] here

McD 230.16 Jay] (McDowell regularizes "Jim" to "Jay".)

McD 230.22 use] *use*

McD 230.24 Jay's] (McDowell regularizes "Jim's" to "Jay's".)

McD 231.2 Oh] O

McD 231.3 giving] given up

McD 231.5 Well,] Well

McD 231.10 here, that] here. That

McD 231.11 most, a good] no it, a good,

McD 231.13 soberly,] soberly:

McD 231.17 *Great*] *Great:*

McD 231.17 *mean*] really *mean*

McD 231.18 *that,*] *that*

McD 231.20 old, old] old old

McD 231.22 said,] said

McD 231.24 terrible] *terrible*

McD 231.25 em] um

McD 231.28 Jay,] Jay

McD 232.6 "Dear,] "Dear

McD 232.11 said, "that's] said. "That's

McD 232.13 said grudgingly] said, grudgingly

McD 232.13 that, Rufus] that Rufus

McD 232.15 said,] said;

McD 232.16 Granpa] Grampa

McD 232.17 fact,] fact

McD 232.20 'Granmaw'] Granmaw

McD 232.22 "Well,] "Well

McD 232.28 "Oh *dear,*] "O *dear*

McD 232.29 landmarks] a landmark

McD 233.3 round] roun

McD 233.3 "What I] (A paragraph break is needed at this point to indicate the switch in speaker. McDowell provides most of these necessary breaks to copyedit Agee's manuscript properly, but misses this one.)

McD 233.6	Oh] O
McD 233.7	hate to] (McDowell properly corrects Agee's "hate too".)
McD 233.7	tonight,] tonight
McD 233.10	long,] long
McD 233.17	it, only] it only
McD 233.19	there were] (McDowell properly corrects Agee's "there was were".)
McD 233.20	said] cried
McD 233.20	that is *hit*] thatn'z *hit*
McD 233.24	said, "Why] said "why
McD 233.25	"There] "there
McD 233.25	was:] was;
McD 233.26	closed] cloven
McD 234.7	low,] low
McD 234.14–17	"Howdy,] "Howdy (There are four instances of this change.)
McD 234.15	grandfather] Grandfather
McD 234.17	"howdy,] "howdy
McD 234.19	"Howdy,] "Howdy
McD 234.20	"Mary,] "Mary (There are two instances of this change.)
McD 234.22	said,] said
McD 234.24	"And this] (A paragraph break is needed at this point to indicate the switch in speaker. McDowell provides most of these necessary breaks to copyedit Agee's manuscript properly, but misses this one.)
McD 234.26	Granma] Granmaw
McD 234.27	"Well, file] "Well pile
McD 235.1	put out] put-out
McD 235.11	*Ayy*] *Myy*
McD 235.13	first,] first
McD 235.16	truth,] truth
McD 235.17	yore] *yore*
McD 235.18	Mary or no Mary] lame or no lame
McD 235.20	Fifth generation] Fift[h] gineration
McD 235.21	you] ye
McD 235.32	be . . .] b—
McD 236.2, 3	post office] Post Office (There are two instances of this change.)
McD 236.6	Panama] Panamaw
McD 236.8	Sadie,] Sadie
McD 236.13	coldly,] coldy:
McD 236.14	threw] th[r]ew
McD 236.15	"Why,] "Why
McD 236.28	"Gracious,] "Gracious
McD 236.28	scatter-brain] scatterbrain (This is a clarification of an end-line hyphen in McDowell's text.)
McD 237.7	"Granmaw,] "Granmaw:
McD 237.7	company] compny

McD 237.9	ever] even
McD 237.17	said,] said
McD 237.21, 25	shyly] (McDowell properly corrects Agee's "shily".)
McD 237.28	deaf,] deaf
McD 238.20	she?"] she,"
McD 238.24	I am] I'm
McD 239.1–2	'Granmaw, I'm Rufus.'"] Granmaw, I'm Rufus."
McD 239.18	color: seen] color. Seen
McD 239.19	through a dot] through the blind gray shining: a dot
McD 239.24	bronze] brown
McD 239.26	ancestor's] uncertain
McD 240.23	quick, soft,] quick soft

TX 5.3, [139] provides a variant for 136.10–138.24 that fits neither into the present nor the McDowell edition. It is a later version of McD 238.9–239.3, but a condensed and earlier version of 136.10–138.24.

[5.3.139]

where she would see him well, and smiled somewhat anxiously. Her face restored itself from the kiss like grass after a light step; her eyes did not alter. Her skin looked like creased, brown-marbled stone over which water has worked for so long that it has become as mild and sleek as soap.

"I'm Jim", his father said, touching his breastbone with his middle finger. "John Henry's boy."

Her hands crawled, and it looked as if she meant to take his hand but she did not take it and her hands lay still again on the blinded gingham. Every white bone and black vein glowed through the varnishlike skin; the flesh at the knuckles was like wrinkled pouches; she wore a red rubber guard ahead of her broad wedding-ring. Her feet were quiet now. Her mouth opened and shut and they heard her low dry croaking, but there were no words, and there was no change in her eyes. It was clear that they were alive in their thin shadow, not blind, but there were no words, and there was no imagining what she saw or did not see, or what, if anything, it meant to her.

"I figger she knows ye," Paralee said quietly.

"She can't talk, can she," Jay said, and now that he was not looking at her it was as if they were talking across a stump.

"Times she can," Paralee said. "Times she don't. Reckon they hain't only so seldom call fer talk, she loses the hang of it." His father shook his head and looked sad. "But I figger she knows ye," Paralee said, "and I'm shore tickled if she does."

His father looked all around him in the shade, sad and unsure, and then he looked at Rufus. "Come here Rufus," he said gently.

"Go to him," his mother whispered for some reason, and she gave his hand a little shove as she let it go.

"Just call her Granmaw," his father said quietly. "Stand close up by her ear like she was your Granmaw Tyler and say 'Granmaw I'm Rufus.' But don't holler. Just say it real plain."

The following original draft of the conclusion to the chapter (TX 5.3, [141.5–14]), even though Agee decided not to use it and substitutes 139.17–140.5 for it, is quite interesting. In it he explores the possibility of Great Aunt Paralee speaking and confusing Rufus for her dead son Jim. The substitution begins with "paper mouth"; however, the complete sentence that contains that phrase is included for convenience.

[141]

Now kiss her," his father said, and he drew out of the shadow of her bonnet and leaned far over and again entered the shadow and kissed her paper mouth, and the mouth opened, and the eyes changed, and the cold sweet breath of rotting and of spice broke from her and her dry croaking said "Jim." And he could hear his mother say "*Oh*" and his father say "Let her be" in a quick soft angry voice, and he felt the hands take him by the shoulders like knives and forks; like ice through his clothes. She drew him closer to her and looked at him almost glaring, she was so grave and so filled with intensity. She seemed to be sucking on her lower lip and her eyes became much brighter, and then abruptly she was not serious any more but smiling so hard that her chin and her nose almost touched and her deep little eyes giggled for joy, and again she said "Jim. Hit's Jim.", and held his shoulders even more tightly, and put her head to one side and smiled and smiled, and with sudden love he kissed her again.

"That was his name," he heard his father say. "His name was Jim, too".

Chapter 22

The following variant is from the Tennessee manuscripts (TN 1A.19, [2.6]). Agee had two versions of his first sentence, which are present in the text below and the note for line 1 below, but these are marked for deletion and replaced in chapter 22. Chapter 22 also expands the scene a good deal.

[2.6]

***

Laura slept very little, during the rest of the night. She felt uneasy, alone in bed; the house itself seemed strangely hollow. The coming of daylight did not reduce this hollowness as she had supposed it would, and she got little good out of reproaching herself for these exaggerated feelings. She had a feeling that a good part of her uneasiness was explained by the fact that she could not feel nearly as deeply involved, in her father-in-law's sickness or death, as her husband did, and as she felt she should. It couldn't be helped, she told herself; after all, if the situation were reversed, Jay would feel much as she was feeling now, and he would feel badly about it, as she was feeling badly. But the more she thought of it the more she was forced to realize that the trouble was, she simply did not particularly like the old man. If Jay's mother were dying, there would be no question about the grief. As it was, she couldn't feel much. She thought of all his good points. He was generous, for one thing. Generous to a fault. But that was a good fault. He was very genuinely kind. A wonderful virtue. And tolerant. He had never once, of that she was sure, joined with most of the others in their talk about her. (On the other hand she could be equally sure he had never stood up for her strongly, and bravely, as his wife had; but she put that out of her mind.) And he never, so far as she knew, complained, about his illness, or his poverty, or made excuses for himself. (And certainly no right to make any; but she put that out of her mind). He had always been extremely nice and friendly to her; and if she had to realize that that was not for herself, but purely because she was "Jim's woman", she certainly couldn't hold that against him; her own best feelings towards him came, as purely, out of recognition of him as Jay's father. Try as she might, that was the best she could do. She could feel very little direct personal concern. Even now at this moment, while he possibly lay dying, or dead (she crossed herself), she could not feel much. Her mind was largely on his son's grief and her inadequacy to it; and she thought gravely of him, merely as she would of anyone who now, it seemed, was near the end. She realized, with surprise, that she thought wholly of Jay's grief, that his mother's had only this moment occurred to her. I must write her, she thought. Perhaps I'll see her soon.

O Lord, she prayed, open my heart that I may be worthy in realization, of this sorrowful thing, if it must happen, and worthy and of use and good to others in their sorrow. And Lord if it be Thy will, preserve him yet a while. Lord God, Lord Jesus, melt my apathy of heart, descend and fill my emptiness of heart. And if he must be taken, if he is with Thee now, may he rest in Thy Peace.

And Lord, if it be Thy Will, I humbly beseech Thee, if this sorrow must come upon him, then through this sorrow open my husband's heart that he may find comfort in Thee, and see Thee more clearly, and come to Thee.

Amen.

But her heart remained troubled and empty as the house; and even when it was time to get up, and the children woke, she did not entirely lose this sense of trouble and of emptiness.

Variant Notes for TN 1A.19, [2.6] (line number cited)

1 slept very little] did not sleep well > slept very little (No choice indicated by Agee.)

3 supposed it would] but rather increased it > supposed it would (No choice indicated by Agee.)

4 little] no > little (No choice indicated by Agee.)

Chapter 23

There are several alternate beginnings to this breakfast scene in the Tennessee archives that occur on a single page (TN 1A.19, [2.10]). The page is rendered below in its entirety because it documents that Agee first developed the material for the opening of chapter 23, then briefly combined the initial ideas of chapters 23 and 25 (see the section after the second three-asterisk separation), but then began again with the content that initiates chapter 25 as a separate entity (the material after third set of asterisks). Of itself, this evidence is ambivalent in regard to Agee's intent to incorporate both chapters into the novel, but does give some support to the fact that there likely are two distinct chapters rather than one chapter (25) and a variant (23) as McDowell assumed.

Another earlier version of chapter 23 (TN 1A.19, [2.9]) follows the four beginnings. This variant is deemed an earlier draft because chapter 23 is more developed and incorporates one of the interlinear additions of this variant into its normal line pattern.

[2.10]

* * *

The children were prompt in asking where their father was, but when Laura told them where he had gone, and why, and when he expected to return, they seemed to be neither disappointed, as she had thought they might be, nor much interested. Since she herself had Jay and his father rather gravely on her mind she was at first a little annoyed, even shocked, by their casualness, and for a moment she was tempted to try to persuade them to realize more seriously what it might mean. Then she realized that they were of course too young to be expected to realize what mortal illness, and death, were, and what the emotions appropriate to them were. There would be time enough to become more serious about it, if the worst happened. She said nothing more[.]

The children were prompt to notice their father's absence, and to ask where he was. But when Laura told them where he had gone, and for what purpose, and when he expected to return, they

* * *

The children were prompt to notice their father's absence, and to ask where he was.

Laura explained: "Daddy was called away in the middle of the night to go to Granpa Agee, because Granpa is very very sick and may not get well. He left you his love, and said to tell you he'll be back—do his best to be—and see you both tonight, before you're asleep."

She had said this in a peculiarly sober and gentle tone because she had slept very little

* * *

Laura slept very little, during the rest of the night. She reproached herself for it, but she felt uneasy in the empty bed, and the house itself seemed strangely empty and momentous.

[2.9]

* * *

The children were prompt to ask where their father was, and Laura explained:

"Daddy had to go away in the middle of the night, to see Grampa Agee, because Grampa is very very sick and may not get well."

"When is he coming home?"

"He told me to tell you both he'll do his very best to get back tonight, before you're asleep. He left you both his love."

That, apparently, was all they cared to know; they kept on eating breakfast; they didn't even look up. She could see that they were not in the least disappointed, as she had thought they might be; and evidently their grandfather's sickness had no meaning for them. She imagined their father, possibly in a great deal of grief, trying nevertheless, doing his best, perhaps with much inconvenience, to get home in time not to disappoint children who scarcely seemed to know he was away. She began to feel anger. Surely by now they were old enough to—but even as she thought this, and watched them, she knew she was wrong. Her impulse had been to talk a good deal more, to impress upon them at least something of the meaning of old age and sickness and death, to work on and waken their sympathies. But now she realized how mistaken her annoyance was. How in the world could they know? Or understand, even if she tried to say? They couldn't. And they shouldn't. She realized that she herself was deficient in her feeling for what was happening, her realization of it. She did not quite realize that this was why she had felt angry, and had wanted to awaken their feelings, but she said to herself, bowing her head, God be merciful unto me, a sinner.

"Huh?"

She realized that she must have whispered the words. "Nothing, Rufus," she said. "And don't say *Huh.* Say 'What is it, Mother.'"

"Oh all right."

"Nor that either, dear, that's very impolite. Say 'Yes, Mother.'"

"Yes, Mother."

"Finish, Emma."

Emma finished.

Chapter 25

The following is a variant beginning to this chapter that is marked for deletion on the bottom third of TX 5.3, [23].

At breakfast, when the children asked where their father was, Laura said:

"Daddy left you his love and said he'll probably see you tonight before you're asleep. Daddy had to go to Jacksboro, very early this morning, because Grampa Agee may be very sick."

"Very very early?"

"Very *very* early. Before you were awake."

"Why did he go so early?"

"Because Uncle Frank called and Daddy thought he ought to come right away."

"Why?"

"Because if he didn't come right away, why then, maybe, he wouldn't get to see Grampa Agee."

"Why not?"

"Because Grampa is old and very sick, Rufus, and God might have taken him away, before Daddy could get there."

There are also four variants of Chapter 25 in the Tennessee collection (TN 1A.19, [2.1–2.2; 2.4–2.5; 2.7–2.8; and finally 2.3, which covers only the last part of the material in the other variants). Because of the complexity of the selection of the chapter for the restored edition, all are recorded. Each has a somewhat different emphasis, and no priority is established among them.

Variant 1

[2.1]

* * *

At breakfast, when the children asked where their father was, Laura explained: "Daddy had to go away, way late last night while you were asleep. He had to go see Grampa Agee because Grampa Agee is, may be, very very sick."

"When's he coming home?"

"He told me to tell you both he'd be home tonight to see you, before you go to sleep, if he possibly can. He left you both his love."

"Why did he go way late last night?"

"Because Grampa is so sick. He wanted to be sure to see him."

Rufus looked at her; obviously he did not understand what she meant.

She said, carefully and gently: "Because if Daddy had waited, God might have already taken Grampa away before he got there."

Away. Sounded to Rufus even more portentous than God; and the tone of Laura's voice bemused Emma.

"Away—where?" he asked, after a moment.

"*Eat,* children. Eat your breakfast. Why to heaven."

They ate, rather sullenly. She explained:

"Sometimes if we're very old or sick, and can't ever get well, why then God is sorry for us and takes us away with Him to Heaven."

"Why?"

"Because He feels sorry for us and doesn't want us to feel sick when we can't get well."

"Why doesn't he just make us well?"

"Sometimes He does. But He makes us well, too, when He decides instead to put us to sleep and take us with him, because then—"

Seeing their astonished eyes and open mouths, she became aware of her mistake.

"Oh, darlings, children," she said, "I *don't* mean like the kitties! Not at *all* like that!"

But Emma was remembering the muted scratching and squeaking of the drowning kittens in the slop jar; her chin worked; and Rufus said: "You mean God *kills* people!"

"*No* I *do not* Rufus!", she flashed at him with a sternness he could not understand. "Nothing like that *in this world* and don't you *ever think* such a dreadful thing!" She took hold of herself and after a moment began again, carefully. "I'm sorry I spoke so, Rufus," she said. "Somehow I've said it all wrong. But children, listen to me, both of you. This is very important so listen very carefully."

She took a hand in each of hers and looked most earnestly from one to the other as she talked.

"It isn't—one bit—like the poor little kitties" (she squeezed Emma's hand, and Emma swallowed). "*We* did that. Not to be cruel, but just because we couldn't keep them. But—"

"We could give them away," Rufus said. "Johnn—"

"*Don't interrupt,*" she said sharply. "God doesn't kill us. When God comes for us to take

[2.2]

us He comes because he loves us, because He's good, and loving, and wants us with Him, and He knows, better than we do, when it's time for us to come to Him. Do you see? Do you understand, children?"

They looked at her.

"When God knows it's time for us to come, He comes and takes our souls, very quietly and lovingly, and when he takes our souls away with Him, then our poor bodies are all that's left. They're asleep. Only now, they never wake up. That's the way I mean that God puts us to sleep. Do you see? It's when he takes our souls away with him. But our souls *never* die.

"Do you see?"

She saw that they were thoroughly confused and by no means satisfied; but how could they understand more, and how could she tell them more?

"It's something for us not to think too much about," she said, "or worry about, one bit. Because with God's Mercy we all have a long, long time to live yet, and as we get older we understand it better and better. All I want to be very sure of now is, Rufus, Emma, that neither one of you thinks for a minute that God is unkind, or kills people. God doesn't kill us. He loves us, and takes us when He knows it's best to. That's all. Do you see?"

They nodded carefully; she thought: Poor things, they don't know what to think. I've said too much, too soon. And she was very sorry. I must watch very carefully, she thought, and come back to it later, when they're older. And she said to them: "Now, hurry with your breakfasts. You specially, Rufus, you'll be late to school."

* * *

Variant 2

[2.4]

At breakfast, when the children asked where their father was, Laura told them:

"Daddy had to go away, before you were awake, to see Grampa Agee, because Grampa Agee is, he may be very very sick. He left you his love, and he said he'll probably be back tonight again to see you, before you're asleep."

They showed none of the disappointment she had expected, or any particular interest. They merely kept on eating their breakfasts. Laura wondered why. She felt a little let down. Yet after all, she reflected, why should they feel either disappointment or interest. They could hardly know what "very sick" meant, for instance. She felt let down, she supposed, because they hadn't answered so much as a word. It was almost as if she had never spoken, and they had never asked where their father was. Then she began to realize that without having been quite aware of her intention, she had spoken in such a way as to forestall questions or even comment. She had said too much at once. She felt silly about it, but the silence made her uneasy. She said: "That is, he *hopes* he can get back tonight."

They said nothing, and continued their eating. She thought ahead, imagining Jay's effort, in spite of inconvenience, to get back in time to see two children who didn't even miss him, and on his behalf she began to feel anger.

"Why?" Rufus asked, startling her.

"Why, what, Rufus?"

"Why is Grampa Agee sick?"

"Do you remember hearing, maybe, he has a weak heart?"

"*I* do," said Emma.

"Well if your heart is weak, why sometimes it suddenly becomes much weaker, and then you have an attack."

"What's an attack?"

"When your heart gets *very* weak, so it hardly beats. Then you're very weak too, and very sick."

"Will Daddy make him well?"

"No, Daddy can't, because Daddy isn't a doctor."

"Then why did Daddy go to see him?"

"Because he's very sick. Because he wants to see him. Like when you had the measles, remember? Remember how you wanted me or Daddy with you, all the time? Well, that's just the way Grampa Agee feels because he's sick too. And so naturally, Daddy wants to see him."

They ate.

"Why did he go before we were up?"

"So he could be sure and see Grampa bef—Because—Because if he waited, and Grampa was very, *very* sick, he might get there too late to see him."

"Why?"

"Because God might have already taken Grampa away."

"Away" sounded even more momentous than God, and neither sounded good. "Away where?"

[2.5]

"*Eat,* Rufus. Eat your breakfast, Emma. Why to Heaven."

"Why would God want to take away him away?"

"Oh I don't mean his body Rufus, I mean his soul."

"Why would God want to take away his soul?"

"Because sometimes if we're very sick, so much we can't ever get well, God is sorry for us and comes to take us with Him."

"Why doesn't he just take away the sickness so we'll be well?"

"Sometimes He does. But he takes it away, too, when he puts us to sleep and takes us with Him, because then we—

"*Puts to sleep!*", both children exclaimed, and looked at her with outrage.

She quickly realized her mistake. "*Not* like the kitties," she said. "It's different from the kitties." But Emma was remembering the drowning of the kittens; her chin trembled. And Rufus said: "You mean God kills us."

"Oh, *no,* Rufus, Emma, it isn't like that at *all,*" she said.

Variant 3

[2.7]

They were prompt to notice that their father was gone, and to ask why. Laura explained: "Daddy was called away, in the middle of the night, to see Grampa Agee. Grampa is very, very sick and may not get well."

"When will he come back?"

"He said to tell you he'll do his best to come back tonight before you're asleep. He left you both his love.". [*sic*]

Although her voice was colored by her trouble, and her sense of dislocation, they did not appear to notice. Now that they knew where he had gone, and why, and how soon he would be back, they said nothing, but simply went on with their breakfasts. They were certainly not disappointed, as she had thought they might be. They didn't even seem to be interested or concerned about their grandfather. They simply ate, without even looking up. Laura felt almost lonelier than before. And as she imagined their father, possibly in deep grief, doing his level best to get back before their bedtime, in order not to disappoint children who hardly seemed to know or care that he was away, she began to feel anger. Surely they ought, they were surely old enough by now, to—but as she watched them, she became ashamed of herself. She had been on the verge of saying a good deal more, of trying to make them realize a little of what old age and deep sickness and dying meant, and meant to others as well; but she had only to look at them to know better. Of course they weren't old enough. Couldn't have the remotest idea of the meaning, talk how she might. And shouldn't, either. And she herself, she knew only too well how deficient her own realization was. God be merciful to me, a sinner.

"Huh?"

She realized she must have whispered the words. "Nothing, Rufus. And don't say *Huh,* dear. Say 'what is it, Mother?'"

"Oh all right."

"Not that, either, Rufus. Say 'Yes, Mother.'"

"Yes, Mother."

"Eat it all, Emma."

They ate.

Rufus asked: "Is Grampa Agee going to die?"

She was startled. She had not even realized that he knew the word.

"We hope not, Rufus. We can't be sure yet."

"What's die," Emma asked.

"Shucks," said Rufus. "Don't you even know what *die* is? Like the rabbits. Like the kitties."

"Rufus!" His head flashed towards her. "Stop that this minute!" She covered Emma's hand with hers; Emma's chin was trembling. "No it isn't one bit," she told her. "Not one bit like the poor rabbits and the kitties. That's entirely different and don't you think of it that way. You either, Rufus. To die is, when you're very old or very sick, and can't ever get well, God is sorry for you because He loves you, and he comes for you and takes you away with Him, and then you don't feel badly ever any more."

[2.8]

"But they did die!" Rufus insisted. "Didn't they die, mama? The rabbits and the kitties died too!"

"But you musn't [*sic.* mustn't] think of that as if that was all of dying. They died a horrible death because they were killed. Most people aren't killed. They just—die, quietly, when God decides it's time for them to, and its nothing ugly or horrible or to be afraid of."

"Does everybody die?"

"Sooner or later, yes Rufus."

"You too?"

"Sooner or later."

"Me too?"

"Yes, someday."

"Even if you don't want to?"

This was just what she had wanted not to happen.

"Nobody wants to, Rufus. But we know that after a while we will, we must, and if we love God and trust Him enough, we are willing to, because we know that He knows best."

"But why do we have to if we don't want to?"

"We have to do ever so many things we don't want to, Rufus. Besides God didn't put us here to do what we want to, or to live forever. He put us here to be good, and worthy of Him, when He comes to take us to Him."

Variant 4

This manuscript page may complete variant 2 ([2.4–2.5]), but is rendered here separately since page [2.5] ends only one-third down that page and [2.3] begins a new page.

[2.3]

"Why?"

"Eat your breakfast, Emma. Why, because, sometimes if we are very old, or sick, or tired, God doesn't want to see us unhappy, or suffering pain, and in His Mercy he comes and takes our souls away."

"Why doesn't he just take the pain away?"

"He does. When He takes the soul away He takes the pain away too and then it's just as if we were asleep. Only then, we don't wake up."

"Why not?"

"Because it was God who put us to sleep."

"Put to sleep, like the kitties?"

"Well, yes, like the kittens, more or less."

"In the slop jar?" asked Emma.

"Huh, that's only for little tiny kitties, isn't it Mama. With big kitties it's cholorform [*sic.* chloroform]. He gives chloroform to big kitties. He gives cholorform [*sic*] to big people, doesn't He Mama, doesn't He."

"That's not the way God puts us to sleep, Rufus. He just takes our souls away with Him to Heaven and then we just shut our eyes and sleep. *Eat,* Emma!"

"Will He put *you* to sleep?"

"Someday, yes."

"Will he put *me* to sleep?"

"Someday He'll put all of us to sleep Rufus, but probably not for a long time to come."

"I don't want Him to put *me* to sleep. Do you want Him to put you to sleep Mama?"

"There's nothing we can do about that Rufus, because it's God's Will."

"Why?"

"Why, what?"

"Why is it God's Will?"

"God—wills us—God doesn't want us to live here on earth forever. We live here only a while. Then God wants us to come and stay with Him."

> "I'd rather stay with you. I'd rather stay with you and Daddy."
>
> "Well now don't worry. We'll probably all be together for a long, long time."
>
> "But not if God wants us."
>
> "No, not if God wants us."

Chapter 27

The following variant recorded at the bottom of TX 5.3, [68], which is marked for deletion, is given here to illustrate that while Agee often expanded when he revised, there are many instances in which he pared his prose as well. When he revises the section below, the result occupies only five lines (212.3–8).

> There it is, Jessie said to herself. She looked back steadily into Laura's eyes. She herself was all but certain that he was dead; and Joel had said it was almost a certainty, or the man would have said more: but now as she gazed into her niece's tormented eyes, she could bear only to realize that it was possible that he was alive.
>
> "Jo—[,] your father said he wasn't going to come up till he heard," she said, "because he knew you wouldn't want him to make a mountain out of a molehill. Not that it's a molehill heaven knows under the best of circumstances."
>
> "That's absolutely sensible of Papa. I understand."
>
> "He said he knew you would. He said the man's probably a complete fool. He said there's no use being sure of anything until you've seen it for yourself."
>
> "That's absolutely right."
>
> "He said we've all simply got to wait."
>
> "Of course we have," Laura cried angrily. "That's what's so *unbearable!*" She drank half her tea at a gulp.

A variant of the conclusion of this chapter also exists (TX 5.3, [90, 76]). Manuscript page [90] parallels TX 5.3, [74–75], which is used in the restored text, and [75] incorporates into its regular line pattern an interlinear comment on [90], making [90] likely an earlier version. The last words of [90] are completed as a sentence on [76] linking the pages, but the top one-third of [76] is crossed out to avoid repetition with the bottom of [75]. The problem is that one cannot readily differentiate Agee's deletion marks from those of his previous editor. Page [90], for example, opens with a leading bracket, but there is no end bracket on the page or on [76]. If this variant is used to conclude the chapter, it would replace [74–76], but would cause additional repetition. Thus the conclusion of this chapter in the restored edition is somewhat cobbled together, but is based upon [75] as a later version than [90], a decision that necessitates the elimination of the top third of [76]. It provides as well a fuller development with less repetition of the scene at hand. McDowell's edition follows this same course. To read chapter 27 with the variant ending, replace 217.14–219.7 with the following text and then read 219.8 to the end of the chapter in the restored text to complete the variant conclusion.

[90]

Yes, it's easy enough for *us* to be stoical, Jessie thought. She felt ashamed of her calm. She wished Joel had come up, immediately, and Emma. "I know," she said, because she was sure that she ought to say something. It seemed, now, incredibly, unimaginative of them, yes heartless, to sit at home waiting.

"I'm sorry," Laura said. "Papa's right. I've just got to hold myself together, that's all."

There was a kind of superstitiousness in their not coming up, Jessie reflected, as there was in Laura's getting the bed ready, and that great kettle of water. And very understandable too. Right, for that matter.

"We're not going to *assume* the worst," she said, and wished that she had not used those words. For they made her think of one of her brother's favorite tropes, Hope for the best and expect the worst, and these words nagged at her so strongly now that she was sure they were in Laura's mind too. At any comfortable distance from trouble they were sound enough; now they were sickeningly trivial and smug.

"Expect the worst," Laura said.

"Nonsense," Jessie snapped.

"We've got to. Whatever else, at least we've got the mercy of fair warning. A little time to compose ourselves in, prepare ourselves. Whatever is, it's over and done with now."

She spoke slowly and with very little feeling, Jessie noticed; she was interested, beyond immediate feeling, in what she was finding out.

"Over and done with." She looked up at Jessie. "Either it's not so serious as the man thought, and he's badly hurt but in time he'll be all right—Or it's fully that serious and he'll die of it or may be dying this minute—Or it's even more than he said and Jay was dead already when he called and he couldn't bear to be the one to tell me, poor soul." Jessie found it hard to keep looking into her eyes but she was sure that she must. "Whatever it is, it's done now, and nothing we can do or think or wish or guess or hope or pray can prevent it or undo it. So it's time just to compose ourselves to accept it as best we can, whatever it may be. That's all that matters. It's all that matters because it's all that's possible."

While she spoke she was opening within Jessie remembrances of hours twenty years past and more, when she had first begun to recognize and to submit to the iron of being alive. She felt as if a huge page were being quietly turned, and the coldness of its breath was upon her heart, and something within her wanted to cry out *yes, exactly, yes, yes. Now you begin to see. Your turn now.*, and she wanted to hold the child away and turn her and admire her, and she wanted to take her in her arms and groan for both of them and for every creature which lived long

[76; the section that is crossed out]

enough to begin to learn what living is. I came up all ready to tell you just such things, she reflected. How glad I am I didn't! How grateful I am that you begin to feel them for yourself.

"That's so, isn't it."

"That and more."

"You mean, God's mercy?" Laura whispered.

Jessie had meant nothing of the kind. She had meant that, if matters were as she believed most likely, Laura was soon to learn such anguish, and how to bear it or fail to bear it, as she could not yet conceive of. But in saying *that and more* she had said more than she intended. Let it come in its own time, in its own way, she said to herself. God forgive me; and she lied. "Of course," she said.

She felt deep confusion and uneasiness. In some way, she was sure, Laura was seeking shelter too quickly; and by her lie she was abetting her. She's going to want to pray, she told herself. It isn't time to yet.

Laura's face became blurred and humbled. She said, shyly, "Aunt Jessie, can we kneel down for a minute?"

Not yet, she wanted to say. She went around the table and knelt beside Laura. We can be seen, she realized; the shades were up. *Let us,* she told herself angrily.

Variant Notes for Manuscript TX 5.3, [90, 76] (page and line number cited)

90.1	Yes] [Yes (A square bracket indicating deletion appears at the start of this page before the word "Yes", but it is unclear if it is Agee's bracket or McDowell's. However, since the thickness of the pencil stroke matches that of subsequent, editorial notation of typescript page numbers on the same manuscript page and elsewhere, the bracket is most likely McDowell's.)
90.22	She] (Paragraph break added)
90.24	"Over] (Paragraph break added)
76.16	shyly] shily

Chapter 29

The following variants (TX 5.2, [84–85] and [84, 86]) are earlier but quite similar versions of the final part of chapter 29 (TX 5.3, [87–89]) and parallel 233.15–236.23 in the text. The number of interlinear insertions and choices on page [84] that are incorporated into the text of the chosen version makes clear that these are earlier drafts with alternative endings ([85] vs. [86]) which Agee then combined and edited. The sections bracketed for deletion in the variant (page [84]) below are labeled as Agee's deletions since those materials do not appear in the corresponding sentences in the final version. A final end bracket (]) after the last word on pages [85] and [86] with no beginning bracket may be Agee's indication that these pages are alternatives.

Variant 1

All brackets in the variant are Agee's.

[84]

Laura's father caught her eye and beckoned her to a corner of the kitchen. "Where can we talk alone for a minute," he asked in a low voice.

She looked at him questioningly and in some kind of fear; then took her glass from the table, said "Excuse us a minute," ushered him into the room she had prepared for her husband, turned on the light, quietly closed both doors, and stood looking at him, waiting.

"Sit down, Poll," he said.

She looked about. One of them would have to sit on the bed. "I had it all ready," she said, "and he never came back."

"What's that?"

"Nothing, Papa."

"Don't stay on your feet," he said. "Let's sit down."

"You sit. I'd rather stand."

He came to her and took her hand and looked at her searchingly; she saw how much his eyes, in sympathy and pain, resembled his sister's. He could not speak at first. You're a *good* man, she said to herself, her lips moving. A good, good man. My father. Her eyes filled with tears and her mouth began to tremble; he took her close to him and, her face on his shoulder, she cried quietly.

"It's hell, Poll, I know," she heard him say. "Just hell. Don't imagine I don't know. It's just plain hell." For a few moments then she sobbed so deeply that he said nothing more, but only stroked her back, over and over from shoulder to waist. God *damn* it!, he cried out within himself; God *damn* such a life! She's too young for this. "But you gotta go through with it," he said.

She nodded, vigorously.

"You've just got to," he said.

"I think I will sit down." With an almost vindictive sense of the violation, she walked away from him and sat heavily at the edge of the bed, next the plumped pillows. He brought the chair and sat knee to knee with her, [and looked at her].

"Drink your drink," he said.

She drank deeply and shuddered, and set the glass on the bedside table, and looked at him.

"Take all you can without getting drunk," he said. "I wouldn't give a hoot if you got blind drunk. Best thing you could do. But you've got tomorrow to reckon with." And tomorrow and tomorrow. [but tomorrow'd be that much worse.]

"It doesn't seem to have any effect," she said, her voice still liquid. "The only times I drank before I had a terribly weak head, just one weak drink was enough to make me dizzy, but now it doesn't seem to have any effect in the slightest." She drank some more.

"Good," he said. "That can happen. [State of] Shock or strain. Take all you want and I've more if you want it, but watch out. Keep an eye on yourself. It can hit you [all of a sudden] like a ton of bricks."

"I'll be careful." She looked sidelong towards the floor and waited for what he had to say.

He had come up full of all that he was sure must be firmly said as soon as possible, but now he was reluctant to begin, unsure of the need, dubious of his or anybody's right to say it even if there were need or use. She's doing pretty well with it, he thought as he watched her. God damned well. But she still hardly even knows what's hit her.

[85]

"It'll take a while to sink in," he said [gently].

She nodded vaguely.

"It's bad now," he said, "and it's going to be a lot worse."

She held her head still and listened without raising her eyes.

Why don't I keep quiet, he asked himself. What earthly use is this. Needless cruelty.

"I don't want to hammer at you," he said. "I just want to warn you."

She was still quiet.

"The worst of it is," he said, "there's nothing anybody can do for you. Except blind animal sympathy, and God knows we all feel that. But there's nothing real that anyone can do. We can't take away one bit of what you'll have to go through. You have to do it alone.

"It's going to be so much worse than this, when it sinks in, you're going to think it's more than you can bear. And more than any human being can bear.

"But you'll bear it. Because you damned well have to. Other people have by the millions. This and worse, and you will too."

He felt sick to death of himself.

"It's just unmitigated tommyrot to try to say a word about it," he said. "Say nothing of brass. All I want to do is warn you, that worse is yet to come, and urge you for *God's* sake to brace yourself for it and try to hold yourself together. The worst thing you can possibly do, to yourself, and everybody else, would be to go to pieces.

"Patty went to pieces you know, when she lost her husband. Tore around like a chicken with its head off. 'Oh, why did it have to be *me?* What have *I* ever done that it has to be *me!*'" He made a sharp fart with his mouth. "Knocking her head against the wall, trying to stab herself with scissors, yelling bloody murder; you could hear her in the next block.

"We're not going to stand for any of *that,*" he said harshly.

She looked up at him with cold, fierce eyes. "Not if I keep my sanity," she said.

"Nonsense," he said. "You'll keep it."

"I think so."

"I know you will.]

Variant 2

Read page [84] above first; the end bracket in the variant is Agee's.

[86]

"You'll have to go through it alone, because there isn't a thing on earth any of us can do to help, beyond blind animal sympathy."

She was gazing slantwise towards the floor in some kind of cold and patient irony.

He felt sick to death of himself.

"That's when you're going to need every ounce of common sense you've got," he said. "I know it's just unmitigated tommyrot to try to say a word about it. Say nothing of brass. All I want to do is warn you, that worse is yet to come. So for *God's* sake brace yourself for it and try to hold yourself together. The worst thing you could possibly do, to yourself and everybody else, would be to go to pieces.

"Patty went to pieces you know, when she lost her husband, a lot later in life and a lot better warning than you got. Tore around like a chicken with its head off. 'Oh, why did it have to be *me?* What have *I* ever done that God picked on *me?*'" With his mouth he farted sharply. "Butting her head against the wall, trying to stab herself with her scissors, yelling like a stuck pig; you could hear her in the next block.

"We got a lifetime bellyful of that," he said. "We're not going to stand for any more of it."

Her eyes were cold and fierce when she looked up. "You needn't worry," she said.

Too rough with her, he thought. "Only worry worth talking about's for you," he said. "And what it would do to the children. I've made a mess of this. It's no wonder you don't quite understand it."

"I think I understand it, Papa."

"See here. It's going to take a while until you know what's hit you, and then it really *is* going to be hell. At the worst of it you'll have every *reason* to want to scream why does it have to be me, and all the rest of it, and nothing else you can tell yourself is going to help very much. You'll think, 'this and a lot worse have happened to millions of other people and they've come through it', but you'll say 'what good does that do *me?* This is *me* this is happening to." Well you've got to bear it in mind with all you've got, that some people are luckier than others, but nobody in this world is specially privileged. You see? Everyone assumes the worst things only happen to other people, never to them. It's silly but it's natural. It's probably the best attitude to have—*until* something happens. That's the only real test, when something happens. Then you have your choice. You start growing up. Or you start to fall apart. That's all."

Her eyes were cast down again. He watched her, and felt great fear.

"I imagine you're counting on your religion," he said.

She nodded, and with a certain pride said "I am."

"Well more power to you," he said. "Get all the help you can from it. I know I can't talk about that but I do say this: take the greatest kind of care you don't just—crawl into a hole and hide with it.]

Variant Notes for Manuscript TX 5.2 (page and line number cited)

84.2 "Where can we talk alone for a minute,"] "I want to talk to you a minute" > "Where can we talk alone for a minute," (Agee subsequently chooses the interlinear statement.)

84.2 asked] said > asked (Agee subsequently chooses the interlinear statement to match the previous interlinear choice.)

84.15 resembled] were like > resembled (No choice indicated by Agee.)

84.27 "You've just got to,"] "No way out of it," > "You've just got to," (No choice indicated by Agee.)

84.32 your drink] up > your drink (No choice indicated by Agee.)

84.36 hoot] whoop > hoot (No choice indicated by Agee.)

84.41 dizzy, but] perfectly squiffy. But > dizzy, but (Agee subsequently chooses "absolutely squiffy. But" for his final version.)

85.5 himself.] himself,

85.22 do, to] do, to > to, do (Agee apparently corrected his inadvertent transposition of words, but forgot to cross out his mistake.)

85.25 'Oh] "Oh

85.26 *me!'"*] *me!"*

85.26 fart] (Agee or a previous editor places a checkmark over this word.)

86.1 "You'll] You'll

Chapter 30

The following variant is located in The James Agee Trust materials at the University of Tennessee (MS 2730, Box 4). This one manuscript page begins with a leading bracket and has a line scored from top left to bottom right across the page indicating its deletion either by Agee or a previous editor. Its content comprises the same material covered in greater detail in TX 5.3, [91–92 (all but the last six lines)] in the restored edition. This page is deemed an earlier version because there is no indication of how it would join the narrative of the chapter on [92] and the pages that follow it and because of the dual deletion marks. The square brackets in the text below are those of Agee or a previous editor.

["Why where—" Laura began; for the kitchen was empty.

"Must be in the living room," her father said, and guided her by the arm.

"More room here," Hugh told her as they came in; although the night was warm, he was nursing a small fire.

"Laura," her mother said loudly, patting a place beside her on the sofa. She sat beside her; her mother took her left hand between both hers, drew it into her lap, and pressed it against her thighs with all her strength.]

Her father and her aunt sat on either side of the fireplace. The morris-chair just stood there by the lamp. Even after the fire was going nicely, Hugh squatted before it, making small adjustments. Nobody spoke.

Finally Hugh straightened, and they all looked at him, trying not to demand too much of him with their eyes, and he looked at each of them in turn. He went over and bent deeply to his mother.

"I'll tell you, Mama," he said, close to her ear. "I'm sorry Laura. That way we can all hear."

"Thank you dear," his mother said.

"Of course," Laura said, and gave him her place beside the "good" ear. They shifted to make room, and she sat at her mother's deaf side. Emma lifted her trumpet; Joel cupped her ear.

"He was all alone," Hugh said, not very loudly but very carefully. "Nobody else was hurt, or even in the accident."

"That's a mercy," his mother said. [It was, they all realized, but that hardly diminished their sense of outrage.] Hugh nodded sharply to silence her.

"We'll never know exactly how it happened," he went on. "But we know *enough*," he said, speaking the last word with a terrible and brutal bitterness.

"I talked to the man who found him; he told me all he knew of course," he said, remembering, with the feeling that he would never forget it, the awed, calm, kind, rural face which had waited so long for what small use he might be to a member of the family, and the slow, careful, half-literate voice. "He said he was on his way home, about nine o'clock, and he heard an auto coming up from behind him, going very fast, and coming nearer and nearer, and he thought 'there's a man that's sure got to get someplace in a [bad] hurry or else he's crazy'" [he had said "or else crazy drunk"]," and all of a sudden there was a perfectly terrific noise, and then silence. He said nothing had come the other way for quite some time so he knew it couldn't have been a collision, though there was noise enough for one, so he knew that whoever was in the car must need help, so he turned around and drove back, about a quarter of a mile he thinks, just the other side of Bell's Bridge. He said he almost missed it altogether because there was nothing on the road and even though he'd kind of been expecting that, and driving slowly, looking off both sides of the road, he almost missed it because just next the bridge on that side the road slopes off quite sharply."

"I know," Laura whispered.

"But just as he moved off the bridge—you come down at a sort of angle you know—"

"I know," Laura whispered.

"Something caught his headlights and it was one of the wheels of the automobile." He looked across his mother and said: "Laura it was still turning."

"Beg pardon," his mother said.

"It was still, turning," he told her. "The wheel he saw."

"Mercy Hugh," she whispered. "Hah!", her husband exclaimed, almost inaudibly.

Variant Notes for The Agee Trust Manuscript Page (line number cited)

AT 20 "Of] (Paragraph break added)

AT 23 carefully] distinctly > carefully (No choice indicated by Agee.)

AT 36 o'clock] oclock

AT 58 It was] (A comma after each of these words has been marked for deletion. Since the restored version does not use commas, this may provide additional evidence that the variant rendered above is an earlier draft.)

Chapters 33, 34

The following variant (TX 5.3, [122–23]) is an example of an earlier draft of parts of chapters 33 and 34 before Agee chose to separate them. Page [122] begins at the same point in the narrative as 277.22 in chapter 33 and ends at the same point as that chapter ends. No previous page that is connected to it apparently survives. Note that the space of one line is skipped and then Agee commences the variant of chapter 34, a complete but shorter version of his final text.

[122]

The silent stars go by, he whispered, in tender awe.

His eyes filled with tears.

Yet in thy dark streets shineth, he sang to himself: the Everlasting Light: and with these words his throat contracted with a sob, which he subdued.

This is crazy, he said to himself incredulously. There's no sense in this at all.

The hopes and fears.

The hopes and fears, he whispered, and said quietly, *of all the years.*

Are met in thee tonight, he whispered: and in the middle of the dark and quiet city, slabbed beneath shadowless light, he saw the dead man, and struck his thigh with all his strength.

Neither his father nor his mother heard, or noticed, nor did any of the three of them speak, throughout their walk. They turned down the steep hill, tightening their knees, and entered their home by the back way. [The variant for chapter 34 begins below.]

"Good night Laura." She kissed her again. "Just call me if you want me. I'm a light sleeper you know."

"I'm all right. I'm all right."

"God bless you."

Laura looked at her carefully, and said, "God help us all."

Jessie drew the door to and went downstairs to her own room. She put on the nightgown, knelt beside the bed, and said an Our Father and a Hail Mary, and found that she could pray no more. May the souls of the faithful, she tried; she set her jaws. May the souls of everyone who ever lived or died, she whispered defiantly, in the Faith or outside it, rest in peace. And especially his.

I can't pray. Forgive me. I'm just too tired and sick.

Thirty-six years old.

Thirty-six.

Into Thy hands I commend my spirit.

She made the sign of the cross, raised the shade, opened the window, got into bed, and turned off the light. The window was gray; the curtains breathed. Against her feet, her hands, and her cheek she felt the cold fresh linen, prepared for another; and it was as if she were touching her dead mother's cheek. She straightened on her back, folded her hands, and closed her eyes.

If it be Thy will, she whispered. Take me now.

And have her find me in the morning!, she thought, with disgust for her weakness.

Lord all-pitying Jesu blest,
Grant them Thine eternal rest.

Laura undressed beneath her nightgown and climbed into bed before it occurred to her that she had not said her prayers: and for such a while she had felt that if only she could be alone, only for that!

It's all right, she whispered to herself; it's all right, she whispered again. She had meant that

[123]

she was sure that God would understand, and forgive her inability to pray, but she found that she meant also that it was all right, the whole thing was really all right. Whatever Thy will may be, she added. All right. All right. She lay and looked up at the ceiling and saw it faintly in the subtly diminished darkness; and it seemed to her that she was falling backward and downward, prostrate, at great speed, yet she felt no concern. Out of the deep have I called unto Thee O Lord, she heard herself whisper; Lord, hear my voice. O let Thine ear(s) consider well: the voice of my complaint.

If Thou, Lord, wilt be extreme to mark what is done amiss: Lord, who may abide it.

The water was low and lukewarm in the large kettle; one by one, along the round wall of the kettle below the level of the water, the last of the bubbles burst and vanished. [Not many stars remained.] [Agee or a previous editor bracketed the previous sentence.]

Jessie lay straight on her back with her hands folded. On her eyeballs the lids were like membranes; the sockets were deep. Her lips were parted and each breath was a light sigh.

Laura lay watching the ceiling: she whispered, who may abide it. One by one, thousand by thousand, in the foreknowledge of dawn, every leaf in that part of the world was silently moved.

Variant Notes for Manuscript TX 5.3 (page and line number cited)

122.1	[top right margin; previous editor's note] 37
122.13–14	[in right margin; previous editor's note?] (A corner bracket is present that may indicate the intended deletion of this section. Whether it is Agee's or a previous editor's cannot be determined.)
122.33	gray;] gray,
122.34–35	[in right margin] glasses [and after a separation and at a different angle] sliding of / feet along the / linen—
122.47	again] aloud > again (No choice indicated by Agee.)
123.1	[top right margin; previous editor's note] 38
123.4	ceiling] cieling
123.4	faintly] (The "ly" is circled.)
123.5	subtly] (The "ly" is circled.)
123.6	great speed] (Both words are circled.)

123.13	round wall] curved firmament > round wall (The word "curved" is over "round" and "firmament" is over "wall"; however, firmament appears to have been added to the manuscript at a different time.)
123.13–14	[in right margin] lid on; / dark.
123.19	ceiling] cieling
123.19	she whispered, who may abide it.] who may abide it, she whispered. (The clauses are marked for transposition in the manuscript and this edition follows that mark, although it cannot be determined whether the transposition was indicated by Agee or a previous editor.)
123.20	foreknowledge] (The word was likely circled by an editor/typist who could not make out the spelling. The previous editor's typescript of this variant originally gave "reknowledge" as the word.)
123.21	moved] turned > moved
123.21	[center bottom of page below final text; previous editor's note] End of Chap 13

Chapters 35, 36, 37

The following variant (TX 5.2, [78–83]) is an example of one of Agee's early drafts. Rufus appears as Richard, and several marginal and interlinear comments are included in the normal text of the greatly expanded versions included in the restored edition. The variant begins with Agee's rough notes focused upon his cap and begins by referring to its purchase (which occurs in chapter 26), but then eventually records versions of chapters 35 and 36 and a small bit of 37. They are all given together below (just as Agee wrote them) as an example of the evolution and development of the novel. The shifts in content from one chapter to another are indicated within brackets in the text of the variant.

[78]

(Did he want to wear it out of the store / wear it home?)

No. I want to wait till Daddy can see it.

Does his mother see it? Does J come up with him. If she does see it she has to be good about it. Well, that's very nice. But also murmurs something, in front of him, about xchange?

From the minute he gets the cap he can think of only one thing: the moment when his father first sees him first really wearing the cap. In the store, & before his mother, he feels, is not real, that is just a try-on. It will be his when he wears it in front of his father.

He waits up for him (& is let wait up a little later than ordinary), but is finally told he *must* go to bed. Yes, if Daddy comes home soon enough, he'll wake you (a lie). Can I have my cap under my pillow? (Thinking of brat-magazine stuff; that seems proper for a treasure.) But that will mash it all up. But you can keep it right by you. So it is put right by him in its tissue paper on a chair. He reaches over in the dark

& feels the long hard carved visor (bill) (His mother calls it a visor; he insists it is a bill; she says visor is a very fine name and was used for helmets by King Arthur and his knights. He says who was King Arthur?) Finally, goes to sleep, determined to sleep so light he can hear the slightest sound (for he is not too sure his father will wake him, because he isn't too sure his mother will tell his father she promised him). But when the telephone rang, not very late that evening, it went across his sleep as faintly, and faded as quickly, as the strafe of a match drawn across a (hot) stove lid; and the talking and footfalls, later, were no more to him than the most remote remorse of thunder; so that never after would he be sure whether he had heard, or imagined the words "no, don't wake them; let them sleep. Let them sleep;" which were always to move him as little as all of poetry could. And so his determination to sleep lightly resulted only in his waking somewhat earlier than usual, but not so early as he might have wished. [At this point, the variant begins to parallel chapter 35.] He saw it was already full daylight and the birds were loud. Something special was on his mind that made him eager and happy and within a second he remembered what it was and, sitting up, his lungs suddenly stretched with immense pride, put his hand with a small smashing noise into the crisp tissue paper and took out the cap. It was light enough that he could see the colors well. He put it on his head and pelted down the hallway, crying "Daddy! *Daddy!*", and burst through the open door into their bedroom, and his father was not here. But his mother lay there, propped up on two pillows as if she were sick. She looked sick, or very tired. Her face was full of little lines he had not seen before, lines as little as those in the mended china cup. She put out her hands towards him. "Where's Daddy," he shouted imperiously, ignoring her hands. "Daddy—isn't here yet," she told him, in a voice like hot ashes, and her hands dropped to the sheet. "Where is he then," Richard demanded in angry disappointment, but she thrust through these words with her own: "Go wake—little Emma, and bring her right here," she said. "There's something I must tell you both together." He was looking all over the room for clues of his father, clothes; the watch. "Right *away*", she said, in a desperate voice. Startled by its mysterious rebuke, and obscurely alarmed because she had said "*little* Emma," he hurried out—and there in the hallway was his aunt Jessie. Her mouth was strong and cold beneath the glittering lenses as she stooped peering forward. "Hello Aunt Jessie," he called with astonishment speeding past her; he saw her go into the bedroom, her hair sticking out in two gray, twiggy braids, and he hurried to the side of Emma's crib. "Wake up, Emma," he yelled. "Mamma says wake up! Right *away!*" And he shook her. "*Stobbit,*" she bawled, her round red face glaring. "Well mamma said so, mamma said so. Wake *up!*" And a few moments later he hurried back ahead of her and she trailed in, two thirds asleep, snuffling with anger, her lower lip stuck out. "*Take off your cap!*", his aunt Jessie snapped with frightening sternness, and

[79]

his hands only just caught it against her snatching. He had never experienced such inexplicable betrayal, and the hardness of her mouth, struggling with self-astonishment and repentance, frightened him. "No, let him wear it if he wants," his mother said in her strange voice. "He wanted Jay to see it so." And as before, she lifted forward her hands. "Children, come close," she said. Aunt Jessie went silently out of the room. "Come close"; and she touched each of them. "I want to tell you about Daddy." But on his name her voice shook and her whole dry mouth trembled like the flaked ash of burned paper in a draft. "Can you hear me, Emma," she said when she had recovered her voice. Emma peered at her earnestly, as if through a thick mist. "Are you awake yet, my darling?" And because of her voice, whether in sympathy or for her protection, they both came much nearer, and she put her arms around both of them, and they could smell her breath, like a dried-up mouse. And now there were even more lines, branching all over her face. "Daddy," she said; "Your father, children": and this time she caught control of her mouth more quickly, and a single tear spilled out of her left eye and ran crookedly across all the crooked lines: "Daddy isn't ever coming home anymore. He's—gone away to heaven and he isn't ever coming home again. Do you hear me, Emma? Are you awake?" She stared at her mother. "Do you understand me, Richard?" He stared at his mother. "Why not," he said. She looked at him with extraordinary despair and said: "Because—God wanted him." And seeing that his was not accepted, continued: "Daddy was on his way home last night and he was—he—got hurt and—God let him go to sleep and took him away with Him to Heaven." She sank her fingers in Emma's springy hair and looked intently from one to the other. "Do you see, children? Do you understand?" They stared at her, and now Emma was curiously awake. "Is Daddy *dead?*" Richard asked. She looked at him, startled as if he had struck her, and again her mouth began to work, uncontrollably this time, and she did not speak, but only nodded her head once, then again, then rapidly, several times over, and suddenly sweeping both of them close against her breasts, tucked her chin tightly down above their heads and they felt her whole body shaken with her breathing, but she did not cry. Emma began to sniffle quietly because everything seemed very serious, very sad. Richard listened to his mother's strange, shattered breathing and gazed sidelong past her fair shoulder to a rubbed place in the carpet; through her breathing he once more heard the birds singing. The streetcar passed below, with a loud iron cry. His mother's breathing became quiet again. With one hand she held Emma closer, and Emma sniffled a little more comfortably; with the other, she put Richard gently away, so that she could look clearly into his eyes. "Neither of you will quite understand for a while," she said. "It's—very *hard*—to understand. But you will," and she repeated dreamily, as if to herself, "*You will*"; and was silent for a few moments. "When you want to learn more—*about* it—just, just ask me and I'll tell you." How did he get hurt, Richard wanted to ask; but he felt that his mother did not want to be asked just now, and kept his silence, nodding to let her know that he understood her. "Just ask," she said again. He nodded again; a strange cold restive excitement was rising in him. "And now you be a good boy," she said in a somewhat different voice, wiping Emma's nose. "Get Emma dressed, and wash and dress yourself, and by then Aunt Jessie will have breakfast ready." "Aren't you getting up Mamma?" Richard asked, much impressed to be delegated to dress his sister. "Not for a while," she said, and by her way of saying it he knew that she wanted them to leave right away. "Come on Emma," he said, and with surprise, took her hand. Emma shook her head. "Go with

[80]

Richard," her mother said, "and eat your breakfast. Mother will see you soon." And Emma, feeling that for some reason she must try to be particularly good today, came away with him without further protest. As they turned through the door Richard saw his mother quietly take a cross and beads from under the pillow and clutch them in both hands, looking passionately at the upright cross.

He buttoned her panties to her underwaist. It was much less easy, he found, than buttoning his own clothes. "Stand still," he said, because to tell her to seemed only a proper part of performing his duty.

"I *am*," Emma said with such firmness that he said no more.

That was all that either of them said before they came down to breakfast. [The variant for chapter 36 begins with the next line.]

Breakfast tasted different because Aunt Jessie had fixed it. She sliced the bananas so thin on the post toasties that they were limp and slimy, and gave each of them a little coffee in their milk, just enough to discolor it. It was a strange meal too because it was so quiet. She did not keep telling them to eat and they did not dawdle but ate steadily and very quietly. The only noise was the very thin dry toast she kept crunching slowly and industriously and the fluttering sipping of the scalding coffee with which she moistened each mouthful of crumbs enough to swallow it. Emma tried to sip her milk with that same noise and Aunt Jessie looked at her in a startled way but said nothing. Richard's fried egg had much less pepper than usual and he and Emma watched with distaste the way the yolk ran. Richard wanted very much to ask questions but he felt sure that his Aunt Jessie would not like it. He turned them over and over carefully in his mind and with the food in his mouth. How did he get hurt? Who hurt him? What did they do to him? Why didn't he fight back? Was he hurt very badly? He must have been hurt *very* badly if God wanted to put him to sleep. How badly is that? Why did anyone want to hurt him? Or did he maybe fall down or get run over. Or was he in the auto. How did he get hurt? When God put you to sleep you woke up right away in heaven but you never woke up again here. How could you do that? His mother had told him he could ask and he would be told, but he felt very shy about asking, as if he would be reproached for bad manners. But why? When would it be all right to ask. He didn't want to be spoken to sharply but he did want to know why. What had happened. How did he get hurt? Was he hurt the way the rabbits were hurt? He tried to imagine how he would look if he were hurt that way, but all he could see was all the torn white fur and the terrible bloody flesh and bowels. The remembrance of this made his face pucker but now the rabbits had no meaning.

[**81**]

It was his father that was hurt. He watched his Aunt Jessie munch her toast and saw how unusually thin the skin was at the outside corners of her eyes, and how sad her eyes were; they were hardly looking at anything. And now his Aunt Jessie folded her napkin, and folded it again more narrowly, and again still more narrowly, and pressed the butt-end of it against her eyes, and laid it beside her plate, where it slowly and slightly unfolded, and, looking just at Richard and then at Emma and then back at Richard, said quietly:

"I think your mother had better not try to talk to you much today, children. I think I'd better tell you just what happened: s'far's we know, that is."

Emma looked at her. "To daddy," she said.

"Yes," said Aunt Jessie: "to your father."

"Who hurt him," said Richard.

"Nobody hurt him, Richard," she said, shocked. "Whatever put that idea into your head?"

"Mamma said he got hurt and God put him to sleep."

"He was hurt but nobody hurt him, Richard. He was driving home, that's all, in the auto, last night, and he had an accident."

Richard felt himself blush and looked warningly at Emma. He knew it could not be *that* kind of accident, an accident in your pants, not with his father a grown man, but Emma might think so. Emma looked at her aunt with astonishment and disbelief.

"A *fatal* accident," his aunt continued, unaware of the disturbance. Her voice was very strange on the strange word, fatal. "That means, that, as your mother said, that he was hurt so badly that God put him to sleep right away. The doctors believe he didn't feel one moment's pain."

She began to realize that what she was saying had almost no meaning to the children, and began again. "One moment he was driving along," she said in a remote voice, "and the next moment . . ." But again she stopped, dismayed to find that words had escaped her which she had never intended to say to them.

"S'far as they've been able to understand it," she said, "it happened this way. Your father was driving, on his way home, it was dark, about nine thirty last night, and something was already wrong with the steering mechanism—with the wheel you drive the car with and keep it going straight where you want it to—Something was wrong with the way the auto steered, but your father couldn't know it, until suddenly one of the front wheels struck a loose stone in the road, and the wheel turned suddenly aside; and when . . ." She paused a moment, then went on, quietly: "When your father tried to make the auto go where it should, he found that he couldn't. And instead, it all twisted aside because of the loose stone, and ran off the road." She paused again. "It seems that your father was thrown from the car," she said, "But they believe he was dead even before that. For the only mark on his whole body," she went on, with strange intensity and resentment, "was"—she pressed one shaking finger to her chin—"right—here!" She looked at them almost as if she were accusing them. They said nothing.

"They are sure how it happened," she said. "The auto gave such a

[82]

sudden *jerk*"—she jerked so convulsively that both children jumped—"that your father was thrown forward. He struck his chin, very hard, against the steering wheel, and from that moment he never knew anything more."

She looked at them. "Do you understand?" she said. They looked at her and said nothing.

"They believe that he was *instantly killed,*" she said. "With that one single blow, because it struck just exactly where it did. Because if you are struck very hard just in that place, it jars your whole brain so hard—just as if, as if you suddenly pulled out an electric light plug. *So hard,* that sometimes people die in that very instant." She let out a long, shaky breath. "Concussion of the brain, that is called, she said; then, almost silently, "The will of God;" and she bowed her head and made a small, private cross on her chest.

She looked up. "Now do you understand, children," she asked. "It's hard to understand. Please tell me if there's anything you want to know and I'll do my best to explain it to you."

They were silent a good while. Richard said: "Did it hurt him bad?"

"He could never have felt it. That's the one mercy. The doctor is sure of that."

"What's instintly?"

"Instantly, is,—as quick as that"—she snapped her finger, more loudly than she had intended; Emma flinched at the noise and did not move her eyes from the finger. "So you can be very sure, both of you, he never felt one moment's pain. Not one moment."

"What's Kuh, Kuh. . . . ?"

"Concussion. Concus-sion of the brain. That's the doctor's name for it. It means, it's as if the brain were hit very hard and suddenly, and joggled loose. The instant that happened, your father was—was—"

"Instintly killed," Richard said.

"Instantly."

"Then it was that that put him to sleep."

She nodded.

"*Not* God." [Chapter 36 ends at about this point but the variant extends the scene.]

"Of *course* it was God," she said with vehemence. "God's will. God's mercy. Whether we can understand it or not. If that wheel had struck your father a little higher or a little lower or a little less hard, nothing of the sort would have happened and your father would be here this minute. If that—cotter pin hadn't worked loose on that dreadful back-country road the whole accident would never have occurred. If that blubbering, drunken fool of a brother of his hadn't called him up at all hours of the night . . ."

She stopped so suddenly they all fell a hundred feet through the silence. "God forgive me—*forgive* me," she said very low, to herself. "Forgive me, children," she said, peering hopelessly into their appalled eyes. "I've been very wicked." And she laid both veined hands along the table. "Let me try to make it clear," she said; "Be patient a moment, and forgive me." She quieted herself.

"When things happen," she said: "When such a thing—just—happens—so suddenly—so much by pure chance, by pure dreadful bad luck—

[83]

with no rhyme or reason to it that we can possibly see—nothing but all that is most wrong—That is just when we have to know, it is God's will, God's own will, we can never *hope* to understand why. We musn't question it or doubt it. Believing it is God's own will is all we have. All we have. Do you see? Do you understand?"

They looked at her.

"For some reason of His own, and we will probably never know what it was, God decided that it was time to take your father away, for you children, and your mother, and all of us. He was a good, good man and you can always be sure that God took him because he loved him. That much we can be sure of. Nothing else. Nothing else. We have to trust in God, and love Him, and—do our best to thank him, however hard that seems to us. You can't understand this now, I know you can't. I've been very foolish to talk so much and only puzzle you. But one day you will. One day we may all begin to understand God's will and His mercy." She stopped and closed her eyes for nearly a minute; then looked at them again and said, in a charged voice: "You're too little to really know yet. Don't try to think about too much. Ask us, any of us, whatever you don't understand. You'll understand it all better by and by." She drew back her chair. [The subsequent two paragraphs are a variant that matches Rufus' actions in the beginning of chapter 37.]

Richard hurried to get his books. "No, you're not going to school today," she told him quietly. "You must stay home, these next few days. No, play quietly, but don't go outside the yard. And be good to Emma. I've got to go upstairs to your mother."

She went to the bathroom and sank her face in the basin of water, blinking her eyes, then hurried quietly along the hall to Laura's room.

Variant Notes for Manuscript TX 5.2 (page and line number cited)

78.2 No. I] (Agee leaves a space of approximately one-half of an inch between "No." and "I".)

78.6–7 [in left margin] Where's your hat?

78.9–23 [in left margin] intercut the / father at the farm? / (was he: intoxicated?) / "those awful roads" / "singing to himself." / wind & high creek & trees / & shapes of hills: night before / he leaves for Knoxville? / Bring in on evening he leaves, / seen & half-remembered / casually?]

78.23 quickly,] quickly

78.28 little as] little in

78.29–30 usual, but] (Agee brackets the following statement that occurs after "usual" for deletion: "[and the day, bright, his delightful & special day: his hand went immediately for the cap and he could see that it was hardly daylight, the birds were hardly beginning yet]"; the reading of the first "his" is conjectural.)

78.39 was] were

78.55 braids,] braids

79.8 [in left margin] very *tired*

79.20–21 [in left margin] hollow, gentle, / remote and dreamy—

79.28–29 [in left margin] his side unslept in / , mother in middle

79.34 tucked] tuched

79.37 [in left margin] cap.

80.3–7 [in left margin] Bell's Bridge, / Ball Camp Pike.

80.14 toasties] stoasties

80.42 meaning.] meaning

81.10 s'far's] (The first "s" is circled by Agee or a previous editor.)

81.21 accident,] accident

81.21 pants,] pants

81.30 moment . . .] moment ___
81.40 when . . .] when __
82.2 that] That
82.22 that"—] that",
82.43 night . . .] night ___

Chapter 37

The following variant (TX 5.2, [87–90]) is Agee's earlier draft of this chapter. See note 295.1 in "Textual Commentary and Notes" for the reasons for this determination. Since McDowell extracts part of the conclusion of this variant for incorporation into the text of his edition, which otherwise uses the correct TX 5.3, [153–64] manuscript, please also see note 308.38 in "Textual Commentary and Notes."

[87]

After breakfast he got his satchel and his hat; then remembered. His new cap must be up in his Mother's room; the last he could remember of it was when she took it off his head. But he felt uneasy about going back into the room for it, and now, thinking more clearly about the cap, he realized that he did not want to wear it. So he put on his hat. He imagined that he ought to say goodbye to his mother but he was reluctant to see her. He went back into the kitchen where his Aunt Jessie stood at the sink and said "Good-bye Aunt Jessie."

"What is it," she said, and turned, peering. "Why Rufus!"

He wondered what he had done.

"You won't be going to school today, child. Or tomorrow. Not until after the, not for the next few days. You must stay home, with us."

"I don't have to go to school?"

"No, you don't have to go to school. Musn't."

But then I can't see them, he realized. It was nice to get out of school. But not today. Today he felt as odd, and special, as if it were his birthday. Something had happened to him which was not happening to any other boy in town. They would all be looking at him and looking up to him. And now he didn't have to go to school.

Musn't.

He strolled along the dark front hall, and he felt so idle that it made him almost tired. He felt as if he were full in some sort of way, remembering his mother's face and her voice and saying over and over within himself, he's dead. He's dead. Just last night he died and now he is dead and he can never come back. Now he has been dead ever since last night and it is already morning. There memories and reflections filled him with a kind of silent whirring, yet at the same time he felt empty, and unendurably idle, and proud, and shy. He put his satchel back on the hat rack but he kept his hat on and quietly let himself out the front door, and walked out to the sidewalk. And now that he was outdoors alone in the blowing sunlight he felt so much more proud and so much more shy that he could feel his face smiling, even grinning, and could hardly control it.

"My daddy's dead," he told the first man who came past him; but the man, who was walking rapidly, did not seem to hear him. "My daddy's dead," he said again, more

[88]

clearly, although he was not speaking to anyone; he walked to the corner and looked down the side street and, in an instant, was overwhelmed with such pride and, even more, with such shyness, as he had never known before. For here they came, several of them, a few his age, mostly older, whose faces he knew so well and whose names he did not know; three together, and two more at a distance, and one alone, and another alone, and some girls, too, whom he scarcely noticed; and he was sure that already each of these boys, and now, he saw, still others, who were coming towards school down Highland Avenue, saw him already, and were still approaching him silently, all looking at him, where he waited. Waiting, daring those many seconds before the first of them came near him, he felt that it was so long to wait, and to be watched in this way, and to watch back, that he wanted to go away and not be seen by any of them or by anybody, and yet at the same time he felt that they were all approaching him with the realization that something had happened to him which had not happened to any other boy in town, and that now at last they were bound to think well of him; so that as they came nearer he once again felt his face break into a wide smile, as if he had nothing to do with it and, feeling that here was something very wrong in such a smile, tried his best to quieten his face and told them, shyly and proudly, "My daddy's dead."

Of the first three who came up, two merely looked at him suspiciously and the third said "Huh! I betcha he ain't," and Rufus, astounded that they disbelieved him, said, "why he is so!", and the boy who had spoken said, "where's your satchel at? You're just trying to lay out of school," and Rufus replied, "I am not, I was going to school and my Aunt Jessie told me I don't have to go to school today or tomorrow or not till, not for a few days. She said I musn't. So I am not."

And while he was speaking two more boys came up and one of them said, "He don't have to go to school, he can lay out cause his daddy got killed."

And the first boy who had spoken said, resentfully, "how do *you* know"?

And the second boy, while his companion nodded, said, "Cause my daddy seen it in the paper. Can't your daddy read the paper?"

And the first boy, interested enough to ignore that remark, said "How did he get killed, then?", and Rufus took a deep breath and began to tell; but the boy whose father had seen it in the paper was already telling, so he listened, instead, feeling as if all this was being said in his praise, and feeling it all the more as he saw that their eyes were on him.

And the boy said: "In his tin-lizzie, that's how. He was driving along in his old Tin lizzie and it hit a rock and throwed him out and run up a eight foot bank and turned over and over and landed on him *whomph,* that's all. And someone came and found him and he was dead already when they got there."

"He was instantly killed," Rufus said. Two more boys came up; they looked questioning. "My daddy's dead," he told them.

"That's what my daddy says,"

[89]

one of them said, and the other said, "what you get for driving drunk, that's what my dad says," and they looked gravely at the other boys, nodding, and at Rufus.

"What's drunk," Rufus asked.

"What's drunk?", one of the boys mocked incredulously; "drunk is full of good ole whiskey"; and he began to stagger about with weak knees. "At's what drunk is."

"He wasn't drunk," Rufus said.

"How do *you* know?"

"He wasn't drunk because that wasn't how he died. The wheel hit a rock and the other wheel, the one you steer with, just hit him on the chin, but it hit him so hard it killed him. He was instantly killed."

"What's instantly killed?", one of the boys asked.

"What do you care," another said. Another boy joined the group.

"I don't know nothing about no chin," said the boy whose father saw it in the paper. "He was adrivin along in his ole tin-lizzie and he hit a rock and the car run off the road and thowed him out and run up a eight foot bank and turned over and over and rolled back down on him *whomp.*"

"How do *you* know," said one of the older boys. "*You* wasn't there. Anybody here *knows,* it's *him.*" And he pointed at Rufus.

"Why?" said one of the two who had just come up.

"Because it's my daddy," Rufus said.

"It's his daddy," others explained.

"My daddy says he bets he was drunk."

"What's *your* daddy know about it?"

"Let *him* tell it."

"Yeah *you* tell it."

"Anybody here ought to know, it's him."

"Come on and tell us."

They became quiet and all of them were looking at him.

"He was coming home from Grampa's last night; Grampa Agee. He's very sick; and he was hurrying to get home because he was late. And there was a cotter pin worked loose."

"What's a cotter pin?"

"A cotter pin holds things together that you steer with. It worked loose so when one of the wheels hit a rock he couldn't steer and the auto ran off the road with an awful bump and they saw where the wheel you steer with hit him right on the chin and he was instantly killed. He was thrown out of the car and it ran up an eight foot embankment and then rolled back down and it was upside down when they found it. There wasn't another mark on his body my Uncle Hugh says. Only a little mark on the chin."

"Heck, how can *that* kill anybody?"

"Uncle Hugh said it was just the way it happened to hit, it was just a chance in a million. It was just concu—con—it was something it did to his brain."

"Knocked him crazy as a loon, that's what," cried one of the boys, and with his forefinger he made rapid blubbery noises against his lower lip.

"Shut up," said an older boy coldly. "Haven't you got no sense at all?"

"Way I heard it, ole tin lizzie rolled right on back on top of him *whomp.*"

This account of it seemed to Rufus more exciting than his own, and more creditable to him and to his father; and nobody could question, scornfully, whether that could kill, as they could of a blow on the chin;

[90]

so he did not try to argue about it. He felt that he was lying, and in some way being disloyal as well, but he said only: "He was instantly killed. He didn't have to feel any pain."

"Never even knowed what hit him."

"Reckon that ole tin-lizzie is done for now. Huh?"

He felt that there was something mean and wrong in calling it an old tin-lizzie; he said only "I guess so."

For some moments now a bell, the school bell, had been weltering in the bright air; now a boy, sprinting along the far side of the street, yelled, "Last bell," and several of these boys cried, "Last bell," and one said "come on. We're goana git hell," and within a second more Rufus was watching them all run away down the street as fast as they could go.

He felt that they had paid him more attention, aside from attention which had been paid unkindly, than ever before. They really listened to him; he was almost one of them; some of them even almost looked up to him. But he also felt that he should have much more clearly contradicted the boy who insisted that his father had been crushed under the car; and that somewhere beneath that lie, there was something far more greatly uncertain, and wrong. He felt somewhat more sure of himself, among the other boys, than he had ever felt before; but there was only one person he wished might know this, and he could not tell him. All morning he felt more sure of himself, pleased and quiet in remembering their crowding, and, when he finally told them how it had happened, their quiet and respectful attention. But by the time school let out, and they were on their way back, he knew that he did not want to talk to them, or see them, or be seen by them; but stayed in the sitting-room, where his eyes constantly returned to the morris-chair. With a sense of deep stealth and secrecy he finally went over and stood beside it. After a few moments, and after listening most intently to be sure that nobody was near, he smelled of the chair, its deeply hollowed seat, the arms, the back. There was only a cold smell of tobacco and, high along the back, a faint smell of hair. He thought of the ash tray on its weighted strap on the arm; it was empty. He ran his finger inside it; there was only a dim smudge of ash. There was nothing like enough to keep in his pocket or wrap up in a paper. He looked at his finger for a moment and licked it; his tongue tasted of darkness.

Variant Notes for Manuscript TX 5.2 (page and line number cited)

88.21	shyly] shily
88.29–41	(Paragraph breaks added)
88.48	(Paragraph break added)
89.4–31	(Paragraph breaks added)

An earlier variant introduction (TX 5.2, [91]) of the first paragraph of this chapter provides additional insight into Agee's construction of Rufus' questions regarding his father's death. It occupies half the manuscript page and is not continued. Agee often drafted and redrafted his opening paragraphs, and this appears to be one such example.

[91]

When breakfast was over he went into the sitting room and looked for a place to sit down, but he did not see any place where he would like to. He felt as if this were his birthday, except that his day seemed even more specially his own day. There was nothing in the look of it which was not ordinary but it was filled with a noiseless kind of whirring. He could see his mother's face as she told them about it and hear her voice, over and over, and over and over, as he looked around the sitting room and out through the window into

> the street, words repeated themselves silently: He's dead. He died last night while I was asleep and now it is already morning. He has already been dead since way last night and I didn't know. He has been dead all night and now it is morning and he will stay right on being dead all afternoon and all tonight and tomorrow. Now he can't come home ever any more but I will see him once more before he is taken away. Where. Away where. Away where they take people when their souls have gone and they are dead. Where is he now and why can't I see him now? He is at Mr. Roberts' and you don't want to see him until he is ready to be taken away; they are getting him ready to be taken away, that's what they do at Mr. Roberts'. What does he look like? He looks just like when he's asleep. What does he feel like to be dead? He doesn't feel it at all but his soul does. Now his soul is at peace. What's at peace? Now he is free and happy, his soul is. All it is sorry about is you and Emma and Mama.

Variant Notes for Manuscript TX 5.2 (page and line number cited)

91.9	silently:] silently,
91.17	Roberts'] Roberts
91.18	away; they] away, they
91.19	Roberts'] Roberts

Chapter 44

Below are the two prayers first given to David McDowell by Father Flye to supply the blank left by Agee and described by him as "(Quote the last half of vespers)." After the novel's publication and upon viewing the context for the prayers, Flye wrote to McDowell to note that these were the wrong prayers and urged him to substitute the ones which he now supplied. The change was never made until the present edition. For more information, please see 350.5–25 in "Textual Commentary and Notes."

The prayers below are supplied from the first McDowell edition, since no other copy of the text that Flye mistakenly provided apparently survives.

> O GOD, the Creator and Preserver of all mankind, we humbly beseech thee for all sorts and conditions of men; that thou wouldest be pleased to make thy ways known unto them, thy saving health unto all nations. More especially we pray for thy holy Church universal; that it may be so guided and governed by thy good Spirit, that all who profess and call themselves Christians may be led into the way of truth, and hold the faith in unity of spirit, in the bond of peace, and in righteousness of life. Finally, we commend to thy fatherly goodness all those who are any ways afflicted, or distressed, in mind, body, or

estate; that it may please thee to comfort and relieve them, according to their several necessities; giving them patience under their sufferings, and a happy issue out of all their afflictions. And this we beg for Jesus Christ's sake. Amen.

ALMIGHTY God, Father of all mercies, we, thine unworthy servants, do give thee most humble and hearty thanks for all thy goodness and loving-kindness to us, and to all men. We bless thee for our creation, preservation, and all the blessings of this life; but above all, for thine inestimable love in the redemption of the world by our Lord Jesus Christ; for the means of grace, and for the hope of glory. And, we beseech thee, give us that due sense of all thy mercies, that our hearts may be unfeignedly thankful; and that we show forth thy praise, not only with our lips, but in our lives, by giving up our selves to thy service, and by walking before thee in holiness and righteousness all our days; through Jesus Christ our Lord, to whom, with thee and the Holy Ghost, be all honour and glory, world without end. Amen.

Marginal Notes

Agee often uses the margins of the manuscript to write phrases, sentences, or paragraphs to be inserted into the text, the position of which he usually indicates with a line drawn to a caret or, in some instances, only a caret. These insertions are incorporated silently in this edition. Other marginal notes and comments unmarked by Agee, and hence not inserted into the text, are often ideas, references, or cues that he may or may not have developed as part of his text and are presented in the following list. Page and line numbers from the present volume followed by a bracketed description give the approximate location of the marginal comments in the manuscript. Agee's marginal comment then follows the bracketed description. A solidus (/) indicates a line break within the marginal note. Agee's underlinings are rendered in italics. Page numbers or letters added by Agee or previous editors to denote the order of the manuscript pages are recorded below; those that refer to pages of the subsequent typescripts produced for the novel are not, unless they reveal significant information about the structure of the McDowell edition. See also 154.1 in "Textual Commentary and Notes."

6.19–23 [in left margin perpendicular to text] more & different on / eyes

8.22–26 [in left margin] facades intricate as / antimacassars / embroiled facades

8.26–30 [in left margin] silver carved / window / in the [illegible—perhaps "small sooty screens"]

17.8–16 [in left margin perpendicular to text] he could hear nothing they said

37.27–38.2 [in left margin] Fountain City? / Park Circle?

42.35–36 [in left margin] upholstery

50.14–15 [in right margin] visors, straps &c / [illegible]ly dressing more?

51.23–27 [in left margin perpendicular to text] does he ask his mother?

57.20–28 [in left margin] he w[oul]d never fight back. / sense of sportsmanship: / such banter [?] beyond him. / They might have on those littler things / but surely on big things like this they wdn't be so mean.

65.33–35 [in left margin] pray for me

70.38 [in left margin] breadbasket.

78.30–31 [in left margin] talking too loud?

88.23–25 [in left margin] popcorn white

88.30–31 [in left margin] E. Tenn [illegible] Fair

89.8 [in left margin] across the gravel

89.20–22 [in left margin] color of popcorn

89.30–31 [in left margin] *sleek* / *sneering* heads / narrow / *black faces*

89.34–38 [in left margin] backs [or "banks"] [illegible—perhaps "meandered"] & damp & you cd see / the green trees ~~by~~ upon the water, / green reflection in shady[space] dark green. / water.

90.1–6 [in left margin] where people went only to spoon—/ (*Jay.*) / (Silly things.) / but right out in the *open.* / They're private as they can.

92.17–22 [in right margin are six randomly doodled stars]

93.26–29 [in left margin] Sometimes I'm up sometimes I'm down / But still my soul seems heavenward / bound

94.28–31 [in left margin roughly perpendicular to text] like a cloud came over / a bright day, or

94.35 [in left margin] slatternly [with line to "slovenly" (the unused interlinear alternative written above "unhappy")]

95.10–11 [in left margin] glass, / RR. Trains with candy

95.11–12 [in left margin beside deleted paragraph] rough people—

95.11–12 [in left margin beside deleted paragraph] cars, / behind the bear pits / smell like horses

96.19–25 [in left margin] big clouds / strings of lights come on in / the daylight gray & pink & blue / cloth rumpling

98.18–24 [in left margin roughly perpendicular to text] a heavy man / with red splotches on his face

98.26–30 [in left margin roughly perpendicular to text] white eyes

123.2–9 [in left margin] Ck electric or / carbide lights? / lamps up at side / of windshield? / 1915 Ford

127.1 [at top of page, left] mother gr.; great great [another "great" above second "great"]; great ["greatgreat" above "great"] / at 16; at 20; at 19; at 17; at 24; / 36; 54; 71; 95,

127.1 [at top of page, center, separated from previous notes by vertical line] Granmaw

127.1 [at top of page, right, separated from previous note by two vertical lines] 3 streaks of us / some live long; some live till round sixty; some die young. That's not counting the babies.

127.1 [top right corner; previous editor's note] 4

127.28 [in left margin; mark in text indicates note refers to "Aunt Paralee"] (name?

128.14 [in top right corner; previous editor's note] 5

130.1 [in top right corner; previous editor's note] 6

131.31 [in top right corner; previous editor's note] 7

133.4 [in top right corner; previous editor's note] 8

134.34 [in left margin next to deleted paragraph] She can hear all right. (apparently three words lined through follow this sentence)

134.34	[in bottom right margin below deleted paragraph; previous editor's note] (to top p. 13)
134.35	[in top right corner; previous editor's note] 9
135.19	[in left margin next to deleted paragraph] knees
135.19	[in left margin next to deleted paragraph] a smooth shining gray
135.20	[in top right corner; previous editor's note] 10
137.20	[in top right corner; previous editor's note] 11
138.25	[in top right corner, at top of page featuring a deleted section; previous editor's note] 13
139.11–13	[in bottom right margin; previous editor's note] (and the / sadness of / time / dwelt—
139.14	[in top right corner; previous editor's note] 14
145.1	[in top left corner; previous editor's note] I
145.1	[in top right margin; previous editor's note] *MOVIE: CORNER*
145.1	[in top right margin below previous marginal note; previous editor's note] chap I
145.1	[in top right corner; previous editor's note] 1
145.1	[in top right corner below previous marginal note; previous editor's note] (to p 7 here)
146.19	[in top right corner; previous editor's note] 2
146.26–27	[in left margin; previous editor's note] (piqué
147.24	[in top right corner; previous editor's note] 3
148.27	[in top right corner; previous editor's note] 4
149.25–27	[in left margin] oriental sword half drawn from / [illegible] ivory scabbard, rows of / blackjacks, mandolin
149.30	[in top right corner; previous editor's note] 5
151.4	[in top right corner; previous editor's note] 6
152.17	[in top right corner; previous editor's note] 7
153.17	[center bottom of page below final text; previous editor's note] END I
154.1	[top left margin; previous editor's note] II
154.1	[top right margin; previous editor's note] Chap II
154.1	[top right margin; previous editor's note] 1
155.16	[top right margin; previous editor's note] 2
156.34	[top right margin; previous editor's note] 3
158.19	[top right margin; previous editor's note] 4
159.22	[in left margin] need any money
160.10	[top right margin; previous editor's note] 5
162.3	[in left margin] forgot coat
162.4	[top right margin; previous editor's note] 6
162.26–31	[circled, in left margin] at home, prefers coffee / but makes no joke / about it
163.29	[top right margin; previous editor's note] 7
164.18–22	[circled, in left margin] you forgot your milk. / need money?

164.31–36 [circled, in left margin] too much of these? or shd there / here be specifications of perhaps / symbolic objects?
165.8 [top right margin; previous editor's note] 8
166.14–17 [in left margin with line to "blesséd spirit" (214.3)] celestial sentinel. / perfected spirit
166.21–23 [in left margin] feeling a baby's cheek
166.26 [top right margin; previous editor's note] 9
168.7 [top right margin; previous editor's note] 10
168.10–11 [in left margin] alley / gate
168.16 [in left margin] hears where too.
170.1 [top right margin; previous editor's note] 11
171.1 [right margin; previous editor's note] Chap 3
172.24 [top right margin; previous editor's note] 12
172.24–29 [in left margin] Ya-up. / Yayup. / Yehu / Yeyup
172.34–35 [in left margin next to Agee's circling of "the brown water widen under the lantern light"] sharpen
173.4–11 [circled, in left margin; circled above this statement is a similar version of the text of the marginal note marked with a arrowed line for inclusion in the text] feeling of hand on breast, / flat craft on bias of / current.
173.12–13 [in left margin] mustard, / pumpkin
173.13 [in left margin] coldness
173.21–24 [in left margin] headlights still / going?
173.34–35 [in left margin apparently in reference to the circled "his own were strangely shy"; the circling may be Agee's, but the marginal annotation is likely that of a previous editor] +?
174.13 [top right margin; previous editor's note] 13
176.1 [top left margin] a "white" sleep
176.1 [top right margin; previous editor's note] Chap 4
176.1 [top right margin; previous editor's note] 14
176.23–26 [in left margin] main barrier between her & Jay
176.26–29 [in left margin] so far as [one or two words illegible] of / understanding of his "background"
177.1–7 [in left margin] a kind of weakness she just / can't like or even forgive, / for it takes advantage through itself / & is unaware of itself
177.34 [top right margin; previous editor's note] 15
179.16 [top right margin; previous editor's note] 16
182.1 [top right margin; previous editor's note] Chap 5
182.22 [top right margin; previous editor's note] 17
184.1 [right margin; previous editor's note] Chap 6
184.20 [top right margin; previous editor's note] 18
184.24–30 [in left margin] took his emotions & woes of voices from his sense of appropriateness to context.
185.37 [top right margin; previous editor's note] 19

187.15–18	[in left margin] his mother, quiet & shy after her terror / almost as if she had had a new body
187.22	[top right margin; previous editor's note] 20
189.6	[top right margin; previous editor's note] 21
190.1–4	[in left margin] afraid of city—too far from home
190.33	[top right margin; previous editor's note] 22
192.1	[right margin; previous editor's note] ch 5
192.12	[centered at bottom of page; previous editor's note] END I
196.1	[centered at top of page; previous editor's note] Chap 7
196.1	[top right margin; previous editor's note] 14
196.11–17	[in left margin] his father got sick about 10[30] the / night before?
196.17–27	[in left margin] build more masculine-vs-feminine, / mountain-vs-city middle class
196.20–30	[in left margin] J. the best of them, but somewhat dangerous and put-off / because of religiousness?
196.29–197.6	[in left margin] ask Jessie's advice / *re* God's will, death, & the children?
196.29–197.10	[in left margin] first to have a Ford; got for family (primitive) reasons? / people askance so poor a man sporting a car?
197.28	[top right margin; previous editor's note] 15
199.17	[top right margin; previous editor's note] 16
201.5	[top right margin; previous editor's note] 17
204.1	[centered at top of page; previous editor's note] Part II / Chap 8
204.1	[top right margin; previous editor's note] 1
204.26–205.2	[in left margin] *anvil / horrid* & *unique / electric shock or shudder*
205.20	[top right margin; previous editor's note] 2
207.33	[top right margin; previous editor's note] 3
208.37	[top right margin; previous editor's note] 4
210.3	[in top left corner of page] Emma, c. 9.
210.3	[top right margin; previous editor's note] 5
211.12	[top right margin; previous editor's note] 6
212.2–3	[in left margin; previous editor's notes in regard to the typescript of a passage marked for deletion by Agee] see / p. 205 / See Insert A, / p. 205a.
212.3	[top right margin; previous editor's note] 7
213.10	[top right margin; previous editor's note] 8
214.16	[top right margin; previous editor's note] 9
215.27	[top right margin; previous editor's note] 10
217.2	[top right margin; previous editor's note] 11
217.14	[top right margin; previous editor's note] 12
217.36	[top right margin; previous editor's note] 13
218.14–30	[in left margin; previous editor's note] *STET* [in regard to passage lined through, apparently by the previous editor]
219.8	[top right margin; previous editor's note] 14
220.1	[top center margin; previous editor's note] Chap 9
220.1	[top right margin; previous editor's note] 1

221.10	[top right margin; previous editor's note] 2
222.10	[top right margin; previous editor's note] 3
223.28	[top right margin; previous editor's note] 4
225.1	[top right margin; previous editor's note] 15
226.19	[top right margin; previous editor's note] 16
227.27	[top right margin; previous editor's note] 17
227.31–32	[in right margin between sections of chapter 28; previous editor's note] end of Chap 8
227.32–33	[in right margin; previous editor's note] Chap 10
229.6	[top right margin; previous editor's note] 18
230.21	[top right margin; previous editor's note] 19
231.14–15	[in left margin; previous editor's note] X?
231.37	[top right margin; previous editor's note] 20
233.15	[top right margin; previous editor's note] 21
234.17	[top right margin; previous editor's note] 22
235.38	[top right margin; previous editor's note] 23
237.1	[top center margin; previous editor's note] Ch 11
237.1	[top right margin; previous editor's note] 6
238.7	[top center margin; previous editor's note] Cha 11
238.7	[top right margin; previous editor's note] 7
239.25	[top right margin; previous editor's note] 8
241.10	[top right margin; previous editor's note] 9
242.28	[top right margin; previous editor's note] 10
244.20	[top right margin; previous editor's note] 11
246.1	[top right margin; previous editor's note] 12
246.1–3	[in left margin] 10-1^{15}
246.4–8	[in left margin] stove: / 4-12 / 9^{30}–
246.11–12	[in left margin; previous editor's note] Tom? / Hugh?
246.28–32	[in left margin] We just got to / laughing so hard we / couldn't.
247.33	[top right margin; previous editor's note] 13
249.15	[top right margin; previous editor's note] 14
249.25–29	[in left margin] 7^{15} stove
249.31–33	[in left margin] 1½
250.30	[top right margin; previous editor's note] 15
252.3	[top right margin; previous editor's note] 16
254.1	[top right margin; previous editor's note] 17
255.18	[top right margin; previous editor's note] 18
256.23	[top right margin; previous editor's note] 19
257.28	[top right margin; previous editor's note] 20
258.38	[top right margin; previous editor's note] 21
260.5	[top right margin; previous editor's note] 22
261.11	[top right margin; previous editor's note] 23
261.24–26	[in left margin] I just—don't—know.
262.23	[top right margin; previous editor's note] 24

263.32	[top right margin; previous editor's note] 25
264.5–6	[in left margin] desolate.
266.6	[top right margin; previous editor's note] 26
267.13	[top right margin; previous editor's note] 27
268.23	[top right margin; previous editor's note] 28
269.17	[in left margin] stunned
270.15	[top right margin; previous editor's note] 29
271.29	[top right margin; previous editor's note] 30
273.10	[top right margin; previous editor's note] 31
274.26	[top right margin; previous editor's note] 32
276.1	[right margin; previous editor's note] Ch 13
276.1	[left margin; previous editor's note] A (The "A" is encircled and has an arrow pointing to "Along Laurel," which was bracketed by a previous editor. A similar encircled "A" with an arrow pointing to "Upon their . . ." at 276.13 is apparently meant to link these sections, perhaps for a typist. 276.13 does not begin with a bracket. The A's, arrows, and bracket are all generated by someone other than Agee.)
276.13	[top right margin; previous editor's note] 33
277.26	[top right margin; previous editor's note] 34
279.1	[top right margin; previous editor's note] 35
280.25	[top right margin; previous editor's note] 36
308.37	[center bottom margin; previous editor's note] End Chapt 16 (This is an earlier editorial judgment, since the McDowell edition subsequently attaches parts of pages 5.3, [164] and 5.2, [90] as the conclusion to the chapter. Please see 308.38 in "Textual Commentary and Notes.")
312.1	[top right margin; previous editor's note] Chap 17
312.1	[top right margin; previous editor's note] 1
313.23	[top right margin; previous editor's note] 2
315.11	[top right margin; previous editor's note] 3
317.3	[top right margin; previous editor's note] 4
317.3–11	[in left margin] have seen a / wedding—J was / best man?
317.12	[in left margin] *earlier* (Here Agee refers to a short deleted section on specific nationalities of orphans that he incorporated "earlier" in the chapter.)
318.27	[top right margin; previous editor's note] 5
318.31–33	[in left margin] hat & jaw?
320.24	[top right margin; previous editor's note] 6
322.6	[top right margin; previous editor's note] 7
323.31	[top right margin; previous editor's note] 8
325.9	[top right margin; previous editor's note] 9
326.23	[top right margin; previous editor's note] 10
327.32	[top right margin; previous editor's note] 11
329.30	[in left margin] //measles
329.30	[top right margin; previous editor's note] 12

332.21	[in left margin; previous editor's note] sunny (The word in Agee's text is difficult to make out, but "sunny" is a logical reading.)
333.29	[in left margin] messengers?
334.1	[top right margin; previous editor's note] 13
335.24	[top right margin; previous editor's note] 14
337.5	[top right margin; previous editor's note] 15
338.27	[top right margin; previous editor's note] 16
340.1	[center; under last section of Agee's drafts of the beginning of the chapter; previous editor's note] Ch 19
340.2	[in left margin; previous editor's note; with an arrow from the marginal notation pointing to the start of the first paragraph] Ch. 19 / variant
340.15–16	[in left margin] solid blue
341.5	[in left margin] he can't look
343.1	[top center margin; previous editor's note] Chap / 19 *con't*
343.1	[top right margin; previous editor's note] 18
344.3	[top right margin; previous editor's note] 19
344.31–33	[in left margin] attendant inside hearse?
345.12–14	[in left margin] (flower auto steals downhill)
345.18	[top right margin; previous editor's note] 20
346.1	[top right margin; previous editor's note] 21 (Another two-digit page number that begins with a "2" that was written by a previous editor is crossed out. This may indicate the previous editor's initial questioning of the placement of manuscript page 5.3, [189].)
346.1	[top right margin; previous editor's note] Chap 20
347.5	[top right margin; previous editor's note] 22
348.18	[top right margin; previous editor's note] 23
350.1	[top right margin; previous editor's note] 24
351.7–8	[left margin] [illegible—one word (foot?; pot?) or abbreviation of three or four characters]
352.1	[top right margin; previous editor's note] 25
353.2	[left margin] horn
353.17	[top right margin; previous editor's note] 26
354.24	[top right margin; previous editor's note] 27
355.28	[top right margin; previous editor's note] 28

Word Choice Where No Preference Is Indicated

Agee occasionally provides two possibilities for a word or phrase within a sentence by writing one above the other, without indicating his choice. In most cases, Agee's initial choice is retained. The following chart lists such instances as they occur in the text. Page and line numbers designate the position of the word or phrase in question and are followed by the editor's choice. After the single bracket, the two possibilities are given, indicating the alternative word or phrase as written above (>) the word or phrase that initially appears in the sentence. For instance, page 4, line 20 contains the phrase "the loose stride inherited from the mountains." In the manuscript, the phrase reads "the loose stride of the mountains" but Agee has written "inherited from" above "of" without indicating a choice. Comments by the editor are contained within parentheses.

4.20 inherited from] inherited from > of

16.3 leaning] leaning > laying

16.27 bore] stretched > bore

16.29 an exhausted] a tired old > an exhausted

17.11 laden] loaded > laden

18.10 worthy] gentle > worthy

18.21 leave] go away > leave

18.23 the hand] their hands > the hand

18.25 rears] rises > rears

18.31 still as] silent and unmoving as > still as (Although it is possible to read "silent and unmoving as" as an unmarked interlinear insertion to the text that yields the phrase "still as silent and unmoving as mountains", Agee's method suggests that they are rather alternative possibilities.)

50.14 powerfully] forcefully > powerfully

50.16–17 others of other groups] others of other groups > each other (The interlinear alternative was chosen since it eliminates the ambiguity of Agee's original statement in which it was unclear if the members were calling to those in their same group or to those in other groups.)

51.12 strange,] extravagant, > strange,

51.26 Then] So > Then
52.33 *Maybe*] But what if > *Maybe*
54.38 great-grandfather] granpa > grandfather
66.5 smartly] crisply > smartly
67.15 went by] went by > passed (The interlinear addition was chosen to avoid the repetition with "passing" in the same sentence.)
85.31 ludicrous] silly > ludicrous
86.24 laid] put > laid
89.32–33 arching above] bending tall > arching above
90.15 biggest] boldest > biggest
90.25 gentle] kind > gentle
94.22 the speed] everything > the speed
94.35 unhappy-sounding] slovenly > unhappy-sounding
95.19 shaft] thing > shaft
105.8 conviction] candor > conviction
109.2 complex] complicated > complex
109.34 we just won't get it."] that's all." > we just won't get it."
115.37 bang] slam > bang
116.9 cryptic] mysterious > cryptic
128.21 teasin] raggin > teasin
128.26 through] among > through
130.15 eleven] eleven > ten ("ten"" is partially crossed out and "eleven" is correct given Jay's statement on 130.13 that she is 103 or 104 years old.)
143.7 would] should > would
145.4 man!"] man!" > Charlie Chaplin!" (Agee's brackets indicating deletion make this his choice.)
146.29 Rufus'] Rufus' > Richard's
147.19–20 fancy vest] fancy vest > mustache
147.36 bright] shining > bright
148.5 fluttering] shaky > fluttering
148.29 grand] lordly > grand
149.6 brag] talk > brag
149.6 son] boy > son
149.23 within] among > within
149.28 exhausted butterfly] moth's wing > exhausted butterfly
150.3 rubbed slick] rubbed > bare ("slick" is written interlinearly below "bare".)
150.6 a high] an > a high
150.6 dirty laundry] dirty laundry > wrinkled cloth
150.28 quiet] idling > quiet
154.7 stilled] quieted > stilled
166.21 gave back] shed towards > gave back
166.22 subsumed] sublimated > subsumed

166.23	blesséd spirit] celestial sentinel. > perfected spirit (in left margin with line to "blesséd spirit")
166.25	dissolving] rapturous > dissolving
166.25	opened] juvescent [*sic*] > opened
166.25	which slept against the sky] whose slumber the sky held as a Madonna. > which slept against the sky
167.31	How's your money?] Need any money? > How's your money?
168.33	machine backed out, crackling] spindly, light on blackness; > machine backed out, crackling
170.7	departed from] abandoned > departed from
185.5	choking] strangling > choking
185.26	terrible] deep > terrible
186.28	hung] slung > hung
189.13	upsetting] capsizing > upsetting
189.19	so] so > as
189.25	path] angle > path
198.4	planting] establishment > planting
204.28–29	"Tell him he can't miss it. We'll keep the light on and a lantern out in front."] "Tell him he can't miss it. We'll keep the light on and a lantern out in front." ("lantern out in front." is written below line) > "We'll keep the light on: Tell him he can't miss it."
207.5	swiftness] hurry > swiftness
207.17	back] spine > back
207.27	soft] stupefied > soft
207.37	right] straight > right
211.1	deep] thick > deep
211.8	circled] turned > circled
212.14	bring] force > bring
214.25	had no business phoning] was a perfect fool to phone > had no business phoning
215.1	It's true] Yes > It's true
219.12	flame] fire > flame
219.25	freezing] paralyzing > freezing
220.26	worked] wrought- > worked
221.34	both ways.] either way. > both ways.
223.9	primping up for] waxing my mustaches for > primping up for
223.30	some] a > some
224.28–29	her immense and unbreakable courage] all the invincible courage of her lifetime > her immense and unbreakable courage
224.30	beside] with > beside
225.3	far] much > far
225.5	in relief] in relief > as if in denial of its gravity ("in relief" is chosen since the original phrase is bracketed for deletion.)
225.6	volubly] interestedly > volubly

225.7	small] weak > small
225.25	enslavements] deceptions > enslavements
228.31–32	face terrible in love and grief,] face terrible in love and grief, > face loving, grieving (The interlinear choice selected by the editor had “face” added later to the rest of the phrase in the left margin, is thus extended into the margin, and is perhaps Agee’s choice. It does seem a better match for his prose in the sentence. McDowell concurs in this choice.)
240.9	came to imagine] imagined > came to imagine
242.14–15	I knew you’d want to be sure just how it was.] of course I wondered the same thing. > I knew you’d want to be sure just how it was.
242.27	Hugh] Tom > Hugh (Agee apparently toyed with changing Hugh’s name to Tom. Hugh appears as “Tom” in several places in the manuscript for the novel. See, for example, note 240.37 for chapter 29 in the “Textual Commentary and Notes.”)
245.34	joke] excuse > joke (Agee marks the inclusion of excuse with a caret, but it makes no sense unless he planned to write “poor excuse for a joke” as his phrase. However, “for a” is not present to complete the insertion.)
246.4	began to dart] became lambent > began to dart
246.5	to become] became > to become
246.9	mouth] cheek > mouth
246.13	thing] soul > thing
247.6	That trumpet’s] That trumpet’s > It’s (“That trumpet’s” is used by the editor for the sake of clarity.)
248.30	fates] fates > fates (Agee likely rewrote the same word more legibly above his original, but it is possible that the original word is different.)
256.7	is not] isn’t > is not
271.1	early] soon > early
272.14–15	which had been so strong about the dead body] which had radiated so strongly from the dead body (This alternative was written in the left margin by Agee, rather than interlinearly.) > which had been so strong about the dead body
285.17	strange] odd > strange
285.35	crookedly across] jaggedly down > crookedly across (McDowell uses “jaggedly down” in his edition.)
285.35	crooked] jagged > crooked (McDowell uses “jagged” in his edition.)
286.18	violent] strong > violent
287.19	ized] ized > ed (Agee writes “ized” over the “ed” of “deputed”; “deputized” is chosen as a word more appropriate for Rufus. McDowell makes the same choice.)
289.19	sharply] sharply > suddenly (“sharply” is chosen for the text because it seems a better match for Jessie’s subsequent wondering if Emma was “trying to be a smart-aleck.”)

290.5 Her mother] Her mother > She ("Her mother" is chosen for clarity.)

291.17 dim] vague > dim

292.23 fell] fell > rolled ("fell" is chosen as a better match for the subsequent explanation that the auto then "turned over" and the repetition of the event in the text at 293.25.)

296.4 any] his > any

299.11 unhappily] unluckily > unhappily

304.3 reverberations] challengings > reverberations

306.23 furious eyes] freezing glare > furious eyes

307.10 malevolence] malevolence > contempt ("malevolence" may also have been meant by Agee to replace "helpless contempt"; "helpless malevolence" is chosen as a likelier representation of Rufus' frustrations at this point in the scene. McDowell concurs.)

307.22 The others] They > the others

314.30 and] so that > and (This is the "and" that precedes "God" in the sentence.)

319.28 left] left > right ("left" is chosen by the editor since the nails of his "right" hand have already been examined. McDowell omits this sentence.)

329.26 home] house > home

330.6 walk] walk > go ("walk" is chosen to avoid repetition with the use of "go" on 434.3.)

339.32 glazing] glazing > glittering ("glazing" is chosen as more appropriate to the rest of the description and because Agee has crossed out the word "on", which follows "glittering" in the original text. He likely forgot to cross out "glittering" in the process of providing an alternative description. McDowell makes this choice as well.)

340.22 disconsolately] disconsolately > heavily ("disconsolately" is chosen to eliminate the repetition with "heavy" in the next phrase. McDowell makes this choice as well.)

341.3 weak, complaining] weak complaining > insecure ("weak complaining" is chosen as a less ambiguous description. McDowell makes this choice as well.)

345.33 think best] think best > like ("think best" is chosen because Agee draws a line from "like" to "think best" and because it seems a more appropriate phrasing for the comment. McDowell makes this choice as well.)

347.1 deceived] deluded > deceived

347.3 crying] weeping > crying

347.11–13 Hearing . . . rocking.] Hearing . . . rocking. > She stopped rocking, less because she felt that the noise was wrong, than because she felt that she did not want to be heard. ("Hearing . . . rocking." is chosen as a slightly less complicated sentence that better fits Emma's thoughts. The choice also places "noises" in closer proximity to "squeaked" in the previous sentence and places her stoppage of "rocking" in closer proximity to the description of her position in the chair after she does so in the following sentence. McDowell chooses the other alternative for his text.)

347.24 straight] tiredly > straight

Paragraphing

Paragraph breaks for changes in dialog, speaker, and occasionally for clarity have been added to Agee's manuscript at the following locations and are cited by page(s) and line number(s) below.

4.12
5.30
6.17
7.35
8.22
9.28
34.16
51.29–53.1
54.5
55.3
56.24
57.15
67.11
67.12
69.2
69.9–21
69.27–71.31
72.11
73.9–74.1
74.22
74.30
75.13–80.7
80.10–26
81.6
84.17
84.19
85.25
85.33–37
86.27–35
87.22–37
91.16
92.5
92.27
94.17
95.34
98.14
99.16
101.1
101.14
102.26
112.17–113.32
113.36–121.21
121.33–122.35
123.14–124.17
124.27–126.20
127.26
128.14–21
129.1–10
129.16–131.13
131.19–132.6
132.29–134.31
135.13–19
136.9–138.22
138.25–139.20
142.10–144.3
149.4
176.18
177.12
177.24
196.19–197.21
198.12–30
201.1–202.11
227.13
229.12–20
230.27
231.19–26
232.18
232.20
232.34
232.35
233.5
234.38
237.27
240.26–31
242.11
243.2
243.15–244.6
245.7–247.4
248.19
248.21
252.30–32
252.37–253.6
255.26
255.31
267.30
273.10
284.21–288.2

289.13–291.3
293.3
296.7
300.7–23
301.7–302.21
302.29–31
303.15–18
304.5
305.21–306.8
306.26–307.5
313.25–28
316.34
317.9
318.37
320.3
322.8
324.11
330.28
331.5
332.22
333.19
344.17
350.31–351.3
353.7
353.29
353.31
355.2

Appendix I

How to Read the Corrected McDowell Edition of *A Death in the Family* from This Text and a Chart of Substantive Corrections to the Library of America Edition of *A Death in the Family*

While the present text demonstrates the significant omissions from and alterations of Agee's intended text for *A Death in the Family* through the editing of David McDowell, it is also designed to allow the reader to read a corrected version of McDowell's Pulitzer Prize–winning rendering of Agee's novel for the purpose of comparison.

This appendix provides two ways in which to read McDowell's version. Method one, by far the more accurate way to reconstruct McDowell's edition from the present restored text, uses the chart and list below. The chart gives McDowell's section and chapter titles in their original order and follows these titles with the appropriate instructions to direct the reader to the corrected equivalent in the restored text and any other necessary information. Below the chart is a list of the proper names that McDowell changed in his editing of Agee's manuscript since so many of the "characters" were still alive at the time of the novel's publication. In the original manuscript, at least for his family, Agee used real names. Be sure also to examine the information available in the "Textual Commentary and Notes," "Major Manuscript Variants," "Marginal Notes," "Word Choice Where No Preference Is Indicated," and "Paragraphing" sections of this edition and its appendix II ("A Structural Comparison of the Restored and the McDowell Editions").

This accurate but cumbersome method reorders the necessary parts of the restored edition to McDowell's chosen structure and corrects any inadvertent errors, usually misreadings of Agee's handwriting, and omissions of words, phrases and sentences, and the like, to provide a text that supersedes all other corrected or emended texts, such as that of the Library of America (2005).

Method two provides a list of substantive corrections to the Library of America edition. That work provides the best extant text of the McDowell edition that one can read without the need to flip back and forth between sections of the restored novel. However, its list of emendations (pp. 811–15) is incomplete and further correction is needed. Therefore, the final part of this appendix is a list entitled "Substantive Corrections to the Library of America Edition of *A Death in the Family.*" It contains more than 275 additional corrections and creates an acceptable reader's text of the novel.

Nonetheless, using the Library of America edition in conjunction with this list does not replicate the accuracy of reconstructing McDowell's text using method one. In general, the list does not record any standardization of spelling, capitalization, paragraphing, quotation, and other punctuation unless used by Agee for matters such as speech patterns, dialect, or emphasis. It also does not record necessary corrections of Agee's or McDowell's errors that would normally be corrected in copyediting. Additional significant differences between the texts that result from using method two that will not be reconciled stem mainly from issues covered in the "Word Choice Where No Preference Is Indicated" section of the present edition, since McDowell simply chose the version of Agee's text—whether word, phrase, or sentence—that he preferred, whereas this restored edition follows a stated methodology and records each choice. Additional differences result from the inclusion of material bracketed for deletion. In several instances in Agee's manuscripts it cannot be ascertained if the brackets indicating deletion were made by Agee or McDowell. McDowell is inconsistent as to inclusion or deletion of the bracketed material, whereas the present edition restores some of these passages and gives the rationale for so doing in the textual notes.

Method One

Corrected McDowell Text	Instructions for Its Reconstruction from This Edition
Knoxville: Summer 1915	Read appendix III, "Knoxville: Summer of 1915" (McDowell italicizes this section.)
Part I	
Chapter 1	Read *Chapter 17*
Chapter 2	Read *Chapter 18, 19,* and *20* as one chapter
Chapter 3	Read *Chapter 21*
Chapter 4	Read *Chapter 22*
Chapter 5	Read *Chapter 25*

Chapter 6	Read *Chapter 24*
Chapter 7	Read *Chapter 26*
[Chapter 7.1]	Read the McDowell variant texts in "Major Manuscript Variants" for *Chapters 1, 2,* and *3* as one chapter (McDowell italicizes this section and presents it as the first of three flashback chapters that are unnumbered.)
[Chapter 7.2]	Read *Chapter 4* (McDowell italicizes this section and presents it as the second of three flashback chapters that are unnumbered.)
[Chapter 7.3]	Read *Chapter 7* (McDowell italicizes this section and presents it as the third of three flashback chapters that are unnumbered.)

Part II

Chapter 8	Read *Chapter 27* and the first part of *Chapter 29* (225.2–227.31) as one chapter
Chapter 9	Read *Chapter 28*
Chapter 10	Read the remaining part of *Chapter 29* (227.32 to conclusion)
Chapter 11	Read *Chapter 30*
Chapter 12	Read *Chapters 31* and *32* as one chapter
Chapter 13	Read *Chapters 33* and *34* as one chapter
[Chapter 13.1]	Read *Chapter 6* (McDowell italicizes this section and presents it as the first of three flashback chapters that are unnumbered.)
[Chapter 13.2]	Read the McDowell variant text in "Major Manuscript Variants" of *Chapter 15* (TX 5.3, [131–35, 140–41]) (McDowell italicizes this section and presents it as the second of three flashback chapters that are unnumbered.)
[Chapter 13.3]	Read *Chapter 12* (McDowell italicizes this section and presents it as the third of three flashback chapters that are unnumbered.)

Part III

Chapter 14	Read *Chapter 35*
Chapter 15	Read *Chapter 36*
Chapter 16	Read *Chapter 37* but alter its conclusion as per note 308.38 in "Textual Commentary and Notes"
Chapter 17	Read *Chapter 38*
Chapter 18	Read *Chapters 39, 41,* and *40* as one chapter
Chapter 19	Read *Chapters 42* and *43* as one chapter
Chapter 20	Read *Chapter 44* (replacing the prayers on 350.5–25 with those listed in the "Major Manuscript Variants" section of *Chapter 44*) and *Chapter 45* as one chapter

Changes of Names

Main Characters

Agee's Manuscript	McDowell's Change
Jay/Jim Agee	Jay Follet
Laura Agee	Mary Follet
Rufus Agee	Rufus Follet
Emma Agee	Catherine Follet
Jessie Tyler	Hannah Lynch
Hugh Tyler	Andrew Lynch
Joel Tyler	Joel Lynch
Emma Tyler	Catherine Lynch
Paula Tyler	Amelia Lynch
Frank Agee	Ralph Follet
Walter Starr	Arthur Savage
Great Aunt Paralee	Great Aunt Sadie
Father Robertson	Father Jackson

Minor Characters

(names that are not changed in or are omitted from McDowell's edition are not cited; those who are given no last name are cited first)

Agee's Manuscript	McDowell's Change
Aunt Maussie (Moss)	Aunt Jessie (Jess)
Aunt Paralee (not the same as Great Aunt Paralee)	Aunt Sadie
Mary Elizabeth	Ettie Lou
Vesta Agee	Sally Follet
Albert Delfrench	Gordon Dekalb
Dr. Delfrench	Dr. Dekalb
Mrs. Delfrench	Mrs. Dekalb
Charley Hodges/Jim Hodges	George Bailey
Maussie Hodges	Jessie Bailey
Ben Goff	Dan Gunn
Bess Goff	Bess Gunn
Hazel Goff	Celia Gunn
Mrs. Goff	Mrs. Gunn
Clifford Glenn	Hubert Kane
Old Mr. Glenn	Old Mr. Kane
Mr. King	Mr. Drake

Miss Knapp	Miss Storrs
Marcia Perkins	Sarah Eldridge
Fanny Salmon	Nettie Field
Lizzie Salmon	Amy Field
Joe Wheeler	Jim-Wilson
Nell Wylie	Ann Taylor

Place

Jacksboro (or LaFollette)	LaFollette

Method Two

Substantive Corrections to the Library of America Edition of *A Death in the Family*

This method allows a reader to use the Library of America (LOA) edition and correct it using the following list. The corrections are noted below by citing the page and line number of the LOA edition. The line count does not include any page headers, printer's devices, chapter titles, or spaces. The text needing correction in the LOA text appears next, followed by a bracket and the necessary correction from the Agee manuscripts for the novel used by McDowell. If needed, further editorial comments on the correction follow in parentheses. Thus "478.20 gnawing] gnashing" indicates that on page 478, line 20 of the LOA edition, the reader should correct the word "gnawing" to "gnashing." Please see the headnote to this appendix for the description of the corrections that are not included in this list.

469 title	*Knoxville: Summer 1915*] *Knoxville: Summer of 1915* (Correction taken from the first appearance of this work in the *Partisan Review*, since no manuscript exists.)
470.38	*gentle*] *gently* (Correction taken from the first appearance of this work in the *Partisan Review*, since no manuscript exists.)
477.26	came in] came, on (Neither is correct. A likely correction is "came on in" and is used in the restored text.)
477.34	absorbed] striking and absorbed (This reading is conjectural. "striking" is indistinct and "and" may be part of the subsequent deletion of "of".)
478.20	gnawing] gnashing
479.10	these] these eyes
480.36	rattled] settled (LOA changes McDowell's correct reading.)
486.9	from thur] frm thur
487.6	exaggerate, and . . ."] exaggerate, do . . ." (LOA changes McDowell's correct reading.)
488.36	said.] said; (LOA changes McDowell's correct reading.)

491.12	and this always, for some reason, still] and always, for some reason, this still
492.28–29	children, unconsciously] children, and, unconsciously
499.37	(obedient] (smug, obedient, (The word "smug" is conjectural; McDowell simply omits it.)
502.8	blacked] blocked (The "o" of "blocked" is unclear, but "blocked" is a more logical reading because it continues the references to shape begun by "skeins" and because "blacked shadows" is redundant.)
514.34	of it] of its sadness
515.1	back and] back in and
515.10	you're a] you're just a
517.24	pains] pain
518.26–27	twice as good] twice the good
523.4	too.] to.
532.9	limp] limpid
533.11	windows] window
535.26	burned] purred
539.1	Gettin] Gettn
539.3	gettin] gettn
539.13	*here*] *how*
540.4	uh-hoooooo] uh-hooooooo
540.9	uh-hoooo] uh-hooooo
541.14	awaitin] awaitn
542.7	*Oh*] *Ohh*
542.18	*Oh*] *Ohh*
542.33	sound] sounds
543.8	*on*] *an*
543.17	*ever*] *even* (LOA changes McDowell's correct reading.)
547.17	would not] wouldn't
552.27	*some*] *same*
552.30	Godd—] God d—
553.29	*you,* would] *you.* Would
556.2	trying] trine
556.3	*em*] *um*
556.8	to em] toom
556.23	*em*] *um*
556.37	waitin] waitn
559.8	standing, she was all] standing, all
559.10	rang.] rang 1115.
559.18	shaking] shifting
561.7	Two, case] Two, in case
561.15	He is] He's
561.33	it would] it'd
562.34–35	the large lenses of his glasses, and] his large lenses, and

563.7	She could hear] And now, she could hear
563.8	and now] (Delete these words.)
564.14	harmonious, don't] harmonious. Don't
565.31	Zuzus] Zuzu's
566.13	soon.] soon now.
566.16	that is] that's
566.33	together, that's] together. That's
569.15	it is] it's
570.6–7	really liked him, or respected him] really liked or respected him
570.30	wasn't a *mistake*] *wasn't* a mistake
570.39	Least of all right now!] *Least* of all *right now!*
573.3	arms'] arm's
574.16	whispered, "strengthen] whispered. "Strengthen
576.11–12	if they were, if he were] *if* they were, *if* he were
576.17–18	conceivable, just] conceivable. Just
579.28–29	And she's trying to work magic by the opposite method. Act as if nothing much is wrong.] (Insert these two sentences as a short paragraph between lines 28 and 29. McDowell chooses to delete it.)
579.29–30	Good a way as mine. Worthless, both ways.] (Insert these two sentences as a short paragraph between lines 29 and 30. McDowell chooses to delete it.)
579.39–580.1	Oh. (paragraph break) "I don't] "Oh. I don't
580.35–36	marriage, making] marriage and brats and making
580.36	Goddamned] God damned
581.39	say that] say, which
582.19	take] took
582.26	she needs that] *she needs that*
582.27–28	I wish I could do more] *I wish I could do more*
584.14	Oh, don't hit me] *O, don't hit me*
584.17	aunt's feet] aunt a foot
585.21	were in labor] *were in labor*
586.3	throat,] throat.
586.28–31	thinking, if she gets drunk tonight, and if her mother sees her drunk, she'll half die of shame, and thinking, nonsense. It's the most sensible thing she could do.] thinking, *if she gets drunk tonight, and if her mother sees her drunk, she'll half die of shame,* and thinking, *nonsense. It's the most sensible thing she could do.*
587.34	it] out
590.33	God*damn* it] God *damn* it
591.8	what Cousin Patty] what Patty
592.20	there is] there's
592.21	she is] she's
592.28	*take* that] take *that*
594.7	the window sills] their sills

595.29	(bless his heart)] , bless his heart,
596.35	breath. There wasn't. After] breath. After (LOA changes McDowell's correct reading. "There wasn't." is bracketed for deletion in the manuscript.)
597.31	here,"] here?" (LOA changes McDowell's correct reading.)
599.10	hand] hands
602.27	an expectation] in expectation
603.33	spirits] Spirits
605.26–28	imbecile." (paragraph break) "Oh, Andrew," Mary burst out. (paragraph break) "The rest] imbecile"—"*Oh, Hugh!,*" Laura burst out—"the rest (McDowell renames "Hugh" as "Andrew" and "Laura" as "Mary" throughout the novel. The correction noted deals with the emphasis placed on what Mary/Laura says.)
605.31	of feeble-mindedness] or feeble-mindedness
607.18–19	death, you *own* it, you] death. You *own* it. You
608.15	it was his father] it was his *father*
609.15	supposed] *supposed*
610.1–2	we? When the—what day he'll—be—] we. When the—what day he'll, h—
611.10–11	Ralph Follet, Ralph, Follet, F, O, L, L, E, T, no, Central, F, as in father—F, O,—have you got that?—L, L, ET. FOLLET.] Frank Agee, Frank, Agee, A, g, e, e, no Central not H. A. The first letter in the—A, g, Have you got that, e, e. Agee. (While McDowell's renaming is consistent and would not normally be noted as a correction, his doing so in this instance eliminates Agee's re-creation of regional dialect as the telephone operator misspells "Agee" back to the speaker because what she has heard sounds like "Hay-gee.")
612.12	Andrew] *Hugh* (Correction is listed because of the change in emphasis.)
614.17	"Why, Andrew] "Why *Hugh* (Correction is listed because of the change in emphasis.)
614.38–39	heart."] heart!
615.23	being,] being.
616.25	room."] room. (LOA changes McDowell's correct reading.)
618.16	'it'] '*it*'
618.40	That] Most
619.15	most] worst
619.17	say] any
621.9–10	good-bye." And] goodbye"; and
621.22	once calm] once a calm
621.34	said,] said: (LOA changes McDowell's correct reading.)
622.8	soul] Soul
622.36	*an*xious] anxious
623.18	business, God] business. God
624.27–28	all, much . . . intended, so that] all, so much . . . intended, that

625.16 as he had first seen him that night.] as he had just seen him.
625.17 first] just
626.11 wheemed] whelmed
626.19 hand] hands
627.1 tonight] the night
627.4 I know] I just know
627.31–32 if—it] if, if it (The inclusion of the second "if" by the present editor, although bracketed in the manuscript, seems better to support Agee's style. These brackets may be a previous editor's and not Agee's, since two subsequent bracketed lines on this page are marked marginally with question marks that are not in Agee's hand. McDowell does not include the second "if" but does include both lines marked with question marks.)
628.14 loud] hard
628.23 "Well if] "Well *if*
630.6 He] Joel (This change is necessary since the sentence immediately preceding this one was deleted by Agee and began with "Joel"; "He" was meant to refer to Joel, but after the deletion would mistakenly refer to Andrew, as the subsequent text makes clear.)
634.3–4 God, years. Seven—] God. Years. Seve—
634.4–5 Shelley, watching] Shelley. Watching
634.27 the everlasting light] The Everlasting Light
634.33 light] Light
636.9 outside it, rest] outside it or defiant of it, rest
637.22 ears] ear
637.25 amiss O Lord] amiss: Lord
639.17–18 others of the groups] others of other groups
640.3 say, "Hello,"] say hello,
641.26 heart and body] heart n body
641.38–39 Maybe . . . *them.*] "Maybe . . . *them.*"
642.5 *soul*] *one*
642.15 nigger's] Nigger's
642.23 word, "nigger,"] word "Nigger"
643.9 said, "Hello, there,"] said hello there
643.23 was led] wanted
643.35 nigger's] Nigger's
643.36–37 turned to him sharply and said to him in] turned on him sharply and said in
644.1 that is] that's
644.5–6 *'nigger'.*" (paragraph break) *But*] *Nigger!*" *But*
644.13 ning-ger] niiig-ger
644.14 ning-ger] niii-ger
644.23 he knew they knew] he honestly knew
644.32 pretending] or pretending

645.7	that;] this;
645.16–17	question. They] question, they
645.22	the rent] The Rent
645.27	the rent] The Rent
645.32	the rent] the Rent
645.37	the rent] The Rent
646.13	go round] surround
646.32	would] could
647.20	where did] where'd
647.29	ignorant] ignernt
650.16	*pecked*] *packed* (The letter "a" is indistinct but likely, since Agee commonly refers to dirt yards as "packed" elsewhere in the manuscript.)
651.2	Lou with] Lou in with
651.17	"Got to] "Gotta
651.19	*ever*] *even*
651.21	"Oh mercy] "O Mercy
651.22	"We are just] "I'm just
651.37–38	till you see your] till your
652.8	it was . . . years since] it's been . . . year sin'ct
653.7	here, that] here. That
653.8	most] no it
653.15	*you* mean *that*] *you really* mean *that*
653.20	*seen*] seen
653.22	*terrible*] terrible
653.24	*em*] *um*
653.39	said, "that's] said. "That's
654.18	landmarks] a landmark
654.22	*round*] *roun*
654.40	*said*] *cried*
654.40	that is] thatn'z
655.6	closed] cloven
655.40	Granma] Granmaw
656.15	Ayy] Myy
656.22	Mary or no Mary] lame or no lame
656.24	Fifth generation] Fift gineration
656.25	*you*] *ye*
656.36	be . . .] b—
657.2	Panama] Panamaw
657.37	company] compny
657.39	*ever*] *even*
659.8	*I am*] *I'm*
659.33–34	color: seen close as this, there was color through a dot] color: Seen close as this, there was color through the blind gray shining: a dot
659.40	red-bronze] red-brown

660.2	ancestor's] uncertain
661.19	brand-new] bran new
662.4	afterwhile] after while
662.7	afterwhile] after while
662.19	*hill*] *hills*
662.22	these] those
664.9	"*Ted!*"] "*Ted Henwrich!*" (In its two occurrences, here and 664.22, the spelling of this surname is questionable. Only "H. . . . rich" seems recoverable after comparing both examples. McDowell simply omits the name (McD 245.10, 23), but that wrongly reduces Mary's/Laura's motherly anger.)
664.22	*Ted.*] *Ted Henwrich.* (See 664.9 above.)
665.6	something. Not] something, not
666.8	pride, he put] pride, put
667.2	"little Catherine,"] "little" Emma, (Correction is listed because of the change in emphasis.)
667.8	twiggy gray braids] gray twiggy braids (LOA changes McDowell's correct reading.)
667.19	this inexplicable betrayal] this betrayal ("inexplicable" is bracketed for deletion.)
669.8	hard] *hard*
669.11	eyes, "You will"; then] eyes, "*you will*"; Then
670.15	of dressing] of the dressing
670.18	her, as] her, again as
671.5–6	it was so still and it seemed dark] it was so still and it was so still it seemed dark
671.33	feel like] feel proud like
672.7	cried, and] cried, and maybe that was why, and (The additional words are encircled by an editor, but not marked for deletion.)
672.10	time she] time these noises meant, you be quiet, and every time she (The additional words are encircled by an editor, but not marked for deletion.)
672.28	around and she] around and wave and she
672.28	right here] here right
673.9	father. Whatever] father," she said. "Whatever
673.38	that, just] that, it's just
674.16	could] *could*
675.4	saw] said
675.29	asked Rufus.] Rufus asked.
676.22	ever] even
677.2	happens] happened
677.3	Instantly] Instintly
678.13	was already] is already
678.35–36	washing dishes] washing the dishes

680.10	then] there
681.28	it, you] it? You
682.32	and be] and to be
682.34	by them] by any of them
682.37	that] which
682.38	town, and] town, and that something had happened to his father which had not happened to the father of any other boy in town, and
684.34	group. Thinking] group. So that was what *instantly* meant. Right off like that. He had thought it meant not feeling anything. Thinking
686.8–9	was not a mark] wasn't another mark
686.28	Goddamn] God damn
689.10	down even harder] down harder
689.13	you busted] you even busted
689.21–22	"You don't] "*You* don't
690.3–4	listening?" she sputtered.] listening?" She squatted.
691.8	Goddamn] god damn
691.11	bibblibblebble] bibblibblebbble
691.12	Goddam] God damn
691.22	that] *that*
694.1	Church] Clinch
695.21	caught] took
698.17	her more] her much more
698.22–27	(See the note on page 814 of the LOA edition. At his point in the manuscript, three lines of narrative are marked for deletion by Agee by his bracketing them in the paragraph. LOA includes the material, even though McDowell does not. However, other evidence indicates that the brackets are Agee's. Another bracketing of the three lines in the left margin of the manuscript emphasizes the selection of these lines, Agee has written the word "*earlier*" just to the left of that bracket, and does, in fact, treat some of this material earlier in the chapter.)
698.28	orphans] orphan
700.32	hat in] hat gliding in
701.8–9	him. But] him. Father Robertson, tilting his head, examined, frowning, the nails of his long, heavily veined left hand. But (McDowell changes "Robertson" to "Jackson.")
703.16	voices: their] voices. Their
704.3	as rapidly] as if rapidly
704.27	had broken] and broken
704.40	now] soon
705.14	would approve] would entirely approve
707.12	didn't] did not
708.33	Gra*mm*-muh-phone] Gra*mm*-mhuh-phone
709.3	learn a little] learn, little
709.27	Catherine] Emmer (Agee's dialect rendering of his sister's name is made unfeasible by McDowell's changing of her name.)

709.40	schooling. Scarcely] schooling, scarcely
710.12	knew] could have dreamed
713.10	unsteadily] crookedly
713.26	head, his arms] hand, his arm
717.7	shuddering] shouldering
718.4	bread. And] bread and
718.4	trespasses, As] trespasses as
718.12	upward. The] upward: the
718.17	bring. That] bring. Grant that
718.31	were streaked and angry, reddish yellow] were a streaked and angry reddish yellow
718.34–35	God, and of his Son Jesus Christ our Lord": His] God." His
719.22	on] in
720.12	only see] see only
720.17	But though] But through
721.11	look over once] look once
722.1	near with Mr. Starr, Rufus] near Rufus
722.7	the house] his grandfather's house
722.15	multitudinous vitality] multitudinous and incomprehensible vitality
722.24	edge] edges
723.16	minute] moment
724.2	they had entered] they entered
724.13	permeated] perverted
734.19	primly] firmly
735.39	now] aware
736.7	giant] great
736.25	if] *if*
736.34	swear] sneer
737.5	even wanted] ever wanted
738.5	briers] briars
814.15	(For 688.16, read 688.23.)

Appendix II

A Structural Comparison of the Restored and the McDowell Editions

Restored Edition	McDowell Edition
Introduction	Deleted
Chapter 1	Earlier draft version used as first part of italicized flash-back [7.1]
Chapter 2	Earlier draft version used as second part of italicized flashback [7.1]
Chapter 3	Earlier draft version used as third part of italicized flashback [7.1]
Chapter 4	Used as italicized flashback [7.2]
Chapter 5	Deleted
Chapter 6	Used as italicized flashback [13.1]
Chapter 7	Used as italicized flashback [7.3]
Chapter 8	Deleted
Chapter 9	Deleted
Chapter 10	Deleted
Chapter 11	Deleted
Chapter 12	Used as italicized flashback [13.3]
Chapter 13	Deleted
Chapter 14	Deleted
Chapter 15	Used as italicized flashback [13.2], but McDowell deletes the middle third of the chapter (see 127.1 in "Textual Commentary and Notes" and see also "Major Manuscript Variants" for this chapter)
Chapter 16	Deleted
Chapter 17	Chapter 1
Chapter 18	Used as first part of Chapter 2

Chapter 19	Used as second part of Chapter 2
Chapter 20	Used as third part of Chapter 2
Chapter 21	Chapter 3
Chapter 22	Chapter 4
Chapter 23	Deleted
Chapter 24	Chapter 6
Chapter 25	Chapter 5
Chapter 26	Chapter 7
Chapter 27	Used as the first part *of* Chapter 8
Chapter 28	Chapter 9
Chapter 29	The first part (225.2–227.31) is used to conclude Chapter 8; the remainder of the chapter forms Chapter 10
Chapter 30	Chapter 11
Chapter 31	Used as the first part of Chapter 12
Chapter 32	Used as the second part of Chapter 12
Chapter 33	Used as the first part of Chapter 13
Chapter 34	Used as the second part of Chapter 13
Chapter 35	Chapter 14
Chapter 36	Chapter 15
Chapter 37	Chapter 16, but McDowell alters the conclusion by substituting from an earlier draft version of the chapter (see 308.38 in "Textual Commentary and Notes")
Chapter 38	Chapter 17
Chapter 39	Used as the first part of Chapter 18
Chapter 40	Used as the third part of Chapter 18
Chapter 41	Used as the second part of Chapter 18
Chapter 42	Used as the first part of Chapter 19
Chapter 43	Used as the second part of Chapter 19
Chapter 44	Used as the first part of Chapter 20, but McDowell never corrects the prayers mistakenly submitted to him by Father Flye (see "Major Manuscript Variants" for this chapter and 350.5–25 in "Textual Commentary and Notes")
Chapter 45	Used as the second part of Chapter 20

Appendix III

"Knoxville: Summer of 1915"

David McDowell prints "Knoxville: Summer of 1915" in italics as a prologue to his edition of James Agee's *A Death in the Family* with the following rationale in his "A Note on this Book": "It was not part of the manuscript which Agee left, but the editors would certainly have urged him to include it in the final draft." Given this statement and that no reference to the piece or its possible inclusion occurs in Agee's manuscripts, notes, and correspondence regarding the novel, it is therefore not included in the text proper of the present edition. (See also the preface to the present volume and the explanation for the restoration of Agee's actual introduction to the novel in "Textual Commentary and Notes.") It is recorded below to facilitate the reading of the corrected McDowell edition (see appendix I) for those who wish to compare the two editions. The text is from the first printing of the work in the *Partisan Review* V (August–September 1938, 22–25). No manuscript or typescript for the work apparently survives.

Knoxville: Summer of 1915

We are talking now of summer evenings in Knoxville Tennessee in the time that I lived there so successfully disguised to myself as a child. It was a little bit mixed sort of block, fairly solidly lower middle class, with one or two juts apiece on either side of that. The houses corresponded: middlesized gracefully fretted wood houses built in the late nineties and early nineteen hundreds, with small front and side and more spacious back yards, and trees in the yards, and porches. These were softwooded trees, poplars, tulip trees, cottonwoods. There were fences around one or two of the houses, but mainly the yards ran into each other with only now and then a low hedge that wasn't doing very well. There were few good friends among the grown people, and they were not poor enough for the other sort of intimate acquaintance, but everyone nodded and spoke, and even might talk short times, trivially, and at the two extremes of the general or the particular, and ordinarily nextdoor neighbors talked quite a bit when they happened to run into each other, and never paid calls. The men were mostly small businessmen, one or two very modestly executives, one or two worked with their hands, most of them clerical, and most of them between thirty and fortyfive.

But it is of these evenings, I speak.

Supper was at six and was over by half past. There was still daylight, shining softly and with a tarnish, like the lining of a shell; and the carbon lamps lifted at the corners were on in the light, and the locusts were started, and the fire flies were out, and a few frogs were flopping in the dewy grass, by the time the fathers and the children came out. The children ran out first hell bent and yelling those names by which they were known; then the fathers sank out leisurely in crossed suspenders, their collars removed and their necks looking tall and shy. The mothers stayed back in the kitchen washing and drying, putting things away, recrossing their traceless footsteps like the lifetime journeys of bees, measuring out the dry cocoa for breakfast. When they came out they had taken off their aprons and their skirts were dampened and they sat in rockers on their porches quietly.

It is not of the games children play in the evening that I want to speak now, it is of a contemporaneous atmosphere that has little to do with them: that of the fathers of families, each in his space of lawn, his shirt fishlike pale in the unnatural light and his face nearly anonymous, hosing their lawns. The hoses were attached at spiggots that stood out of the brick foundations of the houses. The nozzles were variously set but usually so there was a long sweet stream of spray, the nozzle wet in the hand, the water trickling the right forearm and the peeled-back cuff, and the water whishing out a long loose and low-curved cone, and so gentle a sound. First an insane noise of violence in the nozzle, then the still irregular sound of adjustment, then the smoothing into steadiness and a pitch as accurately tuned to the size and style of stream as any violin. So many qualities of sound out of one hose: so many choral differences out of those several hoses that were in earshot. Out of any one hose, the almost dead silence of the release, and the short still arch of the separate big drops, silent as a held breath, and the only noise the flattering noise on leaves and the slapped grass at the fall of each big drop. That, and the intense hiss with the intense stream; that, and that same intensity not growing less but growing more quiet and delicate with the turn of the nozzle, up to that extreme tender whisper when the water was just a wide bell of film. Chiefly, though, the hoses were set much alike, in a compromise between distance and tenderness of spray, (and quite surely a sense of art behind this compromise, and a quiet, deep joy, too real to recognize itself), and the sounds therefore were pitched much alike; pointed by the snorting start of a new hose; decorated by some man playful with the nozzle; left empty, like God by the sparrow's fall, when any single one of them desists: and all, though near alike, of various pitch; and in this unison. These sweet pale streamings in the light lift out their pallors and their voices all together, mothers hushing their children, the hushing unnaturally prolonged, the men gentle and silent and each snail-like withdrawn into the quietude of what he singly is doing, the urination of huge children stood loosely military against an invisible wall, and gently happy and peaceful, tasting the mean goodness of their living like the last of their suppers in their mouths; while the locusts carry on this noise of hoses on their much higher and sharper key. The noise of the locust is dry, and it seems not to be rasped or vibrated but urged from him as if through a small orifice by a breath that can never give out. Also there is never one locust but an illusion of at least a thousand. The noise of each locust is pitched in some classic locust range out of which none of them varies more than two full tones: and yet you seem to hear each locust discrete from all the rest, and there is a long, slow, pulse in their noise, like the scarcely defined arch of a long and high set bridge. They are all around in every tree, so that the noise seems to come from nowhere and everywhere at once, from the whole shell heaven, shivering in your flesh and teasing your eardrums, the boldest of all the sounds of night. And yet it is habitual to summer nights, and is of the great order of noises, like the noises of the sea and of the blood her precocious grandchild, which you realize you are hearing only when you catch yourself listening. Meantime from low in the dark, just outside the swaying horizons of the hoses, conveying always grass in the damp of dew and its strong green-black smear of smell, the regular yet spaced noises of the crickets, each a sweet cold silver noise threenoted, like the slipping each time of three matched links of a small chain.

But the men by now, one by one, have silenced their hoses and drained and coiled them. Now only two, and now only one, is left, and you see only ghostlike shirt with the sleeve garters, and sober mystery of his mild face like the lifted face of large cattle enquiring of your presence in a pitchdark pool of meadow; and now he too is gone; and it has become that time of evening when people sit on their porches, rocking gently and talking gently and watching the street and the standing up into their sphere of possession of the trees, of birds hung havens, hangars. People go by; things go by. A horse, drawing a buggy, breaking his hollow iron music on the asphalt: a loud auto: a quiet auto: people in pairs, not in a hurry, scuffling, switching their weight of aestival body, talking casually, the taste hovering over them of vanilla, strawberry, pasteboard and starched milk, the image upon them of lovers and horsemen, squared with clowns in hueless amber. A street car raising its iron moan; stopping; belling and starting, stertorous; rousing and raising again its iron increasing moan and swimming its gold windows and straw seats on past and past and past, the bleak spark crackling and cursing above it like a small malignant spirit set to dog its tracks; the iron whine rises on rising speed; still risen, faints; halts; the faint stinging bell; rises again, still fainter; fainting, lifting, lifts, faints forgone: forgotten. Now is the night one blue dew.

Now is the night one blue dew, my father has drained, he has coiled the hose.
Low on the length of lawns, a frailing of fire who breathes.
Content, silver, like peeps of light, each cricket makes his comment over and over in the drowned grass.
A cold toad thumpily flounders.
Within the edges of damp shadows of side yards are hovering children nearly sick with joy of fear, who watch the unguarding of a telephone pole.
Around white carbon corner lamps bugs of all sizes are lifted elliptic, solar systems. Big hardshells bruise themselves, assailant: he is fallen on his back, legs squiggling.
Parents on porches: rock and rock. From damp strings morning glories: hang their ancient faces.
The dry and exalted noise of the locusts from all the air at once enchants my eardrums.

On the rough wet grass of the back yard my father and mother have spread quilts. We all lie there, my mother, my father, my uncle, my aunt, and I too am lying there. First we were sitting up, then one of us lay down, and then we all lay down, on our stomachs, on our sides, or on our backs, and they have kept on talking. They are not talking much, and the talk is quiet, of nothing in particular, of nothing at all in particular, of nothing at all. The stars are wide and alive, they seem each like a smile of great sweetness, and they seem very near. All my people are larger bodies than mine, quiet, with voices gentle and meaningless like the voices of sleeping birds. One is an artist, he is living at home. One is a musician, she is living at home. One is my mother who is good to me. One is my father who is good to me. By some chance, here they are, all on this earth; and who shall ever tell the sorrow of being on this earth, lying, on quilts, on the grass, in a summer evening, among the sounds of the night. May God bless my people, my uncle, my aunt, my mother, my good father, oh, remember them kindly in their time of trouble; and in the hour of their taking away.

After a little I am taken in and put to bed. Sleep, soft smiling, draws me unto her: and those receive me, who quietly treat me, as one familiar and well-beloved in that home: but will not, oh, will not, not now, not ever; but will not ever tell me who I am.

(Note: For background information, see Ronald R. Allen's "Knoxville, Tennessee, Summer 1915–Spring 1916 . . . ," Special Collections, University of Tennessee Library.)

Appendix IV

Agee's Memory of His Father's Accident and the Day Before

While the autobiographical nature of *A Death in the Family* is obvious, Agee was clearly concerned with the accuracy of his memories and how they could be integrated successfully into a creative work. He provides his own introduction to his memories below in TN 1A.19, [4.4–6].

[4.4, on back of page]

In most novels, properly enough, remembrance serves invention. In this volume, invention has served remembrance.

[4.4]

Although my remembrance of the matters which will be told of in the following pages is fragmentary, I have thought it best to invent nothing; I have not even asked the help of others, who were part of the same experience.

* * *

Late that night, about two-thirty, my uncle Frank telephoned my father from LaFollete. His father had had a heart attack. He was, Frank said, expected to live no longer than a few hours.

My father dressed quietly in order not to wake me and my sister. I imagine that my mother got into a bathrobe and fixed him some coffee, and probably a breakfast. No doubt he ate it quickly and they said very little. My father thought it likely that Frank was exaggerating—he sounded drunk, he told my mother; but of course it was just possible that his father was as sick as Frank said he was. On that chance, my father preferred not to risk sleeping out the night, annoyed as he was at Frank in advance, on the strong probability that the trip was unnecessary.

Doubtless he tried to be particularly quiet in getting the car out, and doubtless he failed, for those were noisy machines. However noisy this leave taking was, however, it did not wake either me or my sister.

We just realized that he had gone when we woke in the morning. Our mother told us why, and that he was not seriously worried, and thought most likely he would be back in time to see us before we went to sleep. We were interested and concerned about our grandfather, but soon this faded, for our mother, like our father, felt it was unlikely that this was a fatal attack.

That afternoon one of the nicest things happened to me that had ever yet happened in my life. I was taken downtown by my Aunt Jessie on one of her shopping trips, and she bought me a cap.

I had very particularly wanted a cap for a long time. Many boys of my age or size wore them; so did some boys who were smaller than me; all the big boys did: I wore little hats. These little hats I had recognized for quite some time as the badge of babyhood: worse. If I wore a hat at my age and size I was not only a baby, I was a sissy as well. Merely to wear a cap, I felt, would be more than enough to change all that.

But my mother kept saying there would be time enough for that, and to spare, later on, too soon, for that matter, and I had long ago so thoroughly given up hope that I had even stopped wishing for it.

And now that I was downtown with my Aunt Jessie, and she had done her shopping, she turned to me quite casually and said: "And now why don't I get you a cap. Would you like that?" And she even left me considerable liberty in picking out the cap I like best.

I can't be sure I remember rightly, but I think I chose so recklessly, something loud with an enormous visor, that she felt she really had to set a limit, so that what I got was a compromise. If it was a compromise, that made no difference to me. I was all but daft with joy and gratitude—and with anticipation.

For the moment I realized that I actually had a cap, the cap itself became secondary. The thing I wanted, above everything in the world, was to show it to my father, to have him see me in it, if possible, to surprise him with it.

I am pretty sure I remember correctly that much as I loved the cap, I did not even

[4.5]

want to wear it home. I wanted to wear it, for the first time, when he could see me with it. Very likely when he got home, I told my mother about it, with great pleasure, and very likely I tried it on for her, and very likely she said and honestly felt nice things about it, and was touched by my extraordinary pleasure. Quite possibly she realized, as she hadn't before, how much it really meant to me. I don't know. I have no memory of any of this. It can't have meant much to me, one way or the other. What I do remember is the intensity of excitement and joy in which I waited for my father to come home; the kind of all but unbearable excitement that a child feels who is well hidden, in a game of hide-and-seek, and sees the hunter so close he can touch him, still unaware of him. I had the cap by me, ready as a cocked pistol, ready to put it on and rush out to him the instant I heard the car coming.

This kept up all through supper, though we had supper a little late (he had told her not to wait supper), and became more intense with every minute up to our bedtime. We were allowed to stay up a little late, for mother thought it likely that he'd try to get home before we were asleep and if he was a little late, it seemed a shame to wake us—not worth it, for that matter. But finally we were told that we must go on to bed and straight to sleep, and after a great deal of protesting, we knew we were beaten. Would she wake us when he came? If it was not too late. What would too late be? Well she wouldn't say, that would be up to her, but too late would be simply too late. After all, there's *tomorrow,* Rufus, and you can show him your cap first thing in the morning.

So we went to bed, determined to stay awake until he came, and restive with the promise that if he didn't come too late, we would see him. But try as we did to stay awake, we fell asleep—early enough, that we did not hear the phone call which came at about eleven.

* * *

I cannot even remember who it was who found my father. I know only this: just on the north side of Bell's Bridge, on Ball Camp Pike, about thirteen miles out of Knoxville, someone did find him. He lay on the ground in a hollow below the road, on the road's right. The car lay beside him. He was dead.

As they worked it out, this is what had happened:

Those roads were very rough; gradually, a cotter pin had worked itself loose and fallen out, which held the steering gear together. How far back this had happened, they could not imagine, but they thought it likely that for quite some distance he had been driving without it, unaware that anything was wrong because the gear, not being wrenched suddenly, still held in place without the pin. But at this point in the road a front wheel struck a loose stone. The gear was suddenly wrenched and sprang loose, and the car was uncontrollable. They figured that he was probably going at a pretty fair speed, by what the car did from then on. Not that it was a question of brakes—that if he had been going slowly he could have saved himself with the brakes. For with this sudden wrench and jolt, his chin struck the steering wheel, at the exact point necessary, and with enough force, to cause concussion of the brain, killing him instantly; and the car ran wild.

The roadside, near the bridge, dips sharply down towards the creek (name). The car ran off the road into this dip. He was thrown, already dead, from the car, in such a way that he was not touched or hurt in any other way. The car ran past him, and up an eight-foot embankment, nearly to the top. There it lost headway and toppled backward, turning over twice (?), and came to rest beside him. If it had turned once more it would have crushed him.

They found his name in his wallet, called my mother, and told her that her husband was very seriously injured; what should they do? Doubtless she told them to take him straight to the nearest hospital; in which case they said that he shouldn't be moved yet, could a male relative come for him. With this she began to suspect that it was very

[4.6]

grave. She said yes, someone would be there as soon as possible. She telephoned Hugh; he went; my Aunt Jessie, I believe, came to wait with my mother.

They waited a long enough while that they were pretty sure Hugh would have phoned, if it were only an injury, no matter how serious. At about one (?) he came in. He put his arms around Aunt Jessie and embraced her so tightly that she was lifted from the floor.

Notes for Manuscript TN 1A.19, [4.4–6] (page and line number cited)

4.6–7	Frank said,] Frank said
5.33	lay beside] lay [upside down] beside (Agee's brackets)
5.39	it, unaware] it, [surely] unaware (Agee's brackets)
5.50	car ran] ran ran

Appendix V

Unfinished Draft of Agee's Letter to His Father

Internal evidence reveals the date of composition to likely be after Agee's thirty-ninth birthday (November 27, 1948) and before his fortieth, if his statement to his father that "I have lived, now, a year longer than you" is accurate. Agee began this letter (TN 1A.19, [4.8]), perhaps as a companion piece to the draft of his letter to his mother (appendix VI), as one of the ways of examining his early years in regard to their representation in *A Death in the Family.* It also echoes his "Memory of His Father's Accident and the Night Before" (appendix IV) in regard to his method.

[4.8]

If you were alive, and could read this, I cannot believe that you would like it. But if I were to try to make it a thing that you would like, I would fail in that, too, and then I would not even have been true to myself.

My dear father:

This was never my name for you when we knew each other but it has been my name for you for so long, now, that I would be mistaken to try to use the other.

Let me explain what I am trying to do here.

I have lived, now, a year longer than you were given to live. I feel very heavy in the sense of life and death, and very heavy in my sense of uncertainty and of failure in my life so far, and in the work I want most to do and have felt, for a long time, that I was best fitted to do. My way of trying to handle these things is, to try to recall and understand my life, as well as I can, and to try to write it down as clearly and well as I can. And the more I have thought of this, and the more I have tried, the clearer it has become to me that you have had a great deal more to do with it than any of us could easily imagine. In trying to write about my first few years alive, I am bound to be writing, mainly, about you.

There is no use in my hoping that if you were alive
[Agee's letter breaks off at this point in mid-sentence, about two-thirds of the way down the manuscript page.]

Appendix VI

Unfinished Draft of Agee's Letter to His Mother

This letter of Agee's (TN 1A.19, [4.9]), perhaps a companion piece to the draft of his letter to his father (appendix V), reveals his thoughts on how he wished to represent his early years in *A Death in the Family,* at least at the undetermined time of the letter's composition. It shows some vacillation on Agee's part as to whether or not he should utilize the memories of others (see appendix IV: "Memory of His Father's Accident and the Night Before") in writing the novel.

[4.9]

Dearest mother:

I had wanted when I saw you to tell you what I was trying to do, and to ask whether you would feel willing to help me.

I am trying to write a short book, a novel, beginning with the first things I can remember, and ending with my father's burial. The whole closing section is to be as clear an account as I can make, of everything I can remember, from the morning I woke up and learned that he had died the night before, through to the end of the afternoon of the funeral.

Since I'm mainly trying to write the book from inside my own experience at that age, I may write of this, as of most else in the book, only exactly what I can remember. But that may not be the right way to do it. In any case I know that my own memories are so extremely fragmentary, though very vivid in certain patches, that I'm not sure they may piece together into a coherent account without conjecture and invention, and I'm not sure that I want to do much of either, anywhere in the book, and particularly not on this subject.

So I've wondered about asking you, and Hugh, for whatever you can remember about it. I'm asking a good many questions, which I enclose, separate from this letter, because I realize you may well prefer

to have nothing to do with it. If so, don't even bother to look at them. Throw them away. You may not want to remember so distinctly in such detail. And you may have very grave misgivings about my writing about it. In either case I wouldn't want to ask your help.
[Agee's letter ends at this point, approximately halfway down the manuscript page.]

Appendix VII

Letter from Agee's Mother [Mrs. Erskine (Laura Tyler Agee) Wright] Concerning *A Death in the Family*

TX (Box 14, folder 3, 4 pages)
[Postmarked Feb. 3, 1958]

[1]
Sunday
Noon

Dearest Emma:

Your letter was waiting in my P.O. box, and I got it just after mailing mine to you! *Was so glad to hear*—

The other day I rather suddenly wrote what I now feel I can sum up about my feeling about R[ufus]'s book—It has taken me this long to get away from it enough to "*see*" it—

Here it is:—"So much of it drew me straight into it—and yet mingled with it a great deal else that is a writer's privilege: to use his medium to mould and to drive thro[ugh] abstract things, which were not in reality, true. It is a marvellous [*sic*] mixture of these elements, and I recognize it

[2]

as a *great and really universal elegy*—since all of it is the essence of *all* deaths—among mankind—["]

Also I know it as wonderful writing—both poetry and prose—and the complex nature of my son, which always led him to probe the deepest depths, as well as the highest heights his very sensitive soul and mind could take him—(past consciousness for some—but never so for him.)

Every review I've seen sees and comments on some different aspect or fact of this question—and they are *all true!* "We" feel the parts in italics are the most beautiful and true, and are really *Rufus at the very top of his gift*—H.[Hugh C. Tyler] & M.[Mildred H. Tyler] have just read it, & H. was "all in" with being so deeply moved, and also, poor dear, hurt over the thing "Andrew" said, for he knows, as do I, that tho[ugh] we never see eye to eye on religion—yet there was not this bitterness—& we were all *one,* in that day [the day of Jay Agee's funeral]—

[3]

There are still notices about the book coming out. It is run[n]ing first (in fiction) on a list of 4, p[r]esented by a large group of critics, librarians, & book sellers, for the "Book of the Year" (in fiction) award, in March—We shall see—Also it is being much talked of for a *play*—& also for movies—(both here & in England—O I hope *not* ["not" underlined three times]—Also two other scripts he wrote are being sought after—One of them "Noa Noa" about Gauguin was *tremendous*—& he never let it go because he did not approve of the way the movie people wanted to do it—Again—we shall see—I am sad he is not here to know all this—(yet maybe he *does*).

[4]

And he used to say "If I ever did anything that became "popular" or anything that made a lot of money, I would know I had *failed*"—

He made his first Com[m]union at St. John's [Episcopal Church in Knoxville], 39 years ago today—a precious and utterly trustful nine year old—This special month is so full of thought of him—and of Papa [Joel C. Tyler, Laura's father, b. 1860] who died this last day of Feb. '26—and of dear Erskine [Laura's second husband; James Agee's stepfather] who also died Feb. 18—I shall be glad when spring comes along—Had a slight upset this past week—nothing bad—just a prevalent "bug"—dizziness and nausea—over it now—My dear love, as ever—

Laura

Notes

1.1 The address on the envelope is

Mrs. E. A. Hunt,
522 Scenic Drive
Knoxville,
Tennessee

The postmark is South Kent, Connecticut, the place where Agee's mother lived at this time, at 8:30 a.m. on Feb. 3, 1958. Emma A. Hunt is a friend of Agee's mother and purportedly taught James Agee when he attended school in Knoxville.

1.3 Dearest Emma: (Paragraph inserted)] Dearest Emma:

2.11 H. & M.] (" H." is Hugh C. Tyler, a professional artist, the twin brother of Agee's mother, Laura; "M." is his wife Mildred H. Tyler.)

2.13 "Andrew"] (McDowell changed Hugh's name to Andrew in the novel.)

Appendix VIII

Outline and Possible Introduction to Agee's Massive Autobiographical Project and the Place of "This book" in It

At one time, James Agee contemplated writing a huge autobiography of which *A Death in the Family* would form but one part. *A Death in the Family* is referred to in the outline below as "This book." The manuscript page is located in the University of Tennessee's collection (TN 1A.19, [4.1]).

[4.1]

The Ancestors. (Culminate in my mother's and father's meeting in the dancing school).
The Father and Mother. (Ends with my birth: my father coming into the room for the first time.)
This book. (Begins with my first remembrance; ends the evening of his burial.)
Knoxville. (From then until I go to St Andrews to school.)
St Andrews I (From beginning, ending with Maundy Thursday, age 11 or 12.)
St Andrews II. (Then until I leave St. Andrews.)
III (miscellaneous stories?)
Knoxville II (My year at High School and with my grandfather.)
(Europe. My mother's remarriage. Florida.)
Exeter I (First year; summer in Maine).
Exeter II (Second year; Fred Loewenstein; summer in Maine).
Exeter III (Third year; Dorothy.)
Harvard I & II (Mainly the Otto business).
Harvard III & IV (Florence; the Saunders; Via).
Fortune: (Via; writing; first book. Politics).

Florida: (Via, work, the country.)
The Alabama trip.
Via and Alma. (begin with first passes at Alma; end with divorce and beginnings in Frenchtown.)
Alma and the book. (The year in Frenchtown.)
Alma and Mia. (Begin with conception of the child; end with Alma's leaving for Mexico.)
Mia. (Everything since.)

Possible Introduction to this Autobiographical Project

The fourth of the four short fragments printed by Robert Fitzgerald in *The Collected Short Prose of James Agee* and bearing the title "Now as Awareness . . ." ([125]–27) is more likely the introduction to the much larger project outlined above than, as Fitzgerald calls it, "a fresh start on the autobiographical novel." Its last three paragraphs seem to lead directly to the section that in the outline above Agee calls "The Ancestors." The fragment is therefore not included in the restored text of the novel, but is reproduced below from pages 140A–C of Fitzgerald's copyedited typescripts (TX 3, 6–7) since Agee's original manuscripts apparently do not survive. The typescripts for Fitzgerald's volume that survive (TX 3, 6–7) are mainly copyedited typescripts, as is this fragment, but each of the other three of the four fragments that Fitzgerald prints exists as well in an earlier, uncopyedited version at the end of folder 7. (See "Major Manuscript Variants" under the "Introduction" to the novel and chapter 5 for the other three fragments printed by Fitzgerald.) This fourth fragment was apparently found later than the other three since its pagination marks it as an insert into the existing copyedited typescript and its title is a handwritten insertion upon the copyedited typescript page for the "Contents" of the volume. Notes on the corrected text of this typescript are given after the fragment and cited by page and line number as RF 140A.2, for example. The version printed by Fitzgerald is faithful to the corrected typescript, which bears the handwritten correction of three obvious typographical errors which are also noted below. Typeover corrections are not noted.

[140A]

"Now as Awareness . . ."

(Evidently a fresh start on the autobiographical novel. No date)
[Both title and description are Fitzgerald's.]

Now as awareness of how much of life is lost, and how little is left, becomes even more piercing, I feel also, and ever the more urgently, the desire to restore, and to make a little less impermanent, such of my lost life as I can, beginning with the beginning and coming as far forward as need be. This is the simplest, most primitive of the desires which can move a writer. I hope I shall come to other things in time; in time to write them. Before I do, if I am ever to do so, I must sufficiently satisfy this first, most childlike need.

I had hoped that I might make poetry of some of this material, and fiction of more of it, and during the past two years I have written a good deal of it as fiction, and a little of it as poetry. But now I believe that these two efforts were mistakes. This book is chiefly a remembrance of my childhood, and a memorial to my father; and I find that I value my childhood and my father as they were, as well and as exactly as I can remember and represent them, far beyond any transmutation of these matters which I have made, or might ever make, into poetry or fiction. I know that I am making the choice most dangerous to an artist, in valuing life above art; I know too that by good use of fiction or poetry one can re-enter life more deeply, and represent it more vividly, intimately and truthfully, than by any such means of bald narration as I propose; but it now seems to me that I have no actual choice, but am in fact compelled, against my judgment and wish as an artist. Within the limitations imposed by this plain method to which I seem compelled, I shall, of course, in so far as I am able, use such

[140B]

varieties of artfulness as seem appropriate.

Those who have gone before, backward beyond remembrance and beyond the beginning of imagination, backward among the emergent beasts, and the blind, prescient ravenings of the youngest sea, those children of the sun, I mean, who brought forth those, who brought forth those, who wove, spread the human net, and who brought forth me; they are fallen backward into their graves like blown wheat and are folded under the earth like babies in blankets, and they are all melted upon the mute enduring world like leaves, like wet snow; they are faint in the urgencies of my small being as stars at noon; they people the silence of my soul like bats in a cave; they lived, in their time, as I live now, each a universe within which, for a while, to die was inconceivable, and their living was as bright and brief as sparks on a chimney wall, and now they lie dead, as I soon shall lie; my ancestors, my veterans. I call upon you, I invoke your help, you cannot answer, you cannot help; I desire to do you honor, you are beyond the last humiliation. You are my fathers and my mothers but there is no way in which you can help me, nor may I serve you. You are the old people and now you rest. Rest well; I will be with you soon; meanwhile may I bear you ever in the piety of my heart.

They lie down in so many places, as they begin to emerge into domestic legend; in Western England, in Scotland, in Ireland, in

Massachusetts, in New Hampshire, in Vermont, in New York State, in Michigan, in Tennessee, where my own life began: my mother's people. In France, in Germany, in the mountains of a wilderness which became Tennessee: my father's people. And where before that; and where

[140C]

shall my children rest, and their children? We can see, sometimes, a light across a thousand years; we are, perhaps, the eyes of nature, such as they are; stones are hardly more blind, and few creatures are as capricious in their wanderings, or so dice-like in their destinies. Our marriages are imaginations of choice, love, unique desire; we meet and mate like apples swung together on a creek.

Then there are those who come within living memory: my mother's father's father, whom she revered and of whom she has told me; I think well of him, and was burdened by his name, but I never knew him; I doubt I shall ever have occasion to tell my children of him; with this generation he vanishes from the memory of the human race, and only the exceptionally good, or able, or evil survive in memory longer.

Notes

RF 140A.2 (Evidently . . . date)] (This line is a handwritten addition to the typescript. In the published version, Fitzgerald italicizes this line.)

RF 140A.23 truthfully] yruthfully

RF 140B.11 cave] dave

RF 140B.17 no] now